SOMEONE LIKE YOU

By the same author

WOMAN TO WOMAN
SHE'S THE ONE
NEVER TOO LATE

SOMEONE LIKE YOU

CATHY KELLY

HarperCollins*Publishers*

This novel is entirely a work of fiction. The names, characters and incidents portrayed in it are the work of the author's imagination. Any resemblance to actual persons, living or dead, events or localities is entirely coincidental.

HarperCollins*Publishers*
77–85 Fulham Palace Road,
Hammersmith, London W6 8JB

www.fireandwater.com

Published by HarperCollins*Publishers* 2000
3 5 7 9 8 6 4 2

ISBN 0 00 226172 3

Set in Sabon
Rowland Phototypesetting Ltd,
Bury St Edmunds, Suffolk

Printed in Great Britain by
Clays Ltd, St Ives plc

To John, with all my love

ACKNOWLEDGEMENTS

Please forgive me in advance for whoever I leave out because I just *know* I'll leave someone out. People ask what's the hardest thing about writing a book and I always say it's this bit, because when you've put your heart and soul into a novel, you desperately want to remember to thank all the lovely people who've helped you in some way during the writing of it or during the last few books. I tend to think of whom to thank when I'm at the traffic lights in the car and can't write it down. I subsequently forget this vital bit of information in the same way I go into the supermarket to buy milk and come out with four bulging bags of shopping – and no milk. So here goes:

Thanks to my darling John for all your love and encouragement; thanks to my family for being so supportive, to Mum for all the endless things you do; to dear Lucy for being Rupert, to Francis for always being there on the phone to cheer me up, to Anne, little Laura, Naomi and Emer, to Dave and St Lucia, and to my beloved Tamsin who brings sunshine into my day and who appears in this book (thinly disguised).

To Ali Gunn, sweetie, the best agent in the world and the woman who understands that the phone isn't just for Christmas, it's for life. To Deborah Schneider with much gratitude, to Diana, Carol and all at Curtis Brown. To Sarah Hamilton for encouragement, understanding and lovely gossip, to Rachel Hore for gently and expertly doing wonderful things with this book, practically into the maternity ward with baby Leo. Thank you to my wonderful new family at HarperCollins, especially dear Anne O'Brien, Nick Sayers, Adrian Bourne, Eddie Bell, Fiona McIntosh, David North, Martin Palmer, Jane Harris, Phyllis Acolatse, Terence Caven, Jennifer Parr, Lee Motley, Venetia, Moira, Tony . . . just all of you for being so good to me and risking death by hanging those big posters in the atrium! I appreciate it. Thanks to my Irish family, Poolbeg, especially Paul Campbell, Lucy, Suzanne, Philip, Kieran, Conor for all your support, fantastic work and those deadly Poolbeg cocktails.

For advice and support for all sorts of different things thanks to Susan Zaidan, Lola Simpson, Barbara Stack, Lisa Lynch, Patricia Scanlan, Marian Keyes, Kate Thompson, dear Clare Foss, Mairead, Margaret, Esther, all my friends for their help and encouragement, especially all at *Sunday World*.

To the staff at the Animal Welfare Clinic for allowing me to spend some time with them and all their patients, especially to John Hardy, Paul, Grainne, Vanessa, Pamela, Tracy, Juliana and anybody else I'm leaving out. Thanks to Aisling O Buachalla from Sherry FitzGerald for letting me in on the secrets of working as an estate agent. Any mistakes about either being a vet nurse or an estate agent are all mine – probably due to me not being able to read my own shorthand after the event (not unusual).

Thanks to the incredible staff at the Kylemore Nursing Home who looked after my father when he was dying with Alzheimer's and who managed, through a combination of professionalism, compassion and humour, to make that last year a time full of good memories.

Thanks to the booksellers who work so hard selling my books, who have to keep up to date with the phenomenal volume of novels coming out every month, and who are the only people I know who can have wonderful times at parties, drink wine and *still* have intelligent conversations about the new books they're dying to get their hands on. Thanks to you, the people who buy my books and give me such a thrill when you write and say you like them. Without you, none of this would have happened. So thanks.

SOMEONE LIKE YOU

CHAPTER ONE

[illegible]

shaped the fin [illegible] exactly [illegible]

[illegible] herself into the water. [illegible]

It [illegible] that before [illegible]

[illegible] into the water, her hair [illegible]

her [illegible] verbena scented [illegible]

[illegible] reading the Esta [illegible]

[illegible] of the paper [illegible]

[illegible] Hannah [illegible]

[illegible]

[illegible] at the side a [illegible] magical [illegible]

[illegible] The bath was [illegible]

[illegible] making. There [illegible]

other [illegible] Hannah [illegible]

[illegible]

back. That was [illegible]

[illegible] they had [illegible]

[illegible] magic [illegible]

[illegible] The [illegible]

CHAPTER ONE

Hannah stretched one slim, tanned leg in the direction of the taps, clasped the hot tap expertly with her dripping foot and felt hot water flood deliciously into the bath.

'You've done that before,' said Jeff in amusement as she sank back against him in the water, her back slick against his bare chest, nothing but lemon verbena-scented bubbles between them.

'I love reading in the bath and, in the winter, it's horrible sitting up out of the water to turn on the taps, so I've learned how to do it with my feet,' Hannah murmured as the water level rose slowly in the cracked old roll-top bath and the heat flooded all over her limbs. She felt gloriously tired yet happy, every inch of her body satiated even though she'd had practically no sleep last night. Sharing a bath after such a wonderful, marathon lovemaking session had been a brilliant idea. The bath water eased the aches caused by Jeff's very energetic lovemaking. There had been one mad moment when they'd almost fallen off Hannah's bed and she'd just managed not to shriek out loud in agony as a shooting pain had rocketed up her back into her neck. That was obviously the drawback of flings with younger men, she decided gleefully: they had no concept of back problems and were keen to do gymnastic things with mirrors, armchairs and the ties of your dressing gown. The only thing poor Harry had ever done with the ties of his dressing gown was to let them trail behind him all over the kitchen floor picking up bits of fluff, spare cornflakes and dust.

What was she calling him 'poor Harry' for anyway? 'Poor' my eye. Parasitical, Lying Bastard Harry suited him better. Thinking of parasites, she grimly hoped that his year-long trek around South America meant he'd finally met that infamous parasite that lived in tropical rivers and swam up the urine stream of any man stupid enough to pee in a river. Once it swam into your system, you were in big trouble. Hannah hoped eradicating it would involve some agonizing operation where Harry couldn't sit down without wincing for a week. Something like the duck-billed speculum thingy which women had to endure being inserted for cervical smear tests, but much, much worse.

'Is there anything else you can do with your feet?' Jeff asked wickedly, whisking her away from the Amazon and agonizing medical experiments by nibbling her ear provocatively.

'No,' Hannah said firmly, concentrating on letting the water soothe the nagging ache in her right hip. She closed her eyes and began planning the next hour: her small suitcase was neatly stowed on top of the wardrobe in the boxroom and the clothes she wanted to take to Egypt were carefully arranged on the boxroom bed. It would take half an hour to pack, ticking off every item of clothing and every toiletry on her pared-down list. Then she had to empty the fridge. No point coming back to a disgustingly smelly kitchen through carelessness. When the kitchen was linked to the sitting room by badly fitting double doors, limiting bad smells was particularly important. Logistically, Hannah thought as her mind ran through her preparations with the precision of a Swiss watch, she only had a couple of minutes more to soak in the bath.

Jeff had other ideas. His mouth began trailing down her neck on to her shoulders while his hands rippled under the water, stroking Hannah's thighs suggestively. She could feel the muscular chest with its six-pack stomach contracting with desire as he touched her.

She sat up abruptly and turned off the hot tap, her dark hair slicking against her skin like a tangle of seaweed.

'We don't have time, Jeff,' she said sternly. 'It's half nine already. I've got to be at the airport in a couple of hours and I've got some phone calls to make, not to mention the fact that I haven't packed yet.'

Jeff pulled her effortlessly back into the bath with arms used to bench-pressing double her body weight. 'If I was going with you, you wouldn't need to pack very much,' he said, nuzzling her ear. 'Just a couple of G-string bikinis and a sexy dress like that one you were wearing last night.'

Hannah had to smile. The amethyst dress was incredibly daring and unlike anything else in her limited and quite conservative wardrobe: two flimsy spaghetti-strap little slip things worn together, she'd bought it in a designer shop in a sale and it had hung in her wardrobe for a year before she'd felt brave enough to put it on. But last night, for the launch of the hotel's new nightclub, Jupiter, she'd decided to drag it out and wear it.

'There are going to be loads of famous people there. The guest list is like flicking through *Hello!*' one of Hannah's hotel receptionist colleagues had wittered excitedly about the launch weeks beforehand. 'We've got to pull out all the stops, girls. We can't let the hotel down.'

So Hannah had pulled out all the stops, had set her long dark hair in curlers so it rippled down her back like a sheet of raw silk and had shoe-horned herself into the ruinously expensive dress she'd nearly taken back to the shop so many times on the grounds that it was a waste of money. All the other Triumph Hotel receptionists had gasped in shock at the sight of the normally staid Ms Campbell in something other than her off-duty uniform of crisp white shirt, ironed blue jeans, blazer and loafers. She looked phenomenally sexy, they said, stunned. Who'd have thought she could transform herself from a frostily polite receptionist into a siren with just a dress?

Jeff Williams, who ran the hotel's new gym and was as yet unfamiliar with Hannah's reputation as a bit of an ice maiden, had gasped with pleasure at the sight of her gym-toned, curvaceous body clad in a wisp of filmy chiffon that clung in all the right places.

Unlike the starstruck members of staff who spent the night gazing cow-eyed at the various stars knocking back Moët in the roped-off area of the nightclub, Jeff and Hannah spent the evening discovering that they both loved to dance. They drank far more mineral water than alcohol as they moved sinuously on the dance floor, jiving, boogieing, salsaing and even waltzing when the DJ played some slow, jazzy numbers. High on having fun, it only took two glasses of white wine to give Hannah a heady buzz where the idea of letting Jeff kiss her seemed natural really, rather than a complete mistake.

'I'm ten years older than you,' she reproved as they squashed up together on one seat, his muscular arms wrapped around her and his fair head bent over hers. She felt ridiculously like a teenager on a date, but it was fun.

'Thirty-six is hardly old,' Jeff had murmured, kissing the tendrils of dark hair that clung to her cheekbones.

As his bachelor pad was miles across town and sounded like a laddish bombsite shared with three other young men, it seemed more sensible to have that cup of coffee in Hannah's immaculate apartment, a mere stone's throw from the Triumph Hotel.

Sitting on the small, hard sofa-bed, Jeff had admired the unusual brocade cushions that Hannah had hand-stamped with gold fabric paint one weekend, and then attempted a little handiwork of his own, stroking fingers up and down Hannah's arm in a very erotic manner. He hadn't pounced on her. She'd known he wouldn't: used to having women swoon at his gym instructor physique, Jeff didn't have to bother at all to attract gorgeous women, so he always made a point of making sure they knew what they were doing when things got intimate.

'Are you sure you want to?' he asked, his eager and ardent eyes proof that he certainly wanted to.

Hannah, who'd already decided she deserved a celebratory bonk after twelve months of celibacy, had said yes. It had been wonderful, rather like picking up the old tennis racquet you hadn't used since you'd fallen in love with Wimbledon and Ivan Lendl sixteen years ago, and realizing that you could still lob the ball over the net without making a complete fool of yourself.

Jeff wasn't to know that the last time she'd had that much exercise, she'd been in the middle of a class of fellow step-aerobics fans, all sweating like pigs with their T-shirts glued to their backs, their thighs aching and a supermodel-lookalike screaming at them to 'move your arms, girls!'

Neither was she about to tell him that he was the first person other than herself to sleep in the queen-sized bed with the yellow brocade headboard Hannah had re-covered because she hated the original peach Dralon fabric. Men, particularly young men, she always felt, were nervous of the concept of both celibacy and women who made a conscious decision to have sex, instead of just getting carried away by too much vodka and a nice line in flattery. Conscious decisions implied another big C – commitment.

She figured that if Jeff discovered he was the one she'd chosen to break her enforced year of celibacy, he'd probably have run out of the apartment like the clappers, imagining he'd got himself involved with a neurotic bunny boiler. If only he knew.

Life had taught Hannah that men were useful for only one thing, and it wasn't earning money, either. She'd learned her lessons early on, from her feckless father. When you were born in the wilds of Connemara where only the hardiest of livestock could survive, farmers like her father either toiled away until their fingers were gnarled with arthritis and they were old before their time, or they turned to the bottle and let their wives shoulder the burden of feeding the kids and paying the electricity bill. Hannah's father had chosen the second path.

Her mother was the one who'd grown old before her time, her strong-boned face a mask of lines and misery by the time she was forty. Watching Anna Campbell come home white with exhaustion from cleaning out the kitchens in the local hotel and then sit down to knit another piece of the Aran sweater she was being paid buttons to finish, made Hannah vow never to end up in the same position. No man would ever enslave her in unholy matrimony or come home roaring drunk, screaming for a dinner he hadn't contributed a penny to. No way.

She'd earn her fortune and be utterly independent, a career warrior who'd never have to strain her eyes knitting by the lights of a feeble lamp for the extra few pounds to kit her children out in reasonable clothes for Sunday Mass.

Failing her final school exams and the arrival of Harry had been the fatal glitches in this foolproof plan. But, thought Hannah grinding her teeth even though the dentist had warned her to stop doing it, she was back on track now. Sort of. A new job, a cultural holiday to give her some of the education she knew she lacked, and a new life. Jeff, lovely though he was, wasn't part of the new life. He'd get in the way and make her think about love and things. She'd had enough of love to last her a lifetime, thank you very much.

The water was getting uncomfortably cold and she was going to be late if she didn't move soon. Hannah stood up gracefully and climbed out of the bath.

'You're in great shape,' Jeff said, admiring her toned arms and small waist.

'You mean for someone of my age,' she teased, wrapping a towel around her body and rubbing her jawbone where she felt the most pain from her constant teeth grinding.

'For anybody,' he emphasized. 'You must work out a lot. I see so many women who let themselves get out of shape. They think if they're not an athletic build, why bother. But you really work at it.'

Hannah paused in towelling her hair dry and thought of the hours she'd spent on the StairMaster in the past year, jaw clenched as she pounded Harry out of her mind. Getting him out of her life had been difficult enough: eradicating him from her thoughts was another thing entirely.

Before Harry (or BH as she liked to think of it) she'd been in reasonable shape for a twenty-seven-year-old who smoked like a chimney. Of medium height and with a genetic tendency to put on weight, she was still young enough not to bother much with exercise, preferring the Marlboro Light Exercise Plan of lighting up whenever she felt hungry.

But during the Harry years, she'd spent far too long cuddling up next to him on their old sofa, sharing mammoth takeaways and entire boxes of chocolates as they watched videos. Life was one long *Little House on the Prairie* fantasy of delicious meals and lazy evenings toasting their toes in front of the fire while Harry discussed the novel he was going to write and Hannah stopped caring about leaving her dead-end job in the dress shop to pursue her dream of being rich and utterly independent. She stopped caring about her figure and was even persuaded to give up smoking when Harry went off the fags for an article he was writing about nicotine tablets. No cigarettes meant more chocolates and cups of tea with three sugars to make up for the pain of wanting a fag. Harry didn't put on a pound: Hannah put on another twelve.

In cohabiting bliss, her ambition had disappeared along with her waistline. Until that awful August day she'd thrown him out and had started reclaiming her life – and her figure.

'I go to the gym and to three aerobics classes, one toning class, and I walk about ten miles a week,' she told Jeff.

'You can tell,' he said solemnly. 'You gotta put the work in to get the body you want.'

Hannah nodded sagely. It was a pity she was leaving the hotel. It would have been fun to work out with Jeff, even if their fling probably wouldn't have lasted very long.

Men like Jeff were always looking over your shoulder to see who was coming along behind you. One pretty, pouting twenty-something in a thong leotard asking him to explain the lateral pull-down machine and it'd have been all over.

Mind you, if she'd been staying on at the hotel, she wouldn't have gone off with Jeff in the first place. The Triumph Hotel's gossip network was far superior to the actual hotel network. It took over half an hour to have an omelette delivered to a guest's bedroom via room service and only ten minutes for a juicy bit of news to travel all the way from the kitchens to the concierge desk, having reached the business centre and the restaurant into the bargain. The gossiping that would have gone on if Hannah had been seen walking out with the gym's new manager would have been hilarious to behold.

After a year when she had gossiped with nobody, dated nobody and revealed not one item of information about herself to the naturally inquisitive staff, Hannah couldn't have coped with seeing the flood-gates of curiosity come rushing open. But she had her reference, her new job was lined up for when she returned from holiday and nobody could touch her for one carefree fling. 'Indulge yourself,' advised all the women's magazines when it came to getting over unhappy love affairs. 'Have a massage, treat yourself to an aromatherapy session.' Jeff was her first AH (After Harry) treat. More fun than aromatherapy and less painful than a facial, but guaranteed to give you an inner glow that Oil of Olay couldn't manage.

Happily unaware of his status as a reward for a year of celibacy, Jeff let more hot water flood into the bath and lay back in the bubbles. Trying not to let herself get irritated because he obviously had no intention of leaving, Hannah concentrated on rubbing moisturizer into her face.

She had been able to reshape her body with endless hours of exercising but her face remained stubbornly the same as ever: rounded with a pointed chin, slightly too-beaky nose and bright almond-shaped eyes the exact colour of toffee. With a sprinkling of amber freckles scattered across her nose and cheekbones, the cumulative effect of sparkling eyes and the rippling nutbrown hair should have been that of a casually pretty woman. Attractive but no beauty, would be the conclusion if someone had described Hannah to a stranger.

But a simple description would leave out the very thing which transformed her. Hannah glowed with that fleeting, most unbottleable quality that people lacking it did everything to acquire – sex appeal. From the way she walked with that languid sway of her enduringly curvy hips, to the way she drank her tea, wide mouth pursing up softly around the china to take a first sip, screamed of sexuality. She didn't do it on purpose: in fact, she didn't have to do anything. Hannah Campbell, thirty-six-year-old hotel receptionist and spinster of this parish, had been born like that. And it drove her insane.

When her long shaggy hair was tamed into the gleaming knot she wore for work and her small tortoiseshell glasses sat on her nose, Hannah could look as stern as the headmistress of a school for delinquents. Which was why she'd never bothered to get contact lenses. Nowadays she wanted to be able to hide her natural sexuality, to conceal it with sedate clothes, fierce glances and Reverend Mother spectacles.

Sex appeal was all very well in its place but all it had ever given

Hannah was Trouble, with a capital T. Being naturally sexy in her rural home town meant you either got an undeserved reputation as a complete slapper or you aroused rage amongst the local lads who didn't take kindly to being constantly given the cold shoulder.

Sex appeal was all very well for Hollywood starlets, Hannah felt, but for normal women it brought sheer, unending hassle. Well, she amended, with a smidgen of guilty pleasure, her sex appeal had given her the delectable Jeff. But he had overstayed his welcome so it was time for Sexy Hannah to disappear and Ms Cojones of Steel Campbell to take her place.

She expertly coiled her wet hair into a scrunchie and fixed her visitor with the steely look she'd perfected when departing hotel guests insisted they'd had only two drinks in the hotel bar the previous night instead of the ten doubles itemized on their bar bill.

'Jeff, you've got to get out of the bath and leave. I need to be out the door in three-quarters of an hour and I need time to myself. Come on, now.'

Responding to her schoolmarm voice the way he hadn't responded to her gentle wheedling, Jeff climbed out of the bath, stood in front of her and stretched, his splendid naked body dripping water on to the black and white tile-effect lino.

Hannah couldn't help staring. God, he was beautiful: from his short blond hair down to his big feet. Six foot of rippling muscle without a flaw anywhere. Poor Michelangelo would have killed to sculpt something like Jeff Williams.

Hannah gulped as she tried to concentrate on what she simply had to do in the next hour. Packing and sorting out her guide books. She wanted to learn something from this holiday and she'd hoped to spend a while reading her *Let's Go: Egypt* so that she wouldn't embarrass herself in front of all the other people on the trip, people who probably knew about history and mythology . . . Then Jeff smiled a slow, lazy smile and traced one finger along her chest until it hooked under her towel and pulled, tumbling the towel to the floor along with her mental timetable.

Oh, what the hell, thought Hannah, letting her sex drive shift into fifth gear. After all those evenings trying to forget what physical pleasure had been like and watching endless re-runs of *Inspector Morse*, she deserved this. It wouldn't take her that long to pack. She could read her guide book on the plane.

CHAPTER TWO

'Lord! Would you look at the mess in here. I'm all for salads but you've really got to take them out of those awful little white plastic containers when you get them home. They leak everywhere. What's this?' Anne-Marie O'Brien squinted over her glasses at the supermarket label on the tub of couscous which had made an oily puddle in the middle of the otherwise spotless fridge. 'Couscous? Messy, that's what it is.'

Emma Sheridan said nothing as her mother searched for a clean J-cloth, rinsed it out in hot water and then zealously scrubbed the middle shelf of the fridge with the help of a bottle of antiseptic kitchen cleaner Emma had forgotten she'd possessed and had meant to throw out. An overpowering scent of pine disinfectant filled the room. It smelled nothing like any pine tree Emma had ever come across, unless pines were mating with bleach factories these days.

'Much better now,' Mrs O'Brien said, straightening up. She briskly rinsed the cloth out again, inspected the rest of the kitchen with narrowed eyes, then gave the melamine surfaces a quick squirt of cleaner, her every movement the work of an expert with a PhD in Cleaning the Home. Only then did she take the precious Tupperware and tinfoil-wrapped parcels and place them carefully in the fridge, giving her daughter a commentary on her actions at the same time.

'Can't have poor Peter eating that supermarket stuff. Proper dinners is what he should have. I know your father wouldn't touch anything that had to be microwaved, but if I was away from him for a week, it'd be a different matter. Husbands! I've made lasagne that'll last for at least two days, shepherd's pie for tonight and these two are chicken and mushroom pies – I'll put them in the freezer part. Emma, dear! Do you ever defrost this thing? It won't do it itself. Never mind, I'll just sort it out . . .'

Emma tuned out. Thirty-one-years of her mother had taught her that listening to the 'nobody does things the right way, my way' monologue would put you in a mental home if you didn't tune out. Especially when the monologue was designed to tell you what a slatternly housekeeper/student/driver you were and how your poor husband would drop dead from salmonella if you didn't start boil washing both the tea towels and his underpants immediately.

It was immaterial that Emma had spent most of the previous day cleaning and polishing Number 27 The Beeches from top to bottom; immaterial that she'd used up her precious day off work cleaning instead of swanning around the shops buying last-minute bits and bobs for her holiday. She'd toyed with the idea of going into Debenhams to see if she could get one of those black uplift bikinis she'd spotted in a magazine. Even if you were as flat as a pancake boobwise, this bikini would give you a cleavage that'd take the sight out of people's eyes, or so the magazine claimed.

As the only way Emma's cleavage was going to take somebody's eye out was if a wire from one of her AA cups escaped and actually poked them in the eye, she desperately needed a new uplift bikini.

But as usual, the only overdeveloped part of her person, namely guilt, had swung into action and put the kibosh on the shopping trip. Emma's sense of guilt was like a medical textbook description of the heart: a large muscle which contracts unconsciously. Guilt at leaving Peter on his own at home for an entire week while she sailed down the Nile with her parents overcame her desire for a skilfully padded bikini, so she'd given Debenhams a miss and spring-cleaned the house instead. Peter, who wouldn't notice if he had to eat his dinner off the table because they'd run out of plates, would be unaware of her feverish scrubbing. However, Emma's Guiltometer had worked out that an entire day of cleaning would go a long way (fifty-five per cent) to making up for having a holiday without her beloved husband. Buying him an enormous present she couldn't afford and cooking him his favourite dinners for a week after her return would almost compensate for the remaining forty-five per cent.

Sadly, she'd forgotten to buy new rubber gloves for the cleaning fest so her hands were now dry as an overcooked chicken thanks to scrubbing the toilet bowls with bleach. But the house was a veritable palace, with clean carpets, clean loos and not an unironed item of clothing anywhere.

All that and her mother was still tut-tutting over the only visible blemish in the entire premises. Emma could just picture Pete wrenching open the couscous and eating it with his finger beside the fridge that morning, shoving the greasy tub back in carelessly afterwards before grabbing the orange juice carton for breakfast. He adored couscous – and he hated shepherd's pie with a vengeance. Still, what was the point of telling her mother that? Anne-Marie O'Brien wouldn't listen: she never listened to anyone. Except her husband, James P. O'Brien, boss of O'Brien's Heating Contractors, master of all he surveyed and the person who absolutely always had to have the last word on every subject.

Emma sat down wearily on one of her kitchen chairs and examined her newly painted nails. The rosy pink colour she'd bought for her holiday was pretty but still didn't camouflage either the bleach damage or the nibbled bits. She'd chewed her index fingernail into an ugly stub during a long phone conversation the night before where her mother had fussed about the heat in Egypt, the food, the locals, the thought of covering up her shoulders at tourist sites and '. . . would your father be able to get proper milk for his tea.' That idea had summoned up a bizarre mental picture of her father trying to milk a camel, him red and sweating as he stood with his teacup in one hand and a camel teat in the other.

She nibbled a stray sticking up bit of index fingernail. Well, who'd be looking at her bloody nails anyway. She felt too tired to care: she hoped she could sleep on the plane to Egypt. If she could steal one of her mother's Valium tablets, she could blank out the entire journey.

While her mother busied herself with the fridge, Emma surreptitiously touched her breasts through the soft fabric of her denim dungarees. She'd been doing it all day, giving herself a pleasurable thrill that had nothing to do with sex. This thrill was provided by her biological clock heaving a sigh of relief. Nervously, she slid one hand under her T-shirt to reach her bare breast and touched it cautiously. Sensitive, definitely.

They'd looked bigger in the mirror earlier, she was sure of it. The nipples were bigger, weren't they? Yes, yes, yes, she grinned. She was pregnant. It was quite incredible how happy she felt when she thought about the baby, her baby. The glow filled her up inside, like that advert for breakfast cereal where the boy cycling to school was lit from within because he'd eaten his Ready Brek that morning. Emma felt lit from within with a combination of sheer joy and relief. Relief that after so long hoping, it was finally happening. She wanted to dance around the room with delight, but her natural caution advised her to be careful. Say nothing to jinx it. Wait until you're sure and then tell darling Pete the wonderful news, she told herself. All she had to do was get through the hateful week with her parents and then everything would be wonderful. Her secret would keep her going during the next week. It *was* only a week, after all.

Ignoring the 'this place is a mess' monologue, she picked up a pad from the table and began writing a quick note to Pete, telling him she loved him and would miss him desperately.

'Well, madam, having a rest while your poor mother works as usual.'

The sound of her father's voice made Emma jump to her feet guiltily. She felt as if she really was doing something wrong, the way she felt when she passed a police car with a radar gun out the window, even if she was only crawling along at thirty miles an hour. His very presence could plunge her into nervous tension, even now when she was so very hopeful about her precious baby.

'Anne-Marie, there's really no need to be doing Emma's dirty work for her,' Jimmy O'Brien said, treating his elder daughter to a disapproving stare. 'She's big enough and ugly enough to do her own housework. I won't have you skivvying for her.'

'I wasn't skivvying,' said her mother, her voice losing its liveliness and becoming weary.

'Mother was just rubbing up something spilt,' Emma protested, feeling all her good humour fade away as it so inevitably did whenever her father was involved. 'I cleaned that fridge out yesterday . . .'

But her father was no longer listening. Striding over to the bin, he knocked out the old tobacco at the bottom of his pipe and began to fill his wife in on his recent activities.

'I've filled the car with petrol, checked the air in the tyres and put in half a litre of oil,' he announced. 'We're all shipshape, if you're ready to go, Anne-Marie.'

You'd think we were *driving* to bloody Egypt, Emma thought with irritation.

For about the hundredth time since the trip had been booked, she wondered why she was going. It had been her father's idea: the holiday of a lifetime to celebrate his and his wife's thirty-fifth wedding anniversary.

Emma couldn't figure out why he'd picked such an exotic destination as Egypt. Her father was a man who, for the past fifteen years, had been perfectly content to go to Portugal, sit watching sports coverage in a bar and comment loudly on how downmarket the place was getting what with all the football hooligans and brazen young girls running around with suitcases full of condoms looking for men.

'Tarts,' he'd say darkly every time a gang of carefree, tanned girls in skimpy T-shirts and bum-skimming shorts appeared on the scene.

Emma used to gaze wistfully at these modern babes: she was damn sure they wouldn't still be going on holiday with their parents when they were in their twenties, too afraid of the furore to suggest a holiday with their boyfriends. Until she'd been married, she and Pete had only been away to the sun once when she'd pretended to be away with some girlfriends.

His comments about how young people's standards were dropping notwithstanding, her father appeared to enjoy Portugal. But one holiday programme presenter enthusing over a Nile cruise had changed everything. Jimmy had ordered a vast assortment of brochures and spent many happy hours over Sunday lunch reading out the bits he was most interested in.

'Listen to this,' he'd say, blithely interrupting any other conversation with the insensitivity of a despot, '"Enjoy the spectacle of Luxor and Karnak temples. Both monuments are perfect examples of ancient Egyptian architecture. Parts of Karnak Temple date back to 1375 BC." That's bloody incredible, we've got to go.'

Unfortunately, the 'we' also meant Pete and Emma.

'No way, Emma. Why can't they go on their own and just make each other miserable instead of making us all miserable,' Pete complained, which was quite an out of character thing for him to say. Genuinely kind and warm, Pete couldn't be nasty if he tried, but even his legendary patience was strained by her parents. Well, her father, really. Jimmy O'Brien strained a lot of people's patience.

'I know, love,' Emma said wearily. She felt so torn; torn between doing what easy-going Pete wanted and what her domineering father wanted. 'It's just that he hasn't stopped talking about it and he's assuming we'll go too. He'll harp on about how ungrateful we are if we don't go.' Emma didn't need to say any more. Ever since her father had loaned herself and Pete the deposit money for their house, he'd been holding it over their heads like a sword of Damocles.

Going out with friends for Sunday instead of going to the O'Briens' for lunch was seen as a sign of ungratefulness. So was being too busy to pick up Jimmy's new bifocals from that shop in town, or not being able to drive Anne-Marie to the shops because she'd got nervous about driving her own car for some unaccountable reason. The way things were going, the next time Emma refused a liquorice on the grounds that she didn't like the taste, that too would be seen as ungratefulness.

Pete said nothing more about the trip. Emma knew he wanted her to stand up to her father for once and refuse to go so that they could spend the money going away together later. But Emma, who knew she'd feel guilty about leaving Pete but would suffer ten times more if she crossed Jimmy O'Brien, finally figured out a solution.

'Pete can't go to Egypt that week, Dad,' she lied. 'He's got a two-day conference in Belfast. But I'll go – won't that be nice, just the three of us together, like old times?'

The old times reference did the trick. Which was ironic, Emma thought. Her memory of bygone holidays consisted of the feeling that they'd merely changed the setting for her father's daily sarcastic remarks. But, hilariously, he didn't see it like that: Jimmy was delighted with the holiday plan.

Pete was staying at home, sweetly telling Emma that it was all right, he'd go away with the lads for a football weekend later in the year, so she wasn't to worry. All she had to do now was actually get through the damn trip.

'I think I need a cup of tea before I go,' her mother said, dropping the cloth and leaning against Emma's sink, the perfect picture of fatigue. Her mother's put-upon act was like a red rag to a bull where Jimmy was concerned. Somebody had to be to blame for his wife's exhaustion.

Emma knew what would come next: she'd have to make tea and be berated for making her poor mother do her housework. There was no point explaining what had really happened. This particular tableau had taken place so many times over the years, they were all like pantomime characters acting out parts they'd played for thirty years.

You're a lazy, stupid girl, Emma.

Oh no I'm not!

Oh yes you are!

Emma watched her parents dispassionately for a moment, watched them taking over her house as if they owned it. She really wasn't in the mood for a re-run of their familiar power-play game.

She'd recognized what it was ever since she'd bought the self-help books. Her father was a control freak and her mother was passive aggressive, able to slip into her 'poor me' routine as soon as her husband appeared in order to be fussed over. Or so it seemed. All the books had different variations on this type of relationship but Emma could see her parents in each one.

However, while it was all very well knowing what people were, it was a different kettle of fish altogether figuring out what to do about it. As Emma had long since worked out that she was plain old passive and desperately lacking in self-confidence when it came to her family, there didn't seem to be anything she could do about *their* behaviour.

Her problem was herself, she had realized from Chapter Seven: 'Taking Responsibility For Your Own Mistakes'. There was no use spending hours bitterly contemplating her family's behaviour without changing her own. She let them get away with it. Only she could change things.

'The power is within your own grasp,' said guru Cheyenne Kawada, author of *You Only Have One Life To Lead, So Don't Waste It.*

The problem was that she was two people: with her parents, she was clumsy Emma, the elder, less successful daughter – Kirsten was the prodigal – and the one who'd sidestepped a job in her father's business (the only time she'd ever refused him anything). In the office, she was Emma Sheridan, the much admired Special Projects Co-ordinator of the KrisisKids Charity who had several people working for her and who organized the charity's confidential child phoneline as well as two conferences a year.

Her parents had no idea that the businesslike, organized Emma existed, and certainly nobody at KKC would have recognized the put-upon Emma as their capable boss.

'You sit down, love, let me make the tea,' Jimmy O'Brien was saying manfully to his wife as he rummaged through Emma's tidy cupboards for teabags, sending packets of sauce mixes and a jar of soy sauce flying.

Her mother waved the idea away, as if she was dying for a cup but had heroically decided to say no, like someone refusing a life jacket on the *Titanic*. 'We don't have enough time, Jimmy.'

'We would have time if you hadn't worn yourself to the bone tidying up after this lazy madam.' Slamming the cupboard, Jimmy harrumphed and his entire body shook with the noise. His huge cream jumper-clad frame dwarfed everything in the compact room. He was easily as tall as the pine larder and just as wide, big shoulders and flowing white beard making him a dead ringer for Santa Claus.

Luckily for Anne-Marie O'Brien, she wasn't Mrs Claus to her husband's Santa. Tall but melba toast thin, her hair was a carefully dyed fading gold, worn long but with a front section drawn back from her forehead with a large hairclip that sat at the back of her head like an ossified tortoiseshell beetle. In her floral belted summer dress, she looked as trim as the housewife in a fifties commercial and amazingly youthful. Ten years younger than her husband, Anne-Marie had the clear unwrinkled skin of someone who was utterly sure she was going to heaven in the afterlife, thanks to her goodness and her constant devout prayers. She'd never contemplated whether her love of spreading gossip might hinder her immediate path to the Pearly Gates.

Emma, as tall and slim as her mother but with silky, pale brown hair and a sweet, patient face instead of a smug one, watched tight-lipped as her mother meticulously wiped the chrome-plated toaster and kettle, oblivious to the fact that they needed to be polished with a dry cloth if you didn't want to leave big smeary streaks on them.

Pete's favourite present from their wedding three years ago, the chrome appliances were by far the poshest things in their kitchen. Dear Pete. He always told her to 'turn the other cheek' when her father irritated her. Pete's devout upbringing had equipped him with a biblical quote for every situation in life. He was certainly right this time. No matter how hard it was to stoically turn the other cheek when Jimmy O'Brien's famously sharp tongue carved you up, Emma knew it was the only way to cope. Arguing with her father merely drove him into the white-hot rage of 'I'm only doing this for your own good, madam.'

'Turn the other cheek,' she repeated mantra-like, slipping out of the kitchen. She went upstairs to her and Pete's bedroom. Decorated in a mixture of forest green and warm olive, it was the most masculine room in the house.

Emma had picked the colours herself, determined that the first bedroom she slept in as a married woman would be nothing like the frilled, pink chintz girlie rooms her mother had insisted on in the family home. After a lifetime living with more frills than Scarlett O'Hara's wedding dress, Emma had wanted a room that was comfortingly simple. Pete, so laid back décor-wise that he'd have slept happily in a Wendy house, said he'd like anything Emma chose.

So she'd picked simple olive green curtains, a modern blonde wood bed with its stark green duvet cover and had painted the fitted wardrobe unit that surrounded the bed in cool cream. There wasn't a flounce, a ribbon or a ballerina print in sight. The Flower Fairies drawings her mother had donated 'to brighten the place up' had pride of place in the downstairs loo because Emma never went in there except to clean it.

'Are you coming, Emma?' demanded her father from downstairs.

Picking up her handbag and her suitcase, Emma struggled out on to the landing, with one last fond look at her bedroom. She'd miss it. And Pete. She'd miss cuddling up to him in bed, feeling his solid body spooned against hers. She'd miss his sense of fun and the way he loved her so much. Emma could do no wrong in Pete Sheridan's eyes, which was certainly a change from the way her parents felt about her.

They stood at the bottom of the stairs, one impatient, the other anxious.

'You're not wearing that, Emma?' said her mother in a shrill tone as Emma rounded the bend in the stairs, suitcase in hand.

Instinctively, one hand shot up to her chest, touching the soft denim fabric of her dungarees. Cool and very comfortable, they were ideal for travelling. 'I was wearing this when you came in,' Emma muttered, wishing she didn't feel like a teenager being chastised for wearing PVC hotpants to dinner with the bishop.

She was a thirty-one-year-old married woman, for God's sake! She would not be bullied.

'I thought you'd gone up to change,' sighed her mother in martyred tones. 'I'd prefer to travel looking respectable. I've read that people who dress up for travel are most likely to get upgraded,' she added with a satisfied sniff at the thought of being escorted past the riffraff to a luxury bit of the plane worthy of the O'Briens of the poshest bit of Castleknock.

'Well, you'd better go and put on another outfit, hadn't you? Or we'll be later,' Jimmy said impatiently.

Emma decided not to mention that their chances of being upgraded were non-existent because there was no first class on a charter flight.

Her mother's fantasies about an elegant lifestyle never had the slightest basis in reality, so what was the point?

For a moment, she toyed with the idea of saying she wasn't changing her outfit. But the sight of her father's taut face made up her mind. As she'd learned during her twenty-eight years living under her father's roof, he hated 'butch' clothes and women in trousers.

'I'll just be a moment,' she said with false gaiety and ran back upstairs.

In the bedroom, she got down on her knees and banged her head on the bed. Coward! You decided yesterday that your dungarees were perfect for travelling in. You should have said something!

Still berating herself, Emma fished the little red book out from under her side of the bed and opened it on the affirmation page: 'I am a positive person. I am a good person. My thoughts and feelings are worthwhile and valid.'

Repeating those three phrases over and over again, Emma ripped off her dungarees and T-shirt and pulled on a cream knitted long skirt and tunic she sometimes wore to work in the summer when all her other clothes were in the wash.

Today, all her decent summer clothes were in the suitcase at the bottom of the stairs. Bought on a hateful shopping trip with her mother, the cream knit suit made her look like an anaemic café latte come to life – tall, straight as a schoolboy and colourless.

While the soft blues of her denim clothes made her pale blue eyes with the amber flecks stand out, creams and taupes reduced her face to monotones: pale skin, pale hair, pale bloody everything. She sighed; she felt so boring and colourless.

She'd never been good with make-up and, anyway, lipstick only made her thin lips look even thinner. If only she'd had the courage to have a nose job, Emma thought. Long and too big for her face, it was hideous. Barry Manilow's nose was practically retroussé beside hers. Wearing her fringe long was the only way to hide it. Her sister Kirsten had been blessed with the looks in their family. She was vibrant, sexy and a huge hit with the male of the species who loved her unusual sense of style and her *joie de vivre*. The only unusual thing about Emma was her voice, a low, husky growl that seemed at odds with her conservative, shy image. Pete always told her she could have worked in radio with a voice like that.

'What you mean is that I *sound* like a bombshell so I'd be perfect for radio where people can't see me and realize I'm not one,' she'd tease him.

'You're a bombshell to me,' he'd say lovingly.

'Come on,' roared her father from downstairs. 'We'll be late.'

Emma closed her eyes for a brief moment. The idea of an entire week with her parents made her dizzy. She must have been mad to agree to go with them.

She'd always wanted to go to Egypt and take a Nile cruise, longed to go since she'd first read about the dazzling Queen Nefertiti and the beauty of Karnak Temple as a child. But she'd dreamed of going with Pete, Emma thought miserably, tucking her self-help book into her small handbag.

She hadn't planned to bring *Positive For Life – Your Guide To Increasing Your Self-Esteem* by Dr Barbra Rose with her. She must have been off her rocker. On this trip, she wouldn't simply need the book – she'd need Dr Rose herself, complete with a case packed with the most cutting-edge pharmacology to keep her father in a coma. Now *that* would be the holiday of a lifetime.

Satisfied that her daughter was now suitably dressed and wouldn't disgrace the family en route to the pleasures of the Nile, Anne-Marie O'Brien happily kept up her monologue all the way to the airport: 'You'll never guess who I met this morning,' she said cosily, with not the slightest intention of drawing breath long enough for either Emma or her father to guess. 'Mrs Page. Lord Almighty, if you could have seen the get up she was wearing. Jeans. At her age! I wouldn't have bothered to talk to her at all, but she was beside the toothpaste and I wanted an extra tube in case I can't get any when we're away. I can't imagine the Egyptians will be too keen on the hygiene products,' she added.

Squashed in the back seat of the Opel with the luggage threatening to fall on top of her every time they went round a corner, Emma closed her eyes wearily. Was there any point in explaining that the Egyptians lived in a sophisticated, highly civilized society, built the pyramids and studied astronomy when the O'Brien ancestors were still banging rocks together and trying to figure out how to make things with sharp stones?

'. . . If you'd heard her going on about that Antoinette of hers, well.' Mrs O'Brien's voice registered the fiercest of disapproval. 'Scandalous, that's what it is. Living with that man with two children and not a ring on her finger. Does she not think that those little children deserve the sanctity of marriage instead of being . . .' her voice sank to a whisper, 'illegitimate!'

'Illegitimacy doesn't exist any more.' Emma had to say something. Antoinette was a friend of hers.

'It's all very well for you to say that,' her mother said, 'but it's not right or proper. It's a mockery of the Church and the ceremonies. That girl is making a rod for her own back, mark my words. That man'll up and leave her. She should have got married like normal people do.'

'He's separated, Mum. He can't get married until his divorce comes through.'

'That's more of it, Emma. I can't understand young people today. Does the catechism mean nothing to them? At least your father and I never had any problems like that with you. I told Mrs Page you and Peter were so settled and happy, that Peter is Assistant Sales Director at Devine's Paper Company and that you're Special Projects Co-ordinator.' Pleasure at remembering a most enjoyable bit of boasting made Mrs O'Brien smile.

'He's one of the assistant sales directors, Mum,' Emma said in vexation. 'There are six of them, you know.'

'I didn't say anything wrong,' her mother insisted, tart at being corrected. 'And you are Special Projects Co-ordinator. We are so proud of our little girl, aren't we, Jimmy?'

Her father never took his eyes off the road where he was busily making it a dangerous morning for cyclists. 'We are,' he said absently. 'Very proud. Of both of you. I always knew our Kirsten would do well,' he said happily. 'Chip off the old block there.'

Emma smiled weakly and made a mental note to phone Antoinette Page when she got home to apologize for her mother's insensitive remarks, which would no doubt have filtered through by then. If Anne-Marie O'Brien continued boasting about Peter and Emma's brilliant careers as if they were rocket scientists with matching Porsches and millions in the bank, they wouldn't have a friend left. Pete worked as a salesman in an office-supply company and her job involved huge amounts of exhausting work of the envelope-stuffing-and-organizing-shifts variety rather than swanning around at posh charity lunches, which was the way her mother explained KrisisKids to everyone.

Emma's job was administration rather than fund-raising. She organized the phoneline, which abused or frightened kids could phone anonymously, as well as taking care of the day-to-day running of the KrisisKids office. There *were* glamorous lunches where rich, well-connected ladies paid hundreds of pounds for a ticket, but Emma never went to those functions, to her mother's dismay.

Still, Emma thought, determined to see the positive side of things, it was nice to think that her parents were proud of her, even if they only voiced it when they were trying to lord it over other people, and never to her personally. Naturally, they were prouder of her younger sister Kirsten. It was just as well that Emma adored Kirsten, because a lifetime of hearing how clever/pretty/cute Kirsten was could have destroyed any relationship between the sisters. But they were close, in spite of Jimmy's unwittingly divisive tactics.

'Mrs Page was delighted to hear about Kirsten's new house in Castleknock,' Anne-Marie continued. 'I told her there were five *en suite* bathrooms and that Patrick was driving a . . . oh, what's that car called?'

'Lexus,' Jimmy supplied.

'That's it. "Hasn't she done well for herself?" I said. And I told her Kirsten didn't have to work any more but was involved in raising funds for that environmental project . . .'

Emma could have written a book on her younger sister's achievements as dictated proudly by her mother. Kirsten had managed to pull off the treble whammy of marrying an incredibly rich stockbroker, avoiding seeing her parents except at Christmas, and still being the prodigal daughter all at the same time.

Even though she loved Kirsten and, with only one year between them, they'd grown up almost like twins, Emma was sick and tired of hearing about how wonderful Kirsten's charity work was when she knew for a fact that her sister was only interested in environmental charity on the grounds that she might meet Sting and so that she had something to talk about with the other ladies who lunched when they were teeing up at the ninth. Emma was also fed up with the way Kirsten and Patrick managed to wriggle out of all the Sunday lunches, leaving Pete and herself to suffer through at least seven hours of 'What I Think is Wrong With the World – A Personal View by Jimmy O'Brien' every two weeks. Driving home after the last lunchtime rant against emigrants arriving in Ireland looking for work, Pete had asked Emma if there was such a word as 'pan-got'.

'What's that?' she'd asked merrily, happy in the knowledge that their duty was done for another fortnight.

'A person who's bigoted against everything and everyone. You know, the way "pan" means everything.'

'Probably not until Dad came along, but I'm sure we could tape him and send it into the *Oxford English Dictionary* people,' she suggested. 'Pan-got would be in the next edition, certainly.'

Anne-Marie was fretting as they neared the airport. 'I hope Kirsten will be all right for the week; she told me on the phone that Patrick is going to be away.'

Emma raised her eyes to heaven. In direct contrast to herself, Kirsten was one of life's survivors. Put her on the north face of the Eiger with nothing but a tent and a jar of Bovril and she'd turn up twenty-four hours later with a tan from skiing, lots of new clothes and a host of phone numbers from all the other interesting people she'd met en route, who'd all have yachts, villas in Gstaad, personal trainers and Rolexes. A week without Patrick meant Kirsten would have carte blanche to go mad with her gold card in Brown Thomas's and would end up knocking back vodka tonics in some nightclub every evening, with a besotted admirer in tow. Emma didn't think her sister had been unfaithful to her stolid and reliable husband, but she certainly enjoyed flirting with other men.

'She'll be fine, Mum,' Emma said drily.

At the airport, her father let them off outside the departures hall with all the luggage and then drove off to find a parking spot. Anne-Marie went into fuss mode immediately: tranquil when her husband was there and bossing everyone around, she became anxious and hyper as soon as he was out of sight.

'My glasses,' she said suddenly as she and Emma joined the slow-moving queue at the check-in desk. 'I don't think I brought them!'

The note of rising hysteria in her mother's voice made Emma gently take her hand and pat it comfortingly. 'Will I look in your handbag, Mum?' she said.

Anne-Marie nodded and thrust the small cream leather bag at her. The glasses were in the side compartment in their worn tapestry case, blindingly obvious if only her mother had looked.

'They were here all the time, Mum.'

Her mother's anxiety faded a little. 'I'm sure I've forgotten something,' she said. Closing her eyes as if running through a mental list, she was silent for a minute. 'Have you forgotten something?' she said abruptly.

Emma shook her head.

'Sanitary stuff and things like that,' her mother hissed, sotto voce. 'Who knows what you'll be able to buy out there. I bet you forgot. I should have got some for you this morning in the supermarket, but that Mrs Page took my mind quite off what I was doing . . .'

Emma tried to tune out, but her mother's words mocked her. Sanitary stuff. She probably should have brought tampons with her but had hoped it would be tempting fate to bring them.

Her period was due in four days and maybe it wouldn't come this time. This could be it: pregnant! She'd been so tired all week and she was sure her nipples felt sensitive, the way her pregnancy book said they would. They never felt like that normally. So she'd been reckless and left all her period paraphernalia out of her suitcase, hadn't brought even one single tampon or pair of heavy-duty, enormous knickers in case they would bring her bad luck. Emma allowed herself a little quiver of excitement at the thought.

When her father marched up to them, giving out yards about how far away he'd had to park the car, Emma managed to look sympathetic.

'All set then?' he asked. 'Let's queue.'

He put one arm round his wife. 'Egypt, eh? This will be a holiday to remember, Anne-Marie, love. I just wish dear Kirsten could have come along. She'd love it and she's the best company in the world. Still, she's busy with her charity work and looking after Patrick.' He sighed a fond father sort of sigh and Emma started nibbling the thumbnail she'd managed to leave alone up to now.

Calm down, she repeated to herself, using the broken-record technique so beloved of her self-help books. Don't let him get to you. She could cope with him when she had this wonderful feeling of hope lighting her up from the inside. A baby. She had to be pregnant this time, she just knew it.

CHAPTER THREE

Penny lay on the bed with a half-chewed teddy squashed between her golden paws and stared at Leonie balefully. It was hard to imagine that those huge brown eyes could portray anything other than pure canine love but then, Penny was not your average dog. Half-Labrador, half-retriever, she was all personality. Most of it human and all calculated to cause her owner the most guilt possible. Only her frenzied excitement at the rattle of her dinner bowl made Leonie realize that her best friend was actually a dog and not a person. Then again, Leonie thought with amusement, why did she confer ravenousness as purely doggy behaviour? She ate like a pig herself. Dogs and owners invariably looked alike so if Penny was a slightly overweight little glutton who was a slave to Pedigree Chum, then her owner was a carbon copy. A large shaggy blonde with a fat tummy and a propensity for biscuits. Just exchange Mr Chum for Mr Kipling and they were twins.

Leonie extracted an ancient khaki sarong from the back of the cupboard and rolled it into a corner of her suitcase alongside a selection of her trademark exotically coloured silk shirts. Penny, watching sulkily from the bed, snorted loudly.

'I know, Honey Bunny,' Leonie said consolingly, stopping packing to sit on the edge of the bed and stroke her inconsolable dog. 'I won't be long. It's only eight days. Mummy won't be away for long. And you wouldn't like Egypt, darling. It's too hot anyway.'

Penny, seven years of abject devotion and huge amounts of spoiling behind her, refused to be comforted and jerked her head away from Leonie's gentle hand. Another little snort indicated that mere petting wouldn't be enough and that doggy biscuits might have to be involved if she was to be satisfactorily cheered up.

Leonie – who'd only the previous morning told a Pekinese-owning client in the veterinary practice where she worked as a nurse, that dogs were terrible blackmailers and that little Kibushi shouldn't be given human food no matter how much he begged at the table at mealtimes – hurried into the kitchen for a Mixed Oval and half a digestive biscuit.

Like a Persian potentate receiving gifts, Penny graciously accepted both biscuits, got crumbs all over the flowery duvet as she crunched them and immediately went back to sulking. One paw flattening Teddy ominously, she stared at Leonie crossly, her usually smiling Labrador face creased into a look that said, *I'm phoning the ISPCA now, and then where will you be? Up in court on charges of cruelty to animals, that's where. Imagine abandoning me for a crappy holiday.*

'Maybe I shouldn't go,' Leonie said in despair, thinking that she couldn't possibly leave Penny, Clover and Herman for eight whole days. Penny would waste away, despite being cared for by Leonie's adoring mother, Claire, who let her sleep on the bed all the time and fed her carefully cooked lambs' liver.

But Leonie's three children had gone to stay with their father in the States for three weeks and Leonie had vowed to give herself the holiday of a lifetime just to cheer herself up. She couldn't let herself be blackmailed by spoiled animals. Really, she couldn't.

Clover, Leonie's beloved marmalade cat, didn't get on with Claire's cats, hated the cattery and would no doubt lurk miserably at the back of her quarters for the entire visit, going on feline hunger strike, determined to look like an anorexic for her owner's return. And even Herman, the children's rescued hamster, went into a decline when his luxury hamster duplex was moved into Claire's home. All right, so Claire's three Siamese cats had an unnatural interest in little Hermie and did spend many hours staring at his Perspex home in a very calculating manner as if figuring out exactly how yummy he'd taste once they'd worked out how to open the trap door, but still . . . it wasn't abandonment.

Nevertheless Leonie felt guilty leaving her beloved babies while she went cruising down the Nile in the luxury of an inside cabin on the *Queen Tiye* (single supplement £122, Abu Simbel excursion and Valley of the Kings dawn balloon trip extra, bookable in advance).

'I shouldn't go,' she said again.

Penny, sensing weakness, wagged her tail a fraction and smiled winsomely. For good measure, she pounced on Teddy and chewed him in a playfully endearing way. *How could you leave cute, adorable me*? she said, her degree in Manipulation of Humans coming to the fore.

What was the point? Leonie wondered, weakening. She could have her eight days off at home and make herself tackle the bit of overgrown garden down by the river. Why own an artisan's cottage on an eighth of an acre in County Wicklow's scenic Greystones if you let the garden run to rack and ruin with enough floral wildlife for a butterfly sanctuary?

And she could paint the cupboards in the kitchen. She'd been meaning to do that for the entire seven years they'd lived there. She hated dark wood, always had.

Oh yes, and she could clean out Danny's bedroom. He and the girls had been in Boston for nearly ten days already and she hadn't yet touched his pit. No doubt the usual teenage debris was festering beneath his bed: socks that smelled like mouldy cheese and old T-shirts that had enough human DNA on them in the form of sweat to be used for cloning. The girls' room was perfect because Abby had been overcome with a fit of tidiness one afternoon before they'd left and had forced Mel to help her clean up. Together they'd filled a bin-bag with old *Mizz* magazines, cuddly toys that even Penny no longer wanted to chew, old pens with no lids and copybooks with half the pages torn out. As a consequence, their room looked so tidy it was unlikely to be identified as the bedroom of two pop star obsessed fourteen-year-olds – apart from the dog-eared poster of Robbie Williams that Mel had refused to be parted from.

'Don't get upset, Mum,' Abby had said when Leonie had looked into the bedroom and blurted out that it looked as if the girls were leaving forever and not coming back. 'We'll only be away with Dad for just over three weeks. You'll be having such a whale of a time in Egypt and out every night drinking and flirting with handsome men that you won't notice we're gone.'

'I know,' Leonie lied, feeling terribly foolish and sorry she'd broken her golden rule about not letting the children know how terrible it was for her when they spent time with their father. It wasn't that she begrudged Ray time with his children: not at all. She simply missed them so much when they were staying with him and Boston seemed such a long way away. At least when he'd lived in Belfast, it had only been a couple of hours away from Dublin. Leonie wouldn't have dreamed of gatecrashing her children's visit with their father, but she was always comforted by the idea that if she wanted to see them on a whim during the month-long summer holiday, she could.

That was partly why she was off to Egypt on a holiday she couldn't really afford: to stave off the pangs of loneliness while the kids were away. That and because she had to break out of the cycle of her humdrum existence. An exotic holiday away seemed like a good starting point for a new, exotic life. Or at least it *had*.

The phone on her bedside table rang loudly. Leonie sat on the bed and picked up the receiver, straightening the silver-framed picture of herself and Danny beside the roller coaster at EuroDisney as she did so. Nineteen-year-olds didn't go on holidays with their mothers any more, she reminded herself, knowing there'd be no more holidays with the four of them ever again.

'I hope you're not having second thoughts,' bellowed a voice down the phone. Anita. Loud, lovable and bossier than a First Division football manager, Leonie's oldest friend could speak in only two volumes: pitch-side screech and stage whisper, both of which could be heard from fifty yards away.

'You need a break and, seeing as you won't come to West Cork with the gang, I think Egypt's perfect. But don't let that damn dog put you off.'

Leonie grinned. 'Penny's very depressed,' she admitted, 'and I have been having second thoughts about going on a trip on my own.'

'And waste your money?' roared Anita, a coupon-snipping mother of four who'd re-use teabags if she could get away with it.

Leonie knew she couldn't bear another holiday in the big rented bungalow with 'the gang', as Anita called the group who'd been together for over twenty years since they'd met up as newlyweds all in Sycamore Lawns. Gangs were fine when you were part of it in happy coupledom, but when you were divorced and everyone else was still in happy coupledom, it wasn't as easy.

Being the only single member of the gang was sheer hell and would be worse now that Tara (briefly unattached) had remarried and was no longer keen on sharing a room with Leonie where they could moan about the pain of singledom and the lack of decent men. After last year's group holiday where one husband had surprised her with a drunken French kiss and an 'I've always thought you were a goer' grope in the kitchen late one night, Leonie had promised herself never again.

When she and Ray had split up ten years ago, she'd been so hopeful about her future. After a decade of a companionable but practically fraternal marriage, they'd both been hopeful of the future. But Ray was the one who'd come through it all with flying colours, happy with his string of girlfriends, and Leonie was still longing for the one true love who'd make it all worthwhile.

She hadn't been on a date for six years and that had been a blind one Anita had fixed up with a college lecturer who was a dead ringer – in every sense – for Anthony Perkins in *Psycho*. Needless to say, it hadn't been a success.

'Leonie, there's always a bed for you in West Cork,' Anita interrupted. 'We'd all love to have you with us again, and if you're having second thoughts –'

'Only kidding,' Leonie said hurriedly. 'I'm looking forward to it, honest. I've always wanted to go to Egypt. I can't wait to buy some marvellous Egyptian jewellery,' she added with genuine enthusiasm. Her collection of exotic costume jewellery took up most of her crowded dressing table already, filigree earrings tangled up with jangling metal Thai necklaces, most of it purchased in ethnic shops in Dublin and London instead of in their original, far-flung homelands.

'Watch those souks and markets though,' warned Anita, a distrustful traveller who believed that anywhere beyond the English Channel was off the beaten track. 'They love big women in the East, you know.'

'Oooh, goodie,' growled Leonie, instinctively reverting to the Leonie Delaney: wild, sexy, earth goddess image she'd been projecting for years. If Anita guessed that the image was all fake and that most of Leonie's hot dates were at home with the remote control and a carton of strawberry shortcake ice cream, she never said anything.

After a few more minutes' chat where Leonie promised to enjoy herself, she hung up, privately thinking that if any white-slave trader wanted to whisk her away to a life of sexual servitude, he'd have to be bloody strong. At five eight and fifteen stone, she was hardly dancing harem girl material and was powerful enough to flatten the most ardent Egyptian bottom-pincher.

Anita was sweet to say it, she thought later, examining the effect of her saffron Indian skirt worn with her favourite black silk shirt and a coiled necklace of tiny amber beads. Black wasn't really suitable for travelling to a hot country, she knew that, but she felt so much more comfortable wearing it. Nothing could hide her size, Leonie knew, but black camouflaged it.

Rich colours suited her and she loved to wear them: flowing tunics of opulent crimsons, voluminous capes in soft purple velvet and ankle-length skirts decorated with Indian mirrors and elaborate embroidery in vibrant shades. Like an aristocratic fortune-teller or a showily elegant actress from thirties Broadway, Leonie's style of dressing could never be ignored. But black was still her favourite. Safe and familiar. As satisfied as she'd ever be with her reflection, she started on her face, applying the heavy panstick make-up expertly.

If she hadn't been a veterinary nurse, Leonie would have loved to have been a make-up artist. She hadn't been blessed with a pretty face, but when she'd worked her magic with her pencils and her brushes and her eyes were hypnotically ringed with deep kohl, she felt she looked mysterious and exotic. Like the girl in those old Turkish Delight adverts who sat waiting in the dunes for her sheikh. Certainly not too big, too old and too scared of a lonely, manless future.

Her mouth was a lovely cupid's bow that would have looked fabulous on some petite size-eight model but seemed slightly incongruous on a tall solid woman 'A fine hoult of a woman,' as one of the old men who brought his sheepdog into the vet's used to call her admiringly.

Her face was rounded with cheekbones she adored because, no matter how fat she got, they stayed defiantly obvious, saving her face from descending into plumpness. Her hair, naturally rat-coloured as she always said, was golden from home dyeing because she couldn't really afford to have it done professionally any more.

But Leonie's most beautiful features were her eyes. Huge, naturally dark-lashed, they were the same stunning aquamarine as the Adriatic and looked too blue to be real.

'Your eyes make you beautiful,' her mother would say encouragingly when she was growing up. 'You don't need to speak, Leonie, your eyes do it for you.'

Her mother's attitude had always been that you were whatever you wanted to be. Glamorous herself, Claire told her daughter that stunning looks came from the inside.

Unfortunately, Leonie had decided at the age of nineteen that her mother was wrong and that lovely eyes weren't enough to make her the beautiful woman she longed to be, a Catherine Deneuve lookalike. This realization had come about when she went to college after years of being educated in the closeted female environment of the convent school. At University College Dublin, she discovered men for the first time. And also discovered that the ones she fancied in biology lectures were much more keen on her less intelligent but smaller classmates. Her long-distance paramours asked Leonie if she'd join in their Rag Week mixed tug-of-war team, and asked other girls to go to the Rag Ball with them.

Miserably, she concluded that she was nothing more than a plain, fat girl. Which was why she'd decided to reinvent herself. Leonie Murray, shy girl who was always at the back at school photographs, had become the splendidly eccentric Leonie, lover of unusual clothes, wacky jewellery and plenty of war paint applied as if she was ready for her close up, Mr De Mille. As she was physically larger than life,

Leonie decided to become literally larger than life. Vivacious, lively and great fun, she was invited to all the best parties but never asked to go outside for a snog on the terrace.

Her first and only true love, Ray, had seen beneath the layer of Max Factor panstick to see the deeply insecure woman she really was. But she and Ray just weren't meant to be. Their marriage had been a mistake. She'd been grateful to be rescued from loneliness, and being grateful was no reason to get married, as she knew now. Neither was being pregnant. Sometimes she felt guilty because she'd married him for all the wrong reasons and then she'd ended it, after ten years of marriage.

They'd been opposites, she and Ray. He was a quiet arts student who'd never gone to wild parties and who spent every spare minute in the library. Leonie had been the *grande dame* of first-year science. While Ray was reading Rousseau, Leonie was reading the riot act to the impertinent agricultural student who'd teased her about her heavy make-up. (She'd cried over that later but, at the time, she'd been magnificent.)

They met at a screening of *Annie Hall* and ended up spending the evening together laughing at Woody Allen's humour. In the later years of their marriage, Leonie realized that a sense of humour and a love of Woody Allen movies was one of the few things they'd actually shared. Otherwise, they were poles apart. Ray liked non-fiction, political discussions and avoiding parties. Leonie loved going out, disco dancing and reading potboilers with a glass of wine and a Cadbury's Flake in her hand. It wouldn't have lasted but for advance warning that baby Danny was coming in seven months. They got married quickly and were blissfully happy until the honeymoon wore off and they discovered just how unsuited they really were.

It was a testimony to something, Leonie always thought, that they went through another ten years of being civilized and kind to each other, even though there were more sparks in the fridge than there were in their relationship. She'd lived with the knowledge for a long time, enduring it and the barrenness that was her marriage for the sake of Danny, Melanie and Abigail. But finally, something had snapped in Leonie and she knew she had to get out. She felt suffocated, as if she was slowly dying and wasting her life at the same time. There had to be *more*, she knew it.

She didn't know how she found the courage to sit Ray down and ask him what he thought about them splitting up. 'I love you, Ray, but we're both trapped,' she'd said, given Dutch courage by two hot ports. 'We're like brother and sister, not husband and wife. One day, you'll meet someone or I'll meet someone and then this will turn into a nuclear war of retribution, you fighting me and vice versa. We'll hate each other and we'll destroy the kids. Do you want that? Shouldn't we both be honest about this instead of kidding each other?'

It had been a tough time. Ray had insisted that he was happy, that their way of muddling along suited him. 'I'm not a romantic like you, Leonie, I don't expect great love or anything,' he'd said sorrowfully. 'We're happy enough, aren't we?'

Once the doubts were out in the open, it was as if the wound couldn't heal. Gradually, Ray and Leonie drifted apart until, finally, he had said she was right, it was a half-marriage. He'd shocked her by how quickly he found another life, but she was too busy trying to explain things to three uncomprehending children to think about it. Away from her, he'd blossomed. He had scores of friends, went on interesting holidays and changed jobs. He went on dates, bought trendy clothes and introduced the kids to his girlfriends. Leonie had worked hard, looked after the kids and hoped that Mr Right knew he could safely step into her world now that she was a single woman again. So far, zilch.

As she told Penny sometimes : 'I should have stayed married and had affairs. *That* was the right way to do it! True love and romance with a safety net. Trust me to get it wrong trying to do it right.'

She and Ray were still the best of friends and he was a good father.

Now the only people who saw Leonie as she really was were her three children.

With them, she only wore two coats of mascara and a bit of lipstick and they were allowed to see her in her dressing gown. God, she missed them.

Determined not to blub over the kids again, Leonie thought of how she'd always wanted to visit magical Egypt. Fear of flying was no reason to cry off. For a start, she couldn't afford to waste the money the holiday had cost her and, secondly, when did Leonie Delaney balk at anything? She got out her eyeliner brush and fiercely painted on a thick line of dusky kohl that'd have made Cleopatra proud.

How could you jump-start your life if you quailed at the very first fence – a holiday on your own?

CHAPTER FOUR

Four hours later, Leonie stood in the queue at the airport clutching her guide book to her chest and wishing the plane journey was over. Ever since she'd seen that disaster movie about the guys in the Peruvian mountains who'd had to resort to cannibalism to survive after a plane crash, she'd hated flying. Loathed it.

'I'll give you some ketamine for the trip,' joked Angie the previous day, referring to the heavy-duty animal tranquillizer.

'I'd almost take it,' Leonie had replied, not joking. She'd bought a bottle of herbal relaxant tablets, her travel sickness wrist-bands and some aromatherapy oil to rub on her temples, but she still felt more stressed than Mrs Reilly's hyperactive cat when it was getting its claws clipped. A lovely, sweet animal in the home – or so Mrs Reilly regularly assured them immediately after Sootie had mauled somebody – the five-year-old tabby was labelled 'dangerous' in the surgery. Heavy gloves and sedation were required to calm Sootie before even the simplest job. Leonie wished that cabin crew sedated their patients.

She pushed her trolley further along the queue and looked at the other passengers taking Flight MS634 to Luxor. Nobody else appeared to be sweating with fear. Especially not the very slim woman at the front of the queue who had the nervous expression of a purebred Saluki hound. Long, silky, light brown hair that fell over her big saucer-like eyes added to the effect. In an unflattering cream knit outfit, she looked terribly thin and unhappy. She must have been about thirty, Leonie guessed, but she carried herself with the unease of a teenager going on a hated family holiday when she longed to be at home.

An older woman, obviously her mother, stood beside her talking animatedly. The older woman was wearing a very old-fashioned floral dress, the sort of thing Leonie's rather Bohemian mother would have refused to wear years ago because she might have to wear gloves or a pill-box hat with it. A giant of a man with a beard appeared beside them and started arguing with the girl behind the airline counter, his booming voice easily audible along the length of the queue as he roared.

'I'd make a complaint to you, young lady, but I don't see the point,' he thundered at the airline girl. 'I've made my feelings more than plain to the travel people. You mark my words, they won't be taking advantage of me.'

The Saluki Woman looked away, eyes wide with embarrassment, and caught sight of Leonie gazing at her. Abashed, Leonie looked down at her trolley. She loved people-watching but hated being caught. Figuring out what they did and what sort of people they were from peering into their trolleys in the supermarket was her favourite hobby, and she couldn't sit on the train into Dublin for longer than five minutes without speculating on the relationship between the passengers sitting opposite her. Were they married, going out, about to break up? Did the woman with a trolley full of Häagen-Dazs chocolate chip but a figure like Kate Moss actually *eat* any of the ice cream or did she have a fat portrait of herself in the attic?

Up ahead, the woman at the desk said 'Next' with a relieved voice. When the difficult trio finally walked back down the queue after checking in, Leonie kept her eyes averted but risked a surreptitious glance at the younger woman.

As she walked past, carefully stowing her travel documents into a sleek little handbag that wouldn't have held a quarter of Leonie's cosmetic junk, Leonie noticed that the Saluki Woman had pink varnished nails which had been bitten down to the stubs. She looked resolutely ahead, as if she knew the entire queue had heard the argument and was terrified of making eye contact with anyone. Definitely not keen on holidaying with the parents, Leonie decided.

The queue shuffled forward and, with nobody interesting to gaze at, Leonie toyed with the idea of skipping off and driving home. Nobody would have to know: well, her mother would, because that would be her first port of call, to take her beloved Penny and the animals home. But nobody else had to know.

Meaning Anita. Safely on the way to West Cork, Anita wouldn't be in Wicklow for another three weeks and would remain oblivious that her flamboyant, outwardly dauntless, divorced forty-two-year-old friend had cried off from her first single holiday ever because of fear of flying.

'I'm going to the loo. I won't be long,' said a soft female voice behind her.

'I'll miss you,' answered a male voice.

'Oh,' sighed the woman. 'I love you.'

'Love you too,' answered the man.

Newlyweds, Leonie realized wistfully.

She pretended to look around her in boredom and got a glimpse of a young couple kissing gently before the woman, wearing a virginal pale pink short cotton dress that wasn't exactly suitable for travelling in, hurried off in the direction of the toilets, looking back at her husband all the time, giving him sweet little waves and smiling with sheer joy.

He smiled back at her, one hand holding two suitcases on which some joker had written 'Mr & Mrs Smith' in sprawling white Tippex letters.

Had she ever been that happy and that much in love, Leonie wondered, turning back and gazing blankly at the rest of the queue. She didn't think so. Surely she deserved it. Wasn't there someone out there for her, someone who couldn't bear to let her off to the loo without kissing her goodbye and telling her to be careful? There must be. And she wouldn't find him sitting at home weeding the garden. She gave her trolley a determined shove along the slowly diminishing queue. Egypt here we come.

They'd put her in 56C, a window seat at the back of the plane. Leonie winced as she sat down in it and looked longingly at the two empty seats beside her. If only she could swap with one of the other people. But what if they didn't want to move? Hating herself for being so nervous, Leonie peered down the aisle and looked for a stewardess she could accost and ask about changing seats. Instead, she saw a graceful woman striding towards her, confident and slim in jeans and a white T-shirt with a navy cotton cardigan slung casually over her shoulders.

She held her small holdall aloft so she wouldn't bump into anything, but when she collided with a large man shoving a bag into the overhead locker, the woman gave him a dazzling smile, flicked back her long nutbrown hair, and strode on. The man's eyes followed her, taking in the gentle sway of her slim hips and long, long legs. She was aware of his gaze, Leonie was sure of it, from the small smile that tilted up the corners of her full mouth as she progressed up the plane. She looked perfectly elegant and brimming with confidence, the sort of woman who was born to go on a Nile cruise, from the tips of her spotlessly clean deck shoes to the designer sunglasses perched on top of her head. When Leonie stuck her sunglasses on her head, they inevitably fell off.

The woman reached row 56 and smiled in a friendly manner at Leonie, who decided to take the bull by the horns.

'I did ask not to get a window seat,' she gasped up at the glamorous brunette, fear at having to look out the window overcoming her hatred of being a nuisance.

'You can have mine,' the woman said in a gentle voice with just a hint of a West of Ireland accent. 'I hate the middle seat.'

They swapped and Leonie smelled a heady waft of Obsession perfume as the woman arranged herself in the window seat, put on a pair of tortoiseshell glasses, took a very serious-looking guide book from her small bag and settled back to read it. No wedding ring, Leonie noticed. Perhaps she was travelling alone too and they could team up. Leonie felt very grateful to be sitting beside this nice woman. Everything was going to work out.

She tried to relax and peered out of the window from the comfort of the middle seat. She could see the baggage handlers hoisting giant suitcases on to the conveyor belt to the plane's hold.

Practically everyone was on board before anyone arrived at the seats in front of them. Leonie, by now bored looking at the baggage handlers because she could imagine them shaking all her clothes and make-up to bits, watched the late arrivals. The family she'd observed earlier were marching up the aisle towards her. The younger woman came first, her too-long fringe and her downcast eyes ensuring she didn't meet anyone's gaze as she shoved a small rucksack into the overhead bin and sank quickly into the window seat. Behind her came the other pair. Leonie grimaced. From the performance she'd seen at the check-in desk, she could imagine the fun and games they'd have on the flight with Mr Conviviality himself.

'Number 55B,' muttered the older woman. 'There we are. Maybe I should sit on the window seat.'

Silently, the girl got up and let her mother into the seat. She appeared to be waiting to see if her father wanted to sit beside her mother.

'Get in, Emma,' snapped the big man impatiently.

'Sorry,' the girl murmured, 'I just thought . . .'

'Do you want me to put your bag up, Anne-Marie?' he interrupted her rudely.

'No, well, let me see,' began the older woman, 'I'll want my glasses and my tablets and . . .'

Leonie looked out the window again. Family life, what a pain. When she was that age, she wouldn't have gone on holiday with her mother and father for all the tea in China. That girl must be mad – or simple.

When the plane finally took off, Leonie closed her eyes with terror; Hannah closed her eyes and grinned at the memory of Jeff's powerful lovemaking, which was certainly as uplifting as the thrust of a jumbo; and Emma sucked a mint, feeling calmer because of the half a Valium she'd taken in the loo beforehand. She tried to get comfortable but it was hard because her father was taking up a huge amount of space on purpose.

Half a Valium couldn't harm the baby, she hoped, but her father was in a terrible mood and was determined to make everyone else suffer too. Emma had seen several people watching them in the queue when he'd argued furiously with the poor check-in girl over not being able to smoke his pipe on the flight. It was going to be a hellish holiday if he behaved like that the whole time. Why, oh why had she come?

Hannah sank gratefully on to a seat in the air-conditioned bus and decided that the only way she'd ever be cool in Luxor was if she went around naked with a bag of ice strapped to her body. It was half six in the evening and she was roasting after just fifteen minutes outside the airport. She'd have escaped to the cool of the Incredible Egypt tour bus more quickly had it not been for the two porters in Arab dress who fought volubly over who got to haul her suitcase over to the bus.

'Great double act, guys,' she grinned at them, giving them each a tip.

It must be eighty degrees at least and it was nearly pitch-dark. Who knew how hot it'd be during the day. She fanned herself with the itinerary the tour guide had handed out as she greeted her party of thirty-two travellers.

'Make your way to the bus and I'll finish rounding our gang up,' the tour guide had said brightly as she pointed people in the direction of the buses waiting like gleaming silver monsters in the shimmering heat.

Fresh as a daisy in a royal blue cotton blouse and cream shorts, the tour guide was a young woman named Flora who exuded calm efficiency. She'd need to be calm to deal with that horrible man who'd sat in the row ahead on the plane, Hannah thought. He'd complained throughout the journey, saying the meal was cold when it should have been hot and demanding to know if they'd get a refund for taking off an hour late. What a bully, she thought with disgust.

He'd been rude as hell to the sweet, dark-eyed stewardess who'd haltingly told him they didn't serve any sort of alcohol on the flight, and during the scramble for visas in the arrivals hall in Luxor, only the deaf would have been spared his sarcastic comments about Egyptian inefficiency.

'Call this an airport?' he'd roared when the crowds from the plane began milling around the arrivals hall, looking for their tour guides, trying to change money and queuing for visas in disorganized groups. 'It's a bloody disgrace asking Westerners to come into this sort of makeshift place. No signs, no authority, no proper air conditioning, nothing! No wonder these fellas were ruled by foreign powers for so long – couldn't arrange a piss-up in a brewery, if you ask me. I'll tell you, I'll be writing a letter to the *Irish Times* and the Egyptian embassy when I get back.'

Hannah couldn't figure out why he'd bothered coming to a foreign country if all he was going to do was whinge about the heat and make racist and jingoistic comments about the inhabitants.

Taking a gulp from her bottle of mineral water, she watched sweating people haul themselves up the bus steps, panting heavily and repeating 'It's hot!' to each other every few minutes.

'It's hot,' gasped her large blonde next-door neighbour from the plane as she shoved her canvas holdall into the luggage rack and flopped heavily on to the seat beside Hannah.

'That's what we get for not listening to the travel agent who warned it was unbearably hot in August,' Hannah said with a grin.

'Did they say that?' The woman rummaged around in a bulging black suede handbag until she triumphantly extracted a small orange juice carton. She stuck the tiny plastic straw in, drank deeply and then said: 'Mine never mentioned the heat. I just said I could only travel in August and they booked it for me. My kids are away for August, you see. I'm Leonie,' she added.

'Nice to meet you. I'm Hannah.'

Leonie knew her face was pinker than usual, while her shaggy blonde hair was frizzing in the Gas Mark 7 dry heat. On the plane, Leonie had barely talked to her neighbour at all because she'd been desperately trying to concentrate on reading a thriller for the whole flight, hoping that she'd forget the fact that she was on a plane at all if she could immerse herself in a book. Safely on terra firma, she was all talk, loquacious with relief. Hannah didn't look hot at all: she looked as if she was used to the sort of temperatures that could cook a chicken out of doors.

'Wasn't it mad in there,' Leonie said, referring to the arrivals hall. 'These men kept taking my case and trying to stick it on their trolley and I kept having to take it back. I think I ruptured something dragging it off the last time.' She massaged her shoulder.

'They're porters and they're hoping for a tip if they bring your luggage out for you,' Hannah explained.

'Oh. I never thought of that. But I've no Egyptian money yet,' Leonie pointed out. 'I'm going to change currencies on the boat.'

She began fiddling around in her bag to check for her purse, giving Hannah an opportunity to study her. Leonie's uptilted nose was strangely childlike, Hannah decided, and her make-up was a bit heavy for the torrid heat of North Africa. But nothing could hide the vibrancy of Leonie's lively, animated face, which displayed a thousand emotions as she spoke. She wasn't pretty but there was such warmth in her expression that it made her strangely attractive. And her eyes were the most amazing blue, glittering like Ceylon sapphires. Hannah had never seen anybody with such piercingly blue eyes apart from models in glossy magazines advertising coloured contact lenses. Leonie's eyes could have been the result of coloured contact lenses, of course, but Hannah bet her life they weren't. If only she wasn't wearing all that panstick foundation and the heavy eyeliner. It was like stage make-up, a façade behind which she was trying to hide. Hannah smiled to herself. Everyone hid something. She'd been successfully hiding her lack of education for years.

'It'd be lovely if we could have dinner together, maybe,' Leonie was saying, hating herself for chattering away like a blackbird on acid. Terrified at the idea of being away on her own without a single friendly face to talk to, she was thrilled that she'd identified a fellow solo female traveller. But she didn't want to come across as too lonely or too needy: Hannah, who seemed very self-possessed and assured, might not want a holiday companion. 'If you don't mind having dinner with me, that is . . .' Leonie said, her voice fading.

'Course not,' said Hannah, who was perfectly happy on her own but felt oddly protective about the other woman, who was probably five nine in her socks and at least twice Hannah's size. 'It's lovely to have company and we'll be much safer from exotic, handsome Egyptians if we're together. Or is it the male population who should be frightened of us?' she joked.

Leonie laughed and looked ruefully at her sturdy body. 'I think I'm quite safe enough and the male population needn't worry.' For once, she hadn't felt the need to make some crack about men and how she couldn't live without them. Those stupid remarks were only ever covering up her insecurities and she cringed hearing herself say them. Today, she hadn't felt the need to pretend. Hannah was nice, calming. It'd be lovely sharing the holiday with her.

The bad-tempered bearded man, his wife and daughter got on the bus and plonked themselves at the front. Hannah and Leonie watched the trio with interest as the father kept up a critical monologue while his wife fanned herself weakly with a ridiculously out of place Spanish fan. Her long fair hair held back from her forehead was rather girlish for a woman of her age, as if she was acting the ingénue, while her tight-waisted, wide-skirted dress made her look vaguely as if she'd entered a fancy dress competition. She looked displeased, as if Egypt had been examined briefly and found seriously wanting. The daughter sat silently in the seat behind them, her face pale and her expression distant.

'I hope to God we don't end up with cabins anywhere near them,' Leonie whispered fervently. 'They look like the sort of people who complain if they don't have something to complain about.'

'The father certainly does,' Hannah agreed, 'but the person I feel sorry for is the daughter. Imagine being stuck with a loudmouthed tyrant like that.'

Watching the younger woman's taut little face, Hannah was convinced it was sheer embarrassment at her father's behaviour that made her look so distant. 'She looks as if she's going to cry any minute. Maybe we should get her to sit with us,' Hannah suggested, overcome with a desire to save another lame dog, now she'd already saved one.

Leonie winced. 'I'm not so sure . . .' she said. 'What if the other pair insist on making friends with us too and we get stuck with the lot of them for the entire cruise?'

'Leonie,' reproved Hannah, 'you've got to live a little, experiment. Anyway, we'll all end up sitting at tables of six or eight for meals on the boat, so if we're allocated one with them, we're stuck anyway.'

* * *

It was dark as the bus drove through the streets of Luxor on its way to the boat. Flora sat at the front, pointing out sights and welcoming them all to Egypt.

'You'll have a busy week,' she explained, 'because many of the tours start very early in the morning. We make early starts because the temples and sights get very busy with busloads of tourists during the day, and also because it's cooler to sightsee in the early morning. But tomorrow you can have a lie-in as the boat sails to Edfu for the first visit which is after lunch. We'll have a welcome meeting in the bar tonight at –' she consulted her watch '– half eight, which is in an hour, and I'll go through the itinerary. Dinner is at nine.'

Hannah and Leonie peered out the window at the darkened, dusty streets, gazing at the one- and two-storey mudbrick dwellings which looked so different from anything at home. Many looked unfinished, as if another storey was to be built but everyone had lost interest. Scattered among these rural homes were palm trees and, far away from the road, luxuriant green crops could be seen growing several feet tall.

As they drove nearer to the lights of Luxor, Leonie noticed a solitary donkey leaning against a shed roofed with straw. He looked very thin, Leonie thought with a pang of pity. She could see his ribs sticking out painfully. She hoped she wouldn't see animals being treated cruelly: it was bad enough at home seeing homeless dogs brought into the surgery after being hit by cars. At least she could do something for them at home, but here, she wasn't a veterinary nurse: she was just a tourist.

A vision of Penny came to her, suddenly; those melting chocolate eyes filled with abject misery at being left behind. Leonie missed her desperately; she missed all the animals she loved. Poor Clover locked away in the cattery, and little Herman, watched endlessly by her mother's ravenous cats. And she felt so far away from the kids. At least Ireland was nearer to Boston than here. Just a phone call away. Egypt was two continents away and she'd be travelling so they'd never be able to track her down. What if something happened and Ray couldn't reach her and . . .

Stop it, she commanded. Nothing's going to happen. Trying to put portents of gloom out of her mind, Leonie stared out the windows as the countryside gave way to straggly city streets with more traffic. Dust rose up into the air from the other vehicles on the road: battered Ladas with TAXI signs on them and stately old station wagons in bright colours, encrusted with dust. Electric signs in exotic Arabic shone over small shops and cafés, with bright English-language signs over the myriad souvenir shops.

Every few yards, she could see small groups of men sitting outside their houses, drinking coffee or watching football on television. Most wore the long simple cotton robes with white head-dresses tied into a neat hat. Young boys sat nearby, staring and pointing at the tourists in the bus, some waving excitedly.

'I haven't seen any women,' Leonie whispered to Hannah, as if the men watching them from the roadside might read their lips.

'I know,' Hannah whispered back. 'It does seem to be a very male-orientated society. There were no women at the airport either. It's a mainly Muslim country, though, isn't it? And that means the women dress modestly.'

Hannah thought ruefully of her holiday wardrobe, which contained quite a few skimpy clothes for sunbathing on the boat. As the guide books mentioned that women shouldn't wear revealing shorts or sleeveless outfits for visiting temples, she'd brought plenty of cover-up clothes as well. But if the Egyptians frowned upon Western dress, her bikini would be staying in her suitcase. She didn't want to offend people with her clothes. Mind you, she realized with a grin, the elderly parish priest back home in Connemara wouldn't appreciate a pale pink crochet bikini any more than a religious Egyptian.

'On your right is the Nile,' Flora announced and the passengers craned their necks for their first sight of the great river. At first, Hannah couldn't see anything but other people's heads as everyone tried to get a glimpse out of the window.

Then she saw it, a great expanse of gleaming water, sparkling with lights from the large river boats that were moored by its banks. The mystical Nile, the gift of Egypt as Herodotus said – or was it the other way round? She couldn't remember. Egyptian kings and queens had sailed up and down this river in their royal barges, pharaohs sailing to visit their temples and to worship their gods. Tutankhamun, Rameses, Hatshepsut: their names were a roll call of an exotic past world . . .

'Look at the boats,' breathed Leonie, who was dying to know on what sort of vessel they'd be spending the next seven days and who couldn't concentrate on the glories of the Nile until she saw her cabin to see if it had enough room for her vast suitcase. 'That's a huge one,' she added as they drew closer to a floating palace decorated with hundreds of fairy lights. 'I hope that's our boat.'

The bus sped past. 'Oh well . . .' Leonie shrugged.

The bus suddenly shuddered to a halt beside a much smaller boat which was painted French blue and had the words *Queen Tiye* written on the side in huge gold letters. Three decks high, the top deck was half covered with a large canvas awning, the other half open to the skies with wicker seats and sun loungers splayed around. The top deck shone with lots of small lights and they could see a few people sitting around a table, bottles and glasses in front of them. 'Pretty, pretty,' Leonie sighed happily.

Everyone trooped off the bus, identified their luggage for the porters as Flora commanded them, and then climbed carefully down the stone steps at the quay to walk along the narrow wood-and-rope bridge on to the boat.

Leonie held on to the ropes at the side of the bridge to balance herself and beamed back at Hannah who was behind her: 'It's very *Indiana Jones*,' she said, thrilled with the adventure. 'Is this the gang-plank, do you think?'

'Dunno,' answered Hannah tiredly. She was beginning to feel the after-effects of her sleepless night with the energetic Jeff. All she wanted now was to fall into her bed and sleep until morning. But she shouldn't really skip the talk with Flora. Otherwise, she might miss out on what was happening for the voyage – and Hannah couldn't bear the thought of missing out on information. You could never rely on other people to tell you things.

When everyone had filled in a registration card, Flora organized cabin keys. Hannah and Leonie's cabins were opposite each other.

'Isn't this fun?' Leonie asked in childish delight as the two of them walked down a narrow passage to their cabins. She'd never been on a boat like this before.

The big ferries to France were different. Modern and boring. This was all so different, so exotic. The walls were covered in rich dark wood and hung with tiny prints of Victorian watercolour desert scenes offset by filigree gold frames. Even the cabin keys were decorated with little brass pyramids. Leonie wished the kids were here with her to experience it all. Mel would be thrilled at the thought of buying silky Egyptian scarves, Abby would be in raptures at the thought of seeing the temples, and Danny would be pestering the crew to let him steer the ship. She hoped they were having a good holiday.

She opened her cabin door in a fizz of excitement which quickly abated when she saw the room which was to be her home for the next week. The cabin was tiny, not even as big as her bathroom back in the cottage. There were none of the filigree gold paintings or rich wood of the rest of the boat: the cabin was painted plain cream all over with yellow curtains and yellow-striped covers on the two single beds.

A six-inch square ledge served as a dressing table, with another as a bedside table between the beds. There was a small fridge beside the wardrobe, which was really just a niche in the wall with doors. Leonie stuck her head inside the bathroom to find a minuscule room with a sink, toilet and a shower. Her suitcase would barely fit in the cabin, never mind trying to cram her vast store of clothes into the wardrobe, and as for dressing table space – she'd obviously have to use the other bed to lay her make-up and jewellery out.

'Compact, huh?' Hannah put her head round the door.

'Compact is not the word. It's just as well I haven't brought my toyboy lover for a week of passionate thrashing around on the Nile.' Leonie grinned. 'We'd concuss ourselves every time we launched off the dressing table on to the bed!'

'Lucky you with a toyboy,' joked Hannah. 'We must compare stories later.' She disappeared as the porter brought her case along the corridor.

My side of that conversation won't take long, Leonie thought regretfully.

She opened the curtains and let the quayside lights shine into the cabin. Opening the window, she looked down to see the placid dark waters of the Nile. She was really here, she realized with a happy shiver. She hadn't balked with fear and run home; she'd taken her first holiday on her own. That had to be worth something in the independence stakes.

Once unpacked, she showered quickly, thrilled at the fact that the compact shower room had only a tiny mirror so she didn't have to stare at her huge, pinky-white naked self. She spent the usual ten minutes trying on clothes, then ripping them off and throwing them on the bed when she looked awful in the long wardrobe mirror.

Her burgundy velvet embroidered dress was too hot even if it was the nicest thing she'd brought and her other dress, the sleeveless black one, revealed so much of her plump arms she couldn't bear it. Hannah would not be having this problem, she sighed, thinking of what a fantastic figure her new friend had. Slim and elegant, Hannah had looked wonderful in her simple travelling clothes. Leonie would have killed to look that good in jeans.

Eventually, she settled on the sleeveless dress worn with an open pink silk shirt, the long tail covering up her bum, she hoped. She left the cabin full of anticipation for the night ahead.

The informal meeting before dinner in the top-deck bar was in half an hour but Leonie decided to go up now, so she could daydream quietly and watch the world go by.

In her daydreams, she had a vision of herself sitting on the upper deck, glass of wine in hand and a swarm of admiring men surrounding her like something from Scott Fitzgerald. Instead, she caught sight of herself in the smoky mirrors which lined the stairs and saw the familiar reflection: the solid peasant's body and a mass of hair like untamed hay that no anti-frizz serum could help.

Scott Fitzgerald's heroes would probably hand her their empty martini glasses and ask for refills, presuming she was the serving girl.

Wishing she'd stuck to a diet for her holidays, she stomped upstairs to the bar. Decorated in ornate carved wood, it was certainly from another era with its Art Deco furniture and French lithographs behind the counter.

She ordered a glass of white wine from the smiling, dark-eyed young barman and, once she'd signed her room number on the bill, took her glass outside to the bar-level deck where she could feel the night air on her skin and listen to the noises of the river.

There was nobody else there and she breathed in the silence broken only by a distant hum of Arab music from one end of the boat. It was still gloriously warm and Leonie felt herself relax finally as she stared out over the tranquil darkness of the Nile. She wasn't going to obsess about being forty-something and manless: she was going to enjoy herself.

Moored to the other bank, she could see the tall sails of river boats. Feluccas, her guide book had explained. You could rent one and sail down the river for a couple of hours, travelling the way people had for thousands of years. How romantic.

She picked up her glass and was about to take a sip when she heard a hesitant, rather husky voice through the vast open doors order a mineral water with no ice.

Leonie smiled to herself and played one of her favourite games: guessing to whom the voice belonged. She thought of the couple of sedate blue-rinsed ladies who'd climbed on to the coach last of all, twittering with relief that one of their bags hadn't been gobbled up by the carousel but had in fact been rescued from the wrong baggage cart by an apologetic airport official. Definitely one of them. Although that voice was very sexy, very whiskey and cigarettes as it said, 'Thank you so much,' in an anxious manner. Too sexy to be a genteel seventy-year-old, unless she'd had a lifetime of fierce chain-smoking behind her.

Twisting in her seat to see if she was right, Leonie was astonished to see that the owner of the voice was the anxious Saluki Woman with the parents from hell, still wearing her long cream outfit and still looking immaculate. But she looked different somehow.

Instead of her previously distant expression, the woman's face was tired and, no, Leonie wasn't imagining it, friendly. She even carried herself differently: her body was no longer tense and she gazed around as if some weight had been lifted from her. Before, she'd avoided eye contact like the plague. Now, she looked around, spotted Leonie and gave a half-smile that seemed almost apologetic.

Leonie, naturally friendly, smiled back and immediately regretted it. What if the woman and her awful family decided to sit with her and Hannah during dinner? Or attach themselves to them for the entire cruise? What a terrifying thought. Hannah was mad to think about it. Wishing she didn't feel such a bitch, Leonie wiped the smile from her face just as abruptly and went back to studying the Nile as if she was about to sit an exam on What Sort of Objects You Might Find Floating By on a Summer's Evening.

'You look as if someone just pinched your bottom,' remarked Hannah, sitting in the chair opposite and placing a glass of orange juice on the table. 'Or is it because they haven't pinched your bottom you look so glum?' In loose white drawstring trousers and a simple caramel fitted T-shirt, she looked classy and comfortable at the same time. Leonie immediately felt overdressed in her floating pink silk.

'I'm avoiding looking at yer woman in case Ma and Pa Walton decide to join us,' Leonie explained in a whisper. 'She smiled at me when she came in and I'm terrified of starting up a friendship I won't be able to shake off. I can't *stand* people like her father. I never lose my temper except with people like him and then I'm like a bomb, I just explode.'

'I'd love to see you explode at him. Anyway, the poor girl's lonely,' Hannah insisted.

'I collect enough lame dogs at home without collecting a few rabid ones abroad,' Leonie groaned, knowing that Hannah was right. The poor girl was lonely and it wasn't fair to ostracize her just because of the people she was travelling with.

They both sneaked casual glances at the woman, who had positioned herself at a table just outside the bar and was trying to take something from her handbag without anyone noticing. She couldn't have been more than thirty, Hannah decided, and she looked thoroughly miserable, like a cat that had been locked out in the rain. The girl had a long face, Leonie was right about that. But having long straight hair trailing down her face didn't help. Hannah suspected that some unkind person had once told her that wearing your fringe low detracted from a large nose. Probably that obnoxious father of hers. Hannah bet that if the girl smiled or if she wore something less colourless than that hideously old fashioned cream thing, she'd be pretty in an understated way.

'Let's ask her over for a drink,' she said now. 'We're asking her, not Ma and Pa as well,' she added. After all, she thought silently, if she was befriending one lonely soul on this holiday where she'd planned for total solitude, she may as well befriend another. 'I promise you, Leonie, if her father wants to sit with us and they drive us mad, I'll get rid of them!'

Leonie laughed. 'If he annoys me, don't worry, *I'll* do the honours.'

Hannah walked gracefully over to the other girl's table, Leonie watching her new friend enviously. Hannah was so slim and God! so sexy. Leonie would have given five years of her life to look like Hannah for just one night.

'Hello, I'm Hannah Campbell. Since you're on your own, would you like to have a drink with us?'

The girl's face creased into a pleased smile.

Hannah loved being right: the girl was pretty when she smiled. She had a sweet, shy smile and her eyes were a lovely smoky blue colour fringed with fair lashes. If only she'd do something with that hair.

'I'd love to,' Emma said in her hesitant, throaty voice. 'I always feel so self-conscious sitting on my own with a drink. I'm Emma, by the way. Emma Sheridan.'

Carrying her drink, she followed Hannah over to the table and held her hand out to Leonie.

'Emma Sheridan,' she said formally.

Leonie grinned. 'Leonie Delaney,' she replied.

'Do you mind me joining you?' Emma asked.

'Thrilled,' Leonie said.

'Right.' Hannah decided she needed to do something to liven things up. 'We all need a drink. What do you want, girls?'

'I've loads of mineral water left,' Emma said, holding up her glass.

'Nonsense,' Hannah said briskly. 'You need a proper drink.'

The other woman's expression faltered. 'I shouldn't, really. My father, you know . . .' she hesitated, catching herself just in time. Imagine telling these two women that she wasn't going to have a drink because her father disapproved of women drinking more than a sherry and she couldn't face his disapproval. They'd think she was a complete nutcase. 'My father says the beer here is supposed to be very strong.'

'A glass of wine won't kill you.'

Something fell to the floor and Hannah picked it up. It was a small bottle of Dr Bach's Rescue Remedy, the herbal antidote to stress. You took four drops on your tongue to calm your nerves, she knew, having consumed enough of it when she was recovering from Harry's round-the-world bombshell.

Emma gave her a wry look. 'Travelling makes me stressed,' she said bluntly. She left out the words 'travelling with my father . . .'

Hannah handed the bottle back. 'Well, you definitely need one drink then.'

Leonie pronounced her white wine unusual but drinkable, so that was that. The barman brought three glasses of white wine.

Emma, who seemed to be relaxing with every moment, took an enormous sip of her drink. She gasped and gave a happy little shudder. 'I needed that. So,' she said, 'I presume you two are friends.'

'No,' Leonie said, 'we met on the plane. I'm terrified of flying and Hannah swapped seats with me. But as we're travelling on our own, we sort of linked up.'

'I'm here with my parents,' Emma explained, then felt herself redden because she knew damn well the other two knew that.

Everyone who'd been on the plane had known it: you couldn't miss her father. Now they'd really think she was some sort of weirdo who was tied to her parents. 'My husband had to go to a conference and couldn't come with us,' she added. Nervousness made her tactless: 'Do your partners not like cultural trips either?'

Hannah grinned. 'I'm not seeing anyone right now and my last lover' – her full lips curved into a smile at the thought of Jeff – 'well, I don't know if he'd have been into a trip to Egypt.'

'My husband and I are divorced,' blurted out Leonie. 'We meant to come to Egypt on our honeymoon, but we were too broke at the time. I figured that if I waited until I was married again to come here, I'd be waiting a long time.' She slumped in her seat, feeling miserable. It must be jet lag or something.

'Don't be so defeatist,' Hannah said kindly. 'If you want something, you'll get it. If you want a man, go out and get one.'

Leonie stared at her in astonishment. Most of her friends – well, Anita and the female members of the gang, really – changed the subject brusquely if she mentioned her single status. They muttered that men weren't everything and, God, sure didn't they nearly murder Tony/Bill/whoever every five minutes for leaving the loo seat up or for never washing up so much as a spoon. 'Wouldn't you be as well off on your own,' they chorused with fake cheeriness. 'Nobody to act hopeless around the washing machine. And you have the kids, after all . . .'

But Hannah had no such compunction. 'We'll help you find a nice single bloke on the cruise,' Hannah said. 'There's bound to be someone on the boat who's longing for the love of a good woman.'

'It's not that easy,' Leonie protested.

'I'm not saying it is, but you can do it if you want to. It just takes a different approach these days. You've so much going for you, Leonie, you'd get a man no bother if you really put your mind to it.' She patted Leonie's arm reassuringly.

Leonie was still mouthing in shock. How lovely of Hannah to say she had a lot going for her, but how mad as a bicycle to imagine that getting a man was just a simple matter of deciding to do so and accomplishing it. Perhaps that's how it happened to people like Hannah but not to her. I mean, she thought, where had all the available men been over the last few years? Waiting for her to emerge from the chrysalis of having children under the age of fourteen?

'What do you mean by "putting your mind to it"?' she asked finally.

'Dating agencies, magazine adverts, even car-maintenance classes,' Hannah said matter-of-factly. 'You've got to try them all. That's the way to meet people these days.'

'My friend Gwen met her boyfriend through a dinner club,' Emma pointed out.

'A dinner club?'

'It's a club for singles and you all go out to dinner once a month and see what happens. Gwen says she met loads of men. Some strange guys too, mind you. But she met Paul and that's all that matters to her.'

'I'd put any man off me if he saw me eating,' Leonie said, only half joking. 'Or I'd have to do like Scarlett O'Hara and eat before I went out so I'd be able to nibble daintily in front of Mr Right. Women with big appetites put men off, I'm sure of it.'

'I'd probably order the sloppiest thing on the menu and end up with sauce all over my chin and chunks of bread roll flying off to hit other people in the eye,' laughed Emma, getting into the swing of things now that she'd had that wonderful glass of wine. 'I'm so clumsy when I'm nervous.'

'Aren't we all?' Hannah groaned.

Both Emma and Leonie thought that was unlikely. Hannah looked so self-possessed and calm. Even her hair obeyed her. Sleek and perfectly groomed, not a stray dark hair dangled from her neat ponytail.

'Honestly, I am,' she protested, seeing the looks of disbelief on their faces. 'I went for a job interview a month ago and when I was supposed to be reaching into my attaché case to hand them details of this computer course I'd done, I stupidly reached into my handbag instead, and stuck my fingers right into my hairbrush. You know the way you get a bristle under the nail . . . ?'

They all winced.

'It bled like a ruddy artery and I had to get tissue, wrap the finger in it – all while my hand was still in my handbag! – and pretend nothing had happened for the rest of the interview. They must have thought I was hideously tense because I kept one hand clenched up all the time, trying to hide the tissue so I wouldn't look like a casualty victim in need of a transfusion.'

'You poor thing,' Leonie said sympathetically. 'Did you get the job in the end?'

Hannah's grin of triumph lit up her face and the toffee-coloured eyes sparkled. 'Yes. Bloody finger and all.'

She waved at a waiter and tried to order more wine.

'I'll have mineral water,' Emma said quickly, thinking of both the baby and her father. She could still remember that awful moment at

Kirsten's wedding when he'd ticked Emma off in front of all the guests for having too much to drink.

'So what is the job?' asked Leonie. 'What do you do?'

'I was a hotel receptionist but I decided it was a dead-end job. It was a terrible hotel, really, but I took that job to get out of my old one which was even more dead-end, in a shop. My new job is office manager in an estate agent's. I know it's totally different, but I wanted to move jobs. I've done night courses in a management school for the past eight months and I've started an estate agent's course. Not that I think I'd be lucky enough to branch into that part of things, you have to have loads of qualifications from what I can see, but it's good to know all about the business.'

It was funny, Hannah realized. She hadn't talked about herself to anyone for over a year, since Harry. And here she was, practically giving her life story to these two strangers. Holidays certainly had a bizarre effect on you – maybe it was the air.

'Wow,' Emma said admiringly. 'A woman with a mission.'

'I've got a mission all right – to make a career for myself. I got side-tracked for a few years,' she added, not wanting to mention that the side-track had been nearly ten years with Harry, who'd let her sink into the squalor of coupledom before abandoning her for his South American trip.

'And your mission,' Hannah said to Leonie, deciding to change the subject, 'is to find yourself a man, because that's what you want. If I can turn myself into an office manager, you can find a man.'

'Men, the root of all evil,' sighed Leonie, starting on her second glass of wine. 'I don't mean that, really. I love men. That's the problem,' she added gloomily. 'I think I scare them off. But I never thought of a dating agency. To be honest, I always thought only oddballs tried blind dating. Knowing my luck, I'd meet a serial killer or some nut with a fondness for PVC knickers and autoerotic asphyxia.'

Hannah laughed grimly. 'I've met enough nuts without the help of a dating agency. Not PVC fetishists, mind you, but still mad. My last long-term boyfriend should have come with a government health warning and I met him in the safest place in the world: McDonald's at lunchtime. So you may as well try dating agencies, Leonie. At least you get to pick who you'll meet and who you won't bother with.'

'Harrison Ford,' said Leonie dreamily. 'I want a Harrison Ford clone who loves children, animals and overweight blonde divorcées.'

'What about your man?' Hannah asked Emma, who immediately smiled at the thought of Pete.

'He's lovely,' she admitted. 'I'm very lucky. He's kind and funny and I love him to bits.' Pete's face appeared in her mind: the open, smiling face with the brown eyes, big grin and the dark hair cropped close to his scalp. Well, Pete always argued, there was no point wearing your hair long when there was so little of it. She loved his seriously receding hairline, loved kissing him on the top of his head and telling him that bald men were more virile. She wouldn't have wanted Harrison Ford, or even Tom Cruise, for that matter. She couldn't imagine either of them making her breakfast in bed when she felt ill, or massaging her shoulders when she got backache or insisting that she read a magazine while he made dinner on nights when she felt tired. Or leaving a lovely note buried in her suitcase telling her he loved her and that he couldn't wait for her to get home. Pete adored her. Only his dislike of her father meant he'd let her go away for a week without him.

'We've been married three years and he's really good to me,' she said. Then, because she couldn't resist, she told them about the sweet note he'd left hidden between her T-shirts in the suitcase.

'Oooh, that's lovely,' Leonie said.

She and Hannah were half-way down their second glasses of wine and they'd all been talking happily about why they'd decided to come to Egypt when the sound of Jimmy O'Brien's booming voice could be heard from the doorway.

'. . . if this is their idea of a first-class boat, I'll be having words with that young courier woman, I'm telling you,' he was saying loudly to another guest. 'The shower's useless and my towels got soaked because the shower curtain wasn't any good. Call that first class? I don't think so. Rip-off merchants, that's what these bloody fellas are, pretending this is a first-class boat. Hmmph.

'I'm not sitting outside,' he added to his wife, 'we'll be eaten alive. Bloody mosquitoes.'

Hannah watched as Emma visibly shrank into her seat, her eyes briefly filled with an emotion Hannah could identify easily: wariness. Hannah's mother's face had often looked that way, usually when her father rolled home after a day at the races, roaring drunk, bad-tempered and looking for someone to take it out on. He'd been small and ran to fat, mostly beer fat, unlike Emma's father who was a formidable man, tall and strong. A man who could intimidate people and liked doing it. He didn't need alcohol to make him bad-tempered: it was obvious he was like that all the time.

Emma looked as if she'd rather have been keelhauled than face an evening with her parents. A surge of pity made Hannah reach out and touch her arm gently: 'Would you like to sit with us at a separate table tonight?' she asked quietly.

Emma looked relieved at the idea, then shook her head. 'I couldn't, they'll expect . . .'

'Say you're sure they'd like their first evening to be just for themselves, a romantic evening where you're not a gooseberry,' Hannah urged.

Emma stifled the desire to snigger at the thought of her parents having a romantic evening. Her father reckoned romance was for wimps. He'd openly laughed at Pete for buying her a dozen red roses on Valentine's Day.

'Yeah,' said Leonie, getting into the swing of things. 'We need a third musketeer.' Poor Emma was a lovely girl and obviously in need of saving from that obnoxious man. 'Say you know one of us already and you want to chat.'

'They'd never swallow that,' Emma replied.

Mr O'Brien had spotted his daughter with two women he didn't recognize and marched over to their table, his wife in his wake like a tug boat following a liner into port.

'I don't have a wide circle of friends and if we pretended, my father would give you the third degree and soon work out you were lying.'

Leonie tapped her nose enigmatically. 'I happen to be a superb actress. We'll say we know each other through your work. What do you do, anyway?'

'I work for KrisisKids Charity. I'm in special projects,' Emma said.

'That's run by that retired politician, Edward Richards, isn't it?' Leonie insisted. 'His family owns Darewood Castle and the stud farm.'

Emma was pleased that Leonie knew enough about the charity to know who ran the organization. It meant their public relations company were doing their job. But she couldn't see how Edward fitted into this particular evening's equation.

'I'm a vet nurse,' Leonie added. 'Our practice used to be their vets. Very posh, I believe,' Leonie said.

'Hello there,' boomed Mr O'Brien, sizing up the seating arrangements and noticing with displeasure that there was only room for three chairs at the small table.

Emma immediately got up, smiled a nervous goodbye to the girls and led her parents to another table.

'Aren't you going to introduce us to your friends?' her mother asked peevishly.

'I thought you wanted to sit down, Mum,' Emma said, not wanting to ruin her new friendship by making Hannah and Leonie meet her father. Grumpy after the flight, lord only knew what he'd come out with. 'You can meet them later. Will I order you a mineral water?'

Her mother immediately started fanning herself with her hand and looked faint. 'Yes, it's so hot, that would be lovely.'

'Sit down, Emma, and stop fussing,' ordered her father brusquely. 'The waiter will come – eventually. These Egyptians don't seem keen to work. At home, you'd have a drink in your hand within a minute of arriving at the bar, but here . . . oh no, it's a different kettle of fish altogether.' He glared around at the bar where the waiter was busy serving a group of people who'd just arrived and were clamouring for cocktails. 'No bloody concept of service,' said Jimmy O'Brien loudly.

A few feet away, Hannah and Leonie grimaced at his rudeness. Emma cringed in her bamboo chair. This was a disaster. It didn't matter that she was sitting in the balmy night air with the vibrant city of Luxor yards away and the treasures of the Nile waiting to be explored: she was on holiday with her father and he was going to ruin everything.

'I'll get the drinks,' she announced suddenly, thinking she just had to get away before her father said something utterly offensive about the waiter.

Watching Emma practically run to the bar, her face bright pink with embarrassment, Leonie nudged Hannah: 'Poor girl isn't going to have much of a holiday if he carries on like that all the time. The man's a pig and she's mortified.'

'I know,' Hannah nodded. 'But what can you do? He's her father and she's stuck with him.'

Leonie grinned wickedly. 'Maybe not.'

Taking a deep breath, she rose from her seat and sailed across to the O'Briens' table, one bracelet-bedecked hand outstretched.

'Isn't it a coincidence!' Leonie trilled, shaking a surprised Jimmy O'Brien's hand with the grace of a dowager duchess, flowing pink silk shirt rippling around madly. 'Fancy Emma working with dear Cousin Edward in KrisisKids. Now that's what I call a small world. I'm Leonie Delaney, from the Wicklow branch of the family.' She took Anne-Marie's limp hand and shook it gently, trying not to flinch at the cold-kipper sensation of the other woman's handshake.

'We're the merchant banking side, rather than the political side. Daddy couldn't have borne it if we'd gone into politics,' Leonie added in a softer voice, as if this was some great family secret, '*so* low rent. De-lighted to meet you all.'

Hannah watched her in astonishment. One minute, Leonie had been sitting quietly; the next, she was a human dynamo, her collection of brass and enamel bracelets rattling as she twirled her curls in her fingers and pretended to be a merchant banking toff. It was a bravura performance, Oscar-winning stuff.

'Edward Richards,' Leonie was saying to Mrs O'Brien, determined to get the message home. 'Dear Cousin Edward – Big Neddy is what we've always called him.'

Hannah nearly choked as her new friend described as 'Big Neddy' the elegant and aristocratic man she'd seen in the papers when he was a politician.

'Of course,' Leonie drawled in her recently acquired posh accent, 'he hasn't been to Delaney Towers for months. Daddy and Mummy do miss him.'

Realization dawned in Anne-Marie O'Brien's face. This flamboyant woman with the unsuitable heavy make-up and that bizarre metal necklace thing was actually related to Emma's boss, the madly rich and well-connected Mr Richards. He came from one of Ireland's most famous political dynasties. This strange Leonie woman must be one of his cousins on his mother's side. Well, Anne-Marie thought, arranging her face into a welcoming smile, the rich were allowed to be eccentric. Some of those computer millionaires wore nothing but jeans and desperate old T-shirts. You never knew where anyone came from any more.

And if Edward Richards' cousin was on this cruise, then it must be one of the better ones, no matter what Anne-Marie's suspicions had been when she'd seen the size of her cabin.

'So pleased to meet you,' Anne-Marie said in her breathy voice. 'Anne-Marie and James O'Brien, of O'Brien's Contractors, you know. Emma,' she added, as Emma arrived with drinks and a wicked smile on her face at the sight of Leonie sitting with her parents, 'you naughty girl, you should have introduced us to Leonie and told us who she is.' She waggled a reproving finger at her daughter. 'Why don't you and your companion join us?' Anne-Marie added.

'We thought maybe Emma would sit with us,' Leonie said deadpan, 'and leave you and your husband to enjoy a romantic evening *à deux*.'

Anne-Marie blinked at her, while Emma watched in a state of growing puzzlement. Her mother loved using French expressions, yet here she was staring at Leonie as if she didn't understand *à deux*. How weird. Then again, this entire conversation was straight out of the *X-Files* anyway.

She felt bad about letting Leonie mislead her parents, but it would be blissful to have someone else to talk to on holiday. After an entire day with her father and no way of escaping him, she'd have gone off for a chat with someone in a straitjacket if they'd asked her.

'That's kind of you,' said Jimmy O'Brien, who didn't speak French but didn't want to let on.

Emma's mother was still staring at Leonie blankly. 'What were we talking about again?' she asked in a plaintive voice. There was something not quite right about her tonight, Emma felt. Something vague and distant. Her mother was never vague.

Leonie took charge. She relieved Emma of the two glasses of mineral water, put them down on the table in front of the O'Briens senior and slipped an arm through Emma's.

'We'll leave you to it,' she said sweetly.

'What did you say to them?' asked Emma when they were out of earshot, feeling as if she should scold a little bit.

'I lied and said I knew your boss,' Leonie said quickly, not wanting to get into a detailed explanation of her wicked ruse. 'Said we wanted to chat. I mean, I know how it is with parents, they probably feel you'd be lost without them, when Hannah and I both know you'd like a bit of time out. And it gives them a chance to be on their own, second honeymoon stuff.'

Emma raised her eyebrows. Second honeymoon indeed.

CHAPTER FIVE

Leonie stood in front of the Temple of Hathor and knew why she'd come to Egypt. Blazing white heat shone down on her, lighting the dusty scene with a burning white intensity. The temple in front of her, carved by the fiercely proud Rameses II for his beloved queen Nefertari, was beautiful.

Rameses' own temple at Abu Simbel was twice as breathtaking: towering figures of the great king himself looming over the tourists, majestic and exquisitely proportioned. To stare up at the fierce face of the great ruler made the long trip in the bus worth it. Just standing there in the desert sun, listening to the age-old sounds of hawkers trying to sell their wares and the hum of insects droning lazily overhead, Leonie felt as if she could have stepped back in time. She wondered what it must have been like to be one of the archaeologists who'd discovered the fabulous temple after it had lain buried in the desert sands for three thousand years. Or even better, she clutched her golden Egyptian cartouche pendant to her chest, imagining what it would have been like to be the Egyptian queen, Nefertari, honoured by all, beautiful, covered with priceless gold jewellery and awaiting the grand opening of the temple. Lost in her magical world of romance, Leonie felt exhilarated and dazed at the same time.

This was what people felt when they saw the Taj Mahal, she thought reverently. Stunned into silence by the physical proof of what mankind could do. For love. Like the Taj Mahal, built as the biggest love token ever, Nefertari's temple had been built by her besotted husband because he loved his wife so much. No other Egyptian ruler had ever built such a monument, the tour guide had explained as the bus trailed slowly along the road in convoy from Aswan deep into the Nubian desert. They built temples in their own honour or richly decorated great tombs for their journey to the afterworld. But a temple dedicated to one they loved, never.

Imagine being loved so much by such a great king, Leonie thought dreamily. Imagine such a symbol of enduring love in your name . . .

'Leonie, the tour's starting. Are you coming?'

Hannah's clear voice broke into her thoughts. Hannah and a relaxed-looking Emma were following their group towards the temple. As Leonie had discovered during the past two days on the tour, you could easily lose your group in the thousands who thronged around each Egyptian monument. She'd nearly lost them in the giant and confusing Edfu Temple and she was determined it wouldn't happen again. Picking up her canvas bag, Leonie ran after them.

'Wow,' she gasped as she reached the shady spot to the left where Flora was waiting with the others, 'it's too hot to run.'

'Too hot to do anything,' Hannah agreed, pulling a strand of hair away from her damp forehead. 'I don't know if I'll be able to cope with an hour of this.'

'And then the bus journey back to the boat,' groaned one of their fellow travellers, tired after the three and a half-hour bus journey into the desert.

'It's wonderful,' Emma said gaily. Her pale face was flushed in the heat and her hair was tied up in a ponytail to keep it away from her face. Wearing a little blue T-shirt and cotton Bermudas in a pretty madras check, she looked about twenty, and utterly carefree, Hannah thought fondly.

For the first time during the trip, Emma felt about twenty. Her mother was suffering from stomach problems and had decided she wasn't up to the bus journey to visit Abu Simbel. Which meant that her father had cried off too, leaving Emma to enjoy the first Jimmy and Anne-Marie-free day since she'd got to Egypt. It was such a relief, like painkillers after a nagging, three-day toothache.

Neither of the O'Briens were enjoying their trip: her mother because she was in a state of high anxiety the whole time, even more so than usual. She'd behaved very strangely the previous evening at dinner, refusing to eat anything and sitting in a world of her own for the whole meal, staring into space. The heat was getting to her, Jimmy insisted. He, who'd instigated the trip to Egypt, was now telling anyone who'd listen that it hadn't been his idea to come and muttering darkly about how Portugal had always done them very well up to now.

To make the day even more utterly delightful, Emma's period still hadn't come. She was pregnant, she knew it. Every time she went near the loo, she panicked in case a tell-tale trickle of pale pink stained the white loo roll. But nothing. Bliss.

Sighing with happiness, she linked both Leonie and Hannah's arms and led them into the temple after Flora, who was holding a royal blue Incredible Egypt clipboard above her head to make sure her busload of people could see her.

In her state of expectant happiness, Emma was one of the few people who wasn't mildly put out when the bus broke down only half an hour after leaving the temple on the drive home. Crunching to a noisy halt on the outskirts of a dusty little town, it refused to start up despite much swearing and banging on the bus driver's part. Buses and taxis to Abu Simbel always travelled in convoys, Flora had explained earlier, in case one broke down mid-desert. But they were unfortunately the second-last bus in the convoy back to Aswan and the only vehicle behind them was a crowded mini-bus which couldn't take any extra passengers.

'Don't worry, folks, it'll be all right,' Flora said bravely as the mini-bus driver and their driver fiddled around with the engine and talked volubly with much irate hand-waving.

Leonie, fascinated by the exotic signs of life around them, was happy enough to sit and look out of the window, but it did begin to get hot with the bus, and therefore the air conditioning, switched off. Emma was just happy full stop. Nothing could touch the blissful happiness inside her.

They'd get back eventually and she was quite content to sit there, one hand gently on her belly. Small, dark-eyed children waved up at the tourists on the bus and Emma beamed down at them, waving back. Soon she'd have her own darling child. Would it take after Pete or her? She'd prefer a dark-eyed baby, she decided. The vision of a dark-eyed baby in cute denim dungarees lulled her into a contented fantasy.

As well prepared as ever, Hannah had an extra bottle of water in her small backpack and she shared it between the three of them. Emma had boiled sweets, which filled the gap in Leonie's stomach.

'I'm getting used to three massive meals a day on the boat,' she said ruefully. 'I'm ravenous.'

'Me too,' Emma said. 'But don't worry, they'll fix the bus,' she added confidently.

'I doubt it.' Hannah wasn't as confident. She hated disruptions to her routine. The bus was supposed to be back in Aswan at seven thirty in time for dinner at eight. They'd been stopped for at least, she checked her watch, twenty minutes, which meant they'd be late. Shit. She hated being late, hated disorder in her very ordered life. She could feel her pulse increase as the tension got to her. Beads of perspiration that had nothing to do with the heat broke out on her skin. Her nerve ends tingled in that familiar, agitated way. Calm down, Hannah, she commanded herself. If you're late, so what? There's nothing you can do about it and everyone else will be late too. It had been ages since she'd had a panic attack, she couldn't be getting one now.

Flora clambered up the steps into the bus. 'We'll all have to get off, I'm afraid,' she said, still looking calm in the face of mutinous passengers. 'I've phoned the bus company and they'll have another bus here in an hour and a half. I know it's a long time, but it's coming from Wadi al-Sabu which is half-way between here and Aswan. Hassan says there's a lovely little restaurant in the town and I'll buy us all dinner there as we're going to be late back to the boat.'

A rush of angry mutterings greeted her words from the front of the bus, while the people at the back seemed more resigned to the news.

'I'm starving,' Leonie said. 'Let's find this place quickly.' She looked around and realized that Hannah looked strangely put out. Which was unusual because Hannah was always so relaxed, so sure of herself. Hannah never appeared to worry about what to wear, what to eat or what people thought of her. Now she looked as taut as a tug-of-war rope at the news that they'd be delayed by a few hours.

Leonie wasn't sure what to say to calm Hannah down but Emma said it for her, Emma, who was used to people getting anxious over delays.

'There's nothing we can do, Hannah,' Emma said in firm tones they'd never heard her use before. 'We're stuck, we may as well make the best of it. We'll be home eventually, so let's not panic. Food will do us good.'

'I know,' Hannah agreed, taking as deep a breath as she could. 'I hate delays, I'm so impatient. Hanging around for any length of time stresses me out.' She followed Emma obediently off the bus while Leonie went last, forever amazed at people and the chameleon changes they could make. It was a mystery to her that quiet, nervous little Emma could suddenly become the cool, calm one, while Hannah became a wreck. Talk about role reversal.

As the group straggled up the town, people watched them; adorable dark-eyed children giggled and pointed at the foreigners, laughing at Emma's bare legs and her pale skin. Proud-faced men in Arab dress looked darkly at Leonie, resplendent in flowing white silk, her golden hair tumbling wildly around her shoulders, her mouth a vivid crimson slash. With her golden cartouche and several strings of vibrant beads she'd bought locally wound around her neck, she looked utterly exotic in this dusty desert town where the dominant colour was beige.

'Your husband is lucky fellow,' smiled one local man admiringly before proffering some postcards of Abu Simbel.

Leonie tried not to grin but she couldn't stop the corners of her mouth turning up slightly. For once, she was the one getting all the attention. 'Thank you but no thank you,' she said primly and grabbed Emma's arm the way the guide book had warned single women should do to avoid harassment.

'I won't let anyone run away with you,' teased Emma, watching the men watching Leonie. 'You're the big hit around here, and no mistake.'

'Don't be silly,' Leonie said, immeasurably flattered and trying not to show it. 'I'm a mother of three who wears support tights, hardly a siren.' But she couldn't help feeling a little bit siren-ish. People – well, men – were looking at her. Not at Hannah with her cool elegance or at Emma with the milky-white skin and long, coltish grace.

It was the same in the restaurant: a large cool place with rough bench seating and faded cushions, it was staffed by three waiters who were obviously delighted to see a flamboyantly blonde, female tourist.

Flora, with her clipboard and mobile phone, was ignored as the men stared at Leonie appreciatively, treating her like a movie star.

'Pretend you're Madonna,' suggested Hannah, her mood improving. It was ridiculous to get uptight because the bus had broken down. She really must learn to snap out of these moods.

Emma started singing 'Like a Virgin' as the three of them were escorted to their table, a large one in a spacious corner with much softer, more opulent-looking cushions than the rest and an elaborate candelabra.

Leonie, who couldn't sing to save her life, joined in tunelessly, her voice wavering on the long drawn-out notes. She stopped long enough for the oldest waiter to usher her to the best seat, bowing formally as he did so. She bestowed a gracious smile on him and gave him a blast of sapphire eyes. He bowed even lower and hurried off, to return with three fragile painted glasses for them.

'More Ribena,' said Hannah picking up her tiny glass and breathing in the scent of the non-alcoholic fruit drink they'd got used to on the boat.

'I don't need to tell you ladies to enjoy yourselves,' Flora said, arriving at their table when everyone else was settled. 'Just don't forget you have to buy any alcoholic drink yourselves and the bus will be here at around eight.'

'Leave?' said Leonie in mock horror. 'Flora, I may never leave this place.'

Although most local restaurants didn't serve alcohol, when Leonie saw one of the waiters emerge from the back with a bottle of red wine, she said they must order one.

'Now, let's have a real girlie chat,' she said happily when the first course of mezes had arrived and they each had a glass of Cru des Ptolemees.

By the main course – kofta lamb for Emma and Hannah, vegetarian hummus and kebabs for Leonie – they'd gone through men in general and were on to Hannah's story of Harry. It had been quite a relief to tell someone about how devastated she'd been the day he'd announced that he was travelling round South America and that it was all over.

'You think you know someone and then they drop a bombshell like that.' Even a year later, talking about it hurt. She'd felt so betrayed, so abandoned. All the love and time and hope she'd invested in their relationship, and to have it all thrown back at her because he felt stifled and needed a break. He was like all men: feckless and uncaring. But she'd loved him so much. All the aerobics classes in the world couldn't dim the pain of that. At least her new plan to steer clear of men – apart from the odd bit of fun with guys like Jeff – would protect her from having her heart broken again. It just wasn't worth it.

'What is he doing in South America?' asked Leonie.

'I don't know and I don't care,' Hannah said fiercely. 'I haven't heard from him since he left. Not a dicky-bird. He took all his stuff from the flat when I wasn't there and left a note asking for letters to be forwarded to his sister. Huh! He had two chances of me doing that. I threw his new chequebook in the bin when it arrived, and all his tax forms.' She grinned at the memory. 'Then I kept getting phone calls from his boss at the paper because he was supposed to be writing this book for them on political scandals and he'd just left the country without telling them. That was Harry all over: run away instead of face the music,' she said bitterly.

Both Leonie and Emma had been gratifyingly eager to castrate Harry if they ever slapped eyes on him, and Hannah found herself thinking how nice it was to have female friends to confide in again. She'd been too hurt by Harry to seek out all the female friends she'd let go by the wayside when she fell for him first. It was comforting now to have a bit of sisterly outrage and support.

'I doubt I'll ever trust a man ever again,' she admitted slowly 'I shouldn't have trusted Harry in the first place. I should have known.'

'How could you?' Emma asked. 'You're not a mind-reader.'

'It's nothing to do with mind-reading. It's to do with men. They can't be trusted, full stop,' Hannah insisted. 'Well, I can't trust the men I meet, anyway. Your Pete sounds lovely, but I think some of us just aren't cut out for relationships. They mess you up. Some women are better off on their own and that's the sort of woman I am. I can take care of myself and I don't need anyone else. That's my plan.'

'You don't mean that,' Leonie argued. 'You're beautiful, Hannah, you could have any man you want. You simply ended up with a guy who was weak and left you. That's no reason to give up on men in general. You have to dust yourself off when it all goes wrong and start again.'

By dessert – fruit for all of them – they'd moved on to their personal theories on how to get over a man. Emma hadn't had many boyfriends before Pete, so she pointed out that she wasn't much of an expert. 'I met Pete when I was twenty-five and I'd only been out with three men before that. Dad ran the last one off the premises when he arrived smoking a roll-up cigarette. Said he didn't want me corrupted with drugs.'

They all laughed at that.

Leonie admitted that Ray had been her first real boyfriend and that their split had been mutual, more or less, so she hadn't needed to dust herself off. What Leonie couldn't understand was how Hannah had decided to simply give up falling in love until she felt strong enough to cope with men on her own terms. They'd heard about the fabulous Jeff and how Hannah had decided that a post-Harry bonk would be good therapy.

'How can you do that?' asked Leonie, fascinated.

'Do what?' Hannah bit into a piece of watermelon, little squelches of juice slithering down her chin.

'Decide that you won't get involved with any guy but just treat him like a friend who happens to be a lover. I mean, what if you met someone gorgeous and you couldn't help yourself and fell hopelessly in love?'

Leonie wanted to believe that someone gorgeous was always waiting around the corner, that it was a matter of kismet, destiny and the right *Daily Mail* horoscope when it happened. You'd fall in love, it was inevitable. Hannah wasn't convinced.

'Feeling terrible for months after Harry left, that's how I can do it,' she said. 'After the pain I went through, I'm not about to go through it again. If I turn into a heartless cow who uses men, I don't care. That happy, coupley love thing is not for me. I spent years doing that and where did it get me?' she demanded. 'Bloody nowhere. Harry upped and left when it suited him and all I had for ten years of love and affection was a huge spare tyre and a dead-end career. Men are a waste of space, apart from for rumpy-pumpy in the bedroom department.'

Emma broke out laughing at the pair of them. They were a howl. She loved sitting with her feet curled up on the cushioned bench, giggling and talking about men and sex.

She shifted to get more comfortable and felt a familiar ache ripple through her. An ache that turned swiftly from a distant pain into a hard one, gnawing at her insides. Her period. God, no, she shrieked silently. It couldn't be. She was pregnant, she was sure of it.

Emma stared at the others in dread, hoping they'd developed a similar pain, something to do with the lamb or a dodgy shrimp or anything . . . It rippled through her again. An unmistakable pain, the sort teenage girls who'd just had their first period could never adequately explain to their non-menstruating friends. Once felt, it was never forgotten.

Her period. There was no baby, Emma realized. There never had been. Probably never would be. Grief hit her in a wave.

She pushed herself away from the table clumsily, dropping her napkin and spilling what was left of her single glass of wine. 'Must go to the loo,' she said shakily.

In the dusty toilet with no lock on the door, Emma's fears were confirmed. She was numb as she looked at the tell-tale droplets of red in the toilet bowl. Using a wad of loo roll as a make-shift sanitary towel, she walked slowly back to the table, feeling lifeless and drained.

One look at Emma's white face and Leonie and Hannah knew something was wrong.

'Are you sick?' Hannah asked in concern.

'Was it something you've eaten?' said Leonie.

Emma shook her head dazedly.

'It's my period,' she said simply. 'I thought I was pregnant, I was sure I was and now . . .' her voice broke as she started to cry, 'I'm not.'

She sank into her seat beside Leonie, who immediately flung an arm round her. 'You poor, poor thing,' Leonie crooned in the same soft voice she used when the children were sick or upset.

As Emma cried, great heaving sobs that shook her entire fragile body, Leonie was shocked at how thin she was under her T-shirt: not elegantly slim, the way Leonie longed to be. But bony, almost skeletally thin, her ribs sticking out like rack of lamb.

'You poor darling. I know it's awful, but you're so young, you've years ahead of you, Emma,' Leonie soothed, hoping it was the right thing to say. 'Lots of couples take months to conceive.'

'But we've been trying for three years,' Emma said between giant hiccuping sobs. 'Three years and nothing. I know it's me and I don't know what I'll do if I can't have a baby. What's wrong with me? Why am I different? You have children, why can't I?'

Leonie and Hannah's eyes met over the table. There was nothing they could say. They'd both read of women tortured by their inability to have a child: neither of them had ever met anyone in that appalling position. Or, if they had, the women in question had obviously kept it a secret. Leonie dredged her memory for information on infertility. Hadn't she read something about couples who finally had babies when they stopped trying so frantically and relaxed. And Emma being so thin couldn't help. The poor girl was literally wasting away with nerves and strain: she didn't have a hope of getting pregnant while she was like that.

'The stress of wanting a baby so badly may be affecting you,' Leonie said finally. 'You know, some people make themselves ill because they want it so much and then, once they take a step backwards, they get pregnant.' It sounded so lame the way she'd said it, like telling a fairy story about Santa Claus to a knowing and deeply suspicious ten-year-old.

'Why didn't I get pregnant when we were first married?' sobbed Emma. 'We weren't really trying then. Or before we got married. Pete was always terrified the condom would burst and I'd get pregnant. He said my father would kill him. Maybe we're being punished for something, sex before marriage or . . . I don't know.' She looked at them both wildly, her face pink and streaked with tears. 'What is it? I'm not really religious, but I'd pray for hours every day if I thought it'd work.'

'Look at me,' Hannah urged. 'You're not being punished for anything, Emma. Don't be so daft. I'm five years older than you and I haven't even met the man I want to have kids with, so you're doing miles better than I am. If you work on the everything-that-goes-wrong-in-your-life-is-a-punishment theory, I must have done something terribly wrong to get landed with Harry and then get dumped. Now I don't have even one prospective father of my unborn children on the horizon.' She didn't add that children were the last thing on her mind, prospective father or no prospective father.

Emma's sobs subsided a little.

'Maybe you could investigate what's wrong,' Leonie suggested. 'Even if there's a problem, doctors can do incredible things nowadays if you're infertile. Look at all the babies born thanks to in vitro fertilization.'

Emma shook her head miserably. 'I couldn't put Pete through all that. It's a nightmare, I saw a programme about it on the telly. And . . .' she wiped her eyes in despair, 'he doesn't know how I feel, not really. He loves kids, he doesn't understand that if you can't have one after three years, you've no hope. I can't tell him that.'

The others looked at her in alarm.

'You haven't told Pete any of this?' Hannah asked gently.

'He knows I want a baby, but I couldn't really tell him how desperately I want one.'

'Why not?' Leonie asked in disbelief. 'Surely you have to share this with him – he loves you, after all.'

Emma shrugged her thin shoulders helplessly: 'I keep thinking that if I don't say anything, the problem will be in my imagination and I might still get pregnant. If we do something about it, I know it'll be my fault and they'll tell me I can never have a baby . . . I just know it.' Her eyes glazed over, her mind off in some faraway place.

'Ladies, we're going. The bus is here.' Flora's crisp, clear voice startled them and they realized that the other people from the tour were collecting their belongings and wandering out of the restaurant, clutching the inevitable plastic bottles of mineral water.

Hannah waved the waiter over and quickly paid for the wine, shaking off Leonie's suggestion of going halves. Emma didn't say a word.

A subdued trio climbed back on the bus, Emma red-eyed and Hannah staring blankly out into the night. What was wrong with her, she wondered. Why didn't she want children with the same blinding intensity as Emma? Was she abnormal? They'd simply never been a part of her life-plan, a plan that revolved around one facet: security. Making her way in life and being secure so that she'd never have to rely on a man again, the way her mother had had to rely on that feckless lump of a father of hers. Those years with Harry had been a fatal blip in her mission, years when she'd gone all cosy, practically married and ambitionless, and had forgotten that when you most needed them, men had a habit of failing you. Well, never again. She'd build her career up and make sure she never needed a man ever again.

Flings with men like Jeff Williams were allowed: simple physical relationships with people who wouldn't dare to mess with her life. And as for children, they didn't feature in her plans either. Maybe she was heartless, but she didn't think she'd make a very good mother. She still pitied Emma though. She knew how destructive it was to long for something you simply couldn't have. She knew too damn well. Harry's fault, again. Bugger Harry.

Leonie, Emma and Hannah sat on the upper deck in the late afternoon as the boat sailed up the river towards Luxor. With three weak cocktails in front of them, they watched the golden, glowing disc of the sun set on the left-hand side. The rays turned the mountains to the right a deep, mysterious rose gold. Palm trees clustered around the banks, as if planted by a clever gardener who knew how to achieve that artistically pleasing random effect.

'I half expect to see elephants charging from out of the trees, like in Africa,' said Emma dreamily.

'You *are* in Africa,' said Leonie with a grin.

'Oh no, the sun's finally affected my brain,' Emma groaned.

'Sun my ass, it's all those Fuzzy Navels you've been guzzling,' Hannah pointed out. 'I know they're weak ones, but you've had two.'

It was a perfect time of day to sit quietly and watch the valley pass by. The air was cooler than in the early afternoon and as the boat sailed north along the Nile, a refreshing breeze blew against them, rippling Emma's loose hair like a hairdryer.

It was the second last day of their holiday and they were all eager to take in every single detail of the country, determined not to forget a thing. The next day they were going to be busy the whole time, visiting the Valley of the Kings and Queens in the morning, and Karnak in the afternoon. There wouldn't be a spare moment in their exhausting itinerary, Flora had warned, advising everyone to take advantage of their afternoon off.

The girls had been only too pleased to comply. Emma's parents had decided to join in the card game in the inner bar after lunch and Jimmy O'Brien had done his best to get Emma on their team. But she'd refused.

'I'm going to sunbathe, Dad,' she'd said firmly.

He looked genuinely surprised. 'But wouldn't you rather be with me and your mother?'

Hannah and Leonie finished their coffee and began to leave the lunch table discreetly, not wanting to embarrass Emma by being present for what seemed like an inevitable spat with her father. But Emma took strength in their presence. She couldn't imagine either Hannah or Leonie being browbeaten by their father.

'Dad,' Emma said pleasantly, with an unaccustomed hint of steel in her voice, 'of course I like being with you and Mum, but we're not joined at the hip. I want to sunbathe and I don't want to play cards. Enjoy yourself.' She got up and kissed him lightly on the cheek, hoping to defuse her words with the gesture. It worked. Her father remained uncharacteristically silent.

Or plain old shocked because Emma had stood up to him, Hannah guessed shrewdly. If she'd been a psychiatrist, she could have written an entire thesis on Jimmy O'Brien. After five days of watching him, she'd decided he was a horrible man with an inflated opinion of himself.

On Wednesday, he'd insulted the pretty young belly dancer who'd arrived on the boat with a band of musicians by telling her loudly that she 'should put some clothes on and not strut around with everything hanging out like some common floozie'. Only Flora's immediate interference had prevented an international incident, because the lead musician looked as if he was ready to smash his electric keyboard down on Jimmy's head.

'Let's not be hasty,' Flora had said soothingly, placating all around her and gently leading Jimmy and Anne-Marie off to another part of the bar where she had to listen to ten minutes of a lecture on 'Why It Was A Shame These People Weren't Respectable Catholics'. Emma had been crimson with shame and had barely been able to look the belly dancer in the eye.

Somebody as self-effacing as Emma didn't stand a chance of standing up to her father, Hannah realized, taking another sip of her cocktail. Her mother was plain odd. Chatty one minute, she'd lapse into silence the next, staring off into the middle distance with a vacant expression on her face.

'She's not normally like that,' Emma had said worriedly one day when Anne-Marie had broken off what she was saying mid-sentence and begun humming. 'Dad insists the heat is affecting her badly, but she's normally so alert. I can't imagine what's wrong.'

The three women had spent a blissful afternoon sunning themselves on the top deck, reading, chatting, sipping mineral water and listening to the endlessly replayed disco classics record that emanated from the boat's speakers. Whoever was in charge of the music on the boat had a limited selection and veered between seventies disco hits and songs from old musicals.

'If I hear "Disco Inferno" one more time, I'll kill someone,' Leonie said, finishing her Fuzzy Navel and wondering if she'd have another before dinner.

'At least they've lowered the volume,' Emma interjected.

'Only because it was frightening the cows,' Leonie pointed out.

In places where the river widened, there were isolated grass banks surrounded by water, where cows grazed serenely, none of them appearing concerned that there was no obvious way back to the land.

'There must be strips of land back to the bank, a pathway we can't see,' Hannah said, peering at the latest batch of cows on a marshy island, her eyes peeled for a walkway. 'They couldn't swim, surely? The crocodiles would get them.'

'Sobeks would get them – descendants of the crocodile god, Sobek,' said Leonie, who loved hearing about the Egyptian gods and studied her guide book every night to learn more about the sights they were going to see the next day.

'Teacher's pet,' teased Hannah, lobbing her drink's cocktail umbrella over at her.

'You're just jealous,' retorted Leonie good-humouredly, throwing the little umbrella back. It bounced on the table and flew off over the side of the boat. 'I'm going to get a gold star on my copybook for figuring out the great mystery of the fish sacrifice.'

'That was a marvellous piece of deduction,' Hannah admitted.

They'd all laughed heartily the night before when Leonie had come up with a reason why fish were never shown as offerings to the gods on the various temple carvings. Flora, the guide, usually left them with an unanswered question at the end of a tour and told them that she'd explain it the next day.

Yesterday, Flora had answered the question about why Hatshepsut was the only queen buried in the Valley of the Kings and had posed another conundrum – about the fish sacrifices.

Leonie, who was fascinated with Egyptian myths, decided that the answer to the question lay in the story of the god Osiris. Hannah and Emma, sitting in the comfort of Hannah's cabin sharing a bottle of peach schnapps as a nightcap, laughed so much at her solemn explanation that they nearly fell off the bed.

'When Osiris's evil brother, Seth, killed Osiris and dismembered his body, scattering it around Egypt, Osiris's distraught wife, the goddess Isis, found all the pieces and put them back together,' Leonie explained enthusiastically. 'The only part she couldn't find was his penis, which had been eaten by a fish. So that's it.'

Hannah crowed with laughter. 'You're telling us that fish can't be used as a sacrifice because a fish ate Osiris's willy?'

'Yes, it's perfectly sensible to me.'

Emma, who had discovered that she really liked peach schnapps, got a fit of the giggles. 'But we had fish for dinner tonight,' she managed to say, between laughs. 'I think I'm going to puke!'

'You're a right pair of cultural illiterates,' Leonie said loftily. 'I don't know why you came to Egypt at all. You should have gone off to Ibiza with a couple of blokes with tattoos and a ghetto-blaster.'

Emma fell off the bed with a resounding bump. She put a hand over her mouth and giggled at the noise she'd made.

'Your father will be up in a moment to haul you off to bed,' Hannah squealed. 'I'll tell him I'll set Seth on him . . . geddit, set Seth . . .' She roared with laughter and Emma joined in.

'I'd like to see his face with his willy gobbled up by a fish,' roared Emma.

Leonie, who'd been so intent on her ancient Egyptian theory that she'd only had a quarter as much peach schnapps as the other two, gave up. She hauled Emma back on to the bed and then poured herself a huge drink. If you can't beat them, join them, she decided.

'I don't know what I'm going to tell people when I get home and they ask me who I met in Egypt,' she said, downing her drink in three gulps. 'They'll all think I had this cultured time talking about ancient civilizations with like-minded people, when in fact, I've been stuck with two insane, sex-mad alcoholics who think the pyramids are secretly flying saucers.'

'You mean they aren't?' demanded Hannah.

'Shut up and have another drink,' Leonie ordered.

The Fuzzy Navels they were drinking on the upper deck the following evening helped with the hangovers.

'Wave at the waiter and order us another round, will you?' Hannah asked Emma, who was facing the small upstairs bar where the waiters hung out.

'I need to go to the loo,' Emma said, 'but I can hear my father from here. He's downstairs and I don't want to have to go down or he'll try to make me sit with him.'

'He's a bit bossy,' Leonie ventured. She'd love to have said that Jimmy O'Brien was a domineering bully but knew she couldn't.

'You have no idea,' Emma said fervently. The Fuzzy Navels were going to her head. 'He has to be in charge and he has to be right all the time. It's a nightmare.'

'But you stood up to him earlier,' Leonie pointed out.

'And I'll have to pay later. He hates his authority being questioned publicly.'

'Do you see much of your parents at home?' Hannah enquired.

'I see them all the time,' Emma explained. 'They live around the corner from us. Pete and I couldn't have afforded a house on our salaries so Dad loaned us the deposit, then he insisted on our buying this house he liked. It's about five minutes from my old home.'

Hannah winced. 'So he feels he can drop in when he wants to and tell you what to do, on the basis that he's funded you.'

'Bingo.' Emma thought of how her father manipulated things so that she and Pete had Sunday lunch at the O'Briens' every fortnight, and how the question of what to do for Christmas never came up. It was the family do at the O'Briens' and that was it.

'Are you the only child?' Leonie asked.

'I've a younger sister, Kirsten, the one who got away. She's married and her husband is very successful. Dad adores her. But she's managed to get out of all the family stuff. She's managed to get out of having a job, too, because Patrick, my brother-in-law, is loaded. Basically, Kirsten does what Kirsten wants.'

'Sounds good to me,' Hannah remarked. 'My brother, Stuart is the same. When we were growing up, I had to look after my mother's hens in the summer and baby-sit for our relatives. Stuart never had to so much as wash a cup. Lazy pig. He was my mother's pride and joy, now his wife is the same. Pam treats him like he's next in line for the throne. We're not close, I should add.'

'Kirsten and I get on really well,' Emma said. 'She's great fun and I love spending time with her. It's a miracle I don't hate her, really, since Dad is so besotted with her. Do you have brothers or sisters, Leonie?'

'No, just me and my mother. And we get on really well,' she added, feeling almost guilty that she wasn't like the other two, both of whom appeared to have problem families. 'My father died years ago and Mum just gets on with her own life. She works part-time, goes to the cinema and hill-walks, oh yes, she's started playing golf. She does more than me, actually. She's never at home in the evenings, while I catch every episode of every soap on TV. Mum is very easy-going and easy to be with.'

'Like you,' Hannah said.

'I suppose I am easy-going,' Leonie agreed. 'Most of the time. But I do have a ferocious temper which explodes once in a blue moon and then . . . watch out.'

The other two pretended to duck under the table in fear. 'Will you warn us when you're about to explode?' Emma asked in a meek voice.

'Don't worry, you'll see it coming! I'll be sorry to go home,' Leonie said wistfully as they watched the sun sink.

'That's the sign of a good holiday,' Emma said.

'I mean, I'll be happy to be home, but it's been wonderful here. And I'll miss you two.'

Hannah smiled but said nothing.

'Me too,' Emma added earnestly.

Hannah spoke then. 'I know they always say that holiday romances never transfer to the real world when the holiday is over, but it can't be the same for holiday friendships. We've had great fun together. Let's meet up when we get home and try and stay friends. What do you both think?'

Emma grinned delightedly. 'I'd love that. We all get on so well, it'd be great.'

'Yeah, we could have dinner once a month or something,' Leonie suggested enthusiastically. 'We could meet at some midway point between where we all live.'

She thought about it. Her home was in Wicklow, south of the city and an hour's drive from the centre of Dublin. Emma was in Clontarf in north Dublin, which was a forty-minute drive into the centre of the city, while Hannah lived in the city near Leeson Street Bridge.

'My place is pretty much half-way between you two,' Hannah said. 'Sorry. You'll have to do all the driving.'

'I don't mind,' Leonie said. 'This holiday was about starting something new and since I didn't fall in love with some Omar Sharif lookalike, making two fabulous new friends is the next best thing.'

'You mean we're second best?' asked Emma, throwing *her* cocktail umbrella at Leonie.

Leonie laughed and threw it back. 'Only kidding. Right, let's plan the first get-together now. Two weeks after we get back so we still have a bit of a tan to wow the rest of the world. Oh, yeah, we can get our photos developed and bitch about our fellow travellers.'

'It's a deal,' Hannah said.

They clinked their now-empty glasses.

'To the Grand Egyptian Reunion,' Emma said loudly. 'Now, shall I order more drinks?'

CHAPTER SIX

Dragging her suitcase behind her, Emma opened her front door and breathed in the scent of a house where the windows hadn't been opened since she left. The peace lily in the hall looked like a weeping willow, its leaves drooping with thirst, while the newel post of the banisters was armour-plated with a selection of Pete's raincoats and sweaters. Ignoring the mess, Emma abandoned the suitcase at the bottom of the stairs and headed for the kitchen.

There was a note on the kitchen table, lying amid a week's worth of newspapers, supplements and junk mail. Emma put down her handbag, shivered in the chill of the Irish August which seemed so icy after Egypt, and switched on the kettle. Only then did she read the note.

Can't wait to see you, darling. I'm at a match. Back at seven. I've dinner under control. Don't do anything.

Love, Pete

She grinned. Dinner under control probably meant he'd stop off at Mario's on the way home and pick up a giant Four Seasons pizza with a side order of garlic potatoes.

She brought her tea and the luggage upstairs and started to unpack. Out of the suitcase came skirts, T-shirts and underwear, all mingled up with the postcards she couldn't resist and the pretty fake alabaster Egyptian figurines she'd bought in the souk in Luxor. She took one out of its tissue wrapping, marvelling at the detail of the carving on the falcon god, Horus.

It'd fall apart given a sharp knock, Flora the tour guide had warned the Nile cruisers, explaining that real alabaster statues were handmade and built to last, unlike their cheap street-market relatives. Emma hadn't cared. She'd wanted some cheap'n'cheerful souvenirs for the people in the office and, at three Egyptian pounds each, these statuettes fitted the bill perfectly. Happy with her purchases, she pulled the others from their wrapping until all six were uncovered and she began to plan which one she'd give to which colleague.

She took her sandals from the plastic bags she'd wrapped them up in and threw dirty clothes into the laundry basket which was already groaning with Pete's stuff.

Her mind wasn't really on unpacking: she was dying to see Pete and tell him everything; about her new friends and all the places they'd been . . . Then her hand touched something cool, soft and plastic. From under the folds of clothes she hadn't worn, she unearthed the big pack of sanitary towels, an Egyptian brand she'd never heard of with a picture of a dove on the front. She took the packet slowly from the case and the pain hit her again. The pain of knowing that there had been no baby growing safely inside her, wrapped in fierce love and protected from the world by Emma's body. No baby to rest its downy head against her breast, no soft mouth instinctively searching for the nipple, no crying, innocent little creature utterly dependent on Emma for everything.

The pain came from deep within herself. Her chest hurt, her head hurt, it felt as if even the bones of her body ached with the very hurt of it all. She heard a noise and realized it was herself, crying, keening like a woman at a funeral.

After days of holding on, she finally let the heartache out: every twinge of anguish, every pang of loss. It was as if a dam had burst.

Now that she was here, crouched on her own bedroom floor, leaning against the bed, she could cry to her heart's content over her lost baby. Because it was a lost baby to her. Another chance lost, another life she'd been so sure had been inside her gone. Leonie and Hannah had been good to her; they'd tried their best to understand and comfort her. But they didn't understand. Leonie had children, three lovely kids. Hannah didn't seem to want children yet, although Emma would never be able to understand how any woman could not want children. But she didn't. So it was different for them.

But Emma, she wanted her own baby with an intensity that was killing her. It had to be killing her, she thought as the tears ran unchecked down her cheeks, it hurt so much. That much hurt couldn't be good for you. It had to be like cancer, eating away inside you until there was nothing left but a shell, nothing but hate and rage and anger at anyone who had that one simple thing denied her.

Everybody else had children so effortlessly. People had babies by mistake, people had abortions. Emma was always reading about women in the newspapers who said things like: 'Little Jimmy was an accident after the other six, we'd never planned him . . .'

Even worse, her work with KrisisKids meant she was constantly exposed to the stories of abused and abandoned children, defenceless kids who'd been let down by the people who were supposed to love them most: their parents. It was as well, Emma reflected, that her role in the charity was administrative because if she had to personally deal with the crying kids who rang their helpline, she didn't know how she'd have been able to cope. The counsellors found it hard enough, she knew. Sometimes they left abruptly after their shift, white-faced and drained, unable to chat with their colleagues because there was simply no way to go from hearing a child's most terrible secrets to idly discussing the weather or what was on the TV that night. Emma knew she'd have been hopeless when faced with a child haltingly telling her about the cigarette burns or how daddy climbed into her bed at night and told her to keep a secret. Those people weren't parents: they were evil creatures, demonic. What she couldn't understand was why God gave them the gift of a child.

But then, how did God work out who got kids and who didn't? Who decided that Emma would remain childless while some blithe, unconcerned women had families the size of football teams? The rage she felt for those mothers shocked her. She wanted to kill them, women who took it all for granted. Who had no idea what it was like to yearn for a child, who simply laughed when the pregnancy test was positive, and said things like: 'Oh well, another kid for the football team!' or 'We've always meant to start a family, we may as well start now!'

She hated them, hated them with all her being.

Nearly as much as those women who held their children like trophies, proudly and smugly letting the world know that they had babies, even if some poor helpless women couldn't get the hang of it. Emma thought she hated those women most of all: they looked down at her, she knew it.

Like Veronica in the office, who wore her motherhood like a badge of honour, never ceasing to tell all and sundry about little Phil and how cute he was, never forgetting to slyly ask Emma if she didn't want children herself.

Veronica knew. Emma was sure of it. That knowledge was her lever over Emma, her boss.

'Phil is crawling around the house like a little rocket these days,' she'd announced recently as they all sat in the back office having their lunch. Then she'd directed a comment at Emma who hadn't really been paying attention: 'I can't believe you and Pete haven't started a family yet, Emma. You don't want to leave it too late, you know. And then find out you couldn't have kids!' she trilled, her voice grating.

Emma could have killed Veronica there and then. Instead she'd smiled woodenly and managed to get a few words out: 'There's plenty of time, we're in no hurry.'

She thought of Veronica as she sat there silently on the bedroom floor, the tears drying saltily on her cheeks. How would she ever face Veronica on Monday? Phil was bound to have done something miraculous for a toddler of his age during the past week and no doubt Veronica would be discussing whether to ring the *Guinness Book of Records* or not. Everyone would be asked their opinion and Veronica would give the subject far more attention than she ever gave her work. She wasn't a very good assistant. Maybe that was why she hated Emma and was so knowingly malicious. Emma was good at her job and childless. Veronica was bad at hers and was in training to be an earth mother. It was her only advantage and she used it.

Emma shivered. It was cold in the house: Pete hadn't thought to leave the heating on when he'd gone out. Her limbs felt stiff and achey, and she still had that lower back pain she got when she had her period. Finally, she got up and went into the bathroom to wash her face.

A blotchy-faced woman stared at her from the smeary bathroom mirror. A woman who looked young enough if you just took in her unlined face and pale skin dusted with a faint tan, but who looked a thousand years old if you stared at the bruised, hurt eyes.

The familiar pink bottle of baby lotion mocked her from its position on the shelf above the sink. She used it for taking off her eye make-up. Not that she didn't have proper eye make-up removers, of course. But she loved the smell of it, the baby smell of it. Sometimes, she rubbed it on her skin as moisturizer and imagined the smell of a small baby, nuzzling close to her, scented with baby lotion. Today, she shoved the bottle in the medicine cabinet where she wouldn't have to look at it.

Emma splashed water on her face and forced herself to apply some make-up. She didn't want to look like a death's head when Pete arrived home. It wasn't fair to lay all this grief on him, wasn't fair to make him suffer the same pain purely because she wasn't pregnant again. She had to go through too much agony because of her barren, useless womb: why should he have to go through it all too? Sometimes she wondered if she was right to keep her fears from him. Would it tear them apart, her longing for a baby and keeping it to herself? No, she decided. She wouldn't let it.

Just in case, she took one of her mother's Valiums. After a while, she felt marginally better, good enough to shove a load of clothes in the washing machine. She still moved around mechanically, but she could manage.

She was curled up in an armchair watching the costume drama that Pete had kindly taped for her while she was away, when she heard his key in the lock.

'I'm home, darling. Where are you?'

'In the sitting room.'

He was at the door in an instant, the back of his short dark hair still damp from the shower because he wouldn't have bothered to dry it. Solidly built and reliable, he was the perfect defensive player for his soccer team and sufficiently dependable-looking to make a very good sales rep.

His guileless face with the wide-spaced laughing brown eyes and the honest smile was appealing enough to make many a female office manager order far more stationery than she'd originally intended, simply because Pete told her she'd need it. He only said that when it was true. For his guileless expression wasn't a put-on job: Pete Sheridan was one of nature's gentlemen – kind, genuine and nice to children and animals. He'd never cheat on his expenses or walk out of a shop letting the cashier give him change for a twenty when he'd only paid with a tenner. Scrupulously honest was the perfect description of Pete.

Now he threw himself on top of Emma joyfully and kissed her face and neck until she squealed that he was tickling her.

'Missed you,' he said.

'Missed you too.' She held on to him, gaining comfort from his closeness. She loved him so much, adored him. All she wanted, Emma thought, her face hard against the rough wool of his heavy sweater, was his baby. She felt her eyes tear up again and bit her lip harshly in an attempt to stop them. She was not going to break down in front of Pete. She'd promised herself.

'Get off me, you big lump,' she said jokily, trying to make her voice light-hearted. 'You're flattening me.'

'Sorry.'

While her husband levered himself off the armchair, Emma wiped her hand over her eyes, whisking away the tears.

Pete threw himself on to another chair from where he could reach over and hold her hand.

'Tell me everything. How was the trip and how was your father? He didn't get arrested and thrown into an Egyptian prison or anything, did he?'

In spite of herself, Emma grinned. 'No, although I'm surprised the tour guide didn't arrange it. You want to have heard him giving out yards to her when he discovered we had to pay extra to bring cameras into some of the sights.' She shuddered at the recollection and her face burned in remembered shame.

'Oh God, a female tour guide,' groaned Pete. 'That won't have gone down well.' It was no secret that Jimmy O'Brien believed women were less evolved than men. Certainly no secret to his daughter, who'd been brought up hearing the impatient words, 'Here, let me do that. Women are useless at practical things,' all the time. It had never bothered Kirsten because she liked other people doing things for her and had no intention of learning to do anything that involved being practical.

'Tell me about it,' Emma sighed. 'He lost his temper totally in the Valley of the Kings and started yelling at Flora about how we'd paid for the tour and shouldn't have to pay any extra to use our cameras. Then he said that it was obvious the ticket-office people were taking advantage of her because she was a woman and they knew she'd fall for a scam like that, so why didn't he go in and sort things out.'

'Business as usual,' Pete remarked sagely. 'He's quite a character, your father.'

Character, felt Emma, wasn't the word.

'Egypt was incredible,' she enthused, squeezing Pete's hand to show him that she was thrilled to be back, 'but if it hadn't been for these two women I met on the trip, Leonie and Hannah, I don't think I'd have remained sane. Dad drove me mad and Mum is definitely losing her marbles, or losing something.'

'It's your father,' Pete said. 'He has that effect on everyone.'

'No.' Emma shook her head emphatically. 'It's nothing to do with Dad, for once. She's getting very forgetful. She kept wittering on about the foreign currency and trying to work out how many Egyptian pounds there were to Irish ones. Normally she'd leave that sort of thing to Dad, but this time she became obsessed with working it out. She was vague a lot of the time, as if she wasn't aware of where she was. I don't know, I can't put my finger on it but there's something not quite right.'

'Come on.' Pete got to his feet and held out a hand to pull Emma from her chair. 'Let's put the pizza in the oven and you can tell me about these two women you met on the trip. If they can perform the phenomenal feat of keeping your mind off your parents, can they come and stay with us for Christmas?'

'There's a thought,' Emma groaned, thinking of the trauma of enforced festive jollity in the O'Brien house, a place where peace and goodwill to all men was an alien concept. 'You'd love them, Pete. Hannah is really confident and fun. Dad couldn't stand her, naturally. And Leonie is sweet. She's got three kids, she's divorced, and I think she's really lonely. Hannah insists our mission in life is to find a nice husband for Leonie.'

'Neil is looking for a sweet divorcée,' Pete said, referring to one of his old schoolfriends. 'We could fix them up.'

'Neil is looking for a sex-bomb housekeeper whom he doesn't have to pay and, no, I wouldn't dream of setting poor Leonie up with him,' Emma said sternly. 'She's been through enough in her life without getting stuck with Neil, his dandruff and his Newcastle fetish.'

'I'll tell him you said that.' Pete inexpertly cut the plastic wrapper off the pizza and jammed it into the oven, which was so dripping with blackened tomato and burnt mozzarella that Emma knew he'd eaten nothing but frozen pizzas all week. 'We're meeting him down the pub later.'

She groaned. 'Do we have to, love? I thought we'd have a quiet night in now that I'm home.'

Pete completed his cordon bleu preparations by switching the oven on, and then put his arms round Emma.

'I know, but I couldn't help it. It's Janine's birthday and Mike wants us to celebrate with them.'

Mike worked with Pete in the stationery business and the two couples often went out together for dinner. Emma was very fond of them, but wasn't in the mood for being sociable. She wanted to snuggle up with Pete and maybe, just maybe, talk to him about the whole baby thing.

'Why's Neil coming?' she asked.

'He was at the match today and Mike asked him along. Seems that some of Janine's single friends will be there and you know Neil, mention single females and he's drooling to be asked.'

'Mention single chimpanzees and Neil's drooling,' Emma pointed out. 'And you wanted to fix him up with Leonie?'

'I don't know what she's like,' protested Pete. 'They might be perfect together.'

Regretting being so grumpy about the night out, Emma patted her husband's denim-clad bum fondly. 'No, darling, perfect is you and me. Now tell me: did you eat any of the beautiful home-cooked meals I left in the freezer for you, or did you plough all your wages into the frozen foods section of the supermarket?'

The Coachman's was buzzing with a Saturday evening crowd when Pete and Emma pushed their way through to the corner where Mike and Janine were holding court.

'Hiya, guys,' roared Mike, getting up off his barstool to give it to Emma. 'Sit in beside Janine. She's giving out yards to me because it's her birthday and we've been talking footie all night.'

Janine was everything Emma was not. Like a modern Gina Lollobrigida, she had curves in all the right places and favoured sex goddess eyeliner, vermilion lips and clothes from Morgan which she probably had to be sewn into. She and Emma got on like a house on fire, having the same sense of humour and problems with families. Although, in Janine's case, her mother was the domineering one, ruling her family with an iron fist in a floral oven glove. They'd spent many companionable hours discussing home life while their respective spouses discussed the shocking performance at Shelbourne Park the previous day.

'Welcome back,' she said now, planting a pout of Mac's Ruby Woo lipstick on Emma's cheek. 'Tell me everything about your holiday. Was it wonderful?'

It was closing time when they finally left, Janine leading the way because otherwise the boys would never go home, she declared. As Pete had been smiling at Emma all evening, whispering into her ear that he'd missed her and was going to do all sorts of erotic things to her when they got home, she didn't think she'd have any trouble getting Pete to leave the pub.

'I'm shattered and if I don't get to bed soon, I'll collapse,' Janine announced as they stood in the pub hallway waiting for the men to make their way through the crowds. 'We had such a mad day yesterday, Em. Mike's sister was having her baby christened and it turned into an almighty party.'

Beside her, Emma stiffened. Another baby; Jesus, was there no escaping this.

'Honestly, you want to hear Mike's mother when she's got a few drinks in her. She's delirious about being a granny for the first time and she was dropping hints like bricks about me and Mike.' Janine chuckled at the very idea, oblivious to how quiet Emma had gone. She rooted in her handbag and dragged out a Polaroid photo of a smiling baby with huge eyes and not a scrap of hair.

Emma took the photo and made all the right noises as she looked at it. What a beautiful baby, she thought, longing and misery building up inside her. Why, oh why couldn't it be hers?

'It's a lovely baby, don't get me wrong, but God, the mess! That child is only two months old and to bring him anywhere, you need a vanload of stuff. Bottles, nappies, pushchairs! Get off!' she squealed as Mike finally caught up with them and grabbed her from behind. 'I thought you'd be too shagged after today for anything kinky,' she laughed.

'How could he be too shagged?' demanded Pete with a glint in his eye. 'He did nothing on the pitch, failed to score twice and nearly fell asleep when he was marking the other team's winger. He'll have loads of energy!'

They went their separate ways, clambering into taxis and arranging to phone each other during the week. Emma knew she was being very quiet on the way home, but she couldn't help it. All the fun had gone out of the evening thanks to Janine's comments. Someone else with a baby. Mike's sister was only a year or so younger than Mike, which made her around twenty-nine. Younger than Emma. It killed her when women who were younger got pregnant. Was that what women felt years ago when their younger sisters got married before them? Being older and left on the shelf was supposed to be some sort of shame. Now the shame was being childless when girls younger than you were dropping babies like rabbits.

At home, Emma climbed the stairs slowly, still in her baby dreamworld. She was almost surprised when Pete didn't go into the bathroom to brush his teeth but instead pulled her down on to their bed, kissing her passionately. It wasn't his fault, she thought blankly as she let him unbutton her blue shirt. He was telling her he adored her but his words seemed to roll off her.

They'd made such wonderful love in the beginning, she remembered. Neither of them had been exactly experienced – well, Emma didn't count the year dating her first teenage boyfriend as experience. But they'd both taken to the concept of fun in bed like fish to water. Her sister Kirsten had jokingly given them a *Joy of Sex* book as a secret engagement present, and they'd gone through the whole thing from beginning to end, never quite getting the hang of some of the more athletic positions.

But it was changed now. Emma never bought strawberries or chocolate buttons for sexy games in bed; she hadn't purchased any Body Shop massage oil in months. All sex had become trying-for-a-baby sex. Pete didn't appear to notice this change. He still enjoyed himself and did his best to make Emma enjoy herself too. But he didn't know that the passionate moments which used to give her so much pleasure no longer transported her into a world of erotic bliss.

Instead, she was willing each sperm to swim wildly up her cervix, to breach the tiny opening and emerge like brave warriors into the fallopian tubes in search of her all-precious eggs. While Pete was groaning in sexual frenzy, Emma was on an incredible journey, like a documentary camera filming groundbreaking footage inside a woman's uterus, watching the miracle of conception. Sexual pleasure came a poor second to the thrill of conception in Emma's book.

And *The Joy of Sex* no longer gave her the thrill that Annabel Karmel's toddler babyfoods book did. Hidden at the back of her wardrobe, her nest of baby books gave her solace and comfort. Like the few shameful baby things she'd bought on one trip to Mothercare. She'd felt so guilty even going in there, as if she had the word 'impostor' tattooed on her forehead. People would know she wasn't a mother; only experienced women could tell which sort of bootees you should buy for a newborn. She'd planned to say she was buying a present for a friend if any nosy shop assistant noticed her inexperienced fingering of tiny garments. But nobody had come near her, so she'd borne away the small pink velour dress with pride. You couldn't buy baby clothes and not need them, could you? God wouldn't do that to a person. She would need them, of course she would. Maybe not yet but someday, soon.

On Sunday morning, she rang Leonie to say hello. She didn't know why she had this compulsion to talk to Leonie, but she did. There was something comforting about Leonie, and there was the added bonus that she and Hannah knew how Emma felt deep-down about her desire for a child. There was no need to bullshit with people who knew your heart's desires.

'Emma!' Leonie said, sounding delighted to hear from her. 'How are you, my love?'

Emma gasped and let out a little sob. 'Terrible, Leonie. That's why I'm ringing you. I'm a mess, I'm sorry, I'll go . . .'

Leonie interrupted her: 'Don't you dare hang up, you mad thing. It's always depressing to come home and discover everything is exactly the same as it was before. You half expect that the world will have caught up with your renewed sense of purpose and, of course, it hasn't. Is it the baby?' she asked softly.

'Yes.'

'What are you doing today?'

Emma shook her head and then, realizing Leonie couldn't see her, said: 'I don't know. Nothing really. We'll probably go to the cinema tonight and I should spend today sorting out the house and the washing.'

'So you and Pete have nothing planned? Well, will he mind if I steal you away for an hour?'

'No.'

'That's a deal, then,' Leonie said firmly. 'I'll phone Hannah and see if she's free. I'll hop in the car and be with you in an hour, OK?'

'OK,' Emma said tremulously.

'Wait a moment and I'll phone you back.'

Hannah didn't answer the phone until the fifth ring. 'I was

vacuuming,' she explained to Leonie. 'I've been up since eight and, as the place was a disaster, I've cleaned everything, done the kitchen cupboards and most of the hand washing.'

Leonie grinned. 'Will you come and do my house next?' she joked. 'All I've done this morning is walk Penny and toy with the idea of unpacking my suitcase. I'm phoning because Emma rang and she sounds very down. I suggested meeting in an hour for a quick coffee. Are you game?'

'Yes, you can come here,' Hannah suggested. 'The place is clean now.'

'As in, it was a tip in the first place?' teased Leonie.

'Well, it was a bit . . .' started Hannah until she realized she was being neurotically houseproud and Leonie was teasing her. 'Bitch. You bring the biscuits and I'll have the coffee perking, right?'

Leonie got directions, then phoned Emma with them and arranged to meet in an hour.

'Pete, love, I'm just popping out for a few hours,' Emma called to her husband who was engrossed in the Sunday papers in the kitchen. 'I've got a book of Leonie's and I have to give it back to her, so we're meeting for a coffee.' She didn't want to say she was meeting the girls because she needed the moral support they provided her with. It seemed traitorous to seek comfort from them instead of from Pete, but she couldn't tell him how she felt. Not yet.

Hannah's flat was just like her: perfectly elegant with not a caramel velvet cushion out of place. After hugging each other delightedly, Emma and Leonie prowled around the small living room, admiring the modern fireplace with the fat cream candles in their cast-iron holders and the arrangement of cacti in a gravel-filled pot on the small glass-topped coffee table. Everything was airy and contemporary, from the muslin curtains draped over a cast-iron pole to the oatmeal throws Hannah had arranged carefully over her two elderly armchairs. Beautiful black-and-white photos of city streets hung in silver frames on the cream wall, but there were no family photos, no pictures of a smiling Hannah with other members of her family, Leonie noticed. It was as if she'd divorced herself from her past and used arty photos from other people's lives to hide the fact.

'I'm so sorry about the coffee,' Hannah apologized for about the fifth time, as she came into the room with three fat yellow ceramic cups on big saucers. She'd been horrified when she went to make the coffee to discover that she only had instant. She loved it, but it wasn't polite to serve instant, was it? She hated feeling insecure about things like that. At home, they'd only ever drunk tea and their guests had never been what you'd describe as polite society. It was when she was entertaining that Hannah really felt her lack of understanding for things like how to hold a fork or how to introduce people to each other. She longed to be blasé about these matters, longed to know instinctively instead of always carefully watching other people for hints.

'Stop fussing about the coffee,' Leonie said, waving a hand at her. 'Far from percolated coffee we were all reared. We never have real coffee at home or I'd be permanently broke. Danny loves it and uses up a pound in a week.'

'Instant is perfect,' Emma added. 'Your flat is so pretty. You really know how to create a lovely atmosphere. I'd never know how to make those muslin curtains drape.'

'Penny would have them dragged off the pole in a week because she loves going in behind the curtains to sulk,' Leonie said with a laugh. 'That's probably where she is right now, actually, sulking with me. She was thrilled when I got home last night but she wouldn't let me out of her sight all morning, convinced I was going to leave her. She howled when she saw me putting on my good coat.'

'How's poor Clover?' asked Hannah. 'Traumatized from the cattery?'

Leonie nodded guiltily. 'As soon as I got her home, she shot into Danny's room and hasn't come out since. She's probably under the duvet, shivering and covering it with cat hairs. Herman is fine, though. Mum's cats didn't manage to terrorize him for once. In fact, if anything, he's got fat.'

Emma laughed. 'I think Pete must have been eating the same as Herman,' she said. 'He survived on chips and pizza all week and I swear he's put on a few pounds. We were all teasing him about it in the pub.' Her face darkened. 'That's why I was such an idiot on the phone to you earlier,' she said to Leonie. 'Not because of Pete, but . . .' she sighed. 'We were in the pub with our friends Mike and Janine, and she began to tell me about Mike's sister who's had a baby and, I don't know, I went to pieces. It's ridiculous, isn't it? Mention the word "baby" and I become this blubbering fool.'

She took a scalding sip of coffee. It seemed normal to talk about it here. At home, she'd felt as if she was on the verge of a breakdown and wondered if Pete or anyone else would think her unhinged if she said how miserable she felt. But Hannah and Leonie thought it was perfectly natural to talk about your feelings. They seemed to understand how easy it was to have your emotions upended by something.

'Of course it's not ridiculous,' Hannah said kindly. 'I'm like that with Harry. One minute, I'm on top of the world and the next, I see someone walking down the street wearing a jacket like his and I get so freaked out that I don't know if I'm furious or miserable. I start having fantasies about what I'd say to him if I ever saw him again and what sort of garden pruning device I'd use on him . . .'

Emma giggled. 'I have baby fantasies,' she admitted. 'I'm in the car and I imagine what it must be like to be driving around with the baby in the back, talking to her and telling her what we're going to do. You know, "Mummy's bringing you to the shops to buy you some lovely new clothes and then we're going to the park for a big walk to look at the ducks."' She'd never told anyone that before. It was too private.

Leonie patted her arm. 'You can tell us anything, Em,' she said simply, as if she'd known what Emma was thinking. 'That's what friends are for. Maybe because we're new friends and don't have all sorts of histories with each other, we can accept each other for what we really are.'

Emma nodded. 'I know. It's great, isn't it?'

The hour stretched to an hour and a half. More coffee was needed and Emma insisted she make it. 'If we're going to be proper friends, then you can't be waiting on us like a couple of guests,' she told Hannah. 'My God,' she said moments later. 'Your kitchen is spotless.

Are you sure you aren't related to my mother? She'd adore you.'

Hannah stuck on a Harry Connick Jnr CD and they all listened to his mellow voice as they went through the rest of the croissants Leonie had brought.

'He's a fine thing, Harry,' Emma said as Harry sang 'It Had To Be You' in his own special way.

'Yeah, but his name ruins it,' laughed Hannah. 'Anyway, I've gone off dark men. My Harry was dark-haired, so I think I'll go for blonds from now on.'

'Ooh, like who?' asked Leonie. 'Describe him to us, your fantasy man.'

Sitting on an armchair, Hannah hugged her knees to her chest and contemplated him: 'Tall, because I like wearing high heels and I hate men who are smaller than me. Muscular, definitely, and with blue eyes, like yours, Leonie; piercing blue to gaze into my soul. Strong bones and wonderful hands for touching me all over. And golden, honeyed skin and hair to match.'

'That's Robert Redford you're talking about,' Leonie warned, 'and he's mine. If he turns up on your doorstep, you are not to lay a hand on him. Or our friendship will be over.'

'You have to think of your own fantasy man,' objected Hannah. 'You can't just duplicate mine.'

'OK, OK.' Leonie loved this game. She played it all the time herself, picturing the man who'd rescue her from singledom. 'Sorry, Hannah, I'm not copying you, but he has to be tall and strong, really. Otherwise he'll never be able to carry me over the threshold without rupturing some vital bit. And,' she giggled, 'he'll need all his vital bits in perfect working order. Let's see . . . He's got to be over forty and I think I fancy dark men, definitely, but he can have greying temples. That's very sexy, distinguished. You can see yourself running your fingers through the grey bits . . .'

'You can't have sex with him until you've finished describing him,' teased Hannah.

'Dark eyes and a Kirk Douglas chin.'

'What's that?' Emma asked, puzzled.

'With a dent in it,' Leonie answered. 'I used to watch all those old movies when I was a kid and I fancied Kirk something rotten. There was one pirate movie he was in and I dreamed about being the girl in it for months. Oh yes, he has to be filthy rich and love children, animals and women who never stick to their diet. Your turn, Em.'

Emma smiled shyly. 'I know you'll think I'm daft, but Pete is my fantasy man. He's not terribly tall and he's not muscular, although he's fit. He's going bald but I adore him. He's it.'

Hannah and Leonie smiled at her affectionately. 'That's wonderful,' Hannah said.

'True love,' Leonie added. 'You are lucky, you know.'

CHAPTER SEVEN

Hannah had been having a wonderful day until she met the postman when she was on her way back to her front door that evening. He didn't say anything rude or jokingly ask her if she'd joined a convent in her stark grey jacket, long matching skirt, and white shirt, which he'd said one day he met her as she was coming back from a job interview. No, he simply shoved a bunch of letters into the letterbox of the open front door, and the rest of the evening was kaput. Hannah bent to pick them up and realized that two were for her, one in Harry's writing.

His familiar sloping scrawl was instantly recognizable. He never could do joined up writing, they used to joke. Well ha, bloody, ha! she snarled now. It wasn't cute or even amusing. It was plain stupid. Imagine a thirty-six-year-old man who couldn't write properly. She dumped the rest of the letters on the hall table for the other residents and rushed in, shaking her hair to get rid of the light drizzle that had appeared from nowhere. Up till then, it had been a great day.

Her first day working in Dwyer, Dwyer & James estate agent's and she'd arrived early. Parking the car in a space opposite the branch, she sat there for a few moments and began to breathe deeply. She filled her lungs with air, held it and then exhaled slowly. It was a wonderful way of preparing yourself for the day, she found. Somebody tapped on her window and Hannah leapt in her seat. The window was misted up so she instinctively rubbed it to see who was looking in. A strange woman was smiling in at her. Harmless looking, Hannah felt, noticing the good raincoat, pleasant middle-aged face and pearl necklace above a pink pussy-cat bow blouse, but still strange. She rolled down the window.

'Yes?'

'You must be Hannah. I'm Gillian from Dwyer, Dwyer & James. I spotted you from the newsagent's and thought you were wondering if you should park there or not. But you can.'

'That's kind of you,' Hannah answered politely, getting out of the car and thinking that not a lot must happen in Dun Laoghaire if people spent their time peering out of the newsagent's window looking out for the new employees.

'You looked lost in thought . . .' said the woman helpfully.

'Just wondering where to park,' Hannah lied blithely. She wasn't about to tell this person that she never lost a moment's sleep about parking and was sitting there because she was nervous about this new job and needed time to put on her cool, calm façade. Letting people know about your personal life was only asking for trouble, she'd decided. How could she operate as the cool and collected Ms Campbell if the staff knew how she had to calm herself down with yoga breathing? She couldn't, that was the simple answer.

Two hours later, Hannah knew that Gillian had been on reception for years and worked part-time for the senior Mr Dwyer, a kindly faced man who could be seen through his glass-fronted office reading a huge batch of morning papers and getting Gillian to say he wasn't in to phone callers.

'The reception is so busy that I'd prefer to do just one job, looking after Mr Dwyer,' Gillian whispered, as if Mr Dwyer required a lot of looking after.

Hannah also knew that the ladies toilet had an extractor fan problem (recounted in a whisper by Gillian), that the young Steve Shaw would try and chat her up as soon as he saw her even though he was only back from his honeymoon, and that Donna Nelson, the firm's newest senior agent, was a single mother, 'although she seems like a nice enough girl,' Gillian sniffed, as if single motherdom and niceness were mutually exclusive. Hannah said nothing.

Gillian herself had back problems: 'My chiropractor says I shouldn't work, but what would I do with myself at home?' she tittered. Hannah forbore to suggest, 'Contribute to a gossip column?' She was married to Leonard, had one son, a deeply unsuitable daughter-in-law, and a budgie named Clementine, who was a boy.

Hannah, who was supposed to be learning the intricacies of the firm's reception with Gillian as her guide, would have preferred to hear more about dealing with clients and which agents dealt with which areas, and less about how clever Clementine was and what he could do with his mirror. It was soon clear that Gillian, having given so much of herself, was now looking for payback from Hannah in the form of her life story.

Hannah hadn't divulged one bit of personal information all morning, despite Gillian's avalanche of intimate chat. Neither had Hannah mentioned that her job was actually going to be that of office manager but that she'd been asked to start on reception as a way of learning more about the firm. One of her first jobs as office manager would be to train the new receptionist starting the following week. Judging by how Gillian appeared to enjoy her lofty position as Mr Dwyer's assistant, she wouldn't be pleased to find Hannah was actually her senior in the company structure. She'd find out soon enough.

'Are you married?' Gillian asked, pale eyes twinkling in her rosy face, discreet pearl earrings catching the light. She was a monster, Hannah decided. A monster who traded in stories of human misery and who needed Hannah's story to add to her collection of scalps.

'Or engaged . . . ?'

Hannah hadn't grown up in a remote western town where disapproving gossip was the lifeblood of half the residents for nothing.

'Neither,' she said bluntly. Then she gazed coolly at Gillian, holding the other woman's eyes for at least thirty seconds until Gillian looked away uncomfortably.

She'd got the message, Hannah decided.

'I'll make us some tea,' Hannah said warmly. It was vital not to upset Gillian, after all. Just to let her see that Hannah would not be revealing any delicate personal details for the office bulletin board.

It was nearly lunchtime before David James, who had interviewed

Hannah in the firm's city-centre office for the job, arrived. 'He's been busy with the Dawson Street office but he still drops in here from time to time,' Gillian revealed, searching for her frosted pink lipstick when Mr James's Jag pulled up outside the door.

He doesn't drop in often enough, Hannah felt, looking around the rather run-down premises which was a total contrast to the stylish Dawson Street branch. There, the minimalist look ruled with architect-designed furniture, modern prints on the walls and an air of discreet wealth simmered gently in the background.

The Dun Laoghaire branch of Dwyer, Dwyer & James looked like somebody's idea of an elegant office circa 1970. The walls were coffee-coloured, the seats for clients were the sort of low squashy things fashionable when Charlie's Angels were famous the first time, and big brown felt screens divided up the private bits of the office from the public bits. The address was prestigious but the office was a shambles.

In between Gillian's monologues, Hannah had been wondering whether she'd made a huge and hideous mistake in giving up her nice job for this place. Dwyer, Dwyer & James were a big, powerful firm and she'd felt it was a step upwards to work for them as office manager. But this branch was like the office that time forgot.

David James, tall, strongly built and with the sort of commanding presence that reduced the place to silence, walked in, shook hands with Hannah, said he hoped she was settling in and asked to see her in the back office. He threw a raincoat on to the back of a chair and pulled off his suit jacket to reveal muscular shoulders straining under a French blue shirt. He was quite handsome really, she realized. She hadn't noticed it at her interview; she'd been too nervous. But there was something attractive about that broad, strong-boned face and the sleek salt-and-pepper hair. He was probably in his early forties, although the lines around his narrow eyes made him appear slightly older. Immaculate in his expensive clothes, he somehow looked as if he'd be just as at home wielding an axe to chop wood in the wilderness as wielding a Mont Blanc pen in a swish office. He certainly had the colour of someone who liked outdoor pursuits. Not a man to mess with.

'Have you spoken to my partner, Andrew Dwyer, yet?' he asked, settling himself into a big chair, not looking at her as his eyes raked over the papers on the desk that required his attention.

'No. Gillian has been filling me in,' Hannah said.

A flash of brief understanding passed between them, David's dark eyes glinting.

'Ah, Gillian, yes,' he murmured. 'It's not really suitable for Gillian to be doing two jobs. That's why I've hired you. I'm sure you're wondering what you've done, coming from the Triumph Hotel to this place.'

That's exactly what Hannah had been thinking but she was too clever to show it. She kept her face carefully blank.

'This was our first premises and it's ten years since I left,' he said.

Hannah was surprised. Listening to Gillian, you'd have thought Mr James had been gone from Dun Laoghaire for a mere six months.

'My nephew Michael set up the Howth office eight years ago and he was due to come back here to take over but personal reasons prevented him doing it. I didn't have the time to sort this place out. Things have gone downhill here recently since the other Mr Dwyer died. There'll be a lot of changes and I thought we needed a good manager for the place. I need someone who can get on with the existing staff and be able to work with any new ones. That's why I hired you. I know you're a hard worker and I like your style, Hannah.

'We never had an office manager before. Gillian ran the office when it was a small concern, but we've barely been ticking over for a long time. We need a proper office manager, someone who can keep us running smoothly, getting auction brochures printed, etc. From the point of view of security, we need someone who is always aware of where the agents are. When you have people on their own showing houses, you have to be security conscious. I want the female agents to be contacted every hour to make sure they're safe. I'm very confident that you can do it.'

'Thanks,' she said briskly.

'Now, if Donna Nelson's back, perhaps you could send her in. I need to have a talk with her.'

Hannah was glad she was working directly with David James.

Direct and blunt, he clearly didn't waste any time on chatting. He was just the sort of person Hannah enjoyed working for. With someone like him, there'd be no need for extraneous conversations about the state of the weather or how strong the office coffee was.

Gillian was dying to know how she'd got on.

'Isn't Mr James a pet,' she sighed. 'His marriage broke up and he's never really got over it. I mean, he went out with a few women, but nothing worked out. I think he's lonely, don't you sense it too?'

What Hannah sensed was that Gillian would have given poor hubbie Leonard and the talented Clementine the push if she could have comforted Mr James in a very unplatonic way.

By close of business, she'd met all the firm's agents and had liked Donna Nelson best of all. A rather chic woman with a dark bob, navy suit and an efficient air, she was obviously very wary of Gillian and had greeted Hannah with a guarded smile that said, *She's been telling you all about me, hasn't she*?

Hannah responded with her warmest smile and said pleasantly: 'Perhaps we could have a chat during the week and you can tell me how you'd like your calls handled.'

'That would be great,' Donna said, looking pleased. Probably sick and tired of Gillian's sharp manner with clients, she was relieved to find someone who knew how to answer a phone without cutting the nose off someone.

Business didn't appear to be brisk, but Gillian's put-on phone voice, as frosty as her lipstick, wouldn't have enticed cold callers to put their homes for sale through Dwyers.

One caller looking for Donna received a particularly sharp remark: 'If she has time, she'll get back to you.'

'Personal call,' Gillian said disapprovingly, hanging up.

Hannah said nothing again but vowed that when she had sole charge of the office, things would be vastly different. No receptionist she'd train would ever be so rude on the phone.

David James had chatted to her briefly before he left the office that afternoon, balancing his big frame awkwardly on the edge of her desk.

'How are you getting on?' he asked.

Beside her, Hannah could feel Gillian sitting up straight in her office chair, hoping to be noticed.

'Fine. I think I'll have the hang of it in a few days, although it's easy enough to lose calls on this switchboard. The one in the Triumph was more modern and more efficient,' she said frankly.

This time, she could sense Gillian bridling with shock that a new employee had dared say such a thing to the boss, but David James merely nodded.

'We'll talk about it,' he said. 'Goodbye.'

'You're the forward madam, I'll say that for you,' sniffed Gillian when he was gone.

'You said exactly the same thing about the switchboard earlier,' Hannah reminded her gently. 'I was merely telling him.'

'Mr James doesn't want to be bothered with things like that,' hissed Gillian.

Hannah said nothing.

She'd felt pleased as she drove home that evening, pleased that she had made the right choice in moving jobs and confident that she'd do well there. Bloody Harry and his ill-timed letter had ruined that sense of pleasure.

She went into her flat, threw her coat on the hanger and opened the letter.

> *Dear Hannah,*
> *How's it going, babe? Hope you've taken over the entire hotel business in Dublin by now. Knowing you, you have.*
> *I'm still trekking around South America. Just spent a few weeks in BA (that's Buenos Aires to you, babes).*

'Babes!' she snarled, grinding her teeth fiercely. How bloody dare he call her 'babes'?

> *I've been travelling with some guys and we're planning another month here before we go to Chile . . .*

She read lines and lines of chatter about odd-jobbing as a tourist guide and how he'd got a few shifts in an English-language newspaper the previous month. It was all surface stuff; nothing personal, no hint as to why he was writing to her for the first time in a year. It wasn't as if she'd wanted a letter. Not now, anyway. In the first month after he'd left, she'd have killed someone for any news of Harry. Just a postcard or a phone call to say he missed her and wished he hadn't left. If he'd phoned to beg her to visit him, she'd have downed tools and hopped on the first plane to Rio de Janeiro. It was immaterial that she'd thrown him out of the flat when he first announced that he was leaving her to travel abroad, immaterial that she'd roared at him for being a spineless coward who was terrified of commitment and that she never wanted to see or hear from him again. Ever. Because she missed him so much.

And for the first time in her life, Hannah had discovered that when you adored someone and missed them so badly you woke up in the middle of the night screaming out their name, you still wanted them back, no matter what they'd done or said.

Without even reading the final page, Hannah folded the letter carefully and stuck it in a drawer in the kitchen. She didn't want to think about Harry. She didn't want to remember what he even looked like . . .

Eleven years ago, he'd been attractive in a studenty way. Dark hair that reached his collar and curled madly when it got wet; bluey grey eyes that turned down at the corners and made him look constantly forlorn, and that wide, mobile mouth that could smile so mischievously. He always wore big jackets and baggy trousers that looked two sizes too big for him. But then, that was part of the charm of Harry Spender: his little boy qualities made women want to mother him.

Hannah had mothered him for ten long years, from the moment they'd met in McDonald's and he'd spilt his milkshake all over the uniform she wore as a beauty counter assistant in Brown Thomas.

'OhmiGod, I'm so sorry, please let me help you clean it off,' he'd said, his face a picture of innocent remorse as they both stared at the remains of a strawberry shake dripping steadily off Hannah and on to the floor.

And she'd gone with him in the direction of the toilets, not even nervous about going off with a strange man, even when he came into the ladies with her and insisted on using loo paper to soak the shake off.

She should have refused him when he asked her out for a drink that evening. But then, Hannah was her mother's daughter and, at the age of twenty-seven, she was still young enough to be impressed by someone who actually wrote for the *Evening Press*.

At home in Connemara, the Campbell family had only ever read two newspapers: the local paper the *Western People* and the *Sunday Press*. She'd grown up with it, had watched her mother put the previous week's paper at the bottom of the chickens' coop when they were hatched under the kitchen table; had laid it on the floor so that the men coming home from working on the farm wouldn't muddy the floor with their filthy boots. To go out with someone who worked for the same group, well!

Of course, when she finally met Harry, court reporter extraordinaire, Hannah's mother hadn't been that impressed by him despite his job. But it was too late then. Hannah loved him and could already see herself walking down the aisle with him, radiant in white something or other, smiling for the official photo which would appear in that Sunday's paper. Together for richer for poorer, for better for worse. Hannah loved that idea, the notion of stability, security.

Marriage hadn't been on Harry's mind. 'I'm a free spirit, Hannah, you've always known that: I thought that's what you liked about me,' he'd said as she stared at him slack-jawed the day he told her about South America.

'Yes, but up till now your version of being a free spirit meant going to music festivals, buying Jimi Hendrix albums and not paying the phone bill until they threaten to cut us off!' she shrieked, when she finally found her voice.

Harry shrugged. 'I'm not getting any younger,' he said. He was the same age as Hannah. 'I don't want to waste my life. This trip is just what I've been looking for. I've been stagnating, Hannah. We both have.'

That was when she picked up his leather jacket and threw it out the front door. 'Leave!' she yelled. 'Leave now, before you waste any more of your precious life. I'm so sorry I was a waste of time and contributed to your stagnation.'

She hadn't seen or heard from him since. He'd left there and then, and slipping back in to pack up his stuff the following day when she wasn't at home. Rage and fury had possessed Hannah as soon as he was gone, and she'd immediately moved out of the flat they'd shared into another smaller, nicer place, using their deposit money to buy a new bed and sofa. There was no way she was sleeping on the bed she'd shared with that bastard. If he wanted his share of the money back, he could sue her. He already owed her ten years of her life, not to mention all the cash she'd loaned him over the years because he frittered his salary away.

For a year, nothing. And now, out of the blue, came a letter. On the first day of her new job, Hannah sat for a moment at her kitchen table, staring into space. Then she wrenched open the drawer and read the rest of the letter.

Two paragraphs from the end, Harry got to the point: *'I'm sure you're wondering why I'm writing, Hannah. But you can't cut someone out of your life when you've spent ten years with them.'* Oh yes you can, she hissed at the letter.

> *I'm coming home in a few months and I'd love to see you. I've kept in touch with what you're up to, thanks to Mitch. He gave me your new address.*

Damn Mitch, cursed Hannah. One of Harry's old colleagues, she'd told him where she was living when they'd bumped into each other in the supermarket a few months ago.

> *I'd love to see you, Hannah, although I'm not sure if you'd want to see me. I'd understand it, but I hope you don't still feel bitter.*

Bitter! Bitter wasn't the word. Toxic with rage fitted the bill much better, Hannah fumed.

I think about you a lot and feel that we went through so much we've got unfinished business between us. If you're keen, you can e-mail me. Bye, Harry.

His e-mail address was at the bottom but Hannah barely looked at it. She felt dizzy with temper, absolutely straight-up furious. How could he? Just when she was sorting her life out, how dare he try and weasel his way back in. See him again? She'd rather remove her own appendix without an anaesthetic.

The offices of KrisisKids were silent and empty at eight fifteen on Monday morning when Emma let herself into her office and surveyed it with pleasure. Small, really only a cubby-hole, it was plain, simple, and she loved it. The walls were the same restful lemon as the rest of the office, the furniture was blonde wood and the plants that grew luxuriantly on top of her four filing cabinets flourished in the natural light from the huge picture window. Giant posters covered the walls telling visitors to WATCH THE CHILDREN – YOU MIGHT BE THE ONLY PERSON WHO CAN HELP, and giving their phoneline number. Emma had taken over running the phoneline a year ago and had worked hard to develop it from a service which ran during office hours into one which was open round the clock. Staffing a phoneline for such hours was hugely expensive and problematic. But Emma now had a vast rota of qualified counsellors and, although there were times when gremlins got into the system and four people phoned in sick at the same time, it was a big success. Thanks to the phoneline, KrisisKids now received a large state grant and, thanks to a lot of media coverage, the contributions from the public were increasing.

Seeing the phoneline become a success was very rewarding, but Emma often felt it was tragic that there was a need for such a service in the first place. The grainy black-and-white photo of a crying boy on the poster was a set-up. As far as Emma knew, the boy was a happy child model whom the advertising agency had picked because he was small for his age. But the image was powerful nevertheless. His sad eyes seemed to follow Emma around the office, reminding her of how badly people could treat children.

It was ironic, she always thought: she, who was childless, worked in an industry where children were the primary focus.

Emma's desk was just as pristine as she'd left it a week previously: not one piece of paper marred the gleaming wood, her photo of Pete sat at a perfect right angle to her computer monitor, and the painted wooden box she kept her paper clips in was in its usual position beside the phone. Only her overflowing in-tray was evidence that she'd been on holiday. Files, letters and bits of crinkly photocopy paper sat in a perilous heap, towering over the edges of the plastic tray.

'Lovely holiday?' enquired Colin Mulhall, appearing out of nowhere and perching on the edge of Emma's desk, eyes gleaming inquisitively.

The publicity department second-in-command and office gossip, twenty-something Colin was ruthless in his pursuit of personal details. Emma often felt that MI5 had missed out by not signing Colin up for something. He mightn't have been able to speak Russian or Iraqi or even basic English, come to that, but his intelligence-gathering skills were second to none. He couldn't type a press release without hitting the computer spell check at least four times to see if he'd spelled everything right, but if you wanted to know why the new girl in accounts kept coming in with red eyes every morning, Colin was the only man for the job. Except that Emma never wanted to know the gossip. It wasn't her scene. Being brought up by a mother who lived and breathed gossip had instilled in Emma a loathing for dishing dirt about other people. If the girl in accounts had eight lovers, a drug habit and a fetish for wearing fishnet stockings and no knickers, Emma didn't want to know about it.

'Fair enough,' said Finn Harrison, the charity's press officer and Colin's boss, who loved a bit of gossip himself but respected Emma's decision not to get involved.

'I don't know why she's working for a charity when she's not the least bit charitable and hasn't the slightest interest in normal people. She obviously thinks she's above hearing about our humdrum lives,' Colin said darkly about Emma. He resented her managerial position. She was his superior and it rankled. He, Colin, should have been third in command to Edward Richards, not the prim Emma Sheridan. 'Miss Smug with her perfect husband and perfect figure. I bet she has some dark secret. She's probably having it off with the boss. Her door is always closed. Forward planning meetings, my backside.' Under the circumstances, Colin and Emma were not best pals. Emma avoided the photocopier when Colin was laboriously copying out his badly typed press releases. But, because as third in command to the MD Emma had access to lots of juicy, top-secret information, Colin was always trying to engage her in friendly conversation.

This couldn't be it, Emma thought suspiciously. Colin had a tale to tell.

'You'll never guess,' Colin said now, preening ever so slightly in his ridiculous bow-tie (his trademark, he called it) and jaunty yellow shirt that did nothing for his sallow complexion.

'You're right, I probably won't,' Emma replied.

Colin's eyes narrowed slightly. 'Edward is bringing in an outside PR firm to help with the phoneline. He doesn't think we're getting enough good press.'

'That's crazy, it's been working wonderfully,' Emma shot out. 'I can't believe he's thinking of that without consulting me.' Suddenly aware that she'd said too much, she clammed up. 'I better get some work done, Colin,' she said brightly. 'Get rid of those holiday cobwebs.'

'Egypt, was it?' Colin enquired, knowing he was being dismissed but not wanting to leave yet. 'Did Pete enjoy it?'

Emma couldn't resist. She widened her eyes dramatically. 'Pete didn't go, Colin,' she said. 'See you later.'

Leaving an astonished Colin to interpret that bit of disinformation, Emma sorted through her post. At least having a bit of drama at work took her mind off the crises in her personal life.

CHAPTER EIGHT

From her seat near the escalator, Emma could see Kirsten striding along through the afternoon crowds in the shopping centre looking exactly what she was: wealthy, perkily pretty and utterly sure of herself. And she was only fifteen minutes late, which had to be a record, Emma thought, watching her sister's progress through the centre, her step as confident as a supermodel. She looked amazing, as usual. Kirsten's hair, currently a rich chestnut crop, contrasted perfectly with the tiny butter-coloured suede jacket she wore over a tummy-skimming white T-shirt and faded blue jeans. Emma knew she'd have looked ridiculous in an outfit like that, but Kirsten carried it off with ease. People who knew Emma were always amazed to meet Kirsten purely because they looked so utterly different, like the before and after pictures in some glossy magazine feature.

'I'd never have guessed you two were sisters,' they'd gasp, staring at Kirsten, who was the picture of adorable modern chic beside deeply conservative and almost old-fashioned Emma. Kirsten looked at home in cute jewelled hairslides and bounced around in clunky contemporary shoes, while Emma wouldn't dream of using anything other than plain kirby grips to hold her hair back and was a fan of loafers and nice court shoes.

But different hair, clothes and make-up aside, the two sisters actually had incredibly similar features. Both had the same long nose, pale amber-flecked eyes and thin lips. There the resemblance ended.

Kirsten's irrepressible self-confidence gave her an impish beauty that Emma was convinced she'd never achieve. Emma waited until her sister was half-way up the escalator and began waving to attract her attention.

When Kirsten spotted her, she walked over slowly and sat down on the other seat with a sigh, rifling through her small Louis Vuitton handbag for her cigarettes. Like the square-cut emerald on her wedding-ring finger, the bag was genuine.

'Sorry I'm late,' she said, as she always did when they met up. 'I was on the phone to one of the girls on the committee and I couldn't get rid of the stupid bitch. I knew you'd get a coffee and sit down if I was late.' She lit up and inhaled deeply.

Emma couldn't stop herself from looking reproving. She worried about her younger sister and wished she wouldn't smoke.

'They're Silk Cut White, for God's sake, Em,' Kirsten said pre-emptively. 'There's so little nicotine in them you'd get cheekbones like Tina Turner sucking to get any hit at all.' Kirsten grinned evilly. 'Very useful practice for Patrick, all that sucking. Not,' she added thoughtfully, 'as if there's much of that these days. I'm going to have to order some Viagra if he doesn't perk up soon.'

'You're terrible, Kirsten,' Emma said mildly. 'What would poor Patrick think if he knew the things you told me about him? He'd die if he knew you discussed your sex life.' She was fond of her solemn, hard-working brother-in-law and often wondered how the hell he and Kirsten had managed to stay married for four years without one of them ending up in the dock on murder charges.

'I only tell you these things, Em,' protested Kirsten, looking innocent. 'I have to talk to someone or I'd go mad. It's work, work, work all the time these days,' she grumbled. 'He never stops. We never have any fun any more.'

'Well, perhaps if you went back to work, you wouldn't be so bored,' Emma retorted, more sharply than she'd intended.

'I'm not going back to work and that's final.' Kirsten shuddered and pulled Emma's empty coffee cup over to use as an ashtray as they were sitting in the no-smoking section. 'I don't need the money and I'm not cut out for work, Em. I hated that bloody job in the building society, all that getting up in the morning and sitting in the traffic to be yelled at when I got in for being late. Besides, Patrick likes having his dinner on the table when he comes home. I couldn't do that and work, could I?'

'Kirsten, you don't cook. If it wasn't for Marks & Spencer's ready meals, poor Patrick would be a stick insect.'

'Stop nagging,' Kirsten said good-naturedly. 'Will I get you another coffee before we start shopping?'

Over coffee, they discussed their mission: to buy a birthday present for their mother, who would be sixty the following Wednesday.

'It has to be special,' Emma said, 'but I've racked my brains and I can't come up with anything.'

'I never know what to buy for Mum. Come on, let's hustle.' Kirsten stabbed out her third cigarette, got up and led the way to the down escalator. 'She's getting worse to buy things for. I asked her the other day if she'd used that beauty salon voucher I gave her for Christmas and she said, "What voucher?" I swear she's losing her marbles.'

The nagging worry at the back of Emma's subconscious suddenly leapt to the front of the mental queue. 'What did you say?'

'That she's losing her marbles. Well, she is, Em. Before you all went to Egypt, I was on the phone to her and she asked me how Patrick's parents were. I mean, Jesus, his father is dead two years. Do you think she's on something that's making her dopey? That's got to be it. You'd need tranquillizers to live with Dad, after all, so I couldn't blame her . . .'

As Kirsten chattered away, Emma made herself face up to the notion that had been rippling through her head like quicksilver for months: there was something wrong with her mother. Something wrong with her mind.

All that panicking when they'd been away, the way she'd clung on to her Egyptian currency and refused to hand it over when she was shopping, convinced she was being fiddled by the vendors. She kept trying to go into the wrong cabin, which Jimmy had found irritating. And the way she kept losing things – her glasses, the thread of the conversation. It wasn't normal, Emma knew it.

'I think you're right,' she said shakily.

'Really?' Kirsten said, sounding pleased and running a hand through her glossy hair. 'I thought you preferred my hair blonde. Patrick loves this colour, says it's very sexy . . .'

'No, I mean about Mum. I think she is losing her marbles. What a horrible phrase, it's so demeaning. What I mean is that she's confused and acting strangely. That sounds like . . .' Emma hesitated, not even wanting to say the word, '. . . senile dementia.'

'Don't be ridiculous,' Kirsten snapped. 'She's far too young for that. Old people get it, not Mum. Let's not talk about it, right?'

Kirsten hated facing the harder side of life and as a child had often simply refused to talk about things which upset her, like her dreadful exam results and the scathing remarks her teachers made in her homework notebook about her disruptive behaviour in class.

'I'm sorry, Kirsten,' Emma said firmly, 'we've got to talk about it. Not talking about it won't make it go away. That's like having a breast lump and not going to the doctor – the "If I don't see it, it can't hurt me" theory.'

'I'd go to the doctor if I had a breast lump,' Kirsten insisted.

'So says the woman who refused to go to the dentist for three years.'

'That's different. Now come on, we're running out of time, Em. We've got to buy something for Mum and I want to go into Mango first and see if they've any nice things in.'

Emma gave up and followed her sister into the clothes shop. There was no point in arguing with Kirsten when she'd made up her mind. Besides, she was probably right. Dementia was something old people got.

Kirsten strode off to where racks of tiny clothes hung, so Emma headed for the long, suitable-for-the-office skirt department. After a cursory look at some plain grey and black skirts that looked like all the other skirts in her wardrobe, she wandered back to where Kirsten was rifling through a rail of stretchy net tops that looked as if they wouldn't fit an eight-year-old. Selecting two acid pink ones that would either look amazing or desperate with her hair colour, Kirsten mooched on to the next rail.

'Aren't these peachy!' she said, focusing on skinny black trousers with a line of silver beading down each seam.

'Try them on,' Emma said mechanically, the way she'd done for years when they'd shopped as teenagers. Her role had been to hold the handbags and supply different sizes while Kirsten enraged the changing-room queue by spending at least half an hour in the cubicle, discarding things like Imelda Marcos on a shoe-buying frenzy.

'Yes, I think I will try them. But I'll just get a couple of other things. No point stripping off for two tops and a pair of trousers.'

As Kirsten scanned the rails with the narrowed eyes of an expert, Emma thought about their mother. She wished she could be like Kirsten and simply not confront problems, or just put them out of her mind. But she couldn't. Something was wrong with Anne-Marie, she knew it. And she hoped – no, she prayed – it wasn't senile dementia.

She'd read snippets about it, articles she'd half-scanned in women's magazines in between fashion features and the problem pages. She'd never exactly been interested, but that curious desire to read about other people's suffering, if only to thank your lucky stars it wasn't happening to you, had meant she'd absorbed some information about the disease. A slow, insidious intruder, it crept into people's minds and took over, making its presence known gradually with moments of forgetfulness, before leading up to . . . what, exactly? Emma wasn't sure. Did people die from it?

Waiting outside the cubicle for Kirsten, she tried to put the whole thing out of her mind. Kirsten was right. Their mother was too young . . . wasn't she?

'Great Aunt Petra isn't coming, is she?' groaned Kirsten, looking at Emma's rough table plan for their mother's birthday dinner.

'Of course she is,' Emma said, emerging from basting the goose again, her face puce with heat and exertion. 'She's Dad's only living aunt and he'd go mental if she wasn't invited.'

'She's an unhinged bitch and everybody hates her,' protested Kirsten. 'If Dad wants to invite her to their bloody house, that's his business. I don't know why the rest of us have to put up with her.'

'Yeah,' snapped Emma, fed up with the lack of catering help Kirsten had provided since she'd arrived an hour previously with her hair newly blow-dried and no obvious intention of doing anything useful. 'And who'd have to put up with the full-scale row there'd be if she wasn't here? Me, that's who. I'd never hear the end of it.'

'Emma, would you listen to yourself? You're an adult, this is your house and you can invite who you bloody want to. Let Dad throw a tantrum if he wants. Ignore him. I do.' Kirsten ran a lilac fingernail down the list. 'Monica and Timmy Maguire! Ugh, he'll get poor Patrick in a corner and ask him what he should do with his shares, as usual. I told Patrick to ask for a fee next time.'

'You're bloody great at telling people what to do,' hissed Emma, finally having had enough. She was hot, sweaty, tired and fed up with Kirsten. 'Did you come here to help or to simply point out what an inadequate human being I am?'

Kirsten refused to be riled. 'Keep your hair on, Sis,' she answered. 'You're only pissed off because you know I'm right. If you don't stand up to Dad some day, you may as well move back home – because you're totally under his thumb as it is.'

Emma felt her anger deflate like a pricked balloon. Her eyes filled with tears. The goose wasn't half-cooked, the guests were rolling up in an hour and Pete, who'd promised to be home early, was stuck with a client in Maynooth and wouldn't be back until at least seven.

'It's easy for you,' she told Kirsten, feeling hot, angry tears flooding down her face. 'You've always been their pet. You could tell Dad to fuck off and he'd smile indulgently at you. But he hates me; I can never do anything right for him. All I want is some respect – it's not too much to ask, is it?' She tried to rub away the tears but they kept coming.

If fury had no effect on Kirsten, neither did weeping, which was why she so successfully dealt with her father's machinations.

'He doesn't hate you, Sis,' she said calmly, ignoring Emma's tears. 'He's a bully and you've let yourself be his own personal punchbag. I can't help you and neither can Pete. You're on your own. Jesus, Emma, if you can run that bloody office, then you can certainly deal with Dad, can't you? Now, what do you want me to do next? You better go upstairs and make yourself presentable or Petra the Gorgon will have a few choice insults to fling at you about how you're letting yourself go now that you're married.'

If the birthday dinner proved anything, it proved that their fears about their mother were unfounded. Anne-Marie sailed into the house with her husband in tow, face wreathed in smiles and new earrings to be admired. 'Aren't they lovely?' she said coquettishly, pulling back a strand of long, pale gold hair, which flowed loosely around her shoulders. 'They're from your father.' She kissed Kirsten happily.

'Darling Kirsten, I don't know what was wrong with me the other day, I found that lovely voucher you gave me for Christmas. I know it's bad of me, but I completely forgot about it and now it's out of date, but it was a lovely thought. I couldn't see anything with those old glasses, but look –' she produced new glasses with snazzy gold frames – 'I've got new ones and reading is no problem any more. Hello, Emma love, there's a nice smell coming from the kitchen. I hope it's not goose; you know Auntie Petra says it gives her indigestion ever since we had it at her Roland's christening back in 1957.'

Emma and Kirsten shared a conspiratorial grin. 'All the more reason for cooking goose, eh?' whispered Kirsten.

Emma nodded with relief. Her mother was perfectly all right. It was obvious there was nothing wrong with her mind. Nobody who could remember the ill-effects of a goose at a christening in 1957 could possibly have anything wrong with their brain.

Half an hour later, all the guests were there, wandering around the house and chatting. Emma was standing in the kitchen beside the dining-room door, hurriedly ironing the napkins she'd just removed from the drier. Her mother would have had a fit if she'd produced paper ones.

'It's a lovely dining room,' she heard Monica Maguire say. 'I like these pictures,' she added, obviously admiring the Paul Klee prints Emma loved.

'Well, it's not to my taste,' Emma overheard her father say gruffly. 'Still, what can you say. I mean, myself and Anne-Marie gave them the deposit money for it and we'd have liked to have helped them with decorating advice, but you know youngsters, ungrateful.'

Emma stood behind the door into the dining room and felt cold rage flood through her. How dare he tell people he'd given them the deposit money for the house! How dare he! That was their private life. And he hadn't *given* it to them, anyway. She and Pete had insisted on treating it as a loan and were paying money into her parents' account every month. But to casually tell a neighbour about it, as if she and Pete were kids or freeloaders who used and abused . . . That was terrible, awful. A fierce rage for her father burned in her peaceful soul. God she hated that man!

CHAPTER NINE

Leonie was not thrilled with herself. Despite spending many arm-aching hours painting, the kitchen did not look the way she wanted it to. The plan had been simple: inspired by endless television make-overs, Leonie had convinced herself that she too could turn a small cottage kitchen into an exotic Egyptian-inspired room with the aid of midnight blue paint, some artistic stencilling and a can of metallic spray paint. Unfortunately, what looked easy in half an hour on the telly with scores of helpers, expert carpenters, an interior designer and an entire TV crew ready to help out if necessary, wasn't easy in real life. After three evenings and her entire Sunday spent knee-deep in old newspapers with the animals sulking in another room, the kitchen looked desperate. Two of the walls were a frighteningly dark midnight blue with silver stars supposedly reflecting the silver of the knobs she'd bought for the cupboards. The cupboards themselves had been painted primrose to go with both the freshly painted wood-work and the other two walls, but instead of gliding on to the carefully prepared surfaces, the paint had dried in myriad globules so it looked as if the doors had developed smallpox.

Her idea of having stars on the ceiling had been lovely and very celestial, but midnight blue everywhere had made the room – small and, luckily, south-facing – a bit gloomy. So she'd wearily repainted two walls. It took three coats of primrose to cover the blue.

Meanwhile, the stencilled border, which the stencil book she'd borrowed from the library described as 'an Egyptian-inspired motif of birds and animals', resembled something inexpert four-year-olds might daub on their first day at school in between peeing in their seats and sobbing for their mummies.

'It's a bit ambitious, Leonie,' her mother had remarked kindly when she arrived that afternoon with some flowers from her garden and home-made tea brack to celebrate the children's return.

'I like it better today,' Claire said, finding a vase for the off-white roses and putting the kettle on to boil at the same time. 'It was too dark when it was all blue.'

'I know.' Covered with paint and exhausted after forty-eight hours of decorating, Leonie was shattered. Her black leggings were like a Rorschach blot of primrose and blue paint, and Danny's old grey sweatshirt wasn't much better. Every inch of her hands was crusty with emulsion and she needed an hour in the bath at least.

'What have you been up to all day, Mum?' Leonie asked, reaching under the table to pet Penny's silky ears. Penny, who'd been largely ignored during the painting, hummed in bliss.

'I worked on Mrs Byrne's daughter's wedding dress for hours. The pair of them should be strung up. Every time I do something, she changes her mind and I have to rip it. Mrs Byrne insists on hanging around while I sew and the cats keep winding themselves round her legs so she's permanently covered with fluff. I'm going to run out of Sellotape getting cat fur off her dress.' Leonie's mother had been a seamstress and, on retirement, had started her own dressmaking business. She was very good, and her tiny Bray front room was permanently full of hopeful clients wanting a debs dress or wedding outfit knocked up for half-nothing.

Claire took out her cigarettes and lit up. 'I stopped at five and came down here for a break. Will I make us some tea, or are you rushing?'

'You stopped at five o'clock?' Leonie shot up in her seat as the words sank in. 'What time is it now? I've taken my watch off so it wouldn't get covered with gloss and I thought it was only three at the latest.'

'It's half five.'

'Oh, Mother of God, the kids are coming home in an hour,' wailed Leonie. 'I'll never change and make it to the airport on time.'

'Well, I did think you were being very relaxed about getting to the airport. Sure, what do you want to change for? Just go like that,' said her mother sensibly.

'I wanted to look lovely for them coming home,' Leonie said, rooting around under newspapers for her keys. 'I wanted the house to look lovely too . . .'

'They'll be so pleased to see you, they won't mind a bit of paint. I'll rustle up some supper for you all, shall I?'

Tired from the transatlantic flight, the trio emerged half an hour late behind a trolley jammed with plastic bags, rucksacks and bulging suitcases. Mel and Abby were fashionably pale, thanks to many teen magazine articles warning of skin cancer. Danny, on the other hand, was mahogany. All three wore new clothes which made Leonie instantly guilty: their father had obviously decided they were dressed like ragamuffins and had kitted them out from head to toe in new gear. She was a bad, spendthrift mother for frittering away money on a holiday when the kids needed new stuff. The knowledge that at least three-quarters of her clothes came from second-hand shops remained firmly at the back of her mind.

Mothers were supposed to dress in desperate, cast-off rags as long as their offspring had the newest designer clothes and whatever variety of trainers Nike were advertising twenty-four hours a day on MTV.

'You'll never guess,' squealed Mel excitedly as soon as the new clothes had been admired and they were in the car, rattling along the motorway.

'Yeah, Mel's got herself a boyfriend,' interrupted Danny.

'Have not!' shrieked Mel.

'Yes you have,' Danny said, sounding less like a nineteen-year-old and more like his fourteen-year-old twin sisters. Well, more like Mel. Not Abby. Abby was so grown up she wasn't fourteen – she was going on forty.

'Haven't! And that wasn't what I was going to say!' roared Mel.

'Stop it,' said Leonie, wishing they'd waited at least until they were a mile away from the airport before the inevitable row. Danny and Mel sparked off each other like pieces of flint. Every conversation between them turned into an argument. It was because they were so alike. Abby was thoughtful and grave, like her father. Her siblings were the complete opposite.

Mel's favourite sentence when she'd been four was, 'I want Danny's . . .' Danny's dinner, Danny's drink, Danny's toys. If it was his, she wanted it. And he, at the wise old age of nine, had been just as bad. Mel's favourite cuddly toy – without which she refused to go to sleep – had been hidden with Danny's Action Man collection for three whole murderous, sleepless nights before Leonie found it when she was hoovering.

The current argument subsided purely because Danny decided to play with his new Discman and stuck his earphones in with a bored shrug that said, 'Women, huh!' Leonie shuddered to imagine what a Discman cost. Hundreds of dollars, no doubt. Ray must be making a mint.

'Will I tell her?' Abby whispered to Mel.

'Yes.' Mel was sulking now. She stared out of the window with her pointed little face in a sulky pout. The beauty of the family, Mel could even sulk prettily. With her father's big dark eyes, delicately arched eyebrows, translucent skin and full lips, she looked like a teenage catwalk model trying to look moody for a photo shoot.

'Tell me what?' asked Leonie, fascinated and dying to hear every bit of their news.

'It's Dad . . .' Abby began slowly.

Mel couldn't bear it. She had to interrupt: 'He's getting married,' she cried. 'To Fliss! She's gorgeous, she can ski, and we're all invited to Colorado with them – and for the wedding too. She's going to get us dresses made. I want a short one with high boots –'

She shut up at a quick poke in the ribs from her twin.

'I know it sounds a bit sudden, Mum,' said Abby delicately, wise beyond her years and knowing the news might be hard for her mother to take.

Sudden, thought Leonie, struggling to keep her eyes focused on the road. Sudden wasn't the word. Ray was getting married again. She could barely take it in. She was here with nobody and no romantic prospects while he, the one she thought would flounder because he was so quiet, so introspective, so broken-hearted when they'd split up ten years previously, was in love and getting married.

A lump swelled in her throat and she was glad that it was Danny in the front of the car with her, unobservant Danny who was locked into his Discman and some thumping ambient beat. Watchful Abby would have noticed her mother's eyes filling with tears right away.

'Well,' she managed to say, the words nearly sticking in her throat, 'that's great. When is the big day?'

'January,' said Mel wistfully, already imagining herself in groin-level flimsy silk, her long legs in knee-high boots giving middle-aged men heart attacks. 'Fliss's family have a cabin in Colorado and they're going to have a winter wedding in the snow. Imagine! Us skiing. That'll teach snotty Dervla Malone to boast about her holidays. Stupid cow thinks going to France is posh! Huh. She can kiss my ass.'

'Melanie!' Leonie narrowly avoided a daredevil bus driver and shot her daughter a fierce glare in the rear-view mirror. 'If that's the sort of language you've picked up on your holidays, you won't be going anywhere. We don't swear in our house.'

Mel flicked back her straight dark brown hair insouciantly, crinkling up her perfect little nose as she did so. 'Lighten up,' she muttered under her breath.

'I heard that,' Leonie replied tightly.

'Aw, Mom,' pleaded Mel, deciding to be conciliatory in case she wasn't allowed to go to the wedding. 'Sorry. But that's not bad language. In Boston, people say that all the time. I mean, everyone in Ireland says "fuck" every five minutes. All Dad's friends say so. They think we say "super-fucking-market".'

'Mel!' hissed Abby.

'We do not say that word all the time, and I don't want to hear you say it either, got it?' Leonie snapped, wondering why the Von Trapp family reunion wasn't working out the way she had planned. So much for giant hugs and tearful murmurings of: 'Mum, we missed you so much, we'll never go away again.'

One child had become an American overnight and couldn't wait to get back there to see her father's fiancée, another was immersed in music and had refused to be hugged. Only dear sweet Abby seemed vaguely pleased to be home.

'Tell me about this gorgeous fella you're not going out with,' Leonie requested in an attempt to get the conversation back on an even keel.

Both girls giggled. 'Brad is his name,' explained Abby eagerly. 'He's sixteen, tall, with naturally blond hair and he drives a jeep. He was nuts about Mel. He brought us both for a pizza.'

'Brad, mm,' said Leonie with a fake smile, her mind doing cartwheels. A sixteen-year-old with his own transport going out with her little girl! Melanie was only fourteen – a very knowing fourteen it had to be said, but still fourteen for all that. What the hell was Ray thinking of! She could have been assaulted, raped, anything!

'His parents are Dad's friends, and we weren't out long,' Abby added. 'Dad said he'd murder Brad if we were gone more than an hour and a half, and the pizza place is just down the street.'

'I wasn't that interested,' Mel said airily. 'He's too immature for me.'

'He wasn't,' protested Abby and, with a catch in her voice, added, 'he was lovely.'

I wished he'd fancied me instead of Mel, were the unspoken words.

Leonie's heart ached for her much-loved daughter, the one who looked just like her. Abby had none of her twin's effortless prettiness. Abby was as tall as Mel but stocky, with a solid body, mousy brown hair like Leonie's before she got at it with the bleach, and a round, pleasant face that was only enlivened by her mother's startling blue eyes. She was a steady, reliable estate car to Melanie's sleek, capricious Ferrari, and she knew it.

Leonie adored her and saw such beauty and strength of character in Abby's kind, loving face. But fourteen-year-old girls didn't want strength of character: they wanted to look like drop-dead gorgeous movie stars and have teenage boys falling at their feet like flies. Mel did, Abby didn't. And there was nothing their mother could do to even matters up.

At home, the girls rushed out of the car, eager to see their beloved Penny, Clover the cat and Herman.

'Penny,' they squealed in unison as their grandmother opened the front door and Penny sprang out like a caged tiger, hysterical with delight. A huge group hug ensued, with everyone trying to cuddle Penny and have it proved that they were her favourite and had been missed the most. With typical feline indifference, Clover refused to have any truck with cuddles, flicked her tail sharply in disapproval and shot off into the garden.

'She's affected by the paint fumes,' muttered Leonie's mother wickedly.

Luggage was dropped carelessly in the hall, waiting for Leonie to haul it to the various bedrooms.

'Mom!' said Mel, aghast, on entering the kitchen which had been magnolia the last time she'd seen it. 'What have you been doing?'

'Having an orgy with Francis Bacon,' laughed Danny, coming up behind his sister and staring at the brightly coloured disaster area which his grandmother had failed to tidy up completely. 'Were you helping, Gran?'

'No, and don't tease your poor mother. She's been trying to brighten this place up,' she said sternly, heading to the cooker where a chicken stew was bubbling appetizingly. 'Your mother needs a hand to tidy up.'

'I've got people to phone,' said Mel, backing out of the room rapidly at the notion of ruining her nails cleaning up all that horrible newsprint and emulsion. Fliss had given her a French manicure before they'd left for Logan Airport. Domestic work would ruin the effect and she wanted her hands perfect for the next day when she'd pay a visit to her arch enemy and supposed friend, Dervla Malone.

'Me too.' Danny was gone like a shot, leaving Abby, her mother, grandmother and a still joyous Penny amid the endless paint-splattered newspapers and cans of paint.

'I'll help, Mum,' said Abby loyally.

'No, love, we'll eat in the living room,' Leonie decided, looking dismally at the chaos and deciding that she couldn't face a proper clean up. She'd bag all the newspaper and that would be it for the moment. 'Thanks for cooking,' she added, giving her mother a peck on the cheek.

They ate on their knees in the living room with the TV on while Danny controlled the remote and flicked from channel to channel in between wolfing down chicken and rice.

Green, thought Leonie, looking around the small but cosy room with its apple-green walls and profusion of plants. Green was the colour she should have painted the kitchen. Not horrible midnight blue. If they could cope with blue for a week, she'd re-do it all next weekend. Maybe a paler green . . .

Mel's words intruded into her brain, dragging her away from paint.

'. . . Fliss is really nice,' Mel was whispering to her grandmother, who was nodding wisely and trying not to look at her daughter.

Leonie felt her face burn, knowing her mother pitied her and hating it. Claire had loved Ray and had been heartbroken when they'd got a divorce. 'There aren't as many fish in the sea when you're actively looking, Leonie,' she had said gently at the time. 'You love each other: can't you get on with it and stop looking for true love? I'm so afraid you'll regret this.'

Ten years on, she'd been proved right, Leonie thought bitterly. Ray had had several long-term girlfriends while she, the great believer in true love, had had so few dates that flirting with the postman was her idea of romantic excitement. And he was past sixty and grizzled looking.

She pretended to concentrate on the sitcom Danny was watching and surreptitiously listened to Mel telling her grandmother all about the holiday.

'Dad's house is lovely but not big enough for us, Gran, although it had en suites everywhere,' said the girl who'd been raised in a succession of small homes and now lived in a cottage with one bathroom and a constant queue for it.

'Fliss wants to convert one bedroom into a dressing room for herself. She has so many clothes!'

Yeah, snarled Leonie to herself. Probably all band-aid skirts and second-skin leather things. She imagined a cheerleader type, shimmering blonde hair and teeth that had never eaten too many sugar-laden Curly Wurlys as a child. Or maybe she was a hard-bitten businesswoman, another lawyer, all power suits like someone from *LA Law*. Suddenly Leonie stopped, horrified at herself. What was wrong with her, she wondered blindly. She'd wanted to leave Ray, she'd started the whole agonizing process of separation and divorce – so why was she now jealous of this gorgeous Fliss? He was entitled to another life; she'd practically pushed him into it, hadn't she?

What sort of person was she turning into if she begrudged Ray a little happiness? A bitch, that's what. A cast-iron bitch.

Abby was eating very little of her dinner. She normally wolfed it down, eating far more quickly than her twin who nibbled daintily. Now, Abby pushed bits of chicken listlessly around her plate. 'Are you feeling all right?' Leonie asked in concern, staring across the coffee table to where Abby sat beside her grandmother on the sofa-bed.

Abby smiled brightly. 'Fine, Mum, fine,' she replied. 'I'm just not hungry.'

'That'd be a first,' guffawed Danny.

Abby's eyes glistened but she said nothing.

Leonie gave her an encouraging grin and vowed to kill Danny when she got him alone. He wouldn't know how to spell 'thoughtfulness', never mind know what it meant. Abby silently took the plates out to the kitchen while Mel rummaged around in a very trendy vinyl handbag Leonie had never seen before. More holiday goodies from a doting father.

'The holiday snaps,' Mel announced happily, finding a huge wad of photo envelopes. 'I can't wait any longer to show them to you, Mum.'

Leonie cranked her jaw into a steely smile and hoped she could fake a bit of pleasure at the sight of the beautiful Fliss.

Leonie, Claire and Mel squashed up together on the two-seater to view the precious pictures. The first batch of photos were typically Mel – ones where people had their heads chopped off or shots of the glamorous shops in Boston where the reflection from the glass meant you couldn't see anything.

'I don't know how they didn't work out so well,' Mel said in consternation as they all tried to figure out who was who in one particularly blurry picture.

The next batch was better.

'I took them,' Danny said loftily from his position as king of the remote control.

After a couple of photos of the girls and Ray, who looked healthy and tanned, there was Fliss.

'That was the day we took the ferry to Martha's Vineyard,' Mel said wistfully as she passed the photo along to her mother.

Leonie stared in shock. Instead of the young, gorgeous girl she'd imagined, Fliss was at least her own age. But there the similarity ended. As tall as Ray, she was slim with dark, boyishly cut hair and the sort of beautiful unlined face that made Leonie wonder when Revlon would be signing her up for a moisturizer advertisement for stunning women over forty. She wore faded jeans on endless legs and a navy polo shirt tucked in at the waistband. In every picture, she was smiling, whether she was hugging Ray or laughing with Mel and the notoriously camera-shy Abby. Even Danny had been coerced into the photos and had posed, long hair windswept, on the ferry beside Fliss.

'She's lovely and she's very clever, you know. She's a lawyer in Daddy's firm,' Mel prattled on, unaware that Leonie was passing the photos along to Claire with the frozen movements of a robot. 'She has the most wonderful clothes. Daddy teases her for being voted Best Dressed Lawyer in the firm two years in a row!'

Leonie knew she'd never be voted best dressed anything, not unless outsized silk shirts and all-encompassing voluminous skirts suddenly became *haute couture*.

'The most incredible thing is she practically never wears make-up,' Mel added in awe, knocking the final nail into her mother's coffin. 'Mascara and a little gloss, that's all. Although she gets her nails done. Everyone does in America.'

Leonie thought of her own pancake-plastered face and the long minutes she spent applying her goodies every morning. She wouldn't leave the house without lipliner, kohl and blusher, never mind just a bit of gloss and mascara.

The pride in her daughter's voice when she talked about this elegant, glamorous stepmother-to-be made her wonder what Mel really thought of her. Had Mel longed to have a mother just like Fliss, instead of a faux-jolly one who flirted outrageously and laughed loudly at even the most unfunny jokes in order to cover up her insecurities? Painfully, she saw herself through Melanie's eyes: a big fat woman who tried to hide her bulk with ludicrous flowing clothes and tried to make herself interesting with make-up.

'Time for *Coronation Street*,' announced Claire loudly. 'You'll have to show me the rest of your pictures tomorrow, Mel – I can't miss *Coro*. Now, get out to the kitchen and make us a pot of tea. I'm an old woman and I need sustenance. Biscuits would be nice too.'

Mel responded to her grandmother's voice with total obedience. It was Claire's manner that did it, Leonie thought, grateful for the interruption. If Leonie had asked for tea, Mel would have moaned, 'Let Abby do it. She's out there.'

As it was, she collected up her photos and went out to make tea, humming happily to herself.

'Change the channel, Daniel,' ordered Claire imperiously.

He did and the strains of the soap's theme tune filled the room. Claire patted her daughter's knee in a gesture of solidarity. Leonie knew her mother would never speak about Ray's new love unless asked for her opinion, but she would be aware just how raw Leonie felt, simply because she knew her so well.

They sat through two hours of television before Claire took her leave. 'I've got four bridesmaids' dresses to make this week, so I need an early start,' she said as she collected her keys from the pottery bowl in the hall. The girls appeared from their room to kiss their grandmother goodbye; Danny roared 'bye' from the kitchen where he was making a crisp-and-cheese sandwich for himself.

Claire hugged her daughter last of all: a tight, comforting hug. 'Phone me tomorrow if you need to chat,' was all she said, a coded message that meant: If you want to sob down the phone about Ray and Fliss.

After she was gone, Leonie pottered about, tidying up the sitting room and starting on the disaster area that was the kitchen. Mel had left the photos on the coffee table in the sitting room and they drew

Leonie like a magnet. She wanted to look at them again, to see how beautiful Fliss was, how slim, how perfect.

Like a dieter drawn inexorably to the last KitKat nestling at the back of the cupboard, she couldn't resist looking. Danny was engrossed in some cop show and wouldn't notice, she hoped. Quietly, she snatched the photos and brought them into her bedroom. Penny followed her loyally and lay down on the bed with her as she flicked through the envelopes feeling guilty.

Afraid Mel would somehow know which order the photos were in, Leonie carefully went through them so as not to mix them up. There were loads more of Fliss, more than Mel had shown them.

In one, they were obviously all at dinner in some swanky restaurant. Mel was sitting beside Fliss wearing what looked like a very adult sparkly top that Leonie didn't recognize. Abby looked her normal self in a white shirt, but Ray was utterly transformed. He looked as sparkling as Mel's top. The next photo was a close-up of Ray and Fliss, and his face was animated in a way Leonie never remembered it being. He looked utterly content. He'd never looked that way with her, Leonie reflected sadly.

She flicked through the rest of the pictures, feeling more dispirited than ever. After a while, she put them back in the envelopes and stuck them in the kitchen in the old wicker basket on the table where she kept the bills and letters. That way, if Mel had been looking for them, Leonie could say she'd put them in the basket for safekeeping.

In the girls' room, Abby was in bed reading *Pride and Prejudice*, her favourite book, while Mel was at the dressing table painstakingly cleansing her face with cold cream.

This was a new routine, Leonie realized. Normally, Mel didn't bother with any cleansing ritual; she blithely imagined that acne was for other, less naturally pretty girls and never so much as wiped off the mascara she wasn't supposed to wear. Now, she was industriously patting her face with cotton wool pads as if she was a restorer working on a muddy Monet.

Leonie sat down on the edge of Mel's bed. 'It's lovely to have you back,' she said, wishing she didn't feel like an intruder in their bedroom after a mere three weeks' absence.

'Yeah,' muttered Mel. 'Wish we weren't going back to school though. I hate school. I wish it was January.'

Unusually, Abby wasn't in a mood to talk. She often followed her mother into bed, sitting cross-legged at the foot of the bed, stroking Penny's velvety ears and talking nineteen to the dozen until they realized it was half eleven and gasped at the thought that they had to get up at seven. Tonight, she smiled a suspiciously thin smile at Leonie and went back to her book, obviously not wanting to be drawn into any conversation. Maybe she, too, was missing the perfect Fliss, Leonie thought sadly.

Feeling in the way and miserable, she retreated. She turned off the hall light, locked the back door after Penny had been outside for her ablutions, and warned Danny not to have the TV on too loudly. Then she went to bed.

She rarely switched on her clock radio at night but tonight she felt lonely, so she flicked the switch. A late-night discussion show was on and the subject matter was dating agencies.

'Where would ya find a fella in the back of beyond without some help?' demanded one woman, fighting back against a male caller who felt that paying for introductions was the last resort of the hopeless.

'I bet you look like a complete old cow,' the male caller interrupted smugly, pointing out that he was married with four kids.

'And I bet your wife is screwing around on ya, ya old curmudgeon,' retorted the woman.

The radio host intervened, sensing the argument was going to hit the four-letter-word level. 'We'll be back after the news,' he said smoothly, 'for an interview with a couple who found true love in the personal ads.'

Leonie was hooked. An hour later, she turned the radio and her light off and lay in bed in darkness. She wasn't alone after all. There were lots of people who felt lonely and didn't know where to go to meet new partners, people who felt too old for the twenty-something pub scene and too young for tea dances. The woman on the radio had been like Leonie: a lonely woman who couldn't imagine falling in love ever again. Two adverts in her local Belfast paper later, she was dating a lovely man. Now they were getting married and were going to be the subject of a documentary about finding love in unusual ways. Why shouldn't I try that too, Leonie asked herself. If she had a man, she wouldn't feel depressed about Ray and Fliss, or about how Mel seemed bored to be home, or about how fat she was getting, or anything.

She curled her toes up under the duvet at the thought of her exciting plan: she'd take out a personal ad or join a dating agency. Her mission, should she choose to accept it, was to find a man. That was it, she had to have one. And then she'd feel better about herself. Wouldn't she?

'What does GSOH mean?' Leonie asked, staring at her horoscope in the tiny kitchen during the ten minutes they tried to snatch each day between morning rounds and the beginning of surgery.

Angie, the practice's only female vet, looked up from the crossword she did effortlessly each morning in seven minutes flat. 'Good sense of humour,' she replied in her crisp Australian accent. Clear grey eyes scrutinized her colleague. 'Why?'

'Nothing.'

A moment passed.

'You thinking of personal ads?' Angie asked.

Leonie flushed and grinned. It was always a mistake to bullshit Angie, who was one of the smartest women she knew. 'Yes. Desperate, isn't it? I'm never going to meet a man round here, am I?'

'Not unless you want to run off with the postman – who does fancy you, in my opinion. He takes a long time delivering the mail when you answer the door.'

'You're a cow, Angie. He's practically at retiring age. And if he's the best I can do, I may as well give up. It drives me mad, you know. People think if you work in a vet practice the place is a throbbing hotbed of lust with hormones all over the place because we deal with animals. I don't see why,' Leonie said plaintively. 'What's so sexy about staring at Tim's face while he operates on some cat's anal glands?'

'It's the old doctors and nurses thing,' Angie remarked sagely. 'Romantic novels are full of doctors and nurses having if off in between quadruple bypasses. It's fictional fantasy, but everyone thinks it must be the same here. It's the white coat that does it. Women want to be bonked senseless by a guy in a white coat because he's in charge and they can indulge their "I couldn't help it, m'lud, he made me do it" fantasy.'

'Fantasy's all very well, but the reality is very different,' Leonie said, giving up on her horoscope because Virgos were going to have a bad day and fight with everyone. 'Tim's happily married, Raoul is engaged and, unless we both turn gay, you're out of bounds. Maybe if Raoul went back to South America, we could hire a new hunky young vet and our eyes would lock over the operating table when we were neutering a ginger tom.' She sighed at the thought. 'Then again, he'd want to be deranged to fall for a divorced mother of three, wouldn't he? An insolvent mother of three, at that. I'm broke again, Angie, my overdraft is in the stratosphere and Mel is whingeing on about new clothes . . .'

'Personal ads are a great idea,' Angie interrupted before Leonie got carried away on misery. 'Loads of people use them these days and you're not going to meet the man of your dreams in this town, now, are you? What would you say in your ad?'

Leonie extracted a piece of folded-up newsprint from her pocket. 'I got this from the *Guardian* in the surgery waiting room. It's got pages of ads. "Soulmates" they call them. I just don't understand what they all mean. I read it for ages earlier and it's like reading Mongolian. Listen to this: "Zany Slim Blonde F, GSOH, n/s WLTM creative M, preferably TDH for loving r/ship. Ldn."'

Angie translated: 'Zany blonde female with a good sense of humour, non-smoker, would like to meet a creative male, preferably tall, dark and handsome for a loving relationship. Based in London.'

'Ah, gotcha.' Leonie scanned the rest of the ads. 'The only problem is that all these women are slim and all the men want slim women. See: "seeks slim, attractive woman . . ." She could be an axe-murderer, but as long as she's slim, it's OK.'

'Don't be daft,' said Angie, who was tall, attractive in a sporty way and very, very slim.

'It's true. Look at them.'

Together, they scanned the list. The men, who described themselves as anything from 'cuddly' ('That means fat,' Angie pointed out), to 'Not easy to describe in four to five lines' ('Short, fat and often mistaken for a pot-bellied pig,' said Angie).

They giggled over some of the descriptions: the surgical walker who wanted a fun and adventurous companion; and Sir Lancelot who was seeking his Guinevere.

'Would a wimple and chastity belt be necessary?' Angie mused.

'Listen to this: "Shy male, 35, virgin, seeks similar for relationship." How could you be a virgin at thirty-five? That is weird.'

'Not if he's religious,' Angie countered.

'Oh yeah, I hadn't thought of that. What does "seeks for possible relationship" mean?' Leonie asked, bemused.

'That he wants to shag you senseless after a meal where you went Dutch and then he never wants to see you again,' Angie said knowledgeably. 'Happened to a friend of mine in Sydney. She's a veteran of the personals, but even she got badly burned once. He said he was a gorgeous doctor and he wasn't lying, so she forgot her plan to play hard to get and they did it on the first date. Champagne, chocolate body-paint, Polaroid camera, the lot. She never set eyes on him again. Bastard.'

Leonie shuddered at the thought of someone with Polaroid photos of her naked self. She read some more: ' "Seeks classy blonde for fun and games." This is mad stuff. Why doesn't he just hire a hooker?'

'These are hip and trendy ads. You want a nice country ad in a country paper.'

'You sure?'

'Positive. Someone with a cosy hearth who has several animals, pots of money and who looks good in wellington boots.'

'Wicklow is full of blokes like that,' Leonie dead-panned. 'The surgery is probably jammed with a consignment as we speak, all bearing red roses at the news that I'm looking for lurve. Oh yes, and a sick sheep they need looked at. Come on, we'd better get to work.'

They discussed the personal ads some more that morning as Angie whizzed through spaying four cats, two dogs and descaling the teeth on a very old beagle.

Leonie assisted her, shaving the animals' bellies and disinfecting them before Angie got to work. It was also her job to monitor breathing and colour. Older animals were often put on oxygen during operations. Younger ones tended to do well without it, but Leonie kept an eye on their colour to make sure they were getting enough oxygen. At the first sign of a tongue going grey, she'd give them pure oxygen.

'Be honest in your advert,' Angie advised, delicately sewing up a tabby kitten's soft beige belly. 'Say "voluptuous", because you are and you want to make sure whoever wants to meet you knows that. You don't want to end up with some bloke whose aim in life is to make you lose a stone.'

'It's nice to have at least one friend who's honest with me,' Leonie said, keeping an eye on the kitten's breathing. 'If I asked anyone else, they'd lie through their teeth and tell me I'm slim, really. My mother is always telling me I'm beautiful the way I am and not to think about dieting, which is bullshit.'

'Your mother is a wonderful woman and no, it's not bullshit. Half the women in the country are trying to kill themselves dieting. It's a waste of time – you know it. Most people who lose weight put it right back on again eventually.'

'Tell me about it!' Leonie groaned, feeling the waistband of her blue uniform biting into her flesh. 'If I was to put an advert in the paper, what would I say?'

'Voluptuous, sensual . . .' began Angie.

'Get out of here!' shrieked Leonie, secretly pleased. 'Sensual! You can't say that.'

'Why not?' Angie finished the kitten. She gave her a shot of antibiotics and brought her back to her cage.

She returned with a Yorkshire terrier for spaying and took up the conversation as if she'd never been away. 'You are, in every sense of the word. Sensual isn't just to do with sex, you know. It also means someone who enjoys using their senses, and you do.'

'Yeah but saying "sensual" in an advert in the *Wicklow Times* will result in a rush of callers thinking I'm looking for an entirely different sort of man friend, the sort who leaves the money on the mantelpiece.'

'OK then, how about "Blue-eyed blonde, voluptuous, er . . ."'

'. . . loves children.'

'That might put him off,' Angie pointed out, ''cos he'll think you're on the hunt for a sperm donor rather than a man.'

'Well, I've got to mention the children.'

'"Loves children and animals"?' Angie suggested.

'That's it.'

Angie really began to get into the swing of things. She wanted to keep discussing adverts. But Leonie didn't want everyone in the practice to know about her personal life. Louise, one of the other nurses, kept going into the operating room to talk to Angie and Leonie didn't want her to hear.

'We'll talk about it later,' she hissed to Angie.

Operations over, Leonie went back to cleaning out the animals' cages. As a nurse, she worked mainly at the back of the practice where two walls were lined with animal cages for their patients. At any one time, there could be forty animals looking mournfully out at the nurses and vets as they waited for operations or recovered from them. Today, there were several animals scheduled for spaying in the afternoon and three in for blood tests to try and figure out what was wrong with them.

Bubble, a pretty white cat with ragged ears, was vomiting constantly and needed a whole range of tests including liver and kidney function. Bubble had already been through the wars vet-wise. White cats were prone to skin cancers on the tips of their ears and Bubble had already had three operations. A seasoned surgery cat, she was very clever at escaping when her cage was opened, so Leonie had put an ESCAPE ARTIST sign over her cage. 'Escape artist' was better than 'wild', which was the sign they put over feral cats people occasionally brought in. These practically wild cats often tested positive for the feline version of HIV, and more often than not were put to sleep. Leonie had received many scars from being scratched by these poor, unloved creatures.

Below Bubble was Lester, a yellow ferret who was looking for a home. Lester was a bit of an escape artist himself and had managed to wriggle out of Louise's arms earlier and had hidden in the medicine cupboard for ten minutes before he could be recaptured. Leonie carefully took Lester out and tidied his cage. Putting him back with a cuddly toy, she watched him play with it, biting its neck frenziedly. She'd thought of giving Lester a home herself because she could never bear to see animals unloved. Ferrets could bite but, so far, Lester hadn't hurt anyone. Watching him kill the teddy, she reconsidered.

How would Lester describe himself for a personal ad?

> *Sleek, friendly male with an interest in the life of Houdini seeks loving home with someone who doesn't mind being nibbled. Prospective females must enjoy romping in the garden and appreciate strong, masculine scent.*

Leonie grinned to herself. Put that way, Lester sounded irresistible. She must remember to read between the lines of the adverts. Otherwise, God alone knew what would happen.

CHAPTER TEN

The one drawback about being one of the three members of staff who could work the switchboard was that you inevitably had to take over when the receptionist wasn't available. And Carolyn, the girl who'd been working as the Dwyer, Dwyer & James receptionist for the past two weeks, was never available. Hannah was already regretting hiring her. Carolyn had been off sick once the previous week and today, she'd rung in at ten to nine claiming to have the flu.

'Gillian, can you do reception today?' Hannah had asked Gillian, who was still deeply resentful of the fact that Hannah had been brought in as office manager. Gillian had loved knowing where all the agents were and phoning them to check if they were all right. It gave her power over them.

'I can until lunch,' Gillian had snapped. 'I'm on a half-day today.'

Which meant that Hannah didn't have a chance to get on with her own work and had to spend the afternoon at the front desk, fielding calls in between trying to track down a consignment of office supplies which had gone missing.

Naturally, as soon as anybody walked in, the phones went mad. The woman standing at the reception desk didn't look impressed by the fact that Hannah had had to answer four calls before dealing with her. The woman was quivering with impatience, but Hannah waited until she could see the red light on her switchboard go off, indicating that Donna Nelson was off the phone.

'Donna, call for you on line one: a Mr McElhinney about the property in York Road.'

'Thanks, Hannah.'

Swivelling in her new, very comfortable chair, Hannah finally faced the anxious-looking young woman in front of her reception desk. It was a low desk: it had to be, Hannah had explained to David James when he'd discussed refitting the office with her. 'People need to be able to see you, not feel they're queuing up at the post office.'

'I do apologize for all the interruptions,' she said in a conciliatory tone, 'it's been terribly busy today. Now, how can I help you?'

'Number 73 Shandown Terrace, is it gone yet?' the woman said, voice rising with each word, pale freckled face distraught. 'We only realized it was for sale this instant. We've always loved that road and we so wanted to live there. Don't tell me it's sold.'

'Hold on one moment,' Hannah said soothingly. She scanned through her computer files and found the house. Steve Shaw, the agency's obnoxious young agent, was handling the sale. He'd brought two people to view it but nobody had put in an offer.

'Needs twenty thou spent on it before rats would live in it!' Steve had snorted when he came back from his first visit to the property.

'I've good news,' Hannah said, 'it's still on the market. Would you like to speak to the agent who's handling it?'

A few minutes later, Steve was sitting on the reception area's oatmeal couch with the woman – sitting far too close to her, in Hannah's opinion. That was Steve's technique for selling property – invading women's personal space and flirting with them as if they were the most beautiful creatures he'd ever set eyes on.

He'd tried it on with Hannah the moment he'd met her. Just back from his honeymoon and with a mocha Bahamian tan, he thought he was gorgeous. He thought she was gorgeous too and kept calling her that.

'Why'd you join this company, Gorgeous, if you're only going to break my heart?' he'd said the first time she refused his invitation to lunch. This was only five minutes after they'd met. Even peering at him severely from behind her Reverend Mother specs hadn't worked.

'You're very sexy when you glare at me like that,' Steve had said cheekily.

He'd kept up this line of banter for the past three weeks and so far Hannah had resisted the temptation to knock him down to size. So far.

From her position behind the reception desk, she watched him put his hand on the client's knee. Completely out of order, Hannah thought. The woman was clearly so relieved that her beloved house hadn't been sold that she didn't appear to notice the inappropriate gesture and beamed back at him.

It was a busy afternoon. Since David James had taken over the office, the entire place had been buzzing. Fliers about the company had been circulated around the area, two new agents had been hired, and the office itself had been redecorated one weekend. Gone were the coffee-coloured walls and the brown partitions. In their place was a facsimile of the Dawson Street branch, complete with elegant prints, discreet lighting and marvellous furniture. Hannah had been in charge of the transformation and it had been a joy. The reception desk was a curved swathe of bleached maple and the fresh flowers that sat beside the new state-of-the-art computer were replaced every three days. Even the faulty air ventilator in the ladies had been fixed. David James said he wanted the transformation to be very thorough.

Not a man for small talk, he nevertheless noticed every detail. He and Hannah understood each other perfectly. They had a meeting twice a week to discuss the business and Hannah found that she looked forward to these hour-long sessions. In private, David wasn't the tough, silent type he appeared to be. When they'd finished discussing office improvements, he'd order Gillian to bring in coffee and the chocolate-chip biscuits he loved.

'Shouldn't be eating these,' he'd said guiltily at their meeting that morning as he dunked his third biscuit into coffee, 'but I love them.'

'I thought only women were supposed to have a sweet tooth,' Hannah teased. She'd discovered that he had a good sense of humour and enjoyed a bit of banter.

'We can't all be lean fighting machines like you,' he retorted, casting an approving eye over her slim figure neatly dressed in a burgundy silk twinset and grey tailored trousers.

If anyone else had made such a remark, Hannah would have bridled in case it was a sexual innuendo. But she felt relaxed with David James. Despite their close working relationship, she never sensed even a hint of impropriety in his attitude to her. They were colleagues, nothing more.

'If Gillian wasn't so deeply in love with you, you wouldn't be getting those chocolate-chips biscuits,' Hannah said slyly.

'She's not!' He looked up in horror.

Hannah couldn't resist laughing. 'I'm sorry, David, she does have a bit of a penchant for you.'

Not wishing to reveal too much, she clammed up.

'You're kidding, right?' he asked.

'Yes,' Hannah lied. 'Only kidding. I better go and do some work, David.'

She left the office, inwardly amused at how someone as observant as David could totally fail to see that Gillian was obsessed with him. For a brilliant man capable of detecting the slightest nuance in a business conversation, he was clueless when it came to people. Gillian looked at her fiercely when Hannah sat back at her tidy desk. Nobody resented David and Hannah's coffee-fuelled meetings more than Gillian.

It was just before closing time when David rang Hannah from his car phone. 'I've got a client coming in to see me but I'm running twenty minutes late. Tell him that and give him a cup of coffee, will you, Hannah? I hope you don't mind staying late, but it's important. He's an old friend. His name's Felix Andretti.'

How exotic, she thought, writing the name down. At six, the staff who weren't showing houses or meeting clients packed up and left the office.

'Staying late?' asked Donna, passing the reception desk with Janice, one of the two new agents.

'Not really,' Hannah replied. 'I'm just doing something for David.'

'Would you like to go for a drink in McCormack's afterwards?

Myself and Janice have just decided we need a pick-me-up drink. I never normally have the time, but I can stay out a bit tonight.'

'I'd love to but I can't,' Hannah said with regret. 'I'm already going out.'

'Never mind. Next time, OK?'

Tonight was the Egypt reunion. She, Leonie and Emma were going to Sachs Hotel for a drink, then out for dinner, and Leonie kept insisting that they were going to a nightclub afterwards.

'I never get the chance of going clubbing,' Leonie had said wistfully on the phone.

Hannah had grinned at the thought of the three of them dancing around their handbags but hadn't made any promises. However, she'd brought her sexy amethyst slip dress to change into, just in case.

By half six, she had let her hair down, put on more make-up, including the glossy pink lipstick that went well with the dress, and had sprayed herself liberally with Coco. She had to leave in the next few minutes if she was to be in time to meet the girls in Sachs Hotel and she still hadn't changed.

Damn David and his bloody client. When another five minutes had passed and there was still no sign of either of them, she grabbed her dress, stood behind the big filing cabinet so she could still see the door without being seen herself, and undressed. Luckily, she was just wrenching the dress down over her hips when she heard the big solid glass door open slowly.

Struggling to pull the dress down properly, she was about to move forward when she realized that a sexy, tight evening dress wasn't quite the outfit in which to greet the boss's favoured friend, so she dragged her navy nylon raincoat on and was attempting to button it when she first caught sight of Felix Andretti.

It was lucky that it was after-hours, she thought blindly, because she wasn't sure she'd have been able to give anyone else her complete attention and stare at the vision in front of her at the same time. He was breathtaking: not dark, as his Italian name suggested, but all pale golds, like autumn leaves.

His skin was a honey shade, his hair the colour of corn, a mane of silky strands that fell over his dazzling brown eyes and that face . . . Handsome wasn't the word. Wide jaw, long aristocratic nose and cheekbones you could hang your hat on. He'd have given a young Robert Redford a run for his money anytime, she thought in shock. Leonie would have died if she'd seen him. In his cream linen suit, he was as lean and rangy as any cowboy. Hannah could only stare.

'Nice outfit,' he said in a treacly voice, the liquid brown eyes roaming over her opened raincoat, short, short skirt and legs encased in shiny ten-deniers which miraculously hadn't snagged during the day.

For once, Hannah's sang-froid deserted her. She laughed nervously. 'I'm going out and had to change. David's late and he asked me to stay behind for you.'

'I don't know how to thank him,' growled Felix.

She couldn't quite place his accent. It wasn't Irish or British, was it? He sounded posh, as her mother would have said. After years cleaning up after wealthy guests in the Dromartin Castle Hotel, Mrs Campbell was very anti posh people.

'Can I get you a coffee?' Hannah suggested, keen to get the conversation back on an even keel. This man was a friend of David's – flirting with him was not an option.

'Can I have something else?' he asked, arching one golden eyebrow wickedly.

'Er . . . yes, of course.'

'I'll have you, then.'

She blinked at him. 'I'm not on the menu,' she quipped, enjoying the repartee.

'You mean, you were offering me tea?' he asked, eyes glinting.

She glinted back. 'Sadly, only tea. We're out of orange juice.'

He sat on the edge of the reception desk and looked up at her with obvious interest. 'Did David say how long he'd be?' he asked. 'Only . . . it'd suit me if he didn't turn up at all.'

When Hannah threw back her head and laughed her deep, husky laugh, it surprised her most of all.

She, Miss Cold-as-Ice Campbell, the woman who could quell Viking invaders with one sharp glance, flirting like a lunatic with this gorgeous guy! It was unbelievable. But enjoyable.

Maybe the hunky gym manager from the hotel had opened the floodgates and let her trust the opposite sex again, Hannah thought with a rush of excitement. And why not? She'd been on her own for long enough. She deserved a man in her life.

'I suppose it says "professional charmer" on your business card?' Hannah smiled at him and let her cloak of buttoned-up iciness melt away. As she did so, it was as if she had physically changed. Her face relaxed, the tension left her body and her pose became her natural one, an undulating, instinctively sexy one.

'As a matter of fact, it says "actor",' he replied.

'Oh.'

'Disappointed?'

She shook her head, letting her hair ripple gently around her shoulders. It looked good when she did that; she wanted him to notice. 'I've never met an actor before. Not properly,' she amended.

'You mean, you met them improperly?' He grinned.

She waved a reproving finger at him. 'Being smart won't get you anywhere in life.'

'I dunno,' he said, leaning a fraction closer to where she was standing behind the desk, 'it's got me pretty far up to now. Although things have definitely improved since I met you.'

'We haven't met,' she said. 'That's what I meant about meeting actors properly. You and I haven't been introduced, so we haven't met properly. The others I met were never introduced either.'

'They must have been blind not to want to be introduced to you,' he said fervently and held out his hand in a formal manner. 'Delighted to meet you, madam. Felix Andretti, at your service.'

She took his hand, revelling in the feel of his warm skin against hers and the excitement she felt in the pit of her stomach at his touch. 'Hannah Campbell, delighted to meet you too.'

'Now that we've got the proper bit over, can we move on to the improper bit?' he said, dark eyes dancing. 'So what did you mean about meeting friends? Can't you cancel and go out with me instead?'

'No,' she said, smiling at him. 'I can't. This is special, they're good friends and I can't let them down.'

'Male or female?' he asked.

'Female.'

'Goodie. I'll come along.'

'You can't.'

Felix pretended to think about this. '"Can't" isn't a word I recognize.'

'I suppose "no" isn't a word you recognize, either,' Hannah teased.

He grinned in assent.

The phone rang and Hannah grabbed it. It was David looking for Felix. She passed the receiver over and heard them arrange to meet somewhere else as David was still delayed.

'I better get going,' Hannah said sweetly.

'Can I see you again?' Felix asked, leaning against the desk, only a few feet away from her. She breathed in his aftershave, feeling drunk already on this heady sensation.

'Yes. Now, bye.'

'Do you want a lift?' he asked.

'I'm going to take the bus, I left my car at home.'

Felix's smile was almost feral. 'Let me drive you in – we can talk on the way. I want to discover everything about you.'

Hannah thought of Harry's second letter which was burning a hole in her handbag with its pleading for her to answer his previous one. She'd got it that morning and had read it twice. *Please agree to see me, it's important.*

Stuff Harry. She needed to live a little.

Swathed in a flowing cerise dress with nails and lips the same vibrant colour, Leonie sailed into Sachs' bar and tried to look as if she wasn't feeling self-conscious. She was out of her familiar black plumage and had left off a lot of her normal eye make-up, the combination of which made her feel as if she'd come out half-naked or with her skirt tucked up into her knickers. But none of these people would know that. To them, she had to appear confident and relaxed, a woman about to meet her two new friends and to tell them her thrilling news.

She spotted Emma almost immediately. Jammed into a corner by one of the windows, Emma was mouselike in beige office gear, sipping what had to be mineral water. That'd have to stop, Leonie decided happily as she progressed regally through the bar. She'd left her car at home so she could have a few drinks, and she'd insist Emma went home in a taxi if necessary because she was letting her hair down too. On the phone, Emma had sounded depressed even though she'd done her best to cover it up. Leonie had been convinced for many years that while alcohol couldn't cure anything, a couple of glasses of wine made the pain fuzzier and more bearable.

'Emma, love, how nice to see you.'

'Leonie!'

They hugged warmly and Leonie was relieved to feel that her friend wasn't quite as sliver-thin as she had been in Egypt. Emma would never be a candidate for Weight Watchers, but at least she'd lost that skeletal look.

'You look amazing,' Emma exclaimed. 'That colour really suits you. Is the dress new?'

'Old as the hills, nearly as old as I am,' Leonie revealed. 'I've never had the guts to wear it before, but I'm celebrating . . .' She broke off and grinned. 'Can't tell you until Hannah gets here. We need a full coven for revelations.'

'Thank God somebody has good news,' Emma said, sinking back into the banquette, her body flattening against the back of the seat as if all the energy had been drained out of every muscle.

Leonie took a good look at her. Emma was naturally pale-skinned and even a week in the sweltering Egyptian sun hadn't done anything more than give her nose and cheekbones a faint dusting of tan. But she looked paler now than Leonie would have expected. After all, they were only back three weeks. She was still quite freckly herself, an effect she helped along with liberal dustings of bronzing powder.

'What's up?' she said fondly, patting Emma's slender knee.

'Where do I begin?' Emma groaned, thinking of worrying over her mother and of how her father's comments about the loan had been driving her insane with quiet frustration.

'Not without me, you can't spill any beans without me,' came a voice and Hannah appeared, bringing with her several admiring glances and the waiter, who had studiously ignored the other two up till then.

Eyes glittering, Hannah sank into the seat beside Emma and attempted to wipe the enormous dirty great grin off her face. She failed.

'You'll never guess what's just happened, girls!' Her mouth quivered with excitement and she kept moistening her full bottom lip with her tongue, a nervous tic that was clearly having a terrible effect on the waiter's equilibrium.

'Can I get you a drink?' he said in what sounded like a German accent, trying not to drool.

Hannah turned her glittering toffee-coloured eyes to him and breathed, 'Yes,' in a come-to-bed husky drawl. 'I'll have a martini with white lemonade, thank you.'

The waiter looked as if the words 'martini with white lemonade' were code for 'Can you bring me round the back of the bar and shag me senseless,' because he stayed gazing lovingly at Hannah for several moments before Leonie decided she needed to hear whatever exciting thing had happened to Hannah, and that she wouldn't hear it with him hanging about with his tongue around his knees.

'I'll have a glass of white wine and so will you, Emma,' she said loudly.

Emma didn't even protest. The waiter loped off.

'Now,' Leonie turned on Hannah, 'if Mel Gibson walked into your office today and asked you personally to show him a couple of love nests, I want his phone number and his vital statistics or we are never going to be friends ever again, got it?'

Hannah giggled like a naughty convent girl caught out playing hooky from Home Ec so she could have a sneaky fag. 'It's much, much better than Mel Gibson.' She beamed at them and began patting her chest as if to still her beating heart.

'What?' said Emma, agog.

'Yeah, what's better than Mel Gibson?' demanded Leonie, who'd spent a happy evening with Mel and half a bottle of Lambrusco the night before, courtesy of an old *Lethal Weapon* movie.

'Felix Andretti,' breathed Hannah.

'Who?' asked the other two in unison.

'He's an actor, the most gorgeous thing I've ever seen. Older than

Brad Pitt, but with that same golden glow to him and, oh, I can't describe him.'

'Yes, you bloody can!' squealed Emma in excitement. 'The most fun I've had since I last met you two was pushing my trolley round Superquinn wondering whether to splurge on steak or buy special-offer pork again. I need glamour in my life, so tell me,' she commanded, her throaty voice low and vibrating with humour.

'OK.'

They all scooched up closer on the banquette to hear the lowdown on Felix but had to wait until the waiter dispensed their drinks with agonizing slowness.

'Thanks,' they said automatically, willing him to be gone.

'Is he straight, single, or does he have a mad wife locked in the attic à la Mr Rochester?' Leonie asked when they were alone again.

Hannah appeared to think about this. 'You know,' she said meditatively, 'I don't know and,' she smirked, 'I don't care! He's bloody gorgeous and I am seriously in lust. We are talking drop-dead gorgeous, girls.'

She took a sip of martini but barely tasted it: she was high on excitement and didn't need alcohol for any buzz.

'He's half-Spanish and he's been living in London for the past few years. He's making a new TV series in Wicklow for the next six months and he needs a flat. He's a friend of my boss, although I don't know from where. I couldn't imagine two more different people. David is buttoned-up and serious; Felix is exotic, different, a free spirit, a man who doesn't plan life but faces everything on his own terms,' she added dreamily, thinking of how Felix had wanted to drop his plans for the evening to take her out. Just like that. He'd been struck by the thunderbolt of attraction the same way she had.

Emma quietly thought that Felix sounded not unlike Harry, the free spirit who'd broken Hannah's heart when his desire to be different, exotic and to face everything on his own terms meant he'd dumped her unceremoniously to travel to South America. But she said nothing. Hannah was so determined not to get hurt by a man ever again, she'd be careful: Emma was sure she would.

Leonie, meanwhile, was misty-eyed with the romance of it all.

Down to earth in so many ways, she lost all sense of reason when it came to love, Emma realized.

'What did he say in the beginning and how did he get talking to you when it was Mr James he'd come to see?' Leonie asked breathlessly.

Hannah explained how she was changing clothes and had her skirt practically at waist-level when Felix had sashayed into her life and they all roared with raucous laughter at the thought.

'I'd hate to see the sort of guy who'd come marching into the surgery if I was struggling out of my uniform and into a little sexy number,' Leonie joked. 'Probably the local vicar with his poodle, neither of whom have strong hearts. They'd both collapse.'

Emma gave her a gentle shove. 'What are you like?' she said. 'You were the star of the show in Egypt. I hope you're not going to get all negative now you're back home.'

'Only kidding,' Leonie said quickly. 'I'm in a very positive mood, honest. Now Hannah, give us more dirt on the studly Mr Andretti.'

Hannah didn't need any more prodding. Besotted with Felix and still reeling from the heady effect of meeting him, she couldn't stop herself from talking about him. With anyone else, she'd have maintained her usual composed demeanour, but with Leonie and Emma, well . . . they were real friends, not colleagues or relatives or any of the people with some ulterior motive for friendship. She could trust them, so she let herself go.

'I thought you were off men at the moment,' Leonie teased after another fifteen minutes of how beautiful Felix was and how stylish he looked and how he had that long-limbed grace that reminded Hannah of leopards in the wild . . .

Hannah bit her lip. 'I was, but you have to take opportunities when they're presented to you. And he's so presentable. You'd love him, Leonie. He wanted to come here tonight, you know.'

'You should have,' Leonie sighed. 'He sounds amazing. That's probably as near to a man as I'm ever going to get – meeting your Mr Wonderful and touching his suede jacket when we shake hands.'

Hannah immediately felt sorry for wittering on and on about Felix. 'It was only a bit of fun,' she said hurriedly. 'I'll probably never see him again. I'm getting all worked up over nothing. And I did say I was concentrating on my job and not going to get involved with a bloke ever again.'

'You can't limit yourself when it comes to true love,' Leonie declared. 'You have to go with the flow when the time is right. I said you were mad to decide never to get involved with a man ever again, didn't I, Emma?'

'You did. But tell us your news, Leonie. She has something thrilling to tell,' Emma added to Hannah.

'Well,' Leonie hesitated, 'it's nothing compared to Brad Pitt II.'

'Tell us,' hissed Hannah.

'OK, I've put an advert in the personal section of the *Evening Herald*.'

'Yahoo!' yelled Hannah loudly.

'Well done,' said Emma in delight. 'What did you say, when's it going to be in the paper – or have you got any replies yet?'

'I've brought the advert with me,' Leonie said, fishing it out of her handbag. 'It was a nightmare writing it, I can tell you. I mean, how do you describe yourself?'

'Vivacious, funny, glamorous blonde . . .' said Hannah immediately.

'. . . seeks man to be good to her because she's got a gentle soul and deserves love,' finished Emma.

Leonie blushed. 'You're so sweet, both of you. I wish I'd had the pair of you to help me write it. My friend Angie from work helped or I'd never have done it.'

'Give us a look,' demanded Hannah.

Together, they pored over the handwritten copy of Leonie's ad:

> Statuesque blonde divorcée, early forties, loves children and animals seeks warm-hearted man with GSOH for friendship and maybe relationship. Box No 12933.

'It's going in the paper tomorrow for three days,' she said.

'Are you excited?' Hannah waved the waiter over to them.

'Scared and excited,' Leonie admitted. 'Half of me is totally thrilled and the other half is scared stiff.'

'At least you've done it,' Emma enthused. 'That's the important thing.'

'I may as well confess,' Leonie said, 'I only got the nerve to actually put the ad in because of Ray, my ex-husband. I couldn't really tell either of you on the phone because the girls were always there when you rang, but when the kids came back from America, they were all wound up because their father is getting married again. Which is great,' she added quickly, in case they thought she still carried a torch for her ex-husband. 'It's just that . . .'

'It made you feel as if there was something deeply wrong with you because you don't feel you've moved on and he has,' Hannah said shrewdly.

Leonie nodded. 'Ray and I were never really meant to be, I know that and he eventually accepted it, but we went through a lot together, what with the kids and everything. It's an important bond and I care for him. But I always thought I'd survive better than he would, to be honest.'

She remembered how, to begin with, she used to feel so guilty for separating because at least she had the kids and she'd been the one who instigated the break-up.

'I thought he'd be lonely,' she added ruefully. 'Now he's the one who's got his life together and I haven't.'

'You have a great family and a job you enjoy,' protested Hannah. 'That's getting your life together. Having someone to share it with is a bonus, but that's all. I heard that by 2050 or something, thirty per cent of people will live alone. That's normal.'

'So says the woman who's been lit up like a lighthouse all evening because of a glamorous Spanish actor.'

'That's not serious, it's just fun,' Hannah insisted.

'What's she like, this fiancée?' asked Emma, sensing there was more to this than met the eye and knowing the deeply self-critical Leonie would care a lot if Ray's new partner was stunning to look at.

'A knock-out,' Leonie said drily, confirming Emma's hunch. 'Mel adores her and had scores of photos of them all. She's my age, not some bleached-blonde bimbo or anything. She's a lawyer and the exact opposite of me: elegant and slim with short dark hair, no make-up, and she looks amazing in jeans and casual polo shirts. Classy, basically.'

'You're classy,' Emma said with fierce loyalty.

'I'm not putting myself down,' Leonie interrupted. 'She's just in another league.'

'You're only imagining it,' Hannah said and rapidly ordered another round of drinks.

'I'll show you the photos some time. She looks like the sort of girl who was probably asked to be a model when she was seventeen but turned it down to go to Harvard because she'd prefer to be earning a fortune as a brilliant lawyer instead of doing lipstick commercials.' Leonie stared into her empty wine-glass gloomily.

'She's probably crap in bed, then,' Hannah insisted. 'The type of woman who thinks making love with the light on is the last word in perversion.'

'Yeah,' Emma added, 'the sort who thinks oral sex is talking about it! There has to be a fatal flaw in her. Nobody's perfect.'

After ages discussing exactly what could be wrong with the outwardly lovely Fliss – ranging from venereal disease to a sex-change operation transforming her from a male tennis player named Alan – the threesome finally left to hail a taxi and find a nice restaurant before the lack of food sent the wine straight to their heads. On Baggot Street, they went into a little Italian place and got through two bottles of wine with their lasagne, pizza and a wonderful carbonara that Hannah declared the best thing she'd eaten since she'd been to Italy.

'I've never been to Italy,' Leonie said dreamily. 'I'd love to go.'

'It's wonderful,' Hannah said, 'but it'll be a long time before I go away again. I'm completely broke after Egypt.'

'Egypt was great,' Leonie said.

'It was because we met up,' Emma pointed out, 'but I had such wonderful plans when I was there and I haven't followed through on any of them.' She stared miserably at the remains of her lasagne. 'I planned to talk to Pete about IVF and I haven't, and my father completely humiliated me and Pete the other day and I never opened my mouth. I'm such a coward.'

'What happened?'

'I had some relatives over to my house for dinner for my mother's birthday, and in the middle of it all, after I'd killed myself coming home from work early and making this special dinner, my father told some people that he had given myself and Pete deposit money.'

'What?' asked Hannah, not so much confused by Emma's tipsy story as astonished by it.

'He gave us £12,000 when we were buying our house,' Emma said. 'I told you about it, remember. But he didn't really give it to us. He lent it to us, and we're paying him back. But he told this woman – my parents' next-door neighbour – that he had given it to us. He made it sound like loads more money, in fact,' she added bitterly, 'as if he'd paid for the whole house and that Pete and I weren't grateful. That's insulting to Pete.'

'It's insulting to both of you,' said Leonie angrily.

'No, it's worse to Pete,' Emma insisted. 'He works really hard so we'll have a nice home and food and everything, and just because we didn't have enough saved for the house and needed a loan, my father is treating him like some layabout. That's what makes me so angry – I didn't say anything to defend Pete.'

And it had rankled ever since, boiling through her body like lava. She was used to being put down by Jimmy O'Brien, but she wouldn't stand for her beloved Pete being humiliated. Yet she had stood for it. She had said nothing and had let Pete down. The rage burned through her again.

'It's hard to say things to your family,' Leonie said diplomatically.

'No it's not,' Hannah said quickly. 'You've got to stand up to him, Emma. He's a bully and he'll never stop.'

Rubbing her suddenly throbbing forehead, Emma said tiredly: 'Look, can we forget this, please? I don't want to talk about it, I shouldn't have brought it up.'

'But you did,' protested Hannah. 'You need to talk about this and do something . . .'

'OK, but not now!' yelled Emma, startling them all. 'I want to forget about him, right?'

Leonie clasped Emma's hand gently. 'All right, we'll stop talking about it. Hannah, wink at the waiter and see if you can get us some dessert menus. I feel a zabaglione moment coming on.'

It was half two and, feeling deliciously tipsy, Emma crawled into bed beside Pete's sleeping form and snuggled up against him. Normally, she'd never attempt to wake him if he was asleep, but she wanted to be cuddled.

'How are ya, Em?' he murmured, turning over sleepily and putting his arms round her.

'Fine,' she said, wriggling down under the duvet to hold his toasty body close to hers. 'Did you miss me?'

'Loads,' he said, burying his face in the curve of her neck and planting a couple of woozy kisses on her skin. 'Did you have a nice time?'

'Brilliant. We had way too much to drink and I left the car at Sachs Hotel. Will you give me a lift into town tomorrow morning so I can pick it up?'

'For you, anything,' he said. 'Do you know what, Em?'

'What?' She kissed the top of his bald head.

'I love you, even though you stink of garlic!'

She tickled him in retaliation. 'That's to hide the scent of the other fella I was really out with – you know, the six foot four karate instructor. He uses this very powerful aftershave and eating garlic is the only way to throw you off the scent.'

'I'll kill him,' Pete said, his voice getting sleepier. 'Can I go to sleep now, you wild woman?'

CHAPTER ELEVEN

Waiting for Felix Andretti to phone was worse than waiting for Godot, Hannah decided. When he didn't ring the day after she'd met him, she took a deep breath and told herself that such a delay was perfectly normal. He was acting cool, not being too eager. It was perfectly understandable. That didn't stop her jumping every time her phone rang, desperately hoping it was him. She didn't leave her desk at lunchtime that Thursday, either, asking Gillian to buy her a sandwich instead.

'I've a lot to do,' she said vaguely, rifling through files and trying to look too horrifically busy to walk the five minutes down the road to the sandwich shop.

She ended up reading the newspaper and doing the crossword while she ate her tuna sandwich and drank two cups of coffee, longing for the phone to ring.

On Friday, she dressed up in killer high heels, a long lean dark skirt with a split up the side and a kitten-soft cashmere cardigan in a flattering bronze colour. She left her hair loose and wore her contact lenses instead of her glasses, in case they might be off-putting. Wearing her matching coral-pink net bra and G-string, she felt highly desirable and utterly turned on. Felix, she decided smugly, was the sort of man to turn up out of the blue and ask you out to dinner. It would kill her to do it, but she'd have to refuse. As she worked, she toyed with the various ways she'd neatly rebuke him for his audacity in expecting her to drop everything.

'Do I look like the sort of girl who can make a date at a minute's notice?' she'd say archly, making him weep with desire and suffering. 'Sorry, I may be able to fit you in next month . . .' She'd hardly be able to wait that long herself, but she didn't want Felix to think she was desperate.

'Hannah,' interrupted Gillian rudely, 'it's the man about the dodgy plumbing in the gents'. Don't forget to tell him about the problems in the kitchen.' Ripped from her reverie, Hannah applied herself to the task in hand.

'Going anywhere special, love?' enquired the plumber cheekily as he stared at the length of Hannah's shapely leg in her sexy skirt while she showed him into the kitchen.

She shot him a murderous look.

'I was only asking,' he muttered and got to work.

Half five came and went with no personal phone calls. Hannah could have wept.

She stood at her desk, morosely tidying up and thinking that she'd certainly hear nothing from Felix now until next week; if he rang at all, that was. The only way he could contact her was at work.

David James emerged from his office, yawning and carrying his briefcase in one hand.

'Going anywhere special, Hannah?' he asked, eyes roaming admiringly from her clinging cardigan all the way down to her perilous shoes.

'I wouldn't ask that if I were you, mate,' muttered the plumber, passing on his way out to his van. 'She'll have you up on sexual harassment charges, that one.'

He fled past Hannah before she could glare at him.

David grinned. 'Did he try it on?'

'Not really,' she admitted. 'He got me at a bad moment.'

'Fancy going for a quick drink to turn it into a good moment?' David said idly, long fingers drumming the desk.

She shook her head. She was too miserable to be cheered up.

'Just one, and you can moan to me,' David pushed.

She began to relent. One drink wouldn't kill her and while she was talking to David James, at least she wouldn't be moping about bloody Felix.

'Call for you on line one,' yelled Donna. 'Personal.'

A quiver of excitement rippled through Hannah. 'No,' she said to David. 'I'm meeting someone.'

David shrugged. 'See you on Monday,' he said.

Hannah snatched up her phone and punched line one.

'Hannah, it's your mother. I know it's last minute, but can Stuart and Pam stay with you for the weekend?'

'What?' said Hannah crossly, furious that it wasn't Felix phoning her and just as furious at the thought of having her brother and his wife to stay with her for the weekend. The flat was much too small for guests and, what's more, she and Pam didn't get on. Mind you, neither did she and Stuart. 'Last minute isn't the word. Why couldn't they have asked me before now? And why are you phoning, Mum? Has Stuart lost the use of his dialling finger?' she added sarcastically. Her brother was their mother's pet and she did everything for him.

'Don't fly off the handle, would you, Hannah,' her mother said, unperturbed. 'They're up for a wedding and the arrangements for the hotel didn't work out. It's the least you can do. They'll be up by ten tonight, and Pam says not to bother cooking.'

Hannah snorted. She'd had no intention of doing any such thing.

She drove home in a rage. The flat was immaculate as always, although after a weekend of Stuart, it'd doubtless be a tip. Hannah left fresh sheets and a duvet cover on top of the spare-room bed but didn't change the bedclothes – her brother could do that. She wasn't running a damned hotel. In fact, that was probably why Stuart was coming there. Too mean to pay for a hotel, she guessed accurately.

She cooked an omelette for herself and watched television, simmering away at the thought of both her inconsiderate brother and Felix. Why go to all the bother of chatting her up and pretending to be crazy about her if he had no intention of ever seeing her again? *What was the point*? Hannah didn't get it. Was the chat-up a type of sport? Did handsome guys keep scoreboards on flirting so they could gauge how irresistible they were? Probably. She had a mental vision of Felix boasting about how he'd made *'this girl in the estate agent's drool for me! I tell you, lads, she was eating out of my hand.'*

Stuart and Pam arrived at half eleven, waking Hannah who'd fallen asleep in front of the telly after watching *Frasier*.

'Thought you'd be out on a Friday night,' said Stuart, dumping a giant suitcase on to the floor and prowling around the flat speculatively.

'How could I be out if I was waiting for you pair?' demanded Hannah, immediately irritated.

'You could have left a key with the neighbours,' he said.

'You could have booked into a hotel,' Hannah suggested.

Pam, used to the way her husband and his sister got on, made her way to the kitchen and put the kettle on.

'Do make yourselves at home,' sniped Hannah, furious at how her sister-in-law had blithely made herself at home without asking permission.

'We will,' said Pam, a self-satisfied woman who was oblivious to all subtle and not-so-subtle innuendo.

'Nice place,' Stuart said, throwing himself on to the couch and testing how springy it was. 'Got yourself a man yet?'

Hannah remembered why she and Stuart had fought like cat and dog as children. Although they looked alike – he was tall with dark hair and eyes the same colour as his sister – they were utterly unalike on the inside. Stuart was lazy, careless and, as he proudly put it, 'spoke his mind'. In Hannah's book, that meant he was blunt verging on rude. They brought out the worst in each other. She thought he was one of life's takers, while Stuart clearly thought his sister was an uptight cow. When she'd been working for the Triumph Hotel, Stuart had thought nothing of asking for comped rooms for all his pals on wild stag nights, yet if she asked him to have a look at her car – as he was a mechanic – he'd procrastinate until she got angry and paid someone else to do it.

'Yes, I do have a man, Stuart,' she snapped. 'He's an actor, but he's away,' she lied. 'There are sheets in the spare room, towels in the hotpress and I'm going to bed. Good night.'

'Don't you want tea?' asked Pam, appearing at the door of the kitchen with a pot of tea and a big packet of biscuits on a tray.

'No.'

At least they went off early the next morning, after a lot of arguing in the bathroom about who'd steamed up the mirror, and Pam complaining that Stuart never said she looked nice in anything.

Hannah, awake but remaining in bed in case she had to get involved, could hear everything through the thin walls of the flat.

'I got this hat specially for the wedding,' Pam roared at Stuart. 'The least you could do is say that it's nice.'

'It's not!' yelled Stuart. 'You can't wear a red hat with red hair. You look stupid.'

When they'd banged the door loudly on the way out, Hannah finally relaxed. She got up, made herself a cup of coffee and planned her day. Grocery shopping, the gym and a trip to the cinema with Leonie and the twins tonight. It was only then she remembered that she had forgotten to give Stuart and Pam a key to the flat. Tough bananas, she thought grimly. She'd be out until at least eleven and if they wanted to get in before that, they could go hang. Serve them right for being too mean to pay for a hotel bedroom.

She got home at half eleven, tired but relaxed. Mel and Abby had been so funny that she hadn't been able to be miserable. Watching them checking out good-looking blokes in the cinema had been much more fun than watching the movie. When she got to the top of the stairs in the house, Pam and Stuart were sitting outside her flat door looking furious.

'How did you get in?' asked Hannah, not pleased that any of the other tenants had let them in.

'Never mind that,' snarled Stuart, who was obviously plastered. 'Why the hell didn't you give us a key so we could get in? Or why couldn't you be here to let us in?'

'I was out with my boyfriend,' Hannah said sweetly, 'and I didn't think you'd be home so early. The free bar ended, did it?'

She let them in and Stuart immediately threw himself on to the couch, shoes and all, and went to sleep. His drunken snores reverberated about the flat and Hannah looked at him with disgust.

'I don't know why you stay with him,' she said to Pam, staring at her brother's prone figure. 'He's a drunk, like his father.'

'He's not, he's nothing like your father,' Pam protested.

'Isn't he?' said Hannah bitterly. 'He's just the same, if you ask me: useless and bone idle. I'm amazed he's still going to work. I thought he'd have you earning it all by now, with him only venturing out to the bookies.'

'Stuart doesn't gamble any more and he isn't a big drinker,' Pam protested. 'We were at a wedding, after all. I can't remember the last time he got drunk. Just because you've got a hang up about your father, don't tar Stuart with the same brush.'

'I don't,' snapped Hannah. 'I merely see Stuart heading the same way. Like father like son.'

'What about like mother like daughter?' said Pam pointedly.

Hannah whirled round. 'I am not like my mother. I refuse to be tied to some useless lump of a man who's good for nothing.'

'What was Harry?' asked Pam nastily.

Hannah's lip wobbled. That was below the belt.

'You're the one who keeps going for useless lumps of men,' her sister-in-law continued mercilessly. 'At least Stuart married me,' she sniffed. She pulled a protesting Stuart from the couch and dragged him into the spare bedroom, leaving Hannah furious and upset behind her.

She didn't fall for useless men, she didn't. She'd been unlucky. That was all. Pam didn't know what she was talking about. If Hannah had been married to someone as unmotivated as Stuart, she wouldn't have boasted about it. Honestly, some women thought that wedding rings were the be all and end all of life. How stupid could you get?

Tired from two nights tossing and turning, thinking about what Pam had said, Hannah overslept on Monday and woke up to hear the news at eight.

'Shit, shit, shit,' she groaned, dragging herself out of bed, knowing she wouldn't have time to wash her hair. She showered quickly, threw on the first thing she came to in her wardrobe – a plain brown dress that really only looked good with washed, fluffy hair and plenty of make-up – and was out the door in fifteen minutes. She brushed on some eyeshadow and lipstick at traffic lights and cursed for not having time to do her hair. She hated greasy roots.

'Had a nice weekend, Hannah?' asked Gillian loudly, looking at her watch pointedly as Hannah burst through the office door at ten past nine.

Hannah sniffed in reply. She refused to get riled by Gillian.

She grabbed a cup of coffee and sat at her desk, trying to sort her brain out. She'd been so distracted on Thursday and Friday thinking about Felix that she really was behind with work. By half ten, she'd only managed to drink half of her coffee. Ravenous after having no breakfast, she rushed over to the percolator hoping to get a fresh cup and maybe a biscuit. The percolator was empty and so was the biscuit tin. Weary, hungry and miserable, Hannah felt like crying. The whole world was against her.

Her phone rang and she marched back to her desk to pick it up.

'What are you doing tonight, Ms Campbell?' purred Felix.

Hannah nearly dropped the phone with shock.

'Er . . . nothing,' she said, too astonished to revert to her make-him-suffer plan.

'Good. Would you like to go to the theatre with me? We could have a little supper afterwards.'

'I'd love to,' Hannah said, weak with a combination of longing and sheer delight that he'd phoned. 'What time?'

'I'll meet you in the pub across the road from the Gate at seven. Can't wait.' And he was gone.

Her stomach was a mass of butterflies as she thought about Felix actually phoning her. Then the butterflies turned to knots as she realized she had greasy hair, was wearing completely the wrong outfit and wouldn't have time to go home and change before the theatre.

And she hadn't even asked what play they were going to see. Talk about the strong feminist type who thought marriage was for wimps. '*I'll make him suffer*!' Yeah, right. She was like an affectionate cat – rolling over so that someone, *anyone* could rub her tummy. Still, the faintest glimmer of a smile lit up her face. If it was Felix rubbing her tummy, she wouldn't mind.

Determined that thinking about him wouldn't put the kibosh on yet another working day, Hannah did her best to work steadily. She decided to tell David she had to leave early: that way, she could race home, do her hair and find something drop-dead gorgeous to wear.

But Cupid was having none of it. When five o'clock came, David called the senior staff into his office for a meeting. While he discussed sales targets, his master plan, and talked about how well everyone had been doing, Hannah wriggled in her seat. She wasn't listening to a word he was saying. She was mentally running through the contents of her wardrobe, trying to remember if she'd ironed her new silky red shirt from Principles, the one with the tie-waist. And what about underwear . . . ? If the beige lace bra was in the laundry basket, she'd shoot herself. It was the sexiest bra imaginable and looked wonderful with the rich red shirt with a couple of buttons left open so her cleavage could peek out. Hannah didn't usually leave any buttons open, but she'd practised at home in front of the mirror and that particular look was very sexy. She'd even left her glasses off and was wearing contacts for a change.

'I know we're running a bit late,' David said, with a glance towards a fidgety Hannah, 'but an old colleague from the States is here and she's kindly agreed to give us a talk about the real estate business in the USA and what's going on there. Her advice could be useful because of all the clients we're getting from the States who are relocating here. Can I introduce you to Martha Parker . . .'

Normally, Hannah would have been fascinated by the elegant and beautifully groomed Ms Parker, with her bobbed, frosted hair, exquisite fitted cream suit and a shimmering air of self-confidence. Tonight, she wanted Martha to get off the stage so she could race home and primp. Alas, Ms Parker had a lot to say and it took her half an hour to say it. As the staff filed out of David's office, it was five past six. There was no way Hannah had time to go home now. She'd have to do wonderful things with make-up and deodorant, and pray the lights were dim in the theatre. What was that thing she'd read about in women's magazines about talcum powder hiding greasy hair? You shook a bit on your parting, let it get rid of the shine and then brushed it out. Couldn't be easier. She'd buy some en route.

What with asphyxiating herself with deodorant in the ladies loo and having to spend five minutes shaking talcum powder off her dress when she applied it too liberally, Hannah ended up ten minutes late. She was sure she was sweating as she reached the bar, despite all the deodorant and a generous spray of Donna's Opium.

Even in the pre-theatre crowd that thronged the small bar, Felix stood out. His blond, noble head was visible from the door and Hannah could see he was talking to someone. In profile, he was even better looking: the straight nose could have been lifted from a medieval portrait of some arrogant young king, and the strong jaw jutted out in a gloriously masculine way. He threw back his leonine head and laughed. She felt herself smiling in sympathy as she crossed the room. Then he turned and saw her and the velvety mahogany eyes creased up in an appreciative smile.

Hannah felt her insides melt. She reached the group. Instead of taking her hand or kissing her on the cheek, Felix pulled her to him with strong, lean arms. When she was standing in the circle of his embrace, he lowered his golden head to hers and kissed her full on the lips. Utterly unexpected, it was utterly incredible. Forgotten bits of her body moulded against his in excitement. His lips were hard against her full mouth and their tongues entwined in passion.

'Why don't you see if they rent rooms by the hour?' enquired a dry voice.

They broke apart, Hannah red-faced and Felix laughing. 'She's beautiful, can you blame me?' he demanded of the group, keeping one arm round Hannah.

'How are you, my love?' he asked her in a low voice. 'I haven't been able to stop thinking about you.'

Some demon in Hannah's head made her say: 'Really? You took long enough phoning me, then.'

'Ouch,' he grinned, pinching her waist with one hand. 'She bites. I deserved that, I guess.'

Hannah cringed at what she'd said. Talk about clingy and insecure. Why hadn't she just told him she'd spent two days moping by the phone while she was at it.

'I had a couple of hectic days filming,' Felix was explaining. 'That's my excuse and I'm sticking to it. Now, what do you want to drink?'

She was already high and didn't need alcohol, so she asked for mineral water.

'Have a real drink,' said Felix. 'I'd have thought you were the type of tough girl who'd kick-start her vibrator, roll her own tampons and drink straight Scotch.'

The crowd guffawed again.

'I'm only tough with men,' Hannah retorted sweetly, thinking that two could play that game. 'The rest of the time, I'm all woman.'

'Oh, baybee,' growled Felix. 'You're my kind of girl, all right. Mineral water it is.'

He didn't introduce her to the group, which was just as well, Hannah felt, as he seemed different with an audience than he had alone in the office. She preferred having him to herself.

At half seven, they made their way to the theatre. It was the first night of a new production of *Lady Windermere's Fan*, Hannah realized as she saw the posters. She wasn't much of a theatre-goer and felt nervous in case she let this fact slip out. As an actor, Felix obviously went to the theatre all the time. She hated the thought of her lack of culture being made public. Hannah's efforts at improving herself hadn't stretched to the theatre yet. In the Campbell house when she'd been growing up culture was something found in yoghurt. Well, it was with Stuart and her father, anyway, who both felt that reading anything more taxing than the racing results was a waste of time.

Almost as soon as they'd made it inside, Felix said he had to disappear for a moment. 'I see someone I must say hello to. I won't be long,' he said, leaving her in the throng of the foyer.

Feeling a little lost, Hannah looked around her, hoping she could adopt the air of one who fitted in perfectly but was gazing about her with interest instead of nerves. Two women beside her were talking volubly about the arts, braceleted arms jangling as they knocked back white wine.

'. . . I hear the Lubarte Players are thinking of putting on a performance of *Vera*,' one said.

'Really, how terrible,' the other replied. 'What a dreadful play.

You'd hardly believe it was Wilde, I always say.' They laughed.

When Felix returned, they made their way to their seats. 'I love Wilde,' Hannah sighed. 'I'm sure I remember hearing somewhere that some theatre group are trying to put on *Vera*,' she added. 'I've never liked that play; always felt it wasn't really classic Wilde.'

Felix shot her an impressed look. 'I had no idea you were an *aficionado* of the theatre, my love,' he said.

Hannah smiled serenely. 'Never underestimate me,' she said in a mock severe voice.

The play was wonderfully clever and Hannah wasn't sure if it was her heightened sense of pleasure that made it so thrilling for her, or the fact that Felix sat silently beside her, one hand wedged against her thigh, stroking her knee through the fabric of her long dress.

In the interval, they mingled with the other theatre-goers, Felix leading her by the hand as they drifted from group to group, all comers hugging and kissing him delightedly. He was quite the star, she realized, as the fifth person threw their arms around Felix and congratulated him on the wonderful reviews he'd received for his last role. From the comments, she'd established that he'd had a small part in a British/Canadian production set in the 1800s. He was now filming a small-budget British film that was being made in Ireland and it appeared that at least half of the Irish acting fraternity were involved in some way.

'Terrible tosh, but it pays the mortgage,' sighed one elegant man in a velvet suit, who had a small role in the film.

'Wouldn't touch that sort of big-budget brainless rubbish!' sniffed an actress, whom Felix whispered had been sent off after her first audition.

After lots of air-kissing and cries of 'You *must* come to supper with us sometime soon, dear boy,' Hannah and Felix made their way back to their seats for the second half.

'Let's make a speedy getaway when it's over,' he murmured into her ear, his breath caressing. 'I want you all to myself and, if we hang around, we'll have an entourage.'

After the third curtain call, Felix whisked Hannah out of the theatre, into a taxi and across the river to the Trocadero, the traditional after-theatre restaurant and a famous haunt of actors.

Annexing a small table at the back, Felix ordered smoked salmon and champagne for both of them without even looking at the menu.

Hannah wasn't sure what excited her more: the way this fabulous man was gazing at her hungrily, or the way he'd taken charge of everything. There was something so masterful about him, it gave her a *frisson* of erotic excitement to think about being in bed with him. Imagine how utterly in control he'd be then, that hard golden body driving into hers, naked skin on skin . . .

Soft bread rolls came. Felix buttered one thickly for her and fed her small bits, letting her savour the taste of butter melting into the feather-light roll. 'It's soft, liquid and delicious,' he said. 'That's what it's going to feel like when I make love to you, Hannah. Delicious, but –' he grinned wickedly – 'not soft.'

Hannah gulped. This was all moving too fast, yet she couldn't help herself: she wanted him too.

The champagne arrived. Felix never took his eyes off her as he drank from his glass. The liquid exploded in Hannah's mouth, like exquisite pins and needles dancing across her tongue.

'You're beautiful,' he said softly, reaching out with long fingers to touch her face. He traced the high cheekbones, trailed his fingers across her full, quivering lips, letting one finger slide languorously into her mouth. Instinctively, she sucked on it, holding him prisoner while her tongue ran over it, tasting the saltiness of his skin. As moments went, it was more erotic than any she'd ever shared with a man before, and they were in a restaurant! Lord only knew what it'd be like to be alone with him, without a phalanx of waiters and other diners as chaperones.

Felix's wide mouth curved into a wicked smile, one that ignited something deep inside Hannah. Desire surged through her like a bursting dam. He pulled his finger out, then slid it into his own mouth as if tasting her. He put his head to one side consideringly. 'Sweet,' he pronounced. 'Like you. Sweet . . .' his voice lowered an octave until it was the consistency of honey-covered gravel, 'and ripe.'

Hannah breathed out raggedly.

A waiter appeared with two plates of smoked salmon.

Hannah wanted to grab Felix, tell the waiters to forget about the fish, and hightail it back to her flat where she'd show him exactly how sweet she was.

But Felix attacked his plate with the same fascination he'd shown when caressing her. 'I'm so hungry,' he growled, squeezing lemon on to his food with one hand and forking up slivers of smoked salmon with the other. She watched him eat for a while, not hungry herself because desire had elbowed all other primary urges out of the way. She loved the way his blond hair flopped over those hypnotic eyes and the way his huge mouth opened wide, white teeth gleaming as he consumed his meal. He was a man of passion, she thought wistfully, passionate about food, about love, about life and about sex.

'Aren't you hungry?' he asked, looking at her untouched plate.

She gave a wry smile. 'Not really. You've taken my appetite away.'

Felix pulled her plate towards him and attacked that too. Hannah finished the champagne in her glass and poured more for both of them.

'Tell me about yourself,' she breathed.

With most people, that was a difficult request. With an actor, as Hannah was to discover, it was an invitation to declaim a speech as familiar to them as their face in the mirror each morning. Felix loved to talk about himself.

Eating hungrily and drinking big gulps of the champagne, he told her about his career and his hopes. Hannah, trying to keep up with him as far as the champagne was concerned, was enthralled.

He glossed over his youth and family. 'I don't talk about it,' he said, dark eyes soulful as he gazed at hers. But he was happy to discuss everything else. At thirty-seven, he was finally on the edge of huge success. It had been a hard climb, he said, telling her about his stint in an ill-fated British soap and his first film role where his few minutes on screen had ended up on the cutting-room floor. But everything was about to change. A sitcom he had a small part in was growing in popularity and he was suddenly inundated with calls from casting agents. His time had come, Felix said proudly.

It was a life lived in the fast lane, full of parties, premieres, carousing and being one of the beautiful people. But what Felix really wanted, Hannah felt instinctively, was security. He was like her, she knew it. Something in his past had tainted him and made him yearn for a safe haven he'd never had before. She could provide it for him.

The entourage arrived anyway, blowing kisses across banquettes in the Trocadero, waving at friends and waving even more animatedly at enemies.

'We wondered where you two sneaked off to,' said the man in the velvet suit accusingly.

'Privacy is important to me,' Felix replied blandly.

The entourage sniffed and surveyed the tables beside Felix and Hannah.

'Sit somewhere else,' he said rudely. 'We want to be alone.'

Normally, she'd have hated that sort of rudeness, but it was different with Felix. He was so impossibly handsome and talented that people were drawn to him and the only way to get rid of them was to be brusque.

They'd talked their throats hoarse and the second bottle was nearly empty when the waiter came with complimentary Sambuccas.

'I couldn't,' giggled Hannah, eyeing the small flaming glass of liqueur. 'I'm drunk already. I can't imagine what I'd do if I had any more.'

There was an evil glint in Felix's dark eyes. 'Can't you?' he said.

He'd been lounging back in his chair, regarding her possessively as he ran his long fingers around the rim of his glass. Now he pulled his chair forward. She jumped slightly as she felt one of his hands on her thighs under the table, sliding and pushing her long dress up her legs.

Even in her intoxicated state, Hannah tried to stop him. There were other people around, someone might see.

'Someone might see you,' she said, scandalized.

'So what?' he enquired, one eyebrow raised sardonically. 'Let them watch.'

Hannah looked shocked.

'They can't see,' he assured her. 'There's a tablecloth hiding us.'

His hand finally pushed her dress up and with one long arm straining, his fingers moved up the silky skin of her thigh covered only by sheer tights. Hannah quivered as his fingers stroked her skin, only half-way up her thigh and yet, if his fingers slid even a centimetre further up, she wouldn't be able to stop herself from crying out. She couldn't control the erotic feeling that rushed through her. It was like being hooked up to a machine with electrodes delivering unimaginable pleasure to her erogenous zones. His hand crept further up.

'Next time we go out, you'll have to wear stockings,' Felix murmured. She gasped out loud and then, just as suddenly, his hand was gone. 'Let's go,' he said roughly.

He kissed her in the taxi home, nothing more. Just luscious kisses which melted her insides as his tongue explored hers. Hannah could feel her heart beating like a metronome as she led him up the stairs to her front door. She fumbled with her bunch of keys and giggled quietly at her own stupidity. Felix didn't giggle. Finally, she managed to insert the correct key in the door and pushed.

'It's not Buckingham Palace . . .' she began to say as she dropped her handbag on the hall table. She never got any further with her comments.

The front door closed and suddenly Felix was wrapped around her, arms clinging to her, hands probing and trying to pull off her coat. Their mouths were meshed together, lips hard against lips, tongues entwining and twisting in passion. Felix managed to rip her coat off and he began to slide her dress up her thighs. In return, she'd dragged off his jacket and was pulling at his shirt, not caring that buttons were pinging as she pulled, rattling against the floor like hailstones as they fell.

'You're beautiful,' he purred, golden head moving down towards her breasts, fingers burrowing under her dress. Like exquisitely practised Riverdancers, they moved apart long enough to pull off her dress and his trousers. Suddenly remembering that she was wearing that male bugbear – tights – Hannah wrenched them off and thanked some deity she was wearing decent silky black knickers even if her bra was a boring old white cotton one. What a pity she wasn't dressed to thrill in her coral see-through net rig-out. So she ripped off the cotton bra and looked up to find Felix, clad only in striped boxer shorts, watching her. His body was glorious: lean, rangy, golden and perfectly proportioned. She could see the outline of his erection straining against the fabric of his shorts. In one swift move, he'd grabbed her, lifted her up and carried her to the couch. Then he lay down on top of her, grinding his body into hers in triumph, running his hands over her torso, fingers kneading her erect nipples roughly, burying his mouth passionately in her hair.

'You're so beautiful, so sexy, I knew that the moment I saw you,' he said hoarsely.

If he was turned on to some unbelievable level, he'd met his match in Hannah. The sexuality she'd kept under wraps for so much of her life exploded from her, like a bored tiger that had been in captivity suddenly released into a jungle throbbing with life. Their lovemaking was frantic and fierce, not the gentle, sweet lovemaking Hannah had remembered with Harry. That had been placid and comforting: this was fierce, primal and wild. Felix jammed his mouth against hers, plundering her mouth, desperate to taste every part of her. In turn, she dug her nails into his back when he jammed himself inside her, shrieking with relief at finally having his body become a part of hers. Joined together, they moaned and panted, frantic for release and just as frantic for this incredible lovemaking not to end. A sheen of perspiration coating her naked body, Hannah clung to Felix, pulling him deeper with her arms and legs, wrapping her long legs around his waist until she exploded in a firecracker of orgasm that was savage, primitive and utterly blissful.

As if he'd been waiting for her, Felix groaned, his body stiffened and he came, moaning her name over and over again until he fell on to the couch beside her, dank with sweat and exhausted.

They lay coiled together like puppies and breathed deeply. Hannah felt as if every muscle had been stretched to its limit. Her body was suffused with the glorious after-glow of orgasm and yet she felt at peace, as if this wild thing was what she was born for. Or maybe, she thought, with a pang of sheer adoration, it was Felix she was born for.

He brought her hand to his lips and kissed it softly. 'You're wonderful,' he said.

'Look who's talking,' joked Hannah. 'I'm so exhausted, Felix. I'm going to fall asleep here.'

'Bed,' he announced, getting to his feet gracefully and holding a hand out to her.

The birds were singing some exultant song when Hannah woke the next morning with a dull throbbing in her head from too much champagne. She shifted in the bed and her arm touched Felix's warm body. It hadn't been a dream; she beamed with sheer joy. What was a hangover to this feeling of happiness?

Moving quietly so she wouldn't wake him, Hannah padded naked and barefoot into the kitchen and swallowed two headache tablets with a glass of water. After another glass to slake her hangover thirst, she crept into the bathroom. Her hair was a wild bush around her head, tangled curls in all directions. Her make-up, which naturally hadn't seen cotton wool or cleanser the night before, was in patchy scales under her eyes. Her mouth was bruised from a combination of fierce kissing and from Felix's late-night stubble. All in all, the sort of face to normally make Hannah groan. Only, today, something shone out from behind the tiredness, the redness and the panda eyes: something delirious and fulfilled. Her eyes sparkled and her mouth refused to stop smiling. She was happy, in love! She beamed at her reflection. Love, love, love.

After restoring herself to some of her former glory and brushing her teeth until her gums hurt in case she had bad breath, Hannah slid back under the duvet and wriggled over until she was half-lying on top of him. He didn't appear to wake up, yet one hand moved gently to cup her breast, idly caressing the nipple expertly until Hannah sighed loudly. Felix opened one eye.

'Are you a morning sex person?' he asked, his voice hoarse. 'I'd have thought from last night's performance that you were a night owl.'

In response, Hannah wriggled until she was lying completely on top of him, exulting in the amazing sensation of her cool naked body against his sleep-warmed one. 'I think I'm an every moment of the day sort of person,' she said.

'Good,' he replied, pulling her head down to meet his.

Low-angled autumn sun lit up the front of Dwyer, Dwyer & James as Hannah walked towards it, swinging her handbag happily. The office was pretty now that it had been repainted in the firm's trademark crocus yellow and white. Hannah grinned. Everything felt pretty to her today. The dour-faced traffic warden who lingered at the bottom of the road was practically good-looking today, even though he'd given Hannah a parking ticket the week before. Being in love was a wonderful thing, she decided. Better than rose-coloured spectacles any day.

'Morning, Hannah,' said David James, climbing out of his silver Jag.

'Beautiful morning, isn't it?' beamed Hannah.

David eyed her curiously. 'Are you on happy pills or something?' he teased.

'No,' she said, letting him open the door for her. 'Just naturally happy, that's all. You'll never guess who I met last night,' she added, knowing she shouldn't say anything but unable to resist saying his name. 'Felix Andretti.'

David's brow furrowed. 'Where?' he asked.

'At the theatre,' she replied airily. 'He seems like a nice man,' she added, hoping for some titbit of information to drop from David's lips.

'He does?' One eyebrow was raised sarcastically. 'That doesn't sound like the Felix I know and love,' he remarked. 'More of a professional playboy, I would have thought. Nice isn't the sort of word people use about Felix. They either love him or hate him. Women love him until he dumps them, and men sometimes hate him because he's so bloody successful with the opposite sex.'

'Really?' Hannah said idly, shocked but trying to hide it. 'I thought he was nice, anyhow.' She was longing to ask more but daren't.

'Was he with anyone?' David asked, standing at Hannah's desk.

'No,' she said, wide-eyed with innocence.

David grinned and turned towards his office door. 'He must be losing his touch,' he added over his shoulder. 'I've never seen him without a string of beautiful girls glued to him.'

Hannah had all morning to chew this over. Felix and a string of beautiful girls. She was too jealous to be flattered by the obvious fact that she, too, was beautiful if the god-like Mr Andretti considered her worthy of him. Instead, she mulled over the notion that the man she'd slept with on the first date was something of a lady-killer and always had a few women in tow, women he'd dump whenever the mood took him.

What had she expected, she thought jealously. Felix was thirty-seven, he must have had scores of girlfriends before this. What if he'd gone out with her to try and bed her and, once that had been accomplished, he'd no longer be interested? Perhaps that was why women hated him. For the second time in twenty-four hours, Hannah felt her heart skip a beat with shock. How stupid could she be to sleep with him on their first date. What sort of woman would he think she was?

She cast her mind frantically back to his departure that morning.

All he'd said when he left was, 'Adios, bebe,' giving her a passionate kiss on the doorstep and the promise that he'd phone. Well, not so much of a promise, more of an: 'I'll call.'

Feeling like a woman whose lottery numbers have just come up but who forgot, for once, to buy a ticket, Hannah sat gloomily at her desk all morning. What sort of an imbecile are you? she was mentally asking herself for about the hundredth time when a messenger boy appeared at her desk, hidden by a huge bouquet of the palest pink roses.

'Oh!' gasped Hannah. 'For me?'

'If you're Hannah Campbell, then yes,' said the messenger. 'Sign here.'

She buried her nose in the flowers, trying to breathe in the fragrance but finding them curiously scent-free. Still, they were beautiful.

'Who are they from?' demanded the rest of the staff.

Hannah opened the card. 'To Hannah, my beautiful, ripe peach. See you tonight. I'll pick you up at home at eight.'

Happiness saturated every pore of her body. He didn't think she was a stupid slut; he wanted to see her tonight after all. Bliss.

CHAPTER TWELVE

Leonie stared into the cage at the heavily drugged cat. He lay like a soft marmalade cushion, belly curled up and fat paws lifeless on the post-operative sheepskin blanket. Poor Freddie. Removing the elastic bands he'd swallowed had been touch and go, and Angie had been understandably nervous about operating on such an elderly cat.

'He's fourteen, he might die under the anaesthetic,' she'd said worriedly to Leonie.

But there'd really been no option once Mrs Erskine was told what Freddie's chances were. She'd broken into sobs as she held her beloved cat in her arms, saying he was her only comfort in life since her husband had died. 'Please operate. I know he's old, but so am I, and I'd be lost without him.'

Leonie had a lump in her throat as Angie patted the old lady on the arm, firmly helping her from the surgery into the waiting room, while Leonie held on to the distressed cat. But Freddie had come through the operation with flying colours, his intestine yielding five small elastic bands which would have certainly killed him if they hadn't been removed.

She reached into the cage and patted his soft fur gently. 'You're a fighter, aren't you, Freddie?' she said softly, watching his body rise and fall with deep breaths. Louise, the other practice nurse, had a few phone calls to make to other anxious owners and she'd volunteered to phone Mrs Erskine to tell her the good news. The old lady would be so happy. But Freddie wouldn't be going home for a few hours until he'd slept off the anaesthetic.

Leonie checked the cages next door. Freddie's neighbours were two female cats who'd been spayed that afternoon. Both were still knocked out. But three cages down, the inhabitant was wide awake. He was a black tom who'd been enjoying life as a feline Don Juan in his neighbourhood for many years, fathering countless litters. The knife had finally fallen on Tommy, who'd just been neutered as part of Angie's Wednesday afternoon surgery. Hissing from the back of his cage, he glared at Leonie fiercely, as if he knew exactly what had been done to him and was determined to wreak revenge for the loss of his cathood.

'Is tonight the night for romance?' enquired Angie, coming out of the cramped surgery toilet having changed into her going-home clothes.

'Be quiet,' whispered Leonie in horror. 'Somebody might hear you. No one else knows – and yes, tonight is the night.'

Leonie was already regretting everything about her blind date. She regretted having put the personal advert in the paper in the first place, and she regretted telling anyone about it. So far, the only people who knew were Hannah, Emma and Angie. But they were quite enough. The girls had been sweet about the whole idea, while Angie kept mentioning it with increasing excitement, as if Leonie would be announcing her engagement any day. If it hadn't been for Hannah's calm and sensible encouragement, Leonie might well have thrown all the replies in the bin.

Her 'statuesque blonde divorcée' advert had warranted ten replies, two of which were from men who obviously assumed she was a hooker offering a bit of French polishing under the guise of respectability. One respondent had sent a note in splotchy Biro, telling her 'a mother of children should be ashamed to be throwing herself at men like a brazen hussy'. She considered framing it for posterity but decided against it on grounds of decency. The other seven sounded reasonably normal. Well, semi-normal. But then, as Leonie had spent a month deliberating, what exactly was 'normal'?

Was the man who said he liked golf going to be the type who

talked of nothing else but handicaps and would refuse to spend any summertime daylight hours with her when he could be out on the course? Or would the 'good-humoured professional, loves the theatre and literature' turn out to be a card-carrying snob who'd spit at the sight of the copy of *Hello!* on Leonie's kitchen table and insist on reading Kafka in bed?

Hannah had been thrilled at the number of replies Leonie had received. 'I told you there were scores of lonely single men out there who just want to meet someone,' she said proudly when Leonie had phoned with her exciting news. 'Which ones are you going to contact?'

'I thought just the best one,' Leonie answered, still hung up on the idea that she'd only need to meet one and that would be it.

Hannah said nothing to that but asked Leonie to read out a couple of them. They both agreed that Bob – 'tall, forty-something, losing hair but not my sense of humour' sounded the best.

'Hold on to the rest of the replies,' Hannah advised sensibly. 'And if Bob turns out to be a complete nutter, then you can phone up the others.'

Leonie agreed but secretly thought that Bob sounded as though he might very well be the man of her dreams. His answer to her advert had been everything she'd ever fantasized about: '*I've never done anything like this before. Help! I'm forty-something and my last relationship broke up a year ago. I don't have a clue how to get into this dating thing – it's all changed since I was young. I love children, animals, hill-climbing and the cinema. This is the first advert I've ever answered and I hope that it's fate that we should both meet the first time we try this. So should we actually meet?*'

The second-last sentence had sealed things for Leonie. She lived for the idea of fate, kismet and destiny; the idea of lovers who lived worlds apart but met by chance, purely because they were destined for each other in the great cosmos of love . . .

'Where are you meeting Mr Wonderful, then?' Angie asked, putting on lipstick.

'The China Lamp,' Leonie said. He'd said he'd be sitting on the left-hand side, wearing jeans and a tweed jacket. He'd had a lovely voice on the phone too: soft and cultured. She'd thought that the Chinese restaurant in Shankhill was far enough away from Greystones for her not to meet anyone she knew, but she might. To do so would be terminally embarrassing.

'OhmiGod, am I mad to be doing this?' she said out loud. 'I mean, I'm forty-two-years-old and I'm going on a blind date. This is insane, isn't it?'

'No it's not. It's perfectly normal, modern stuff,' Angie said, unperturbed.

'What if he's some weirdo? Maybe I should cancel, or simply not turn up.' Panic was beginning to set in. This was the final step, much more final than sending off an advert or answering letters sent to an anonymous post office box. That was practically child's play. Nobody knew you, nobody could contact you unless you wanted them to. This was something else.

'Relax, will you. He's probably telling all his pals he's scared out of his mind in case he's going to meet this sex-starved woman who links up with unsuspecting men via the personals for wild rampant sex.'

Leonie shuddered as she changed out of her nurse's blue tunic. 'I'm beginning to feel like that. Normal people don't have to meet up like this, do they?'

'They do if all their friends are living in married or co-habiting bliss and the only offers they get are from bored husbands who think they're game for an uncomplicated quickie,' Angie retorted. 'You haven't told anyone else about this, I assume?'

Leonie grinned ruefully. She hadn't breathed a word to her mother. Not that Claire would have disapproved of the idea. On the contrary, she'd have been delighted to see her daughter actually do something to change her life if it meant escaping from the endless loneliness of divorced parenthood. It was just a tad embarrassing to tell your nearest and dearest that you'd resorted to the personal ads for . . . well, a personal life. Which was why she hadn't said anything to the kids either. They thought she was going into Dublin for dinner with Emma and Hannah. It would be too humiliating for them to discover – and subsequently to tell the blissfully happy Ray – that their mother was going on blind dates, when her ex-husband was about to marry the Best Dressed, Cleverest, Most Beautiful lawyer in the greater Boston area. God, she hated that bitch.

'Give me his phone number,' Angie commanded.

'His phone number?'

'In case he does turn out to be a weirdo, stoopid. Then when you don't turn up for work tomorrow, I can notify the police and your whole sordid personal life will come out in the tabloids.'

Angie's joke had the desired effect. Leonie started laughing helplessly.

'I don't know what's so bloody funny,' said Tim, the senior vet grumpily, arriving with a limping Great Dane the size of a large pony. 'I've got to stay late and operate on Tiny here to get a splinter out of his paw. Can you stay late, Leonie?'

'No, she can't,' Angie answered sharply. 'She's worked late twice already this week. Get Louise to do it.'

Leonie waved gratefully to Angie and, grabbing her coat and handbag, hurried out the door.

Back home, World War Three had broken out and Leonie was dragged in to referee before she'd even taken her coat off. The previous day, taking advantage of Leonie's rare plans for an evening out, Mel had asked could she and Abby have some schoolfriends over for dinner. No problem, Leonie had said, and then dutifully trudged round the supermarket in order to buy the vegetarian sausages and veggie grills that were currently the most popular food group with figure-conscious Greystones' teenagers. However, Danny had arrived home with uninvited guests – two equally large, gangling students from college – and as it had been hours since their last enormous meal in the student canteen, they'd rampaged through the fridge, eating all Mel and Abby's dinner along with the potato salad Leonie had earmarked for her lunch the next day.

'He doesn't even like vegetarian food!' shrieked Mel to her mother, eyes glinting with a mixture of tears and sheer rage.

'It's my home too and you should have said if you wanted to keep your girlie food for your girlie friends,' sneered Danny, who was being ultra-cool because he had pals in the house to impress. He'd then stomped off into his room, slamming the door so hard that the entire cottage shook. Loud music began emanating from the room and Mel had burst into tears.

'I hate him,' she sobbed. Leonie hugged her, wondering how she was ever going to find time to doll herself up for her blind date. Penny, who hated rows, was curled up miserably in her basket beside the dresser, her dark retriever eyes two great pools of distress. Catching her mistress's eye, she whimpered softly. Leonie blew a kiss to the dog over Mel's head. Penny had that miserable, unwalked look about her.

'Now come on,' she said to her daughter. 'We'll race to the shops and buy something else for the girls, OK?'

Mel sniffled and wiped her nose on her sleeve. Despite wearing one of her very adult American costumes – a teeny pink long-sleeved jumper and baggy, faded denims – Mel looked younger than her fourteen years when she was upset. 'OK,' she said grudgingly.

Just then, the doorbell rang loudly.

'They're here,' Mel wailed, breaking into fresh sobs.

A chatter of excited female voices could be heard and then Abby, the peacemaker, stuck her head round the kitchen door cheerily: 'Liz and Susie say they want chips tonight, Mel. Is it all right if we go to the chipper, Mum?' Abby asked. 'We'll only be fifteen minutes, twenty max.'

'You can, but don't be long. I want you all here before I go out,' warned Leonie, relieved that the threatened tantrum had been bypassed.

'Thanks, Mum,' said Mel, with a dazzling smile, her good humour restored. 'Can I borrow some money?' she wheedled.

'Take some change from my purse,' Leonie said. 'But don't touch the twenty-pound note.'

'I promise I won't,' Mel said. She danced out of the room and a chorus of, 'He's gorgeous!' could be heard.

'Is he one of Danny's friends?' asked a breathless voice that Leonie identified as Liz. One of Danny's pals – the Ricky Martin lookalike, she guessed – had obviously briefly stuck his head out of the bedroom door to see what all the noise was about.

'Yeah, I'll introduce you to him when we get back,' Mel replied, as if she hadn't been threatening murder and destruction to her brother and his pals just seconds before. The front door slammed and the loud music went up a notch in Danny's room.

Peace more or less restored, Leonie sighed and wondered if she could risk a speedy bath. When Mel came back she'd be bound to wonder why her mother was getting all dolled up for a mere dinner with two female friends. Mel only bothered with serious beautifying for the male of the species and would be suspicious at longer than normal time spent getting ready for a girls' night out. Fifteen minutes was enough for a soak, Leonie thought longingly. But Penny had other ideas. Now that there was nobody shouting, she emerged from her basket and stretched languorously in front of Leonie, arching her golden back and then shaking herself, blonde dog hair flying everywhere.

It was obvious she was ready for a walk, and equally obvious that none of the children – all of whom adored Penny and bickered over whom she loved most – had no intention in hell of bringing her out. Leonie relented and said that one magic word: Walkies? She knew that Penny pretended not to comprehend sentences like, 'Get off the couch!' or 'You're a bad dog for eating the remains of the chicken dinner.' But Penny instantly understood the word 'Walkies'.

Danny reckoned she could even spell it, because saying things like, 'Did anyone take the dog for a W.A.L.K.?' made her yelp delightedly.

'Come on, Penny,' Leonie said, bending down to give her most adoring friend a cuddle, 'let's go.'

She pulled her old anorak from the peg inside the back door, took Penny's lead from the pocket and went out into the October evening. It was nearly six fifteen and it was still light, but a very wintry breeze rushed up the valley, rattling the leaves on the beech trees along the road. Thrilled to be out, Penny bounced along, pulling Leonie with her as she danced into puddles and joyously scattered piles of leaves. They hurried along the cottages on the road, the wind whistling through Leonie's anorak. They crossed over the main road and turned left into a winding country lane which went away from the suburban streets of Greystones. The lane was perfect for walking Penny when it was too dark for their field walk. In the summer, Leonie thought nothing of trekking along the fields, with Penny off the lead, bounding enthusiastically to the edge of the ditches that circled the field and into the trees which bordered it. But when it was growing dark, she preferred the laneway where at least you had somewhere to run to if you met a dark menacing figure. She never let Mel and Abby walk Penny in the field: it was too isolated and you never knew who you'd meet.

Tonight, she and Penny walked quickly along the lane, Penny snuffling piles of leaves where the local dogs had left their mark. At every interestingly smelly point, she simply had to pee, looking apologetically at Leonie as she did so, a 'sorry, but this has to be done' look on her smiling face. Usually, Leonie didn't mind what Penny did or how long it took her. But tonight, she was a bit tight for time.

'Come on, Honey Bunny,' she said reprovingly, 'you can't pee at every spot. Mummy is in a hurry to go home. We'll have a long walk tomorrow, I promise.'

'Hello.'

Leonie nearly jumped out of her skin. She hadn't noticed the man coming out of the big black gates accompanied by two collies straining at their leashes. Mortified at being caught talking baby-talk to her dog, she mumbled, 'Hello,' in reply and hurried on.

How embarrassing. He didn't look as if he'd call his dogs honey bunnies or even let them on the bed for cuddles at night. A gruff, big bear of a man who'd bought the old house in the woods that used to belong to the doctor, he probably kept his poor dogs outside in freezing kennels. Leonie marched on. She couldn't very well turn back yet or she might catch up with him and then he'd think she wasn't much of dog owner, giving Penny such a short walk. It was half six but she kept going with Penny straining delightedly at the lead in front of her. After another ten minutes, Leonie realized she'd never get to have a shower at this rate, never mind a bath, so she turned for home, walking as fast as she could.

When she opened the kitchen door, a blast of warm air greeted her and the pungent aroma of fat, greasy chips from Luigi's made her realize she was ravenous. The girls were sitting around the kitchen table, all eating daintily. Recently, Mel had been picking delicately at her food, eating in an exaggerated fashion like a supermodel determined to make a lettuce leaf last ten minutes. But at least she did eat, Leonie thought. Abby, on the other hand, didn't appear to be eating at all. She was pouring orange juice for everybody, listening while Liz told a convoluted story about her impossible French homework and how the teacher ought to be shot.

'Hi, Mrs Delaney,' chorused Liz and Susie, the French story drying up immediately.

'Hello, girls,' Leonie said, repressing the impulse to steal a chip. 'You're not eating, Abby?' she asked.

'I've had mine,' Abby said quickly. 'I was starving.'

'OK, girls, I'll leave you to it.'

Fifteen minutes later, Leonie was driving down the road, hoping she didn't look a complete fright. Bob would be expecting some glamorous type rattling with jewellery and confidence, no doubt. And he was getting a dishevelled Earth Mother who probably smelled of chips, perspiration and eau de veterinary surgery, thanks to nothing but a speedy scrub in the bathroom with a flannel. The last squirt of Opium in the bottle had definitely not been enough.

The China Lamp in Shankhill had opened a few months ago but, looking at the redbrick building which seemed strangely familiar, Leonie realized she remembered it aeons ago when it had been the Punjab Kingdom. She'd been there when she was still married to Ray. Aeons indeed. She parked outside and got out of the car, willing herself not to look in the mirror to primp. The remains of her early-morning make-up would have to do. She was a normal, modern woman who was going on a blind date. Lots of people did it; there was no need to be nervous, really.

Once inside, her courage vanished and she nearly bolted out the door. How did you ask for a man you'd never met before? March up to a waiter and purr: 'Can you tell me, where's the single bloke in the tweed jacket and jeans? I'm his date for the night. The name's Desirée.' She felt herself go weak with embarrassment at the thought.

This was a ludicrous thing to be doing. She should be at home watching the telly, chatting to Mel and Abby's friends, finishing up the remaining few chips and washing up after Danny's next commando raid on the fridge, not here, waiting to see a strange man –

'Leonie?'

She blinked and focused on the man in front of her. He was indeed wearing a tweed jacket and jeans, along with a very nicely ironed pale blue shirt. She looked up. He was tall, too. Very tall. And he hadn't been joking about the going bald bit, either. His sparse hair was confined to a fast-disappearing tonsure. But he had a kind face, thin and tired perhaps, but still kind. Not *Psycho* material, thankfully.

'Bob?' she said with a strained smile.

'That's me!' He kissed her awkwardly on the cheek. 'So nobody knows we're meeting for the first time,' he said cautiously. 'I thought it'd be a bit obvious if we shook hands, you know, classic signs of a couple who've never met before. Let's sit down.'

He darted over to a table in a corner and held a chair out for Leonie, as if he was very keen to get her seated. She didn't think they stood out like a personal ad sore thumb. Neither of them had a red rose clamped between their teeth or a copy of *Time Out* under their arm.

She sat obediently and the waiter arrived with menus, the same waiter she remembered from the Punjab Kingdom days, Leonie thought in surprise. When he was gone, she looked at Bob and tried to remember what you said on first dates.

'So,' she said brightly. 'Nice to meet you. Finally.' She knew she was smiling again, a big fake grin.

'You too,' Bob said, a similar smile painted on his face. 'Er, will we look at the menus first?'

'Yes!' Leonie responded. Anything to avoid having to start the conversation. She pretended to look at the set menu details and surreptitiously tried to study her date. He looked fifty-something instead of forty-something; maybe it was all that teaching. His hair was greying and his face was quite lined. Then again, she couldn't talk. Every morning when she studied herself in the mirror, her face looked a little more like a road map of Paris, complete with *peripheriques* in red.

Bob had nice dark blue eyes, friendly but a bit anxious. She could easily imagine him at the top of a classroom, gravely trying to educate young minds into the arcane mysteries of . . . what?

'What do you teach?' she asked, delighted to have hit upon a line of conversation.

Bob's eyes lit up. 'Maths and physics.'

Leonie's smile faltered. If he'd said biology or history, she'd have a hope of making sensible conversation. But physics and maths . . . A vision of Sister Thomas Aquinas came to her, standing at the blackboard and waiting for a clueless fifteen-year-old Leonie to recite Theorem 2.3. Sister Thomas Aquinas had had a long wait, if Leonie remembered correctly.

'Gosh,' she said helplessly, 'I'm not exactly the most mathematically minded person in the world –'

'It's OK,' he interrupted her. 'Most people aren't. Particularly the kids I'm teaching right now.' He grimaced. 'Anyway, let's not talk about my job. It's so boring compared to yours. My ex always says I could enter the Olympics in the Most Boring category when I get started about my job. Tell me about yours instead.'

Leonie filed away the bitter mention of his ex (girlfriend or wife?) for further analysis and went into a spiel about her job and how one minute you were holding some sweet little animal and the next, you were squealing with pain from a bite from the cuddly successor to Jaws. Laughing about it broke the ice and Bob was soon telling her about his beloved terrier, Brandy, a charmer with a fondness for fig rolls and licking the remains of Bailey's Irish Cream liqueur out of glasses.

'He sounds lovely,' Leonie said. If Bob had a dog, then things were looking up. She could never go out with someone who didn't adore animals.

'Of course, he's not with me any more,' Bob added with a sigh. 'He lives with my ex and her husband. She has more space and it's only fair. I'm out all day, you see. She's there with the baby.'

'Oh.'

The waiter never knew how close he came to being kissed for arriving precisely then.

'We're ready to order,' Leonie said brightly.

'I'm not sure what I want,' dithered Bob.

The waiter began to move away.

'NO!' Leonie said loudly. 'It'll only take a moment to decide.' At least ordering would get them off the subject of ex-partners.

But there was to be no joy on that score. Bob wasn't to be deterred. Obviously labouring under the opinion that any new inamorata had to know all about the previous ones, he considered it his duty to tell Leonie as much as he possibly could about Colette. By the time the crispy duck had arrived, Leonie knew more about Colette than she did about Bob. Colette was also a teacher but had taken a career break to have her first baby. She lived in Meath, was doing an aromatherapy course in her spare time and had been extremely gifted at the violin, if only she'd kept it up.

'You've got to move on, though, haven't you?' Leonie announced firmly when she'd had enough of both Colette and the duck. 'That's why we're here, Bob. To move on.' She gave him an earnest look, the one she saved for telling children in the surgery that pets were a responsibility and had to be looked after, not just cuddled once and dumped back in an unclean cage.

'Yes,' Bob said passionately, as if he spent endless hours thinking about the concept of getting on with your life. 'To move on, to meet other people who understand just what it's like out there on your own: the pain, the hurt, the sleepless nights. I can tell that you understand, Leonie,' he added heatedly, eyes roving over the purple velvet tunic that made her look even more bosomy than usual. 'You look like the sort of person who understands things.'

Nodding, Leonie wondered whether he assumed this type of understanding would involve her pulling his head towards her bosom and letting it rest there, comfortingly. Probably, she decided. Colette had been cast in the role of the perfect partner, the one who'd got away, while Leonie was the Motherly Stand-In, who'd be good for a bit of affection to stave off pangs of loneliness.

'Not many people understand what it's like to be just dumped and left there, all because you've changed from the sort of person you were in the beginning,' Bob said, staring at the remains of his dinner. 'People change, I know that now, but you can change together. It's a challenge, but you can do it. You just need the chance.'

'You mean, Colette didn't give you the chance?' Leonie asked, abandoning the attempt to have a Colette-less conversation.

He shook his head sadly.

Leonie sighed. It was perfectly obvious that Bob didn't want a partner; he wanted a support group: the Been Dumped, Now Talk About It Group. He'd blindly assumed that a voluptuous blonde divorcée must fit into the same emotional category and that was why he'd answered her advert. He wasn't looking for love. He *was* in love. With Colette.

The only positive side of Bob's descent into emotional misery was that he stopped being so jumpy. Leonie realized that if she was a bit nervous about being seen on a blind date, Bob was positively phobic about it. Every time a waiter appeared within his range of vision, he jerked, as if expecting to see the parents' committee descend upon him and mutter something about blind-dating teachers not being suitable role models for impressionable young minds.

What was he doing here, Leonie wondered, idly crunching up another prawn cracker. They did manage to talk about Bob's supposed other hobbies: cinema and hill-climbing.

'I'm not much of a climber, although I walk Penny every day. But I love the cinema. I don't really have anyone to go with because my mother prefers the theatre and the kids want to see James Bond or things with teenage actors I don't recognize.'

'We can go together,' Bob said, sounding pleased. 'How about this time next week? You pick the movie.'

At least she had a date of sorts for the following week, Leonie reflected as she drove home, stuffed to the gills with Chinese food yet feeling deflated. Bob certainly wasn't suitable partner material, but he was a new friend and wasn't that what agony aunts always advised: meet new people, new friends, and, when you're least expecting it, a partner will appear. It looked good written down, anyhow.

What a strange evening. She realized she'd even talked about Ray. Well, when you were with somebody who was passionately interested in the concept of ex-relationships, you couldn't help putting in your thruppence-ha'penny worth. And Bob had been interested too, although astonished when he realized that she had instigated her marriage break-up. 'You simply decided it was over?' he said, shocked.

Leonie shrugged. 'What was the point of staying married if we weren't right together?' she said. 'Too many people do, purely for convenience, because the other person is there. I don't understand that. It's like you're too scared to do anything different even though you'd secretly like to do it. That's fear of the unknown, not real love. I couldn't cope with a life like that. I believe there's somebody perfect out there for all of us.'

Bob had looked at her so blankly that it was obvious he couldn't comprehend what she was getting at. Mind you, Leonie thought as she parked outside the cottage, her mother had never been able to understand it either. Every once in a while, the normally orange-juice drinking Claire would have a couple of glasses of wine and start gently berating her daughter for divorcing Ray.

'You'll never find a man like Ray,' she'd mumble sadly.

Leonie thanked the man above she hadn't revealed anything about her blind date to Claire. Because Bob certainly wasn't a man like Ray – husband material, in other words.

Mel's good humour appeared to have evaporated when Leonie got home.

'Danny's a spanner-head,' she said crossly, emerging from the sitting room before her mother had time to struggle out of her coat.

'Don't use that type of language, Melanie,' Leonie said wearily. 'What's he done now?'

'He was watching videos all evening and we couldn't bring Liz and Susie in to see *ER*,' sniffed Mel. 'And he let them smoke in the house, too,' she added triumphantly.

'You can't keep your mouth shut, can you?' roared Danny, who could hear what was going on from the sitting room.

'Well, you let them smoke,' roared Mel back.

'Oh yeah, and you're Miss Goody Two Shoes who'd turn her nose up at a cigarette if she got the chance, right?'

Mel clammed up like a shot. She must have been smoking herself, Leonie realized. That'd have to stop. Mel could forget about ever getting pocket money again if she started smoking. But that was an argument for tomorrow. Leonie felt she'd had enough tonight.

'Would the two of you stop this bickering,' she said firmly. 'I'm not in the mood for it. Try and act your age for once.'

Abby was in the kitchen with Penny and her plain face lit up with a grin when Leonie went in.

'Well done, Mum,' she said. 'They've been at it since you went out. I nearly rang Gran to ask could I go round to her house to escape. By the way, Hannah rang and asked you to give her a buzz when you got in.' Abby's eyes twinkled mischievously. 'I never pointed out that you were supposed to be with her and Emma.'

Leonie grinned back. 'I'll let you in on my secret if you promise to keep it to yourself.'

'Mum!' Abby looked wounded. 'You know I can keep a secret.'

'Of course, I know you can.' Abby would carry a secret to the grave, unlike her sister, who'd promise not to breathe a word to anyone but wouldn't be able to keep it to herself for longer than a day. Leonie didn't like asking Abby to keep something from her twin, but she knew that while Abby would be pleased her mother had had a date, Mel wouldn't. Capricious and demanding, Mel liked to be the centre of her mother's world and wouldn't have coped well with news of a rival for her affection, even if it was Bob.

'I was meeting a man for dinner. Hannah set me up with a friend of hers,' Leonie improvised. 'He's very nice and she thought we'd get on. We did,' Leonie paused delicately, 'but as friends, really. We're going to the cinema next week, but we'll just be friends, nothing else.'

'Do you still love Dad? Is that why you haven't got a boyfriend?' asked Abby suddenly.

Leonie felt as if she'd been punched in the stomach. 'Is that what you think?' she asked. 'That I still love Dad like that, that I'm upset about Fliss?'

Lips clamped together as if she was scared she'd said the wrong thing, Abby nodded mutely.

'It's not like that at all, darling,' Leonie said. 'I'm happy for Dad, and I'm not in love with him in that way. I love him . . . but as a friend, as your father, not as anything else.' God, she thought blankly, what else could she say to convince her daughter that she wasn't in bits over Ray and Fliss's nuptials?

'I'm not upset about the wedding . . .'

'But you looked as if you were,' blurted out Abby.

'Did I?'

Abby nodded.

'It was a shock, that's all,' Leonie said, floundering. She must have looked terrible the day the kids came back from America. She thought she'd hidden it well. Obviously she hadn't. 'I didn't want to go out with anybody when you were younger,' she said in a rush. 'It was too hard to think about men when I wanted to look after you all.' She reached out to touch Abby affectionately.

'I want you to be happy,' Abby said, her face crumpling. 'If Dad is happy, I want you to be too. Is he nice, this man you met tonight?'

For the first time since the strained conversation had started, Leonie smiled genuinely. 'He's nice, but he's not Brad Pitt.'

Abby giggled. 'Mel would kill you if he was.'

'He's a teacher and he's a lovely man, but I think going to the cinema is as far as we're going to get. Still, it's nice to have some new friends. It's a bit boring going out with the people your father and I knew twenty years ago.'

'Dad told me he'd love you to come to the wedding,' Abby said.

Leonie was astonished. 'That's sweet of him but . . . I don't think it would be a good idea.'

Abby wasn't finished. Now that she'd broached the subject, she was determined to finish it. 'We had a big talk one day when Fliss had taken Mel off shopping. He wanted to know how you are and if you're happy. He says he's happier than he's ever been.'

'Great,' Leonie said faintly. 'Of course I'm happy, Abby. I have you three and Penny and Clover. I don't need a man to make me happy, you know that. Granny lives alone and she's happy, isn't she?'

'Granny's different. She doesn't need anybody.'

Which was true, Leonie reflected. Her mother was one of life's loners, content with the company of her beloved cats and pleased to dip in and out of her daughter's life every few days, staying for a cup of tea and then returning to the sanctuary of her own home. Her mother was a solitary woman. Leonie wished she'd inherited that trait.

'I was thinking the other night about what happens when me and Danny and Mel are gone and you're here on your own with Penny,' Abby said. 'You'll be lonely. I know I would.'

'Abby . . .' Leonie kissed her daughter on the forehead. 'That's a long, long way away. Let's not even think about a time when you're not living here, OK? Now, you better hit the hay, love, it's a school day tomorrow, although your sister seems to have forgotten.'

While Abby went off to tell Mel it was time for bed, Leonie sat down at the kitchen table and phoned Hannah, who was deeply apologetic for having rung while Leonie was still out.

'It was eleven before I rang and I thought you were meeting him at half seven, I was sure you'd be home. It must have gone well,' she added, a knowing tone to her voice.

'Er . . .' Leonie hesitated, 'that depends entirely on your definition of "gone well",' she said.

'Oh.'

'Oh, is right. I would not expect a wedding invitation to land on your doormat any time soon, let's put it that way.'

'Well, I didn't think you were angling for a white dress anyway, but I take it that Bob didn't turn out to be the answer to any maiden's prayers?'

'Only if the maiden in question was a psychiatrist specializing in post-relationship trauma who needed a subject for her doctoral thesis.'

'You're kidding.'

'I wish I was. He is a sweet, kind man, but he is obsessed with his ex-girlfriend. On our next date, I'm expecting to see a photo of her,' Leonie joked.

'You mean, you're having a second date!'

'Not really. We're going to the cinema together. Probably to something black and white and Swedish,' she shrugged, 'but it'll get me out of the house.'

'Phone the next guy on your list,' Hannah urged.

Leonie shook her head and then realized she was on the phone and that Hannah couldn't see her. 'I think I've had it with blind dates for a while,' she said. 'I've dipped my big toe in the water and I'm testing the temperature.'

'Leonie,' pleaded Hannah, 'you can't back out now. Think of the other guys who answered your ad. They could be wonderful – Mr Wonderful,' she corrected herself, 'waiting to happen.'

'Mr Wonderful can wait,' Leonie said firmly. 'I need a chance to get over my first great date with Bob. And who knows,' she said, even though she did know, '*he* could turn out to be Mr Wonderful. He may simply need time.'

'Time in therapy, more like,' declared Hannah. 'OK, you win. I'll keep shtoom about your next date, but there's a time limit on my silence. I want the romance of the century happening soon and I'll keep nagging you until you get it!'

Hannah got back into bed and began to flick through her copy of *Understanding Property: Your Guide to Real Estate*. David James had given it to her and she was half-way through it, consuming it greedily in order to know as much as possible about her new career. After talking to Leonie, she found she couldn't concentrate.

Leonie was a wonderful raconteur. She could make the silliest stories utterly hilarious, especially when she was being self-deprecating. Her version of the date with Bob was a classic but, Hannah thought, it was a pity it hadn't worked out. Leonie deserved a nice bloke. Like Felix. She dropped her book and hugged her knees to her chest. Felix, Felix, Felix . . . Even his name was thrilling. He was an incredible guy, dripping with charisma and talent. You name it, he had it. There weren't words for all the qualities he possessed.

And he was so ambitious, like her. That was one of the things they shared.

'You're like the other half of me,' he'd murmured only the night before. They'd been lying in her bed, Felix on the side where Hannah usually slept, sprawled carelessly on the newly changed sheet, his naked body inviting her to caress it. 'We have this connection, Hannah: you want the whole world and so do I. It's a dangerous obsession.' He played with her hair, curling the strands with his long, sensitive fingers. 'My career isn't the only thing I'm obsessed with,' he added. 'I'm crazy about you, do you know that?' he said suddenly, gazing at her, dark eyes brooding.

She was afraid to speak in case she broke the spell. It would be wrong to say she was crazy about him too, although it was true. She could think of nothing else. These last few days, it was a miracle she'd been able to do any work at all for losing herself in a daydream of Felix. She couldn't understand it really. How she'd miraculously changed overnight from being wary and suspicious just because of him. If Emma or Leonie could see her now, they wouldn't recognize her: this adoring woman who used to be so in control, who now quivered whenever Felix merely glanced in her direction. Ms Cojones of Steel had turned into a woman in love, and she adored the sensation.

He sat up in the bed and leaned over her, his gaze trailing lasciviously over her nakedness.

'You're very sexy,' he growled, the timbre of his voice rich and deep.

As usual, Hannah felt every bone in her body melt. She'd never met anybody with a voice like that. What would he sound like on stage, his rich, resonant voice reaching the back row, capturing every member of the audience in his spell?

'I'd love to see you on stage,' she blurted out.

'I haven't done much theatre,' he said, fingers idly trailing designs on Hannah's bare shoulder. 'I prefer the cinema. If this TV series really works, it could be the big time for me, darling. If I make it big, will you come with me? To London?'

Hannah was still. She couldn't believe he'd said that. Felix's lifestyle meant he had to be the ultimate free spirit. With that in mind, she'd tried to keep things deliberately light. She never expected to see him and treated each phone call or date as an enjoyable bonus, half-knowing that Felix wouldn't have tolerated a woman who clung to him. And now he was the one making plans for the future. She'd have to be careful, she knew. Love could hurt with greater accuracy than hate. She was scared to get too close to Felix in case he dumped her just when she'd given herself body and soul to him.

'That's a flattering thing to say, but I've never expected us to be a permanent fixture,' she said, choosing her words carefully. 'I can't think of anything more wonderful than living with you, Felix, but we both have our hopes and dreams and I don't believe in tying someone down.'

He buried his face in her shoulder and licked her skin, moving off to her mouth and kissing her deeply.

'That's what I love about you, Hannah. You're so independent, you're your own woman,' he said admiringly when his lips left hers. 'It's refreshing, different. We're made for each other, darling. You're the sort of woman I need. An actor needs a strong partner, like you. Not some namby-pamby little hausfrau who has a nervous breakdown every time he performs a love scene with his leading lady. You're a star, Hannah.'

He grinned at her triumphantly and she returned his smile, thanking God she hadn't blown it all by squealing with delight at the very notion of living with him. Felix liked his women independent and in control: that was the way he'd find Hannah Campbell. Not for her the role of clinging, limpet girlfriend consumed with anxiety about her handsome lover. Strong and independent were her middle names. She let her fingers slide under the duvet where they encountered Felix's muscular stomach.

'One hundred sit ups a day,' he'd told her proudly, the first time she commented on his physique. Wash-board wasn't the word for it. Tonight, that wasn't what she was interested in.

'Is that a pistol in your pocket or are you just pleased to see me?' she murmured, fingers sliding down further.

'I haven't got any pockets,' said Felix huskily, 'but I'm certainly pleased to see you.'

'Have a nice night out, did you?' asked Gillian tautly, when Hannah arrived into work the following morning, still glowing from the night before. She'd slept well. Felix insisted on a good night's sleep.

'My skin looks terrible in the morning if I don't,' he said apologetically when he asked her to turn out the light. But they'd made up for lights-out at midnight by waking up at dawn to a very erotic interlude. The things that man could do with his mouth, that perfect made-for-TV mouth . . . Hannah sighed.

'Lovely, yes,' she answered Gillian automatically, ignoring the bite to the other woman's enquiry. 'How about you? Has Leonard got over his cold?'

Gillian, as she had discovered, liked morning chit-chat and enquiries about her health. Otherwise, she sat at her desk all day in a tight little knot of resentment, icily deflecting all subsequently friendly remarks. After a few days of that, Hannah had realized that a bit of conversation first thing made the atmosphere in Dwyer, Dwyer & James much cosier.

'I meant to watch that Jane Austen thing on BBC last night, but I was out and forgot to tape it. What did you think of it, Gillian?'

'I prefer real-life documentaries, to be honest,' sniffed Gillian. 'It was on in the background but I didn't really watch it,' she added and then proceeded to give Hannah a blow-by-blow account of the first episode of the costume drama.

As she talked, Hannah listened with one ear and began organizing her desk for the day ahead. The office had been so busy the last few days, 'the last flurry before the season dies down,' David James remarked. Last flurry or not, Hannah wanted to hire a new photographer before too long. The current guy could make a glorious multi-million-pound stately home in rolling parkland look like a two-up, two-down in need of renovation. He was hopeless and she was determined to get rid of him before the new influx of clients began to sell their homes elsewhere. Of course, bad photography worked when it made people arrive at a house they'd thought was hideous from the photo only to discover it was really a bijou residence with buckets of potential. But when it put them off viewing altogether, bad photography was a major disadvantage. He had to go, that was it. Today, she'd start phoning around for replacements.

'Where were you last night that you weren't in watching telly like the rest of us?' Gillian asked archly, removing a bit of imaginary dust from her desk.

'Out.' Hannah had no intention of telling Tell-All Gillian about her actor boyfriend. She relented, however, seeing Gillian's mouth metamorphose into a prune. 'With my girlfriends. We went to an Indian restaurant for a meal.' Well, they'd eaten Indian, after all, though she could hardly tell Gillian that her lover had licked cucumber raita off her nipples because they'd been eating their takeaway in the nude.

'I can't stand Indian food,' Gillian muttered.

You would if it was served on six foot of blond sex god, Hannah thought with a secret smile.

By noon, she'd been in touch with four photographers who were going to visit the office with their portfolios and she'd arranged for a stand-in to replace their own photographer, whom she'd fired.

'You can't do this to me,' he had sputtered on the phone when Hannah rang him to politely tell him that she was giving him a month's notice. 'I've been working for your boss for years. I'll go over your head and have you sacked, you bitch. You can't fire me.'

'Actually, I can,' Hannah said calmly. 'You work for us on a freelance basis, which means that I don't even have to give you a month's notice. I was doing that out of respect for the years you've worked for us. It's not necessary. And you may phone my boss if you wish. But you'll find that this decision is final.'

'It's so sudden,' he roared, 'not a clue you were going to do this. When I think of the work I've put in for you people, out in all weathers, trying to make crappy dumps look nice. This is the thanks I get, being dumped by some whippersnapper who's probably screwed somebody to get the job. Or have you some boyfriend in mind for my job? Is that it, eh? Nepotism?'

Hannah had had enough. 'If you haven't seen this coming, you must be living on another planet,' she said. 'Ever since this branch has been renovated, I've had to phone you about bad photos. Remember the property on Watson Drive? You had to go back twice because of how terrible the photos were. The house was a total blur the first time. It was impossible to tell where the house ended and the garage began. The owners wanted to go to a different estate agency and only a promise that we'd give them a discount in their fees, as well as taking the photo again until they were satisfied, made them stay with us. You must have realized that we were not pleased with your work. And, no, I'm not firing you so I can conveniently hire one of my relatives. I have four total strangers coming in tomorrow to apply for the position. As office manager, it's my job to make sure this business runs smoothly. If you were doing *your* job properly, you'd still have one. Good day to you.'

She put down the phone to find David James and at least half of the office staring at her. Gillian looked outraged. David looked amused, his dark eyes shining at her and a smile curving up the dead straight line of his mouth.

'Well done,' he said. 'I've been wondering how long it would take you to do that. His shots are so obscure that they practically qualify as modern art.'

Hannah let herself indulge in a small smile. 'Nobody likes firing people, but it has to be done if we want the company to grow,' she said seriously. Not that I've ever fired anyone before, she added to herself. But nobody here had to know that.

She may have come from a background where her family took orders rather than gave them, but she was determined to hide the fact. Hannah knew she could play to the manor born as well as the best of them.

Her phone buzzed. Hannah jumped, hoping it was Felix but it was David James. 'Can you drop into the office?' he asked.

He was staring at an open file on his desk when she arrived but Hannah had the funniest feeling that David wasn't paying any attention to it. He looked distracted, tired even, which was unusual for him. He was such a powerhouse of a man, she often felt that if the electricity went off, they could power the office from the energy emanating from him. But today he had shadows under his eyes and there were new lines etched in his already craggy face. He had the weary air of a man who'd spent the night with a sick child, although she knew he didn't have any kids.

Gillian often mentioned David's ex-wife, with whom he had a

strained relationship. According to Gillian's intelligence-gathering machine, they'd separated a few years ago but weren't divorced yet. David was still in love with her, insisted Gillian wistfully, although his love wasn't returned. Unlike some of Gillian's wilder bits of gossip, this titbit made sense: why else would a clever, attractive man like David James still be single?

Hannah wondered briefly if his miserable love life was the reason David looked tired or if it was something to do with work. She'd never dream of asking, though. Anything other than business was taboo between them for all their easy-going relationship.

They talked briefly about the type of photographer they needed and, when the conversation was over, Hannah stayed in her seat. 'Is there anything else, David?' she asked, sure there was something he wanted to discuss.

'No.'

She rose gracefully to her feet.

'Actually, there is.'

He looked ill at ease and he fiddled with his pen as he spoke. 'I know it's not exactly any of my business, but I believe you're seeing Felix Andretti.'

Hannah stared at him, taken aback by this personal remark. 'It isn't really any of your business, David,' she said formally, 'but I am seeing him. Is there a problem with that in relation to my job?'

David sighed. 'Come down off your high horse, Hannah,' he said in exasperation. 'I'm not playing the heavy-handed boss and there's no law that says you can't go out with a friend of mine. I'm just asking. I've seen Felix a few times lately and he never mentioned it to me.'

Hannah stared at him. How strange. Felix had said nothing to her about seeing David. Stranger still that Felix hadn't mentioned her to David, but then perhaps he was trying to be discreet for her sake.

'Another friend of mine who's a film producer mentioned that Felix was dating you. I was surprised, that's all. I didn't think Felix would be your type.' David looked up from his desk to gaze at her. His expression was, as usual, unreadable. He had to be a superb poker player, Donna always said. You'd never know what he was thinking behind that cool, detached exterior.

'Who knows what sort of person is anyone's type,' Hannah said dismissively, trying to remain calm even though a maelstrom of emotions were stirred up inside her at the thought of her lover's secretiveness. How could Felix meet her boss and say nothing to her? What else had he been hiding? He was so damn enigmatic, so insistent on keeping parts of his life shrouded in mystery.

'Of course, I appreciate that,' David was saying slowly and painfully as if he was pulling teeth. 'I was merely concerned about you, that's all. You're my star employee and I don't want to see you being hurt because I've inadvertently introduced you to someone . . .'

Hannah finally tuned in. 'Because you've inadvertently introduced me to someone who's what?' she demanded hotly at the implied criticism.

David's face was impenetrable as he ground his pen nib into his desk until it left a mark.

He must hate doing this, Hannah thought suddenly, aware of how tense he was. Every muscle in his face was taut. Getting involved in personal matters was obviously distasteful to him, but he seemed to have an old-fashioned feeling that he had some duty to his workers. Victorian wasn't the word for it.

'Someone with a reputation for being a playboy,' David said finally, as if it was vitally important that he pick his words with care.

'I'm a big girl, David. I can look after myself,' Hannah said with finality. The conversation was over as far as she was concerned. 'Is there anything else?'

David shook his head and stared at her for a moment before looking back at his paperwork.

The rest of the morning sped past. Hannah tried not to think about Felix's odd behaviour in meeting David and not mentioning it to her. It was nothing, she was sure of it.

Dismissing the idea that he was sly from her mind, she began to plan their dinner tonight. Felix was coming round after his first day's filming in Wicklow. She'd told him she'd cook, as distinct from ordering pizza, although her nerve faltered at the idea of making something edible that didn't involve chicken breasts and a tin of supermarket sauce.

Normally, she didn't take a full lunch break, preferring to eat a sandwich in the office before going for a brisk ten-minute walk to clear her head for the afternoon. But today, as soon as the clock hit one, she nipped down to the main street in Dun Laoghaire to buy something special for dinner. A bottle of really good wine, she decided, browsing through the wine shop and wondering if the most expensive wine was the best. David would know something like that, she thought, staring blankly at racks of bottles. She'd meant to ask his advice earlier, but after this morning's strange discussion it had seemed best not to. In the light of his remarks about her inability to look after herself, she hated to show her lack of savoir-faire when it came to wine. No, she'd ask the guy in the shop.

'I'm not much of an expert on wine,' she said, 'but I want a Spanish red . . .' she tried to remember what wine Felix had picked that first time they'd gone out to dinner. Spanish, definitely. But her accent was atrocious. 'Marques de . . . ?' she said hesitantly, thinking she'd probably said it totally wrong.

'de Caceres,' finished the wine shop man confidently.

Admitting you didn't have a clue was a novelty for her but it had certainly worked out well, Hannah decided as she strolled back to the office carrying her two bottles of wine, some horrifically expensive Parma ham and a Provençal tart. Felix would be impressed, she was sure of it. Cooking was not her strong point. When she'd lived with Harry, they'd existed on a diet of chicken with supermarket sauces or takeaways.

'Press the redial button on the phone and you'll get the Kung Po Palace,' Harry used to joke. He thought it was a howl telling people that. But then, he was hardly king of cuisine himself. His idea of a home-cooked meal was putting the little tinfoil containers back in the oven when he got home to re-heat them.

Felix, on the other hand, said he loved cooking. 'I'll cook you my special veal parmigiana soon,' he'd told Hannah. She couldn't wait. In the meantime, she was going to show him that she too could cook, even it that wasn't strictly true. The Provençal tart was straight from the deli, but what Felix didn't know couldn't hurt him.

That afternoon Hannah was so busy, she barely had time to think about Felix. She still managed it, though. By half six, she was home, singing to herself as she carelessly arranged the arum lilies in her glass vase. She put her *Carmen* CD in the player, poured herself a glass of wine and started getting dinner ready. He'd be there by seven thirty at the latest, he'd said.

By eight, the edges of the Parma ham were beginning to curl from being left out on the carefully laid table, so she put the plates back in the fridge. She poured another glass of wine and waited.

At ten, she listlessly ate her part of the meal and watched the second half of *Romancing the Stone*. She'd seen it so many times she didn't need to see the first three-quarters of an hour to know what had happened. As she watched, she unconsciously listened for the sound of footsteps outside. One of the paving stones on the path to the front door made a very distinctive noise when anybody stepped on it. Even from her first-floor flat, Hannah could hear people walking to the red-brick Victorian villa. She sat up eagerly when somebody stepped on it at half ten but sank back into her seat dispiritedly when she realized it was the couple from the flat downstairs coming noisily home. The bottle of wine was empty by the time Michael Douglas and Kathleen Turner were kissing on board his new yacht as it was towed along a New York city street. Hannah switched off the television, threw Felix's dinner in the bin and went to bed. She wasn't sure why she'd bothered going to bed as she lay wide-eyed in the darkness. She couldn't sleep, but going to bed was automatic. Like getting up and going to work the next day.

Nobody in Dwyer, Dwyer & James noticed the dullness in Hannah's usually sparkling toffee-coloured eyes. She was determined they wouldn't. She chatted idly with Gillian about inconsequential things, interviewed four photographers with her usual polite skill and even had a quick tuna sandwich with Donna Nelson in the little coffee shop around the corner. She talked, smiled and worked, all on automatic pilot. Inside, she was screaming. Screaming at herself for being so incredibly stupid as to ever trust a man, and screaming at

Felix for treating her like this. If she ever saw him again, she'd kill him, so help her.

She wasn't the only one in the office in a raging bad mood. David James was in a foul temper.

Most uncharacteristically, he'd roared at Steve Shaw over some deal that had fallen through and later the walls of his glass office rattled as he was heard yelling down the phone at someone. Hannah knew how he felt. She could have contributed a bit of screaming herself.

When he threw open his office door and yelled that he wanted coffee – now! – all the staff flattened themselves into their seats and hoped they wouldn't have to brave his temper by being the waitress.

'You go,' Gillian begged Hannah. 'I'm having one of my turns. I couldn't face him in this mood.'

Anything for a quiet life. Hannah made coffee and put four chocolate-chip biscuits on the tray before carrying it into David's office. He glared at her, taking in the heavy make-up to hide her exhausted eyes and the bright red shift dress she'd worn to try and lift her mood that morning. Severely tailored though it was, the dress couldn't hide Hannah's slim curves and, as the skirt ended just above the knee, it showed off a length of slender leg in elegant high heels. She'd left her hair loose today, hoping to make herself feel like a desirable woman instead of a dumped cow who couldn't keep a man longer than a few weeks. The long, lustrous curls rippled around her face prettily, half hiding her elegant pearl stud earrings.

David was not impressed. 'I'd prefer if your private engagements didn't interfere with your obligations to this office,' he snapped, staring at her grimly. 'I don't think that outfit is really suitable for Dwyer, Dwyer & James.'

The Vesuvius inside Hannah erupted. 'What do you mean?' she demanded. 'I've worn this outfit into the office many times before and I am not wearing it because I'm going on a date. In fact, I'm wearing it for exactly the opposite reason. You bloody men are all the same,' she hissed.

David's chilly eyes grew a few degrees warmer.

'What do you mean, "for the opposite reason"?' he asked mildly.

Hannah had had enough. Always controlled and calm, she'd have preferred to be dragged naked over hot coals than to let her professional demeanour drop in a business situation, but today, exhausted and heartsore, she let everything drop.

'I'm wearing it to remind myself that I'm a clever, powerful woman who doesn't need a bloody man around, especially not anal-retentive bosses who can't cope with the sight of a woman in sexy clothes in case she emasculates them, and,' she paused, her voice quivering with rage, 'because I've had it up to here with men, full stop. You're all insecure, unreliable and utter liars!'

She slammed the tray on to his desk and the coffee slopped out of the cup and on to the tray. Picking up two of the biscuits, Hannah dropped them venomously into the cup. 'Here's your coffee, your lordship. I hope you choke on it!'

She slammed the door on the way out and marched into the ladies, where she allowed herself a few moments leaning against the cool tiles of the wall to get herself back to normal. She wasn't apologizing, no way. David had been out of bounds with his comments. He had no right to make such personal remarks, and if he thought he had, then he'd better start looking for another office manager because she was leaving. Her only regret was that she'd revealed as much as she had. Unless David was thick as four short planks, he'd figure out that things weren't going too well between her and Felix. Damn him, anyway.

'I don't know what you said to him, but he's in great form now,' Gillian whispered as Hannah sat at her desk, head held high, daring anybody to say a word of reproof to her. 'He's laughing so loud you can probably hear him half-way down the street.'

Hannah peered in through the glass partition and there was David, phone jammed against his ear and his head thrown back as he laughed uproariously, eyes crinkled up with amusement.

'Like all men, he needs to be kept on a tight rein,' Hannah said grimly. 'That's all they understand.'

An hour later, David, briefcase and coat in hand, left his office and stood in front of Hannah expectantly. Normally, she'd have smiled back, admiring the Italian grey wool suit that hung so well on his large frame, the clever tailoring emphasizing broad shoulders and hiding the slight thickening around the waist from too many business lunches. Today, she glared at him.

'I've told you I was flying off to Paris for a long weekend,' he said to her.

Hannah's eyes were frigid. He could go to Kathmandu overland on a limping camel for all she cared.

'I think we need to talk, so I'm sorry I'm going,' he added, looking at her almost regretfully.

Hannah didn't give a damn if he was feeling guilty and wanted to apologize. Let him feel guilty: let every man on the planet feel guilty. They deserved to.

'I'll be back on Tuesday and maybe we could go to lunch?' His face had lost that impenetrable look. He appeared hopeful . . . yes, that was definitely the word. Hopeful that she wouldn't resign, Hannah decided.

'Fine,' she said with the frosty manner of a duchess.

He left smiling and, as he shut the door behind him, David turned and gave Hannah a rowdy wink that could clearly be seen by everyone else in the office. Honestly, he was incorrigible, she thought crossly.

The rest of Friday passed in a blur and, at the thought of facing a Felix-less weekend at home, Hannah decided to work on Saturday morning. It was that or spend the day feeling like a balloon with the air let out of it. Hannah didn't know why she felt so empty without him. She'd lived quite happily on her own for the past year and a half, so why now, a mere month after meeting Felix Andretti, had he become such an important part of her life? Why had all the things she enjoyed doing up to now, like going to the gym or sitting in her small, cosy sitting room reading, seem dull and hopeless?

'I thought you'd given up working weekends now the place is shipshape,' commented Donna when Hannah arrived in the office at eight-fifteen on Saturday morning.

'I have a few things to get organized and it's so busy during the week that I never have a chance,' Hannah replied, bending over the bubbling percolator so that Donna wouldn't see her tired eyes and the dark circles under them. She'd planned to camouflage her misery with make-up in the ladies' loo, thinking that she'd be the first in. But now that Donna was here, she'd have to talk. Donna was one of those people who noticed things. Hannah didn't want her noticing the palpable misery she knew was emanating from her like radioactivity from plutonium.

Yawning deliberately to make it look as if she'd had a late night, Hannah picked up her coffee and her handbag and made for the loo. 'Must tart myself up or I'll frighten the clients,' she said nonchalantly. 'Remind me never to drink too much Spanish wine again!' she added ruefully.

'Drowning your sorrows?' Donna said gently.

Hannah stopped and looked at her. Donna wasn't inquisitive or the office gossip, for that matter. Just someone intuitive.

'That obvious, is it?' Hannah said finally.

'Only that you looked pretty wretched yesterday. Not that anyone else would pick up on it,' Donna added hastily. 'You hide it well. But I recognize that look; I've had it often enough myself. If you want to talk, be my guest. I won't be broadcasting to the Gillian Network. And if you don't feel like talking, that's fine too. I thought you might need a shoulder to cry on yesterday when we went out to lunch, but I can understand you wanting to keep your private life private.'

Hannah put down her handbag and her coffee and sank into the nearest chair. 'You have to have a life to keep it private,' she said, trying to joke.

'Is it David James?' Donna asked gently.

For a moment, Hannah was startled out of her misery. 'David?' she repeated in astonishment. 'Whatever gave you that idea? He behaved like a complete asshole yesterday, but, God, that's all. Nothing I can't manage. Typical boss.'

'Oh,' Donna said. 'I'd rather got the impression that there was something between the two of you . . .' Her voice trailed off as Hannah gaped at her.

'Where did you get that idea?' demanded Hannah. 'He's good to work for, but there's nothing between us.' She cast around wildly for words to describe her relationship with David, words to explain how platonic it all was. 'He's a nice man and all that, but, really . . . And he's still besotted with his ex, isn't he?' she added.

Donna raised one eyebrow. 'I don't know where you got that idea. I don't think there are two people on Earth who were happier to get shot of each other. A marriage made in hell was how I heard it described, by someone who knows them both.'

'Gillian said he was still in love with her.'

'Gillian desperately hopes he's in love with his ex because then he can't fall in love with anyone else . . . like you, for example,' Donna said shrewdly.

This time Hannah laughed out loud. 'How ludicrous.'

'It isn't ludicrous at all,' Donna protested. 'I'm not the only one who thinks David is keen on you and Gillian wouldn't be able to stand it. She hates you, you know and it would kill her if her beloved Mr James fancied you.'

'Well, she's safe from instant death because he doesn't fancy me,' said Hannah jokingly.

'I think he does, actually,' Donna said quietly.

Hannah couldn't hide how jolted she was. 'I . . . I . . .' she stammered. 'I'm in love with someone else,' she managed finally. 'David is just a colleague, the boss. He knows my boyfriend, he knows I'm going out with someone,' she said.

'And this boyfriend is the one giving you sleepless nights, then?'

Pleased to have the uncomfortable subject changed, Hannah nodded wryly. 'I like having some trauma in my life,' she said caustically. 'Heartbreak and romantic nightmares are my hobbies. Mind you, at least I'm not in love with David. God,' she shuddered, 'imagine being in love with the boss. What a nightmare that would be!'

Talking to Donna had helped, Hannah realized, as she climbed on to the stepper in the gym that afternoon and began entering in her weight and what programme she wanted to use. This would help even more. Nothing cleared her head like pounding away on the step machine, working up a sweat until her muscles ached from the exercise. It had worked on Harry; it'd work on bloody Felix, the bastard!

Up down, up down, she ground away like a machine, letting the intense and repetitive action work the fury out of her system. What she'd do to that bloody Felix-fucking-Andretti if she ever met him again. Pound, pound, pound. He'd be lucky if he was able to walk when she was finished with him. Disturbingly, David James's face kept shimmering into her subconscious mind. He'd been telling her only a few days ago that he hadn't been to the gym in two weeks because of work.

'When you get to my age, you've got to try harder,' he sighed, patting his stomach. 'You wouldn't think I once ran three marathons, would you?'

'You're very fit looking,' Hannah had protested.

'I'm a stone heavier than I was when I ran the marathon,' he pointed out. 'I've got to get to the gym three times a week. But the way business is right now, the only way I'm going to get any exercise is if I install a running machine in my office.'

Hannah increased the intensity of the stepper. David couldn't possibly fancy her, Donna must be wrong about that. Yet the look on his face when he'd left the office the day before kept coming back to her. He wanted to talk to her about something on Tuesday, but what? And he'd cheered up out of his black mood when she'd screamed at him about how unreliable men were. He'd known she meant Felix, must have figured out it was over between them. Perhaps he wanted to tell her he was interested in her after all. She felt a hot flush that had nothing to do with exercise flood through her. What an awkward mess. There was no room for anyone in her heart but Felix, damn him.

Pulling her gym bag out of the car was an effort after two solid hours of working out. Hannah's body ached pleasurably from it, her limbs feeling leaden. She was ravenous and wondered if she had the energy to cook anything or if she'd simply stick a curry in the microwave and pig out on that.

She was trying to recall exactly what was in the freezer section when she saw the blond head. Lounging beside the front door, all in black and wearing the expression of a child who has just seen his kitten run over and was considering whether to cry or not, was Felix.

He'd been leaning against the red-brick wall, staring off down the road as if waiting for Hannah to arrive from the other direction. With his head turned slightly, she could see the exquisite profile in perfect detail. Probably what he'd planned, Hannah was surprised to find herself thinking. His nose was chiselled like a Greek god's, while strands of golden hair fell over eyes staring morosely into the middle distance. It was a pose that must have looked wonderful through the lens of a camera, she thought grimly. Well, if dear Felix had arrived with the intention of acting his way out of this one, he was in for a big surprise.

She banged the front gate viciously and flakes of blue paint fell off on to the weeds between the paving stones.

'What do you want?' she said coldly, stopping a few feet away from him.

Felix looked at her and his eyes filled with misery. He said nothing but stared at her mutely, expressing so much emotion in that tortured gaze that Hannah felt her iciness melt away. God, she'd missed him. It had been like a pain, a physical pain. And now he was here . . . waiting for her, looking like he'd been in pain too.

Sensing the change in the way she felt, Felix took a step forward and crushed Hannah in his arms. At that first touch, she dropped her gym bag and clung to him, letting his mouth bury itself in her hair, letting him murmur endearments to her. The scent of his aftershave filled her nostrils, that dear familiar spicy smell which warmed her heart and sent little shivers up and down her spine. Shivers of erotic excitement. After their third date, she'd considered buying a bottle of it, just to be able to smell him when he wasn't around. Today, she'd smelled it on some bodybuilder in the gym, a tantalizing waft of Felix that had made her knees go weak with longing and misery.

And here he was outside her door, longing for her too. She pulled away briefly, to stare up at him questioningly.

'I couldn't get away, my love. The director . . .' he paused, eyes flickering over her face as if memorizing every detail of a beloved painting. 'I thought you'd never forgive me for the other night but it was so late when I finally got out of his trailer and then I almost lost my nerve. I was scared you'd never forgive me. You're so determined, so brave, so sure of everything. But I missed you terribly, I had to come, even if you throw me out.' He hung his head and Hannah couldn't bear it.

'Course I forgive you, silly,' she said, half-laughing, half-crying. 'I missed you too, so much. I was worried when you didn't even phone me. I couldn't get in touch with you.'

'I'm sorry, the director kept me late going over scenes. He's a slave driver, I told you.' Felix grinned at her, his laughing golden beauty restored now that he was forgiven. 'Let's go inside so I can show you exactly how much I've missed you.'

Afterwards, they lay lazily in bed with Felix indulging in his secret vice: smoking. He even smoked beautifully, she thought, propped up on the pillows and watching his long fingers hold the white cigarette languorously as curls of smoke drifted from his lips. 'Everybody is becoming terribly anti-smoking,' Felix grumbled, inhaling deeply. 'I daren't say I smoke any more or some bloody casting director will complain about how it ruins the skin and gives you lines around the mouth.'

'You don't have any lines around your mouth,' protested Hannah, looking at the lush mouth in question.

'Thankfully. I'm going to have dermabrasion at the first sign of them,' he said, feeling for lines.

'You goose! Men look better with lines,' Hannah said. 'It's actresses who have to stay young forever. Actors turn into Clint Eastwood. Although you're much better looking.'

He kissed her. 'You're so good for my ego, darling,' he purred.

'Tell me what happened on the set,' Hannah said in what she hoped was a non-accusatory tone of voice.

She wanted an explanation of sorts. To be absent without explanation for one day was one thing; to miss a dinner they'd planned was another thing entirely. He could have phoned. Wicklow wasn't Outer Mongolia.

Felix sighed. 'The director and I were having very different views on my character. Radically different. He thinks I should be playing Sebastian as someone without sophistication, a callow innocent, if you like. While I know he's supposed to be a complex character who pretends to be unsophisticated, do you see?'

As Felix had originally explained his role in the First World War drama as that of a blindly patriotic young officer who was sent off to fight as nothing more than cannon fodder, Hannah couldn't see how the character had metamorphosed into a sophisticate. The innocence of his character, Sebastian, was what had drawn Felix to the role in the first place. It was totally different from the street-wise, knowing roles he'd always played on television previously. Or at least, that's what his agent had said, according to Felix.

'Sebastian understands what's really going on but feels it's his duty to fight, even though he knows he's going to be killed,' Felix said fiercely. 'That's his motivation – duty not stupidity.'

'Have you and the director resolved the problem?' Hannah enquired delicately.

'I don't know. Not really, not yet.' Felix threw the covers from his body and climbed out of bed. He stubbed out his cigarette and immediately lit another one. 'I can't play this guy as a fool, it'd be so bad for my profile. Felix Andretti playing some bloody stupid idiot. I'd be stuck playing half-wits from now until the year dot.'

His face was dark. It was evening and the pale October sun had long since disappeared, leaving the bedroom cast in shadows.

Hannah watched him from the bed. She wasn't sure what to say. Pointing out that he'd fought to play this character in the first place would be a mistake. Actors' egos were such fragile things, as she was discovering daily. Yet, if Felix argued with the director, he could be thrown off the series. That happened, she knew. He wasn't the star, he was replaceable.

An idea struck.

'What about your agent – couldn't you ask her opinion?' she said.

'I'll have to use your phone,' Felix said thoughtfully. 'My mobile's broken.'

'I didn't know you had one.'

He shrugged, his mind already miles away. 'That's because it's been broken for so long.'

She left him dialling his agent, Billie, in London and went into the kitchen to see what she could rustle up for dinner. A Spanish omelette was being browned under the grill half an hour later when he danced into the kitchen, his depression gone and his face animated. Felix slid his arms round Hannah's waist as she stood at the grill, peering in at the omelette. 'You're a miracle worker, do you know that?'

Thrilled he was happy, she smiled. 'No, why?'

'I phoned Billie, and she agreed with me. Said Sebastian was obviously a more intelligent and aware character than they're giving him credit for. But she says we've got to give the director his shot at it. Says he'll discover he's wrong but we've got to do it all as per the script. The director had already rung her and told her my scenes were dynamite, so I'm going to give him a chance. I phoned him now and he's delighted.'

'Phoned the director on location?' Hannah enquired innocently, taking two plates out of the cupboard. So there were phones on the set. Hannah felt a knot of unease in her guts. Felix could have phoned her if he'd wanted to. The way he could have told her he'd met David James if he'd wanted to. She looked down. The hand holding the plate was shaking. Stop it, she commanded herself. Remember your middle names: Hannah – Strong Independent – Campbell.

'Yeah, he was happy.' Felix didn't appear to notice her comment. 'This smells great. Let's eat, then we're off into town to Lillie's. There's a gang from location going out on the town tonight. It'll be fun, are you up for it?'

'You bet,' Hannah said automatically.

She'd never been to the Grafton Street nightclub before. Harry had been more of a pub sort of bloke and their nights of wild revelry had been confined to drinking sessions in Ryan's of Parkgate Street, which was near their old flat. She loved dancing and put on her designer strappy dress with glee, thankful that she'd washed her hair earlier in the gym. Felix was crazy about the dress and, after looking at the mainly conservative garments in her wardrobe, said she needed lots more like it. In the taxi into the city centre, he was so turned on by the outfit that he nearly made the driver turn around again and take them back to Hannah's flat.

'I thought you were mad to go partying,' said Hannah, slightly embarrassed by his touching her up with the taxi driver pretending to keep his eyes on the road.

'You mean, you're a party animal after all?' Felix murmured, fingers burrowing under her hem.

'Raring to go,' she replied primly, removing his hand and giving him a jokey smack on the wrist.

But by the time she and Felix left the Shelbourne after a few quick drinks to go to Lillie's, Hannah, who'd been up at seven to get into the office early, was feeling the effects of both her early morning and her energetic gym workout. It was only ten forty-five and she was already tired. Felix, on the other hand, was like the constellations in the sky – he came alive at night.

'I'm crazy about you, babe,' he crooned at her as they walked down Grafton Street, clicking his fingers to some inner beat. He was wired, almost as if he'd taken something, Hannah thought worriedly. But he couldn't have, he'd been with her the entire time.

Queues of people thronged the small entrance to the nightclub, all eager to be seen in the place where rock stars and models let their hair down. For a brief moment, Hannah wondered how they were going to get in but she'd reckoned without her boyfriend. Even though he'd only been living in Dublin for six weeks, the bouncers obviously knew Felix and welcomed him in with open arms. Within minutes, they were being led into what the blonde waitress had described as 'the library' where a gang of people lounged around on armchairs with ice buckets and glasses splayed on the tables in front of them. Despite the music and the booze, everyone looked studiedly bored.

'Felix, honey!' squealed one lean and rapacious redhead in a leather dress, unwinding herself from the arm of a sofa to wind herself around Felix.

'Carol,' he said, giving her a long kiss on the cheek, one long-fingered hand resting on her sinewy hip. 'Said I'd come, didn't I?'

'Not that you'd be bringing company,' Ms Leather Dress said, giving Hannah the once over.

Hannah recognized competition when she saw it. And she knew how to deal with it too.

She let her full mouth curve into a feline smile and, as extravagantly as possible, let her coat slip from her shoulders to the seat behind her. With the amethyst dress moulded to breasts already shoved into a breathtaking Wonderbra'd cleavage, she was a match for any skinny redhead.

'Felix and I go everywhere together,' she said to Carol.

Felix pulled himself away from the other woman's grasp and moved towards Hannah.

'Got yourself quite a babe there, Felix, my man,' said one of the onlookers appreciatively.

'I know,' drawled Felix, draping one arm protectively around his property.

Hannah gave Carol a loaded smile. Don't mess with me, it said.

More champagne was ordered, packets of cigarettes were circulated and nobody appeared to want to dance. They were all far more interested in posing in the exclusive section of the club, looking coolly distant each time anyone unconnected with their party was given admittance. Hannah was sure she recognized a couple of guys from an American rap band in one corner but as nobody gave them a moment's notice she reckoned she was wrong. It was only when a fan sneaked past the library security to get an autograph that she realized she'd been correct all along. It was just that the gang of actors she was with refused to recognize anyone else. Hoping to be recognized themselves, they feigned ignorance of any other vaguely famous people. Her first insider glimpse into the world of showbiz made Hannah realize that there was only one thing more important than fame to this lot: looking coolly unconcerned. It was an art form that they all practised desperately. Hannah was pretty good at looking coolly unconcerned herself.

She drank champagne and sat calmly beside Felix, who was more animated than a Duracell bunny. She'd have loved to have asked him who everyone else in their party was. Who was playing which part, or even, were they all actors? They all appeared to work on the TV series with Felix but were quite vague about their jobs, apart from Carol, who told everyone within a fifty-metre radius that she was playing a nurse and had trained in RADA.

'What do you do?' she asked Hannah beadily, sinking into Felix's seat when he'd gone off to the loo.

Without blinking, Hannah lied. 'I run a property business.'

Carol looked upset at this information. Obviously Carol had hoped she was a bimbo, Hannah smiled to herself.

'How did you meet?' Carol wasn't giving up yet. Watching her prey from narrowed eyes, she looked like a magpie about to launch itself on an unsuspecting worm. Hannah was no worm. She could bullshit with the best of them.

'Carol was giving me the third degree while you were gone,' Hannah told Felix later.

'What did she want to know?'

'What I did for a living and what my social security number was – you know, meaningless stuff.'

'What did you tell her?' he asked idly, eyes suddenly opaque.

Hannah nibbled his ear. 'That I ran a property business and we met when I was showing you my most valuable property, a duplex overlooking the harbour in Dun Laoghaire.'

He smiled with satisfaction. 'That's my girl,' he said. 'Everybody in this business lies. It's all about deception and perception. The more they think you have, the more they want you,' he added. 'They're all impressed with you. We're a good team,' he said, before locking his mouth over hers.

CHAPTER THIRTEEN

Felix had Monday off and persuaded Hannah to do something she had always vowed she'd never do: phone in sick.

'We could spend the whole day in bed,' he said, nuzzling her ear as if he was sucking chocolate off an almond. 'It's only one day, after all, and I'm working all next weekend.'

Guiltily, Hannah phoned Gillian, lied about recovering from a twenty-four hour bug, and crawled back under the covers with a delighted Felix.

Saturated with love, exhausted from a weekend of lovemaking, Hannah sauntered into the office on Tuesday. She was an unheard of half an hour late and didn't care: she felt insulated by love and gloriously weary from sex. Even the dark circles under her eyes couldn't hide her white-hot radiance of sexuality.

Despite having almost no sleep, Hannah's face glowed and not even her Visa bill could dim the sleepy smile that lifted the edges of her full mouth so enticingly.

'Did lover boy come home to roost?' enquired Donna, as Hannah put her bag beside her chair and sank on to it, crossing long ten-deniered legs and smoothing down the flirty black skirt she'd never before worn into the office.

Hannah laughed throatily. 'Is it that obvious?'

Smirking, Donna replied: 'It couldn't be any plainer if you had a sign over your head that had "This woman has been well bonked" written on it. That man sure is good for your complexion. Can you bottle some of whatever he's giving you, because my skin could do with an instant boost.'

They both burst out laughing at the thought.

'Hannah,' said David James, 'have you got a moment?'

She sashayed into his office, utterly unable to stop herself glorying in the wonderful feeling of being in love. Her body felt so alive, so vibrant. That was the effect Felix had on her: he was like a drug, a life-enhancing, erotic drug.

'You look . . . different,' David said as Hannah sat down and ran a languorous finger through her curls in a way she never normally did.

Hannah grinned at him. 'I had a good weekend,' she said happily. 'Did you?'

'Well, yes, all right.'

He didn't look as if he'd had a good weekend, she decided. He looked a bit peaky really, almost uncomfortable.

'What I wanted to say . . .' he began.

Hannah had to interrupt. She just knew he was going to apologize for saying what he did about Felix, and she was far too happy and full of love to let him embarrass himself by doing it. She was happy, they should let bygones be bygones.

'David,' she interrupted, 'I know what you're going to say and I'm sorry, too, about Friday. I was upset because Felix and I had had a row and I shouldn't have said what I did to you. That was unforgivable. And it's kind of you to look out for me,' she went on earnestly, 'but there's really no need, David. Felix and I are both grown-ups and we can take care of ourselves. I know he's a friend of yours, but I'd prefer it if we could keep the office and my personal life separate, OK?'

David seemed unable to meet her gaze. 'So it's back on, is it?' he asked gruffly, suddenly interested in opening up the e-mail on his computer.

'Yes,' she beamed.

He exhaled slowly, almost painfully. 'If you ever want a shoulder to lean on,' he said, 'mine is available.'

'David, you are a pal,' Hannah said fondly.

'Yes,' he said grimly, 'I am a pal.'

She danced out of the office. Life was wonderful.

As November drifted into December, a pattern developed to their days together. Felix would arrive late most Friday nights, sometimes in a taxi from the set; sometimes in a limo with a crowd of actors, all half-drunk and eager for Hannah to climb in with them and head off to a wild party or nightclub. Hannah liked the taxi nights best. Then, Felix was hers alone and after drinking whatever bottle he'd brought with him – usually some variety of champagne, vintage or non-vintage depending on how broke he was – they retired to bed where their noisy lovemaking paid Hannah's downstairs neighbours back for their constantly over-loud TV. On Saturdays, they spent the mornings in bed, consuming brown toast and honey with the strong Colombian coffee Felix loved. Then in the afternoons, they went to the gym together. Nobody could accuse Felix of having a beautiful body without working at it, Hannah thought, marvelling at how long he could spend on the weights machines, honing each muscle with almost obsessive precision. She'd never met a man who could spend longer working on his body, consumed by making it better and taking care of it. Felix had more body lotions than she did and he was far more assiduous in his application of body scrub than she'd ever been. But, she got used to his vanities.

She also got used to the girls in the gym blatantly chatting him up while she was away working on the stepper. Well, she almost got used to it. Her glutes weren't the only muscles clenching when some nymphet dawdled around the lateral pull-down machine, chatting earnestly to Felix as his muscles rippled under the show-off T-shirt he deliberately wore.

She once snapped that she wasn't surprised he was ogled by all and sundry, seeing as how he went in for the type of T-shirt only male strippers wore with the intention of having them ripped off. Felix had laughed loudly and long to that one.

'Jealous, are you, my pet?' he said, in unconcern. 'You'll have to get used to it. Women chat up actors all the time: fame is a huge lure, you know.'

Conversely, he preferred Hannah to work out in more conservative work-out clothes. Keen on being admired by the opposite sex, he disliked the same thing happening to her. When she'd worn her shiny lycra thong-leotard with the sleek purple leggings and had been chatted up by an earnest body builder who was at least two inches taller even than Felix, he hadn't been impressed.

'I don't like strange men hanging around you,' he said possessively, before casually adding that he preferred her wearing T-shirts and shorts to the gym instead of her second-skin leotard.

Emma had thought this was odd when Hannah had laughingly told her about it over the phone.

'What's sauce for the goose should be sauce for the gander,' Emma said. 'I mean, if Felix is allowed to dress to thrill, why can't you?'

Hannah had immediately wished she'd kept her mouth shut. She'd been trying to explain to Emma – who hadn't met Felix yet – that he adored her, was crazy about her and couldn't bear other men to so much as look at her. But Emma had picked it up all wrong and more or less said Felix was possessive.

Emma didn't understand, Hannah thought impatiently. She didn't understand that there was a difference between possessiveness and real passion. Anyway, look who was talking: Emma wouldn't stand up to her father if her life depended on it.

In these halcyon days, the only fly in Hannah's ointment was David James. For some reason, their relaxed relationship had vanished to be replaced by a stiff-necked formality that had Hannah wondering exactly what had gone wrong.

It wasn't that David wasn't polite or friendly to her: on the contrary, he was both. Yet nothing more. They didn't indulge in their chocolate-chip biscuit passion any more: meetings in his office were brusque and utterly businesslike, and without the distraction of dunking biscuits in coffee.

Hannah tried to convince herself that it was something else bothering him, something that had nothing to do with her. But she couldn't rid herself of the sneaking suspicion that Donna had been right and that David did like her in a way that had nothing to do with work.

The day Felix rolled up in a borrowed Porsche to collect her didn't make things any clearer. Abandoning the car in his usual reckless manner right outside the door, Felix sauntered into the office and went bang into David who was leading a client out.

'Felix, hello,' said David shortly when his client was gone. The urbane, charming manner he'd displayed for the client was gone. From her desk, Hannah watched the proceedings nervously.

'Hi, my man,' said Felix, clapping David on the shoulder, seemingly impervious to the chilly atmosphere. 'I'm here to collect Hannah.'

'Sorry, I'm going a bit early this evening,' Hannah apologized to David, appearing beside her boyfriend. Damn Felix for being early.

David's frosty face cracked a bit and he managed a smile. 'That's fine,' he said, almost jovially. 'Look after my top employee,' he added to Felix.

'What's up?' Felix asked as he opened the car door for her.

'Nothing, just a bit of a headache,' lied Hannah. Felix, jealous as he was, could do without being told that Hannah suspected her boss fancied her. Or perhaps he didn't. David hadn't appeared lovelorn at the sight of Felix. Hannah shook her head as if to loosen the thought. She really was imagining things.

'Thank God you're in.' For once, Gillian looked delighted to see Hannah.

'Why? What's wrong?' Hannah knew she was late but it was only ten past nine. What disaster could have befallen the office in that twenty-five minutes?

'Donna's daughter has had to go into hospital, something to do with an asthma attack,' Gillian said.

'Poor Donna, poor Tania,' Hannah gasped. Donna had often confided in her about seven-year-old Tania and the severity of her asthma attacks. But she hadn't been in hospital with one since she'd been very young. Donna had been hoping her daughter had out-grown the really vicious attacks. Obviously not.

'. . . and she's got three appointments this morning and nobody else is around to fit them in,' Gillian was muttering, staring at the appointment book with the horror of the easily flustered.

'Somebody is bound to,' Hannah said impatiently. 'It's not the end of the world, Gillian. Let me see.' She stared at the book, rapidly assessing where the other estate agents were and working out who could deal with Donna's clients. Three minutes on the phone to the other agents solved two of the problems. But nobody could fit in her first client in Killiney at nine forty-five. Hannah knew the house in question: a rather ugly semi owned by a couple who were trying to buy a house in Drumcondra. They desperately needed to sell their home because they couldn't afford bridging finance and a previous sale had fallen through. If they couldn't get a sale agreed within a day or so, they'd lose the house in Drumcondra. Donna had liked the couple and hoped this morning's viewers would make an offer after seeing it again. If it had been any other house, Hannah would have cancelled the viewing but she knew this was important. David James was unavailable so she couldn't ask his advice.

Briskly, she shut the appointments book. 'I'm going to take Donna's nine forty-five myself,' she told an open-mouthed Gillian.

On the way, she left a message on Donna's mobile asking if there was anything she could do to help with Tania. 'I'm so sorry to hear about what's happened, Donna. Ring me if you need anything,' she stressed, 'and don't worry about work. Concentrate on getting Tania better. We're all thinking of you.'

A gleaming four-year-old BMW was waiting for her at the house when she drove up. Conscious that her elderly banger wasn't the ideal vehicle for a thrusting, would-be estate agent, Hannah parked a few doors away, pleased that at least she looked the part even if her car didn't. The burgundy trouser suit from Wallis worn with her high-heeled boots was perfectly suitable for this unexpected change of job.

The clients were waiting impatiently at the door and the woman looked pointedly at her watch when Hannah walked confidently down the driveway.

Blonde, expertly made-up and dressed in expensive casual clothes, Denise Parker obviously thought she was the last word in yuppie chic and liked to give the impression that her time was very valuable. Her husband Colin, a less impressive looking sandy-haired man in a suit, appeared equally impatient.

'We are in a rush, you know,' Denise said, before Hannah had a chance to say hello.

'Of course,' Hannah said soothingly. 'Ms Nelson told me all about you both. I know you're very busy people.'

She couldn't actually see how a hairdresser and a computer salesman were any busier than anyone else but realized that flattery would be a balm to this self-important pair.

'A pleasure to meet you both,' she said, shaking hands. 'I'm Hannah Campbell. I don't normally do viewings,' she added gravely, 'but Ms Nelson couldn't make it and as we wouldn't dream of cancelling your viewing, I said I'd come.' She hadn't actually lied, Hannah knew, just implied that she was far more important than she actually was in the hope that the Parkers would be impressed. They were.

Denise sniffed. 'Thank you,' she said graciously.

Inside, the couple strolled speculatively around, Denise rubbing an unimpressed finger along walls to see if the darkened colour was damp or dirt. Colin screwed up his nose at the chipped marble fireplace that no amount of trailing ivies could camouflage and grimaced at the porridge-coloured curtains that were included in the asking price.

Prepared to wait for them to go through the entire house with painstaking slowness, Hannah sat down on a sofa and calmly looked through the list of properties she'd brought with her as if she didn't have a million things waiting for her back at the office. It was important to look as if you had all the time in the world for your latest clients, explained the psychology bit in her real estate manual.

'Make them feel special, as if finding the precise home for them is your mission,' said the book. Hannah tried not to roll her eyes to heaven. Doing anything for this pair of surly customers was a mission, all right. Mission: Impossible.

She remembered talking to Donna about the psychology of showing a house.

'Some agents praise everything, tell the clients that it's wonderful and that it's perfect for them,' Donna explained. 'I don't do it that way. I'm very matter-of-fact about a house, I point out that they're going to need to spend money on it. They want to know what needs to be done, especially the three most expensive things in a house: wiring, windows and heating. Honesty, that works for me.'

Honesty, Hannah thought, nervously. She could do this.

When the Parkers finally arrived back in the room, Hannah tried her best to look as though she was surprised they'd been so quick.

'It has buckets of potential, doesn't it?' she said in a matter-of-fact voice. 'I'd rip out the fireplace, naturally. But imagine how good it'd look with a modern black slate one.'

The Parkers looked wonderingly at the fireplace, as if astonished that the estate agent was pointing out a negative feature of the house.

'Well,' Hannah added with a casual shrug of her shoulders, 'some people would probably like that fireplace; they'd leave it here, in fact. But anyone with an eye for interior design would see it has to go. I could see you hated it.' She allowed herself a small smile. 'But not everyone has your taste.'

Denise looked pleased. 'No, you're right. I was just saying to Colin that the fireplace was the first thing I'd rip out.'

Hannah nodded approvingly. 'And change the bathroom suite. Navy is so eighties.'

'Lord, yes,' rushed Denise. 'That's just what we said.'

Hannah began organizing her papers. 'I'd love to see what you two could do to this house,' she said conversationally. 'I'd say you've great ideas and it's a nice area.'

'Isn't it,' agreed Colin, looking much less po-faced.

'I'll just check all the windows upstairs are closed,' Hannah said, escaping to give them a moment alone. When she came back down the stairs, they were waiting for her in the hall with smiles on their faces.

'We'll take it,' Denise said triumphantly. 'I can just see that living room done in greys and greens with a slate fireplace. We've got to have it.'

'That sounds fantastic,' lied Hannah before congratulating them and asking for a deposit cheque.

Ten minutes later, the BMW sped off down the quiet road and Hannah allowed herself to squeal with delight.

She was good at this! Bloody good! The Parkers were the sort of people who expected to be bullied into doing things and their instinctive belligerence meant they were always poised to fight back. She'd taken them totally by surprise by pointing out the bad features of the house, treating them as if they were naturally more intelligent than your average client, and so they'd never had the chance to be aggressive.

The only sour point was that poor Donna's misfortune was the reason she'd been given this wonderful chance. She switched on the mobile she'd taken from the office and rang Gillian, anxious to see if Donna had phoned in with an update on poor little Tania's condition.

'No,' said Gillian, sounding put out. 'Mr James rang in and he said to tell you it was a great idea to take over Donna's client yourself.'

Hannah grinned at the little sniff with which Gillian finished this sentence. Obviously Gillian had delighted in telling the boss that Hannah had stepped out of line, hoping Hannah would get her knuckles rapped. How irritating for Gillian to have her plan backfire.

'Thank you for telling him what I was doing, Gillian,' she said calmly. 'That was efficient of you. I'll be back shortly.'

Hannah knew it would only have taken her fifteen minutes to get back to the office, but the sense of achievement inside her was so heady that she felt she needed to sit back and enjoy it.

She made a detour to a small coffee shop, bought a takeaway cappuccino and sat on a bollard on Dun Laoghaire pier, watching the hustle and bustle of the busy port. She loved looking at the sea. Back home in Connemara, the sea wasn't too far from her parents' house, although the rocky shore leading down to the tumultuous Atlantic Ocean was a million miles away from the Victorian splendour of Dun Laoghaire's harbour where order seemed to reign. The elegant hotels behind her looked as if ladies in tea gowns holding parasols could emerge at any moment, while the pretty yachts moored side by side along the marina could have come from another era if you narrowed your eyes and ignored the modern innovations like radio aerials.

The two giant arms of the pier encircling the harbour like a lover's embrace made the sea look safe and comfortably tame. At home,

Hannah always felt the sense of dangerous nature prevailed. Small boats were tied up firmly against ancient stone jetties and when the waves lunged violently over the sea walls making the boats rattle, Hannah remembered thinking she would never get in a boat as long as she lived. The sea was much safer here, she decided, sipping her cappuccino pleasurably.

'It was wonderful today,' she told Felix that night when he rang her. He still hadn't taken his mobile phone to get it fixed so it was a rare treat for him to call her during the week. 'Donna couldn't believe I'd sold the house to that pair. She rang in to say Tania's getting out tomorrow and she was delighted –'

'That's great, darling,' Felix interrupted. 'I've only got a minute to talk. I'm on Leon's phone. I was just ringing to say I won't be up this weekend as we're moving the set to Waterford for the final two weeks before we break for Christmas and we're on slave duty.'

'Oh.' She couldn't hide the disappointment in her voice: she'd planned a special lunch with Leonie, Emma and Pete. The girls were dying to meet the delectable Felix they'd heard so much about and Emma had been promising to bring Pete along for months.

'We'll do that another time,' he said impatiently.

When he'd hung up, Hannah gazed at the phone despondently. Being in love with an actor was like being in love with a married man, she thought despairingly. You could never make plans.

CHAPTER FOURTEEN

Her mother ran a hand over the floral fabric in the centre bolt. Pale blue with yellow and blue flowers, it was very Laura Ashley and very pretty. Just the sort of thing her mother adored, Emma knew. She could imagine the brief her mother would give the curtain-maker: 'Frills, frills and more frills.'

Anne-Marie O'Brien's hand moved to another bolt of fabric, also blue but with only a small cream design in it. 'Lovely,' she said absently.

They'd been in Laura Ashley's fabric department for ten minutes and, so far, that was as much as Emma's mother had said about anything. Normally, on a trip to buy material for her spare-bedroom curtains, she'd have been on a high of excitement, in raptures at the thought of re-doing yet another room in the house. Pete swore the O'Briens redecorated the entire house from top to bottom every two years. 'Your mother is a decorating nut,' he said each time the 'What colour shall we paint the woodwork?' shenanigans began.

Emma didn't know why her parents didn't buy their own wallpaper stripper. They paid so much in hire fees that they could have owned one twice over. This time, the spare bedroom was being done up because her mother's second cousin was visiting from Chicago and, naturally, the spare bedroom was in such a state that nobody could be expected to sleep in it. Certainly not someone from Chicago, Anne-Marie would have said in scandalized tones.

Only she hadn't said it, hadn't suggested redecoration: her husband had. Although once she'd got the idea, she was all for it.

'You'll come with me to buy the curtain material, won't you, Emma?' she'd pleaded with her daughter.

Emma wouldn't have dreamed of refusing. Another Saturday morning wasted, she thought with irritation. She and Pete had planned to start their Christmas shopping that day. Christmas was barely three and a half weeks away and they didn't want to spend endless hours at the last minute trying to get into crowded city-centre car parks as the entire country went mad buying gift sets, novelty ties and other useless Christmas presents.

Perhaps if she and her mother weren't too long looking for wallpaper and fabric today, she could nip down to Alias Tom's and see if they had anything nice for Pete, Emma thought. A really nice sweater or a designer shirt, maybe. It'd be splashing out, but he deserved something special. He'd been working so hard lately, making lots of overnight trips because of the overtime money he got paid for them.

Emma had never mentioned her father's horrible comments about how she and Pete had borrowed their deposit money from him, but it was as if Pete had somehow sensed what had been said and was now doing everything he could to pay it back. She sighed. Darling Pete. He was so good to her and yet she'd been like a bear with a sore head for the last few weeks.

'Where's your father?' enquired her mother suddenly, breaking into Emma's thoughts.

'What?'

'Your father. Where is he? I can't see him anywhere.'

A moment passed as Emma stared uncomprehendingly at her mother. What had she said . . . ?

Anne-Marie's eyes, so like Emma's, were pale with amber flecks. Always alert and watchful, looking for things she didn't approve of. Now, the pale eyes were filled with some secret fear. She was looking anxiously around them, pupils darting here and there, blinking rapidly.

'Dad's not here,' Emma said slowly, watching in horror as her mother's mouth wobbled and she began to cry.

'He must be, where is he? He was here. You're lying to me!' Anne-Marie's voice got louder.

She was panicking, Emma realized.

Quickly, she took her mother's arm, hoping to comfort her and remind her that Jimmy O'Brien was working that day. But her mother shook off Emma's arm with surprising strength and started to run away from her, calling, 'Jimmy, where are you?' in an increasingly frantic voice.

Still in shock, Emma ran after her and, because she couldn't think of what else to do, grabbed her mother again. They were beside a display of cushions and Anne-Marie seized one and started hitting Emma with it.

'Get away from me! Get away from me! Where's my husband?'

She must be having a stroke or an aneurysm, Emma thought wildly as she dodged the blows. Something terrible, something that had affected her mind in this way. She didn't even seem to recognize Emma. Her face was distorted and her expression was quite manic, utterly frightening.

'Mum, Mum, it's OK. It's me, Emma. Stop hitting me. We'll find Dad, I promise. OK, Mum?' Emma begged, unable to control the sheer terror she was experiencing. What was happening, why was her mother behaving like this? Anne-Marie kept roaring, her shouts overpowering the gentle shop muzak.

'Where's my husband? I have to find him!'

Emma kept a grip on her mother, scared that, if she let go, Anne-Marie might run away again. The screams and the frantic bashing with the cushion continued. Emma did her best to pull the cushion out of her mother's hand but couldn't. She was so strong. People were watching them now, a crowd had gathered in a wide circle around them, and one of the shop assistants approached tentatively.

'Is everything all right?' she asked.

As abruptly as she'd started, Anne-Marie stopped hitting Emma with the cushion. She stared at it in astonishment, as if bewildered as to how it had found its way into her hand in the first place.

'Emma?' she breathed.

'I'm here, Mum. I'm here.' Emma hugged her mother's rigid body gently, afraid to hold her too tightly in case she started screaming again. 'It's OK. We'll find Dad.' With one hand, she took the cushion and dumped it back on the display.

'I'm sorry,' she said to the shop assistant, 'I don't know what happened . . . She got confused or something.' The girl looked at Anne-Marie, whose face was now quite normal, and then back to Emma. She clearly didn't believe a word Emma was saying. Who would, Emma thought. This perfectly normal-looking woman and her daughter must have had some sort of row. What else would people think?

Her mother patted Emma's cheek briefly, then smiled brightly and turned around to admire the cushions she'd been using as weapons only moments before. The onlookers drifted away and Emma was left, her legs like jelly with shock, her heart pumping like the drums in a techno-music song.

'Nice,' said her mother happily, holding up a tapestry cushion.

'Let's go, Mum.' Terrified the whole procedure would start again, Emma led her mother out of the shop and into a café. Still holding Anne-Marie's arm, she bought two coffees at the counter and a Danish pastry for her mother.

Emma found them a table, keeping up a stream of meaningless conversation about Christmas and buying fabric for the bedroom, like a parent trying to amuse a fractious toddler. She put a spoon of sugar in her mother's coffee and pushed the Danish in front of her.

Not saying a word about how she could put her own sugar in her coffee, thank you very much, Anne-Marie took the cup and drank deeply before starting on her pastry. Emma, barely able to swallow a sip of coffee, watched her.

'Will we look at wallpaper now?' her mother asked in a normal, contented way.

'I don't know, Mum,' Emma replied weakly. 'I've got a migraine,' she lied, anything to avoid more shopping.

'Will we go home?' her mother said eagerly, like a child.

Emma nodded. She couldn't speak. Seeing her mother reduced to someone she didn't recognize was the most terrifying experience of her life. As Anne-Marie drank her coffee, Emma ran through the list of possibilities behind her bizarre behaviour in the shop. Each time, she came painfully back to the one answer: Alzheimer's disease. There could be no other explanation. It was warm in the coffee shop, almost tropical, to ward off the early December wind outside. But despite the heat, Emma felt a shaft of pure cold slice through her. Her very bones felt chilled, touched by an icy grip that had nothing to do with the actual weather. Her mother was ill. Very ill. Whatever could they do now?

'Kirsten,' Emma said with relief into the receiver. It was so comforting to hear her sister's voice, the voice of normality. 'I don't know what to do. You'll never believe what's happened.'

'Can you be quick?' came the reply over the phone, 'I'm just going out to the manicurist to get a nail fixed. We're going to a ball tonight and I snapped my thumbnail on a tin of Diet Coke.'

Emma raised her eyes to heaven. No matter what domestic disaster was unfolding, Kirsten would be bound to have some much more urgent matter awaiting her attention. If the world was ending in a giant fireball, Kirsten would insist on getting her roots coloured first.

'You won't feel much like going to any ball when you hear what I've got to tell you about Mum,' Emma said soberly.

'Don't be ridiculous,' Kirsten said brusquely when her sister had finished the story. 'There's nothing wrong with Mummy. You're imagining it. You know how she frets when Dad isn't around, how every little incident becomes a full-scale disaster. That's all that's wrong.'

'No,' protested Emma. 'That isn't all. You didn't see her, Kirsten, she was . . . she was crazy, hitting me with a cushion and yelling at the top of her voice. It was terrifying, I thought she'd lost her mind. I know what it is, I think. Alzheimer's. Oh God, I even hate to say it.'

There was silence at the other end of the phone. 'You can't be serious,' Kirsten said finally.

'This is hardly a joke. Who'd make something like that up?' Emma demanded.

'Well, she's fine now, isn't she? It's all over, so there's nothing to worry about. You're panicking about nothing.'

'Kirsten!' exploded Emma. 'Will you listen to me. Mum didn't know who I was. She's been acting a bit strange recently, you know she has. She can't remember words to things. She tried to tell me last week that the washing machine had broken down and she couldn't remember the word for it.'

Emma recalled the phone conversation: 'The thing's broken,' her mother had wailed. 'There's water and it won't work. I don't know how to fix it.'

'What thing?' Emma had asked gently.

'The thing, the big . . . thing,' her mother had yelled in frustration. 'Kitchen thing, for clothes, I don't know what you call it, just stop annoying me. It's broken.'

But when Emma had called round that evening, her mother seemed in perfectly good form and the washing machine was trundling away in the kitchen.

'I keep telling myself there's nothing wrong with her,' Emma told Kirsten now, 'but I can't do that any more because I've seen it for myself: she's not well. She's got something, some dementia, something like Alzheimer's, I know it.' Emma stopped, weary from trying to convince Kirsten. 'We've got to decide what to do about it. I didn't say anything to Dad. I dropped Mum off and came back home. I didn't know what to say to him. That's why I'm phoning you. We've got to decide what to do together.'

A snort from the other end of the phone told her that Kirsten had no intention of doing anything of the sort. 'There's nothing to figure out. We all forget things. I can't remember people's names half the time. Mummy's fine, I know it. You think I wouldn't know if my own mother was sick?'

'This isn't a competition, Kirsten,' stressed Emma. 'We're not having a game to see who diagnosed it first, to see who is the better daughter. We've got to do something. Maybe Dad doesn't know, maybe this has never happened before, but we've got to take some action.'

'You can, I'm not going to. I think you're over-reacting. Now, I can't talk, I told you.'

With that, Kirsten hung up.

Emma stared at the phone in amazement. She knew Kirsten didn't like facing painful things, had known it for years. Kirsten had taken two days to tell their parents she'd been suspended from fourth year in school for smoking; only the arrival of the official letter from the principal had forced her hand. But to deny there was anything wrong with their mother when it was so patently obvious there was . . . It didn't make any sense.

CHAPTER FIFTEEN

Rampant kennel cough had affected what seemed like half of the dogs in the area. Leonie felt she would scream if she had to listen to one more painful canine cough or see the accompanying look of bewilderment on the poor animal's furry face. Most owners were so good about bringing their dogs to the vet but there were always those terrible few who thought that animal healthcare was on a par with tearing up fifty-pound notes for fun. They'd paid out for the initial parvo-virus shots when their dog was a puppy and had never been seen over the threshold of the surgery since. They'd seen four cases of kennel cough that morning, although because it was the most infectious thing imaginable, Angie had examined the dogs in the surgery hallway. They never admitted a dog with kennel cough.

The latest patient was very bad with it. Leonie didn't know how the owner could have let it go on for so long. It was such an unmistakable cough, you couldn't listen to your dog coughing in that way without your heart breaking.

'She's never sick,' the man had explained off-handedly when he'd brought in a spaniel who was obviously in agony with kennel cough. Her eyes were rheumy with 'flu-like symptoms and each time she coughed, her small body was racked with what had to be painful spasms. 'The last dog never got anything,' the owner complained as Angie examined the dog with Leonie helping. Bloody miracle, Leonie thought venomously, if this was how well they looked after it. This poor little dog must have been sick for days and these bloody pigs wouldn't bother their backsides bringing her in. Money couldn't be the problem, either. The man dangled Saab keys in one hand and the sheepskin coat slung over his Lacoste shirt was hardly bargain basement. Leonie longed to let him know just what she thought of him, one swift prong with the bovine rectal thermometer and he'd know all about it. *She's never sick.* What a load of old . . .

'Leonie,' said Angie, who recognized the signs of rage in her friend, 'would you hold Flossie for a moment while I listen to her heart and lungs?'

Flossie, dear little thing that she was, wagged her feathery tail in a friendly manner as Leonie held her expertly. 'You're a lovely girl, aren't you,' she said softly. 'All you have to do is wait here for a moment and we'll soon have you better. Good girl.'

The owner stood back and leaned against the wall. He looked bored, as if this entire trip had been a waste of his valuable time.

He even managed to sigh once and look at his watch. Leonie and Angie's eyes met over Flossie's liver-and-white back. Angie's eyes were just as narrowed as Leonie's.

When the examination was over, Angie faced him.

'I'm afraid your dog is very sick with kennel cough,' she said icily. He didn't react. 'In fact, I'm surprised you didn't bring her sooner. Most people come in at the first sign, your dog has been ill at least two weeks.'

The man stopped leaning against the wall. 'Well, you know, Christmas and all that . . .' he stuttered.

'Yes. It's easy to neglect animals because of Christmas,' Angie said pointedly. 'But a few more days and this would have become very serious. And she's quite thin. Has she been wormed recently?'

The man had the grace to look shame-faced. 'I'm afraid we never think of things like that.'

Leonie couldn't help it. 'Why do you have a dog, then?' she snapped.

Angie shot her a fierce look. They weren't supposed to say things like that. Furious owners might never bring their poor dogs back to the surgery again if they were given grief when they *did* come.

Flossie's owner was looking shocked.

'How often you worm your dog or otherwise is your business,' Angie said formally, ignoring Leonie for a moment. 'To clarify matters, we are only obliged to inform the authorities when we think a dog is being neglected.'

He paled at the word 'neglected'.

'She's a sweet little thing and the children love her,' he mumbled. 'I didn't mean to neglect her or anything.'

'I'm sure you didn't,' Angie interrupted smoothly, 'but she'll need a course of antibiotics and I'd like to see her back here in a week to see how she's doing and to worm her. Would that be possible?'

'Of course, of course.' He began patting Flossie anxiously and Leonie was pleased to see that the dog liked him. At least he wasn't beating the poor little thing.

He was the last client and when he left, Leonie tidied up as Angie wrote up the dog's medical file, noting the antibiotics they'd used. As they'd both suspected, Flossie had been to the surgery four years before for her initial vaccination shots as a puppy and she'd never been back.

'Too expensive, I bet,' Leonie said with disgust. 'Like that man with the pub.'

Angie nodded wearily. Every vet and nurse in the surgery had been horrified by the fabulously ostentatious owner of two city-centre pubs who'd refused to have his pet dog's cataracts operated upon because it was 'too bloody expensive'.

They'd all known that he could have easily afforded it, even though it wasn't a cheap operation, yet he preferred to let the lovely German Shepherd go on banging clumsily into things until she'd stumbled out on to the main road and been killed. A regular in the gossip columns, he'd even had the nerve to mention he was upset about his beloved dog because he 'adored animals and would do anything for them.'

'Hypocrite. He'd have paid that much to get the headlights fixed on his bloody Rolls,' Leonie had howled with fury when she'd heard. None of the staff members had felt themselves able to speak to the man again, even though he drove past the surgery on his way to work every day in his flashy ice-blue Rolls Royce.

Angie swore she was going to throw broken glass in his way to see him get a puncture. In her angrier moments, Leonie said they ought to blindfold him and let him see what it was like trying to live in the dark.

'Well, why the fuck don't people like that get a goldfish?' Leonie said now, wiping the examining table with disinfectant. She never swore, only when she was really angry or upset. 'Then they could throw a few crumbs on top of the water every week and forget about the bloody things.'

'Fish require lots of care,' Angie reminded her mildly.

'Yeah? I don't care for fish, except on a plate with white wine sauce on it,' Leonie replied. She couldn't help it: she was furious with all these pigs who pretended to love animals and wouldn't bother to care for them properly. No, they weren't pigs. Pigs were animals and no animal would ever treat another creature in that way. When she thought of some of the lovely animals who came into the surgery, hobbling on fractured limbs, bitten out of their minds with fleas or half-starved, all because of sheer neglect, it was all she could do not to hit their owners, those feckless, useless people who thought that owning a pet was like owning a car that didn't need petrol, water or oil.

'Calm down, Leonie,' Angie said gently. 'You're having a bad day. Go home, have a big glass of wine and forget about it. When the revolution comes, we'll put all those crappy pet owners up against a wall and shoot them.'

Leonie managed to smile. 'Only if I can pull the trigger,' she agreed.

She and Angie closed up the surgery and she drove home, not particularly looking forward to that, either. Home was not the refuge it normally was, mainly because Abby and Mel were squabbling. Leonie sighed. A mere month ago, she'd have said it was hard to imagine Abby squabbling; the usual suspects in a grudge match were Danny and Mel, who fought like warring Medicis over everything from the last piece of toast to the control of the television remote. Abby was the peacemaker, pacifying all parties in the endless war that went on between her siblings. But for some reason, Abby hadn't been getting on with her twin for the past few weeks and their rows were frightening to behold.

Yesterday, they'd had a screaming match in the bathroom because Mel had dared to wear Abby's glittery, bought-specially-for-the-Christmas-disco T-shirt.

Leonie was used to hearing Mel squealing like a four-year-old. But she'd been shocked to hear Abby doing it: 'You cow, I hate you, hate you!' followed by door-slamming, loud music, more shouting and more door-slamming.

Tonight, not feeling ready for a repeat performance, Leonie parked the car outside the cottage and walked slowly to her front door. The paintwork was peeling again, she reminded herself as she did every evening. It was two years since she'd last had the cottage exterior painted and the lovely rich dark green of the door was getting shabby. You didn't notice it as much in the summer because the climbing roses hung so prettily over everything, hiding flaking paint and chipped stonework with a cluster of pale pink, glorious-smelling buds. But in the bleak winter, the place was starting to look shabby, Leonie decided. Dear little Flossie wasn't the only thing to be neglected, she thought ruefully.

Inside, it was blissfully warm and blissfully quiet. Nobody was screaming 'spannerhead!' at anyone else and Penny didn't race frantically to greet her mistress, meaning somebody had kindly taken her for a walk. One more chore ticked off the list, Leonie smiled to herself.

'Hi! Mel, Abby and Danny, I'm home.'

Silence. A note in the kitchen explained that the girls had brought Penny out.

Danny rang, he's home late. Save dinner for him. Mel had added in her nicely rounded handwriting.

As if she'd cook dinner and not save any for Danny. When did she not save dinner for him, Leonie asked wryly. She had a waste-disposal unit for a son and all he did was eat. In the peace and quiet, she decided to do exactly what Angie had suggested: she opened a bottle of wine (£5.99 special from Superquinn) and poured herself a glass.

Dinner was going to be the chilli she'd taken out of the freezer that morning, baked potatoes and salad. Switching the oven and the radio on, Leonie sipped her wine, and scrubbed the potatoes under the cold tap. She half-listened to news updates and traffic reports, enjoying the rare solitude. When Penny erupted into the kitchen via the back door twenty minutes later, barking delightedly at finding her beloved mistress there, a green salad was crisping in the fridge, the potatoes were beginning to sizzle and Leonie had laid the kitchen table for the three of them.

'Hiya, Mum,' said the twins in unison.

Mel hurried in without taking off her anorak or runners and threw herself on to the chair nearest the radiator. Her heart-shaped face was flushed with the combination of exercise and cold air, her big dark eyes were shiny and the biting wind had coloured her lips ruby red. Even windblown, she was so pretty.

Abby hung up both her anorak and Penny's lead before hunching down beside the radiator with her sister. You'd never have believed they were twins, Leonie reflected, looking at Abby's round, open face with its solid chin so unlike Mel's pointed little one. Although Abby was looking a little thinner, she suddenly realized. Nothing major, just a faint thinning of her cheeks. It suited her, Leonie decided with a jolt of pleasure. Perhaps Abby wasn't destined to look like her, with the peasant's face that no amount of make-up could really hide. Nothing would give Leonie greater pleasure than to see Abby turn into a swan. Being an ugly duckling was such a difficult burden to bear. Well, perhaps not an ugly duckling, she told herself. But large, solid and sensible-looking as distinct from petite, dainty and Bambi-eyed.

'You're both in good form tonight,' she said, smiling at them.

'Yeah, sorry about last night,' Abby said apologetically. 'Dunno what got into me.'

'Steven Connelly!' smirked Mel evilly. 'Or you wish he'd got on to you.'

Abby pulled her sister's hair in retaliation. 'Cow.'

'Ouch,' yelped Mel. But it was a good-humoured yelp.

They were friends again, thankfully.

Leonie sat down on a kitchen chair and sipped more of her wine. God only knew what year it was, but it certainly tasted like a good one.

'Who's Steven Connelly?' she asked, knowing she wasn't supposed to ask but unable to resist.

'Who cares about him,' Abby said primly. 'He's someone Mel thinks I fancy. We've much better news.'

'You *do* fancy him,' Mel said simply.

'I don't. Now shut up. Dad phoned,' Abby went on.

'About the wedding,' Mel finished for her, sloe-black eyes glittering excitedly. 'He wants you to come.'

'Fliss and he want you to come,' Abby said, emphasizing Fliss.

It was their mother's turn to mutter 'ouch' to herself.

'That's kind of him,' she said as nonchalantly as she could, 'but I don't think so, girls.'

'What did I tell you?' Mel said to her twin. 'I knew you'd say that, Mum.'

'Did you now?' Leonie got up and bustled around at the cooker to hide her distress. 'You're great at knowing what I'm going to say, aren't you? What if I said you've got to run the Hoover over the sitting room before dinner – were you expecting that?' She spoke lightly, hoping to deflect them from the conversation at hand.

Mel groaned. 'I hate hoovering, Mum. It's Abby's turn, anyway.'

'He wants you to go and so do we,' Abby spoke up.

Leonie got a packet of green beans she hadn't intended cooking out of the freezer and slowly put them in a microwaveable bowl.

'It's bumper to bumper on the Stillorgan dual carriageway,' trilled the traffic reporter on the radio, *'and in Cork, the Douglas area is a no-go zone because an articulated truck has jack-knifed . . .'*

'Mum? You'd love it, you know you would. Dad wants you to phone him. You will, won't you?' Abby pleaded.

'Of course I'll phone him, girls, but I really don't think it's such a good idea. I mean, it'll cost a fortune and your dad doesn't really want me there, does he?'

'He said he does,' Mel pointed out. 'It'll be fun, Mum. Dad says he'll pay your airfare. He's paying for ours too.'

He must be making a bloody mint, Leonie thought. 'I'll phone your father, but that's all. I'm not making any promises.'

'Please,' begged Ray. 'I'd love you to. You always said we had to stick together for the children's sake and show them people can divorce in a civilized fashion.'

Three thousand miles away, Leonie grimaced. Hoist by her own petard. She *had* said that, and not just for the children's sake. She hadn't wanted the kids to be used as pawns in the sort of vicious break-up most people had; used as blackmail in a fight that was all about power and blame, where parental responsibility counted for nothing.

Leonie had seen too many marital break-ups disintegrate into a litany of whose fault it was and why the kids couldn't possibly see 'that bitch' or 'that bastard'. It was all so unhelpful and childish, she felt.

She'd wanted to be able to talk calmly with Ray about the welfare of Abby, Mel and Danny, to do what was right for their family even though they were splitting up as a couple. And they had, always had. This very adult and mature state of affairs suited Leonie too because she'd instigated the break-up and she couldn't face years of Ray's venom bouncing off the kids and back at her simply because he resented what she'd done. It would have been devastating for them, and acutely painful for her. But there had been no venom. Ray had been as good as his word and their divorce had been civilized, just as she'd hoped.

Now, ten years later, her own words came back to haunt her.

'If it was you getting remarried, I'd be there for you, Leonie,' Ray pointed out. And he wasn't lying, she knew.

Leonie wondered if she'd have wanted her ex-husband there if she got married again. She would, she decided. It would be nice to have him there, smiling, encouraging, giving his blessing. Proof that she hadn't ruined his life. Which was a joke, she thought wryly. The only life she'd ruined in her attempts to find true love had been her own. Ray was happy, the kids were happy, and she was the one who longed for the passionate encounter she'd dreamed about since she was old enough to watch black-and-white movies on the telly on Saturday afternoons. Unfortunately, she was turning into a facsimile of Stella Dallas instead of an episode of *Dallas*.

'What does Fliss think about this, about me coming to the wedding?' she asked.

'She's as eager as I am,' Ray said happily. 'She had a wonderful view of the whole thing. Her parents are divorced and see each other all the time. They both own this skiing lodge in Colorado and share holidays with their new partners. It's very civilized here. Fliss wants you to be there because she's going to be the kids' stepmom and she wants you to meet her. It'll be great, Leonie. A holiday. We've got two extra cabins booked, so you and the kids could share one. I'll pay your fare.'

'Nonsense,' Leonie said automatically. 'I'll pay my own fare.' She had said it before she realized what it meant: capitulation by mistake.

'So you're coming! Great! It'll be wonderful to see you, Leonie. Thanks, I really appreciate it,' Ray said enthusiastically.

They discussed arrangements briefly but, because Ray was at work, he couldn't talk for long. 'I'll call during the week, when I've got everything planned,' he said. 'I can't wait to see the kids. And you.'

How different America was from Ireland, she reflected as she hung up. Americans had it all sorted out in their heads. Enlightened, that was the word. People broke up and went on with their lives, ex-spouses met current spouses and nobody threatened to beat anyone senseless because they all hated each other's guts and resented the hell out of each other. Leonie tried to think of one wedding she'd heard of where the ex-spouse turned up to watch the proceedings – well, other than weddings where the ex turned up uninvited to try and *wreck* the proceedings. She couldn't think of any. It was all too civilized. She'd heard of people who refused to go to their *children's* weddings because their ex-partner would be there. How pathetic.

Now she was getting in on the enlightened act by going to Colorado to the January wedding of her ex-husband. How very modern. What a pity she would be going on her own. She'd have loved to have a partner to bring along: someone to act as a personal talisman, to remind her that she was a lovable person. Her talisman would also be proof to the rest of the world that she wasn't some lonely has-been who had scoured the personal ads looking for love and come up with nothing.

Mel was on a high during dinner, volubly discussing what she'd bring to the wedding.

'Liz thinks I should go dramatic in black,' she said, nibbling salad and chilli daintily. 'I don't know. Black makes me washed out; white would be good because it'll be snowy, but it's bad manners to wear white to weddings, isn't it?' she chattered away. 'I'll have to phone Fliss to check what she's wearing. Or maybe a clingy shift dress would be nice. Susie's older sister has this chiffon mini-dress. It sounds deadly.'

'You're not wearing anything clingy, white or chiffon,' Leonie said firmly. 'You're fourteen, Melanie, not eighteen. If I'd wanted you to turn into Lolita, I'd have named you Lolita.'

Mel groaned but took no notice. 'I have to look fab, Mum, that's all. Who knows who'll be there. All the movie stars have houses in Vail.'

'It's not Vail, is it?' her mother asked, horrified.

'Yes,' Mel said happily.

'God, we'll all have to dress up,' Leonie said, 'won't we, Abby? Can't let Ireland down by turning up like a gang of down-and-outs.'

Abby was very quiet with all this talk of outfits and clingy shift dresses. Poor thing was undoubtedly fed up thinking that Mel would look like a superstar while she melted into the background yet again, put in the shade by her much prettier sister.

'Are you not hungry?' Leonie asked Abby, noticing she was only picking at her dinner. 'You have been off your food lately.'

Abby shook her head quickly. 'I'm fine,' she said and began to load up a fork with chilli, as if to prove that she was hungry. 'Fine, really.'

Abby closed the bathroom door quietly. It didn't take her as long these days but it was still good to get in there quietly, before anyone realized how long she'd been gone and that she was actually in the bathroom. That had been a dodgy moment earlier when Mum had asked if she was feeling all right. Abby had been sure she'd managed to hide the fact that she'd been dieting. Over the past few weeks, she'd fed Penny surreptitiously under the table and had hidden bits of dinner in her napkin at mealtimes, anything to avoid eating too much. It had been so difficult and it hadn't worked. She was always hungry and she wasn't getting any thinner, she was sure of it. The ancient bathroom scales weren't exactly accurate so it was hard to check. Nobody ever used them any more. Mum just ate what she liked and didn't seem to worry about her figure; Mel was skinny no matter what she ate and Danny only cared about how muscular he was getting. He was always admiring his biceps in the hall mirror when he thought nobody was looking.

Abby's only other option for weighing herself was the speak-your-weight machine in Maguire's chemist and it was so hideously embarrassing to have to stand on that with all the other girls from school wandering in and out, buying nail varnish and spot concealer, that she never used it.

Either way, she wasn't thinner, despite all her efforts at avoiding chips and lasagne, her favourite. Dieting had seemed hopeless until she'd come up with the perfect way to lose weight. She'd read about it two weeks ago in one of her mother's magazines. You could eat all you wanted and still be thin. It hurt the back of her throat, though. But it would be worth it if it meant she became as thin as Mel. That was all she wanted really: to be beautiful like Mel, just for once, for Dad's wedding. Then she'd stop. Abby tied her hair back in a scrunchie so it wouldn't get in her way and leaned over the toilet bowl.

Only Penny's pleading eyes made Leonie grab her anorak and brave the hideous December weather. It had rained solidly for three days, great sheets of rain that defied any raincoat, scarf or hat. No matter how well wrapped up you were, the rain insinuated itself under some hem or other, soaking clothes until the wearer was wet and freezing.

The girls were cuddled up in the sitting room with the heating on full blast, pretending to revise for their Christmas exams but really watching a crucial episode of *Home and Away*. In the oven, a lemon and herb basted chicken was roasting succulently for dinner. Leonie's plan had been to read the paper and, exhausted after a busy day in the surgery, veg out until dinner. But Penny, who hadn't been walked for the entire water-logged three days, looked so mournful that Leonie finally gave in.

'If they gave Oscars to animals, you'd get one for sure,' she muttered as Penny sank to the floor in abject misery, resting her nose miserably on her fat golden paws. 'Nobody can look more depressed and abandoned than you. Skippy, Flipper and Lassie wouldn't have a hope.'

Wearing waterproof leggings, her big waterproof anorak and with a pink knitted hat under the hood, Leonie hoped she'd stay dry.

Penny danced around her mistress's feet, singing in her high-pitched canine voice, thrilled with herself. Shivering, Leonie trudged down the road, wondering if she was stone mad to be doing this.

It was ten days before Christmas and every house along her road had candles or small lights in their windows. The brightly coloured gleam of Christmas tree lights shone through windows and glass porches, and the atmosphere of cosy warmth inside made it feel all the more cold and wet outside. Leonie huddled into her anorak.

Even watching Penny delightedly bouncing in and out of the myriad enormous puddles didn't make her laugh the way it usually did. Ten minutes, that was all she was doing. After ten minutes on an evening like this, she'd be a drowned rat. Once they'd left the main road, she let Penny off the lead and followed slowly, hating the sensation of needles of rain hitting her face with ferocity. She was so cold.

Penny buried her nose in a puddle and whisked it up joyfully, splashing water over her laughing face. With her rainproof fur coat, designed by nature for all kinds of weather, she didn't mind the rain, although she always quivered when she was being hosed after a particularly dirty walk, as though the cold water she'd leapt into moments before was painfully cruel when it was coming out of a hose instead of a big puddle.

'You're lucky I love you, Penny,' Leonie grumbled to her gambolling dog, 'otherwise I'd never bring you out on an evening like this.'

She moved to the other side of the narrow road because it was more sheltered from the rain.

She was so busy trying to cover as much of her face as possible from the icy rain that she never even noticed the giant pothole beside the big forbidding black gates. As Penny bounced about the gates, sniffing excitedly and peeing, Leonie stepped on a cracked bit of asphalt, her foot in its wet wellington boot wobbled and she fell heavily, barely managing to protect her face with her hands. She was up to her knees in the water-logged pothole and her elbows ached from landing heavily on the road.

'Ouch!' she cried with pain, tears flooding her eyes. Penny instantly ran back and started barking. Feeling jarred and shocked by her fall, Leonie didn't know what to do for a moment. She could feel the water seeping into her clothes, and her knees and elbows stung, but shock meant she couldn't move.

'Are you all right?' said a masculine voice. She moved her head, only then noticing the car lights behind her. Suddenly someone was putting arms around her and helping her gently to her feet. She swayed in this person's embrace, feeling unsteady and shaky. Penny hopped anxiously from paw to paw, knowing something was wrong but not able to do anything.

'You're in no fit state to go anywhere,' the man said decisively. 'Come with me and we'll get you dried off and see whether you need the doctor.' He half-carried her over to a big Jeep with headlights blazing.

Normally, Leonie would have resisted and said she'd be fine, really, and that Penny couldn't get into the Jeep because she was filthy and wet, but she was too shocked and tearful to say anything. The man helped Leonie into the passenger seat as if she were light as a feather and then opened the back door for Penny to leap in.

Leonie closed her eyes wearily, still in shock. The pain in her elbows was getting worse. She felt them gingerly, sure she'd torn her anorak in the fall.

'Don't,' he advised, 'you'll just make it worse. Wait till we're home and then we'll have a look at you.' He paused. 'Maybe I should bring you straight to the doctor's house now.'

Leonie shook her head. 'No,' she mumbled tearfully, 'don't. I'm OK, really.'

Suddenly she realized where they were going: in the gates where she'd fallen. It was his house, he was the big bear of a man who she'd seen walking the two exuberant collies.

'It's my fault,' he said. 'That pothole's been getting bigger all the time and I should have done something about it.'

'It's the council's fault really,' Leonie said, trying to feel if her leggings were ripped.

The Jeep bounced along a winding drive and stopped at a house that Leonie had never seen before. A small wood hid it from prying eyes on the road, which was just as well, she realized, because if people could see it, they'd want to come in and gawp. It was beautiful: an elegant Palladian villa, perfectly proportioned with big windows and graceful columns on either side of the wide front door. Painted a soft honey colour, the house was surrounded by beech trees that nestled protectively around it.

'It's beautiful,' breathed Leonie, the pain receding somewhat as she gazed at the most lovely house she'd ever seen. 'I had no idea this was here.'

'Seclusion is one of the reasons I bought it,' the man said, getting out of the car.

He helped Leonie to hobble to the door.

'We shouldn't go in the front door, Penny's filthy,' she said suddenly.

'It's fine,' he said. 'The floors are all wood so there are no carpets to muddy.'

A cacophony of barking greeted them and two glossy black collies jumped on the man excitedly when he opened the door. They then spotted Penny and all three dogs went into a frenzy of excited tail-wagging, plumy tails competing with Penny's damp blonde one.

'They're males and they're very friendly,' he said. 'They never fight.'

'Good,' said Leonie, feeling sick. 'Do you have a cloakroom?' she asked weakly.

He quickly showed her to a small, pristine bathroom and, as soon as she'd locked the door, Leonie threw up. Shock and adrenaline, she diagnosed, as she sat shivering on the floor beside the toilet bowl, still in her wet, torn clothes. She sat there until the nausea passed, trying to breathe deeply. After a few minutes, she felt well enough to admire the room, which was decorated entirely in caramel Carrerra marble. It was very European and spotlessly clean. Even the white towel edged with caramel braid was as white as snow. She wished there was another bathroom in the cottage: if somebody fell into a pothole outside her house, she'd have to rush in with the bathroom cleaner and spend half an hour in there before she could let a stranger loose in it.

'Are you all right?' he said from outside the door.

'I am now.' She got to her feet and unlocked the door. There was no sign of the man, but the three dogs immediately tried to rush into the small room, tails wagging and tongues lolling happily.

'I've left some dry clothes outside,' he called.

She couldn't get the dogs to leave the bathroom. The collies wanted to sniff her, shoving inquisitive wet noses everywhere, and Penny wanted to be petted and be assured that she was still the favourite. Furry heads jostled for attention and they banged happily into Leonie, the sink and the loo, cannoning off each other.

Leonie obliged with petting for a minute, then picked up the bundle of clothes and tried to eject her admirers. 'Shoo,' she said, shoving the dogs out and trying to shut the door on three disgruntled wet noses.

He'd left her a white T-shirt, a huge grey woollen jumper, a pair of men's jeans and black socks. Gingerly, she peeled off her wet things, wincing with pain as she pulled off her anorak, which had a big rip in one elbow. Amazingly, she wasn't cut anywhere, although her elbows were already bruising and there was an ugly dark mark on one of her legs where she'd banged her shin painfully on the asphalt.

Everything ached, but Leonie was so relieved that she hadn't cut herself to ribbons that she didn't mind. Nothing was broken, although she knew she'd be stiff and sore for a few days.

Just as well I'm not planning on wearing a little flirty outfit to Ray's wedding, she told herself, looking at the hideous purple colour of one elbow. She used the towel to dry her hair and wipe the mud from her face and neck. When she was finished, she left it and her clothes in a neat pile. She'd bring it home and wash it: she couldn't leave it here filthy.

The dogs whirled around her when she opened the door again and she followed them through the parquet-floored hall, down a half-flight of stairs into the kitchen. All wooden flooring and old wooden units, it was a warm, friendly room with two comfy dog baskets beside an ancient, squashy russet couch in one corner. He was standing near the sink and didn't turn round when she spoke.

'Thanks for the clothes.'

'How are you? Do you want to go to the doctor?' he said, still not turning round.

'No, I'm all right. Sore though, and my career as a photographic model is finished, obviously,' she joked. 'I look like I've done a few rounds in the ring with Mike Tyson.'

He turned with a half-smile on his face. It was the first time she'd got a proper look at him. He was perhaps ten years older than her with a shock of dark auburn curly hair that was streaked with grey and a bushy beard to match. A huge man well over six foot, he had broad shoulders yet his clothes hung from them, as if he'd lost a lot of weight from his big frame. His face was curiously hollowed, dark russet eyebrows beetling across opaque, hooded eyes. The smile lifted his face miraculously, made him almost handsome: without it, his expression was cold and grim.

'I've got some painkillers, if you want them,' he offered. 'I got them for my face,' he added bluntly.

Leonie looked at him. She could see the scars on one side of his face, dark and angry purple spreading from his jaw up to his cheekbone yet hidden by the thick bushy beard. They were like marks from a fire, she thought. He kept looking at her, as if daring her to look away. But Leonie was made of sterner stuff. She'd seen animals hurt in fires, their skin a mass of cooked flesh and their agonized eyes begging for the pain to disappear.

It was torture to look at. She was much better coping with injured people than injured animals.

'You're healing well,' she said in a matter-of-fact tone. 'Was it a fire?'

'Yes,' he said, as if stunned that she'd mentioned it at all. 'Two years ago.'

She held out her hand. 'I better introduce myself. I'm Leonie Delaney and this is Penny.'

Penny, stretched happily out in one of the collie's baskets, wagged her tail at the mention of her name.

'I better be going,' Leonie said, 'my two daughters are at home waiting for dinner and, although they probably wouldn't miss me if I disappeared, I better get home to them.'

'I made you a hot whiskey,' he said. 'I thought it would help. They help me. I don't know if it's advisable to have one with painkillers or not, but I daresay it won't kill you.'

'I'm a glutton for drugs and alcohol,' Leonie said wryly, sitting down on the couch where she was immediately surrounded by dogs. 'I'll stay for one whiskey.'

She didn't know why she'd agreed to stay. She must be mad. This guy was obviously shy and anti-social. He was also blunt and very edgy, as if he wasn't used to company and felt uncomfortable having someone in his home. And he was utterly hung up about his injuries. He hadn't even told her his name . . .

'I'm Doug Mansell,' he said, handing her a glass wrapped in some paper towels. 'This is very hot and quite strong.'

'You mean I'll be so plastered after this that I'll fall back into the pothole on my way out,' she remarked, taking the glass.

He laughed, a deep, hoarse laugh that sounded as if it hadn't had a good airing in months. 'I promise to drive you,' he said. 'I also promise to get that hole filled in. Can't have the neighbours killing themselves outside my property.'

He sat on one of the kitchen chairs, a few feet away from her, so that she couldn't see the scarred right-hand side of his face. The collies sat either side of him, arching their heads back for him to pet them. He had huge hands, she noticed as he fondled the dogs. They quivered ecstatically under his touch, obviously adoring him.

She remembered seeing him walking the dogs and thinking that he looked like the gruff sort who'd keep them in a shed and never let them inside the house or call them honey-bunnies. Grinning, she realized that she'd been as wrong as you could be. They clearly had the run of the house and their baskets were stuffed with dog toys. Although she still couldn't see Doug being the sort of man who went in for cute pet names.

'What are they called?' she asked.

'Jasper,' he said, nodding to the dog with the silky, all-black coat, 'and Alfie,' petting the one with white socks and a white blaze on his chest. 'Alfie is Jasper's son. He's two and Alfie is eight.'

They talked about dogs for a time, while Leonie sat back and drank her hot whiskey.

'The only problem with dogs is having to walk them when it's raining and freezing,' Leonie remarked, petting Penny's silky ears. She drained her glass.

'Let me get you another one,' Doug said.

'No, it's OK. You've done your good Samaritan bit,' she said. 'I don't want to intrude any longer.'

'You're not intruding,' he said abruptly. 'I'm not used to having visitors; turned into a bit of a hermit, really. But it's been nice talking to you.'

'Oh.' She sat back and let him take her glass.

'I think I'll join you,' he added.

'You must come to dinner some night,' Leonie found herself saying. 'I only live over the road and you'd like the kids. It's bad to turn into a hermit.'

'It's your turn to be the good Samaritan, is it?' he said caustically.

'I'm only offering dinner, not emergency rescue services,' she replied easily. 'And my humble abode isn't a patch on your palace, so I can understand if you say no.' She got up to go.

'I'm sorry,' he looked humble. 'I didn't mean it like that. It's just . . . I've forgotten how to behave in polite society,' he said. 'Forgive me. Please stay. I'll show you round. I'm sure you'd like to see the rest of the house, although it's no palace, I promise.'

Leonie treated Doug to the sort of don't-mess-with-me look that Danny, Mel and Abby were familiar with and would have instantly recognized as teasing. 'Bribing me on the grounds that women are terminally nosy and can't resist a sneaky glimpse of other people's houses, eh?'

He nodded.

'It's a deal.'

Clutching her second hot whiskey, Leonie followed the procession of Doug and dogs around the downstairs. It was a truly beautiful house, but somehow unloved. Graceful, airy rooms with large windows, exquisite marble fireplaces and cornices picked out in subtle gold leaf looked lonely without any homely clutter.

'I pretty much live in the kitchen,' Doug confessed, as they trailed from one cold room to another, 'and in my studio. I'm a painter.'

'It's a lovely house,' Leonie said truthfully, but she'd have liked it much better if there'd been plants spilling out of tubs or newspapers flung carelessly on the low tables. It was like a museum exhibit: a perfect recreation of a regency villa yet with only paying guests passing through, gazing at the huge white couches and the armchairs upholstered in pretty striped fabrics, yet never actually sitting in them. There were no paintings anywhere. She decided that Doug was so reclusive he didn't like anybody seeing his work.

'You live in one of the cottages on the main road, don't you?' Doug said, when they returned to the kitchen after their tour of the ground floor.

'It's about an eighth of the size of this house and there isn't a spare inch of it that isn't given over to teenage clutter, empty crisp wrappers and videos that haven't gone back to the shop yet,' she said. 'You obviously like the minimalist look; you'd hate my house.'

'I don't like the minimalist look, as a matter of fact,' Doug remarked. 'I bought this place as an investment. I didn't intend to live here. The . . .' he paused, 'the accident changed my mind about that. It's secluded enough to be suitable. I just never did anything with the rest of it when I moved in. I haven't been in the mood for making it more homely.'

'Buying stuff for a house can be a pain in the neck,' Leonie agreed, deliberately misunderstanding what he was implying. If Doug thought he was too hideous to be seen out and that was why he hadn't been shopping, that was his problem. She wasn't going to go along with it.

He shot her an amused glance. 'When is this Samaritan's dinner on, then?' he enquired. 'As I haven't met any of the neighbours up to now, I may as well start with your family.'

'I'll have to check their diaries,' she said. 'Boring old mother is always in, but the three of them are always out. I'll get back to you. I better go home,' she added. 'Doubtless the girls won't have missed me yet, but in case they are wondering where I am, I should push off.'

'I'll drive you,' Doug said. 'It's still raining and you'll be drenched.'

They drove in silence until Leonie told Doug which house to stop outside.

'See you soon,' she said, opening the door. 'I meant it about dinner. No hassle, just a neighbourly evening.'

'I'd like that. I hate people asking me things,' he said awkwardly, 'and you haven't.'

Leonie shrugged. 'I hate that too. People like *placing* you,' she said ruefully. 'You know: are you married, single, divorced, interested in golf, whatever. As a divorced mother, I'm fed up to the back teeth of nosy people trying to figure out where I fit into the grand scheme of things, if I've got a boyfriend, why my marriage ended, all sorts of personal stuff. As an attractive, apparently single man living in isolated splendour you would be a five-course banquet for all the local gossips. I am not one of them, so if you want an uncomplicated dinner with us, you're welcome to take pot-luck any time. And I won't be hitting on you, either.'

He laughed again. 'You're refreshingly frank and an awful liar at the same time, Leonie. I can't imagine anyone hitting on me ever again.'

'Nonsense,' she said brusquely. 'You're not Quasimodo, you know. Pity is short on the list in my house. I'm offering food not counselling, but why don't you roll up with some red roses and let's really get the locals talking?'

He was still grinning when he drove off. A nice man, Leonie thought, as she and Penny ran up to the cottage front door. But he was deeply scarred both on the outside and the inside. She wondered what had happened to make him so suspicious and hostile. It was more than the accident, she was sure of it. A woman, definitely. Someone who hadn't been able to cope with a fire survivor who'd become introspective and untrusting.

Telling herself to stop trying to analyse people, she stuck her key in the lock. Her clothes were dry and she didn't feel like trudging round to the back door, having to bypass all the dripping evergreen bushes.

The telly was blaring and the smell of burned chicken filled the house.

'Girls,' called Leonie mildly, 'didn't you smell anything?' Anaesthetized after two hot whiskeys and a Ponstan, she couldn't summon up the energy to get angry.

'Oh er, we forgot,' said Mel shamefacedly, sniffing the air in the kitchen. 'Sorry. Mum, what *are* you wearing?' she added, finally noticing that her mother was clad in unfamiliar and far too big men's clothes.

'I was abducted by aliens crossing the road and they took me to their planet, performed experiments on me and then sent me back in these clothes,' Leonie dead-panned.

'Oh, Mum, what are you like?' Mel rolled her eyes to heaven.

'What happened?' Abby demanded.

'I fell into a pothole down the road,' Leonie began, and explained the whole thing. 'It's lucky I wasn't really abducted by aliens because you pair wouldn't even notice. I said I was only going out for ten minutes and I've been gone an hour and fifteen minutes. I could have been raped and murdered and you two would just change the channel and start watching *Coronation Street*, completely ignoring the sounds of wailing police sirens in the background!'

'We were watching something good on TV,' shrugged Abby.

'What are we going to do about dinner?' Leonie wondered aloud as she peered into the fridge. The chicken, dried up like it had been charcoaling in a kiln all day, sat on the worktop. Even Penny, who usually slavered over any food left out, turned her head away in disgust.

'I'm not hungry,' Abby said quickly.

'Me neither,' Mel said.

'Toasted cheese sandwiches, then,' Leonie said decisively. 'And you two can make them.'

Two days later, she met Doug as she trudged along past his house in the late afternoon, walking Penny in yet another downpour. Even the holly bushes slumped miserably in the rain, prickly leaves cast down. There were no bushes with berries left: festive locals had denuded all the berry-bearing bushes for Christmas decorations.

'Nice weather for ducks,' Doug said, stopping the Jeep beside her. 'When are you having the grand dinner?'

'Tonight, if it suits you,' Leonie replied, peering up at him from under her sopping baseball hat. 'I've done my pre-Christmas grocery shopping and the freezer is full. You can have lasagne, mushroom and chicken pasta or chilli.'

'Lasagne, definitely,' Doug said.

'I'll see you at seven,' she said and trudged on, secretly pleased. It was nice to have a new friend and she felt a certain *frisson* that Doug had befriended her when he'd blatantly ignored all attempts at camaraderie from his other neighbours. Subtle questioning of the woman next door had revealed that, in his eighteen months in the area, Doug had rudely slammed the door on the outraged emissaries of the Best-Kept Village group and he'd told the curate to 'bugger off' when he'd bicycled up with the Easter dues envelope.

'Really?' said Leonie, enthralled.

'Why are you asking?' enquired her neighbour.

'No reason, I just wondered who lived in that house,' Leonie lied blandly. 'What does he do, anyway?'

'Something arty-farty,' sniffed the neighbour. 'Painter or some such. Wouldn't hurt him to paint those gates, if he's so good with a paintbrush. They're peeling something rotten and it's letting the whole tone of the neighbourhood drop.'

As she bustled around getting ready for dinner, Leonie wondered about Doug's career. She'd never heard of him, but then, she liked watercolours of roses and baskets of fruit, things that the artistically inclined Abby thought were naff.

She defrosted a big lasagne, made a crisp, green salad, put baked potatoes in the slow cooker and bustled around tidying the house. After half an hour, she realized it was a waste of time. The house was too small to contain four people, one dog, one cat and a hamster, and remain even vaguely minimalist. Remaining tidy would be a miracle. At least it was clean.

She began to change from her old leggings and sweatshirt into something a bit glammer, when she stopped herself.

Poor Doug was obviously traumatized over a woman and would run a mile if he spotted her all tarted up and reeking of Samsara. She'd promised she wouldn't hit on him and even though that was the last thing on her mind, because he wasn't her type in a million years and she was damn sure she wasn't *his,* he'd be bound to suspect it if she dolled herself up.

So she brushed her hair, put on a slick of lipstick and exchanged her old sweatshirt and leggings for a baggy denim shirt and cotton skirt instead of the silky purple blouse and velvet pants she'd planned to wear. Now, she thought, staring at herself in the mirror, nobody could accuse her of setting her cap at Doug. With her face almost devoid of make-up, except for eyeliner and mascara, she looked very natural. Not her femme fatale, Mata-Hari of the make-up counter self. She settled on a gentle squirt of Body Shop vanilla perfume as an alternative to overpowering Samsara, and then went back to the kitchen to check on dinner.

It was nearly half seven before Doug arrived. Danny had given up watching television with the twins in order to moan at intervals about how ravenous he was and how it was bad for your body to be denied food for so long.

'You had a pizza three hours ago, you human dustbin,' his mother replied crushingly. 'You'll just have to wait until Doug arrives.'

'Did you buy crisps?' Danny demanded, opening cupboard doors and banging them shut in his attempts to find something edible.

'Doug's here,' announced Mel, bringing him into the kitchen. He was carrying two bottles of wine. 'Can I have wine, Mum?' asked Mel. 'It is nearly Christmas.'

'Did you buy beer?' demanded Danny, having waved hello at Doug and now searching the bottom cupboards systematically for Budweiser.

'I have hidden all the goodies because you know you'll wolf it all down in one go and I am not shopping again before Christmas. And, yes, there is beer,' Leonie said, rolling her eyes. Everything yummy was hidden at the back of the cupboard which held Penny's dog food. They'd never think of looking for it there. That way, she could magic chocolate Kimberlys out of nowhere when the kids thought everything nice was gone. 'Bet you're sorry you came,' she said to Doug.

'Not at all,' he smiled, sitting down at the table and petting a delighted Penny. 'If you give me a corkscrew, I'll do the wine.'

Nobody had looked at his face or paid him much attention at all, Leonie realized, which was probably just what he needed.

Dinner was great fun. Buoyed up by a glass of wine, Mel and Abby were chatty and giggly. Danny clearly enjoyed having another man at the dinner table, muttering about how he felt outnumbered normally. 'Even the dog is a female!' he groaned.

They all ate lots of lasagne, and Doug even asked for seconds.

There was only one sticky moment when Mel looked wonderingly at Doug and said, 'Your poor face, does it hurt?'

Leonie felt her stomach disappear. But Doug wasn't upset by the ingenuous question.

'Not any more,' he said. 'Plastic surgery is next on the list, but I don't think I want to go through with it.'

'I would, I'd love plastic surgery,' said Mel artlessly, eyes shining. 'I'd have my boobs done.'

'What boobs?' demanded Danny. 'You have to have some in the first place to have them done.'

'Shut up, smart arse,' Mel retorted. 'That's why you'll never need brain surgery, not having any brains to start with.'

Leonie was relieved to see the corners of Doug's mouth lifting.

After dinner, Abby announced that she wasn't studying because there was only one more Christmas exam left and it was art, so no studying was required. 'Let's get a video,' she said eagerly.

Leonie didn't think that Doug would be impressed by that idea and half-expected him to say he was going home. Instead, he surprised her by offering to drive the girls to the video shop.

'I better come too,' Danny said, 'in case you pair get some romantic shit.'

'Danny!' said Leonie. 'Language.'

'Sorry, some romantic rubbish,' he corrected himself.

The four of them came back with a comedy, proof that a truce had been reached because Danny and the twins never agreed on any sort of video. Mel made coffee while Abby broke open a tub of ice cream and they all had dessert while watching the film.

Abby and Doug began discussing art history quietly and Leonie pretended not to notice. If he wanted to discuss what he did for a living, he would. She certainly wouldn't pressurize him.

It was a relaxing, enjoyable evening. When the film was over, Leonie was surprised to find that it was nearly eleven o'clock.

'Come again,' Danny said as Doug put on his coat.

'Yeah,' said the twins enthusiastically.

'I had a nice time,' Doug remarked as Leonie saw him out.

'Evidence that not all neighbours are inquisitive busybodies who spend their lives peering out from behind their net curtains,' Leonie laughed. 'We must do it again. See you, bye.'

'He's a painter,' Abby announced. 'He's going to show me his studio.'

'Really?' Leonie said, with what she felt was Oscar-winning astonishment.

'He's a cool guy,' Danny said as he passed her on his way into the kitchen for refuelling. 'D'you fancy him?'

In response, his mother slapped his behind. 'No you big lump, I don't fancy him. I reckon he's a bit lonely and I thought it'd be nice to have him over for dinner, that's all. You can be friends with someone without it being romantic, you know.'

'Just wondering, that's all.'

It would be so simple if she did fancy someone like Doug, Leonie thought as she tidied away the dishes. Imagine how handy it would be to date the man who lived around the corner. But Doug, though a decent guy, really wasn't her type. Too moody and difficult to live with, she felt. And she hated men with red hair. Although his was more tawny red, the colour of darkening beech leaves. He'd been great tonight because he enjoyed the relaxed family atmosphere, but she reckoned he'd be a nightmare in a relationship: tense, uptight and very high-maintenance. Not her type at all. Leonie wanted a man who lived life with passion and vigour, someone who would grab her in a giant bear hug every morning, not one who looked as if he could be grumpy and who had locked himself away like a prisoner in a fairytale because he couldn't face the world.

CHAPTER SIXTEEN

'We deserve a treat,' Hannah had said once she'd finally convinced the other two to come with her to the hairdresser. 'We've been working so hard and we have to look nice for Christmas. You've got that big party,' she reminded Emma of Kirsten's big New Year event which was hanging over her like a sledgehammer, 'and you've got the wedding,' she said to Leonie, who hadn't forgotten either.

And I, thought Hannah silently, have a wonderful Christmas with the handsome, soon-to-be-a-big-BBC-star Felix Andretti. Of course, Felix hadn't finalized their plans yet. He was so forgetful, he'd forget his beautiful head if it wasn't stuck on.

'A revamp,' she told the others. 'That's what we need.'

Leonie had been getting her hair cut in the same small hairdresser's for years. 'Cheap and cheerful,' she admitted, touching the ends of her golden hair, which were dry as kindling from two decades of home dyeing in an attempt to look like the Nordic blondes on the hair-colour box. 'It'd be nice to look slightly different for the wedding,' she added. Her hair had been the same for aeons: shoulder-length, curly and more than a little wild. 'No hairdresser can tame this.'

Emma wasn't too keen on having anything done. The long, silky strands had hung poker straight around her face for years, concealing her ears and falling over her eyes. 'I like my hair like this,' she said defensively. 'It camouflages my nose.' Her father had told her that when she'd been small. Kirsten, the apple of his eye, had never needed to grow her fringe long to conceal a nose like Concorde.

'You'd swear you had a nose like an elephant,' Hannah said briskly. 'Honestly, you've a nice nose: distinctive, strong. Why hide it? You don't want one of those retroussé little things you see on insipid girls, do you?'

'Yes,' laughed Emma, 'I do. You weren't born with a conk like mine.'

'I'm not doing too badly,' Hannah retorted, rubbing her own slightly beaky nose with a slim finger. 'But I use mine for sniffing out wickedness in the office. It's especially useful for when Gillian is bullshitting me about the amount of work she's supposed to have done.'

'What are you getting done?' Leonie asked her.

'The chop,' Hannah answered. 'I've worn it long for years because it's handy to tie it back, but I'm ready for a change. I want it cut to my shoulders with some reddish brown lowlights put in.'

'Get you!' Leonie said. 'Getting ready for the BAFTAs, are you?'

Hannah grinned infectiously. 'No, the Oscars!'

Leonie had expected the colourist in a trendy hairdresser to be equally trendy. She'd had visions of nose piercings, ultra-hip clothes and hair that had been sliced, chopped and treated with the latest cutting-edge gels to make it fashionably messy. Instead, the colourist turned out to be a pregnant woman in her thirties who wore black dungarees with a hot pink T-shirt, and had dark, bobbed hair as shiny as glass. Her only piercings were small pearl studs, and she wouldn't have been out of place behind the maths teacher's desk at a parent/teacher meeting. Her name was Nicky and as she ran her fingers through Leonie's bleached mop in a professional manner, she said: 'You tell me what you would like me to do and I'll tell you what I think.'

Leonie looked at herself critically in the mirror. Heavily made-up in preparation for the onslaught of harsh hairdresser lights and the big, cruel mirrors, Leonie thought she'd looked quite reasonable when she'd left the house. Somehow, now, she merely looked over made-up, tarty almost. Her hair was awful, she realized in desperation. Bottle-blonde meets Amsterdam's red-light district with a detour into a Soho sex shop.

'I don't know, Nicky,' she said sadly. 'It's terrible. I've been dyeing it myself for years and the ends are dry, over-bleached and well . . .' she sighed, 'a mess. Maybe I'm too old to be blonde.'

'Nonsense.' Nicky was brisk. 'The colour's wrong for you; you need a more subtle blonde to tone in with your skin. Skin fades as we get older, so you've got to go for a more toned-down hair colour. What you need are lots of tawny browns to break up the golden blonde, with some pale golds running through it. You may have to rethink the make-up too,' she said appraisingly. 'Heavy eyeliner will be too strong for your new look.'

'You think so?' Leonie was unsure. 'I've always done it this way. My eyes are so indistinct without kohl and lots of mascara.'

'Nonsense, you've beautiful eyes. I've never seen anyone with such blue eyes,' Nicky said earnestly. 'While you're under the drier waiting for the colour to take, I'll get one of the girls from the beauty salon upstairs to come down and do your eyes for you. You won't believe it when I've finished with you. Now, do you want tea or coffee?'

Emma, who was only having her hair cut, was finished first.

'What do you think?' she asked Leonie anxiously, angling her head in the mirror to look at her new haircut from every angle. The long strands which had hidden her amber-flecked eyes had been cut back and, although Emma had only allowed two inches to be cut from the longest layers, the whole effect was very different. You could see Emma's sweet, patient face properly and she didn't need to pull strands of hair out of her eyes any more. She looked older without the schoolgirl hair, although you'd still never guess she was thirty-one.

'It's fantastic!' Leonie said warmly.

Hannah was finished next. Her once-long hair had been cut to shoulder level and low-lighted, so that cinnamon and chocolatey strands rippled through her own dark brown colour. Glossy and bouncy, it swung as she walked, framing her face elegantly. Her full lips glistened with bronze gloss and she looked like a supermodel.

'Get you,' said Leonie, feeling very ugly in comparison, as her hair was now adorned with scores of tinfoil flaps which looked like some sort of medieval headdress perched on her head.

The new colours made Hannah's almond-shaped eyes even more striking and matched the smattering of amber freckles across her cheeks.

'Do you think it's all right?' she asked, running her fingers through the glossy strands apprehensively.

'Fantastic,' Leonie said. 'And if you wonder will Felix love it, he'd want to be mad not to.'

Emma and Hannah arranged to come back in an hour.

'If my hair isn't cooked by then, it'll never be done,' Leonie said gloomily.

They left and Leonie returned to her magazines. Fed up with looking at impossibly gorgeous people in the social columns of *Tatler*, she got her hands on a tattered *Hello!* Everyone in that was stunning, too. There had to be scope for an 'Ordinary People's Weekly', Leonie felt. A magazine with normal people in it, normal people with big backsides, blocked pores and clothes that looked as if they'd been purchased in the 'two-blouses-for-fifteen-quid' section of a chain store and put on in the dark.

She was marginally cheered up when the beautician arrived and turned out to be a pretty but plump girl who was bursting out of her white beautician's dress.

'Oh, you've lovely skin,' cooed the girl in a lilting Cork accent. 'And your eyes are amazing. I've just the colour for you.'

It was a shock to see her heavy kohl and pancake foundation being removed. Leonie closed her eyes and reminded herself that she could run into the nearest pub loo when she left the hairdresser's and reapply her heavy-lidded glory.

Only she didn't need to. When she opened her eyes, the face that greeted her looked like a stranger. Gone was the heavy smoky kohl and the lipstick line that had circled her mouth since she'd been twenty. In its place was a subtle mélange of golds and fawns. Her eyes stood out, thanks to beautiful shading and a slender line that opened them up. Her usual sooty black mascara had been replaced with rich brown and her mouth was a full pout thanks to a caramel shade with no visible liner.

'Gosh,' was all she could think of to say.

'It'll be better when the tinfoil is gone,' said the beautician sagely.

When the tinfoil was gone, Leonie thought her hair looked quite dark.

'It's still wet,' said Nicky comfortingly. 'Wait till it's dry. You won't recognize yourself. You'll look amazing.'

And she did. After half an hour of expert blowdrying, the golden brassy colour had vanished and in its place was a mop of wavy hair, a mass of honeys, pale golds and hazel browns. Leonie touched it in wonder. She looked like another version of herself, like the rich, elegant twin of her old brassy self. All she needed now was a wardrobe of subtle cashmere clothes, some discreet but expensive jewellery and a BMW, and she'd be a lady who lunched. She grinned at her reflection.

'Never mind my friends not recognizing me, I don't think my kids will!' she joked.

CHAPTER SEVENTEEN

Hannah laughed loudest and smiled the most at the Dwyer, Dwyer & James staff Christmas party in McCormack's. She roared with laughter when the stripping vicar turned up as a surprise for Gillian because it was her birthday the day after Christmas, and when the vicar was down to his boxer shorts and looking for somebody else to kiss, Hannah gave him a cheeky grin and earned herself a big hug. Nobody watching her glowing face lit up with mirth would have imagined that, inside, Hannah felt about as festive as a turkey in a poultry farm.

'Goodness, what are we doing here?' gasped Donna at half ten, throwing herself down on the banquette beside Hannah after they'd queued for half an hour to go to the ladies because the pub was jammed with festive drinkers.

'Yes, we're mad,' Hannah agreed, doing her best to make her eyes sparkle happily as she said it. It would be too, too humiliating to admit to Donna that once again Felix had let her down. 'I've still got a load of Christmas shopping to do and I don't fancy getting up first thing in the morning to brave the city-centre shops. I know I should be home in bed but I feel like having fun.'

'Buying presents on Christmas Eve is murder,' agreed Donna, 'especially with a hangover. I've got everything already, thankfully. Believe me, it's so much harder when you've got kids to think about. You daren't leave buying Santa's presents until Christmas Eve in case there's been a run on Barbie's pony or whatever. Tania would go berserk if Santa didn't come up trumps.'

Hannah nodded. She'd lied about the Christmas shopping as she'd already bought presents for everyone she needed to buy for. She'd been holding off buying anything for Felix because she wanted to buy him something utterly perfect. Now there was no point going near the shops, but it sounded so sad and single to say so.

'What are you up to for the day, anyhow?' asked Donna, pouring tonic into her vodka. 'I'm so glad I'm staying at home this year. Every Christmas we trek to my mother's in Letterkenny. This year, I told them all to come to us. The house will be full, mind you, but it'll be fun. I get nightmares at the thought of cooking for ten!'

Hannah grinned. 'I can't see you getting nightmares at anything so simple,' she joked. Donna was one of the most organized people she knew and probably had the entire dinner pre-cooked and already frozen, waiting to be defrosted half an hour before the meal was due to begin.

'My kitchen is so small it's hardly designed for large-scale catering,' protested Donna. 'What about you? Staying here with the glorious Felix, or do you go home to the West?'

For a millisecond, Hannah considered her options. She *could* sit at home, eating a solitary Christmas dinner and pleasing herself about what to watch on the box, fortifying her spirit with plenty of wine. With no Felix to share it all with, she couldn't face cooking the pheasant she'd bought, and what would be the point of decorating the table with fat beeswax candles, gleaming holly sprigs and intricately tied red and gold ribbons if there was nobody to admire her efforts? Or she could do what had seemed unthinkable before – go home to Connemara with her tail between her legs. Her mother hadn't given up asking Hannah to come home for Christmas even though she'd been absent for the past two years. Hannah had claimed she was working in the hotel the previous year, the year she'd been Harry-less and embarrassed by the fact. Her family all knew Harry and, even if they weren't incredibly impressed by him, having him was better than being without him. Everyone she'd grown up with at home was now married with kids, so Christmas was like a parade of accomplishments from the returning thirty-somethings. Outside the church on Christmas Day was reminiscent of a beauty pageant with proud locals showing off their spouses and kids. Hannah had allowed herself to dream of future Christmases when she'd roll up with the famous Felix Andretti and really get people talking. So much for that idea.

In late November, she'd told her mother she had plans for the holidays. Which had been true at the time. She'd planned a gloriously romantic idyll with Felix, a time where they could take long walks in the icy afternoons after spending sensuous mornings in bed giggling over *Willie Wonka* and watching re-runs of *Little House on the Prairie*. They wouldn't see anybody or go to any parties: it would just be the two of them on their own. Sheer bliss. Felix had put the kibosh on this darling plan by saying point-blank that he was going home to his mother in Birmingham. He hadn't invited Hannah or even appeared to consider that she might be hurt by being left out of his festive arrangements.

'Family problems,' he'd said blandly on the phone, as if that absolved him from having to think about anything or anyone else. 'I'll call you when I get there.'

But he hadn't. Left to simmer in her own misery, Hannah decided that she'd just joined the ranks of Felix's ex-girlfriends, another one to add to the not-so-select band of those who hated him. Three days had elapsed since that final phone call and she'd retreated into herself in depression. She couldn't bear to think about him, to remember the wonderful times they'd shared. It was so painful, like having a tooth extracted without an anaesthetic. Felix had been the one. She was sure of that. But it now appeared that while he was her one, she wasn't *his*.

More numb than she'd been at any time since Harry had left, she existed on automatic pilot and tried to stop herself wondering why she picked men who dumped on her and then dumped her. That was a no-go area, one for another day, another century, perhaps. Hannah didn't want to look into her subconscious and work out what was wrong with her. She wanted to get incredibly drunk instead, and the office party was providing a pretty good opportunity for this.

She threw her eyes to heaven at Donna's enquiry about her Christmas plans. Hannah's current Christmas arrangements were non-existent. Unless . . .

'Going home to the West, I'm afraid. Felix is furious with me because he wanted us both to visit his mother, but I promised *my* mother last year that I'd be there this time . . .' Hannah broke off and sighed deeply to give Donna the impression that being a good and dutiful daughter was tough but that Hannah simply had no option. 'I'll miss him but I couldn't let Mum down. My brother, my sister-in-law and their little boy are going to be away for Christmas so my parents will be on their own. Anyway, Felix and I will see each other for New Year,' she lied. Who knew what Felix was up to for New Year? Probably bungee-jumping from some Australian bridge or something equally wild. Maybe partying with honey-skinned models turned actresses who longed to hang out with real actors. Whatever he was doing, he hadn't discussed it with Hannah.

'You deserve a medal!' exclaimed Donna. 'If it was me, I think Felix's charms would win and I'd be telling my poor mother she'd have to live without me for one more year.' Donna laughed. 'You're a hell of a woman, Hannah Campbell. Your word is certainly your bond.'

'I know, I'm a saint.' Hannah drained her drink, hating herself for lying to someone as good and kind as Donna. 'I'm going to brave the bar again. Do you want another?'

'Go on,' Donna groaned. 'Just one more and then make me go home, please!'

'I promise,' grinned Hannah.

She felt almost happy, bizarrely enough, now that she'd decided to go home for Christmas. Lolling around in misery since Felix had delivered his bombshell three days previously, Hannah hadn't been able to manifest any enthusiasm in anything. She'd felt adrift, unmoored. But with the notion of going to her home in Connemara, she felt like a part of something again. She wasn't a lonely woman destined to a solitary existence of Lean Cuisines, single pots of creamed rice and the television guide. She was Hannah Campbell, a person with roots and a family, even if she didn't see them a great deal. It was as if a punishing weight had been lifted from her and she bounced up to the bar, insinuating herself into the anxious crowd yelling for drinks before closing time kicked in.

A couple of good-looking guys in rugby shirts smiled at the pretty woman with the glittering eyes and the provocative smile on her face. Hannah had worn a silky pewter-grey blouse to the pub and she'd deliberately unbuttoned it so the top of her black lacy bra was just barely visible. Subtle but sexy as hell. It had made her feel better to dress up.

'Go ahead, love,' said one of the rugby blokes, making a space where Hannah could squeeze past him and get nearer to the bar.

'Thanks,' she breathed, giving him a blast of unrestrained Hannah. If Felix didn't want her, there was no reason not to flirt with other men. Her confidence needed a lift, she decided firmly.

'Maybe I can buy you a drink,' he said hopefully.

Hannah shot him a wicked glance. 'I don't see why not,' she said.

'I see you're enjoying yourself,' said a dry voice. She looked around to find the big figure of David James looming over her. Still in his suit from the office, he looked out of place among the casually dressed and very merry gang in the pub. His grey eyes were tired and more crinkled up than ever, giving him a rumpled bloodhound look.

'Where did you spring out of?' she asked, mildly discomfited to be found flirting with strangers when she was supposed to be deeply in love with Felix.

'I've been working late and dropped in for half an hour,' he replied, eyes taking in her flushed face, the coral lipstick that was smudged off her full lips and the silky blouse with three buttons open.

'So, what are you having, love?' asked Mr Rugby Shirt.

'Nothing,' said David coldly. 'She's with me.'

'Suit yourself,' Mr Rugby Shirt said huffily to Hannah.

Her colour ripened to that of a peony, bright red and embarrassed.

'I thought perhaps you needed rescuing,' David said pointedly.

'No, I didn't,' she hissed, wriggling out of the throng for the bar.

He followed her and grabbed her by the shoulder, turning her round to face him.

'I'm sorry, Hannah,' he apologized. 'I saw that guy chatting you up and I thought you wouldn't like it . . .'

'David, I'm sick of people taking it upon themselves to know what I'd like and what I wouldn't like,' she said wearily. 'I'm going home. Have a nice Christmas.'

She turned and left, stopping only to pick up her coat and wave bye at an astonished Donna. As she pushed her way out of the pub, she could feel David's eyes upon her and knew they were probably hurt by her curt behaviour. But she hadn't been able to help it. An entire evening pretending to be happy and smiling until her jaw ached had been too much for any woman to bear. She'd apologize to David after Christmas. He'd been so good to her since she'd taken over from Donna that day. He had even said he'd train her in as a junior agent in January, which was an incredible opportunity. Hannah knew she should be delighted at this chance, but she felt depressed and low. Bloody Felix.

Early the next morning, she stopped in Rathmines long enough to buy edible goodies, booze, a few presents from Dunnes and a big bottle of ludicrously expensive perfume for her mother, before taking the road west. At ten on Christmas Eve morning, the roads were still busy but the line of traffic that would soon clog up all the main routes out of the city hadn't yet materialized.

Fortified with toffees and with the radio blaring carols, Hannah drove west, ignoring the steadily falling rain that made travelling such a pain. She amused herself by listening first to a radio play and then a current-affairs programme where the guests analysed what had been happening politically during the year. Talk radio was better than music, she'd discovered. It was too painful to listen to chart music that she'd heard with Felix. The same thing had happened to her when she'd split up with Harry. A fan of opera, he'd often played his precious Maria Callas records when they'd been making love. Even now, Hannah couldn't listen to a single bar of an opera on the radio without getting a lump in her throat and having to change the channel immediately. Those tragic throaty sounds were all too tied up with loss and misery in her mind; the loss of Harry, the loss of Felix. Was her life always going to be about losing things?

Four hours later, it was still raining. The scenery had changed utterly. Houses were few and far between on the winding Clifden road once she'd passed the postcard-pretty village of Oughterard with its pastel-coloured houses. Prettiness gave way to the desolate, angry beauty of the inhospitable grey mountains which loomed out of the mist on her right. The rolling foothills were crisscrossed by drystone walls, with small houses dotted here and there in the wilderness, trails of smoke drifting from their chimneys. She could smell the peat in the air, the scent of burning turf that would forever symbolize home to her. Hardy mountain sheep grazed by the road, ignoring the traffic that passed as they chewed grass methodically. To the left, she could see the Atlantic peeping from between the myriad gorse-covered peninsulas. God, it was beautiful, but so remote.

She reached Maam's Cross and waited to turn right at the crossroads while a very modern tractor progressed steadily past her. The tractor driver waved energetically but Hannah didn't respond because she didn't recognize him. She'd moved away twelve years ago: it was hard to recognize people she'd been to school with since they'd all grown up and now looked totally different. *She* looked totally different, that was for sure.

She'd always worn her long hair tied back when she'd been growing up and her daily uniform had been sloppy cardigans and jeans. Now her hair was shoulder-length and loose, waving gently around her face. She'd abandoned the loose, shapeless clothes she'd habitually worn to hide her curvy figure and now favoured classic, fitted clothes.

Her Felix wardrobe – a selection of party-ish clothes he'd helped her buy – was another matter entirely. She wouldn't dream of wearing any of them here. Her mother would have a fit, not to mention what everybody else's reaction would be. Fifteen years ago, anyone stupid enough to wear a mini-skirt near the environs of Macky's Pub got catcalls, 'Gerrup ya girl, ya!' and the odd cry of 'Shameless hussy' roared at them. Once done it was never repeated. Hannah doubted if the local young fellas had changed much. Nor the old fellas, for that matter.

After another twenty minutes on minor roads, she reached the familiar gate-posts. There hadn't been gates there for as long as Hannah could remember: just the big concrete gate-posts with the hinges still attached, blackened with ancient rust. Her father had spent years promising to get gates but, like most of his promises, it had been unfulfilled. Hannah swung down the potholed drive and feared for her suspension.

The Campbell home, like many homes in this most beautiful and remote part of the world, was situated half a mile back from the road. The little Fiesta bounced and jiggled along the drive, past the windbreak of pine trees her grandfather had planted thirty years before, until she turned a bend and could see the house. Imposing, it wasn't. Originally a one-storey building with two windows on each side of the front door, the house had been extended over the years the Campbells had lived in it. Now the whitewashed façade was lopsided with a bit added on to the right side, a flat-roofed extra room which housed the bathroom and back scullery. A stranger might have wondered how they'd got planning permission for a bathroom leading on to the kitchen, but when Hannah's grandfather had been building his extension, planning permission hadn't crossed his mind.

Beyond the house were the outbuildings: a piggery now used as an all-purpose shed and a selection of rickety little buildings where the hens and the geese used to live. Hannah's mother hadn't bothered with hens for years. Cleaning them out was such a nightmare and they were always getting killed by the foxes. The hens had been Hannah's pets when she was a kid; clucking inquisitively and angling their red-feathered heads sideways when she talked back to them, the twenty or so Rhode Island Reds were better companions than the rest of her family.

It was six months since she'd been home but nothing appeared to have changed. The water barrel was still peeling away outside the corner of the house, white paint stripping off it like flakes of scurf. The patch of garden was as barren as ever, but the family's old Ford wasn't parked where her father always abandoned it, with a big puddle at the passenger door so anyone getting out that side would be soaked. Good. She didn't fancy meeting him right now. If the car wasn't there, he was out on the booze instead of sleeping off the previous day's excesses.

Hannah could see the kitchen curtains being pulled back as she parked. She hadn't even opened her car door before her mother was at the porch.

'This is a surprise,' Anna Campbell said, a small smile on her worn face. 'I hope you brought your sleeping bag. Mary and the children are here too.' Hannah gave her a small peck on the cheek. Mary was Hannah's cousin and she wondered briefly why Mary had rolled up here for Christmas. Her mother was looking very tired. But then, Anna had been looking tired for years. They looked alike, mother and daughter. Both had the same oval-shaped face, the same toffee-coloured eyes and the same dark hair that curled wildly and refused to be tamed with hairdryer or spray.

But while Hannah's lush, high-cheekboned face had an inner light and her beautifully plump mouth was often curved up in amusement, her mother's face was wary and worn. Her bone structure was clearly visible under the thin skin.

Anna Campbell wore no make-up except for a bit of lipstick when she was going out and the brown eyes under strong, never-plucked eyebrows were hard. She was thinner too, from a lifetime of having to work hard to keep her family fed and from the cigarettes she could not do without. That there wasn't an ounce of spare flesh on Anna's body had nothing to do with any exercise plan Jane Fonda had come up with. Her daily life was a hymn to the dual efforts of hard work and nicotine. Hannah knew that her mother had to walk to McGurk's supermarket up the valley most of the time because her father had taken the car and ended up sleeping the booze off in the back seat up a boreen somewhere, leaving the family carless and clueless about his whereabouts. But they were used to that. Keeping their elderly house clean, tidy and damp-free was a job for more than one person and the years of doing it on her own had taken their toll.

Today, in old navy cords and a faded blue print blouse under a bottle green hand-knitted cardigan, Anna looked older than her sixty-two years.

'Give me your things,' she said now, reaching into the car and effortlessly pulling out Hannah's suitcase with strong arms. 'Mary said she needed somewhere she and the kids could come for a couple of nights. She wouldn't say why, but Jackie lost his job in the factory and I bet he's taking it out on her, screaming and roaring all the time. She says she had to get away and I didn't want to interrogate her.'

And she came *here*? Hannah wanted to ask incredulously. Christmas in a damp old house in the wilds with a drunken eejit was hardly ideal for a woman and two small children, but then again, maybe it was better than spending the holiday with Mary's husband, Jackie, whom Hannah reckoned was living evidence of the missing link between humans and apes. She knew that Mary Wynne, her mother's niece who lived in a pretty bungalow outside Galway, had nowhere else to go with her two small kids. Her parents were dead and her brother lived in the UK.

'How did they get here?' asked Hannah, scooping up the rest of her belongings from the car.

'She got a lift. She says she's going to leave him. About time too. That man can't hold down a job for more than six months without getting the sack. He'd just been promoted too, but he had to go and screw it up. He's an *amadán*,' she said, using the Gaelic word for fool.

Hannah said nothing. It struck her as surreal sometimes that her mother was the emotional mainstay of her female friends and relatives, advising wisely on matters of bad husbands, when her own spouse was a raging alcoholic who hadn't earned an honest penny in years. Hannah was relieved that, for all his addiction to booze, Willie Campbell had only ever hit his wife in a once, never-to-be-forgotten incident. Bad poteen, he'd said cravenly in his defence when Anna was in hospital having her arm plastered up. Her mother would have thrown him out instantly if he'd been violent, Hannah knew. It was a pity that he wasn't aggressive when drunk. At least then she'd have dumped him.

Jackie Wynne certainly wasn't violent but Hannah found him intensely irritating. As for his devotion to football, it'd drive a sane person mad. If his team lost a match, he was inconsolable. Hannah had long ago decided that, if she'd been married to him, she'd have walked out years before. She couldn't handle the unreliability.

'Mary insists she's going to go back to work as well. I don't know how she'll manage with the children.' Anna sighed. 'Don't say anything to her. She gets so embarrassed by Jackie and, well, you know she's always looked up to you and thought you had your life sorted out, Hannah. She'll be mortified that you'll know she had to leave him at Christmas. If you read about something like that in the papers, you wouldn't believe it.'

'Of course I won't say anything,' Hannah said, silently thinking that if Mary knew precisely how well Hannah had sorted out her life, she wouldn't feel in the slightest bit embarrassed by her own predicament. They were the same age, although they'd never been close. At least Mary had two kids she adored out of her mess of a marriage. All Hannah had as proof of her thirty-seven years on the planet were a string of failed romances and a rapidly developing sense of cynicism. Oh yes, and a disgruntled boss because she'd been rude to him the night before. Hannah still felt guilty over poor David.

There was one advantage in Mary's being there: nobody would be that interested in details of Hannah's abortive Christmas plans when they could be discussing what a bastard Jackie was and what sort of lawyer Mary needed to take him for every penny he didn't have.

The huge kitchen was the heart of the Campbells' house. Anna still loved floral prints and the walls and the big armchairs were all covered in a variety of rosy patterns, the walls blue and yellow, the armchairs pink and gold and awash with cushions. A profusion of potted plants stood on all surfaces as proof of Anna's green fingers.

It was all very pretty for a house that looked so cold and lacking in comfort from the outside. Hannah had long since worked out that her mother needed her flowery nest to help her cope with the rest of her life, which was more than a little bleak.

The house was warm after the icy grip of the Atlantic breeze. Curled up on an armchair beside the big cream stove that heated the entire house, was Mary, pretending to read a magazine. Her mouth wobbled when she saw Hannah, who went over and gave her a hug.

'Hannah, did your mother tell you?' said Mary tremulously, big baby-blue eyes filling with tears.

'A bit,' lied Hannah, perching on the edge of the chair, pleased to see that misery hadn't ruined Mary's looks. She was still very attractive with her short curly dark hair, rosy, freckled cheeks and eyes like saucers fringed with long lashes clogged with mascara.

Two little girls who were the spitting image of their mother erupted into the room from the spare bedroom, dressed in grown-up clothes that trailed clumsily after them. The younger one, who had to be about four, Hannah reckoned, was wearing purple eyeshadow and a splash of bright lipstick all over her rosebud mouth.

'Look at me, Mummy!' she squealed happily. 'I'm going to the dance.' She twirled and nearly fell over in her trailing outfit.

'Me too,' said the older one, whom Hannah remembered was nearly six and who was wearing Anna's old black weddings-and-funerals hat with the grey feathers curling limply down instead of jauntily up the way they had when it had first been purchased twenty years ago.

'Courtney and Krystle, don't you remember your Auntie Hannah?' Mary said.

Whatever had happened at home didn't seem to have left any lasting impression on the two children, Hannah decided hours later, when they'd played dressing-up games for hours, followed by half an hour of stories from a big blue book of fairytales. They loved Hannah and fought over who got to sit on her lap in front of the fire as she read to them about Cinderella's adventures and how she married the prince but got a wonderful job just so she could keep her independence. Hannah was determined that her fairy stories should have a modern, realistic twist.

'You're great with children,' said Mary fondly. She seemed much cheerier after another pot of tea and a slice of Anna's fruitcake.

Hannah grinned at her. 'Nobody's ever said that to me before.'

By seven, the two girls were finally fast asleep in Anna's bed and Hannah felt worn out. Driving all the way from Dublin and playing with two energetic children had exhausted her. But Mary didn't appear tired at all. Or even very emotional, for that matter.

'Will we drive up to the pub for a quick drink?' she asked Hannah.

'What about the girls?' Hannah asked in surprise.

'I'll look after them,' Anna said. 'I've never set foot in that pub all my life and I'm not going to start now. I'll put the camp-bed up in the spare bedroom for the girls. We can move them from my bed later. I didn't air the bed in your old room, Hannah, so I'll do it now. You two go off and enjoy yourselves for an hour.'

Hannah shrugged. It was obvious that Mary wanted to tell her all the grisly details of the break-up with Jackie. But she felt too tired of driving to take the car out and, besides, with the stringent drink-driving laws, she wouldn't be able to have even one drink if she brought the car.

'Let's walk,' she said. 'It's only a mile and it's stopped raining.'

She pulled on a pair of old flat boots of her mother's and, with a raincoat on, just in case, they set off up the drive.

'The pub'll be crowded, I suppose,' Mary said, sounding remarkably enthusiastic for someone who was theoretically fleeing from misery. She'd painted on another coat of mascara and her lips gleamed with glossy pink lipstick.

'Always is on Christmas Eve,' smiled Hannah. 'You'd swear nobody was going to get a drink all Christmas the way they go mad for it this night.'

Hannah was welcomed into the pub with delight, which was just as well, because otherwise, they'd never have got a seat in the crowded lounge. They refused all the kind offers of drinks and ordered their own, Mary deciding she needed to visit the loo before their glasses of Guinness had arrived. Hannah rarely drank the black stuff any more, but going home made her long for the bittersweet taste.

'Won't be a minute,' Mary said cheerfully, slipping into the crowd.

A lively session was starting up in the corner beside the fire. Several people pushed an elderly man to the front and roared at him to take down the fiddle from its place on the wall and play.

'I've not a note in my head,' said the old man sweetly as he took the fiddle and began to expertly play a lively foot-tapping tune. The bar exploded into roars of laughter and a few of the hardier souls started dancing a jig in the centre of the room, amazingly not cannoning into each other although they were very drunk.

Hannah sat back in her seat and tapped her feet to the rhythm, keeping an eye out for Mary. She was surprised to see her cousin emerging not from the loo but from the left-hand side of the bar where the telephone was. Mary had a glow on her rosy face as she wound her way over to Hannah.

'Why didn't you use the phone at home?' Hannah asked, puzzled.

Mary went brick red. 'I didn't feel as if I could use Auntie Anna's phone,' she said shamefacedly.

'Why? You're not going back to Jackie, are you?'

Mary shook her head guiltily. 'Promise you won't tell?' she pleaded.

'I won't.'

'It's not Jackie that made me leave. I'm in love with someone and Jackie found out.'

'*What?*'

'You promised you wouldn't tell anyone.'

'I won't,' said Hannah. 'Now tell me.'

She could see her cousin's eyes shining like candles in a dark night as she recounted the tale of the handsome fitness instructor she'd met one day at a parent–teacher meeting.

'Jackie always left those meetings to me,' Mary protested. 'He never went to one of them. If Krystle had been a boy, he'd have been there, all right, trying to get him into the school soccer scheme before he was seven, but Jackie isn't interested in girls. Now Louis,' she breathed his name reverently, 'is different. His wife is a bit strange. That's why he was there without her. She works all the hours God gives and he has to look after their little girls while she's away. The oldest one is in the class ahead of Krystle. It just went on from there.'

'How long have you been seeing each other?' asked Hannah.

'Six months. He's going to leave her for me, but Jackie found out yesterday and there was war.'

'I can understand why,' Hannah said mildly. 'But why didn't you tell Mam what had happened? It's not fair to leave her in the dark like that. Jackie might turn up, you know, screaming blue murder, and Mam will be in a rage when she finds out that you've lied to her.'

'I haven't lied.'

'OK,' Hannah said, 'lied by omission.'

Mary scowled. 'I couldn't tell her because you're the perfect daughter. She's *always* talking about you and how well you're doing. Now you've got some famous boyfriend and I couldn't very well break it to her that I've been carrying on with this man and that my husband had found out, could I?'

'If she finds out, you'll wish you had.' Hannah was amazed. Imagine her mother telling everyone that she was the perfect daughter. Hannah had assumed her mother wasn't too interested in her life. That's how things had been when she was growing up. Then, Stuart, Hannah's older brother was the one Anna had involved herself with. Stuart had only to get reasonable results in an exam for Anna to bake him a special cake in celebration; when he announced he was getting married after his girlfriend, Pam, became pregnant, you'd have thought he'd been awarded the Nobel prize for Biology instead of screwing up on the most basic bit of human biology. Anna had gone crazy trying to buy the perfect wedding outfit and had knitted enough babyclothes for quadruplets. Now here was Mary telling her that Anna spoke about her reverently. It was all too hard to believe.

'I suppose you'll advise me to give him up and go back to Jackie like a good little wifey,' Mary added sharply.

Hannah laughed. 'Are you mad?' she demanded. 'It's not up to me to advise you, Mary, and I'm not the sort of woman who believes the answer to every question is: a man. You're a grown-up. Just look after yourself and the girls. Don't rely on any man too much, that's all I'll say.'

'I thought you were in love,' her cousin remarked. 'You're not sounding like it.'

Taking a sip of Guinness gave Hannah a moment before she had to respond. She didn't want to discuss her own life, and saying that all men were lying, cheating scum might give Mary some hint that everything in Hannah Campbell's garden was not rosy. 'Men are all right,' she said. 'I'm very fond of them but I'm not in love right now.' Her nose would grow longer any minute, like Pinocchio's. 'I've been seeing somebody, that's all.'

'Real love is wonderful,' Mary said, eyes glowing again. 'You were in love with that Harry, weren't you? What went wrong there?'

'I trusted him,' Hannah said bluntly. 'Don't make that mistake, Mary. For your sake and for the girls'.'

* * *

Christmas Day dawned cool but dry with a pale sun casting watery light along the front of the house. There was still no sign of her father. Hannah didn't ask where he was. She could guess. Sleeping off a gallon of porter in the back of the car, still half out of his skull. By ten thirty, the girls were tiring of their presents from Santa and they all trooped to morning Mass in Hannah's car. Hannah, who hadn't been in a church for ages, kept standing up in the wrong places and sitting down when she should have been kneeling, earning herself a reproving stare from six-year-old Krystle.

'That's wrong,' she hissed at Hannah with the piety of a child who was in training for her Holy Communion.

'Sorry,' said Hannah meekly, holding on to Courtney's small hand and trying not to laugh at Krystle's stern face. Courtney had taken a shine to her auntie and insisted on sitting beside Hannah, holding on to her new crying, nappy-wearing doll with the other chubby little hand. Occasionally, she'd give the doll to Hannah and would sit, thumb in her rosebud mouth, leaning against her new friend, utterly content. It was nice to sit there with Courtney's little body against hers and look around at all the people, Hannah thought.

She felt vaguely guilty about not having been to Mass for so long. Religion hadn't seemed important in her life and yet, today, with Anna, Mary and the children beside her and with the hard-working people she'd grown up with united in worshipping God, she felt as if she'd been missing something. She was what Leonie called a submarine Catholic – they only came up when there was trouble. It might be nice to go more often, she decided.

The elderly Ford was parked outside the house when Hannah drove up. He was back.

'Don't be giving out to your father, Hannah,' warned her mother in a low voice so that Mary wouldn't hear. 'I don't want a row. This is Christ's day, so let's pretend to be a normal family.'

Once, Hannah would have fought with her mother for even daring to say that to her. *He's as bad as he is because nobody ever says anything to him*, she'd have hissed. *If he didn't get away with spending every penny he gets on drink, then we'd all be a lot happier.*

That was a different Hannah. This one didn't want a fight today, she wanted peace and goodwill to all men, and if that meant managing a cold smile for her father, then she'd do it.

The children rushed into the house and stopped in fear at the sight of Willie Campbell slumped in the armchair beside the fire. As fat as his wife was thin, he was an almost comical figure with his threadbare tweed jacket and a shirt that had probably been white when he'd put it on but was now stained with beer. He still had a full head of thick dark hair but it was growing grey now, the same colour as the eyes that roamed over the visitors. Guilt and remorse were written all over his face.

'Mary,' he said slurring his words slightly. 'Welcome. And little Hannah. Have you got a kiss for your old father?'

Hannah looked at the hopeless creature in front of her and wondered why she'd made him into such an ogre in her mind. He wasn't bad, she realized. Just weak. Weak and a drunk. It wasn't his fault he'd given her a lifelong distrust of other men. It certainly wasn't his fault that she was so hopeless with men that she kept picking ones who'd let her down just like he'd done all her life.

'Hello, Dad,' she said, making no move to embrace him. 'Long time no see. Happy Christmas.'

'Happy Christmas, Uncle Willie,' said Mary, dragging the two girls over to their uncle. She hugged him but they were not keen to do the same.

'Come on, girls,' said Anna firmly, taking them by the hand and leading them away. 'Let's go up to your bedroom and take off those coats. Willie,' she said to her husband, 'go and have a wash and change your clothes. This is Christmas Day and you could do with a fresh shirt. If you want to have a rest, we'll wake you for dinner.'

Nothing had changed, Hannah thought. Her mother carried on as usual, giving her father a way out with the usual coded messages, messages telling him he could sleep his hangover off and that he'd be welcome at the table when he was clean and sober. It was her version of see no evil, hear no evil. When she'd been growing up, Hannah had raged against this, what she saw as her mother's blind acceptance of his alcoholism. *Stop making excuses for him. Leave, get out! Or make him leave!* she wanted to scream in frustration. But her mother wouldn't. Her marriage was all she had and she'd been brought up to accept what she'd been given in life.

Perhaps it was having been away from home for so long, or maybe it was because she'd changed too, but Hannah no longer felt the need to fight with either of them.

'I'll make you a cup of tea to bring to bed, Dad,' was all she said now. Her father looked at her gratefully.

'Thanks, love.'

When he'd shuffled off to the bedroom he shared with her mother, Hannah heaved a silent sigh of relief. She felt as if she'd passed some sort of test. Not his test but one of her own making. Accepting who you were in life meant accepting your parents for what they were. She'd managed it, just about.

They had dinner at five and it was great fun thanks to the presence of the two small girls. Getting Courtney to eat anything green was a trial and Hannah was in charge of that mission.

'Don't wan' it!' Courtney would say petulantly, throwing her Winnie the Pooh fork across the table with great force when presented with a bit of broccoli.

'Me neither,' declared Krystle.

'I'm surprised at you, girls,' Willie remarked, 'not eating your dinner when you know that Santa is watching.' He'd said very little during the meal, merely mentioning that everything was lovely and eating ravenously.

'We've got our presents already,' Krystle said smugly.

Willie raised his eyebrows. 'But he can always take them back, can't he, Mary?'

The broccoli was consumed with great zeal after that. Nobody was more amazed than Hannah at her father bothering to get involved with the children. He'd never been much good with kids, had he? She tried to remember and somehow a hazy memory came back of when she'd been little and had loved sitting on his knee listening to him tell stories. He'd had a big rust-coloured armchair and she used to curl up in it when he wasn't there, missing him. She had to pretend to sneeze to conceal the fact that her eyes had brimmed with tears.

'You're not getting a cold, are you, Hannah?' asked her mother.

'No, Mam, I'm not.'

There was never any alcohol in the house, but her father still seemed to sink into a tipsy haze that evening, although Hannah never saw him with a drink in his hand. He must have some hidden somewhere. The following day, he went off at lunchtime and didn't come back. The three women had a lovely day, playing with the children, talking, and going for a long walk up the mountain before returning home in the dusk to make steaming hot cups of tea and rest their aching legs in front of the fire.

That night, Hannah woke up at half two to the sound of someone at the front door. She shivered, feeling as if she was a kid again at the sound of her father's key in the lock. You could never tell what sort of mood he'd be in: happy and giggly, or in one of his dark sombre moods when he blamed everyone but himself for the fact that he had no job and no future.

'What about us? We're your future and you're not looking after us or Mam,' Hannah always wanted to scream at him. 'Stop feeling sorry for yourself and do something.' She hated the way he'd wasted his life in a haze of alcohol.

Afraid he'd make noise and wake up the kids, she got up silently and went into the kitchen. She found him sitting on the floor, trying to take his shoes and socks off quietly.

'Hannah,' he said in a stage whisper, 'will ya make me a cup of tea? I'm dying for one. It'll kill the hangover for the morning.'

He looked ridiculous on the floor, and harmless, his big face smiling and his legs splayed out like a child playing with his toys as he struggled to unlace his shoes. He was hardly a role model, she thought wearily, putting a few extra sods of turf on the fire and switching on the electric kettle. But he was her father, not the devil incarnate.

'Sit on the chair and I'll do your laces,' she commanded. 'And be quiet.'

'Yes, Hannah,' he said obediently. 'You were always like your mother, a great woman to have in charge.'

The following morning, she packed her suitcase into the boot of the

Fiesta feeling like a different person from the uptight woman who'd arrived three days previously. Real life courtesy of the West of Ireland always did that to her. It shifted the world on its axis somehow, made problems look differently when the backdrop was different.

Her mother stood beside the car in the misty morning air with her arms full of oddly shaped packages and jars wrapped in newsprint.

'There's rhubarb jam – four jars of that – and some free-range eggs from Doyles up the road. I've put in a loaf of brown bread and some of yesterday's bacon because nobody would finish it and it'll go to waste here. Mary'll be gone tomorrow.'

'Where's she going?' Hannah asked, stowing the packages carefully in the boot.

'Off to her fancy man, I've no doubt.'

Hannah straightened up in shock. 'So she told you. I thought you'd be furious with her.'

Her mother shrugged. 'No point in that. What can't be cured must be endured. Did you ever hear that one?'

'You never cease to amaze me, Mam,' Hannah said finally. 'Just when I think I know how you're going to react, you do something else.'

'Like what?'

'Like telling Mary that I have my life all sorted out and how proud you are of me . . .' Hannah's voice trailed off. She was sorry she'd started this now. All through the holiday, she'd wanted to ask her mother about what Mary had said and now that she had, she regretted it.

'Did you not think I'd be proud of you?' demanded Anna harshly. 'When you've got out of this place and made another life for yourself? Wouldn't I have loved to do that myself if I could? Of course I'm proud of you, but you could never see it.'

'You were always so tough on me,' protested Hannah. 'Stuart was your golden boy.'

Her mother snorted. 'Lads will always be golden boys because they have it both ways. They're men and they get what they want in life. If a woman gets what she wants, she's seen as some tough old bird who couldn't get a man. Stuart didn't need help, you did. I didn't want you turning out soft. I treated you hard to *make* you hard, so you wouldn't go through what I did,' explained Anna.

'Oh.'

They stood there for a moment. Anna had never been an affectionate woman; it wasn't in her nature to grab people just for the hell of it. Today, Hannah decided to ignore that. She put her arms around her mother's stiff frame and held her tightly. Anna Campbell relaxed and stayed there for at least a minute before pulling away.

'You better be off, Hannah,' she said gruffly. 'The world and his granny will be on the road today heading home, so you should leave now.'

'I'm going,' Hannah said with a grin. 'Phone me, won't you?'

'You're never there!' her mother said. 'Always out gallivanting. That's my girl.'

The journey wasn't any shorter on the way home, but it flew past. Hannah drove with a song in her heart. The trials and tribulations of the weeks before had vanished and she felt reborn, revitalized. So what if Felix had a commitment problem? It was his problem and not hers. She didn't need him. She was a strong, intelligent woman who came from a long line of similar women. What did a handsome playboy actor matter to a woman like that? Driven with the desire to forge ahead, she began planning her new life and career.

It was time she put down roots, time she bought her own home. If she hadn't wasted all that money buying stupid party dresses so she'd look nice for Felix, she'd practically have her deposit money now. Well, it wouldn't take too long to replace the extra cash. If hard work and long hours were all it took, she could manage that. She'd have a career, her independence and a place of her own. Felix could go hang.

CHAPTER EIGHTEEN

How Kirsten got out of Christmas dinner, Emma would never know. But whatever the combination of words were, they convinced Jimmy O'Brien that his dear, sweet younger daughter was ill and couldn't possibly leave her sick bed simply for a bit of roast turkey and stuffing and a bit of family bonding.

'Poor love, she's worn out,' he said, hanging up the phone and coming back into the kitchen where Emma, hair stuck to her forehead with perspiration, was basting the turkey for the tenth time that day. 'I think she's . . .' Jimmy winked at his wife, 'you know. Pregnant. She doesn't want to say anything yet, but I'm sure of it. She did say she was feeling nauseous.' He swelled up like a bullfrog with pride.

Emma slammed the oven door shut venomously. If there was one thing she was certain of, it was that the deeply unmaternal Kirsten wasn't pregnant. Hungover, more likely. Every Christmas Eve, she and a crowd of her old friends hit the Horseshoe Bar for a riotous evening of champagne cocktails, followed by a party in one of their houses until the wee small hours, or at least until Santa was at home in bed, having delivered his wares. One poor mug had to be designated driver to ferry the plastered revellers from the Shelbourne to their homes. Usually, Patrick drew the short straw.

Emma would have bet the very nice lilac mohair jumper Pete had given her that morning that her sister was lying in bed at that precise moment, gulping down Alka Seltzer and whining that she'd never drink another cocktail ever again. The cow. Kirsten knew that Emma was dreading the ritual O'Brien Christmas.

Every year, they all went to Anne-Marie and Jimmy's house for dinner, along with Great Aunt Petra and Jimmy's unmarried brother, Eugene. Torturous at the best of times, it was going to be worse this year, Emma was convinced of that. Her mother had been behaving quite normally for the past few weeks and there'd thankfully been no reoccurrence of the Laura Ashley incident. But Emma was sure it was only a matter of time until it happened again. It couldn't have been a one-off, she was painfully sure of that. Christmas, with all the fuss and excitement, was bound to be the trigger for another attack.

In her usual ostrich fashion, Kirsten had refused to discuss it at all, but she'd known how nervous Emma was about the family party. It was pure meanness on her part to cry off at this late stage. It wasn't as if she'd have had to do anything either. Emma had gone with her mother to the supermarket three days previously and bought all the food for Christmas. It was unheard of for her mother not to have ordered her turkey a month in advance, complete with spiced ham and a load of sausages. But this year, she had nothing organized and Emma had ended up doing everything. Her father wouldn't notice that the Christmas pudding wasn't home-made, she decided, if enough brandy was poured on to it. Kirsten could have helped a bit if she'd been there, even if it was only to put their father in a rare good mood.

'I'll phone Patrick,' Emma announced suddenly, 'ask him how she is. You know Kirsten, complete hypochondriac. She's probably just got a cold.'

'You'll do no such thing,' growled her father. 'Your poor sister is in her sick bed and you think she's just got a cold. And all because you don't want to help your mother cook the dinner. Laziness, that's what it is. In my day, we were damn lucky to get a Christmas dinner, never mind be complaining about having to cook it.'

Emma opened her mouth to protest that, actually, *she* was the one doing all the cooking while her mother had been fiddling about with a tin for ages. Turning away from her father, she caught a glimpse of Anne-Marie's face: it was a picture of confusion. In one hand, she held a tin of the mushy peas Uncle Eugene consumed by the bucketful.

In the other, she held the egg whisk. The tin-opener lay abandoned on the counter. She was trying to open the peas with the egg whisk, God love her.

'Forget it, Dad,' Emma muttered. 'I won't phone Patrick. You're right.' It was easier to placate him. She'd phone later, secretly.

He stormed off and Emma gently took the tin and the whisk away from her mother.

'Mum, you've done everything so far, why don't you sit down and talk to Auntie Petra for a while? I'll bring you both a nice glass of sherry and you can watch the carols on the telly.'

Emma wasn't sure whether sherry was good for people with problems like her mother's, but if it calmed her down and took that sad, bewildered look off her face, then a good glass of sherry was ideal. A strong drink might also dilute the effect of Petra's caustic tongue.

She left the two women sitting happily listening to some sweet child soprano singing 'Hark, the Herald Angels Sing' on RTE1, each with a giant glass of sherry. In the kitchen, she checked that everything was cooking away nicely and then phoned Pete's home. He was having dinner with his family. The festive theory was that every second year, they had dinner with one family but Emma was tired of Christmas in the war zone of the O'Briens'.

Last year, they'd promised each other they'd break the Christmas cycle by having their dinner together in their own house, ignoring the plaintive demands from their families. The plan would have worked, because Pete's parents perfectly understood their son's desire for a break with the tradition. But, naturally, Jimmy O'Brien hadn't been pleased.

'Have Pete here,' he'd commanded, 'then you'll be together.'

'That's not the point,' Emma had tried to explain, in vain. To make life easier for her, they'd compromised again this year.

Pete hadn't said anything about not letting her father boss her about. He'd kept his peace and had hugged her tightly that morning when she'd said goodbye to him and had driven to her parents' house. Next Christmas, she vowed fiercely, it'd be different.

'Hi, Pete,' she said now, wishing he was beside her for a cuddle.

'Hi, my darling,' he responded. 'Wish you were here. I miss you.'

'Oh, don't,' she groaned. 'I can't wait until tonight. You're sure your mum doesn't mind me only popping over later?'

'No, she's dying to see you. She's told me what she's got you for Christmas and you'll love it.'

Emma couldn't stop her eyes brimming over. How she wished she was with Pete now, laughing with the rest of the Sheridans as they stood around in the kitchen, chatting and generally hindering Mrs Sheridan with her dinner preparations. They usually sat down at around half five after an afternoon playing Scrabble or charades. There was rarely any alcohol at the Sheridans', but their Christmas party didn't suffer because of the lack of it. The small, close-knit family got on so well that they didn't need anaesthetizing. They didn't need to watch TV to enjoy themselves, either. Emma's favourite part of Christmas Day in her parents' was when dinner was over and they all sat down to watch whatever big movie was on the box. With nobody given the opportunity to argue with anybody else, and with a few glasses of wine inside them, peace reigned briefly. Jimmy loved the telly and loved films and, while he was watching one, he managed to keep his temper under control.

It was no accident that Emma had bought him four classic videos for Christmas. If there was nothing good on after lunch, she'd stick on *Dr Zhivago*. He loved that and it was at least three hours long. She yearned for those three hours of peace, but first, they had to get through dinner.

Having said a tearful goodbye to Pete, Emma dialled her sister's house. Patrick answered.

'You sound miserable,' Emma remarked.

'I am. Madam is in bed with a brutal hangover and there's nothing in the house for Christmas dinner,' her brother-in-law said gloomily. 'I'm having four sausage rolls, a pizza and oven chips. She's not eating anything because she says every time she opens her eyes, her head spins.'

'I'd make her head spin if I was anywhere near her,' Emma said crossly. 'I'll throttle her for wriggling out of dinner here. It's like Chateau Despair. The turkey would kill itself if it wasn't already dead.'

'Happy days, as usual?' Patrick asked.

'You said it. I'm worried that Mum will have another turn and I don't know if I can cope on my own, that's why I wanted Kirsten here.'

'What sort of "turn"?' Patrick asked, sounding puzzled.

'You know, like in Laura Ashley's.'

'I don't want to sound dense, Em, but I haven't a clue what you're talking about.'

'You mean, Kirsten never told you!' Emma was utterly shocked. She couldn't believe her sister hadn't mentioned their mother's problem. Kirsten was unbelievable. 'I can't talk now,' Emma whispered, 'but ask Kirsten to tell you what happened earlier this month when I brought Mum out shopping. I'm worried about her – really worried . . .'

Dinner was hellish. Great-Aunt Petra dubbed the turkey too tough, the sprouts inedible and the gravy lumpier than an old mattress. Jimmy agreed, conveniently deciding that it was all Emma's fault. Anne-Marie had listlessly picked at her food, more interested in chasing sprouts round her plate with the knife than actually eating any of them. Only Uncle Eugene had eaten everything uncomplainingly, with the delight of a bachelor who rarely had home-cooked meals.

'You're a great oul' cook, Emma,' he said gratefully as he shovelled another forkful of mushy peas into his mouth.

At least she could get mushy peas right, Emma thought, with gritted teeth. She brought all the dishes out to the kitchen and couldn't help noticing that, for all her aunt's protests about rubbery turkey, she'd managed to eat enough of it.

She loaded the dishwasher on her own, made tea, custard for the pudding, and delivered the next course into the dining room in time to hear her father talking about Kirsten as though he was discussing the Second Coming.

'She's a great girl,' he said fondly. 'Did that Ballymaloe cookery course with Darina Allen and, boy, can she cook. She's something of a whizz in the kitchen, all right. What was that thing she made last time we were in Kirsten's house, the dinner she learned how to make?' he asked his wife.

Anne-Marie shrugged blankly.

I'm surprised he can remember that far back, Emma growled, putting the teacups down with a clatter. Kirsten wasn't known for the regularity of her family dinners. She wasn't known for the regularity of any dinners for that matter. Poor Patrick was never in any danger of putting on weight from his wife's cuisine.

Thanks to that two-day course in the famed Ballymaloe House, which she'd only gone on because some of her charity lunch pals were organizing it, Kirsten could conjure up a roasted pepper salad, make organic *boeuf en croute* and whip up a nice frozen yoghurt dessert. But there was no point asking her to roast a chicken, cook an omelette or prepare any sort of vegetable that didn't come washed and trimmed in supermarket packaging with instructions on how to microwave it.

'Fish thing, was it?' her mother was saying, her face puzzled. 'No, not fish but, that thing, you must know what I'm talking about!' She turned in frustration to Emma. 'You *know* what I'm talking about, Emma. I can't think of it . . .'

'Beef, that was it. You should have tasted it,' said Jimmy, waxing lyrical. 'Pity she wasn't here today.'

Emma wasn't listening. She was staring sadly at her mother's baffled face. She knew that her mother could remember what Kirsten had cooked, she remembered everything her darling Kirsten had ever done. Yet it was as if she couldn't find the words for it. They were lost in her head. She tried to smile bravely and encouragingly at her mother, but Anne-Marie was staring into her plate, silent and confused.

'Emma has made us a great dinner,' said Uncle Eugene loyally.

'Well, yes,' Jimmy said. Then catching sight of his daughter's tired face and the apron she wore over her new lilac jumper, he seemed to relent. 'She's a good girl, aren't you, Emma. Now, I hope this custard isn't too lumpy and not out of a packet. You know I like proper custard.'

'Of course, Dad,' Emma said automatically. In the kitchen, she tried to make sense of her mother's problem. She knew what it was, what it had to be. But she hated to face up to it. How could Anne-Marie cope with the loss of her mind? How could anyone?

'Have you got the pudding ready yet?' roared her father. 'Our stomachs think our throats have been cut!' He laughed uproariously at his own joke.

Emma gave the custard a vicious stir, relishing her small victory by virtue of the fact that it wasn't real custard: it wasn't even custard you had to add boiling milk to. It was instant – the just-add-water variety.

Tough bloody bananas, Dad. She'd poured a huge dollop of brandy into his bowl when she was dishing up the pudding earlier: she didn't want to bring it in and light it in case anyone copped on that it was a M & S special instead of Anne-Marie's own secret recipe. She gave everyone a bowl and they tucked in.

'Lovely,' Jimmy said as he dug in. 'There's nothing to beat your pudding, Anne-Marie,' he said proudly. 'I'd recognize it anywhere.'

The brandy had the desired effect. Emma shooed them all off into the sitting room afterwards, ostensibly to watch *Dr Zhivago*. 'I'll be in soon,' she sang cheerily, having no intention of joining them. She was going to tidy up, scrub all the pots and pans, and then retire to the conservatory for a rest. Her relatives could pass out in front of the box without her.

However, the best-laid plans and all that . . . Jimmy found her sitting quietly in the conservatory and chivvied her back into the fold, like a bull driving a solitary cow into his herd. She quite liked *Dr Zhivago* but not when she was already feeling emotional and depressed. The haunting 'Lara's Theme' echoed through her mind with each fresh tragedy. Only the knowledge that she had to drive soon and couldn't drink kept Emma from diving into the sherry herself. She could barely watch the film any more when salvation came in the unlikely form of the doorbell.

'I'll get it.' She leapt to her feet and ran into the hall. To her utter surprise, Patrick and a green-faced Kirsten stood outside.

'We couldn't leave you to face the whole day on your own,' Patrick said grimly.

'Oh yes we could have,' grumbled Kirsten, pushing past her sister and hurrying into the kitchen to get a glass of water to slake the ever-present hangover thirst.

'I got her to tell me what had happened to your mother,' Patrick whispered to Emma. 'It sounds terrible.'

'You and Pete are the only people taking this seriously,' Emma said, relieved Patrick was there. He was a very capable man. Her father never bullied him, although Kirsten did all the time. Still, having Patrick on her side was a bonus.

'Where's Pete?'

She rolled her eyes. 'I was supposed to go to his parents' this Christmas but Dad insisted we come here. Under the circumstances, we decided to split the celebrations. I'm going to his house later.'

'Why don't you go now?' Patrick said kindly. 'We'll stay here for the evening. And if your father wants to roll out the fatted calf for Kirsten, she can cook it herself!'

'You can't leave,' hissed Kirsten, who'd emerged from the kitchen and had heard the last bit. 'I'm not sitting here all night with bloody Great-Aunt Petra . . . Hello, Aunt Petra! How are you? I love your outfit,' she cooed, straight-faced as Petra and their father appeared in the sitting-room doorway.

'Kirsten, my love! Happy Christmas!' said Jimmy O'Brien.

It was hugs and kisses all round. Even Anne-Marie seemed to come out of her trance-like state to greet the new arrivals.

'I've got your presents under the tree,' Anne-Marie told her daughter happily. 'And I haven't forgotten you, Patrick.'

Emma watched and wondered if her mother's problem really existed except in her own imagination. Earlier, Anne-Marie had been sitting quietly, not really taking part in the conversation, merely nodding and saying 'yes' when her husband spoke to her. But now she was the life and soul of the party, happy and laughing. Did she enjoy Kirsten's company so much that she only came to life when her younger daughter was around? Was Emma imagining some horrible illness purely because she couldn't come to terms with the fact that both parents preferred her sister?

Confused and tired, Emma got her coat and handbag. 'I'm going to Pete's,' she said quietly to Patrick.

He gave her a sympathetic hug before she slipped away without anyone really noticing. No doubt her parents would be angry that she hadn't gone through the palaver of kissing everyone goodbye, but she couldn't face it today. She'd played the dutiful daughter for most of the day. Now she wanted to be with her husband.

'Is it me?' she asked him an hour later when she'd been welcomed with open arms by his family and they'd exchanged more gifts and drunk yet another pot of tea. 'Could I be imagining that Mum's sick? She seemed OK today and when Kirsten arrived, she was absolutely normal. God, maybe I'm the one who's losing my marbles.'

Pete scooched up closer to her on the bench seat in his mother's kitchen. 'Don't be daft, love. You're the sanest one in your family. And you said she tried to open a tin with the whisk. That's not exactly normal behaviour, is it? The thing is, your mother adores Kirsten. She'd go to hell and back not to upset her. I think she's trying very hard to cling to normality when Kirsten's around and it's only when she's with you that she can lapse into how she's really feeling.'

Emma didn't think it could be that. 'You don't choose the times when you feel confused and when you don't, do you?' She rubbed her eyes tiredly. 'I wish I knew more about things like Alzheimer's. Should we get a book on it? There's bound to be one with a guide to what to do if someone you know has it. Or should we go to the doctor and talk to him?'

'Talk to the doctor about what?' enquired Mrs Sheridan, coming into the kitchen to see if they wanted to play Scrabble.

'Nothing.' Emma smiled brightly. It was bad enough that her mother's problems had ruined the festivities in her home, without the spectre of it hanging over someplace else.

Patrick and Kirsten turned up at Emma and Pete's home the following day, bearing a bottle of champagne and a huge box of hand-made chocolates.

'Peace offering,' said Kirsten with an irrepressible grin as she marched into the kitchen, leaving the men on their own. 'Let's open them now.'

The only green thing about her today were the emerald studs she wore, one of her presents from Patrick. 'They match my engagement ring,' she said, angling her small head so that Emma could admire the earrings.

'Lovely,' Emma said truthfully, taking out wine glasses for the champagne as she and Pete had never found it necessary to buy champagne flutes. 'Is the coat new, too?'

'God no, this is ancient,' Kirsten said, flicking a disdainful hand over the full-length black leather coat Emma had never seen before. 'My other present is a week in a health farm, which isn't much of a present, really.'

'You're greedy and spoiled, you know that?' Emma reproved her. 'Patrick is too kind to you.'

'It's not greediness. It's just a useless present for me. I don't want to lose weight and I'm not stressed.'

'Give it to me then,' said Emma shortly. 'I'm stressed out of my brain.'

'I know, sorry. Patrick nearly murdered me when he found out about Mum. But I mean, Emma, we don't know anything for sure and I think you're over-reacting . . .'

Emma snatched the bottle out of her sister's hands. 'Don't tell me I'm over-reacting! If you want a drink, bring those glasses into the sitting room.'

Pete, Patrick and Emma were all agreed that something was obviously wrong with Anne-Marie O'Brien. 'My grandmother went like that before she died,' Patrick revealed. 'In those days, they called it senility. Now they've lots of names; dementia, Alzheimer's – I saw a TV programme on it and it was pretty terrible, I must say.'

They were all silent for a moment, even Kirsten, who had been sipping her champagne as if she hadn't a care in the world.

'What do we do?' Emma said finally. 'If we're wrong, Mum or Dad will never forgive us. And if we're right, and we don't do anything . . . Mum could hurt herself or have an accident driving – who knows what could happen. I'd never forgive myself if she got hurt and it was because I'd been too nervous to tell Dad.'

The three of them were all agreed on one thing: Kirsten would be the best person to broach the subject to her father. 'Just tell him you're worried about Mum and maybe you could bring her to the doctor to get her checked out. Who knows,' Emma said, clutching at straws, 'it could be something they can operate on. We could be barking up the wrong tree entirely.'

There was only one flaw with the plan: Kirsten refused to do it. 'No way!' she said. 'I think you're all mad. There's nothing wrong with Mum and I'm not going to say there is.'

'Kirsten!' said Patrick angrily.

'Well, you didn't notice anything wrong with her yesterday, Patrick, did you?' Kirsten pointed out. 'You said so yourself: she was pretty normal all evening.'

'Yeah, and I also said that I wasn't the best judge and that if Emma thought there was something wrong, there was. Don't quote me if you're only going to quote half of what I say.'

He looked furious and Emma wondered exactly what was going on between Kirsten and Patrick. He normally wouldn't say boo to his wife, letting Kirsten do and say what she liked without comment. But something had changed, definitely.

'I don't care what you all think,' Kirsten said stubbornly, 'I'm not saying anything to Dad. Mum has behaved perfectly when I've been around her, and that's enough for me. If you think she's going nuts, Emma, then *you* tell Dad. Come on, Patrick, we've got a party to go to.'

Later that evening when she and Pete were cuddled together in front of the fire chatting, Emma brought the subject up again. 'You don't think I should say anything to Dad, do you?'

'I don't know, love. Your father would certainly be the sort of man who'd kill the messenger who brought him the bad news. It'd be your fault she was sick, you know that. He'd never forgive you.'

Emma nodded in agreement. 'You're right. I just wish someone else had experienced Mum acting strangely and not just me. If Kirsten had seen –'

'Forget about Kirsten,' interrupted Pete. 'I know she's your sister and everything, but she's so flaky it's unbelievable. Kirsten wants everything in her garden to be rosy and this doesn't fit in with her plans. If she didn't have Patrick to look after her, God knows what'd happen to her.'

Remembering how angry Patrick had appeared with her sister earlier and how furious he must have been the previous day to drag her out of bed to spend time with the O'Briens, Emma had the feeling that the worm was beginning to turn.

And if Patrick did decide he'd had enough of Kirsten's histrionics, then life was going to be very rocky in their household.

Stop it! Emma told herself crossly. Stop worrying about Kirsten. Kirsten wouldn't give ten seconds to thinking about anyone else's problems. It was a skill Emma wished she could develop.

She was sick of worrying about her family: let them look after themselves. She was going to enjoy her time off with Pete. She stretched her bare feet out towards the burning coals and yawned languorously, snuggling up closer to Pete.

'How do you fancy going to bed early?' she murmured.

In response, he nibbled her ear gently and slid a hand down to open the top button of her blouse. 'Or how about we don't bother going to bed early but stay in front of the fire?'

'Brilliant idea,' his wife replied. There was something so sensual about lovemaking in front of an open fire. It reminded her of when they'd been engaged and never managed to get any time on their own together. Back then they used to wait until everyone in the Sheridan household had gone to bed and then they'd cuddled up in front of the huge fire, growing more and more passionate but too scared to let go and make love in case someone coming downstairs for a drink of water caught them in a compromising position. They'd never tried that in Emma's home: she'd have been in a state of constant fear that her father would appear at the sitting-room door with a shotgun and a Bible in his hand. But they'd had some wonderfully torrid sessions in Pete's house.

Time to rekindle that old, easy-going lovemaking, Emma thought as Pete gently opened her buttons. That had been a time when her only worry about impending motherhood had been that she'd get pregnant before the wedding. She was determined to let go of her constant thoughts about a baby: that was to be her New Year's resolution. She'd never have a baby if she became obsessed with it. From now on, that obsession was in the past. She and Pete had to enjoy whatever their marriage brought. If that meant no babies, then so be it.

CHAPTER NINETEEN

It was ten days after Christmas and Leonie was used to her new haircut now. Mind you, she thought, running a hand through the shorter, layered style that seemed to sit better, she'd never be able to afford to have all that done again. Having your hair cut and mesh-dyed cost a bloody fortune. Still, it was nice to have honey-gold hair with tawny brown streaks running through it. It looked almost natural. The girls had been most impressed.

'Mum, it's beautiful,' Mel had said, almost in surprise.

To go with her new hairdo, she'd bought some new clothes. Hannah had been great advising her about what to bring, especially for travelling.

'Don't waste something dressy on the plane,' she'd advised. 'It's Fliss and Ray you want to impress, not the people on the jumbo. Change when you get to Denver if you want to, but wear something baggy and comfy for the trip across the Atlantic.'

Hannah was very shrewd, Leonie acknowledged. She instinctively knew that looking good when she met Ray and his fiancée was of paramount importance to her. Pride was a terrible thing, Leonie reflected, as the air stewardess ran through the safety checks and the twins sat clutching each other delightedly.

They were so excited about the trip, it was contagious. Leonie found herself sitting back happily, content because she had a nice fat detective novel in her handbag for the flight and had got the doctor to give her four tranquillizers to cope with her fear of flying. They were working – so far.

Danny had somehow managed to get himself allocated a seat apart from the rest of the family, one row ahead, beside an attractive girl in faded jeans. Just so he wouldn't get above himself, Mel and Abby had been making loud remarks about how his girlfriend must be missing him and how he'd promised to save himself for her.

He had to keep turning back to shoot them daggers looks and the naughty pair convulsed with mirth every time, keeping silent for about one minute before resuming their conversation about how lovely his fictitious girlfriend was. Leonie grinned but told them to keep their voices down. What a pair.

She hoped they'd calm down a bit in Colorado or she'd have a manic time trying to keep an eye on them. With the twins behaving as hyperactively as if they'd been slugging down fifteen cans of Coke each, she couldn't see them giving her much time for relaxation. Well, their father and their new stepmother could take over for a while, Leonie decided, opening her handbag and extracting her P.D. James novel.

She was going to relax. And if she felt stressed at any time, Emma had given her a little bottle of herbal Rescue Remedy. Leonie remembered Emma having it with her in Egypt. She swore by it. Just to be on the safe side, Leonie put a few drops of the remedy on her tongue, wincing at the slightly alcoholic taste.

In the toilets in Denver airport, Leonie decided against another dose of Rescue Remedy. She'd taken so much, Ray and Fliss would think she was drunk if she had any more. The flight to Atlanta had been a nightmare. It didn't matter how calmly Danny had explained that turbulence wasn't dangerous, it was merely the plane flying through a particular type of air current or something like that, she still felt as if she was going to have to scream with sheer terror every time the plane wobbled. It felt like being in a whale's belly, a whale who was in training for one of those public aquariums where they jumped up and down through hoops for the audience. Did whales do that, or was it only sharks and dolphins? Leonie didn't know. All she knew was that if she had to endure any more turbulence, she'd die. She hated flying. Why the hell had she allowed herself to be convinced to come on this trip? Amazingly, the twins and most of the rest of the passengers had slept through the storm. After dinner and a Bruce Willis film, they'd all happily dozed off, making the most of the night-time flight to sleep. Leonie had sat rigidly in her seat, unable to read, sleep, or even listen to the moronic comedy hour on the airline headsets. Three little bottles of wine hadn't helped at all: if anything, they'd made her feel even more paranoid and convinced the plane was about to drop like a stone from the sky.

Half an hour before they arrived in Atlanta, the turbulence disappeared and people woke up. 'Are we nearly there?' asked Mel, stretching sleepily.

They'd had a wait of an hour and three-quarters in Atlanta before boarding the plane for Denver, and Leonie spent most of that time convincing herself that air travel was the safest in the world and that it'd be stone mad to even *think* about hiring a car to drive to Colorado.

'Jeez, Mum, relax will you,' said Danny, who wasn't impressed by this lack of cool from his mother.

Thanks to Mel's frantic desire for even more new clothes, they had nearly missed the plane. Five minutes before boarding, she had disappeared and Leonie had to double back and look in all the shops for her. She'd found Mel in a chic boutique investigating designer sunglasses that cost more than Leonie's entire outfit.

'God, Mum, they're lovely. And much cheaper than back home. Couldn't you lend me the money, pleeease? Dad'll give it to you.'

'No,' hissed Leonie. 'Everyone else is on the plane. They're calling our names, so come on!'

It was, therefore, a tired and weary woman who arrived with her charges in Denver. They were all happy and excited; Leonie felt as if she'd been dragged through a hedge backwards and, looking at herself in an unforgivingly enormous mirror in the luggage hall ladies' loo, she discovered she looked like it too.

What had Hannah suggested to her? *Bright lipstick and throw on that silky red sweater so you'll look vibrant no matter how tired you are*. It had sounded great when Hannah said it but, under the current circumstances, Leonie decided that messing around with lipstick and red sweaters would merely highlight her exhausted, red-rimmed eyes. Then again, perhaps matching your eyes with your sweater would be seen as a plus. A sort of colour-coordination thing.

Fliss and Ray were meeting them. Originally, Leonie had protested that of course she and the kids would get to Vail on their own.

'It can't be that difficult,' she'd told Ray loftily. 'There are shuttle buses, I believe. I'm sure we can manage.'

But she was glad now they were being picked up. She couldn't face negotiating another journey, sorting out which bus they wanted and piling luggage on to it.

Unfortunately, being collected by the soon-to-be-happily-marrieds had its disadvantages: they'd see her in this state. She unscrewed her lipstick and slicked some on before struggling into her red sweater. It was a small improvement, she decided wearily.

Danny had manfully collected all their luggage. 'What have you got in there, Mel, a dead body?' he grumbled, hoisting the final suitcase on top of the overloaded trolley.

'We don't all want to look like backpackers, you know,' Mel replied snootily. 'I've just brought a few things.'

'Oh yeah, like a few trowels to slap all your make-up on,' he retorted.

So it was squabbling as usual that the family emerged from customs into the bright glare of the arrivals hall.

'Dad! I see Dad!' squealed Mel excitedly. She ran through the crowds with Abby, and Danny pushed the trolley rapidly after them. Reluctantly, Leonie followed.

She slowed down. Let them all say hello to each other before she got there. She needed a few moments to prepare herself. A group of people barged in front of her, momentarily separating her from the others. Leonie waited patiently for the group to pass. She hadn't seen Ray for two years and felt a bit anxious about meeting him now. A large man in front of her moved and, through the gap in the crowd, she could see her children finally reach their father and his fiancée. The joy with which they all greeted each other took her breath away. Ray looked happier than she'd ever seen him: he'd filled out, wasn't as thin as he used to be. His dark hair was greying, but he was tanned and looked wonderful, just like the slender, vibrant woman at his side. Fliss was even better looking in the flesh than she was in the photos from the kids' summer holidays. Dressed in denims and a butter-coloured suede jacket, she was lightly tanned and, when she smiled, her teeth were gleaming white against her glowing skin. The short dark hair that had looked like a boyish cut in the photos was now longer but still casually chic. That was the word for Fliss, Leonie decided: chic. Watching them all from her hidden vantage point, Leonie felt like the interloper, the spectre at the feast.

Ray and Fliss could have been the kids' parents, not Leonie and Ray. They were all laughing and smiling, hugging each other. Ray was saying, 'You've got bigger, Danny, I swear!' Mel even looked like Fliss: the same long limbs, the same careless beauty. Fliss rested her hand on Abby's waist and Leonie was horrified to see that Abby was smiling radiantly. Jealousy curled around Leonie's heart like a starving boa constrictor clutching a small animal. They were her children, yet they were smiling at this woman with love and affection. And yes, Leonie could see it in all their eyes, admiration.

'Leonie! There you are!' Ray bypassed the group in front of her and hugged her warmly. 'You look wonderful. It's so great to see you. Come and meet Fliss.'

He must need to visit the optician, Leonie thought grimly as she was led round to meet Fliss. *You look wonderful,* my ass.

Fliss didn't grab Leonie in a bear hug. Instead, she smiled what seemed like a very genuine smile, held out her hand and said: 'It's lovely to meet you at last, Leonie. I'm so glad you could make it.'

Leonie smiled back and said, yes, it was lovely to meet her and what a lovely place Denver was and God, but she could kill a cup of tea or the chance to put her feet up, she was so exhausted.

Listening to herself, she realized with disgust that she sounded like some cardboard Irish woman from a terrible play, the stereotypical solid old bag with an emerald-green headscarf and an Aran sweater who kept saying, 'Begod, America's a fine spot and sure, put the kettle on there and boil up some spuds.' What was *happening* to her?

Where was the sophisticate she'd planned to be? Why had she been replaced by an auto-pilot parody of an Irishwoman?

'I'm so sorry, forgive me. You must be exhausted, Leonie,' Fliss said instantly. 'Come along, guys, we've got to give your mom a rest. Danny, there's a vending machine over there. Here's a dollar, get your mom a hot drink.' She handed him some change and he obediently went off.

Leonie stared at him. Getting Danny to do anything without a ten-minute interval of grumbling was impossible. How had Fliss managed it when she, his mother, couldn't?

'Ray, honey, we're parked a long way off so if you get the Jeep, Leonie and I'll wait for you with the luggage – that way she won't have to walk all the way round the lot to get to it,' Fliss commanded.

He rushed off to do her bidding too and Leonie found herself standing with Fliss at the entrance to the parking lot, sipping a plastic cup of something that didn't taste as if a tealeaf had ever even swum through it. The girls chattered nineteen to the dozen to Fliss while Danny lounged beside her, only saying anything when a particularly nice car drove past.

'Wow, a Pontiac Firebird,' he exclaimed as something red and sporty appeared.

Ray pulled up in a huge off-road vehicle and they dumped the luggage in the back and climbed in.

'Are you OK back there, Leonie?' Fliss asked in concern from her position in the front seat beside Ray.

'Sure, it's lovely,' Leonie said. *Stop with the begorrah act*! she hissed at herself. 'Marvellous,' she added, determined to get the blarney out of her voice. 'It's cold, isn't it,' she said, as Ray fiddled with the heater. 'There must be quite a wind-chill factor. I don't think any of us knew how cold it would be here. Usually on holiday, I end up going somewhere hot.' Shit. That made it sound as if she was the sort of vacuous woman who liked baking herself to a crisp on the Costa Del Whatever and couldn't cope with any other sort of holiday. 'It's wonderful to be here in Colorado,' she continued brightly.

'We're glad you could come,' Ray said. 'Wait till you see Vail. It's breathtaking. The skiing is marvellous, you guys.'

The talk turned to skiing and, as Leonie had no intention of trying it, she sat back in her seat and looked out the window as the lights of Denver swept past. Even the ever-laid-back Danny was excited about skiing for the first time and, as the other five talked, Leonie stared out into the inky night. Denver had a marvellous natural history museum with a planetarium, she'd read in a guide book borrowed from the library. And lots of bookshops and plenty of historic sights like the Unsinkable Molly Brown's Victorian house.

If the wedding fever got too much for her, she'd get a bus back to the city and do her own thing, she decided. Vail was only a hundred miles away and there was daily transport to and from the city.

After the trauma of the flights, Leonie surprised herself by falling asleep for the journey.

'Mom, we're here,' said a voice. Mel, calling her 'Mom'. Americanized already, Leonie thought sleepily.

She got out of the off-roader to find herself outside a selection of wooden cabins and one small hotel, all of which could have come straight from the pages of *Heidi*. Windows with adorable carved shutters, sweetly carved porches complete with wooden curlicues and window boxes with little conifers gave the cabins an authentic Tyrolean look. Not that she'd ever been to the Tyrol, but Leonie had looked at enough holiday programmes in her time to recognize the Austrian experience had been uprooted and replanted in Vail. Every little detail, including the hanging wooden signs proclaiming the cabins' names, was picture-postcard perfect. Only the phalanx of gleaming and expensive four-wheel drive vehicles parked carelessly to one side of the hotel showed that this was wealthy Vail and not nineteenth-century Heidi-land.

'Isn't it adorable?' sighed Fliss. 'The hotel has a dining room, bar, sauna, hot tub – everything you could want – but each cabin is self-contained. The best part about the complex is that we're only two miles outside Vail village itself. They'll shuttle you into town anytime you want, or it's a mile by the back path. Ray checked you in earlier so you don't have to bother with registering; you can do that tomorrow. I'm sure you're dying to get into bed.'

'Yes,' Leonie said. 'I could sleep for a week.'

'Sleep!' exclaimed Mel. 'How could you want to sleep, Mom? I'd love to explore right now.'

'I thought you'd want your beauty sleep, young lady,' Fliss said, affectionately ruffling Mel's silky hair.

Another dart of jealousy nipped Leonie. She was surprised at how much it hurt her to watch them together. It was ridiculous, being jealous of your children enjoying themselves with someone else. Honestly, what was she like?

'Thank you so much, Fliss,' she said, being over-friendly to compensate for how bitchy she felt. 'This is lovely. It's a truly beautiful place for a wedding. Which cabin is ours?'

The word cabin was a bit misleading, she felt as Ray let them into it. Leonie had been expecting something practical and spartan in a homespun way. That's how skiing cabins looked on holiday programmes normally: roomy enough for skiing paraphernalia and with a basic kitchen fitted out for cooking enormous après-ski dinners. This one was obviously the deluxe version.

Decorated in a warm, dark umber colour, the huge sitting room was a shrine to American Indian art, complete with wall-hangings, a driftwood sculpture of a bison and two giant watercolours of rock drawings on pale stone. 'They're Anasazi paintings, from the Mesa Verde,' explained Ray. 'The Anasazi were native Americans from over two thousand years ago. Fliss's mom is thinking of getting a trip together to visit Mesa Verde some day. It's hard going in winter, but it's worth it, she says.'

'Great!' said Abby, who loved history.

'Knew you'd like that, Pumpkin,' her father said lovingly. 'I better leave you to it. I'll phone you in the morning to see what you want to do, kids.'

Danny threw himself down on a huge couch in front of a big fire and admired the room, while the girls rushed to investigate the bedroom facilities.

'This one's huge, it should be yours, Mum,' Abby said.

'But there's two of us and we need more room. And it's got an ensuite,' wailed Mel, who wasn't as giving as her twin and clearly fancied herself in the master bedroom.

Leonie went in to referee.

'This room's prettier,' said Abby, peering into a second room. 'It's got twin beds, a fireplace and patio doors.'

'Oh, lemme see,' squealed Mel.

Leonie toured the premises. A well-equipped kitchen leading on to a dining area, the sitting room, a huge bathroom with an enormous tub big enough for three people, and three bedrooms.

Danny could have the third room.

She got her luggage, dragged it into the double room – which was very nice really, with a huge bed, and striking dark green décor – and left them to it.

Nine hours of sleep later, Leonie felt well enough to get up and think about breakfast. The girls were gone but Danny was still in his bed. Some things never change, she thought fondly, peering in his bedroom door at the giant lump huddled up in a stripey duvet.

Somebody had kindly left coffee, milk, sugar, bread and a few other necessities in the kitchen, so Leonie made herself coffee, delighted to have figured out the complicated coffee machine so easily. After fixing herself toast, low-fat spread and some sort of grape jam labelled jelly, she retired to the sitting room and looked out of the window to see what sort of place they were in.

Magnificent, she realized, having to stop munching mid-slice as she gazed at the stately snowy mountains all around her. They were huge, they made the mountains back home look like hills. The sun shone off the snow, lighting the valley with bright glorious sunshine. The Colorado light was legendary, Leonie's guide book had said. The guide book was right. The whole place was fantastic. Leonie felt a *frisson* of excitement. This was such a glorious place, they'd have a wonderful holiday.

Ray phoned to say the girls were with him and that he hoped to bring them all to lunch in Vail at one o'clock to show them where everything was. 'It's terribly pretty, Leonie. You'll love it. There's lots to do if you don't want to ski: shopping, sleigh rides, eating out. The list is endless. I'm going to take the kids ice skating in Beaver Creek tomorrow,' he added, 'if you'd like to come. By the way, Fliss has dinner organized with her parents tonight, and I hope you can come. Apart from that, and the wedding, of course, you're free to do what you want.'

'Which cabin are you in?' Leonie enquired.

'We're staying at Fliss's parents' place, half a mile away. That's where the wedding is going to be held,' Ray explained.

It must be a small wedding then, Leonie thought. Funny, she'd been expecting some big, showy affair.

'How many are coming?' she asked.

'About two hundred,' he replied.

'Jesus, that must be one hell of a cabin,' Leonie gasped.

There was an embarrassed silence 'That's what I thought at first,' Ray said finally. 'They all insist on calling it a cabin. It's really a big house, split-level with masses of room. It's the same as the way they all call those huge houses in the Hamptons "cottages" when they're mansions.'

'I better not mention my *cottage* then,' Leonie grinned. 'Everyone will think I'm loaded.'

Vail was beautiful, she had to admit, hours later when she and the girls were tired from going from shop to shop, admiring the designer clothes and everything you ever needed to ski in style.

The twins adored the picturesque Bavarian-style buildings and Mel was in seventh heaven as they trekked from boutique to boutique, looking at clothes.

But it wasn't a cheap place. Fliss's parents must be seriously rich if they owned a place here.

'Did you meet Fliss's mum and dad during the summer?' she asked the twins.

Abby shook her head: Mel was too busy drooling over a beaded micro-dress in one of the few shop windows that didn't have skiing clothes in it.

'It's cold,' Leonie said, shivering. It began to snow gently, soft fluffy flakes, perfect for skiing on, Abby explained.

'Let's sit down somewhere,' Leonie begged. 'These boots are killing me.'

Over mugs of steaming cinnamon-topped hot chocolate, Mel stared out the window at the passing pedestrians and Abby read the Vail guide book her father had given her. She was fascinated by the skiing section: Ray was taking them all out the next day and Abby couldn't wait. Leonie sipped her sweet chocolate and hoped the simple dinner tonight wasn't going to be some fiercely dressed-up affair. Everybody in Vail was beautifully, expensively dressed. She'd seen more fur here than she'd ever seen before. The anti-fur lobby obviously hadn't reached this corner of the world.

They'd watched two women in ankle-length minks, snow boots and wrap-around sunglasses sashaying across the street in exquisite full make-up. Mel had been convinced they were movie stars and had craned her head for a better look. Leonie had even seen fur-lined skiing clothes. She didn't feel as if she fitted in. Had it been a horrible mistake to come?

Ray didn't pick them up in his Jeep that evening for dinner: a short man who respectfully called her Mrs Delaney came instead.

'I drive for the Berkeley family,' he explained when Mel artlessly asked him who he was.

'How lovely,' smiled Leonie, wincing on the inside. Now she knew for definite that it was going to be a very posh evening.

Any family who had their own driver were in a different league to the Greystones' Delaneys. Doubtless, dinner would not be lasagne and baked potatoes eaten at the kitchen table. Her old reliable, the copper velvet trousersuit, was not going to cut the mustard with the super-rich Berkeley family, even if she was wearing her best Egyptian jewellery and had gone easy on the kohl. It'd probably be the sort of night where even the maid wore Gucci. Gulping at the thought, Leonie pulled on her warm woollen coat and climbed into the back of the Jeep.

The Berkeleys' cabin would have made a super B & B, she decided as the driver steered the car into the drive where two Mercedes were already parked. Mel was most impressed by the size of the house.

'Wow,' she said in awe. 'This is amazing.'

'Yeah,' Danny agreed. 'They must be loaded.'

'Danny!' hissed his mother. 'Keep your voice down. We're not here to assess their net worth. Don't turn the plates upside down to see where they came from.'

Everyone giggled.

Fliss and Ray were waiting at the door for them and Leonie was struck once again by how much a couple they seemed; every time Fliss moved, Ray watched her, his eyes following every gesture, every smile, as if he couldn't bear to tear his gaze away from this beautiful creature. And Fliss did look beautiful.

She wasn't showily dressed. In fact, her grey tailored trousers and silvery V-neck sweater were simple in the extreme. But they were beautifully cut, elegant clothes. The sweater was probably cashmere, Leonie thought. And definitely expensive. It was the combination of the clothes and Fliss's own simple, understated beauty that made you stare at her. She really did wear practically no make-up apart from lip gloss and mascara, as Mel had explained that first time. Still, she looked wonderful. Leonie felt like she'd escaped from the clowns' caravan in the circus by comparison.

This time, Fliss hugged her. 'I'm so glad you're here, it means such a lot to Ray,' she confided as Ray led the others into a large reception room. 'I don't know if I'd be able to go to my ex-husband's wedding, I'm so possessive. But it's wonderful that you and Ray get on so well. It's great for the kids, and I wanted you to meet me and know they'd always be safe and happy with me.'

It was the longest speech she'd made to Leonie, who wasn't quite sure what to say in response. Leonie felt that it might be a mistake to reveal that seeing Fliss with her children cut her to the quick, so she smiled and limited herself to saying, 'I'm happy to be here, Fliss. I'm glad Ray is happy.'

Which was true, more or less. Well, it wasn't that she wished him to be *un*happy, but it was hard to see him marrying someone he adored while she remained so spectacularly single. If he'd been a teensy bit less happy, it might have been easier to bear all this wedding stuff. Sheer joy was very hard to cope with at such close quarters.

But Leonie could hardly let that slip. So she patted Fliss's arm and added that people were very civilized in Ireland these days and remarriages were commonplace now.

It was a very civilized evening all round. Fliss's parents were there with their new spouses, and when Leonie was first introduced to them, she couldn't imagine how the original Mr and Mrs Berkeley had got together in the first place. Opposites must certainly attract.

Fliss's mother, Lydia, was a taut-faced, elegant brunette who spoke in a genteel voice and looked as if she never lifted a finger to fetch a tissue when she could summon a minion to do it for her.

Fliss's father, Charlie was a big blond bear of a man with a weather-beaten face, hands like hams and a marvellous sense of humour. He spent most of his days on his cattle ranch in Texas, a place where Leonie couldn't imagine the immaculate Lydia ever setting foot. His current wife, Andrea, was a down-to-earth, country-loving woman with Bo Derek bone structure and a mane of silvery blonde hair. She and Leonie hit it off immediately. Fliss's stepfather, Wilson, was a lawyer and he and Ray were obviously good pals.

Andrea, Charlie and Wilson were incredibly friendly, and all did their best to make Leonie, Danny, Mel and Abby feel at home. Clever, warm people, they were good company and made Leonie relax. The guests were plied with food and drink and everyone made a big effort to include them in the conversation. Only Lydia, Fliss's mother, was aloof. It was most disconcerting, but every time Leonie looked up, she found Lydia watching her. Probably wondering how her future son-in-law ever married me, Leonie thought grimly. She couldn't warm to the ex-Mrs Berkeley, even when Lydia insisted that Leonie sit beside her at the dinner table so they could talk.

Leonie suspected the only thing Lydia wanted to talk about was how much alimony Ray was paying her, so she could ascertain whether her beloved Fliss was getting her fair share. Not that Fliss appeared to need any money. Between her wealthy parents and her job, she obviously didn't go short.

During the first course, Lydia questioned with the subtlety of a NASA probe. But with the entertaining Charlie on her right, Leonie managed to enjoy the meal.

Charlie kept the conversation going with stories about his ranch and life in the Panhandle.

'You should visit us there,' he told her. 'You'd love it, particularly as you're not partial to skiing. Texas is hot, believe me.'

Once he discovered that she worked as a veterinary nurse, they were friends for life. Charlie had dabbled in every type of farming, from dairy to horses. Now, he had what he described as a small herd of cows and a few horses. Andrea laughed and told Leonie that her husband's notion of a 'small herd' meant six thousand head of cattle.

'Ours is mainly a small-animal practice,' Leonie explained when Charlie began getting into the intricacies of modern breeding techniques and embryo transplantation. 'I haven't seen a cow for a long time. We handle a lot of dogs, cats and hamsters, with the odd lizard thrown in for good measure. Oh yes, one client breeds African Greys. They're parrots,' she added, 'so we care for them too. They're lovely, so affectionate. There's nothing quite as sweet as a parrot nuzzling up to you and gently grooming your hair.'

Even the uptight Lydia relaxed after a few glasses of wine and unbent enough to chatter idly with Leonie about the wedding.

Leonie kindly listened to fifteen minutes of minutiae about placements, the difficulty of getting caterers who could do a really exquisite lobster thermidor, and how Fliss had always said she wanted a Calvin Klein wedding gown.

Leonie felt that if she said, 'Oh really?' one more time, she'd choke on the words. To vary her responses, she tried asking about the actual gown. 'Is it Calvin Klein? What's it like?'

Lydia looked as shocked as if Leonie had suggested a gang-bang with the staff on the snow-covered terrace. 'I can't talk about it with Ray here,' she whispered. 'It's unlucky. I'll show it to you now, shall I?'

Leaving Leonie no time to say that, actually, she could live quite happily without seeing her ex-husband's fiancée's wedding dress in advance, Lydia had loudly announced that coffee would be served in the library.

There was a *library* too? Leonie sighed. And this was only the holiday home. God alone knew what sort of mausoleum Fliss's actual childhood home had been. Palace-sized, no doubt. No wonder she was so slim – all that running between rooms would keep you fit.

'Fliss,' whispered Lydia, 'I'm going to show Leonie your dress.'

'What a wonderful idea,' cried Fliss.

The female members of the party set off en masse to see the dress, leaving the men alone with the coffee. Mel and Abby, who'd both been allowed a glass of wine with dinner, were giggly and linked hands conspiratorially with Fliss as they all marched through a long corridor to the bedroom where the gown was displayed on a dress-maker's dummy. Everyone was suitably silent with approval at the sight of the dress.

It was very Calvin: an oyster silk, bias-cut sheath with a gently draped neckline. Leonie could just imagine Fliss wearing it, looking gloriously sophisticated and giving the young supermodels a run for their money.

'Oooh,' sighed Mel in designer delight. 'It's beautiful.'

'Gorgeous,' said Abby.

'Do you like it, girls?' asked Fliss anxiously, as if their opinion was the most important of all.

'Of course,' they chorused and hugged her.

Leonie felt a lump in her throat at the touching tableau. Fliss was wiping her eyes with the emotion of it all, while the twins kissed her and told her she'd look stunning in the dress.

Andrea gave Leonie a comforting smile. 'I'm sure it's hard to see your ex getting married again,' she whispered, giving Leonie's arm a squeeze.

'Not at all,' protested Leonie honestly. What was killing her was seeing Mel and Abby so utterly in love with their soon-to-be step-mother. *That* was what hurt, not the idea of Ray and Fliss walking down the aisle looking like an advert for forty-something love.

'Beautiful,' Lydia said proudly, looking at both the dress and her beloved daughter.

'Beautiful,' echoed Leonie, smiling so hard she thought her foundation would crack.

Everyone was being so kind to her, so warm and welcoming, yet she felt like the spectre at the feast. How could the children not want to be part of this gilded, privileged family when the alternative was their boring old life back in Wicklow?

'Would you look at that. Isn't it beautiful?' said the girl sitting next to Leonie on the little gilt chair in the Berkeley sitting room which had been transformed into a chapel of *lurve* in honour of Fliss and Ray's nuptials. Pale orchids drooped in the almost tropical heat of the room and subtle saffron-coloured ribbons were trailed around them, creating a display that was both elegant and beautiful.

'Yes, it's beautiful,' said Leonie dutifully. Her bum hurt from half an hour on the chair, which was not built for anyone with the vaguest hint of arthritis. Since she and the children had arrived half an hour previously, people had been murmuring, 'Isn't it beautiful!' to her constantly. It was all bloody beautiful, from the morning-suited men right down to the posies of orchids clinging to every conceivable spot. The string quartet were beautiful; the pre-ceremony glass of pink champagne had been beautiful; and Fliss's sister, Mona, a raver in approximately one metre of cream leather who clearly wasn't having any truck with being a bridesmaid in yards of frills, was also beautiful if a little underdressed. Leonie was fed up to the back teeth with the whole beautiful thing.

'Mum,' breathed Mel, sliding into her place beside Leonie, 'she's coming and she looks . . .'

'Don't tell me,' said Leonie between gritted teeth: '. . . beautiful.'

Mel was overawed. Her mother could recognize the signs. For the past three days, Mel hadn't stopped talking about the Berkeleys' house, all the lovely things they had and how nice it must be to live here. Ray had taken them skiing, on a sleigh ride, to dinner in a quirky steak restaurant and ice skating. Leonie wondered if Mel would ever again adapt to life in a small cottage in Greystones. At home, the house needed painting, the tiles in the bathroom were slowly disconnecting from the wall, the library consisted of the bookcases in the sitting room, and the only time they ever used linen napkins at dinner was when Claire came round and gave them out because she hated using kitchen roll.

'Don't forget, Mel, this is lovely but it is a different world to ours,'

Leonie couldn't help saying. 'It's Fliss's parents who have all this money. Neither Dad nor I do, so our life isn't like this.'

'I'm not stupid, Mum.' Mel looked scathing. 'It's nice to enjoy it. Can't you let me do that without trying to ruin everything!'

Which was why Leonie's eyes were filled with tears when Fliss walked slowly and gracefully down the aisle to meet Ray. Through the tears, Leonie saw that Fliss did indeed look stunning in her Calvin Klein dress: a tall, slim vision in cream with a small bouquet of creamy orchids in her hands.

Andrea, who was on the other side of the aisle, shot Leonie a sweet, poor-you look. Leonie wanted to scream out loud that she didn't give a flying fuck who Ray married but she'd had it up to her tonsils with the Berkeley family's obvious wealth, which was being shoved down their throats.

After the ceremony, Mel shot off, leaving her mother, Abby and Danny in their seats, wondering what to do next. They weren't left wondering long. The two hundred guests were ushered into the dining room. Double doors which opened into a huge conservatory had been taken off, making one huge ballroom-sized room. The conservatory faced an expanse of snow-covered mountain, so the vista from the room was magnificent. So too was the huge table laden with an extravagant buffet, and at its centre an ice sculpture of two swans beside a huge bowl of oysters.

There was lobster, salmon, what looked like a side of beef, and more Parma ham than you'd find in Italy, not to mention every sort of salad on earth and the more unusual varieties of lettuce. Tuxedoed waiters flew about noiselessly, bearing champagne, mineral water and gold-edged plates for the buffet. It wasn't long before the party began in earnest, with lots of laughing, joke-telling and even a moment of madness when a sprightly octogenarian dragged Mona up to dance while the entire wedding party clapped on the sidelines.

Lydia couldn't resist sidling up to Leonie and boasting about everything. 'The ice sculpture had to be flown in from LA,' she said smugly. 'It's keeping the oysters cold.'

With great effort, Leonie resisted the temptation to say they didn't need an ice sculpture to do that: stick the oysters beside Lydia herself and they'd remain suitably frosty. Instead, she nodded gravely and said she was always nervous of serving shellfish at parties because of the salmonella risk. It was worth it to see Lydia's eyes widen with horror as she rushed off to the kitchen, no doubt to harangue the poor caterers to make sure nobody died in a hail of food poisoning.

'Great, isn't it, Mum?' said Danny, arriving with a plate already piled high with food. He had a glass of beer too. 'Dad got it for me,' he said, taking a slug of beer. 'He knows I'm not into wine. You all right, Mum?' he asked. 'You're a bit quiet. Mel driving you mad, huh?'

Leonie felt herself tear up again. This was ridiculous. She was developing incontinent eyes. It was just that having Danny being unusually intuitive was so sweet. It was normally Abby who understood exactly how her mother was feeling. These last few days, however, Abby had been superglued to Fliss's side, chatting and smiling up at her, apparently happier with her new stepmother than with her real mother.

'I'm fine,' Leonie said briskly. 'I keep having visions of the place at home and comparing it to this place. I'll never be able to eat off our fifty-pence-in-the-sale plates ever again after eating off these gold ones.'

Danny snorted. 'This is all show, Mum,' he said dismissively. 'It's Fliss's mother's idea. She's a real show-off and she's full of crap. Everyone else is nice,' he added, 'but she's the one who wants this big party. Dad told me that he and Fliss wanted a small wedding but she begged to have this funfair.'

Leonie felt a momentary twinge of pity for Lydia. Having an ostentatious wedding for her daughter was obviously her way of dealing with a life of boredom.

By nightfall, Leonie was bored herself. She'd talked to endless kind couples and had eaten far too much, but even the wonderful food and vintage champagne couldn't make up for the ache she got in her heart when she saw Mel and Abby fussing around their new stepmother so delightedly. Or compensate for how out of it she felt as the only unaccompanied woman there.

Every time Leonie looked in their direction, Fliss was laughing and giggling with the twins. The newlyweds circulated graciously as a couple with their ready-made family tagging along behind them. And it was Abby, once her mother's stalwart, who appeared happiest with Fliss. Her face was animated as she laughed at Fliss, who patted her arm and fixed Abby's hair with the affectionate gestures of one who had done this often. Mel hung on her father's arm, seemingly delighted to be part of this laughing, gorgeous group. She was so pretty: her cheeks were flushed a pale rosy pink and her dark hair swung silkily around her heart-shaped face. Fliss had lent the twins some expensive make-up and they'd had a ball that morning doing themselves up in the bathroom. Watching them all together, Leonie couldn't help but feel a pang of fear deep inside.

Fliss obviously loved the twins and would be a fabulous mother to her own kids. But what if she became so close to Mel and Abby that she took them over as hers? What if the twins decided they preferred this wonderful American lifestyle to their own simple life with her in Ireland? What would Leonie do then?

Kirsten and Patrick's New Year's Day party was going brilliantly. Even bad-tempered Great-Aunt Petra, had she been asked, would have had to admit that they knew how to throw one hell of a do. But because Kirsten hated Petra, no invitation had been issued to her.

'I'm not having that old cow at our party,' she'd told Emma forcefully. 'Let her sit at home and mix up eye of newt and wing of bat in her cauldron, the old witch.'

Emma wished *she* was as forceful when it came to keeping Petra off her invitation list.

At least a hundred and fifty people were crammed into their large modern Castleknock home, stuffing their faces with the oriental food Kirsten had insisted on. The wine was flowing and if some of Patrick's fellow brokers were growing a bit rowdy in one corner, it all added to the general air of merriment which was helped along by a CD playing kitschy Christmas tunes at full belt.

Kirsten sailed around the house in a gold Karen Millen crochet dress, flitting from conservatory to dining room to kitchen, chatting with guests and draining vodka after vodka. She'd left Emma in a corner of the dining room with Anne-Marie and Jimmy, both of whom were looking unimpressed at the plateful of dim sum they'd been given. Pete had gone off to get a refill of wine for himself and Jimmy. In his absence, there was silence in their little group, a direct contrast to the loud, excited chatter going on all around them as Kirsten and Patrick's pals exchanged Christmas horror stories and groaned about the thought of going back to work after such a long holiday.

Emma, who wasn't drinking because she was designated driver, crunched into a spring roll and stole a surreptitious look at her watch. Nearly six. She and Pete had decided to invent another party that evening so they'd have an excuse for leaving early.

'You know that Kirsten will dump your parents on us,' Pete had groaned. 'We may as well have a contingency plan so we have some hope of escape.'

Their real plan was a quiet evening at home. A trickling sound made Emma glance over at her mother who was sitting at the table between Emma and Jimmy. She had stopped pushing food around her plate with her fork; her glass had fallen sideways in her hand and she was slowly spilling her red wine on to the floor as tears ran heedlessly down her face. Emma stared at the slowly spilling wine, too shocked to do anything for a moment.

'Mum!' hissed Emma.

As her mother's red eyes turned to face her, Emma was frightened by what she saw in them: Anne-Marie's expression was of sheer, anguished fear.

'I'm afraid, Emma,' she sobbed. 'Afraid. I don't know what's happening to me. I don't know anything any more.'

Her mother's hand jerked and the trail of red liquid started splashing on to her lap, soaking the floral silky skirt with a growing crimson stain. It was like blood, Emma thought in horror.

'Mum,' she said in distress, trying to take the spilling glass from her mother. Anne-Marie's hand was clenched tightly around it and more wine slopped on to Emma and the carpet before she could wrench it away. Crouching down on the ground beside her mother's chair, she threw her arms around Anne-Marie.

'Mum,' she crooned, 'it's OK, I'm here and Dad's here.'

'But you're not always here and I can hear the voices and I can't remember things,' moaned her mother.

Emma kept hugging her, but her mother couldn't stop crying. And why wasn't Jimmy doing anything?

'Dad,' whispered Emma, 'look at Mum. Can you help her.' She felt powerless to do anything, but so was Jimmy. His face froze as he saw his wife with tears sliding down her face.

'Help me, help me, help me!' shouted Anne-Marie suddenly, her voice loud and carrying across the room.

Emma could see Pete arriving from the kitchen with wine, his mouth an astonished oval. He seemed to be walking slowly towards them, as if in slow-motion.

The entire scene seemed as if it was being played in slow-motion, Emma felt. She could sense her father's eyebrows lifting slowly in shock, could feel people's heads swivelling at a leisurely pace towards them and mouths opening at a snail-like pace.

'Mum,' she soothed, 'please don't get upset. We'll help you, I promise.'

'You won't, you won't! You're all against me,' screamed her mother, clambering to her feet abruptly.

'No,' she roared, so loud that nobody in the house could miss hearing her, despite the sleighbells of Kirsten's Christmas album jingling loudly in the background. 'No, no, no, no!' She was screaming now, lashing out wildly and shoving plates and glasses across the table. Crockery crashed to the floor. 'How could you say it? What are you trying to do to me?' she roared. 'You don't understand, do you hear me? You don't understand. I won't go there, I won't!'

Pete dumped the glasses of wine and together, he and Emma tried to put their arms around Anne-Marie to calm her.

'Mum, it's OK. We're here with you, nobody's trying to send you anywhere.'

'You are,' wailed her mother, still trying to shove plates from the table. 'You're all in on it!'

'It's all right, Anne-Marie,' said Pete soothingly, 'all right. We'll look after you.'

His calm voice seemed to do the trick. She stopped struggling and sat heavily down in her chair. Pete and Emma squatted on either side of her.

'Mum, it's me, Emma.' Emma tried to keep her voice steady. It was hard: she was shaking so much she felt as if her very bones were rattling. 'Dad, can you help?'

Hearing Emma speak to him, Jimmy O'Brien seemed to come out of the astonished trance-like state he was in. 'Yes,' he gasped.

He shoved Pete out of the way and grabbed his wife.

'Anne-Marie, I'm here with you, love. Don't worry about a thing. It'll be all right.'

She collapsed against his bulky figure, her long, pale golden hair escaping from its butterfly clip to stream untidily down her back.

'Let's get her home,' Jimmy said firmly, holding his wife's frail body tenderly.

Kirsten insisted on staying with her guests but Patrick drove Jimmy and Anne-Marie home in his BMW, with Pete and a terrified Emma following behind.

'We've got to call the doctor,' Emma said, still shaking.

'Absolutely,' Pete said.

But Jimmy O'Brien was having none of it. 'We don't need a doctor!' he roared. 'She's perfectly fine. A bit stressed, that's all.'

Upstairs, where she was helping her mother to change her dress, Emma cringed at the fury in his voice.

Pete and Patrick exchanged a glance. 'I'm sorry, Jimmy,' said Pete firmly, 'you're over-ruled on this one. Anne-Marie is more than just stressed. She's not well, she could have something serious wrong with her. I'm phoning the doctor. I can't live with my conscience if something serious is wrong and we've done nothing.'

Emma strained towards her parents' bedroom door, desperate to hear what would happen next. Her father spoke, only it didn't sound like him really. This voice was tired and weak, not the obstreperous man she'd known all her life:

'What if they want to put her in a hospital, what will I do then?'

'I'm sorry, dear,' Anne-Marie smiled at her daughter, clumsily trying to close the buttons on a clean dress and failing. 'I was angry, wasn't I? I am sorry, I didn't mean to be. I don't know what came over me.'

'It's all right, Mum,' Emma said, gently taking over the buttoning. Her mother, who would once have been outraged if anyone had tried to help her with her toilette, sighed with relief as Emma buttoned her up. 'Tell me,' Emma began, 'you said you forget things, Mum. What things do you forget?'

Her mother blinked at her. 'Where I put things: I can't find things any more. And I can't seem to read. I have to get my glasses changed, they're not strong enough. The words, you see,' she explained earnestly, 'the words are too small and jumbled up. I tried using your father's magnifying glass, but it doesn't help. Will you bring me to get new glasses, Emma?'

Her daughter had to bite her lip to stop herself bursting into tears.

'Of course, Mum. But first, let's get the doctor to look you over.'

The family doctor, an elderly gentleman with the kindest, gentlest hands and a charming manner, examined Anne-Marie from top to toe but could find nothing outwardly wrong. She chatted away to him the way she'd always done, saying she was sorry he'd been dragged out on New Year's Day and adding fondly that her dear son-in-laws fussed too much.

'Fit as a fiddle, my dear,' he told her as he left her room.

'It sounds as if she's very depressed from what you tell me,' he said thoughtfully to Pete, Emma, Patrick and Jimmy downstairs. 'That could make her lash out and get so worked up that she'd shout. But it could be some sort of seizure. We'd need tests to see what's really wrong . . .'

'No tests,' Jimmy said angrily. 'She's under a lot of strain, that's all.'

'It's more than that,' Emma said. She ignored the fierce look her father shot at her. 'She says odd things at odd times, she loses things all the time, she tried to open a tin with an egg whisk the other day.

They're all small things, but I know there's something wrong, Doctor. Now she's after telling me that she can't read any more and she thinks it's her glasses. It's not, it's more than that.'

'This is the first time this type of strange behaviour had occurred? She's been perfectly normal until now?' the GP asked.

'No. She got very upset with me a few months ago when we were shopping,' Emma said quietly. 'In a fabric shop. She began to shout at me and she didn't know who I was. I couldn't calm her down and she was calling for Dad, even though he wasn't actually with us.'

'You never told me,' said her father accusingly.

'I'm telling you now,' said Emma with an edge to her voice.

'My wife is stressed and a bit depressed,' Jimmy maintained. 'A few tablets, that's all she needs. Like the time she was on those tablets before, when Kirsten was sick with glandular fever. They sorted her out. That's all she needs now.'

'Bring her to the surgery next week and we'll have a chat,' the doctor agreed. 'If she's depressed, we can help her, but without tests, we won't know what happened today.'

'She was overwrought, Doctor, nothing more,' Jimmy said. 'She's fine now, isn't she? If it had been serious, would she be able to chat to you now as if nothing had happened?'

'True. She's only young, too. Just sixty you tell me. Well, Jimmy, I can't think what could be wrong with her at this age, but we'll keep an eye on her, I give you my word.'

'He's an old fuddy-duddy,' hissed Pete as Jimmy let the doctor out. 'Your mother could have a brain tumour and that man wouldn't recognize it. She needs to see a specialist.'

'She'll be fine,' announced Jimmy, slamming the front door.

Emma sent Pete and Patrick home. She didn't fancy staying with her father any longer, but felt she should be there for her mother. Jimmy didn't appear to know how to handle Anne-Marie.

The three of them sat in front of the television for a while before Anne-Marie said she was tired and wanted to go to bed. It was only half past eight.

Her mother didn't quibble when Emma accompanied her upstairs and helped her with her clothes. Instead, she seemed happy at the company. When she was tucked up in bed, Emma sat down beside her and smoothed her mother's long fair hair gently.

'I'm sorry you were so upset earlier,' she said softly.

'You were telling me I had to go to that bad place again,' Anne-Marie said sleepily, one hand holding Emma's tightly.

'I didn't mean it,' Emma said, thinking that it was probably kinder to pretend that she knew what her mother was on about.

'Talk to me, Emma,' murmured Anne-Marie. 'I like to hear your voice.'

Emma started a soft, gentle monologue about what she was going to do the next day and how she'd come over in the evening and see Anne-Marie. Her voice certainly seemed to soothe her mother, who drifted off to sleep, still clutching her hand.

Emma remembered being a child and how the roles had been reversed: whenever she had a nightmare, her mother, wearing one of her lovely soft brushed-cotton nightdresses with lily-of-the-valley-scented handcream on her soft hands, would hurry in once she'd heard Emma's screams and sit comfortingly beside her, stroking her fevered forehead and telling her that the hobgoblins had all gone.

Now *she* had taken the role of the mother comforting her child instead of the other way round. How strange to have someone to mother after so long dreaming of a baby; only now, her baby was a sixty-year-old woman who'd sunk into childhood again. But why? And would she get worse in the future?

She wished she had a night-light to leave on the bedside table, something dim and soothing in case Anne-Marie woke up suddenly and couldn't remember where she was.

Emma could recall the tiny light with a caterpillar inside that her mother had bought when Kirsten had been small: his green glowing body let off enough light to scare away the bad dreams. Maybe that was why Kirsten never had nightmares. She'd had Mr Caterpillar to keep her safe at night.

Her mother was breathing easily now. Emma got off the bed and silently tidied up the room. She folded clothes and sorted out the jumble of toiletries on the once-immaculate dressing table. That was proof in itself that things were amiss: Anne-Marie had always been incredibly house proud. She'd never have allowed any surface in her home to become dusty and untidy. Cotton buds lay scattered around and talcum powder had been spilled and not cleaned up. Emma vowed to tidy it soon.

Her mother's handbag was dumped carelessly under the dressing-table stool, its gilt clasp open, displaying the contents. Sitting down on the stool, Emma looked into the handbag. Instead of the usual neat array of glasses, lipstick, powder compact, purse and linen handkerchief, there was a tangled mess with lots of little scrunched up bits of paper. Emma took a bundle out and slowly unfolded them. 'Teabags in blue tin,' read one. 'Glasses on dressing table. Don't forget!' read another. One had Emma's home phone number, with the digits written slightly wrong in two separate places and then scribbled out. It was as if her mother had tried to write it down but couldn't manage to do it correctly until the third try.

Slowly, she unfolded each pathetic scrap of paper, reading each sad message that Anne-Marie had written to herself. Reminders about where the milk was kept and what day the window cleaner came round. Most poignant of all was one with her mother's name and address carefully written on it. As if she could conceivably get lost and not know who she was or where she lived.

Emma used a tissue from the dressing table to wipe her wet eyes.

At the bottom of the handbag were buttons, lots of buttons. She counted out fifteen of them, ranging in size and colour from tiny mother-of-pearl ones to bigger navy ones that looked as if they'd been cut from Jimmy's big overcoat. God love her, Emma thought wearily. Collecting buttons. Perhaps she thought they were coins.

'Is she asleep?' asked her father, appearing at the bedroom door.

Emma nodded. She couldn't talk to him just then. He angered her so much. Today, he'd done what he always did: bulldozed over anyone who had a different opinion to his and insisted that he was right. Anne-Marie was seriously ill but, as usual, Jimmy refused to see any viewpoint other than his own.

He could face the reality on his own tonight, then. Emma wasn't going to hang around and help him deny his wife was sick. She grabbed her things and left. She could walk home; it wasn't far.

The phone call woke her and Pete at six thirty the following morning. Emma reached groggily over to the small table where the phone sat. 'Hello?' she mumbled. She could feel Pete dragging the covers over his head to block out the noise.

'Emma, it's your father,' said a voice. 'Can you come over? I can't cope.'

CHAPTER TWENTY

There was nothing to beat the satisfaction of a job well done, Hannah thought with pride, as she phoned the office to tell them 26 Weldon Drive was finally sold. Nothing. Not that first glass of wine after a hard week, not amazingly orgasmic, earth-shattering sex, nothing. Well, she allowed herself a faint grin, not that she'd had much experience of the orgasmic, earth-shattering sex thing lately. Not for over a month. A month and two days to be utterly exact.

Celibacy had its good points, she conceded. You didn't have to bother with uncomfortable G-strings sliding into the crevices of your body in an attempt to look permanently ready for sex, nor did you have to worry about whether your bikini-line resembled a hippie with a shaggy perm instead of a smooth expanse of hairless flesh. Nobody saw these bits when you were celibate, except the women in the showers in the gym, so why bother?

Hannah reckoned you could always tell the desperately in love women in the gym by the state of their bikini-lines. Women with perfectly waxed pubic mohicans were in the throes of a love affair, madly exfoliating, plucking and manicuring so that their beloved would think them perfect examples of womanhood. While women hairier than Demis Roussos were either single or in a very long-term relationship where they were in such an advanced state of intimacy – sitting on the loo while their beloved was in the bath – that they didn't bother with waxing or plucking.

Still, it was a disgrace not to bother with these feminine things, Hannah decided. There was no excuse to be slovenly. She'd book a beauty salon session later. Just because Felix wasn't hanging around like a male rabbit on heat, there was no reason to let her standards drop.

She shut and locked the front door of number 26, admiring the garden, which was awash with crocuses of every colour. Vermilion ones drooped beside vibrant yellows, with a few shy, creamy white flowers bending their bell-like heads beside the privet hedge as if overwhelmed by the gaudy glory of their friends. The woman who'd been selling the house loved her garden, that was for sure. If only she'd taken as much care of the interior, it mightn't have taken four months to sell the place.

On the market in November, it was now nearly February and the office had despaired of ever flogging this particular des res. It didn't matter how many coffee beans or loaves of bread you stuck in the oven or what sort of fragrant lilies you displayed on the hall table when buyers were coming round, the most outstanding smell in number 26 was of unneutered tomcat and unwashed clothes.

Hannah had been given the house as one of five properties in her portfolio. David gave senior agents at least fifteen each, many of which were for auction, but as she was only a junior, she had five for sale by private treaty.

She loved her new job. She loved the freedom of driving around from property to property, organizing viewings and seeing clients. Normally, David would have put her working on customer service for at least a year before letting her manage properties as a junior agent. But he had a lot of faith in her.

She was studying auctioneering part-time now, one night a week and some weekends, and had vowed to pass her exams in record time. Donna had been a great help, giving her advice on tricks of the trade, telling her how to handle any lone viewer who made her nervous ('Stand near the door,' Donna warned. 'I know you're supposed to be keeping an eye on the place to make sure they don't steal anything, but you're more valuable than any trinket they can pocket.')

There was so much to learn, about negotiating, the legal aspects of the job, and how to deal with difficult clients. 'Most people are so incredibly grateful when you sell their home,' Donna explained. 'That's a huge part of the buzz of the job, it's very rewarding. But there are difficult ones too, and you've got to know how to deal with them.'

Donna grinned. She had lots of hilarious stories about her years in the business. There was the one about the man who'd been drunk and goosed her as she led him upstairs to see a flat, another about a wet dog who'd been inadvertently let into the property when the owners were out. 'I gave that dog an entire pack of biscuits to get him back into the garden!' Donna laughed. 'The viewing was due to start at half two and I had this huge wet animal running around the house like a lunatic, throwing himself on to beds and destroying the place.'

She'd even come across one couple making love on a dining-room table when she let herself into a house. 'The woman was one of the owners,' Donna recalled, 'but the man wasn't her husband. I bit my lip to stop myself laughing. They were so embarrassed.'

Hannah had a few stories of her own now. Like the awful occasion when she'd lost a set of keys to a house. She'd searched high and low and hadn't been able to find them.

David had grinned when she came to tell him, cringing in case he'd be furious.

'You can't qualify as an estate agent if you haven't lost at least one set of keys,' he said kindly. 'Tell the client we'll get the locks changed at our expense.'

Her mobile rang, blistering the quiet of the mid-morning suburban street.

'Hannah, urgent message for you,' said Sasha, the office manager who'd been appointed when Hannah began to work as an estate agent full-time. 'Mrs Taylor, from Blackfriars Lodge in Glenageary just rang up in a complete panic. Her daughter's got measles and she can't take her out of the house for the viewing. She wants to know if there's any way we can let people see the house but stay out of that room. I know,' Sasha added, 'it's crazy. But she asked me to ask you.'

'Does she not realize that the viewers will be at risk of getting measles into the bargain, not to mention the fact that they'll all want to explore every centimetre of the place, the under-the-stairs cupboard included?' Hannah laughed. 'I'll phone her back, don't worry about it.'

Once she'd persuaded Mrs Taylor to stop panicking and promised to reschedule the viewing for the following week, she phoned Leonie to make sure she was still on for lunch. Hannah had to drive to Enniskerry in County Wicklow for a viewing that afternoon, so she had arranged to meet Leonie for a quick sandwich half-way.

'Can you make it?' Hannah asked, once she finally got through after waiting five minutes with a canine barking chorus in the background in place of 'Greensleeves'.

'Yes,' sobbed Leonie.

'What's wrong?' asked Hannah in alarm. 'Is it Abby again?'

'A guinea pig just bit me and, ouch, it's sore.'

Giggling erupted from the other end of the phone. 'Is that all?'

'You want to get bitten by a guinea pig some time, sweetie,' Leonie retorted. 'They've got teeth like chisels. And now he's squealing like an Italian tenor – you'd think *he* was the one who'd been bitten! Cuddly little thing, my backside! You won't believe his name: Peaches. Honestly, the names people give animals. They should have called him Pavarotti, the way he sings. Or maybe Fang.'

'Will you be recovered enough from your encounter with Peaches to join me for a sandwich in half an hour?' Hannah enquired.

'Only if I can have a slice of cheesecake too,' Leonie bargained. 'I'm celebrating.'

'What are you celebrating?'

'You'll have to buy me the cheesecake first.'

'Spill the beans, Ms Delaney,' Hannah ordered, plonking the tray with their lunch on it down on the table in the corner of the pub. 'What are you celebrating? If it's a man, I don't want to know. Poor single old dears like me don't want to hear about other people's sex lives.'

Leonie laughed. 'That's moving a bit fast, even for me,' she joked. 'Particularly as I haven't actually met him yet.'

'So it *is* a man,' Hannah said triumphantly. 'I knew it. You are a terrible tart! You know, Leonie, you only ever light up when it's something to do with a man.'

'I might be unlit when I meet him, because it mightn't work out,' Leonie pointed out. 'He's one of my personal advert men and I got the courage to phone him the other day. He sounds amazing, so friendly and clever and sensitive and . . .' She grimaced. 'Then I get the collywobbles when I think about Bob and what a disaster that turned out to be. He sounded lovely on the phone too, so this guy could be terrible.'

'Nonsense. He's probably wonderful.' Hannah took a bite of her tunafish sandwich.

'I'm hoping for a six foot blond Adonis with a body to die for and healing hands,' Leonie said dreamily. Then gasped. Talk about putting your foot in it. That was almost a perfect description of poor Hannah's Felix. Leonie had finally seen him on a sitcom on ITV and he was gorgeous. Gorgeous and somewhere else. 'Sorry,' she mumbled.

'Sorry about what?' Hannah didn't appear perturbed; she continued eating her sandwich. 'I've got to be at the next house in half an hour,' she apologized, 'so I've got to wolf this down. Spill the beans on the new bloke.'

'His name's Hugh.'

'Wonderful name,' Hannah said delightedly. 'You can sing that Whitney Houston song now: "I Will Always Love Hugh"! Geddit? Hugh and not You?'

'I'm glad you're an estate agent and not trying to break into the comedy circuit,' Leonie said calmly. 'But I digress. Hugh –' she shot Hannah a stern look – 'works in a bank. He's an investment advisor and he's separated too.'

'That's good.'

'He's older than me and he's mad into dogs. He's got three: a spaniel, a Jack Russell and one Heinz 57 variety. Ludlum, Harris and Wilbur, after the novelists. He's into adventure thrillers.'

'And you discovered all that over the phone? He must be some talker.'

'He is,' Leonie said happily. 'Imagine if we got married and at the wedding we had to talk about how we met and what we remembered about it. I'd have to say I fell in love with him when he told me he rescued Wilbur from certain death when someone tried to drown him as a puppy. Someone had put him in a sack and thrown him into the Grand Canal. If not for Hugh, poor Wilbur would be dead.' Her face had that moony, dreamy quality that said she was in fantasy land. And she was.

Leonie was picturing the wedding, complete with four dogs in their Sunday best as bridesdogs (Penny) and groomsdogs (Wilbur, Harris and Ludlum) with beribboned sachets of Mixed Ovals on the tables instead of pastel fondant sweets.

It was Hannah's turn to deliver a stern look. 'Leonie, stop confusing people who love animals with people you're going to fall in love with. It's not the same thing. And I wouldn't mention weddings to him, either. Men aren't as keen on the idea as women are, I think.'

Leonie finished her sandwich and started on the cream-laden slice of cheesecake. 'You're right. I have become a bit obsessed with weddings since Ray and Fliss got married. I can't help it. That Calvin Klein dress haunts me. Every time I pass Madame Lucia's Bridal Boutique in town, I peer in the window to see if there's anything suitably elegant that I should put a deposit down for. I mean, it's mad. Mel caught me looking in one day and I had to pretend I was straightening my rain hat in the window.'

'When's the big date?'

'Saturday night.'

'That's good, because at least you know he's really separated and not just married but pretending to be separated to get women,' Hannah said without thinking.

Leonie looked shocked.

'Some people do use personal adverts to spice up their life when they're actually already involved,' Hannah explained, sorry she'd started this. 'But a date on a Friday or Saturday is a good sign.'

'I'm not sure any of it's a good sign,' Leonie said, still looking startled.

'Sorry. I really am, Leonie. I'm so anti-men right now I'm turning into an embittered old cow. I should just stay at home and write a feminist polemic and be done with it. Hugh sounds really nice, and well done you for getting the courage to phone him. Ask him if he has any brothers,' she joked. 'No! Only kidding, don't. I'm not in any condition to see a man. I don't want a man, either. They're nothing but trouble.'

'No word from Felix, then?' Leonie asked delicately.

Her friend shook her head. 'Not a whisper. He left a very nice Paul Smith T-shirt behind in the laundry basket and I only found it the other day buried right at the bottom. I cut it into pieces and now I'm using it to clean the bathroom,' Hannah said with quiet satisfaction.

'Anyway, I'm over him. Felix was proof that I'm not the sort of woman who should get involved with men. It's too messy. Maybe I should be ultra modern and become a mistress. I was reading this article in the *Daily Mail* about a woman who says she's got her career and a bloke once a week and it suits her fine. His wife gets the dirty socks.'

'You'd hate that,' Leonie argued. 'You're an all-or-nothing sort of person.'

'Yeah, you're right. So I'm sticking to nothing,' Hannah said firmly. 'No men, ever again.'

She was sitting quietly at her desk later that afternoon when the phone rang. Hannah picked it up absently, her mind on her paperwork, and then she froze. She would have recognized that voice anywhere. Low, soft and light-hearted, as if something had amused him and he was quietly laughing at it while he was speaking to you.

'Hannah, great to talk to you.'

She slammed the phone down with such force that Sasha, Steve and Donna all looked up from their respective desks in surprise.

'The phone went dead and I got that high-pitched squealing noise,' Hannah lied blatantly. She was not about to say that Harry-fucking-Spender had phoned her out of the blue, after eighteen months in South America, eighteen months of swanning up and down the bloody Amazon having a whale of a time while she tried to pick up the pieces of her life again. *How dare he? How bloody dare he?* The computer document she'd been working on disappeared and the monitor darkened into screensaver. Everyone in the office had a different one. Hannah's was a kitten chasing after a ball of wool. Normally it amused her, watching the kitten pounce excitedly on the wool only to see it bounce away. She slapped the return key sharply and the kitten vanished. Her phone rang again. Without betraying the knot in her stomach at the sound, Hannah picked up the receiver and cradled it between her neck and chin the way she normally did.

'Hello, Hannah Campbell speaking,' she said for the second time in sixty seconds, her voice professional.

It was him.

'Don't hang up, Hannah,' he begged, not sounding quite as amused this time.

Tough titty, she thought victoriously as she put the receiver down again without speaking another word.

'Must be something wrong with my line,' she said to the others, wide-eyed.

When the phone finally rang for the third time, it was one of the people to whom she'd shown the Enniskerry house earlier that afternoon.

Relieved that it wasn't Harry, Hannah heaved a sigh of relief. He'd got the message, thankfully. He wouldn't be ringing back. She wondered briefly how he'd got her work number but realized that people gossiped and that one of their group of friends – Hannah's ex-friends – was bound to know where she was working and had passed on the information. Dublin was such a small city: you couldn't hiccup without someone remarking on the fact a month later.

She stayed in the office until six, trying to catch up on paperwork. The business was booming, turnover was up by three hundred per cent, David James had announced proudly. Which was wonderful, but it also meant there really weren't enough hours in the day. Sipping the coffee Sasha had brought her, Hannah kept her head bent and worked. But at the back of her mind remained niggling thoughts about Harry. She'd been so heartbroken when he'd left. After ten years together, she'd never have imagined that he could leave her, but he had, to find himself 'because he was being stifled by their relationship,' apparently. At the time, it felt like the worst thing in the world, but the passage of time had dimmed the pain. Guys like Jeff and Felix had helped, except that she hadn't meant to fall in love with Felix. She hadn't planned to fall in love ever again. Harry should have cured her of that. Felix certainly did.

As she worked, she thought about Harry, about how he used to spend hours wandering around in his dressing gown, something which had irritated her beyond belief. He'd been such a slob. If he didn't have to get up and go into work, Harry would slouch around half-dressed all day, phoning Hannah at work and asking her to buy milk/fags/bread on the way home. And she used to do it, she remembered with shame. She'd been a bigger eejit than he was to let him get away with it. He never washed a cup or emptied an ashtray if he could help it, and she'd rarely remonstrated with him about it either. More fool Hannah.

Oh yeah, and the novel. Harry's great opus. He'd been talking about it for years, how he was going to be able to give up the day job when it was written and how it'd win literary prizes left, right and centre. He was worse when he got drunk, telling her he'd be famous some day, famous and filthy, stinking rich. *Oh yes, you mark my words, incredibly rich and famous.* Thirty seconds later, he'd ask her for a loan of a tenner so he could run out to the twenty-four-hour garage and buy cigarettes and Pringles.

Donna was still at her desk when Hannah finally switched off her computer and tidied up the manila folders on her desk.

'Fancy a drink?' Hannah asked, suddenly overcome with the desire to talk to someone about Harry's phone call. She liked talking to Donna: the other woman never judged, never jumped to conclusions and never breathed a word of their conversations to anyone else.

'I'd love to,' confessed Donna, 'but I'm picking Tania up from a friend's house in an hour and I've got some paperwork to finish first. Sorry.'

'That's fine, no sweat. I'll see you tomorrow. I've got an early start anyway, I don't know why I'm even thinking about the pub.' Hannah laughed. 'See you tomorrow.'

As she walked out into the cool evening air, she didn't notice the car parked opposite. She certainly never thought it might be Harry's car. He'd driven a battered old Fiat that was verging on the antique it was so elderly. This car was a very respectable saloon with not a bit of rust in sight. Hannah barely looked at it. So she was astonished when the door opened and Harry got out, calling her name.

She stared at him, wondering if this was a mirage and knowing it wasn't. For what felt like hours but was actually only a minute, she stared silently, unable to summon up an intelligent sentence. Then her brain reasserted itself.

'What the hell are you doing here?' she demanded.

'I came to see you, Hannah. We have to talk,' Harry said, as if it was the most natural thing in the world to turn up on the doorstep of the woman you'd dumped a year and a half previously for a trip to find yourself.

'You've seen me. Now fuck off,' she replied, marching towards her car.

'Hannah, don't be like that. You can't walk away from ten years, you know.'

She glared at him. 'That's supposed to be *my* line, Harry. *You*, if I remember correctly, were the one who walked away. Now you can do it again – out of my life, and don't ever set foot near me again or I'll report you as a stalker, got that?'

Boiling like Mount Etna, she reached the Fiesta, unlocked it, wrenched open the door and threw her papers in. Harry followed her and stood behind her. She knew he was standing with his hands falling limply by his sides: that was what he always did when he didn't know what else to do. She ignored him, amazed at the rage she felt. It was as if he was Harry and Felix rolled into one, deserving of all the fury she'd directed at both of them.

'Hannah,' he said again, hesitantly this time, 'please stop and talk to me, that's all I want. Please. I'm sorry.'

It was the 'I'm sorry' that did it. At no time during his rapid departure from her life had Harry ever apologized. He'd never looked embarrassed as he bluntly told her he had to get out or he'd stagnate. He'd never asked her forgiveness, not even when she sat down on the end of their bed, her legs gone from under her with shock and weakness at his announcement. Even his bizarre letter from South America the year before had been full of inane chatter about what he was doing and lacking in any mention of their life together and how sorry he was he'd destroyed it.

Hannah put her handbag on the passenger seat before facing Harry.

'You're sorry?' she said calmly. 'Now? Isn't it a bit late to be sorry? I thought the time for apologies was when you dumped me like a sack of old potatoes, not when you return nearly two years later, looking for . . .' She put her head on one side and surveyed him with narrowed eyes. 'What, I wonder. Somewhere to live, perhaps? Or a loan of money? You must be looking for something, Harry, if you're back.'

He looked pained. 'You obviously have a terrible impression of me, Hannah, to think I'd only come back for money or something like that.'

'And you haven't given me any reason to have a bad impression of you, is that right?' she said caustically.

He lowered his eyes first. 'I am sorry, Hannah, though you obviously don't believe me. I know I can't make it up to you, but I just wanted to talk to you, to explain.'

Weariness flooded Hannah's limbs. She hadn't the energy to fight with him any more. Let him try and explain what she found inexplicable.

Hannah knew there was nothing he could ever say that would explain what had happened. She'd recovered from it, though. She'd suffered and come out the other side, stronger – she hoped – than ever. But if he had to tell her, then so be it. 'I'll meet you in McCormack's in half an hour,' she said abruptly. 'We can talk then, for about fifteen minutes. Then, I'll have to go.'

Without waiting to see whether this suited Harry or not, Hannah jumped into her car, slammed the door and drove off down the street like a possessed Formula One driver with the rest of the grid on her tail.

There was nothing she needed to do that would take half an hour.

But Hannah had needed some time alone to get to grips with Harry's reappearance in her life. She drove quickly to the pub and then sat in her parked car outside, with the newspaper spread on the steering wheel in front of her. She was too tired to read and no matter how many times she stared at any particular paragraph her eyes glazed over and she saw Harry's face instead of newsprint. When he'd suddenly appeared in front of her, she'd known what to say. Driven by pent-up fury, she'd bitten his head off. But now, after thinking about it all, Hannah couldn't think of a word to say. All those missile-shaped words had deserted her. If only she'd taped the late-night drunken speeches she'd declaimed when she was on her own, ones where she'd told Harry exactly what he could do with himself. Fuelled by Frascati, they'd been eloquent, if tearful, and they'd be so useful now. She could simply press 'play' on her tape recorder and let him listen to a perfectly encapsulated, very emotional précis of how she'd felt and what sort of a bastard she thought he was. Thinking of Harry forced to listen to a drunken speech made Hannah smile for the first time in hours. He was looking good, she had to give him that. Still long on boyish charm, but his body had filled out and the sprinkling of fine lines around his eyes suited him. So did the tan. He'd always tanned well, going a coffee colour while Hannah's freckles were merely joining up.

And he looked very presentable, not his usual slacker self in droopy trousers and some type of ancient sweatshirt that no self-respecting charity shop would let past the front door. In its place, he wore chinos and a cream cotton sweater that looked brand new. Stylish almost; very unlike the Harry she used to know.

Well, Hannah smiled grimly, if he was different, so was she. She wore a severely tailored Jesiré suit with a knee-length skirt to show off toned-up legs in barely black seven deniers. Nothing under the jacket – just a bra. And perilous fuck-me stilettos from Carl Scarpa. Her hair, instead of the taut knot she'd worn during the Harry years, was a glossy shoulder-length mane that swung when she walked. She'd finally dumped the granny glasses for contacts and her lips gleamed sexily in strawberry lipgloss.

This look of restrained, business-like sexuality still drove men mad.

Let Harry suffer a little, Hannah decided, getting out her strawberry gloss to give her mouth that PVC look.

When she saw Harry drive up in his distinctly unrusted car, she hopped out of hers and ran inside, grabbing a table at the back. Immersed in her newspaper, she pretended not to notice Harry's loping progress towards her until he said her name.

'Oh,' she looked up in astonishment, as if she'd completely forgotten she was to meet him. 'Harry. I'll have a soda and lime with ice.'

He returned with their drinks and sat down heavily, as if the weight of the world was on his shoulders. 'Thanks,' Hannah said cheerily. She'd decided that emotionally she wasn't up to a huge row with yelled recriminations that could be heard half-way across the bar. Far better to behave like a benevolent friend talking to a younger pal who's always in trouble. A sort of 'You scamp, what have you done this time?' type ploy with a smattering of 'I couldn't care less, really,' thrown in for good measure.

'You look wonderful, Hannah,' Harry said earnestly.

Her savoir-faire took a direct hit and she had to grind her teeth hard not to screech that break-ups were good for the figure on account of all the stepping you had to do in the gym to pound your ex out of your mind.

'Thanks,' she replied evenly. 'Harry, I haven't got all night. Can you get to the point?'

'You've got a date, then?' he asked idly.

She blinked at him steadily before replying: 'None of your business, OK?'

'Fine, fine, I was just wondering . . .'

'Stop wondering. Why are you here? I thought we didn't have anything to say to each other any more.'

'I do,' he said. 'I wanted to apologize, Hannah. I've thought about you so much, about the fun we had together. I feel,' he hesitated, 'that it's all unfinished. That we shouldn't have done it, do you understand?'

'No.'

'But you must – you said yourself, Hannah, we were good together.'

'Harry, if you remember correctly, you'll remember that *I* said that when you were collecting up the CDs you were afraid to leave in the flat. *I* was telling you we were wonderful together and *you* were scanning the room for valuable personal objects I might destroy in a rage when you'd gone because you'd dumped me. Things have changed since then.' Harry looked as if he was about to speak but Hannah kept going. 'You have had eighteen months of adventure where you could occasionally think fondly of *the girl you left behind*,' she said with heavy irony, 'because you did the leaving. You had what the Americans call "closure". You made the choice to leave and you did. I, on the other hand, didn't have closure because I was the person to whom it all came as a big shock. A massive bloody shock. Since then, I have got over it, over you, and have reached, acquired, whatever the damn word is, closure. So why exactly do you think I'd welcome you with open arms? Was I really that stupid that you'd imagine I'd be thrilled to see you?'

He grabbed her hands with his. 'No, you're the least stupid person I know.'

Hannah pulled her hands away roughly. 'Don't touch me!' she said.

The couple at the table next to them looked round. Harry flashed them an apologetic half-smile. Hannah resisted the impulse to slap it off his stupid face.

'Are you here to convince me to go out with you again?' she asked bluntly.

'No. Yes. Sort of. I want us to be friends,' he said lamely.

'I have enough friends,' Hannah announced. 'I don't need any more.'

She was about to grandly throw her untouched soda and lime all over him when some inner force made her look up and she saw Felix approaching the table.

There must be hallucinogens in the air-conditioning unit in work, Hannah decided, her mind in slow-motion, as she watched Felix coming nearer. There really was no other explanation for today. I mean, to meet one ex-boyfriend was misfortune, to meet up with two . . .

'Hello, Hannah,' Felix growled, looking at Harry with dislike. 'I hoped you might have come here for a drink after work because you weren't at home when I phoned.'

'Hello, Felix,' she said calmly, as if she hadn't just spent the past month in silent misery over him, wondering where he'd got to and asking herself if she should buy one of those self-help books for women who love bastards.

She peered around as if expecting a *Candid Camera* host to appear suddenly and tell her she was the star of the latest show. The coincidences that were piling up were way off the Richter scale and there had to be a reason.

'I hope I'm not interrupting anything,' Felix said, sitting down on Hannah's other side, quite clearly not giving a damn if he was interrupting anything. In fact, he was pleased to be interrupting it, Hannah deduced, if the cool smirk he'd directed at Harry was anything to go by.

'What brings you here?' Hannah asked. 'I didn't know you were back in Ireland.'

'Aren't you going to introduce me to your friend?' Felix said, ignoring her question and placing substantial emphasis on the word 'friend'.

Hannah ground her teeth some more. 'Harry Spender, Felix Andretti,' she said.

'How do you know each other?' said Harry pointedly, looking at Felix as if he were Hannah's father and Felix was a particularly unsuitable boyfriend who'd just rolled up.

'We went out together, Harry,' Hannah explained kindly. 'But it didn't last.'

'Oh,' said Harry, pleased. He reached for Hannah's hand again.

She moved out of his reach and encountered Felix's long, muscled thigh against hers. He stared at her, smouldering in his own special way. If smoulderability could be marketed, Felix would be a billionaire.

'How long since you broke up?' asked Harry, piqued.

'We haven't,' hissed Felix.

Hannah arched an eyebrow. Talk about *l'embarras de richesses.*

One minute, she had no man on the horizon. Suddenly, she had two and they wanted to fight over her, like medieval knights jousting in a tournament for the hand of the fair lady. Well, she had news for them: the fair lady had to be game before there was any point in jousting for her hand. And this lady wasn't keen at all. She'd finished with both knights and they could get stuffed.

'Enough chitchat, boys. I'm afraid I have a date and I've got to go. Nice talking to you, Harry, and you too, Felix.' She gave them a bright smile and got up.

Both of them looked dismayed, although on Felix's handsome face, dismay was wedded with displeasure.

'You can't go,' he said, flicking back his golden hair, his trademark gesture.

The little creature who stoked Hannah's inner rage got out the bellows and gave things a huge blast of air. She felt the fire inside her grow into an inferno of fury.

If she thought she'd been irritated to see Harry, that was nothing to what she felt at the sudden reappearance of Felix. A month and nothing. At least Harry had actually dumped her. Felix had just vanished and his mobile number had bleated that it was no longer valid when she'd rung it in tears. And here he was again, behaving as if nothing had happened despite his mysterious absence.

'You've got a date?' Felix said hotly, as if he disapproved of this idea.

Etna erupted.

Hannah turned on him. If the eyes were the window of the soul, she hoped he'd see flames in hers.

'What I do is none of your business, Felix,' she breathed. 'Don't forget that. I'm leaving, goodbye.'

She stormed out, daring either one of them to follow her. If they did, she'd *kill* them with her bare hands, so help her God.

The rage left her before she reached home and by the time she was sticking her key in the lock, she was grinning at the lunacy of the whole thing. It was official: she had yo-yos for boyfriends. They kept coming back, in spite of their best efforts to keep away.

Within an hour, Felix yo-yoed back again. He rang the doorbell continually for ten minutes and, when Hannah stuck her head out of the window and told him to piss off, he started ringing everyone else's doorbells. Finally, she stomped downstairs and let him in.

'What are you doing here, Felix?' she demanded as he followed her up to her flat. She was irrationally pleased that she hadn't changed out of her work clothes, which meant that Felix was getting an eyeful of swaying hips and long legs as he walked behind her.

'To see you, Hannah. We need to talk.'

Déjà vu or what? she thought grimly, remembering Harry saying those very words to her only hours before.

'Is this International Ex-Boyfriend Day?' she enquired. 'Was there something about it on the news? No, don't tell me. You were stuck in a time machine for four weeks and have only just come back to this century. Am I right?'

'I've been so stupid, Hannah,' murmured Felix. While Harry had relied on verbal reasoning to put his case for disappearance, Felix used much more carnal means. He slid his arms round her waist and began to kiss her, his soft lips scorching hers. Hannah felt her stomach contract with sheer, animal lust. Felix was a superb kisser. If he ever decided to leave the world of acting, he could undoubtedly make a fortune as a gigolo.

Momentarily, she let herself sink into his kiss, leaning her body against him, feeling his hips grind against hers erotically. It was wonderful, glorious, so sexy. After a month without him, Hannah felt like a thirsty Saharan traveller faced with a rippling, icy-cool stream. Her hands roamed eagerly over his back, one pulling his head down to hers, the other moulding him closer to her. And then she stopped. What was she doing? If she wanted cheap sex with no strings, all she had to do was hit the nightclubs and pick up a bloke who'd hidden his wedding ring in his back pocket. Why succumb to Felix when all he was doing was lulling her into a false sense of security? He'd have her eating out of his hand again and then, when he felt like it, he'd leave. Dump her. Like Harry had.

She imagined them sharing notes once she'd left the pub. Stupid Hannah, what a pushover.

Give her the puppy-dog eyes and she's putty in my hands, Harry would say smugly.

No, no, Felix would smirk, *she is sexy, she loves making love. Tease her with kisses and wonderful sex and she'll fall into my arms.*

Hannah pushed him away forcefully.

'Hannah?' he gasped.

'Felix, you left me without a word. I can't forgive that. It's over,' she said, panting with a mixture of desire and temper.

'I know, but it's because I'm weak, Hannah,' he said. 'And scared. I was ashamed to phone you after Christmas, I knew you'd be so angry with me and I couldn't . . . You're so strong, you're my rock. I need you.'

'What a load of old crap!' she hissed, not sure who she was most furious with: Felix for waltzing back into her life unannounced, or herself, for falling for his tactics and kissing the face off him. 'You knew I'd be angry, I'd every right to be. But I'd have forgiven you. I loved you. One week, two weeks, I'd have forgiven you after that long. But four is pushing it, Felix. And at Christmas into the bargain. The season to be jolly, my backside. I'm sorry. Get out. You wanted to talk and we have. You've got what you came for.'

'I came for you. You're my rock, Hannah,' he repeated. It sounded so corny, like a line from a second-rate TV movie.

'Tom Stoppard not writing your lines, then?' she said bitchily. 'You need something snappier than that, Felix.'

'Nobody I know is as funny as you, Hannah,' he said fondly.

'Not even all the bimbos you've been fucking since you left me?' she spat. 'I saw the piece in *Hello!* about you and "your lovely companion" at that horror movie premiere. She looked like girlfriend material from the way she was clinging to you. Either that or she's an aspiring actress practising for a role where she plays your girlfriend. Or maybe she's someone important's daughter and you're dating her as a favour, although it isn't much of a trial going out with some babe in slashed to the waist Gucci. Was she someone helping your career, Felix?'

The photo had cut her to the bone, the sight of Felix mid-laugh with one arm around a blonde vision in barely there jungle-print silk, the picture of twenty-one-year-old beauty. He was described as the handsome actor who'd been a big hit in the TV sitcom *Bystanders*. She was an unidentified blonde, but they were *two* fabulous blondes really, glamorous other-worldly creatures. Hannah had felt like a bog-trotting beast by comparison.

A woman not given to self-criticism when it came to her looks, she'd felt ugly as she looked at *Hello!* No wonder he'd left her, she'd thought in misery, when he could have a woman like that.

'I can't imagine you were missing me too much that night, eh, Felix?'

He hung his head in sorrow. 'I know. I don't deserve you, Hannah. But please –' he sank on to her couch and put his face in his hands – 'please don't send me away. I need you, so much. You can't tell me you haven't missed me too.' He turned beseeching eyes up to her.

Christ, he was handsome, she thought irrationally. Almost impossible to resist. She had to.

'I have missed you,' she said slowly. 'You have no idea how much. Which is why I won't have anything to do with you any more, Felix. I'm not a masochist. Please leave.'

He uncurled his long body from the couch, graceful as ever, and gave her another heart-rending look with those soulful eyes. He was going.

'I want to explain one thing before I go,' he said softly. 'You don't understand; I didn't want to fall in love with you. Having a person I loved wasn't part of my career plan. I didn't want to be in love, I wanted to play around and have fun, but I met you and it went haywire. I fell in love with you, Hannah.' His face was strangely bleak as he spoke, the lines around his eyes more noticeable than usual. He *did* look weary and anguished; it wasn't an act. 'I know it doesn't show me in a very good light if I admit that I tried to fight what I felt about you, Hannah. I wanted you to be like all the others, to be with me for a month before we both got bored with each other. But it didn't work that way. I love you, in spite of myself. I'm not proud of how I've behaved, but it's the truth. I wanted you to understand and I'm sorry I hurt you.'

Hannah said nothing, she couldn't trust herself to speak. She hoped she could keep her face stony for as long as it took him to leave the flat. He didn't say anything else as he left, closing her door behind him quietly. Watching him leave without calling him back was one of the hardest things Hannah had ever done.

She wanted to desperately but she couldn't, wouldn't. She waited motionless until she heard the front door slam shut and then she broke down.

Tears flowed down her face as she wept with grief. She'd been kidding herself. She wasn't over Felix, not even a little bit. She was still crazily, horrifically in love with him. She longed for him, longed to hold him and kiss him and let him make love to her. And the sensation of holding him earlier had been such bliss . . . It was agony to think he was gone from her life, that she'd never hold him again, never touch him, never feel his hot breath on her skin. It was as if he was dead to her. Imagine a life where Felix existed but she couldn't see him or talk to him ever again, never hear his voice husky with love, never touch his face tenderly. Waves of sheer misery swept over her as she cried helplessly, standing alone in her flat, with nobody to love her or care about her ever again. She cried for what felt like hours. For once, the tears simply wouldn't stop. She cried thinking of all the wonderful times they'd had together and she cried because she knew Felix would have stayed with her, if only she'd let him. She didn't care what he did, whether he had ten women as well as her, as long as she could be with him sometimes. In her hubris, she'd sent him away and now she was paying for it. Alone, alone forever.

Finally, she forced herself to stop sobbing. Mechanically, she went into the bathroom to wipe her face and almost didn't recognize the stranger staring back at her from the mirror: a hollow-eyed woman with mascara trails running blackly down her face. She looked a hundred, not thirty-seven. No wonder Felix had wanted to date a carefree blonde child. He wanted a woman who was girlish and pretty, not a neurotic hag with enough emotional baggage to fill an airport. She listlessly removed her make-up and then washed her face with a flannel, scrubbing her skin as if to punish herself. Then she stripped off her work clothes and pulled on the most comforting thing she could find: old soft jeans that had been washed so often they were the palest blue imaginable, and a giant sloppy grey jumper she'd had for years. Barefoot, she padded into the kitchen and looked around. She'd been making dinner when he'd arrived: pasta with tuna, garlic and onions. The garlic she'd been chopping scented the air enticingly, but Hannah didn't have an appetite any more. She never wanted to see food again.

She scraped the garlic into the bin and threw the plastic chopping board into the sink. Meals for one, that was her life from now on. She'd never cook up a delicious feast for two again. Not that she'd ever been much of a cook, but Felix had always been so appreciative of her meals.

'I love the things you can do with pasta and a tin of supermarket spaghetti sauce,' he'd tease her when she was assembling a meal with the help of a tin-opener.

Everything came back to Felix, she sighed. Why had she fallen in love with him? Why hadn't she been able to resist? It wasn't as if she didn't know the problems men brought with them, but she hadn't taken her own advice. She'd fallen for him hook, line and sinker. All she was left with now was a sense that a huge part of her life was over forever. The things she'd valued so much seemed curiously hollow – her job, her flat, her independence. They paled into insignificance beside love. Or lack of it. Loving somebody shouldn't be important, that had been her mantra. True love was such a pile of rubbish, she was sure of it. The only person in life who truly loved you was yourself. Nobody else could be trusted. People like Leonie, who longed for love with incredible intensity, were mad.

Leonie. A picture of her friend's laughing, kind blue eyes came to her suddenly. Yes, she'd go and see Leonie. Hannah couldn't bear the thought of spending the rest of the evening alone in the flat. Her heart ached and she couldn't think of anyone better to comfort her. Leonie understood pain, heartache and love. Hannah looked at her watch: it was only ten to nine. How strange that her life should receive such a mortal, shattering blow, yet a mere two hours had passed.

* * *

Leonie's sympathy on the phone was like a balm to Hannah's wounded heart.

'Come and stay the night,' Leonie urged. 'You can go into work from here tomorrow and that way you can have a couple of glasses of wine with me. Have you eaten?' she asked, practical as ever.

'I couldn't eat,' Hannah said dully.

'Yes you can.' Leonie was firm. 'I've just the thing for you: seafood chowder. I made it earlier and there's loads left.'

Hannah couldn't imagine eating a single morsel of food. Drinking was another matter, however, so she stopped at an off licence en route and recklessly bought three bottles of wine. But when she arrived at Leonie's, the scent of fragrant hot chowder made her stomach leap with hunger.

'I didn't think I could manage a single mouthful, but that smells wonderful,' she said, peering into the saucepan where the soup bubbled invitingly. Leonie's lovely golden dog leaned against her legs, eager to have her ears rubbed.

'Aren't you a good girl,' Hannah crooned at Penny, after crouching down on the floor to hug her properly. Penny basked in this new source of adoration.

Mel, Abby and Danny all trooped into the kitchen to say hello but Leonie shooed them away after a few minutes.

'You were all grumbling earlier that I wanted to watch *The Bodyguard* and you hated it,' she informed them. 'Now you have the telly to yourselves and you all decide you want to be in the kitchen. Scram.'

'You're not going to drink all that wine, are you?' said Danny, mildly scandalized at the thought of his mother and Hannah consuming three bottles between them. He and his pals wouldn't think twice about drinking that much, but his *mother*. He was sure he'd heard that women shouldn't drink as much as men.

'Yes, we are,' she said with a wicked grin, shutting the kitchen door firmly behind him.

On their own at last, she hugged Hannah tightly. 'Don't cry,' she warned. 'Wait till you've had your chowder and then we'll get the wine going and you can sob till you drop. But you need something in your stomach.'

Hannah nodded tearfully. It was lovely being mothered like this. She sat at the table while Leonie ladled up a huge steaming bowl of chowder. Hannah buttered a soft roll and tucked in. Penny sat by her side, looking mournfully at Hannah as if to say she never got a bite in her life and would dearly love just a teensy, weensy little crumb.

'That was gorgeous,' Hannah said appreciatively when she put down her spoon finally after finishing the whole lot. 'I wish I could cook like that. Felix joked that I should start my own cookery school – the Tin-Opener Cook.'

Her mouth trembled. Felix again. He was haunting her thoughts. She began to cry softly and Leonie whisked away the dishes, produced a box of tissues and opened the first bottle of wine.

'Tell me everything,' Leonie said gently, pouring glasses for them both.

Half-way through the second bottle, Leonie was groaning that she'd regret it in the morning and Hannah was feeling a lot better. Good food, nice wine and the comfort of her dear friend had helped immeasurably. So had the presence of the lovely golden retriever, who seemed to understand that Hannah was heartbroken, and had sat loyally near the table all evening, distributing licks to both women at intervals.

When Hannah was worn out talking about Felix, Leonie talked about Ray's wedding and how insecure she'd felt when she watched the twins with their new stepmother.

'You should see her,' Leonie sighed. 'Fliss is incredible, your basic nightmare. Clever, gorgeous, slim, nice. That's the killing thing, you know. She's a lovely person, genuinely lovely. If she was a conniving bitch it would be much easier to hate her, but she's kind, warm and wonderful. The twins adore her and Danny would do anything for her.'

Hannah poured Leonie another glass of wine.

'I shouldn't,' said Leonie, taking a deep slug. 'She and Ray phoned three times from their honeymoon. Now, I know Ray loves the kids, but I also know that *he* wouldn't have phoned three times. It was Fliss's idea. She told me on the phone it's vitally important that the kids don't think she's taking their father away from them. She wants them to be more a part of his life than ever before.' Miserably, she took another huge gulp of wine. 'How can you hate someone like that? *And* she keeps sending the most incredible presents to them all. Donna Karan denim jackets for the girls because they liked her one, and some new MP3 thing for Danny. Oh yeah, stacks of perfume and silly things like sparkly nail varnish. I'm too busy cooking dinner to think about buying them sparkly nail varnish,' she finished gloomily.

'That's all very nice,' Hannah said tipsily, 'but you're their mother, Leonie. You shouldn't feel so threatened by her. They're not going to forget that for a designer denim jacket, are they?'

Leonie snorted. 'They're teenagers! They'd go off with Jack the Ripper if he came up with the correct designer wear.'

'Well,' comforted Hannah, 'they don't see her that much, do they?'

'That's the thing,' Leonie said, draining her glass and holding it out for a refill, 'she wants them to go to Boston as often as they can. Am I being selfish in not wanting them to go?'

'Don't be too hard on yourself,' advised Hannah. 'It's a difficult situation. Do you have any crisps?

'I'm so tired,' Hannah said after just one glass of the third bottle she'd insisted on opening. It was half past twelve and she felt limp with exhaustion, the way she felt after a mammoth session in the gym. 'I think I'll go to bed. If you show me where the blankets are, Leonie, I'll make up a bed on the couch.'

'No you won't,' Leonie said. 'I've got a double bed and you can bunk in with me. According to Danny's mates, sleeping on that couch is like sleeping on a bed of nails; I wouldn't put you through it. My bed's lovely, as long as you don't mind . . .'

'Don't be silly,' Hannah said, a fresh crop of tears welling up in her eyes at Leonie's kindness. 'You feed me, take care of me and now you're letting me sleep in your bed.'

'Only if you don't mind a big lump jumping into the bed in the middle of the night,' Leonie said, trying to make Hannah laugh. 'Penny sleeps on her bean bag for half the night and then gets lonely by about four a.m., when she dives on top of me. If you're very good, she'll lick your make-up off in the morning!'

They both laughed at this and Penny joined in, barking delightedly.

'Come on,' Leonie added, opening the kitchen door and leading Hannah to her room. 'You sort yourself out and I'll let Penny into the garden for her ablutions.'

'You're finally out of the kitchen?' Danny said, popping his head round his bedroom door. 'I'm starving and I didn't want to interrupt the boozing session.'

'I think he has a tapeworm living inside him,' Leonie remarked to Hannah. 'It's the only explanation I can come up with for why he eats so much and stays like a whippet.'

'Well, if you've got a tapeworm inside you, Mum,' Danny laughed minutes later, when Leonie returned to the kitchen to see him making a ham sandwich, 'it's drunk after all the wine you've had. Three bottles, you old alco!'

'Ha ha,' she said, giving him a mock slap on the bum. 'I'm still the boss round here, sweetie-pie. I'll withdraw your fridge privileges if you keep slagging off your old mother, right?'

'Yes, wonderful, non-alcoholic mother,' Danny mumbled with his mouth full of sandwich. 'Your wish is my command.'

Hannah's head throbbed when she woke up, instinctively knowing she was in a strange place. The bed felt different and she didn't have dusky pink sheets, surely? Just then, another pink thing loomed: a long pink tongue began affectionately licking her face.

'Penny,' said Hannah fondly, remembering where she was and why she had a hangover. 'You darling. What a nice way to wake up, with someone kissing you.'

Penny threw herself down beside Hannah and waited to be petted. Hannah did so mechanically, that ache at the back of her eyes telling her that being licked awake by a dog was the nearest she was going to come to affection in the morning for the rest of her life. She gulped fiercely, determined not to cry again. Penny squirmed and made growly noises which Hannah correctly interpreted as meaning, *Pet me some more, on my belly*. Maybe she should get a dog. She'd love one, but it would hardly be fair to the poor dog seeing the hours she put in at the office. You couldn't leave a dog on its own all day. Or maybe if she got two dogs, they could keep each other company.

'Maybe I'll steal you, Penny, and bring you home with me,' she said, sitting up and playing with the dog.

Penny replied with more delighted growly noises, rolling on to her back for more comprehensive adoration.

'She's a shameless hussy,' Leonie said, arriving with breakfast. 'Rub her tummy and she's anyone's. I brought you some toast, juice and coffee. Danny is actually making bacon sandwiches, but I didn't think you'd be up to anything that advanced.'

'Quite right.' Hannah's stomach lurched at the thought of greasy congealed bacon. But toast and coffee she could manage. 'You're spoiling me, Leonie,' she said. 'I don't know how to thank you.'

'Ah, shut up, would you,' Leonie replied. 'Wait till you get the bill. Get off the bed, Penny. She'll spill your coffee if she decides to move,' she told Hannah. With a disgruntled Penny off the bed, Leonie laid the tray on Hannah's lap. 'It's half seven, so you don't have much time if you want to be in work by eight forty-five,' she warned. 'I'm going to have a quick shower to make myself presentable. It's all your fault I'm hungover, Campbell, you brat. I'll have to use the liquid cement make-up this morning to cover up the ravages of last night.'

Hannah grinned and attacked her orange juice gratefully.

By eight forty-five, she was parking her car near the office, feeling a damn sight better than she had any right to. Leonie's kindness, not to mention the hysteria that ensued in the Delaney household in the morning as three teenagers all vied with each other for bathroom time, had cheered her up immensely. Listening to Mel and Danny sparking off each other like two comedians would have to make you laugh. It was all part of the rich tapestry of post-Felix life, proof that life moved on no matter what.

She breathed deeply a few times, trying to fill herself with calming energy, as the yoga-teaching aerobics instructor in her gym advised. Then she marched into the office, determined to get through this day as best she could.

It wasn't easy. Gillian had a grievance about Carrie, the receptionist, something to do with the pecking order, Hannah knew.

'Honestly, I wouldn't mind, but it's the second time this week she's told someone I wasn't at my desk when I'd just nipped to the loo,' Gillian droned, having hopped on Hannah as soon as she'd arrived, determined to get her side of the story to as many people as possible in case of repercussions.

'What did you say to Carrie?' Hannah asked wearily, knowing she should really tell Gillian that it was no longer her job to referee office squabbles. That was Sasha's bailiwick now, thankfully. She was office manager, not Hannah. But she wasn't up to a full-scale fight with Gillian.

'I said she should mind her job because she wouldn't be here long if she couldn't tell the difference between someone being in the loo and not being at their desk,' Gillian said hotly.

Hannah tried to make sense of this bewildering sentence. 'Well, you weren't at your desk, were you?' she said, giving up her attempts to remain neutral. Gillian was *so* bloody irritating. 'So Carrie was right to say you weren't there. It's better than saying you're in the ladies, isn't it?'

Gillian swelled up in indignation. 'I might have known you'd take *her* side,' she hissed. 'It's outrageous. You've had it in for me ever since you came here! I know your type, Hannah Campbell. You're nothing but a jumped-up, bog-trotting culchie from the back of beyond and I can see through you, even if nobody else does!'

Big mistake, Hannah thought icily. Gillian had picked the one day in a million when it wasn't wise to argue with Hannah. Slowly and quietly, like a lioness selecting which impala she'd kill, Hannah moved closer to Gillian until she was standing a mere two feet away from her. The rest of the people in the office, who'd all heard Gillian's last outburst, held their breath.

'This sort of unprofessional behaviour is why you've been bypassed for promotion every time, Gillian,' she said, making sure she was speaking loud enough for all the onlookers to hear. 'You fail utterly to see that it's your fault you haven't been made office manager because the reality is that you are lazy, slapdash and determined to do as little as possible with maximum fuss. If you spent half as much time on your job as you do on manufacturing personal grievances against other members of staff, you might be worth something to this company. But you can't see that, Gillian. You're hyper-aware of everyone else's faults and blind to your own. If you're not at your desk when your phone rings, then Carrie is correct in saying you're not at your desk. That's not personal, that's doing her job. And because I pointed that out to you, you decided to launch a vicious personal attack on me with everybody listening. Not very wise, if you want to keep your job.'

Gillian paled.

'I will be writing a memo on all of this to Mr James, although I've no doubt he heard most of it.' She gestured towards the reception where David stood listening, briefcase and newspaper in hand, an unforgiving expression on his face.

Gillian went even whiter under her orangey panstick. She hadn't heard him come in.

'Finally, Gillian, I am proud to come from the country, and if that makes me a "culchie", then so be it. At least I don't try and disguise my roots by adopting a false accent.' She'd been professional up to then, but Hannah, tired, angry and heartsore, couldn't resist one low jibe at Gillian, who did her best to hide her normal Dublin accent with a posh twist when she was trying to impress anyone.

'Hannah, would you be so kind as to join me in my office,' David James said, walking past. 'We need to have a discussion on staff.'

Gillian clutched the chair behind her weakly. Hannah walked into David's office and the level of conversation in the open-plan office went back to normal.

'What was all that about, Hannah?' he asked, settling himself behind his desk and phoning Sasha to bring him a coffee. 'No, make that two – I guess you need it, Hannah.'

She sat down in front of his desk, glad that she had the sort of relationship with her boss that meant she could be completely honest with him. 'Gillian resents me,' she explained. 'She was furious about Carrie this morning and wanted people on her side of the argument, so she started telling me all about it as soon as I got in. When I pointed out that Carrie hadn't done anything wrong, Gillian flipped and it got very personal.'

'I heard that,' he remarked drily. 'I understand the problem, Hannah. My difficulty is that I have a vision of the same scene if a client had been in the office. Gillian is a stupid, lazy woman and she was wrong to say what she did, but you shouldn't have let it denigrate into a slanging match in the front of house. It's unprofessional and' – he looked at her searchingly – 'most unlike you.'

Sasha arrived nervously with two coffees. When she was gone, Hannah sipped hers and hoped the caffeine would start to kick in soon. 'This is no excuse, David, but a personal problem came up yesterday and I'm ashamed to say it affected my behaviour today. That's no excuse, I know,' she repeated. 'It's hardly intelligent management style to bawl out someone like Gillian with an audience.'

'Will I sack her?' he asked. 'She certainly deserves it. Her work is mediocre at best and she behaves as if she owns the place.'

'No,' Hannah said. 'I couldn't have that on my conscience. She'd be fine if she'd stop believing that she's hard done by and actually got on with her job. Gillian's problem is that she feels everyone else is plotting against her all the time, trying to undermine her. If she recognized that they're not, she'd be OK. But she's blind to her own faults. I think she feels she'd be running Microsoft if other people didn't keep ruining her opportunities.'

'She's got a second chance, then,' David said, 'thanks to you. Not that she'd believe it if I told her. I'm relying on you to make sure there are no more ugly scenes in the office and, if there are, or if she steps out of line again, I want to know. We're not running a charity. Now that Dwyer is retired, she's working for me, and if she can't pull her weight or refuses to co-operate with the rest of the staff, she's history. Right?'

'Right,' Hannah agreed.

'I'll get Sasha to send her in now and,' he paused, 'if you have any problem I can help you with, Hannah, my door is always open.'

'Thanks.' She got to her feet to leave.

'I know my old pal Mr Andretti is back in town,' he added carefully, eyes searching her face for something. 'We've known each other for years and I'm fond of him, but as I've said before, he's a bit of a lady-killer.'

Hannah grimaced, not wanting to blub again but feeling the tears threatening. 'I think I've figured that out already,' she said hoarsely.

'Just be careful. I don't want him messing up the most talented trainee estate agent on the block,' David said lightly.

'It doesn't matter any more, David,' Hannah said dully, misery making her not care what she said. 'It's over between us.'

'Oh.'

Hannah wondered, had she imagined it or had David's eyes lit up momentarily?

'Tell you what, how about I bring you out to lunch to drown your sorrows?' he said brightly.

Hannah was about to say no when she changed her mind. Might as well. After all, who knew when she'd next get invited out to lunch by an attractive man, even if he was her boss and was doing it out of pity?

'Why not,' she said, summoning up a smile.

Outside, Gillian shot her a daggers look as they passed in the hallway leading to David's office. Hannah ignored her and went to her desk.

Whatever David said to her in the twenty minutes she was in his office, it must have been lethal. A subdued Gillian emerged, red-faced and silent. Hannah glanced at her and realized she really didn't give a damn about Gillian and her neuroses. She had enough problems of her own.

Nevertheless Gillian approached: 'Mr James said I was to apologize to you for what I said,' she said stiltedly. 'It was wrong and it won't happen again, I promise.'

She sounded like a ten-year-old reciting a poem she'd learned by rote.

'Apology accepted, Gillian. I'll take your word for it that nothing like that ever happens again. This is too small a company for feuds.'

Duty done, Gillian stomped back to her desk. Hannah sighed. She'd made herself an implacable enemy.

* * *

She'd almost forgotten their lunch date when David appeared in front of her at twelve forty-five, drumming his long fingers on her desk. He'd splashed on some cologne, she noticed with a grin, smelling that soft scent redolent of musky, spicy nights.

'Did you get a better offer for lunch?' he enquired, eyes glittering.

Hannah laughed. 'No,' she said. 'I'll just be a mo.'

They walked to a small pub around the corner and ordered soup, sandwiches and a glass of wine each. David attacked his chicken sandwich hungrily, consuming half of it before Hannah had managed one bite of hers.

'I'm ravenous,' he said apologetically. 'I was up early for a run in UCD and I didn't have time for breakfast.'

Hannah pushed half of her sandwich over towards him. 'Have this,' she offered. 'I'm not hungry.'

'I hope it's not Felix putting you off your food,' David said lightly, eyes meeting hers.

Hannah looked away first.

'Sorry, I didn't mean to pry,' he said gently. One big hand crept over the table and landed on hers, clasping it in a comforting manner. It felt nice to be touched. Hannah missed that, even though Felix, for someone so sensual, wasn't that affectionate. Tactile when love-making was involved, he wasn't much of a man for little kisses or gentle, affectionate strokes as he walked by. David's big warm hand enfolding hers felt lovely. Only he didn't leave it there long. Clearing his throat, he removed his hand and took a gulp of wine. 'I do put my size twelves in it sometimes,' he remarked. 'I didn't mean to upset you, Hannah. That's the last thing I'd want to do.'

She forced a grin to her lips. 'Size twelve feet? How ever do you get shoes?'

David laughed, a deep throaty laugh that made several people look over at their table. One nearby diner gave a squeal of delight and got to her feet, hurrying over to where David and Hannah sat.

'David James,' she purred, pleasure written all over her pretty face.

The woman was probably around Hannah's age but with a modern crop of dark hair and clothes far trendier than anything Hannah ever wore. Hipster lycra jeans, a childish-looking bright T-shirt and a fitted French Connection denim jacket clung to her slender frame.

'Roberta,' David said, getting chivalrously to his feet to shake hands with the woman. Roberta wasn't into hand-shaking: she threw her arms around him. Hannah watched it all with interest.

'I thought it was you, David! How lovely to see you,' Roberta cooed. 'You're a terrible man, David James. I invited you to our Christmas party and you never turned up. All my single girlfriends went into mourning because I told them I'd found a gorgeous man for them and then you don't show, you bad boy.'

The woman was flirting with him and Hannah found herself taken aback. She'd never seen David in that light really. It wasn't that she hadn't thought he was attractive. He was. Some women loved that sort of big, solid bloke with the rumpled face and the crinkled up eyes. And he had a commanding presence.

David was the sort of man who made everyone from waiters to managing directors dance attendance on him. He was very calm and relaxed, and treated everyone the same. In control, methodical and shrewd, he saw everything and forgot nothing.

But as a romantic possibility – never. Roberta obviously didn't agree. She was actually twirling a bit of short dark hair in her fingers. Hannah began to get irritated.

'We're thinking of selling up again,' Roberta said gravely. 'Perhaps you'd come out and do a valuation for me . . .'

If it's like you, honey, it's cheap, Hannah glowered. Honestly, talk about throwing yourself at a man. What if *she'd* been involved with David and this cow turned up, ignoring Hannah and flirting like a sex-starved nymphomaniac. She sat there primly, eating her sandwich and pretending to ignore the other woman.

When David finally managed to pry Roberta's French-manicured claw from his arm, he sat down wearily and rolled his eyes at Hannah.

'She's a bit intense,' he whispered.

'Not your type, huh?' Hannah enquired nonchalantly, astonished to find that she actually cared.

'You can say that again,' he winced. 'I sold a house for her a year ago and she's been on my case ever since. I thought if I didn't turn up at her Christmas soiree she'd get the hint.'

'Are you not interested in meeting all her lovely single friends?' prodded Hannah archly.

His head still bent over his sandwich, David raised his eyes to hers, dark eyebrows giving him an ironic gleam. 'I'm not interested in them,' he said, heavily emphasizing the word 'them'. Their eyes locked, toffee-coloured orbs meeting the shrewd grey eyes that were suddenly warmer than Hannah had ever seen them before.

A laser beam of awareness pierced through her. David fancied her. It was so obvious! How come she'd never noticed before? That was why he wasn't interested in any other woman the irritating Roberta could set him up with. To hide her shock and confusion, she quickly drank a spoonful of soup. To further discomfit her, the soup went down the wrong way and she began to choke.

As soon as she began to cough and splutter, David threw down his sandwich and started slapping her on the back.

'Are you OK?' he asked anxiously.

'Yes,' spluttered Hannah, coughing into her napkin. Her eyes had watered madly, so she wiped them and wished she could think of something to say, something to defuse the situation. She didn't need to. As if aware that he'd stunned her with his revealing statement, David sat back in his seat and resumed eating his sandwich.

'Roberta's house was beautiful. A genuine Georgian townhouse. They'd put a lot of money into it,' he remarked, as calmly as if they'd been discussing business a minute before instead of romance.

Embarrassing subject avoidance was something Hannah was becoming an expert at. She'd had enough experience every time someone asked her how Harry – and later Felix – was. 'Really?' she said brightly, as if she was enthralled in what sort of stately pile the nauseous Roberta had lived in. 'What did it go for?'

They talked business for another fifteen minutes before Hannah said she really should get back to work.

'Me too,' said David.

As they reached the office, he touched her arm briefly. 'Let's have a proper lunch soon,' he said. 'The full works: not just a quick sandwich.'

'Sure,' Hannah agreed. She might possibly feel more normal in a week or so and capable of having a meal with a man who fancied her. Right now, she simply wanted to cry over the man who clearly *didn't* fancy her.

It was an exhausted Hannah who drove home that night, worn down by the combination of a lingering hangover, a huge workload and Gillian sitting close by with a face like a thundercloud. She'd tried not to think about Felix all day but it had been hard. That afternoon, she had sat in the pine kitchen of a Dalkey cottage while a man and his wife ooh-ed and ah-ed over the cottage's alpine garden and hardwood deck, and her thoughts had run to Felix. She could just imagine them living together in this house, she realized sadly, gazing around at the pretty kitchen. Two bedrooms with a split-level sitting room that had a mezzanine containing a tiny dining room: it would be perfect for the two of them.

Airy and stylish, wonderful for entertaining Felix's friends and throwing marvellous dinner parties where guests from their various worlds mingled successfully. She loved the real fire in the bedroom. How nice to light it and snuggle up in bed on cold nights, watching the flames leap up until their own flames ignited . . .

She parked the car outside her flat, happy to find a space that wasn't four blocks away for once. It was chilly even for January and she wrapped her red wool coat tightly around herself as she walked to the gate. And stopped. It looked as if someone had transplanted an entire florist's shop to the garden. At least fifteen bouquets confronted her: giant white lilies trailing greenery, vast armfuls of red roses, with myriad pinks, purples and yellows dotted here and there. In the midst of this riot of stephanotis and blossoms sat Felix, scrunched up on the doorstep and looking as if he was freezing in just his suede leather jacket and jeans.

'I didn't want to come to the office so I waited here,' he said with chattering teeth.

'You poor love,' Hannah said instinctively, rushing towards him. 'You must be freezing. Did you bring all these flowers?'

He nodded. 'I wanted to show you how much I loved you, and I know you adore flowers. I didn't know which ones to pick, so I got them all.'

'Are you here long?' she asked.

'Only half an hour. I knew you'd be home soon. Can I come in?'

While he sat with a cup of whiskey-laced coffee and warmed up, Hannah brought her flowers up to the flat, blushing puce with embarrassment when the people in the downstairs flat arrived and stared in wonderment at the blaze of colour in their usually barren garden.

'Isn't it more traditional to plant actual flowers and not just leave a load of bouquets out here?' said the man waggishly.

Once the bouquets – twenty in total – were installed in the flat, most of them in the bath as Hannah certainly didn't have enough vases for them, she sat down beside Felix on the couch.

'I didn't expect to see you again,' she said softly. It was hard to be angry with someone who'd just brought you twenty bouquets, especially when you'd spent the whole day thinking of them, missing them desperately.

'I wanted to think of a way to make you see I was serious, Hannah,' Felix said, taking her hands in his and giving her the full effect of his soulful eyes. 'I missed you so much . . . I need you, you've got to understand that.'

Hannah gulped. She knew she should say something about flowers being no substitute for trust in a relationship, but the words froze in her mouth. She couldn't help it: she was so in thrall to Felix, she could refuse him nothing.

'I know,' she said, biting her lip, 'I missed you so much too, Felix. I just can't let you hurt me again.'

He nodded and kissed her. It was like coming home after years away: lovely, gentle and caring. His mouth was soft on hers. A tender, loving kiss quite unlike the passionate ones they usually enjoyed. When he finally pulled away, Hannah sat with her eyes closed, feeling glorious peace flood through her.

Then she felt something cool on her fingers. She looked down to see Felix sliding a ring on to her wedding finger, a modern gold band with a cabouchon diamond set grandly in the middle. She gasped in astonishment.

'You will marry me, Hannah, won't you?' Felix said, slipping the ring over her knuckle until it rested properly on her slender finger. 'Say you will.'

Of all the things Hannah had expected, an engagement ring was not on the list. She stared at it, stunned. She'd never owned anything like it: a large diamond had hardly been on her must-buy list. 'It's beautiful,' she breathed. And it was. It suited her slim hand perfectly.

'Well?' Felix asked.

Hannah's face lit up, her toffee-coloured eyes gleaming as if the gods had sprinkled stardust in them. 'Yes!'

This time, their kiss was the passionate variety, with Hannah only breaking away to warn Felix of what she'd do if he left her again: 'I'm never going through that again, ever. You hear me?' she said fiercely.

'No, no, darling,' he said, busy undoing the buttons of her work blouse, his lips sliding sensuously down her neck into the soft velvet of her cleavage.

'I mean it, Felix. If you ever run away on me again, that's it. Finito. No matter how much I love you, I won't let you destroy me.'

'Never, darling,' he said gravely. 'Never. I promise, I promise with all my heart that I'll never hurt you again. I love you too much. Let me show you how much.'

Hours later, satiated with sex and nicely fed, thanks to an Indian takeaway, Hannah lay entwined with Felix in bed, glorying in the sensation of his body next to hers. Only yesterday, the flat had seemed barren and lonely with just her there. Now it was a home: lively, warm and comforting. She snuggled up beside him, listening to his slow, easy breathing. Imagine it: she was engaged to Felix.

She couldn't wait to tell the girls. Leonie and Emma would be delighted, she knew it. Of course, there were things to be ironed out – like where they'd live, for a start. She knew that a lot of Felix's work was in the UK, but with more and more films and television series being made in Ireland, there was surely a case for them living here. He could always commute on those occasions when he needed to be anywhere else and, anyway, Ireland was such a Mecca for international actors and musicians, Felix would feel right at home. He'd love it.

She felt a brief moment of regret about David James. He was a nice man, sexy really, if she thought about it. It would be easy to fall in love with him: he was a wonderful mixture of dependability and drive. A self-made man. And he certainly liked her. But he couldn't compare to Felix, movie-star handsome and passionate. Nobody could compare to Felix, Hannah beamed. And he was all hers.

The flowers had been lovely, she thought dreamily, managing to forget how much she'd have liked even one bouquet on her thirty-seventh birthday the week before. But Felix hadn't known about that, she thought forgivingly. Next year, it'd be different. Twenty bouquets on her birthday, she was sure of it.

Leonie put the phone down. Hannah hadn't answered and that was the fifth time she'd tried since seven o'clock. She just hoped her friend was all right. Hannah had been so devastated yesterday, her world ripped apart by love. Or the lack of it. Normally, Hannah was the positive, optimistic one of their little group, teasing Emma when she went all maudlin about her father's moods, cheering Leonie up by telling her the perfect man was out there for her, it was just a matter of finding him and nailing his feet to the floor. It was a shock, therefore, to see Hannah hollowed out with misery, a slave to love like the rest of us, Leonie thought gloomily. She wondered did men suffer the same pangs about love. Probably not. They wouldn't waste valuable time thinking about whether they were hopeless specimens because they didn't have the right partner, or worrying about whether the size of their feet might put off would-be suitors. This last bit was getting to Leonie quite a lot lately, ever since she'd gone shopping for a new pair of 'going-out' shoes only to discover that dainty mules didn't exist in size nine.

Her feet had never really bothered her before: she was tall, statuesque, end of story. A big woman, in plain words. Which meant large feet. The problem was that she'd never had any trouble buying shoes up to now because she'd always stuck with low, sensible ones, not wishing to make herself look any taller.

Exposure to the glam crowd in Vail had changed this. Tall, short, built like supertankers or famine victims, they went for fierce glamour in all social situations. So Leonie had decided that she needn't bother hiding her size in voluminous velvets and low boots. No way. It was going to be high-class elegance all the way from now on, complete with hair by the actual hairdresser, instead of by Leonie herself wearing rubber gloves to protect her hands from dye, and shoes by Cinderella's fairy godmother. Except Cinderella shoes didn't exist in sizes over seven. She was in love with those spindly things that looked as if you'd twist your ankles in them, sex-on-stilettos she called them. But after size seven, dainty spindly things vanished and you were left with granny shoes.

'Would Madam like to see those in her size?' enquired the male assistant in the last shoe shop, holding up a pair of cushioned sandals you could conceivably hike up the Himalayas in.

Not unless Madam also buys long thermal drawers, American tan support tights, a floral pinny and a zimmer frame, Leonie wanted to hiss at him. She was forty-three not eighty-three!

She came out of the shop with a pair of court shoes that looked like every other pair of court shoes in her wardrobe: plain, black and unlikely to set any man on fire. They were also a smidgen too tight, but she planned to stretch them with her trusty shoe trees.

Sighing, Leonie tried Hannah's number one more time. It rang out.

'Mum, are you off the phone yet? I want to ring Susie,' yelled Mel.

'Yeah,' Leonie answered.

Feeling miserable on Hannah's behalf, she went into the kitchen and started on dinner. She was half-way through chopping up bits of chicken when Danny arrived home from college, obviously in a foul temper about something. Leonie figured this out because normally he and Mel had at least ten minutes' grace before they started killing each other on any given evening: tonight, he was barely in the door when roars could be heard from the sitting room.

'You can't be on the phone *and* be watching television at the same time,' yelled Danny. 'I want to watch *Star Trek*, not some crappy soap.'

'Bugger off, you big pig!' hissed Mel.

'Bugger off yourself,' screamed back her brother.

The advantages of paying a fortune for private education, Leonie thought grimly as the four-letter words flew. She yelled that they'd better stop fighting or they could cook their own dinner.

Moments later, Danny barged into the kitchen, having obviously lost the battle of the remote control. Mel could be tough as old boots when the need arose.

'What's up?' Leonie asked.

'Nothing,' he said, wrenching open a cupboard and poking around inside it aggressively. Finding a packet of crisps, he slammed the door shut, slumped on a kitchen chair and crunched moodily.

Leonie knew better than to say anything else. Even when he'd been a toddler, waddling around the house with his Dinky cars, he'd been happiest with his own company, not appearing to need anyone except the family's dog, then an elderly and sadly incontinent bitza named Otto. When he was older, that solitariness had developed into a fierce need for privacy. Once, when he was ten, he'd stopped talking to her for days because she'd cleaned out his wardrobe. Experience had taught her that giving Danny time was the best way to deal with him. Eventually, if the need to discuss the subject was strong enough, he'd tell her.

She browned the pieces of chicken in her casserole dish, chopping up button mushrooms and grabbing a handful of chives from the window-box in between stirring. The scent of sizzling meat filled the room and Penny gave up begging crisps from Danny to sit at Leonie's feet longingly, hoping in vain that a stray bit of chicken would hop out of the dish into her drooling mouth. The casserole was finally in the oven and Leonie was measuring rice into her most invaluable piece of culinary equipment, the rice steamer, when Danny decided to spill the beans.

'Remember that exam I had last month?'

'Yes,' Leonie said absently. Sounding as if you were half-listening was the best trick, she'd learned. If you became immediately intense and interested, Danny would change his mind about telling you.

'Well, I failed it, and my tutor says if I don't pass all the others over the next term, I'll fail this year.'

Leonie felt her stomach lurch. Fail the year! Oh Lord, don't let this be happening. She knew plenty of families who were at their wits' ends with third-level students who dropped out when the going got tough. Please, please, let this not happen to Danny.

'That sounds pretty severe,' she said as nonchalantly as she could. 'Is he serious about it, or is it just an attempt to scare you?'

Danny considered this. 'Think it's serious. Nobody else in my group failed.'

Leonie's heart sank further. 'How exactly did you fail?' she asked, trying to make it sound like an innocent question and not the terrified probing of a shocked parent.

'It was fermentation, a section I hate. I think I hate the whole fucking course.'

For once, she didn't correct him for swearing. There was a time and a place for everything.

'Fermentation's all maths and I hate that. I'm good on stuff that isn't so mathematics-related. It's all about how the vats work and the amount of mixing and air,' he muttered, more to himself than to his mother.

Leonie didn't say anything about how, on a personal level, Danny was keen on fermentation. Access to lots of home-made wine was the sole reason she could see for membership of the college Microbiology Club. He'd brought home a bottle of the club wine one night. Stronger than paint stripper, it tasted roughly the same, but Danny loved it.

'I mean, medical micro might be a better major for me . . .' he was saying.

'Danny, look,' Leonie interrupted, 'if you hate the course right now it's probably because it's not working out. Why don't you put your head down and work hard for the next month – ask for extra tutorials, perhaps. And if you fail, we'll look at your options then. You could always repeat the year with a view to specializing in another area, like medical micro. You liked the virology section, didn't you?' She knew she sounded a hundred times calmer than she felt, but giving Danny the impression that they could cope with this calmly was vital.

She patted his shoulder encouragingly. 'Don't let this get to you, Danny, love. There's nothing so awful that we can't face it realistically and without panicking. You're an adult and you know you have to deal with whatever life throws at you. If that means more studying, then I know you'll do it. You're too bright to let one section of the course mess up your chances.' She smiled and ruffled his hair, the way she used to when he was smaller. 'I bet that tutor doesn't have a clue what he's up against with the Fighting Delaneys! He'll pass out with shock when you get the best results for your year in the exams.'

Danny grinned and didn't give out to her for messing up his hair. 'Yeah, Mum, I'd love to see his face if I did. Tim has great notes. I'll give him a ring and ask can I photocopy them at the weekend. I was hoping to go to Galway with the lads tomorrow morning, but I better give it a miss now. Shit.'

Leaving his empty crisp packet on the table along with the crumbs of his snack, Danny ambled off to use the phone. Leonie only hoped Mel had finished whatever conversation she'd been having, because another argument might wreck the fragile ceasefire. Feeling shattered, she sank on to the chair Danny had vacated and put her head in her hands. This was when she missed having Ray or anyone else around: when some crisis erupted and she felt hopelessly alone.

That was the difficulty of single parenthood: not worrying about childminding, fitting in doing the grocery shopping, or working out how to rob Peter to pay Paul, but the gut-clenching trauma of a crisis when there was nobody else to turn to.

Leonie always acted on instinct when it came to parenting. In this case, she'd felt that giving out to Danny would have been totally counterproductive. He'd desperately wanted to confide in her, but had been afraid she'd be furious to learn he might fail the year. So she'd decided to act very calmly, to treat him like an adult who had to take responsibility for it himself, hoping he'd actually do that.

But maybe she should have yelled at him like a fishwife, demanding to know what he'd been doing to fail the most vital part of the year and telling him he could forget about pocket money until he upped his grades.

She rubbed her temples, feeling a low-grade migraine percolating. Noise in the hall made her jump to her feet. She didn't want to ruin the 'let's all be ultra laid-back' effect by letting Danny see her moping at the kitchen table. So she was peering pointlessly into the oven at the casserole when Abby meandered into the kitchen, with her French grammar book.

'What's for dinner?' Abby asked, perching on a chair and pulling her tracksuit-covered legs up under her.

'*Coq au vin* with a twist – the twist being there's no *vin* in it.' Leonie rarely cooked with alcohol. When she bought a bottle of wine, she preferred to save it for those nights when she needed a restorative glass or two.

'Yuck,' Abby said. 'Do I have to eat it? I'd prefer a baked potato.'

'Yes, you do have to eat it and we're having rice tonight, so there's no baked potato option.'

'Mum! Nobody should have to eat what they don't want. Meat is murder,' she added as an afterthought.

'Meat has only become murder recently in your mind,' Leonie remarked, thinking that tonight was turning into one of those restorative glass of wine nights. 'You ate sausages on Tuesday.'

Abby sniffed. 'Can't I have a veggie burger?'

'Darling, I've made dinner. If you wanted veggie burgers, you should have said so before I started cooking. And anyway, I can't spend the evening making different meals for everyone. This isn't McDonald's.'

Abby said nothing but stomped off sulkily. Leonie closed her eyes and counted to ten. Abby had become so difficult about food lately. She was drinking loads of water, apparently to improve her skin, and she was so fussy about what she ate it was like running a health farm. Nowadays Abby insisted on fruit and cereal for breakfast, shunning Danny's inevitable bacon sandwiches although she used to love them. Leonie was spending a fortune in the supermarket buying exotic fruit because Abby said she'd love starfruit and mango salad in the morning. Then, Abby would decide she didn't actually like mango and the poor thing would sit in the fridge going off until Leonie had to throw it out.

She remembered those marvellous days when they'd all eaten everything she put in front of them. Abby particularly had always had a great appetite, probably too good really, because she was overly fond of dessert and anything with chocolate sauce on it. Leonie had watched her putting on weight and had cringed at the thought that some cruel kid would come along and taunt her about her figure and she'd feel fat forever.

If *she* had told Abby to cut down on desserts, it would have given the poor girl the impression that even her mother thought she was too big. So Leonie had held her tongue and tried to serve healthy foods, hoping that Abby would lose her puppy fat sooner rather than later. But now Abby appeared to have made the connection between dessert and being plump. At least the new healthier diet was having a good effect on her figure. She'd been much heavier than the dainty Mel for years, but now the difference was lessening. Abby still didn't possess her twin's sleek limbs and tiny waist, but she was much slimmer than she had been.

Leonie hoped she wasn't being *too* careful about what she ate. Both girls were still growing and needed plenty of protein, vitamins and minerals. They'd discuss it over dinner, she decided.

Come dinnertime, Leonie had succumbed to the lure of a glass of wine and Mel was back on the phone, squealing excitedly to Susie about 'this amazing thing that happened . . . !'

'Whatever marvellous thing it was, could you talk about it later?' Leonie said, poking her head into the sitting room where Mel was perched on the arm of a chair, one eye on *Home and Away*.

'And could Susie phone *you* next time,' Leonie added, 'because the last phone bill was the size of the national debt.'

Mel raised her eyes heavenwards.

There was more raising of eyes when Abby slouched into the kitchen and looked at the dishes on the table.

'I told you, I'm not eating that,' she said shrilly, pointing to the bubbling casserole.

'I'll have yours, then,' said Danny, loading up his plate.

'You won't,' Leonie said patiently. 'You have to eat some dinner, Abigail. And you're not leaving the table until you do. Tomorrow, I'll make you veggie burgers but, today, this is what we're eating.'

She missed the look of panic that crossed Abby's face before she sat down and helped herself to a minuscule portion of chicken and a slightly bigger spoonful of rice.

'That's hardly enough,' Leonie said, turning back to the table with a steaming bowl of mangetout and broccoli.

'It's loads.' Abby helped herself to a huge portion of vegetables. She then got a large glass of water and drank it down before filling another one.

Dinner was a silent affair. Danny just wolfed his down in ten minutes while Mel picked at her food delicately, reading the magazine she'd hidden on her lap. Leonie hated people reading at the table when they were all eating together.

Abby ate slowly, endlessly rearranging the food on her plate until Leonie told her to eat it all. 'I know you're trying to eat carefully, Abby,' Leonie began, 'but you are still growing and your body needs nutrients. I don't want to see you on a diet,' she warned. 'You're too young to diet. Eating sensibly is one thing, but missing meals is another. If I get you both some multivitamins, will you take them?'

'Mmm,' said Mel, engrossed in her magazine.

'I suppose,' answered Abby in a tight little voice.

She continued to fiddle with her food. Leonie knew she shouldn't say anything but couldn't help herself.

'Abigail, stop playing with your dinner and eat it!' she said, much more sharply than she'd intended.

'Stop telling me what to do!' shrieked Abby in retaliation. 'I'm not a child! Stop treating me like one. Fliss and Dad don't!'

Everyone looked at her in surprise. Abby never got into a rage, ever. But she was in one now.

'I hate this sort of horrible food, and I hate you for making me eat it!' she roared at her mother. 'When are you going to learn that I'm not like you? That I'm different, a different person. Not a bloody child!'

Leonie stared at her beloved daughter in shock; not just shock at Abby using bad language, but shock at the whole thing. 'Abby, stop it,' she said weakly.

But nothing could stop Abby now: 'It's my body and I can do

what I want with it!' she said fiercely. 'You don't understand what it's like, Mum. Nobody does.'

Shoving her chair back violently, she ran from the room.

'Hormones,' said Danny sagely.

'Must phone Louise about homework,' Mel said, before racing off.

It was their turn to do the washing up, but Leonie was too shell-shocked to say a word.

What was happening to them all?

Chicken casserole was horrible, especially the way Mum made it, with olive oil and stuff. It was bound to make you huge if you ate it. And as for rice, that couldn't be good for you. She'd have to look it up in her calorie book, Abby decided, as she leaned against the bathroom door, taking a few deep breaths to calm herself before she started. She hadn't meant to shout, but she had felt so tense, it had just happened. It was important that Mum didn't cop on to what was happening.

Veggie burgers were her favourite meal now; there was only just over two hundred calories per burger and it looked like a big meal to everyone else, particularly if you ate it with a baked potato. No butter on the potato, though. Butter was a killer. And lots of water with the meal. Abby had told everyone she was drinking plenty of water because it was good for your skin. Mel had even started joining her, trying to outdo her in the eight-glasses-a-day stakes. The only thing was that Mel had no idea the real reason her twin consumed so much water with meals: it made throwing up easier.

It was handy in school because there was less time to spend in the loo after lunch, so drinking lots of water meant Abby could simply rush into the upper years' bathroom, wait for someone else to flush and then puke quickly and efficiently. She always saved her apple and ate that afterwards; otherwise, her stomach rumbled terribly all afternoon. It had been quite noticeable in History one day. Luckily, the history teacher, Miss Parker, had such a loud voice that her droning on about Lenin quite drowned out Abby's intestinal rumbling. Mel had given her a funny look at one point, though.

She'd have to be careful in case Mel copped on to what she was doing. That was the problem with a twin: they noticed stuff that other people didn't. Like Mum never noticed her giving her cereal to Penny in the morning, and she didn't seem to realize that Abby never ate the chocolate biscuits she brought out at night when they were watching the telly. Instead, Abby would hide them in her sleeve and put them back in the cupboard later, although once she'd kept some under her bed and ate eight of them in one go. Puking them up had been horrible; her throat hurt like hell and she was sure she hadn't got them all up.

But Mel was cute enough. Even though she always seemed more interested in herself than in anyone else, she just might notice what Abby was up to. Anyway, it was none of her business if she did. Mel was so bloody lucky to be naturally thin, like Fliss. She didn't need to puke four times a day to lose weight. So she'd better keep her mouth shut if she did cop on. This was Abby's secret.

As for Mum, she'd apologize to her later. She hated upsetting her mother but she had to do this, *had* to.

When she was finished, she sat on the floor of the bathroom, shattered from retching, her stomach aching and her throat burning. She felt terrible. Hot tears ran down her face and, as she wiped them away, her jade bracelet rattled. Fliss had sent it to her as a present from the honeymoon in China. Abby loved it. It was so pretty. Fliss was kind and knew exactly what things she liked without having to ask. Fliss would understand about this, Abby thought darkly, even if her mother didn't.

CHAPTER TWENTY-ONE

By six the following Saturday, Leonie wondered why she hadn't had her tubes tied years ago. Children were a *nightmare*. Well, her lot certainly were. She could remember the far-off happy days when they'd confined their energies to drawing on the wallpaper, eating clay in the garden and hitting other small children over the head with their wooden alphabet bricks. She'd thought *those* days were difficult. How wrong could you be? Small children were a joy compared to three teenagers. At least when Abby had been sweet and amiable, there had been some let-up in the constant warfare that made up the Delaney household but since Abby had turned into a cranky, health-food obsessed creature, it had been sheer hell all the way. They'd made up after Abby's outburst the other night, but Leonie still felt as if she was walking on eggshells with her.

Today had started well enough: Leonie, happily thinking about her first date with investment-banking Hugh that evening, had bounced out of bed early, enjoyed a peaceful breakfast with Penny and the pair of them had gone for a wonderful three-mile-walk, buffeted by brisk January winds. As the rain started just when they reached home again, she was delighted they'd escaped a drenching. At half twelve, she left the house to do some grocery shopping and had bought herself a pair of pretty pink glass earrings in a local dress shop for her date. With a nice juicy magazine thrown into the shopping trolley along with a pack of her favourite low-cal chocolate drinks, Leonie decided she had a relaxing afternoon sorted out for herself. Saturday was the day when the kids did their bit of housework, which meant ten minutes of bickering over who did the kitchen, who did the bathroom and who did the hoovering and dusting. Leonie never minded the bickering. She'd long ago stopped herself from entering into the fray by screaming that she'd have the whole place clean in the time it took them to argue over who did what. That type of involvement got you on the slippery slope of doing it yourself anyway. Now, Leonie let them argue.

However, when she got home, it was apparent that the vacuum cleaner hadn't moved from the last time Leonie used it. The inevitable layer of Penny's blonde hairs was still scattered all over the hall carpet and the kitchen was unswept. Worse still, the remains of teenage breakfasts still littered every surface and an empty carton of milk stood on the worktop beside the bin. Whoever had emptied it hadn't bothered to move it the eighteen inches required to put it into the bin. Furious, she dropped her grocery bags on the floor and went in search of the people responsible. Unfortunately, this meant passing the bathroom. The door was open and a pile of towels were clumped damply on the floor. The toothpaste, squeezed in the middle, was abandoned in the hand-basin and there was so much water in the soap dish that the soap itself, carelessly abandoned, was melting slowly into a puddle of sludge.

The lazy so-and-sos, she thought furiously. They expected her to do bloody everything. Well, it wasn't good enough. They weren't getting away with it this time.

'Melanie, Abigail and Daniel!' yelled Leonie. 'Why is this house such a pit? It's your turn to tidy up. Twenty minutes each, that's all I'm asking for.'

She flew into the twins' room but there was nobody there. Danny, looking outraged at being interrupted, was rubbing gel on his wet hair when she knocked brusquely and entered his den without waiting for a reply.

'Have you got the slave's wages?' she demanded.

Danny looked understandably blank.

'Because you and your sisters insist on treating me like a slave, so

I presume I'm going to get paid some sort of pittance.' Leonie glared at her son.

He began to look mildly ashamed.

Leonie ploughed on: 'I work hard all week *and* I cook, clean and tidy up after you lot. Saturday is the only day when I expect some serious help keeping this house clean, and what do I get? Nothing!'

'Cool it, Ma. I'll start now,' Danny said.

'Where are your sisters?' she demanded.

'I'm here, Mum,' said Mel meekly, appearing in her dressing gown with what had to be the remains of Leonie's last bit of avocado face mask plastered all over her face.

'Is that my face mask?' Leonie asked.

'Er yes, I'm going out in half an hour and my skin's a mess . . .'

'Going out in half an hour? So when exactly were you going to help clean the house?' Leonie demanded icily.

'Well, I didn't think it'd matter . . .'

' "Didn't think it would matter," ' her mother said angrily. 'No, let stupid old Mum do it all, that's all she's good for, isn't that what you thought?'

'No,' protested Danny and Mel in unison.

'Where's Abby?' Leonie asked suddenly.

'Gone jogging.'

'Jogging! It's pouring from the heavens, what's she jogging in this weather for?'

'Dunno. I'm sorry, Mum. I'll do my share now,' Mel said, remarkably docile for her. 'I'll hoover and dust, Danny, if you do the bathroom. You did mess it up,' she began, then stopped when her mother shot her a fiery glance.

'I don't want to have this conversation again,' Leonie said, still angry. 'You all expect to be treated like adults, yet none of you will actually behave like adults. I'm not a skivvy, remember that!

'You can put the shopping away, Danny,' she ordered. Bringing Penny, who hated the vacuum cleaner, with her, Leonie marched into her room and slammed the door.

When she came out later, Abby had returned and cleaned the kitchen in a very haphazard fashion. Even though Leonie's rage had passed, she still had some harsh words for Abby about duties and how they all had to pull together to keep their home running smoothly.

'Smoothly?' shrieked Abby. 'If this is what you call smoothly, I want to leave. I'm sure Dad and Fliss would like me to live with them! I hate you.' With that, she ran into her room and slammed the door. Too shocked to go after her, Leonie stood like a statue for a few stunned minutes then did the only thing she could think of in her distraught state; she drove to her mother's house.

Claire was in the garage practising her golf swing when she arrived. She'd only taken the sport up in the last month and was keenly going to the driving range with her friend, Millie, at least twice a week.

'You should try golf,' Claire advised, putting her eight iron back in her bag and escorting her daughter into the house.

'I have enough trouble coping with all the things I do now,' Leonie said tearfully, 'without taking up something else I'd be useless at.'

'Nonsense.' Claire was brusque. She raked her eyes over Leonie's flushed face, spotting the tell-tale signs of impending tears. 'What's Mel said now?'

'It's not Mel, that's the awful thing, it's Abby.'

When she'd recounted the whole sorry tale, Leonie felt somewhat better. Tash, one of Claire's beautiful Siamese cats, had deigned to sit on her lap and Leonie always felt better when she had an animal to hug. Her own cat, Clover, wasn't the sitting-on-laps variety, so her animal comfort normally came in the form of cuddling Penny. Tash rewarded her with a few rumbling purrs and arched her graceful neck.

'Abby sounds a bit like you when you were younger,' Claire said reflectively.

'I was never like that!' Leonie protested.

'Yes, you were,' her mother pointed out, 'when you were about sixteen and decided you were huge and ugly. It was awful, but there wasn't much I could do. You blamed me in the absence of anyone else to blame.'

'But Abby is miles prettier than I was then and she's always been such a sweet person,' Leonie said helplessly. It was totally different. She did everything she could to make Abby feel serene and secure in herself. Not that Claire hadn't tried to do that with her, but, well, it was different. Wasn't it?

Claire took a tin of catfood from the fridge and Tash leapt off Leonie's lap, claws tearing into her skirt as she left. The other two cats mysteriously appeared, all trying to look uninterested in the catfood, but eyeing each other warily all the time, as if determined that the others wouldn't get any more than they did.

'She is pretty and growing prettier, but don't forget that you didn't have a beautiful twin sister to compete with all the time,' Claire pointed out.

'I had you to compete with,' Leonie said wryly, looking at her mother's petite and trim figure, slim in navy trousers, a matelot jersey and a jaunty red scarf round her neck. Claire had Gallic style, the ability to make the simplest outfit look chic. 'You looked miles better than me when I was a teenager. Remember that awful striped crochet bikini I insisted on buying for that holiday in Spain?'

Her mother laughed. 'You donated it to me.'

'And you looked fantastic in it,' Leonie said. 'Ursula Andress, compared to me as Two Ton Tessie.' She watched the cats circle their respective dinners, tails aloft as they assessed the food like disgruntled restaurant critics trying to ascertain whether the pesto oil was home-made or not, purely by sniffing it. 'Life was easier then, wasn't it?'

'Life is always easier in retrospect,' Claire said. 'What else is wrong? You hardly drove over here on a Saturday afternoon just for that.'

Leonie shook her head. 'There's nothing else wrong, apart from the fact that Danny's failing college, Mel isn't even vaguely interested in school, except when it comes to getting the bus there so she can bat her eyelashes at boys en route, and now Abby has turned from the best, most well-adjusted person I know into this prima donna I barely recognize who never stops talking about her stepmother. I'm sick of dealing with it on my own,' she said in an unguarded moment.

Her mother sniffed. Leonie groaned inwardly. She knew what that meant.

'If you hadn't broken up with Ray, you wouldn't be on your own and the children wouldn't have a fairy godmother for a stepmother,' Claire said primly.

'Mum, I don't want a lecture.'

'I'm not going to give you one. But if you come over here and ask my advice, you have to expect to get something. It's tough bringing them up all on your own, but that was your choice, Leonie. You decided you wanted true love and that Ray didn't measure up. You're living with that choice now,' Claire said heavily. 'That's all I'm saying. End of lecture. So, what are you up to this evening? Myself and Millie are going to the cinema. We can't decide whether to go for improbable thriller, improbable courtroom drama, or something with Sean Connery in it. Do you want to come? It might do your terrible offspring some good if you leave them to their own devices for once. They've got so used to having meals cooked for them and the house magically cleaned that they'll die of shock if you're not there to dish up some cordon bleu meal.'

'I'm . . . er, actually going out this evening,' Leonie stuttered.

'With the girls?' asked her mother absently, then catching sight of Leonie biting her lip, she pounced. 'With a man! I'm right, aren't I? Good woman, Leonie. About time you got yourself a man. Who is he and where did you meet him?'

It was either the Spanish Inquisition or the How to Live Your Life lecture, Leonie realized. 'He's a friend of Hannah's,' she lied.

'Really. Tell me all about him – or will that jinx the entire enterprise?'

'No, his name is Hugh Goddard, he's an investment advisor with the bank, he's separated and he loves dogs.'

'His CV sounds wonderful, but what's he like as a person and what does he look like?' demanded her mother.

Leonie paused. She could hardly admit that beyond knowing he was sensitive – well, he'd rescued a poor dog from the Grand Canal, so he must be – she hadn't a clue what he was like and no idea what he really looked like. *Solid, one-time rugby fanatic, works with money, no spring chicken but GSOH. Prospective partners must be animal nuts* might be very descriptive as far as personal ads were concerned but didn't yield the private nuggets to describe the person in detail to interested parties. She went for the vaguely impatient approach: 'Really, Mum, he's just an ordinary guy, honestly. We met at Hannah's and he seemed very nice, so I've agreed to meet him for a drink, that's all.'

'OK, don't get your knickers in a twist,' Claire said. 'I was only asking. Will I ever get to meet him?'

'If he turns out to be the love of my life and we decide to emigrate to the Bahamas leaving you with the kids, then, yes, you will meet him. It'll be the least I can do. Must dash, Mum.'

Hugh had suggested meeting in a pub in Dublin so Leonie decided to take the DART into town rather than drive. Hobbling a bit in her new and slightly tight court shoes, she left the house at a trot after giving explicit instructions on how to reheat lasagne and on how she didn't want to return and find Danny had gone out leaving the girls on their own.

'Where you going to in your finery, anyway?' Danny enquired, taking in her best ruched velvet skirt, the silky red shirt with the top three buttons opened and her Egyptian scarab necklace.

'Out with the girls,' his mother fibbed, dragging on the black suede jacket she only wore on special occasions. As Abby had been sulking all day, she didn't want to start another row by mentioning that she was going to meet a man. Who knew what sort of extreme reaction that would provoke? In her current emotional state, Abby would probably race for the airport to fly to Boston, stopping only to phone the ISPCC to report her mother for child cruelty.

Having timed her departure to coincide with the passing of a bus, Leonie was soon on her way to get the DART into the city centre. However, by the time she'd got to the Greystones train station, having hobbled from the bus, every step agony, Leonie was tempted to throw her new shoes in a bin and go into town in her stockinged feet. People might point and stare, but surely not any more than they were going to do on seeing a tall woman limping along with little yelps of pain at every step. She took a seat on the right-hand side of the carriage so she could look out of the window at the sea. Easing her feet out of the shoes, she realized at last just how apt the Cockney for feet was.

Plates of meat suited hers perfectly, both visually and realistically. She rested the plates on the empty seat opposite, hoping a train employee wouldn't appear and remind her that 'seats aren't for feet'. He'd get a court shoe in the gob if he did.

Pain notwithstanding, Leonie enjoyed her train journey, peering into gardens and lit-up houses from the vantage point of the carriage, and watching people walking delirious dogs along the strand at Sandymount. That was her favourite bit of train journeys: the insight it gave you into other people's lives. It was fun looking into curtainless kitchens, watching people at the sink with saucepans or wandering around drinking tea, oblivious to the fact that the passengers on the DART could see them.

The only flaw in this form of entertainment was the fact that the train went too fast for her to have a thoroughly good look.

At Tara Street station, she realized that taking the shoes off had been a serious error. Cramming her feet back into them was like stuffing an anaesthetized rodent through a narrow cage door. Hobbling even more painfully on now swollen feet, she trudged slowly along to the hotel in Temple Bar where she was meeting Hugh.

She was ten minutes late, her feet felt as if they required urgent amputation and she knew her 'banish the blemish' corrective foundation was sliding down her cheeks with the heat of struggling along in painful shoes and a heavy jacket. Her spirit of romance felt deeply absent. Perhaps he wouldn't turn up and she could go home. There was a Richard Gere film on the telly and if the kids were all sulking madly, they'd probably stay in their respective bedrooms and sulk there, leaving her with control of the remote.

One foot in the door of the hotel and she spotted Hugh immediately. It would be hard not to. He was the only person in the premises over the age of twenty-five, apart from herself, that was. Standing by a pillar with a glass of beer and an uncomfortable expression on his face was a man of medium height with big shoulders, the bullish neck common to sporty blokes, and plenty of short nutty brown hair that was greying at the temples. He was good looking, she realized with a pleasant shock; he had a healthy outdoorsy colour, strong features and a solid, reliable sort of chin. In a casual open-necked shirt and tweedy jacket, he looked as out of place in this youthful emporium as a dowager duchess at a rave. Busker's was clearly the in spot for the city's bright young things on a Saturday night, because it was jammed with huge gangs of guys and girls, all dressed up for partying.

Overpowering wafts of hairspray competed with pungent after-shaves and perfumes. It was an asthmatic's idea of hell. Minxy girls in snippets of lycra giggled into their bottles of beer and eyed up newly shaved blokes who attempted to look cool by smoking too much.

Leonie couldn't help but grin at the stupidity of meeting in such a place and when his eyes met hers across the throng of exquisite twenty-year-old flesh, Hugh grinned back in agreement. He wound his way to the door, his face apologetic. He had nice crinkly eyes – laughing eyes, she could see up close – and a scar in the aforementioned reliable chin.

'Leonie?' he said loudly so she'd hear him over the music. 'This is what I get for pretending to be trendy and suggesting we meet in Temple Bar.'

'If it's any consolation,' she said, eyes shining, 'I'm just as untrendy or I'd have known that this isn't our sort of place. Will we find somewhere for geriatrics where we don't have to semaphore our conversation? My hearing-aid battery is running low.'

He nodded, put his half-full glass down and they went outside.

In the disco-beat-free atmosphere, Leonie half-expected that their instant easiness with each other would disappear. But it didn't. She liked this guy, mad though it was to make such a decision after a few minutes. But she did.

They walked slowly along Temple Bar and laughed at how stupid otherwise mature, intelligent people became when they started dating via the personal ads. 'The first time I tried it, I suggested dinner in this ultra-posh restaurant to impress her and she said she hated pretentious restaurant bores so much that she left after the first course,' Hugh recalled. 'This time, I thought I'd be sort of trendy and with it by suggesting Busker's.'

Leonie didn't bridle at the mention of other personal ad dates on the grounds that he might be a serial dater. He wasn't, she was sure.

There was something comfortable about him, as if she'd known him for years.

'My dating sin tonight is wearing new shoes to impress you,' she said, struggling on the cobblestones that were considered part of the Left Bank-ish charm of Temple Bar. 'Consequently, my feet are in agony and these cobblestones are hell.'

'You should have said,' Hugh declared, taking her arm. 'I'll drag you over to the footpath, milady, and we shall find a suitable hostelry where you can take the shoes off and nobody will notice.'

'I need somewhere I can lie down,' she joked, then blushed at what she'd said.

Hugh took no notice. 'This is too advanced in the personal ad dating department for me,' he said blithely. 'Sex in the first ten minutes is too confusing, don't you think?'

Leonie laughed. 'Definitely. But a drink would be nice.'

'Or how about something to eat?' he said. 'I'm actually ravenous and didn't want to suggest dinner in case we hated each other and needed to escape quickly.'

'That's *exactly* what I thought,' Leonie said. 'I'd even invented a fictitious private party I'd have to get to by ten, in case you were as dull as ditchwater, but I'm starving.'

'Right. Dinner. Lean on me. And if you suddenly need to leave at half nine, I'll get the picture.'

Finding a table for two on a Saturday night when you haven't booked is the Holy Grail of modern dating. But they managed it without having to hobble too far. Installed in a tiny booth for munchkins in a Chinese restaurant – the only place with a table – Leonie slipped off her shoes and moaned with relief.

'You can't do the fake orgasm scene from *When Harry Met Sally* without food,' Hugh warned her. 'Otherwise we'll be thrown out for fondling each other under the paper tablecloth. The police may even be involved. It won't be nice. I'm a respectable man.'

She giggled. He was very funny, which was refreshing. Bob, whom she'd met twice since in a platonic way, was about as amusing as piles – and that was on a good day.

'Ethnic restaurants are a good way of establishing if you can bear each other or not,' Hugh remarked, putting on a pair of half-moon reading glasses to peruse the menu. 'If one person starts laughing like a drain when they ask for "flied lice", then you either know you've met your soul mate or not.'

'If you're a flied lice merchant, then I'm off,' Leonie said. 'Those glasses are great, by the way. I can just picture you peering at someone over a big desk and telling them they've been very bad.'

Hugh raised his dark eyebrows questioningly. 'I think you've got your personal ads mixed up,' he said. 'I'm the investment advisor person; you're thinking of Mr Whippy, who advertises on the next page as being good at punishment.'

Leonie smiled. 'You mean, you're not Mr Whippy?'

He appeared to consider this. 'As long as it never gets out, I'd be prepared to consider it. No fee, seeing as it's for you.'

She grinned with delight. This was marvellous, this was *flirting*. Ah, remember that. Smiling and making jokes with wicked innuendoes.

The waiter appeared and took their order. When Hugh got to the bit where he said he wanted fried rice with his beef, Leonie felt the giggles bubbling up inside her. She *couldn't* laugh now. It would be too, too rude to the nice waiter who'd think they were making fun of his accent when it wasn't that at all.

Hugh sent her a stern look. 'Behave yourself,' he mouthed. 'She goes berserk after a few pints of shandy,' he told the waiter.

She laughed seriously this time.

'What is it about you that makes me keep laughing?' she asked when the waiter had gone, unperturbed by the strange antics of diners.

'My bald patch?' he offered, bending forward so she could see it.

'I think it's relief because you've turned out to be so normal,' Leonie declared. 'Well, a bit abnormal really, but my sort of abnormal. I feel as if I've known you for years.'

He nodded. 'Ditto. I never joke around with people I don't know: I'm actually quite shy and when I don't know someone, I'm very formal to cover up. Handy in my line of work, mind you. You can't discuss investing money for someone and keep making cheap jokes. But with you, I feel very comfortable.'

'Me too. So, you weren't the life and soul of the party when you brought your last blind date to the posh restaurant?' she asked slyly.

Hugh raked a bit of hair back with one hand and looked pained. 'Hell, no. It was like a job interview. I told her what I did, where I did it and what my hobbies were. That was all before we'd ordered our first drink. If we'd had time, I'd have probably moved on to my career strategies and where I hoped to be in five years. Horrible. It's a miracle I tried this again, after that fiasco.'

'What was she like and why did you answer her ad?' Leonie asked. 'Actually, why did you answer *mine*?'

'She said she worked with money and I thought it might be nice to meet someone in the same line of work,' he explained. 'That was a big mistake because I'll probably spend the rest of my professional career hoping I'm never allocated to a branch where she works. She's a tough cookie. It takes some nerve to stand up and say that we obviously weren't suited and she didn't want to waste the evening.'

'Ouch. Maybe she's a Miss Whippy,' Leonie said evilly.

'Wouldn't be at all surprised. I'm afraid I was Mr Wimpy to her Miss Whippy. It's not nice sitting on your own in a restaurant when your date has left abruptly. Everyone probably assumed we were married and I'd just told her I was having an affair or something.'

He looked so forlorn at the memory of that restaurant scene, that Leonie had to bite her lip to stop herself smiling.

'That was in November,' he said, 'so I've been sitting at home licking my wounds for the past couple of months.'

Food and wine arrived and they tucked in.

'You're not getting off that easily,' Leonie said, when she'd sated the first pangs of hunger with satay chicken. 'Come on, spill the beans: why did you answer my ad?'

'You sounded lovely and friendly, and you said you loved animals. Obviously, I do too and that was it. Also, I'm a sucker for statuesque blondes and my friends told me I was getting too big for my boots and needed another strange woman walking out on me on a blind date to knock me down to size. Only kidding,' he added. 'Although not about the first bit.'

'If you're hoping to get out of paying for your half of dinner with flowery compliments, stop right there,' Leonie warned.

'Not guilty, miss,' Hugh said honestly.

He gazed straight at Leonie. 'You've the most beautiful eyes I've ever seen,' he added softly. 'They're so blue, beautiful. And I'm having a wonderful time. Honest.'

Leonie's belly quivered. Or at least *something* in her nether regions quivered. Maybe it wasn't her belly after all, but some of the long-since rusted up sexual bits that hadn't been out of dust sheets since Adam was a lad. Yes, definitely a quiver. She breathed deeply and said: 'That party at ten o'clock has been cancelled, by the way.'

'Good. When my friend rings my mobile at nine forty-five pretending to be locked out of his flat, to which, incidentally, I have the only spare key, I'll tell him it's OK, you've turned out to be wonderful.'

Chinese food had never been more fun. They laughed and talked their way through far too much Peking Duck and Sizzling Beef, until Leonie said she'd have to open all the buttons on her skirt or she'd burst out of it. She couldn't imagine making such a statement with any other man, but she felt so relaxed with Hugh, it seemed natural. Of course, the second bottle of plonk helped.

'I'm not really a heavy drinker,' Leonie said, holding up her glass for another refill. 'I like wine but it doesn't take that much to get me drunk.'

'I hope you haven't copped on to my fiendish plan,' said Hugh, dead-pan. 'I've got a van out the back and I'm taking you on to my place to have my wicked way with you.'

'Not *that* drunk yet,' said Leonie, waving a reproving finger at him. 'The worst I ever was when I was drunk was in college,' she said, shivering at the memory. 'It was a medical students' party and they'd made ferociously strong punch with poteen and God knows what other booze. I mean, I was plastered after about four glasses, and I got talking to this guy who was a gynaecologist.' She giggled at the memory. 'Of course, I just *had* to ask him that fatal question.'

Hugh looked blank.

Leonie leaned forward and lowered her voice: 'You know, how they can look at women's bits all day and then go home and make love to their wives or girlfriends.'

Hugh's eyes were dancing now. 'What did he say?'

'I can't remember. I was too drunk! God, I was embarrassed the next day. People kept coming up to me and telling me things I'd done, all of it terrible. I was mortally embarrassed. The only reason I'd got drunk in the first place was because I desperately wanted to fit in and I thought booze would help.'

'Your poor girl,' Hugh said, petting her hand kindly. 'I am ashamed to say that at the age of forty-seven, I'm not much better. The night of my ill-fated date with Ms Whippy, after she left the restaurant I finished the bottle of wine that we'd only just started and then had three brandies. At least you were a mere child when you did it.'

It was Leonie's turn to pet his hand. 'That's perfectly understandable, Hugh,' she said indignantly. 'I'd have had two bottles in misery – or else I'd have pretended to go to the loo, climbed out the window and never gone back out of sheer embarrassment.'

He nodded. 'Being a grown-up with kids doesn't make you immune to the same pangs you went through as a teenager, does it?'

'You've got kids?' said Leonie delightedly. 'You never told me.' This was great. A separated man with children was perfect because he would understand how important they were to Leonie.

'Jane, who's twenty-one and Stephen, who's eighteen. He lives with his mother, but Jane lives on her own in a flat near here. They're terrific,' he said warmly. 'I don't know what I'd do without them.'

'Tell me everything,' Leonie said.

Everything involved two more coffees on the grounds that they shouldn't have any more to drink for health reasons. 'I'd like to be able to get out of bed for some of the day tomorrow,' Hugh said, 'and not be hopelessly hungover.'

He didn't say why he and his wife had separated three years ago and Leonie didn't like to ask a question as personal as that. If he wanted to tell her eventually, he would. But he loved talking about his kids; his eyes lit up when he told her all about them.

Jane was 'beautiful. I don't know whose side of the family she got it from, but she's a corker.' She worked in an insurance company as a clerk. She was very clever and a wonderful artist. 'I keep telling her to visit galleries with some of her paintings but she won't.'

Stephen, on the other hand, sounded like a bit of a wild child and was currently saving up to take a year off his business studies degree to travel round the world. 'Every time he mentions the Far East, Rosemary, that's my ex, has a fit.'

'I can understand that,' Leonie said, sympathizing with Rosemary. If Danny had announced he wanted to travel to the Far East, *she'd* have had a fit. Only the week before she'd read another article about vulnerable young Westerners getting duped into the shady world of drugs in Thailand through having all their belongings 'stolen' by drug gangs, who then roped them in by lending them money and new luggage – luggage with a street value of a few million dollars in hidden heroin.

She recounted the most recent article to Hugh, pointing out that she'd read about young business people who'd never been involved with drugs in their lives ending up in jails thanks to having drugs planted on them by corrupt local police looking for protection money.

'Nonsense,' he said. 'That's all hype and hysteria in the press. Young people need to spread their wings and travel. That's what life's all about. I'm only sorry I never had the chance to do it myself. I'm fully behind Stephen on this. I've told him I'll pay his air fare and give him a thousand pounds when he wants to go.'

Leonie was stunned. If Danny had wanted to take a year off to travel, she'd make damn sure he paid his own way. What was the point of taking a year to mature and broaden your mind if you were relying on hand-outs from your parents to do it? He'd learn nothing about being independent if she was bankrolling him.

'Wouldn't it be better if Stephen earned his fare?' she said tentatively.

'I have the money, it's the least I can do,' Hugh said, his jaw tensing. 'I'd give my kids anything. Anyway, I helped Jane buy her little runaround, a Mini, so Stephen deserves something to even it all up.'

'Oh,' Leonie said, smiling. Guilt money from an over-indulgent father. She'd bet a month's salary that he'd left Rosemary and was now indulging his children like mad to make up for it.

'Were they very upset when you left home?' she asked.

'I didn't leave home,' he said, surprised. 'Rosemary did. She left me for someone else, but it went sour. Then we decided she should have the family home and I moved out. It made more sense that way as both the kids were still living at home.'

'Sorry, I didn't mean to be nosy,' Leonie said quickly. So much for the home-spun analysis, Dr Freud.

'No, it's fine. We should get this sort of stuff out in the open so we understand each other. Tell me about your family.'

It was after twelve when they finally left the restaurant after some mild quibbling over who'd pay the bill. Hugh had wanted to pay for everything but Leonie said no, she preferred to pay her own way, thank you very much. They walked to a taxi-rank in silence. Their date had been wonderful and Leonie wanted to see him again, but she didn't know how to say that without coming across as pushy. And what if she said it and he didn't want to see her again? The ground would open up and swallow her, she hoped.

They joined the taxi queue but it must have been a quiet night in the city because they were at the top of the queue within minutes. Leonie could see a taxi approaching. Hugh lived in an entirely different direction to her, in Templeogue, so they couldn't share one. This was goodbye. The taxi cruised to a halt and Hugh opened the door for her.

Disappointment flooded through her. He wasn't going to ask to see her again. Then, she felt his lips brush her cheek gently. 'What are you doing next Saturday night?' he asked.

She beamed at him. 'Painting my toenails, unless I get a better offer.'

'You've got one now,' he said, thrusting a business card into her hand. 'Dinner same time next week. I'll book somewhere exotic and you can phone me on the mobile.'

The taxi drive home took nearly an hour. Normally, Leonie would have been taut as an elastic band watching the meter rack up the fare with the speed of a slot machine in Vegas. Tonight, she felt as if she was sailing home on a thermal breeze, like a yacht racing around the Caribbean. Inviolate from the pain of everyday life, including huge taxi fares.

She whispered his name to herself a couple of times; Hugh Goddard, Hugh Goddard. It was a nice name and he was a nice man. Mind you, she could see them arguing over how to bring up kids, but then, that was hardly the issue here. She was hardly planning on having any more, so their wildly different views would not matter. What *did* matter was the way he made her feel. He was funny and attractive, and in his company she felt funny and attractive too. In other words, the perfect match.

'No, we haven't set a date, but we want it to be soon,' Hannah said, holding her hand out as Emma and Leonie bent over and admired the rock. 'Felix is up in the air for the next few months because he's auditioned for two series and he won't know if he's been successful for ages. Which means,' Hannah sighed, 'that we daren't book anyplace for the reception.'

They were having coffee in Hannah's kitchen, a hastily convened conference to discuss life, the universe and men.

'Oh,' Emma said. 'I thought Felix would be crazy to hold on to you now you've agreed to marry him. I was expecting you to say the pair of you were off to the Seychelles for a beach wedding in the morning.'

'I'd like that,' Hannah admitted. 'I'm not into big family weddings, to be honest, and the thought of a party with seventy elderly relatives I haven't seen in aeons doesn't appeal to me. Not to mention what my father would probably do if he got drunk.' She corrected herself: '*When* he got drunk. We'll have to see what happens about the wedding. A beach one would be nice . . .' she added.

Leonie was in fantasy land. 'It'd be so romantic, Hannah,' she sighed wistfully, thinking of Hugh. 'Barefoot on the beach, coconut trees everywhere and the sound of water lapping the shore.'

Emma didn't appear quite so happy at the news, Hannah thought. She must be imagining it: Emma was one of the sweetest people she knew. She'd be thrilled to see Hannah happy.

'Are you sure you're doing the right thing?' Emma asked bluntly.

Both Hannah and Leonie gaped at her in shock.

'You don't think you're rushing into it, do you?' Emma went on. 'I know you love Felix, but wouldn't it make more sense to live together for a year and then decide. Just to be sure,' she added.

'I am sure,' snapped Hannah. 'We were made for each other. I'm crazy about him –'

Emma interrupted. 'Don't get cross, Hannah. I'm not saying that for a moment. I know *you* adore him, but marriage is a big step, you want to be absolutely sure. And Felix did go off before Christmas and not tell you where he was going. You have to be certain he's not the sort of guy who does that on a regular basis.'

Hannah's jaw tightened. 'I don't need to be reminded of that, thank you very much,' she said icily. 'He explained why. It's complicated, and I didn't invite you here to question my judgement, Emma.'

The other woman flushed. She'd gone too far and had hurt Hannah, which was the last thing she'd intended. 'Please don't get angry, Hannah. I only wanted to say, I'm afraid you're rushing into it and that you'll get hurt. I'm not saying it to be horrible. He's lovely, I know that, and he said he was sorry. I'm sorry too, I'm just being cautious. That's me –' she gave a brittle laugh – 'too cautious.'

She sounded so genuine, but Hannah was hurt by the inference that Felix wasn't really in love with her and that it was a one-sided relationship. She was also still smarting from Felix's disappearing trick at Christmas, and to have Emma bring the subject up as though she *pitied* Hannah – well, that was too much to take. How dare Emma say those things?

'I know you *think* you're helping, Emma, but you're not,' she said in a tight little voice. 'I'm getting married to Felix and I hoped you'd be pleased for me.'

'I am,' protested Emma.

'Girls, let's not fight,' begged Leonie. 'With you two at each other's throats, it's like being at home again while Danny and Mel are having a fight.'

Hannah allowed herself to smile briefly. 'You're right,' she agreed. 'Let's get off the subject of weddings, shall we?'

They had more coffee and tried to talk naturally, but the tense atmosphere remained, like the lingering scent of nicotine long after the cigarette had been put out. Eventually, Emma couldn't take it any longer.

'I have to go,' she muttered. 'I'll phone you both during the week.' And she was gone.

Hannah and Leonie sipped their coffee in silence, Hannah staring moodily at the fireplace.

'She's trying to be a good friend, that's all,' Leonie said, ever the pacifier. 'Emma cares for you and she's cautious. We all know that Felix adores you.' Which wasn't exactly true, because neither Emma nor Leonie had met Hannah's Mr Wonderful. But they had heard Hannah's version of events: that he was perfect and that he adored her.

'Yeah, I know,' sighed Hannah. 'I suppose I over-reacted a bit. Let's forget about it, shall we?'

But even though she wanted to forget what Emma had said, she couldn't.

It was like a bad omen or a blight hanging over what was supposed to have been a lovely day. When Leonie had gone, Hannah pottered around the apartment, tidying things and straightening cushions. Emma's words niggled at the back of her mind. How sure was she of Felix, really? He'd left suddenly without worrying about her. Could that happen again?

'Hannah's insane to get married to Felix,' Emma said to Pete that night when they were washing up companionably.

'Why do you think that, Em?' Pete asked.

'I don't know, there's something about Felix I don't like. His name for a start. I mean, Felix! Come on, he comes from somewhere outside Birmingham. Felix Andretti is a bit exotic for Brum.'

'He might have parents who weren't born in the UK,' Pete said mildly.

'And I'm Dutch,' his wife replied. 'He went off and left Hannah without a word for a whole month and then swans back into her life, expecting her to welcome him with open arms! He's a bastard. And I saw a photo of him in *Hello!* with someone else. I didn't tell Hannah – I couldn't.' Emma's eyes narrowed. 'Who knows what he was up to when he was away for that month. I bet Felix thinks fidelity is something to do with a stereo system.'

Pete laughed. 'You're a panic when you're angry about something, you know that?'

'Well, it's just that I'd feel like a useless friend if I didn't say something, Pete.' Emma rinsed the last saucepan and started wiping the sink fiercely with a J-cloth. 'I don't trust him and I tried to tell Hannah what I felt. But she got so angry that I chickened out at the last minute and backtracked.'

'If you feel that strongly about it, try again. Phone her and say you care about her and don't want her to be hurt, so is she sure she knows what she's doing,' Pete suggested.

'Yeah,' Emma said. 'I suppose I could. But she's already furious with me for bringing the subject up in the first place. She'd never talk to me again if I went for a repeat performance.' She gave a little sigh. 'Come on, *Father Ted* is on in three minutes. I'll make the tea and you get the biscuits.'

She had the baby dream again that night. It was so real, so utterly intense. She was standing in the shopping centre, trying to push a trolley into the supermarket. But she was tired and she was afraid of hurting the baby. A baby! she realized in astonishment. Then she looked down and saw that her belly had swollen to this small, neat bump. A three-months pregnant bump. She spent the next while gently holding on to it, as if something would fall out if she let go. How she caressed the bump, talking to it, loving it. It was a wonderful feeling, knowing that she was pregnant and sensing this tiny creature inside her, a creature she had to protect. Her little girl. How Emma knew it was a girl, she wasn't sure. But it was a girl. She walked around and talked to people, Pete and her mother among them, but she didn't say she was pregnant or anything, in case it would jinx things. So she decided to do a pregnancy test, but when she walked – barefoot for some reason – to the chemist to buy one, the chemist's had strangely become a grocery shop.

Emma knew she had to do the pregnancy test, she panicked about it. But she couldn't find one and she needed to sit down in case all that walking hurt the baby, and it started to rain and then . . . she woke up. Lying in her bed, she felt for a few moments as if she was still pregnant, it had all seemed so utterly real. Then Pete shifted in the bed and started snoring. The faint dreamworld faded as the real one came into focus. She looked at the clock: six thirty, it would soon be time to get up. And she wasn't pregnant. Emma didn't need to touch her belly to confirm that.

She climbed out of bed, knowing she wouldn't go back to sleep now and not wanting to. She couldn't bear to drift back into that dream and fool herself that she was pregnant again.

She slipped downstairs and made herself a cup of tea, all the while conscious of a huge sense of loss inside her. If this was what it felt like to lose a dream baby, what must it be like to lose a real baby, she wondered bleakly. How would your life ever go back to normal after that? It wouldn't. You'd ache for that child every day.

Feeling empty and hollow, Emma sipped her tea and watched breakfast television for half an hour. She couldn't cope with being alone with her own sad thoughts.

Pete walked into the sitting room as she was turning off the TV. His eyes were bleary with sleep and his hair, what little there was of it, stood up straight.

His very presence irritated her, she thought irrationally, as he leaned over and kissed her on the mouth.

'What has you up so early?' he asked, throwing himself down on to the couch and closing his eyes.

'Couldn't sleep,' she snapped. Honestly, couldn't he *tell*? Had he any clue what was wrong with her? Men!

CHAPTER TWENTY-TWO

The weeks flew past. As April gave way to one of the warmest Mays in recent years, Felix amused himself learning his lines for a film being made in September, while doing commercial voice-overs to keep his bank account in the black. He still hadn't heard back about the two series he'd auditioned for and the phone bills were horrendous as he rang his agent in London daily, alternating between optimism and sheer angst over the length of time he was forced to wait.

Hannah worked hard at the agency and was thrilled when David James came to her with the news he was opening another branch, in Wicklow this time, and would she like to move there in a more senior position?

'It's a fantastic opportunity,' she told Felix that evening as they meandered along Dawson Street to meet some of his actor pals in Café En Seine. 'I can't believe how much my life has changed in this year. The job, you, everything . . .' She beamed at him. 'It's wonderful. You're wonderful, Felix Andretti. David said we could talk about the new office next month, to give me time to think about it. You do think I should go for it, don't you?'

'Sure, baby,' Felix answered absently as they arrived at their destination to find his band of beautiful people sitting outside, shades on despite the fact that the evening sun had all but sunk. 'Here's the gang. Hiya, guys.'

* * *

On Thursday morning, Hannah was to think of the wry little comment Emma always made whenever they were talking about plans. 'We plan, God laughs,' Emma would say. 'That's the story of my life.'

Personally, Hannah had always thought this was a bit defeatist. She felt that life was there for the taking. What happened was up to you, not anyone else, a deity or otherwise. If you believed that sort of rubbish, humankind would still be stuck in the Middle Ages, terrified that a vengeful God would wreak havoc if they started messing around with the world of science.

That wasn't Hannah's motto at all. No. *You* make it happen – that was how she lived her life.

Her faith in this credo faltered on Thursday morning as a direct result of Felix feeling amorous. Early morning lovemaking was her favourite and she was still feeling delicious orgasmic ripples running through her body after a glorious romp when Felix withdrew from her and said, 'Shit!'

'What's wrong?' she asked lazily, still smiling.

'Bloody condom burst,' he said.

'Did it?' She sat up.

He examined the pack. 'That's the second time that's happened with these ones.'

Hannah grabbed it from him. 'These are out of date, Felix,' she howled. 'Where did you get them?'

'We were out of them and I had these in my sports bag.' He shrugged.

'Two years out of date,' Hannah said, feeling herself get nervous. 'And you're saying another one burst. I don't remember that?'

'It's only a bloody condom,' he snapped. 'Honestly, you do get in a fuss about the smallest things, Hannah.'

'The smallest things can cause the biggest problems, like a baby, Felix,' she said in a high, staccato voice.

She scrambled out of bed and threw herself into the shower, still in shock. She'd thought they'd been so careful having sex. Emma was always saying that women's fertility decreased after the age of thirty-five, so she felt sure she had less of a chance of conceiving at the age of thirty-seven. They always used condoms . . . She winced under the powerful jet of water. Using condoms was no good if the condoms in question were out of date. It was on a par with jumping out of a plane with a badly ripped parachute.

She dressed and didn't bother with breakfast. She didn't feel hungry somehow.

As she drove to her first job of the day – a bungalow in Killiney – Hannah tried to recall her last period. She never wrote it down and only ever remembered it in relation to certain events. She'd got a terrible one on New Year's Day, she remembered, with murderous cramps, and she'd been out of tampons, too. But that was the last time she could specifically recall when it had arrived. There had been others since then, but when? Furious with both herself and Felix, she stopped at a chemist and bought a hateful pregnancy tester. Why hadn't she gone on the pill? There was no point in relying on men for that type of thing: your fertility was your problem.

At the bungalow, Hannah was delighted to see that the vendors had gone to work. She hated doing it, but she had to use their loo for her test. What they didn't know wouldn't hurt them, she thought, admiring the corner bath with the jacuzzi jets. She'd read reports where some irresponsible estate agents admitted to having sex in clients' houses. Hannah was appalled at the idea. She didn't think having a discreet pee would be considered unprofessional.

The test done, she shoved the apparatus back in her handbag and opened the door to the viewers, a fixed smile glued to her face. They wandered around the house for nearly half an hour, but it didn't take nearly that long for the second blue line to appear in the pregnancy tester window.

Alone in the house again, she looked at the tester and cursed Felix, condom manufacturers and herself, in that order. 'Bloody, bloody pregnant!' Hannah howled to the empty house.

It was ironic. Poor Emma would kill to be in her position now, she thought gloomily. Emma longed for a baby with all her heart. And now Hannah, the most unmaternal of the three friends, was pregnant. Hannah imagined that creatures who ate their young were more maternal than she. She had no interest in babies or kids. Well, she conceded, her cousin Mary's two were sweet enough. Krystle and Courtney were nice girls, but that didn't mean she wanted them to live with her.

As she drove back to the office, Hannah railed out loud, bitterly asking someone to tell her why she, of all people, had to get pregnant. Here she was with an exciting new job opportunity, a wonderful fiancée and a great life, and now it was all going to be ruined by some squalling, screaming brat. Bloody wonderful.

Carrie, the receptionist, waved a sheaf of phone messages at her when she went in. 'Felix just rang,' said Carrie, her face flushing. She'd met Felix a few times when he'd come to meet Hannah after work and obviously had a thumping great crush on him. Which Felix didn't do anything to neutralize, Hannah thought crossly, recalling the way he'd sit on the edge of Carrie's desk and chat to her.

'He says it's important,' Carrie added.

Wait till he finds out what important news I've got for *him,* Hannah thought grimly.

'Babes!' yelled Felix jubilantly. 'You'll never believe it!' He was obviously stuck into the drinks cabinet already, so it had to be good news. 'I got *A Moment in Time*. I can't believe it, the starring role. We're made, it's a career part. BAFTAs here I come! You wouldn't believe the money I'll be on. Bill says they really want me and I can name my price. Edwin Cohen, the director, is a huge star in the States. He never does TV – you can't imagine what it means to be working with him.'

'That's fantastic, darling,' Hannah said, pleased for him. But her joy was dimmed by the presence of a positive pregnancy test. 'I've got something to tell you too. Hold on a mo, I've left something in my car,' she lied. 'I'll phone you back.'

Outside, she rang him on her mobile. 'Felix, that's the most incredible news ever, but I'm afraid I've got news too which may not be so good.' There was no point beating around the bush. She had to tell him straight up: 'I'm pregnant, Felix.'

'Fantastic!' he yelled.

Hannah blinked. This was not the reaction she'd been expecting. She'd anticipated groans about how it wasn't the right time in either of their careers and how a baby would interrupt his sleep and inhibit last-minute party-going. Instead, Felix whooped like a small boy who'd just won a conker match.

'Darling, I'm so pleased! We'll have to get married straight away – the Seychelles, I think. This is fabulous news. Bill is going to look for a house for us in London, I'll have to tell her to make sure it's got a nursery. And,' she could practically hear him grinning, 'Edwin Cohen is very much the family man. His wife is expecting their fifth kid and they'll be leaving LA to live with him during shooting. You can make friends with her, it'll be *brilliant* for my career. Gotta go, honey, there's a call waiting. I'll talk to you tonight about plans. Ciao.'

Hannah pressed the end button on her mobile and stood stock-still, trying to absorb everything Felix had just said. Moving to London? Making friends with the director's wife who just happened to be pregnant also? What about her job and her life and her friends, she thought helplessly. This was ridiculous, she was being swept along on some moving walkway, propelled in a direction she didn't want to go.

She loved Felix, obviously, but did she want a baby and to follow him to London? She didn't know. A baby had never fitted into her plans before.

She rang Leonie before lunch. 'I'm going mad and I have to talk to someone,' she said. 'Have you got a free twenty minutes for a sandwich?'

'I've got an hour,' Leonie said. 'Is everything all right, Hannah?'

'I'll tell you when I see you.'

'It's not Felix, is it?' Leonie asked anxiously as they met outside the coffee shop they liked that was equidistant from both places of work.

'Sort of.' Hannah groaned. 'I'm pregnant.'

'That's wonderful news!' squealed Leonie, before realizing that Hannah wasn't smiling. 'Isn't it?' she asked. Hannah was silent. 'You mean, you don't want it,' Leonie said slowly.

Her friend bit her lip. 'I don't know what I want, Leonie. I've never thought about children, as such. I never felt my biological clock ticking like a bomb or anything. And I know,' she raised her eyes, 'that makes me unnatural and strange. But that's genuinely how I felt. Some people are really into kids but I wasn't, I'm not.'

'So it's unplanned?' Leonie asked gently.

Hannah laughed sourly. 'Does Dolly Parton sleep on her back?'

'What does Felix say?'

'He's over the moon, curiously enough. I thought he'd be bundling me on to the first ferry to Harley Street to get an abortion, but he's actually thrilled.' She didn't add that, being Felix, he had instantly spotted how useful a pregnant missus would be for making pals with his new director. 'He wants us to get married immediately too,' she pointed out.

'That's sweet,' Leonie said.

'Yeah, but he's not the one who has to spend nine months looking like a whale, and he's not the one who has to give up her job and hightail it off to London to be a bloody earth mother while he's got an interesting career.'

'You don't have to give up work just because you're pregnant! It's a baby, not a disease,' Leonie said in exasperation.

'That's the other thing,' Hannah said gloomily. 'Felix has landed this wonderful new part in London and we've got to move.'

'Oh.'

They ate their sandwiches and discussed the notion of Hannah leaving Ireland and her burgeoning career to be with her fiancé. Finally, Hannah said that she just wished it hadn't all happened *now*.

'I did think about an abortion, but I don't know, Leonie,' she said, toying with her coffee. 'Could I go through with it? I remember when I was a teenager growing up, I would have had an abortion like a shot if I'd got pregnant. Mind you, then, I wouldn't have known how to go about it. There was such a veil of secrecy over the whole thing and "taking the boat to England" was this big, secret shame. But that was then and it seems selfish to do it now just because it's inconvenient.'

'I can't advise you, Hannah. It's up to you.'

'I know.'

* * *

By the time she got home that evening, she was weary from thinking about her pregnancy and what she was going to do.

'Darling!' whooped Felix, sweeping her into his arms as she opened the flat door. 'The mother of my unborn child!'

She sighed and pushed him away. 'Oh, Felix, I don't know. Is this the right time for a baby? We're not prepared, we've never discussed it and I don't even know if I want it.'

'You mean, you're thinking about a abortion!' Felix looked at her coldly. 'I can't believe you'd even suggest that, Hannah,' he said. 'You can't do that to our child. I thought you loved me?'

'I do,' she said miserably. 'I just feel as if I have no choices left. Yesterday, I was a woman with promotion looming and a great future ahead of me. We were going to buy a house here . . . and today, I'm this brood mare who has to follow you wherever you want to go.'

Felix got up and opened a packet of cigarettes. Then he put them down again and turned to her, his expressive eyes bright with enthusiasm.

'Hannah, I know women's hormones go bananas when they're pregnant and everything, but this is ridiculous. Yeah, you're upset and emotional at the thought of leaving your job, but they've got estate agents in London too, you know. It's not an end – it's a beginning. With the money I'm earning, we can get a nanny and you can go back to work. You'll have a life, you'll have independence.' He pulled her down to the couch with him. 'You'll have me and our baby, Hannah. Won't that be wonderful?'

She let herself see their future through his eyes.

'Imagine, Hannah, a lovely Georgian house with a garden – we could do it up together, a cute nursery. Dinner parties. You'd be the perfect hostess. And we'd make a great couple. When I saw that smug bastard Harry with you, I just knew. I had to have you, to marry you, if needs be. Well, I didn't want Harry to get you,' he said.

Hannah's heart missed a beat.

'What do you mean?' she asked.

Felix raised his eyebrows. 'When you left that night, he had the nerve to say he was going to ask you to marry him, the little bastard.'

She blinked. 'Harry said *that*?'

'Yeah,' said Felix unconcerned. 'Imagine him thinking that you'd prefer him to me. I ask you! I told him where to get off, I said we were already engaged and were having a row, so he could bugger off if he knew what was good for him.'

'But we weren't engaged,' she said evenly. 'You'd left me, Felix. You had no right to say that to Harry.'

Felix's response to this was to slide one warm hand up under her top, long fingers burrowing into the lace of her bra. 'We've all got a past, love,' he said. 'Harry was your past and I've got mine. But that's what they are: the past. Forget him, you're with me now.'

CHAPTER TWENTY-THREE

Emma sat at her desk and opened the second drawer. Like everything else in her pristine office it was scrupulously tidy, with a box of spare staples, another of spare paperclips and several pens and post-its neatly arranged on top of a couple of ring notebooks. Emma reached into the back of the drawer and took out a small toiletry bag. Her emergency kit, as she called it, contained tampons, a spare pair of knickers, a pair of barely black tights, an old foundation compact and some make-up in case she ever needed to go anywhere after work and forgot her make-up, and painkillers.

She needed them now. Her period had only just started but already she could feel the agonizing cramps she suffered from every three to four months. She'd barely popped the pills in her mouth when Colin Mulhall appeared at the door with an 'I'm bored and want to chat' expression on his face.

Emma took a swig of water and swallowed, mentally cursing the fact that Colin was the one to catch her self-medicating. By lunchtime, it'd be round the office that poor Emma had a headache/period ache/brain haemorrhage/whatever. Colin liked to exaggerate. When the receptionist was off for three months with glandular fever, Colin had had her diagnosed as dying with cancer, until she came back and quickly scotched the rumours by appearing healthy. Whoever said that women were the worst gossips had obviously never met Colin, Emma thought grimly.

'Not well?' Colin enquired silkily, perching on Emma's spare chair. He was wearing a red spotted bow-tie today. It looked ridiculous.

'Headache,' Emma said sharply.

'I find meditation really helps,' Colin said. A devotee of anything New Age, he never stopped telling everyone exactly how they could improve their life the way he had. All you needed was time and an open mind, he'd say piously, as though he was open-minded and the rest of the office were cretinous oiks.

'I find paracetamol helps,' snapped Emma. 'Was there something you wanted, Colin?'

'Yes. Finn isn't in and Edward came to me about the plans for the conference.'

Emma bridled. Finn was the charity's press officer. He and Emma often worked closely together planning the yearly conferences. If Finn wasn't in, the last person Emma expected Edward to approach about it was the odious Colin, who couldn't type four lines without making eight errors. Imagine asking him about the forthcoming conference on child safety. The words 'piss-up' and 'brewery' came to mind.

'Did he?' was all she said. Her head ached with the desire to tell Colin he was a jumped-up little idiot who wouldn't do himself any favours trying to leapfrog over her to a senior managerial position in the company. But being a bit sharp with Colin was about as forceful as Emma had ever been, so she held her tongue.

'He wanted to see what we'd been planning publicity-wise and I took the opportunity of putting my oar in with regards to how long the conference will last,' Colin said smugly.

Irrationally, Emma found herself taking offence. Working out how long conferences lasted and organizing every detail was *her* job. Helping Finn as publicity officer was Colin's job. Not that he did that very well, Emma thought crossly.

'Isn't that a bit beyond your remit?' she said.

'Well, you see,' Colin's beady little eyes looked earnest, 'I've been talking to journalists and they say if we want to really get the message across that we're a serious agency concerned with children, then we should be having week-long conferences, maybe outside of Dublin, you know. So people can go away for a week and concentrate on them.' He was getting into his stride now. 'It'd be a wonderful idea, maybe go to Limerick or Galway and take over a small hotel where we can have guest speakers . . .'

'Go away for a week?' Emma was incredulous. 'How is KrisisKids supposed to finance that sort of conference? The costs would be ruinous. And I don't know which journalists you've been talking to, but it's difficult enough to get one full day out of most of them because they've so many other events to cover. Only a small percentage will make the second day of the conference this time – and you want them to go away for a week! You've no idea, Colin, really you don't.'

Colin sniffed and got to his feet, tossing his head back in pique. 'Edward thought it was a wonderful idea,' he said. 'He said he'd talk to you about it, but I thought I'd mention it first so you wouldn't be surprised. I wish I hadn't bothered. I remember when you were a nice person, Emma. I don't know why you've changed, but you have – and not for the better, either! You've turned into a jealous bitch.' With that, he swept out of Emma's office.

Emma stared at the door open-mouthed. Had she been awful to Colin? Had she been professionally sharp or merely unprofessionally bitchy because she felt threatened? Was Colin right – had she changed so much? It was hard not to when life was so difficult, she reasoned. Everyone and their granny had what they wanted and she didn't. One baby, just one small baby, that's all. Was that so much to ask for? How could anyone expect her to be serene and happy when this crippling need for a child was taking over her whole damn life! Crack. Emma looked down and saw that she'd broken one of the pale green KrisisKids pencils. Snapped it right in two.

Horrified, she realized she'd just gone off on to another baby rant in her head. Thinking about her baby was taking over her entire life. Work, home, play, sex: you name it, longing for a baby drowned every other emotion and overwhelmed all other parts of her life. Now it was affecting her at work to the point where she had lost her temper with a junior member of staff who was doing nothing more than trying to come up with new ideas. Colin was a terrible gossip, for sure, but he wasn't a bad person. Perhaps he did have a problem with Emma being his superior, but it was up to her to make sure that her subordinates worked with her and not against her. If Colin didn't like having a woman boss, or if he was genuinely trying to make her look foolish, Emma should have dealt with it in a professional way and not by snapping his head off. It had to stop, she decided.

Edward was on the phone when she knocked on his door but he motioned her to come in anyway.

When he had finished the call, he smiled at her a tad nervously and said he was glad she'd come in because there was something he wanted to discuss.

'Colin Mulhall came up with quite a good suggestion earlier and I wanted to talk it over with you,' he said hesitantly. He was never usually hesitant. Edward was the most direct and uncompromising person she'd ever met. But she instinctively knew he was wary of telling her this because he was afraid she'd go ballistic. How awful that she'd changed so much and nobody had told her.

'I know you see the conference as solely your baby,' Edward said.

She winced at his choice of words.

'And for that reason, I don't want you to get upset at this, but we must consider all ideas, you understand?'

Emma put him out of his misery. 'Edward, I know what you're going to say because Colin told me a few minutes ago – and I'm ashamed to say I was angry with him. I blew his suggestion out of the water because I was jealous and felt threatened, and I'm on my way to apologize to him. I just wanted to drop in to ask if you think I haven't been doing my job properly lately, or if I've been difficult to work with . . .' It was a tough question to ask but Emma's high standards demanded it.

Edward's momentary hesitation told her everything.

'I'm sorry,' she said before he could speak. 'There really is no excuse, Edward. I'm going to see Colin now, then I'm going home. When I come in tomorrow, I'll be my old self again.'

'Promise?' Edward said.

She nodded.

Colin was sulking and immediately picked up his phone to make a call when Emma walked slowly to his desk. However, when Emma began to apologize profusely and explain that she was under a lot of strain about something entirely unrelated to work, he cheered up.

'I thought you must be stressed out about something,' he said. 'I said to Finn only the other morning that you weren't your lovely, smiling self and we couldn't imagine what it was. We all know what it's like to be under strain too, and if you ever feel like an old chat over a cappuccino, talk to me. You know I'd never breathe a word about anyone's personal business.'

'I know you wouldn't, Colin,' Emma agreed, thankful that she still had a sense of humour. 'We'll talk about your idea tomorrow, but I'm going to take a half-day today, so I'll see you in the morning.'

At home, Emma threw her self-help books in the bin and then cleaned out her secret hoard from the bottom of her wardrobe. It broke her heart to throw out the pregnancy guide, the how-to-feed-your-baby guide and the lovely baby clothes she hadn't been able to resist buying. The tiny yellow bootees were the worst: hand-made chenille from a craft shop, they were exquisitely made. So dainty and small. When she'd bought them, she'd wondered how any baby's feet could ever be that tiny to fit inside the little shoes. It had been ages since she'd taken them out and touched them. She allowed herself one brief caress, then she bundled them into the bin liner with the other things. She threw the baby lotion she used as make-up remover into the kitchen bin and dragged her bag of goodies outside. Double-parking at the Oxfam shop, she left the bag just inside the door and then hurried off. She cried as she drove away. It was so final, so absolutely final. There was no hope for her and she was only tormenting herself by thinking that there was. Apparently, she was tormenting other people too. If she couldn't have a baby, then she couldn't and that was that. What was the point of destroying her life and Pete's into the bargain because she couldn't come to terms with it?

She went to the supermarket and bought her groceries, including stacks of cleaning equipment. It was odd, being in the supermarket in the early afternoon. Usually, she went at the weekend or late at night when the place was full of harassed career women and men flinging microwaveable meals into trolleys. Today, there was a different type of harassment in the air: that of exhausted mothers with young children, trying to drag youngsters in primary school uniforms away from the chocolate biscuits while simultaneously consoling the sobbing toddler jammed in the trolley seat.

Emma pushed her trolley to the check-out with the shortest queue. Ahead of her was a petite Chinese woman with a small baby in one of those chunky carry seats. Emma tried not to look at the baby as the woman threw groceries on to the conveyor belt. She couldn't help it. Dark, slanting eyes stared solemnly at her from a tiny face topped with a bright pink hat.

The baby waggled her fingers at Emma imperiously, demanding attention. Tiny fingers ending with minuscule translucent nails. It never ceased to amaze Emma that a creature so small could be such a perfect version of an adult, with fingers, toes and a little button nose that was scrunched up now in dismay because nobody was paying her enough attention.

'Isn't she lovely,' said an elderly voice behind her.

A fragile old lady with just a few things in her trolley was smiling at the baby, making coo-coo noises. 'They're lovely at that age,' she said to Emma.

'Yes,' Emma replied faintly. Talk about attacks from every side.

'Do you have any yourself?' the old lady asked.

Emma wondered how rich she'd be if she had a pound for every time she'd been asked that particular question. She'd also wondered how astonished the questioner would be if she were to scream, 'No, I'm infertile, you nosy, insensitive bastard!' at them. But you couldn't say that, especially not to a little old lady who was probably lonely and wanted company.

'I'm afraid I don't,' she replied.

The old lady smiled. 'There's plenty of time, love, you're only young.'

'Why don't you go ahead of me in the queue,' Emma suggested to her. 'You've only got a few things and I've loads.'

'That's kind of you, love,' said the woman. 'I can't hold those baskets any more and I have to get a trolley no matter how few things I want.'

She moved ahead of Emma and began chatting to the baby's mother. Emma picked up a magazine she hadn't wanted from the rack beside the check-out and started reading. She didn't really want to know how to transform her house with painting techniques as seen on TV, but anything was better than talking about babies nonchalantly, as though every fibre of her body didn't long for one.

Once she'd unpacked the shopping at home Emma changed into old clothes and started on a frenzied clean up. She'd scrubbed their bathroom and the main bathroom, and was busily thrusting the Hoover nozzle into the corners of her wardrobe when she heard the phone ring. It was Hannah.

'Hi,' said Hannah guardedly. 'Are you ill? I rang the office and they said you'd gone home early.'

'No, I'm fine,' Emma replied. 'How are you? Are you still on for next week?'

They'd planned a trip to the theatre to see *Les Liaisons Dangereuses*.

'Yes,' Hannah said slowly. 'It's just that I wanted to tell you something beforehand. I didn't want to land it on you next week.'

Emma was intrigued. 'Felix is playing Valmont as a surprise?' she said, amazed to find she could make a joke despite how depressed she felt. 'You've won the Lotto?'

'No.' Hannah sounded so serious.

'What is it?'

'I'm pregnant. I wanted to tell you myself, I didn't want Leonie to have to tell you. Because I know how hard it'll be for you . . .'

Emma made a harsh sound that she managed to turn into a little hoarse laugh. 'Why should I be upset, Hannah? I'm delighted for you. You must be so thrilled, and Felix, of course. When's it due?'

The words stuck in her throat like lumps of stone but she had to say them, had to say the right things to dear Hannah who'd been such a friend to her.

'The beginning of December. Actually, I'm scared stiff, Emma,' she revealed, unable to help herself. 'I know it sounds terrible, but I'd never thought that long about having a baby and, now that I am, it's wonderful and all that but . . . I'm terrified. What if I'm not the maternal type? What if I'm hopeless at it? Everyone seems to think it comes naturally, but people are always telling you certain things come naturally and that's rubbish.'

'Stop panicking,' Emma said reassuringly. 'Hannah, you're a competent, intelligent woman who can run an office, who has successfully changed careers and who's well able to apply herself to anything. Are you trying to tell me that you'll fall to pieces at the sight of a nappy, or collapse when you have to purée a carrot?'

Despite herself, Hannah laughed.

'It's common sense, Hannah,' Emma continued. 'It's going to be your baby and of course you're going to love it. You may not turn into Mrs Earth Mother in floral frocks who grows her own organic rhubarb, but you'll be great. You'll do it your way, right?'

'I suppose,' Hannah said. 'It's just that Felix seems to think that now I'm pregnant, this maternal glow surrounds me like some madonna in a medieval painting. I don't even think he fancies me any more,' she admitted.

'That's not unusual either. Some guys can only cope with one concept at a time. It's that madonna/whore balance. You were the whore – not you personally, Hannah, but because you were his sexual partner. Now you're the mother of his child, so you're off-limits sexually.'

'You'd make a great psychiatrist,' Hannah remarked. 'I just thought Felix was being his moody old self.'

'Hey, you're his fiancée. You should know. Perhaps I've been reading too many self-help books,' Emma said drily, thinking of the pile of books she'd dumped a few hours previously.

'You're a great pal,' Hannah said warmly. 'I was dreading telling you about all this. Listen, I've got to go. I've got to show a house to two morons who haven't a clue what they really want. I'll see you and Leonie next week, OK?'

'OK,' Emma answered automatically and hung up.

She was glad she'd thrown away all the baby stuff. She didn't want it in the house, mocking her by its very existence. But she still allowed herself to cry bitterly at the irony of it. Hannah, who didn't want children, was unexpectedly pregnant. And she, who did . . . What was the point of going over it all again? At least she'd managed to lie convincingly to Hannah about her true feelings. She wouldn't make much of a psychiatrist, but she was a good liar.

The notion of psychiatry hit her – why didn't she see a counsellor? Everybody went to therapists these days. It might help her deal with how she was feeling, it might unlock the painful knot that threatened to take over her whole body. It might be a complete disaster, of course, but she'd give it a try.

Checking the phone book for registered counsellors, she came upon a list of names. Several lived nearby and she closed her eyes and picked one.

Elinor Dupre. It sounded exotic and French. Maybe she didn't speak English and it'd be very easy, Emma thought, therapy where neither party understood the other. She dialled the number, expecting an answering machine or a secretary and a waiting list at the very least. To her surprise, a woman answered in crisp, received pronunciation tones:

'Elinor Dupre speaking.'

'I . . . er, hello, my name is Emma Sheridan and I got your name from the phone book,' stammered Emma. 'Do I need to get a referral from a doctor or anything . . . ?' she broke off.

'No, you don't. It would help if you told me why you wanted to see me, though. I may not be able to help.'

Her voice was soothing, calming. Emma had this ridiculous desire to spill out everything over the phone, but confined herself to saying: 'I can't have children and it's taking over my life, that's all.'

'I think that's a very big problem in anybody's life,' replied the calm voice as if she understood everything instantly. 'I certainly wouldn't dismiss it as "that's all",' she added gently. 'When would you like to see me?'

Emma didn't know why but she began to cry into the phone. 'So sorry,' she blubbed. 'This is stupid, I don't know why I'm crying or why I'm calling you.'

'Because it's the right time to do so,' said the woman firmly. 'You have made a decision and when that happens, there is a certain release experienced. I have an unexpected cancellation tonight at six thirty. Would you like to come then?'

'Yes, please,' Emma said fervently. She didn't know how she'd even wait until half six. Suddenly, talking about how she felt to someone who could understand was the most important thing in the world.

Elinor Dupre's home was a tall Georgian house at the end of a small cul-de-sac. Her office was in the basement and Emma could see a light shining in one of the basement windows as she parked the car. Before she'd had the chance to knock on the door, it was opened.

'Do come in,' smiled Elinor Dupre, her natural warmth belying the formality of her words. A serene-faced woman in her late fifties, Elinor wore a striking, richly patterned kimono and her long dark hair was tied up in a simple knot. She wore no make-up and her only jewellery was a watch hanging from her slender neck on a long chain.

She led Emma downstairs to an airy room with a fireplace, book-cases and two armchairs in it. On a small table beside one of the armchairs was a box of tissues.

Elinor sat down in the other chair, putting a notebook and pen on her lap, leaving Emma to sit beside the tissues.

She arranged the cushion behind her so that it felt comfortable, then sat looking around anxiously, suddenly not wanting to meet Elinor's gaze. Now that she was here, she didn't know why any more. What was she going to say? Was this all a ridiculous waste of time and money? And why didn't Elinor speak? She did this all the time; it was her job; she knew what came next. Emma hadn't a clue.

As if intuitively knowing what was going on in Emma's mind, Elinor finally spoke: 'There are no rules to these sessions,' she said. 'It seems strange at first when you're waiting for something to begin, but psychology is not like that. You've come here because you needed –'

'Your help,' interrupted Emma.

'Actually, you will be helping yourself, Emma,' Elinor said gravely. 'There are different types of psychoanalysis, but I practise cognitive therapy, whereby you will really be solving your own problems. I will be a guide, a helper, that's all. Sometimes I will ask you questions to help me understand but, for the main, you are in the driving seat.'

Emma laughed hoarsely at that one. 'I wish,' she said bitterly.

Elinor said nothing but angled her head slightly, as if asking why.

'I don't know why I said that,' Emma said quickly.

'Because you feel it is true?' Elinor asked.

'Well, yes . . . sometimes . . . I don't know.' Emma stared around her blankly. She didn't know what to say.

'There are no right or wrong responses,' Elinor said. 'Say what you feel, how you feel, why you think you're not in the driving seat.'

'Because nobody ever listens to me!' said Emma, astonishing herself with the ferocity of her answer. 'Nobody. No, Pete does but he's the only one. My mother, Kirsten, my father – never! He just walks on me and thinks I'm stupid. I hate that, I hate him!'

She stopped in shock. She'd said it and the sky hadn't fallen down, nobody had looked horrified and said she should be ashamed of herself. In fact, Elinor was merely listening quietly, as if many other people had sat in her armchair and said terrible things about the people they were supposed to love most in the whole world.

'I can't believe I said that,' gasped Emma.

'But you've wanted to?' Elinor asked in her low, soothing voice.

'Yes. You've no idea what it's like living with them. I love Kirsten, really I do, but she's their pet and I'm not. I'm not even close. It's not jealousy,' she said helplessly, wanting to explain properly. 'Kirsten is amazing, she's so pretty and funny, I'm not jealous of that. But I don't understand what I have to do to make them accept me for what I am. For him not to bully me or make little of me – does that make sense?'

Elinor simply nodded.

'I'm thirty-two years old and they still treat me like a child – a stupid child at that. I can't seem to break out of it. You know,' said Emma, sitting back in her chair and looking up at the cornice behind Elinor's chair, 'I envy those people who emigrate, because they can leave all the hassle behind. Nobody treats them like a child, people respect their opinions. I thought of telling Pete – he's my husband, by the way – that we should emigrate, I don't know, to Australia or America. But it wouldn't be fair. I mean, he loves his family. I love mine too,' she added hastily, 'it's just . . .'

'You don't have to qualify statements here,' Elinor smiled. 'This room and this hour in your week is for saying what you really think.'

'I never do that,' Emma said. 'Except at work, and I'm a different person there. But I can't imagine ever saying what I really think to my parents, never. I feel so stupid and sad.'

She began to cry and, for once, wasn't embarrassed at crying in front of another person who she hardly knew. It was obvious what the tissues beside her chair were there for.

By the end of the hour, Emma was shattered. She sat quietly for a moment while Elinor looked in her diary to make a firm appointment for the following week.

'This was a cancellation,' she explained. 'You'll have to come at a different time next week. Would half-past five on Monday suit you?'

Just over an hour after she'd arrived, Emma found herself outside the front door, feeling a little shell-shocked by the whole experience. She'd spent an hour with a stranger and yet still knew nothing about Elinor. Meanwhile, seamlessly and expertly, Elinor had elicited information about Emma's life. There had never been a sense of being questioned, just of telling someone who needed to know. Occasionally, Elinor wrote something down in her notebook, but she did it so unobtrusively that Emma barely noticed.

And she hadn't talked about wanting a baby at all, which was weird. That was the most important thing in her mind and it hadn't come up.

She drove home feeling more drained than she ever had in her entire life. Watching the soaps on telly would be beyond her, she felt so weak. And sad. Which was also weird. She'd thought that therapy was supposed to free you from past demons and make you into this wonderfully strong person. All she felt was miserable and exhausted. It could only get better.

It got worse. The following week, Emma was a bit more prepared for the emotional upheavals of talking to Elinor and determined not to cry. How pathetic to sob like a child. It was wasting valuable time when she could have been working on making herself stronger and more positive.

'It's about power, isn't it?' she said. 'I have power but I don't use it, or I let them take it away from me.'

Elinor angled her head. She did that a lot, Emma thought with a grin. It meant 'elaborate on that statement', without actually saying anything.

'I could say to my father to piss off but I don't because, as soon as I see him, he makes me feel about four again.'

'Would it make you feel better to say "piss off" to him?' Elinor asked.

Emma rotated her right ankle as she thought about this. 'Maybe not. He'd go ballistic but would it be worth it . . . ? My friend Hannah's father is an alcoholic and she's told him to piss off on numerous occasions, but I think they have a very different relationship from my father and I.'

'Hannah is one of your friends from the holiday?' Elinor asked, pen poised to write down some factual information.

'Yes,' Emma said. 'She's pregnant.'

With that, the tears started rolling down her face. She wasn't sobbing or weeping hysterically, just crying in silence as if the word 'pregnant' had been a signal to open a dam. 'I don't know why I'm crying,' she said stupidly. But she did know, of course she did.

'You must go through a lot of tissues,' she whispered, grabbing a handful.

Elinor let her cry. Eventually, she asked: 'Have you cried about this in front of anyone else?'

'Hannah and Leonie when we met on holiday. I was sure I was pregnant . . . Everybody asks do I have children,' she said hoarsely. 'In the supermarket last week, a woman asked me. On Sunday at my mother's house, a relative arrived and she asked me when would I think about having children. I'm sick of it. I want to tell them all to fuck off.'

'I think you need to work on saying what you want,' Elinor said slowly. 'You have to feel confident enough to say "this is what I want" and to know that if your needs upset other people or surprise them, that's not your problem. How *you* feel is your problem. And how they react to that is *their* problem. You cannot be responsible for other people's feelings.'

Emma sat in wonder. She never said what she felt. Then she realized that she had to say this out loud.

'I never say what I feel or need, or only rarely and to certain people. I don't know why.'

'You're trying to be approved of,' Elinor said. 'Even when it's about something desperately painful to you, you say nothing. You wait and gauge what other people want, then you adjust your needs to that. So you know that when you speak, you'll be saying what they want to hear. But why should you do that? What does that gain for you, other than making you sublimate your needs and desires for others? Think about it this way: do you know anyone who simply says what they think, no matter what? Someone who wouldn't dream of saying they wanted a glass of white wine, purely because the white was opened, when they really wanted red?'

'Kirsten. That's Kirsten to a tee.'

'Do people approve of her?'

'Yes, people adore her. She's mercurial but she says what she wants.'

'Which means that you can do that and be loved and approved of. So why can't you do it? Do you think you're somehow less loveable than Kirsten? That she can get away with it but you can't?'

'Actually, yes. I do think that,' Emma admitted. 'That's wrong, isn't it?'

'Right and wrong don't come into it,' Elinor explained. 'But it's not good for you. Being like that is having a negative effect. Tell me one thing: what did the doctors say about your infertility?'

Emma sat very still. 'I haven't seen any doctors,' she confessed.

'No?' said Elinor in that pleasant, almost uninterested tone.

'Well, it's just that I haven't ever wanted to talk to anyone about it . . .' Emma tried to explain.

Elinor was still looking at her with a hint of expectation on her face.

'Nobody has ever said I was infertile,' Emma said finally. 'I know

I am, it's simple. Some women can tell the moment they get pregnant; I know that I can't ever be. I can't explain it.'

'Is that the reason you've never seen a doctor about it,' Elinor asked, 'because you know without any tests?'

'It's obvious I can't have children,' Emma said stubbornly.

'Why?'

'Because I can't, because it's been years and it hasn't happened, that's why,' Emma replied in exasperation. 'Didn't you ever know something, Elinor? Know it without having to be told.'

'Sometimes,' Elinor said noncommittally. 'Do you often know things without being told?'

'Not really,' said Emma tetchily. She felt irritated by this line of questioning. It was as if Elinor doubted what she was saying. She'd kill to be able to have a baby. She just knew she couldn't.

Elinor's clock struck the half-hour. Their time was up. She was glad to leave today.

Emma mulled it all over in her mind as she drove home. The one thing which struck her as odd about the whole experience was the fact that Elinor didn't treat the whole baby thing as the main reason why Emma was seeing her. She hadn't said, 'Eureka, now we're talking about the real subject!'

She obviously felt that there was much more to it than that. Emma sighed. Anybody who thought talking about your innermost fears was enjoyable must be off their trolley.

She told Pete about her therapy sessions the following Sunday morning when they were in the car on the way to her parents for lunch.

'I don't want you to think I'm cracking up or anything,' Emma said, staring straight ahead at the red traffic lights.

Pete's hand found its way from the gearshift on to Emma's lap and round her tightly clenched hand. She clung to his fingers.

'I don't think you're cracking up, Emma,' he said gently. 'I know you're under a lot of strain with your mother and . . . everything.'

Even now, it was unspoken between them, her hunger for their child. She didn't know which of them was worse: her for becoming obsessed with it, or Pete for being so scared of upsetting her that he never mentioned children at all.

'I just want you to be happy, love, and if talking to someone helps, then that's great. I'd just hate to think you couldn't talk to me. You're the most important person in the world to me and I love you.'

He had to take his hand away to shift into second gear. Emma nodded, too emotional to say anything for a moment.

'I *can* talk to you, Pete,' she managed finally. 'It's just that there are some things I've got to sort out in my head and it's easier to talk to someone who doesn't know me or isn't involved in any way. I don't want you to be angry with me for doing it in the first place. It's not about you and me, Pete. I love you to bits, you know that.'

He put his hand back on hers. 'I know, you big dope. If I thought for a minute we were having problems, I'd be the one dragging you off to marriage guidance counselling. I'm not going to lose you, Em. I know you're finding it hard to cope with your mum and dad, and,' he paused, 'the whole baby thing.'

'How did you know?' she asked in a low voice.

'I'd want to be blind not to notice you're dying to get pregnant, Emma. I know you love children, it just takes time, that's all.'

She nodded, not sure if she was relieved or not. Pete knew she wanted a baby but hadn't a clue of the desperate, agonized longing she had for one. Or of her conviction that she couldn't have one because it was all her fault, that the worst-case scenario was just waiting to happen. She wasn't simply slow getting pregnant: she was infertile, barren, hopeless and useless as a woman. She knew one thing: she didn't want to talk to him about this deep-seated fear, not yet.

'Pete,' she interrupted, 'we have to talk about it, but I don't think I can do it yet, please? Soon, hopefully but not now.'

'If that's what you want, OK. But we've got to talk about it soon, Em. We're young, we've got loads of time. I promise.'

Emma couldn't speak. She sat with her lips pressed tightly together, almost not believing they were having this conversation. Pete thought he knew how she felt, but he didn't. He was trying his best, but nobody could understand this except another woman. That was the tragedy. It would pull them apart if she let it.

She reached over and kissed him on the cheek. 'Thank you. I don't know what I've done to deserve you, Pete.'

Her mother was polishing the brass knocker on the front door when they arrived. 'Hello, dears,' she said vaguely. 'I'm polishing.' She went back to her task, ignoring them.

Pete and Emma exchanged glances.

Inside, Emma was surprised to see Kirsten there, although not surprised to see her sprawled on the couch reading the beauty supplement to one of the Sunday papers. Her sister was not the sort of person to help out with cooking lunch if she could possibly get away with it. The roast could ignite in the oven before Kirsten would stir from her prone position.

'Oh, hi, guys,' she said, looking up briefly.

'Have you seen what Mum is doing?' Emma asked.

'Polishing something, isn't she?' Kirsten said, focused on her magazine again.

'Polishing the front-door knocker, Kirsten, which is strange behaviour for her on a Sunday morning. Mum never does housework on Sundays, apart from cooking. Don't you think she's behaving oddly?'

Kirsten sighed heavily and laid down her magazine, as if to say it was obvious she wasn't going to be left in peace to read it. 'Not really, Emma. She's ridiculously house-proud, you know that. I wouldn't be surprised to see her doing any housework.'

Emma began to lose her temper. 'Kirsten, do you ever notice anything except what's going on in your own private little world?'

Her sister sniffed. 'I don't know what your problem is, Emma. I'm the one in the middle of a nightmare.'

'What do you mean?' Emma perched on the edge of the couch.

'Patrick and I are fighting. He's such a bastard. You don't know how lucky you are, Emma.' Kirsten looked meaningfully at Pete, who had taken up one of the papers and was pretending to be immersed in the sports section so he wouldn't get roped into any argument.

'What happened?' Emma said flatly. She wasn't interested in Kirsten's histrionics today. As a result of the usual skyscraping Visa bill, Patrick had probably made a mild comment about her shopping addiction and how she'd have to cut back. He never lost his temper, amazingly for someone who lived with Kirsten. 'I suppose you've been shopping like there's no tomorrow as usual? You should have shares in Gucci by now.'

'You can mock, but it's serious this time,' Kirsten retorted. 'Very serious.'

Emma couldn't believe this. 'Describe "serious" to me,' she said acidly.

'He's talking about going to stay in his brother's house for a few weeks.'

'Bloody hell!' Emma was shocked out of her coolness.

'You can say that again,' Kirsten said moodily, getting up and leaving the room.

Emma followed her. 'Where's Dad?' she asked, seeing no sign of him anywhere.

'Some emergency at Aunt Petra's, apparently. She's probably just found the remains of the gas man she locked in the garage when he went to read the meter ten years ago. I hope Dad hurries back soon, I'm ravenous.'

She gazed into the oven with the helpless expression of a time-travelling Victorian faced with the space-shuttle controls.

'You are so useless around the house, Kirsten.' Emma checked out the roast and, seeing as it was nearly done, turned the temperature down and started preparing the vegetables.

'I better learn, then. Patrick says he has no intention of keeping me in the style to which I've become accustomed and that I can get a job. Sorry, the exact words were "bloody job".'

'What did you do, Kirsten?'

Kirsten blinked a couple of times. 'Slept with someone else.'

'Oh. Do you love him?' Emma asked tentatively.

'No. I was pissed, it was a mistake really. Well, not totally because he was very good,' she added reflectively.

'You stupid cow!' Emma was furious with her sister. Talk about reckless behaviour. Imagine doing that to poor, trusting Patrick.

'What people don't know about doesn't hurt them,' Kirsten retorted, 'and what do *you* know about it anyway?' she added sarcastically. 'Miss Bloody Perfect! Just because you've never had the urge to have a fling doesn't mean the rest of the world feels the same.'

'I'm not Miss Perfect,' shouted Emma. 'I'm upset because I care about Patrick and because you don't give a shit about this guy. If you loved him, then I'd stand by you every step of the way, but you don't. He was nothing more than a quick drunken shag. You just don't give a shit about other people, do you, Kirsten?'

It was all coming out now. Emma couldn't stop herself. Her mouth was running away with her, saying all the bitter, resentful things she'd been thinking ever since Kirsten had blankly refused to even discuss their mother's condition. Together, they could face whatever was wrong with Anne-Marie and tell their father what they feared. But without Kirsten's help, Emma was afraid to take that first step. 'Self-absorbed doesn't come close with you – you're self-obsessed!' she hissed.

They glared at each other across the kitchen, Kirsten's eyes blazing.

'You think you're the sensible, dutiful one, don't you?' spat Kirsten. 'For sensible, read "walked on"!'

'I don't want to break up the heavyweight boxing final of the year, but I think one of you should come and get your mother inside,' said Pete, peering round the kitchen door as if expecting to get hit with a flying saucepan.

'What's she doing?' Emma asked, row forgotten.

Pete grimaced. 'Listen,' was all he said.

The sisters could hear their mother shouting, roaring really: 'Get away from here, you bastards! Get away!'

'Jesus,' said Kirsten shocked.

'I tried to make her come in but she won't,' Pete said.

They rushed to the front garden where Anne-Marie was standing at the gate, waving her fists belligerently at bemused passers-by. 'Get out of here!'

'Oh, Christ, I can't look!' said Kirsten and rushed back into the house. Pete touched his wife's hand briefly and then they both approached Anne-Marie.

'Come on in, Mum,' Emma said in her softest voice. 'Let's have a nice cup of tea, shall we?'

Hannah had spent the past month practising what she'd say to David James.

I'm leaving because I'm pregnant, so thanks but no thanks to your fantastic job offer in Wicklow. And thanks for all your faith in me, promoting me from office manager and giving me a real career.

No matter how she said it, it still sounded terrible. Half-hearted and ungrateful.

She was getting used to the idea of being pregnant, and was secretly thrilled at the idea. She'd been reading pregnancy books and was policing her daily intake of calcium and all the right foods. Although he too was delighted at the idea, Felix still kept trying to give her glasses of wine in nightclubs and couldn't understand why she didn't want him smoking near her. Telling people was the difficult part. The rigorous self-control bit of Hannah hated having to tell anyone she was unexpectedly pregnant. An unplanned pregnancy smacked of some flibbertigibbet who let things happen to her rather than made them happen.

Her mother had been delighted at the news and they still had to brave a visit to Connemara where her father would be let loose on poor Felix.

'Your father will be delighted,' Anna Campbell had insisted on the phone. 'He loves children.'

Felix wanted to get married before they went visiting the various in-laws, and Hannah, who had visions of her father yelling blue murder about being denied a big bash for his only daughter, was inclined to agree with him. Anna Campbell wouldn't mind being presented with a *fait accompli* as far as the wedding was concerned. Stoic was her middle name. Hannah would have quite liked to have met Felix's family first, but he was strangely reticent about them and Hannah, who understood that, didn't push him.

But before weddings and family reunions, Hannah simply had to tell her boss. For some reason, she hated doing it.

She'd picked a Friday evening so she could skive off afterwards without having to face David's disappointment for the rest of the day.

'Can I talk to you for a minute?' she asked him at five thirty that evening.

'Sure. Come into my office in five minutes,' he said.

He was still on the phone when Hannah went in and stood, feeling like a schoolgirl about to be bawled out for faking period pains for the second time in a month in order to miss games.

David smiled at her as he listened to the person on the phone and gestured to her to sit down. Oh hell, she thought miserably, sitting. She felt terrible. He must guess what she was going to say. Surely guilt shone out of her like a beacon. But what did she have to feel guilty for? She was pregnant and engaged to be married. What was wrong with that. Absolutely nothing!

David put the phone down and sat back in his chair with a sigh.

Temporarily buoyed up, Hannah launched into her spiel at breakneck speed: 'David, I'm pregnant. Felix and I are getting married and we're going to live in London.' There. Done it.

'Oh,' was all he said. Hannah had expected more. She wasn't sure what, but more . . .

'So I won't be able to take the job in Wicklow, even though you were so good to offer it to me,' she rushed on, frantic now to fill in the gaps in the conversation and get out of there.

David steepled his fingers and looked at them thoughtfully as if trying to figure out some arcane puzzle that lay hidden therein. 'That's a pity,' he said, without looking at her. 'We will miss you round here and I had great plans for your future. You're a natural at this game.'

'Sorry,' she said lamely, looking down at her own hands now. She was sorry she hadn't worn her engagement ring to give her confidence, but she deliberately hadn't been wearing it into work until she'd officially announced it.

'Felix is a lucky man,' he added lightly. 'Do I get asked to the wedding because I inadvertently introduced you?'

Hannah instinctively felt that the last thing David wanted was to be at her wedding to see her marry Felix.

'We're probably going to get married abroad,' she said, avoiding eye contact. 'I'll work out my month's notice here, naturally.'

'Naturally,' he said. 'Hannah . . .'

The way he said her name, softly, caressing, made her look up at him. He normally sat up so straight in his chair, ramrod straight in an almost military way. Now he was leaning against the desk with his arms resting tiredly on it and the lines on his face made him look suddenly old. He needed a holiday, Hannah thought fiercely. He worked so hard and never took time off. A few weeks away, letting the sun tan the strong, hard planes of his face and lifting the lines that seemed ingrained around his dark eyes: that's what he needed. But she wouldn't be around to suggest it in a half-bossy, half-motherly fashion, the way she might have before.

'Don't lose touch, will you?' he asked, his eyes boring into hers. He looked sad somehow, terribly desolate.

'I won't.'

She got up to go and he did too, walking towards her to open the door.

Impulsively, Hannah threw her arms round him. It was the closest she'd ever come to him before, apart from that strange pub lunch when he'd held her hand. As her arms went around his shoulders, his closed round her waist, pulling her closely to him.

Suddenly, he lowered his head to hers and kissed her gently on the lips, his five o'clock shadow grazing her chin. It was a kiss redolent of regret. Not hard and sensual, the way she'd imagined he'd kiss, yet intensely moving all the same. For some strange reason, Hannah wanted it to go on: she wanted to feel his huge hands circling her waist as if she were a slender little thing; she wanted to feel his body crushed against hers and to run her fingers through the salt-and-pepper hair. She wanted to bring him home and tell him he needed a day off, a week off, and . . .

He pulled away slowly. 'I meant that,' he said. 'Don't lose touch. I'm your friend, Hannah, and I'm here if you need me. There'll always be a job for you here.'

Nodding, Hannah hurried out the door, scared that if she didn't get away, she'd say something she'd regret.

* * *

'What did he mean there'll be a job for you?' said Gillian, who'd been standing conveniently beside the photocopier which stood outside David's office. For a second, Hannah was horror struck at the notion that Gillian might have witnessed the kiss, but then she realized that David's blinds were down.

'I'm leaving, Gillian,' Hannah said far more pleasantly than she felt. She may as well tell them all now.

'Leaving?' asked Donna, who was tidying up her desk.

Hannah nodded. 'Felix and I are getting married. We were going to anyway,' she said with a sidelong glance at Gillian, 'but I got pregnant, so we've pushed the date forward.'

Gillian was magnanimous in victory. Her most hated enemy was leaving and she could afford to be nice.

'I'm *soo* delighted for you, Hannah,' she said, eyes roving over Hannah's belly speculatively to figure out how pregnant she was. 'When's the happy date? The wedding, I mean?' she said with a little tinkling laugh.

'The baby's due in December and we haven't organized the wedding yet.'

Thankfully, Gillian's phone rang so Hannah was spared more questions.

Donna gave her a congratulatory hug. She was happy for Hannah, but her reservations showed in her eyes.

'You don't think I'm doing the right thing, do you?' Hannah asked quietly.

The other woman shrugged. 'You're pregnant, in love and about to get married. What could be wrong with that?' she said wryly.

'If it's not too personal a question,' Hannah said tentatively, 'why didn't you stay with Tania's father. Don't feel you have to answer.'

'I did for a while,' said Donna, speaking quietly so Gillian wouldn't hear. 'I thought you had to make a go of it with the father of your child, but he wasn't worth it. She was, but he wasn't. I'd made a mistake so I got out of it. Tania and I are better off without him.'

'Is that what you think about me and Felix?' Hannah asked fearfully.

Donna shook her head. 'It's not my place to say what I think is right or not, Hannah. You're a grown woman. I respect you and I respect your judgement. You have to do what you think is right. Tell me, are you allowed even half a glass of wine? With enough mineral water added, we could make you a spritzer to last all evening.'

But their plans for a quiet drink went awry as soon as Hannah went out to her car. She was going to meet Donna in McCormack's and had just phoned Felix on her mobile, leaving a message on *his*, to say she'd be a bit late. She'd only just unlocked the door when someone said, 'Hello, Hannah.'

Whirling around, she saw the last person she'd expected: Harry. 'How dare you creep up on me like that!' she said, her heart rate belting along with the shock.

'I didn't mean to scare you,' he said apologetically. 'I wanted to talk to you and I was afraid if I went into the office, your fiancé,' he said the word with heavy irony, 'would be coming to pick you up and would thump me.'

'Brave as ever, eh?' Hannah said sharply. 'So you decided to scare *me* instead?'

She briefly wondered what Felix could have said to make him so frightened. Probably stole the lines from some gangster movie and told Harry he'd be wearing concrete shoes and swimming with the fishes if he didn't leave her alone.

'Don't be like that, Hannah. I wanted to talk to you, that's all,' Harry said, going into his sweet little boy mode. He brushed back a lock of long hair and smiled engagingly.

It didn't work. The bits of Hannah that would have once trilled with excitement at the sight of Harry, trilled no longer.

'Why?' she said wearily. 'I'm meeting someone and I'm too tired to stand up here arguing with you, Harry. I thought I told you I didn't want to see you again.'

'You look tired,' he remarked.

Hannah glared at him. 'Ever the charmer. Have you thought of giving lessons?' she asked sarcastically.

'I didn't mean it like that.'

Hannah wanted this conversation to end. She didn't want to be standing by the side of the road talking to a man who'd put her through so much pain. Harry was the past. She had a future and it involved Felix and a baby – she pushed David James and his distracting kiss out of her mind.

'I *am* tired, as it happens. It's called pregnancy,' she said coldly. Let him put that in his pipe and smoke it.

Harry's mouth dropped open so wide that she could see his fillings. He had loads of them, she noticed. He'd always had terrible teeth. Hannah couldn't help smiling to herself. This was the man who'd driven her to distraction when he left her and now she was looking coolly at him, utterly unmoved by his presence and noticing the state of his dental work. Time, and the love of a sexy man, were great healers.

'Pregnant?' he repeated.

'Not the sort of thing you'd be keen on, Harry,' Hannah said bitchily. 'Pregnancy is the ultimate in – what was it you said? "Stagnation", that was it. Aren't you lucky you escaped without me ever getting pregnant. Then you'd really have been trapped with me.'

Harry stopped trying to look boyishly lovable. 'You must really hate me, Hannah,' he said dully.

She leaned against the car, no longer bothered that it was dusty and would mark her suit.

'I don't hate you, Harry,' she told him. 'I gave up hating you a long time ago. It was too exhausting. I've moved on with my life and I wish you'd do the same. What's the point of coming to see me all the time? I'm with Felix and that's not going to change. I'd love to be one of those people who stayed best pals with their exes, but I'm not. I'm too black and white for that and, anyhow, the way you left more or less ruined that little idea. I have my pride, you know.'

Harry grinned sheepishly. 'Yeah, going out to dinner with the guy who ran off on you doesn't fit in with the "let's all be pals" scenario,' he said. 'We were good together, though, weren't we?' he added wistfully.

'Great,' Hannah said, thinking of what a bone-idle, daydreaming creature Harry had been when they were living together. He'd done her a favour by dumping her. Otherwise, they'd still be together: him making grandiose plans about the big novel he was going to write and her, adoring as ever, washing and ironing his clothes and playing second fiddle to his ego.

'I must go,' she said. 'Take care, Harry. I mean it,' she added. She kissed him lightly on the cheek, then got into her car and manoeuvred out of the parking space. In her rear-view mirror, she could see him loping off down the street. She'd told him the truth: she didn't hate him any more. Harry was out of her life, like David James, she reminded herself firmly. It had been a day for ending things. Closure all round.

The Egypt reunion was due to take place in a Japanese restaurant because none of them had been there before and it had been getting rave reviews in the papers. But Hannah had phoned on Tuesday, the day before, to explain that she dare not eat anywhere raw fish was part of the menu because it might be dangerous to the baby.

'Dangerous to the baby,' Emma repeated bitterly as she marched from the bus stop to the Italian bistro where they were now going. It hadn't taken Hannah long to change from irate career girl into earth mother extraordinaire, had it? One minute, she was afraid a child would cramp her style – now, she was talking about her baby as if nobody on earth had ever been pregnant before. Emma walked faster, panting at the speed she was going at.

There was no need to walk so quickly, but the bitterness that was fuelling her forced her to march at a fierce pace. Emma had promised her father she'd spend the next two nights looking after Anne-Marie, who now got incredibly upset if she was left on her own or with the neighbours. Emma wasn't looking forward to it. She felt guilty when she thought about how much she'd prefer an evening with Pete to an evening following her mother around the house, closing cupboards and tidying up the things Anne-Marie wrecked. Tonight, stressed out because an all-day KrisisKids conference was being held in Burlington on Friday, she could have done with a quiet night at home rather than an evening of forced jollity. Now she'd have to sit and make congratulatory noises all night after a day of endless phone calls and problems. She had cried off from their last reunion, a trip to the theatre to see *Les Liaisons Dangereuses*, so she *had* to be there tonight. Leonie would have been so upset if she didn't come.

She was the first one at the restaurant and sat down in a banquette. *La Traviata* playing on the sound system, the waft of garlic from the kitchens, red-check tablecloths and candle-grease-splattered wine bottles as candleholders all contributed to the effect of a wonderfully Continental restaurant. Emma ordered a glass of house wine, hoping that it might have a sedative effect on her. Calming down was what she needed.

Half-way down the glass, she was breathing normally and beginning to relax. Leonie and Hannah arrived together, wreathed in smiles as they gave their coats to the waiter. It was nearly six weeks since Emma had seen Hannah and she was astonished to see that Hannah's belly was gently swelling. She must have been well over two months pregnant and Emma hadn't expected there to be any obvious signs at all. But, incredibly, in a soft olive-green tunic top and matching clinging skirt, her pregnancy *was* just visible. Wicked darts of jealousy pierced Emma's heart as she watched the waiter smile charmingly at Hannah and offer congratulations on her pregnancy in true Italian style. She couldn't imagine a waiter of any other nationality doing such a thing, or even graciously leading them over to their table as if Hannah was about to give birth en route, extravagantly pulling out the table so that Hannah could slide into the banquette seat with Emma.

'Emma! Hello, love,' said Hannah, kissing her.

'Hi, pet,' said Leonie warmly, leaning over the candle to kiss Emma and nearly setting fire to her cardigan in the process. 'Sorry we're a bit late.'

'My fault,' Hannah said apologetically. 'I've finally had to realize that you cannot get by with ordinary clothes when you're growing as fast as I am.' She smiled serenely. 'I was wearing a pair of jeans with a jumper over them, but I couldn't do the top button, so I had to keep poor Leonie waiting while I found this outfit.'

Under the table, Emma balled her left hand into a tight fist, nails digging into her palm. Anything to stop herself saying something vicious and bitter in response.

Hannah was glowing. Her face, always luminous, glowed with

some hidden joy. Her dark hair was luxuriant and she looked, in short, like a woman deeply in love. Emma was horrified to discover how much she resented her friend for all this. It should have been *her* glowing in the early stages of pregnancy, not Hannah.

Finally getting a grip on her feelings, Emma attempted small talk. 'You do seem to have expanded since the last time I saw you,' she said, trying to keep her tone light and pleasant. 'I didn't think you'd look this pregnant yet.'

Hannah groaned. 'Neither did I,' she revealed. 'Felix says it's like sharing the bed with a baby elephant.'

Through two courses, and a lot of debate on what Hannah could and couldn't eat on the menu, they discussed her pregnancy in fine detail. As Emma prodded her tagliatelle listlessly, she discovered that Hannah didn't have morning sickness and, apart from two weeks when she was unaccountably tired and could barely get out of bed in the morning, she felt fantastic. Her nails were growing at a terrific rate, she was determined not to get stretch marks so was obsessively rubbing Body Shop stretch-mark lotion into herself twice a day, and Felix was being very funny coming up with the most bizarre baby names.

'Honestly,' giggled Hannah, 'imagine calling a child *Petal*! My poor mother would disown me if I landed any grandchild of hers with a name like that. But Felix loves it. He's mad.'

Emma thought her head would explode if she heard one more word. She felt as if she knew Hannah's doctor intimately and, thanks to a lengthy discussion on expanding clothes sizes, could picture exactly what Hannah would look like naked: that elegantly curvy body now swollen in the most feminine way, breasts full and heavy, a precious swelling in her belly where the baby nestled.

Hannah, joy making her insensitive, continued rhapsodizing over being pregnant.

'I never thought I'd feel this way about the baby,' she said earnestly. 'It's like nothing else I've ever experienced. Half the time I'm paranoid in case I'm doing something that'll be bad for the baby, the other half, I'm reeling around happily.'

Leonie smiled at her friend and then noticed Emma's stricken face.

She was white, her eyes like two hollows in a skull. Poor, poor Emma. Hannah had forgotten how awful it was for her, Leonie realized with a pang. So had she, really. They'd both been so tied up talking delightedly about the happy event that they hadn't remembered how devastating it must be for their friend. She felt terribly ashamed.

'Girls, I almost forgot!' she said brightly. 'Hugh brought me to his house the other night and cooked me the most amazing dinner. Crab cakes to start, minute steak and stuffed aubergines and then,' she paused for effect, 'this sinful chocolate cake he'd bought. Eating it was like having a multiple orgasm.'

This revelation had the desired result. The other two laughed.

'Trust you to think chocolate was orgasmic,' chuckled Emma, thrilled at the change of subject.

'It's the only thing that *is* orgasmic,' Leonie protested. 'I've forgotten what sex is. My idea of sexual delight is a half-bottle of wine and a decent novel.'

'You mean you haven't gone to bed with him yet?' Hannah was astonished. 'You've been going out for ages.'

'When you're my age, you don't rush into bed with people,' Leonie said equably. 'You have to wait three months for the anti-cellulite cream and the Weight Watchers dinners to work.'

'I don't know why you're so keen on having people jumping into bed at the first minute, anyway, Hannah,' Emma said hotly. 'Not everyone is like you. There's more to life than sex.'

'I know there is,' Hannah said in surprise. 'I was joking, that's all . . .'

'Not all your jokes are funny,' snapped Emma and, getting to her feet, she rushed off in the direction of the loos.

Hannah blinked back tears. She was so emotional these days. 'What did I say?' she asked plaintively.

Sighing, Leonie patted her hand. 'It's nothing you've said, Hannah. You know I'm utterly thrilled that you're pregnant, but you've got to understand, it's tough on Emma. She loves you but it's got to hurt her to see you so blissfully happy about the baby when she'd do anything to be in your place.'

'That's not my fault,' Hannah said stubbornly. 'She could go and do something about it but she won't. She probably still hasn't told Pete she thinks she's infertile. There's IVF, fertility drugs, ICSI – there are loads of things they could have done.'

'I know, I know,' Leonie comforted. 'Emma has this mental block about the whole thing. You know she's convinced that if she has tests and they say she can't have children, then she'll have no hope left.'

'That doesn't explain why she won't discuss it with Pete,' Hannah said.

'I know. But we could make it a bit easier on her and not talk so exclusively about the baby.'

'If she didn't want to come tonight, she shouldn't have,' Hannah said. She was hurt that Emma couldn't share her joy about the baby. She understood wanting something and not having it, but she wouldn't begrudge Emma if *she* had something Hannah didn't. When Hannah had been Felix-less, she hadn't been jealous that Emma had Pete to come home to every night while she was stuck with the remote control and a dinner for one. How *dare* she bitch at Hannah now?

'Don't get upset,' Leonie begged, seeing the anger glittering in her friend's dark eyes. 'We have been a bit insensitive talking about the baby all night. Give her a break.'

Her face set darkly, Hannah nodded. 'I don't want to bore anyone,' she sniffed.

'You're not boring anyone,' Leonie insisted. 'I love hearing all about the baby and so would Emma, if only it wasn't so painful for her. In your heart you know that. Quick, talk about something else. She's coming back.'

'Tell us more about the wonderful Hugh,' Emma said tightly when she sat down.

Hannah said nothing but her full lips were pressed firmly together. Leonie said a silent prayer that they wouldn't try and kill each other over dessert.

'Hugh,' she began cheerfully, 'is wonderful . . .'

Normally, the Egypt reunions ended much later than originally planned because they all loved sitting talking, but this time the waiter had barely placed the cafetiere of decaf on the table when Emma announced that she really had to get home.

'I've a busy day tomorrow,' she said abruptly. 'We've got two guest speakers coming in for the conference and I'm looking after them.'

She drank her coffee quickly, left money for the bill and then got to her feet.

Hannah gave her a brief, cool smile and leaned forward for a kiss on the cheek. The result was a classic air kiss, neither touching.

'Bye, Leonie,' Emma said, giving her a genuine hug.

She hurried away, snatching her coat from the waiter, not wanting to hang around in case she either burst into tears or screamed. Emma felt so emotionally charged that she didn't know quite which emotion would emerge: rage or misery.

As she waited for the bus, she wondered how she'd explain why she was home so early to Pete. He'd be bound to notice that this dinner had been half the length of all the previous ones. He'd even teased her about it earlier, joking that if she came home plastered again, he wasn't undressing her and putting her to bed.

'I'll be sending you to the Betty Ford Clinic for your next birthday if you keep up with these reunions,' he laughed, his voice crackling on the mobile phone line. 'I know you're secretly out on the tear looking for men, I know your type Mrs Sheridan, leaving your wedding ring in your handbag . . .'

'Pig,' she chuckled into the receiver. 'I must go, love. My other line is ringing. There's a pizza in the freezer. I'll see you later, Pete.'

Emma leaned wearily against the bus shelter, wanting to be home so she could feel Pete's arms comforting her. Hannah was so pregnant, looking so blissfully maternal that it hurt. But, of course, she couldn't explain that to Pete. What would he think of her if she revealed that a green-eyed monster raged through her every time she had to look at Hannah's burgeoning belly? All evening, she'd had to look away or bite her lip to hide the intensity of her feelings. She was ashamed of herself. What sort of a friend was she? When the chips were down, she was more concerned about herself than about anyone else. Shame washing over her, Emma vowed to phone Hannah the next day and apologize. It was only fair. They were supposed to be friends.

She let herself into the house. The hall was in darkness. Good. Pete wasn't home yet. He'd mentioned that he might go for a drink with Mike after work. At least his absence gave her a chance to go to bed. And if he came in after a few drinks, he wouldn't be intuitive enough to notice her downcast eyes.

Emma left the hall light on and went upstairs to bed. She got as far as taking off her blouse when the wave of utter hopelessness hit her and she had to sit down on the edge of the bed and weep. Great gusts of sobs came from her, her chest heaved with each breath and she cried until her face was red and raw. Would she ever get over this pain of being childless? She'd stopped wondering if she'd ever have a child: that seemed too hopeless now. All she wanted was for the pain of wanting to abate somewhat, so she could cope.

'What's wrong?'

Startled, Emma looked up to see Pete standing in the doorway in his ancient leather jacket and faded jeans.

For a brief moment, she thought of lying. Then Elinor Dupre's voice sounded in her head: '*What's so wrong about saying what you want, Emma*?'

Elinor was right. She couldn't hide it any more. 'Hannah's pregnant and it's killing me. I can't bear to think I'll never have my own baby. I think I'm infertile,' she said bluntly.

'Oh Em,' said Pete. 'I'm so sorry, my love.' He looked at her helplessly, his normally merry face miserable.

Suddenly, Emma regretted telling him. As if it wasn't bad enough that she was upset, now he was too.

'It doesn't matter,' she backtracked. 'Let's forget I ever said that.'

'Forget it?' Pete said incredulously. 'Why should I forget it? This involves me too, Emma, in case you've forgotten. There are two of us in this marriage, you know. Nothing annoys me more than the way you feel you have to shoulder all these things on your own,' he said fiercely. 'You've never let me stand up to your father, even though he bullies you; you insist on keeping secrets like this to yourself and you let Kirsten away with murder when it comes to family responsibilities. You just won't let me help. Why the hell are you pushing me away? You're destroying our marriage, in case you hadn't noticed. Stop locking me out of your life!'

She'd never seen him so angry. He grabbed her by the shoulders and shook her. 'Why can't you see that I love you, Emma? I love *you,'* he yelled. 'Not the person you think you have to be to be loved!'

'I know,' she stammered. 'I didn't want to tell you . . .'

'In case I'd be angry with you,' he roared, 'like your bloody father?'

She flinched at the rage in his voice. 'No,' she protested, 'not because of that. Because . . .' she faltered.

He waited angrily.

'Because I thought that if I said anything, it wouldn't just be in my head, it would be real: I couldn't have a baby. It would be the worst possible result, I just know it.'

'Jesus, Emma, that's stupid,' he said, but she could see the anger fading from his eyes. 'That's superstitious rubbish. Did you really think that saying the words would jinx us? Because if you do, then there's no point in us seeing an ordinary doctor about this. We might as well see a witch doctor or a voodoo queen. Or, better still, I'll buy tarot cards and use those to work out why you haven't become pregnant.'

'You can't buy tarot cards for yourself,' Emma said in a small voice. 'They only work when somebody else has bought them for you. I read that somewhere.'

Pete laughed and pulled her into his arms. 'As you read so much, have you ever read about all the medical stuff they can do for childless couples?' he asked.

She nodded.

'Right. If they can clone sheep, pigs and the Boys from Brazil, they can help us have a baby. Infertility isn't half as complicated as cloning, so I think we're in with a chance. We're young, we're healthy – we'll do anything, right?'

'I hated the thought of putting you through all that investigative stuff,' Emma said, her face buried in his shoulder.

'You mean being locked in a room with a paper cup and the entire back catalogue of *Hustler*?' he asked wickedly. 'You may have to come in and help me with that, Em. But we can do it. Hey, who knows, there may be nothing wrong with either of us. You could be panicking unnecessarily. It takes time to make a baby, you know.'

'It's over three years,' Emma reminded him. 'That's a long time to be using no contraception and still not be pregnant.'

'OK, OK, maybe there is a problem, maybe there isn't. But let's find out for definite before we jump to conclusions. First thing tomorrow, phone the doctor and make an appointment. He can refer us to the specialists to get checked out, both of us.'

'You . . . you don't mind?'

Pete took her thin face in his hands, staring deep into the anxious pale blue eyes. 'I love you, Emma. I'd love us to have children. And if there's a medical reason why we can't, then we'll try our best to sort it out. But if nothing works and we can't have them, I can live with that. I've got you, we've got each other. Right?'

Emma nodded tremulously.

'Promise me one thing, Em. Don't keep secrets from me any more. Promise? It's been tearing me up, knowing things weren't right but not able to get close to you.'

'I promise I won't keep any more secrets. It was just so hard for me to tell you . . . to talk about it. I wanted to keep it to myself . . .'

'That doesn't work, Emma,' Pete interrupted. 'Do you think I haven't spent months worrying about you getting more and more introverted, worrying that I was doing something wrong, that you didn't love me?'

'You know I love you,' she protested.

'How can I know that when you keep this most important thing from me?' he demanded. 'I'm not very good at working out what people are thinking, Em, I'm sorry. I'm not a mind-reader. I need to be told. I was nearly going to ring Leonie and ask her. I mean, you tell her more than you tell me.' He sounded so bitter.

'Oh, Pete,' Emma said, feeling worn out, 'I love you. And, no, I don't tell Leonie everything. I did tell her about how I felt about the baby,' she admitted. 'That's all. I can't explain why I couldn't tell you.' She sighed miserably. 'Everything's always my fault. I thought this would be too.'

'Cut the bullshit,' snapped Pete fiercely. 'That's your bloody father speaking. He'd love everything to be your fault, but that doesn't mean it is. It simply means he's a spiteful old bastard who wants to control your every thought by making you feel useless. If you want that therapist to give you your money's worth, get her to exorcize your father's malignant presence from your head!'

'I never knew you felt that way,' gaped Emma.

He smiled, looking like her good-humoured Pete again. 'We're both learning things tonight. The most important one is that we have to stick together, Emma. Don't you agree?'

She nodded.

'You know what, Pete?' she said, eyes shining with unshed tears. 'I love you.'

When you were older and falling in love, the problem wasn't meeting your beloved's parents, Leonie mused. Difficult prospective in-laws were no longer the major obstacle. Wary, exacting children were. She was about to meet Hugh's two kids and she'd heard so much about them that she was as nervous as a vasectomy patient letting the doc touch his nether regions for the first time. Terrified was not the word.

It must have been the same for Fliss meeting Danny, Mel and Abby, she realized wryly as she got ready that momentous Saturday afternoon. Although that might have been easier. At least if you had children, you knew how territorial they could be and you could gird your loins for a certain amount of dislike/sheer naked hatred when Daddy or Mummy brought home a new 'friend'. But if you were childless like Fliss, you probably laboured under the misapprehension that children were dear little things too busy thinking about their own prospects with the opposite sex to worry about anything their wrinkly old parents were doing. Wrong. Children who felt they were being sidelined could hate far more effectively than any estranged, bitter spouse.

Luckily for Fliss, the kids clearly adored her. She was briskly chatty and too confident to be affected by teenage prejudices. There hadn't been any option but for them to adore her.

They were adoring her now, for sure. What kids wouldn't adore a stepmother who had whisked them off for a thrilling long weekend in Cannes and all the shopping Mel could dream of?

Ray had begged Leonie to let them all go for a week. 'We'll be in France for a fortnight and it seems crazy not to have the kids with us for at least one week,' he'd said.

'Mel and Abby have school,' Leonie replied. 'They can't just take a week off like that in the middle of May. They'll be getting their proper holidays in a month. And Danny has important exams coming up, so he can hardly go for a week.' She didn't mention anything about Danny's conviction that he wouldn't pass half his exams.

'Well, a weekend, then,' Ray had pleaded.

Leonie had been working late in the surgery on Thursday evening and couldn't drive the twins and Danny to the airport. She'd planned to book a taxi but Doug insisted he'd drive them.

'Only if I get a 101 Dalmatians mug as a present,' he told the twins.

At least she was footloose for the weekend, even if it did mean that the twins had more time to become besotted with their stepmother.

Leonie wondered how Hugh's kids would view *her*.

'They'll love you,' Hugh had said as he set about arranging a quick drink between the four of them.

Despite his assurances, she had a premonition of disaster. It wasn't particularly to do with Stephen, who sounded a bit like Danny with the same GameBoy thumb and a penchant for spending entire weekends in bed finding personal meaning in the lyrics of Oasis songs. But Jane, beautiful, talented Jane, sounded like Trouble. Leonie couldn't quite put her finger on why she thought this: something to do with the way Hugh spoke about his twenty-two-year-old daughter perhaps? In tones of pure adulation, as if Jane was Marie Curie, Mother Theresa and Julia Roberts all rolled into one adorable package. You didn't need an IQ in the stratosphere to figure out that Jane could do no wrong. Which, conversely, meant that if Jane didn't take an immediate shine to Leonie, it was curtains for Daddy's new friend.

The meeting was a quick one on a Saturday afternoon in the National Gallery. A suitably innocent venue.

Thinking of how Fliss would have played it, Leonie dressed in her usual clothes – Prussian-blue silk shirt, black velvet trousers and an embroidered violet angora shawl she'd picked up in a charity shop in Dun Laoghaire – and did her best to feel nonchalantly confident. Not trying too hard, because that would be a mistake both for her personally and for Hugh. She dearly wanted his children to like and approve of her, but it had to be approval on real terms.

She didn't want to transform herself into something she wasn't just so she passed muster with a teenage boy and his twenty-something sister. Well, that was the theory, anyway.

It was only 'a quick drink to meet the kids', as Hugh had put it. Not a grilling in the High Court. But her theory wasn't working very well and she still felt worried. I mean, she thought, desperate to bolster herself with courage, she had kids and she knew how to handle them. If she knew how to deal with the dizzying combination of Mel and Abby, surely Jane would be a doddle. Older and more mature, obviously . . . ?

Hugh was waiting in the National Gallery restaurant when she arrived, hot from rushing from the car park and mentally berating herself for never going to the gallery normally except when she was meeting people in the restaurant. She must try harder to fit some culture into her life. Hugh was sitting at a small table at the back and there was someone with him, Leonie realized: a young woman in denims.

Her first thoughts were that he'd met someone he knew while waiting for all of them. It couldn't be the fabled Jane.

Jane was, in her father's words, 'beautiful, stunning,' and Leonie had had a mental picture of a girl with her father's confident, laughing gaze and the bone structure of a gazelle.

This dumpy young woman with a denim jacket welded unflatteringly on to her could not be Jane. Short dark hair, not even washed, plump features and small eyes under over-plucked brows. This was not gazelle material, unless gazelles were blessed with suspicious eyes and a scowl.

'Leonie!' Hugh got to his feet and greeted her as though he'd just spotted a distant acquaintance and, after racking his brains for ages, had finally remembered her name. He patted her back energetically. Normally, he kissed her.

'Meet Jane, my pride and joy. Jane, this is a friend of mine, Leonie.'

Leonie had been struck dumb on very few occasions in her life. Such a thing was unheard of in a woman who so hated gaps in the conversation that she would babble ceaselessly in company when there was an awkward silence just to fill in the blanks. Now, she smiled gormlessly at her boyfriend and his daughter, wondering how in the hell even a besotted father would describe Jane as 'stunning'. But then, how awful of her to judge the poor girl on looks alone. Perhaps Jane lit up with some inner flame when she spoke and laughed.

'I've heard so much about you, it's lovely to meet you,' she said, finally finding her voice and shaking Jane's hand warmly.

'I've heard almost nothing about you,' Jane replied primly, shooting a look at Hugh.

She shouldn't purse her mouth like that, Leonie thought absently. She'd have terrible lines when she was older.

'Oh dear,' Leonie said jokily. 'Am I your father's big secret?'

She intercepted a glare from the girl to her father. 'I think so,' Jane said sharply.

Hugh smiled helplessly at Leonie. 'It's no big secret at all,' he said with the false bonhomie of a man facing the firing squad and turning down the use of a blindfold. 'Leonie is my new friend and I wanted you and Stephen to meet her. It's simple. We've only been out three times but you know I wouldn't want you to feel left out, Jane, sweetie.' He shot an imploring look at Jane.

Leonie felt that now wasn't the time to point out that they'd been on ten dates and one heavy petting session where only the presence of her period and a pair of horrible big knickers had stopped them getting naked on the couch in Hugh's apartment. She had long-range plans for a romantic scene that included bikini waxing, nice, non-grey underwear and fake tan to camouflage the flabby bits with a nice golden glow. These plans seemed very long range at this present moment. She'd thought she was his girlfriend, but he hadn't made that clear to anyone else.

On the phone, he'd been murmuring sweet nothings and saying things like, 'You're incredible, Leonie.' Now, in the presence of the Inquisitor General, he was a squirming mass of manhood who'd deny his romance with a 'Makin' Whoopee'-singing Michelle Pfeiffer herself if it would keep him in his daughter's good books. Leonie felt betrayed. What was more, she felt like getting up and leaving them to it. But she didn't. It would be unfair. As a mother, she knew how hard it was to draw the line between living your life for your children and giving them the ultimate power over your life. There was a balance, and poor Hugh needed help finding that balance.

She would help. If it was the last thing she did.

'Don't be silly, Daddy,' Jane said. 'I don't feel left out at all. It's just that I know all your friends. If I'd known you were meeting work people, I wouldn't have bothered to come. Which branch are you working in?' she asked Leonie.

Those last two sentences clarified matters for Leonie. It was obvious that Hugh hadn't told his kids who she was or that they were going to meet her today. Either that, or Jane was determined not to acknowledge the existence of any woman in her father's life and was therefore casting Leonie in the role of an unattractive colleague her father took pity on and brought out occasionally. And calling him 'Daddy'! Most kids got over the Daddy stage when they went to big school and moved on to a bored-sounding Dad.

Leonie smiled at Hugh.

He was gazing at her hopefully, hope-you'll-lie-fully she reckoned.

'I'm a veterinary nurse. And I'm not one of your father's colleagues,' she said pleasantly, 'I'm a friend.'

'Oh.' Jane's mouth pursed into a little moue of disapproval.

'Your father has been telling me all about you,' Leonie went on gamely. 'He says you're getting on brilliantly in work and are up for promotion. Well done.'

'Daddy!' hissed Jane furiously. 'That's private.'

'Oh, look,' said Hugh in desperation. 'Here's Stephen.'

Tall and solid like his father, Stephen had a smiling face, wore clothes that looked as if he'd dressed in a hurry, and seemed to know who Leonie was.

'Nice to meet you at last,' he said, throwing himself into a chair. 'About time the old lad found himself someone. Has anyone ordered? They do great cakes here.'

Jane glared at him instead of her father. 'You might have told me,' she said fiercely. 'I feel as if I've been hijacked.'

It was Hugh and Stephen's turn to exchange meaningful looks. What a family! Leonie wished they'd talk instead of staring intensely at each other. People said what they thought in the Delaney house, especially Mel, who'd be the person most likely to feel put out by Hugh's existence.

At least with Mel, you'd hear how she felt, normally at eighty decibels. She wouldn't have just sat there simmering in silence and glaring at people.

'Don't be daft, Sis,' said Stephen. 'What's the fuss? I told you. You're here to meet Leonie. What's the big deal?' He turned to Leonie. 'Will I go up and order us something? I'm ravenous. Would you like coffee or cakes?'

He was sweet, she decided. Aware that his sister was furious, he was doing his best to defuse the situation.

'I'd love some,' she said. 'I'll come up with you and carry a tray. Coffee, Hugh?' she asked pleasantly, determined not to let her expression betray the fact that she thought Hugh was acting foolishly by kowtowing to the awful Jane.

'Yes,' he said, looking her straight in the face for the first time in ages.

Leonie and Stephen examined the cake counter with interest. Normally, Leonie wouldn't have allowed herself anything. But today, she wasn't in the mood to deny herself.

'I could murder some of that carrot cake,' she said to Stephen, pointing out some fabulously succulent cake that probably contained the exact amount of calories a marathon runner needed in an entire week.

'Me too,' he agreed. 'I bet Jane would love it too. She's on this no-fat diet, but I can usually persuade her to give it up when she's with me.'

Leonie wasn't sure she could imagine anyone persuading Jane to do anything she didn't want to.

'She'll be fine,' Stephen said as if he could read her thoughts. 'She's a bit possessive about Dad. She's his favourite and she doesn't really get it that he needs someone in his life.'

'I understand,' Leonie lied. 'But your mum has a new partner, doesn't she? Isn't that hard on Jane too?'

Stephen put three fat slices of cake on his tray. 'Yeah, but Jane isn't the same with Mum. They are, like, exactly the same. That's why Jane doesn't live at home any more. They kill each other. She's cool about Kevin – he's Mum's boyfriend.' They moved slowly along the queue towards the coffee machines. Stephen put a chocolate bar on his plate as well.

'I worry about the old boy. He gets lonely. He's happier since meeting you.'

'Thank you,' Leonie said sincerely. 'It's lovely of you to say that. I'm so very fond of your father and I wanted you both to know that. It's hard that Jane seems set against me.'

It's 'cos you've got kids,' Stephen said sagely. 'She's terrified Dad'll end up liking them more than us, or end up leaving them something in his will if you two get married.'

'How do you know this? Jane didn't seem to have heard anything about me before today.'

'I know Jane,' he said simply. 'And she does know about you. I knew Dad would bottle out of telling her about you, so I did it for him. She's pretending not to know just to get at him. Don't be hard on her,' he said suddenly. 'She's a bit . . .'

Spoilt, Leonie wanted to say.

'. . . insecure,' Stephen finished. 'She adores Dad and he adores her back. If you were on the scene, it'd be a different ball game.'

'Well, thanks for being so honest with me,' she said. 'Should I simply go home now?'

Stephen laughed. 'Don't be daft. Jane will be fine, eventually.'

They arrived back at the table with trays laden down with goodies. Jane and Hugh had been talking animatedly until they arrived, whereupon all conversation ceased. They all drank their coffee in stony silence. Leonie could hear her own jaw clicking as she ate her carrot cake.

Finally, she couldn't take the silence any more.

'I was thinking we could go to the cinema later,' Leonie said brightly. 'Why don't you two come?' Did I say that? she asked herself in horror. Please say no.

'Why not? I've nothing else on tonight,' Jane said ungraciously.

Leonie, Hugh and Stephen all wanted to see the new Bond movie but Jane wanted to see the latest art-house sensation, a grim, black-and-white production about youngsters getting involved in the murky world of international drug-smuggling. Leonie would rather have cut her front lawn with nail scissors than watch that type of film. However, it was Jane's choice and, as Leonie was discovering, Jane liked to get her own way.

At least they had something to talk about afterwards, when they shared a pizza in Temple Bar. Stephen chatted happily about the film while Jane, who'd forced them to sit through it, decided she hadn't liked it much at all.

Leonie's palm itched with the desire to slap Jane's sulky little face.

After an hour, when it became plain that Jane had no intention of leaving before Leonie did, Leonie gave in and announced that she had to go home.

'I'll walk you back to your car,' Hugh said. She shot him a grateful look. Free from the horrid Jane at last.

'Dad,' Jane said in a childish voice, 'can I ask you a favour?'

'Yes, darling,' he said fondly.

'Could I use your credit card to book my holiday? Mine is maxed out and if I don't book on Monday, I'll lose my place. I'll pay you back, of course,' she added, giving him a beseeching, big-eyed look.

Leonie's right hand clenched up into a fist.

Hugh ruffled Jane's hair. 'You don't have to ask, pet, you know that.'

For the first five minutes, Leonie and Hugh walked in silence.

As they reached Nassau Street, Hugh took her hand in his.

'Well,' he said tentatively, 'how do you think it went?'

'It might have gone better if you'd told Jane about me,' Leonie suggested. 'It's not easy meeting someone who's under the impression that you're nothing more than a colleague. I thought we were going out, Hugh, but listening to you earlier, you'd swear we were old, platonic friends on the verge of getting our bus passes.'

'Sorry. It's difficult, you know. Jane is . . . well, she's sensitive.'

About as sensitive as a rhino, Leonie thought grimly.

'I should have told her, Leonie. Please forgive me.' He squeezed her fingers. 'I'm afraid I'm one of those indulgent fathers who can't deny my children anything. Jane expects nothing short of adoration.'

'And the use of your credit card,' Leonie remarked. 'Jane mustn't be very good with money if she's got this wonderful job and still has to beg from you.' As soon as she'd said it, Leonie regretted it. Criticizing your beloved's children was a dating no-no, on a par with saying you'd got a letter from the clinic and the warts were practically all gone. She could have kicked herself. 'Sorry,' she said quickly. 'That was rotten of me.'

'I thought you of all people would understand,' Hugh said tightly. 'Children are there to be nurtured and taken care of.'

Leonie nodded. She agreed with him. But Jane wasn't a child. She was a manipulative grown-up and Hugh wasn't doing her any favours by not seeing this. Treating her like an adored child was a recipe for disaster.

'I know you love them to bits and I shouldn't have said that,' Leonie apologized. 'I guess I'm a bit upset because Jane obviously didn't approve of me.'

'Silly,' said Hugh sweetly. 'She'll love you when she gets to know you. It just takes time.'

Now where had she heard that before?

'How did it go?' asked Hannah when she rang the next day.

'I am compiling research for a book called Dating Divorcés,' announced Leonie, 'and the longest chapter is going to be about meeting horrible, self-obsessed children who think you're after their father for his money and who make it perfectly obvious that they hate you.'

'You mean you're *not* after him for his money?' joked Hannah, trying to inject a note of humour into things.

'Hugh has less money than I do,' said Leonie hotly, not seeing the funny side of it. 'And now I know why. He gives it all to Jane, although I can't think why, because she has a perfectly good job. She had the nerve to ask him if she could book her holiday using his credit card. I ask you – a twenty-something with a good job! It's ludicrous.'

'It didn't go well, then?' Hannah said tentatively.

'His son is a darling and was very sweet to me, but the daughter, Jane,' Leonie paused, 'is hideously jealous. As if he can't love her *and* me.'

'Maybe she's afraid that if you're there the cheques will dry up,' said Hannah pragmatically.

'It's more than that. It's weird. She's nuts about him, like a small child.'

'Girls and their fathers,' Hannah pointed out. 'Somebody wrote a song about their heart belonging to Daddy.'

'I don't know any grown woman whose heart belongs to Daddy,' said Leonie crossly. 'Yours doesn't and neither does Emma's. Mel and Abby love Ray but they didn't go into a flat spin when he married Fliss.'

'That's because they're well-adjusted kids.'

'Hugh's well adjusted,' Leonie argued. 'How could he have a daughter like this?'

'What's his ex-wife like?'

'Sounds perfectly normal. They get on well and the split was as amicable as any I've ever heard of.'

'Ah well, that's it,' Hannah said sagely. 'No split is ever amicable. It's an oxymoron: the words "split" and "amicable" just don't go together. Do you think Mummy is poisoning little Jane to loathe every woman who ever tries to replace her?'

Leonie gave a mirthless laugh. 'I don't think Jane needs anyone to poison her. She's poisonous enough on her own. Hugh is so wonderful, but I can't bear the thought of having to put up with Jane's bitchiness for the rest of my life.'

'Hugh thinks you're wonderful,' Hannah comforted. 'That's all that matters. Jane will come round, you'll see.'

Leonie liked Hugh's home. A three-year-old townhouse on the edges of Templeogue, it was pristine, still new looking and without any peeling paintwork or teenage detritus. Inside, it was wall-to-wall magnolia, enlivened by Hugh's collection of old film posters, the bookcases that lined the walls and lots of curious collectibles like a wind-up gramophone and a huge marble chessboard with marble pieces fashioned into jungle animals. It was all very quirky and Leonie liked it. In fact, there was only one thing Leonie *didn't* like in the house and that was the plethora of pictures of Jane all over the place. The mantelpiece was a veritable shrine to her, with seven separate photos of Jane looking winsome as a First Communicant, sulky as a teenager, and even sulkier on a variety of other occasions. There were only two of Stephen. Leonie hoped he didn't mind, although he probably did secretly. Nobody could remain untouched by the fact that their parent preferred their sibling. Leonie hoped she'd never made one of her children feel they were less loved than the other two.

The small back garden was like a rugby pitch, thanks to the antics of Wilbur, Harris and Ludlum, Hugh's dogs. Leonie kept meaning to bring Penny on a visit to Hugh's house but hadn't got round to it yet. It seemed forward to bring her dog there, because investigating whether their animals got on was tantamount to discussing whether they should live together or not. Leonie was crazy about Hugh, but she didn't think they were anywhere near that stage yet.

Tonight, they were reaching an important point in their relationship, however. Going To Bed Together. In Leonie's mind, this event was in capital letters. It was immense, huge, a giant hurdle to be crossed.

They had been going out for four months and, although there had been some erotic moments, like that time in the Savoy Cinema watching a modern film *noir*, or the evening at Leonie's when Danny and the girls had been out and they'd ended up getting very hot and bothered on the couch, they'd never been that intimate with each other.

It wasn't that Leonie didn't fancy Hugh. Far from it. She found him very sexy. He was actually slightly shorter than her, but she didn't mind that. There was something virile about him. How virile, she planned on finding out tonight. That tonight was the night was an unspoken arrangement between them. Leonie had asked her mother to stay at the cottage with the girls, ostensibly because she was going away for the night with Emma and Hannah.

Claire – whom Leonie suspected knew exactly what was really going on but was too discreet to say 'about bloody time!' – had said she'd be delighted.

The girls taken care of, Leonie had splurged money she didn't have on matching knickers and bra in silky coffee-coloured lace. She'd spent so long scrubbing herself in the bath that she reckoned she'd probably lost a pound in skin alone, and she'd massaged scented body lotion into every centimetre of her body.

Determined not to reproach herself for forgetting to rub the anti-cellulite cream into her bum and thighs, Leonie didn't look at herself too long in the mirror. She was a forty-three-year-old woman, not a supermodel. Hugh liked her for what she was. She couldn't change what she was, no matter how much she'd secretly like to.

Hugh had obviously made a similar effort in the cooking department. When she arrived, the three dogs chorused a delighted greeting and then raced back into the kitchen to stand guard over whatever delicious-smelling thing Hugh was cooking.

'Beef?' said Leonie, sniffing the air in the hallway and getting an enticing mix of garlic and onions with some subtle herbs.

Hugh, looking good in a cream cotton sweater over chinos, shook his head before kissing her hello.

'It's a surprise,' he said.

'I love surprises,' she replied archly.

He kissed her neck too. 'I've got another surprise for you later,' he purred, making her giggle.

Dinner was wonderful, but Leonie found it hard to eat too much. She didn't want her belly to be hanging out over her sexy new knickers purely because she'd stuffed her face with boeuf bourgignon and summer pudding with cream.

'You don't like it?' Hugh asked anxiously when she insisted on only having a small portion of dessert.

'I love it,' she said. 'You're so good to cook for me, darling. I'm just er . . . not that hungry after the lovely beef.'

They shared a lingering kiss over the coffee and danced in the kitchen to the mellow sounds of Frank Sinatra. With her arms wrapped round Hugh's neck, her body meltingly close to his, Leonie closed her eyes and thought how perfect it all was.

'Shall we go upstairs?' Hugh said thickly.

She murmured assent and, holding hands, they climbed the stairs. Leonie had only been in Hugh's bedroom once when he'd shown her around the house. It wasn't as tidy as it had been that day: obviously the strain of cooking up a cordon bleu feast meant he hadn't had time for too much housekeeping. Clothes hung carelessly on the back of a chair by the dressing table, a towel graced the back of the door and a single sock peeped out from the half-open wardrobe. But the double bed was perfectly made up, with fresh smelling navy striped sheets reeking of flowery fabric softener. Leonie grinned until she saw the small table beside the bed.

A blue painted picture frame with a carved teddy anchored on one side sat beside a high-tech clock radio and inside the frame was a picture of Jane. The frame was more suited to a nursery than an adult's bedroom.

'Isn't it lovely?' Hugh said fondly, noticing the direction of her gaze as he hastily tidied up. 'Jane gave it to me last week. She's such a pet, always giving me gifts.'

Leonie gritted her teeth and vowed to dispose of some item of clothing so that it covered up Jane's picture. There was no way she could make mad, passionate love with Hugh and have Jane's smirking face watching every move.

Having Jane in the room with them was good in one way. It meant that Leonie didn't have a moment to feel nervous about Hugh lovingly peeling off her blouse or helping her out of her skirt. She couldn't concentrate on the awfulness of her thighs because she was thinking that it was as if Jane was in the room with them, *watching, looking, sneering.*

It was only when Hugh was down to his boxer shorts and led her over to the bed that Leonie decided she had to do something. While Hugh pulled the duvet back, she carefully moved the picture till it was facing the other way. When she turned back to Hugh, he was watching her.

'Sorry, I feel uncomfortable being watched,' she said nervously. 'Having one's children watching doesn't feel right.'

'Is that all?' he smiled.

'Mothers can be very prudish about things like that,' Leonie said.

What they did next wasn't prudish at all. Hugh buried his head in her cleavage and moaned happily as he nuzzled her breasts. Leonie stopped feeling upset and began to enjoy herself again. She enjoyed it when Hugh stroked her all over, telling her she was gorgeous and that he adored her beautiful, sexy underwear. She enjoyed touching a man erotically again, feeling him grow aroused because of her. And she adored it when she finally guided Hugh inside her, remembering how wonderful lovemaking felt and asking herself why it had been so long since she'd experienced it.

'Oh, Hugh,' she moaned as the tempo of their lovemaking increased.

'Leonie,' he murmured hoarsely, his naked body hard against hers.

Suddenly, Hugh's body spasmed and he came, shuddering and calling, 'Oh God, oh God,' before slumping motionless on top of her.

A religious orgasm, Leonie thought unexpectedly, her own excitement quenched with his lack of activity. There were four types of orgasms, Hannah had gigglingly told them in Egypt: Religious, Positive, Negative and Fake.

Religious was 'Oh God,' at the moment of orgasm. Positive was 'Yes!' Negative was 'No!' And fake was the name of whoever you were with. 'Oh, Hugh!' in this case.

Leonie waited a moment, feeling Hugh heavy on top of her. She waited for him to murmur something about being sorry for coming too soon, she waited for him to insist on pleasing her. She'd read all the articles in magazines and newspapers: modern men knew what was expected of them in bed. The days of wham, bam, thank you, Ma'am were over. Men were sensitive creatures with instincts finely tuned to the needs of their women. Leonie had expected multiple orgasms, she'd read all about them in women's magazines. Moments of such exquisite pleasure that she'd squeal like a turkey at Christmas and possibly wet the bed into the bargain. Men knew how to do that type of thing nowadays. The G-spot was as well known now as the offside rule in football.

Hugh moved. Leonie smiled with expectant pleasure. Now it was her turn. Hugh planted one sloppy, sleepy kiss on her shoulder and slid off her to lie on the other side of the bed. One leg was still resting heavily across hers. He moaned and began to snore gently. In the darkness, Leonie blinked fiercely with rage. He was asleep. Hannah would murder her if she knew Hugh had dropped into the Land of Nod without making even an attempt to satisfy her. Hannah only went out with New Men. Leonie got Neolithic Men.

Boiling with a combination of rage and unfulfilled desire, she lay beside the sleeping Hugh.

'It's all right, Jane, sweetie,' she muttered, glaring at the turned-away photo. 'You'd have been proud of your old dad tonight. There wasn't anything for you to be jealous of.'

It was better in the morning. Leonie woke to find Hugh gently stroking her naked back. She stretched languorously but didn't turn to face him. Let him turn her on this time. She didn't want a repeat performance.

This time, when their naked bodies fused, Leonie was ahead of Hugh. With enough stored-up sexual energy to power the national grid, Leonie focused on making herself orgasm. When she screamed with pleasure, thrashing around in ecstasy, Hugh was the one who had to do the catching up.

'That was amazing,' he said afterwards.

Leonie just grinned.

'It was better than last night.'

She couldn't help herself. If they were to have a proper relationship, he had to know: 'Last night, Hugh, you fell asleep as soon as you'd come and I didn't come,' she said.

He was contrite. 'I didn't know you hadn't,' he protested.

How could he not know? Still, she could teach him.

Leonie snuggled up to him. 'Don't worry,' she said. 'We've got lots of time to get to know each other in every way.'

CHAPTER TWENTY-FOUR

Leonie was tidying when she found them. It was Friday morning and she was having a much-needed day off. The house was like a tip and she'd promised herself that if she could spend two hours on housework, she'd have lunch out as a treat. Danny's room was a complete nightmare and there wasn't much she could do there except pick up all the dirty clothes from the floor and hoover the bits of carpet uncovered by college books, sports gear and stacks of CDs. The bed looked as if Penny had been rolling in it after a particularly dirty walk.

'How did I rear such a piglet?' Leonie wondered out loud as she stripped the sheets and duvet.

Herman the hamster, who somehow managed to survive in the murky ecosystem that was Danny's bedroom, climbed into his hamster wheel in shock at all the domestic activity and started running furiously. 'You're next, Herman,' warned Leonie. 'Your house smells. It's clean-out time.' Herman ran faster.

When Danny's room was done and the bathroom was gleaming, it was half eleven and Leonie was beginning to wane. The thought of a leisurely lunch in the Delgany Inn with a glass of wine and a magazine made her feel wearier than ever. But the girls' room needed a quick whizz with the Hoover and, as she'd ironed duvet covers the night before, she decided to change their bedclothes too. Normally, the girls changed their own sheets but she might as well do it while she was cleaning. Mel still hadn't unpacked after the weekend in

Cannes and her suitcase lay on the floor, clothes spilling out of it. Mel's method of unpacking was to slowly remove things from the case as she needed them. Eventually, it would be emptied out.

She stuck their radio on and found some uplifting music before pulling out each twin bed and ripping the covers off. Mel's bed was soon freshly made with the hot pink cover she loved. It didn't go with the pale coral stripey wallpaper, but the girls didn't appear to mind. Leonie turned to Abby's bed. As she leaned over to tuck in the pale pink sheet close to the wall, she found them: a large red pack of laxatives.

Leonie stared uncomprehendingly at the packet for a moment as if the lettering on the front was Swahili instead of English. Laxatives. Whatever did Abby need them for?

The answer came to her in a blinding flash – Abby *didn't* need them.

Neither did any of the thousands of schoolgirls who bought them, and consumed far more laxatives than was safe. They did it in order to be thin. Laxatives in teenage girls' bedrooms meant eating disorders.

Leonie sank abruptly on to the bed as if someone had just taken her ability to stand away. She opened the pack to find that half the laxatives were gone. Half of a pack of twenty-four. God alone knew how many more packs Abby had already gone through. God knew how many were hidden under the bed even now, emptied and waiting to be dumped when Leonie wasn't looking.

She fell to her knees on the floor, pulled up the duvet and stared under the bed. Old magazines, a couple of tennis balls and a shiny blue doll's suitcase stared out at her. Balls of fluff and scrunched-up tissue paper reproached her for not hoovering there often enough. For once, Leonie didn't feel upset at signs of dust. She used a tennis racquet to poke around under the bed, discovering an old cuddly rabbit, some pens and an odd blue sock. Nothing else. Then she dragged out the doll's suitcase. It had come with a travelling doll, an ugly black-haired witch of a thing that Abby had unaccountably loved when she was seven. Leonie remembered Mel teasing her twin about her secret hiding place and knew without doubt that the suitcase was it. A perfect place to hide things from prying eyes.

Opening it was like reading your children's diaries or bugging their telephone calls or something awful, Leonie was sure. Child psychologists would have a field day telling her what she was doing was totally wrong and would be betraying her daughter's trust. But right now, Leonie didn't give a damn about child psychologists and their version of child–parent relationships. What did they know? They hadn't just been presented with the evidence that their fifteen-year-old daughter had an eating disorder. They weren't the parent who felt guilt creeping up on her because she'd never noticed what had been going on.

Leonie wrenched the suitcase open. Inside lay a hideous treasure trove of Abby's goodies: empty sweet and chocolate wrappers, a half-eaten packet of chocolate biscuits, several bags of crisps and at least eight more bright red laxative packets, all empty. She touched them lightly, running her fingers over the scrunched-up foil wrappers the tablets had come in. Poor, poor Abby. She had visions of her daughter doubled up with pain in the bathroom, trying to cope with horrific cramps from taking an unhealthy amount of laxatives.

Guilt hit her painfully. How could she have not known? What sort of a mother was she when she hadn't noticed what was going on? Her mind flew over the events of the past few months, desperately trying to piece together evidence of Abby's problem, evidence that seemed painfully obvious now but imperceptible then.

She remembered Abby losing weight and becoming picky about her food. She thought of the fuss and bother when Abby insisted on eating only vegetarian products, and how happy she'd been that Abby was growing prettier and slimmer, convinced her daughter wouldn't have to cope with the pain of being large and dull the way she'd had to. Now those happy thoughts turned sour in retrospect – Abby had been getting thin because she was taking laxatives and . . . Leonie paled at the thought of what the 'and . . .' might be.

If only taking these things was the extent of her problem, if only she wasn't developing anorexia or bulimia.

The phone rang and she let it ring out. Leonie sat on the floor of the twins' bedroom and stared blankly at the posters of the boy bands on the walls, not seeing their bronzed and toned torsos; seeing instead sweet little Abby coping with this awful thing on her own. Leonie cursed herself for not noticing. She'd been so obsessed with her own problems, worrying about the effect Fliss would have on their lives, getting caught up in her romance with Hugh, that she'd completely missed all the signs.

Leonie had felt a lot of emotions in her life but never had she felt like a bad mother. She did now. Schoolgirls who didn't look much like schoolgirls made their way out of the big silver gates of St Perpetua's at four that afternoon. Trailing schoolbags and sports bags, sleek, grown-up looking girls wandered out, regulation navy coats unbuttoned, royal blue A-line skirts hitched up as soon as they'd passed the watchful eyes of the nuns. The older ones all looked far too old to be in secondary school, Leonie thought, as she sat in the car and watched for Mel and Abby. Some lit up forbidden cigarettes as they walked towards the bus stop, others applied mascara and lipstick as they waited for lifts, chattering nineteen to the dozen, delighted to be free for the weekend.

The bus to Bray had come and gone before Mel and Abby appeared in the middle of a group of other transition years, laughing like drains at some magazine they were all craning their necks to read.

Mel saw their mother's car first and hurried over to it. She looked startled to see her mother for they usually got the bus home from school.

'Mum! What's wrong? Is it Gran or Danny? What is it?'

'Nothing like that,' Leonie replied.

'But you never pick us up any more . . .' began Mel.

'I need to talk to you both,' said Leonie grimly.

'Oh.' Gloomily, Mel got into the front seat and fastened her seat belt. 'What have we done now?' she asked.

'What's up?' Abby asked blithely, opening the back door. She threw her bags into the back seat and fell in. 'I'm knackered, Mum. This is a nice treat. Did you have a good day off?'

Leonie looked intensely at her daughter through the rear-view mirror, searching Abby's face for some sign of illness or bulimia, as if it would be written on her forehead.

'Er yes, I did,' she stuttered.

'We're in trouble, Abby,' announced Mel. 'What have we done now, Mum?'

Leonie drove down the hill in a quandary. At the bottom, she braked a little too late and had to jam her foot to the floor to bring the car to a halt at the stop sign. How did she say it? Should she wait until they were at home, or should she only say it to Abby?

'Spill the beans, Mum,' said Mel, exasperated and keen to find out if whatever misdemeanour would result in her not being allowed out all weekend.

'I found some laxatives in your room today, beside Abby's bed.' Bluntly was the only way to say it. Leonie looked at Abby again in the mirror.

Abby's face closed over. She said nothing.

'I wasn't snooping,' Leonie said. 'I was changing the sheets and I found a pack beside your bed, Abby.'

'So?' Abby said sullenly.

'I know I shouldn't have, but I looked in your blue case and I found all the others,' Leonie added.

'You what! You had no right to look in my private things!' screeched Abby. 'How would you like it if someone did that to you? They're my things and I'm entitled to my privacy.'

'I know, love,' said Leonie, trying to placate her, 'but I'm worried about you. I wasn't looking for diaries or anything. I needed to see if you'd taken more of those awful things. They're so bad for you,' she protested.

'It's my business if they are or not!' yelled Abby. 'I hope you didn't read my diary.'

'Of course I didn't, I didn't even see a diary. But *you're* my business, Abby,' said her mother heatedly, 'that makes it my business. I have a right to know what you're doing because I'm your mother and I want to look after you. Taking laxatives is bad for you, it's stupid. You're lovely, darling, you don't need to change how you look. There are other ways to be slim, if that's what you want,' she said pleadingly.

'Oh yeah, and you'd know about that, would you?' snarled Abby with vicious accuracy.

Even Mel, who liked rows and was never fazed by rudeness, gasped.

Leonie found herself mouthing helplessly like a goldfish out of water.

'She didn't mean that, Mum,' Mel said.

'I did!' howled Abby.

It was Leonie's turn to howl. 'How could you say something so nasty?' she asked. 'Is that what you really think of me?'

Abby didn't answer.

They turned into the drive and as soon as the car had stopped, Abby leapt out and rushed into the cottage. Mel ran after her. Feeling weary, Leonie got out and followed them.

'Abby, we have to talk,' she said loudly, standing outside the girls' bedroom. There were scuffling noises and whispering. Leonie didn't want to barge in but it looked as though she might have to. 'Abby!' she called again. 'We have to talk.'

Cheeks flushed and eyes suspiciously bright, Abby emerged after a moment, looking less upset. No doubt she's been checking to see that her diary was there, unopened. Leonie had never even noticed a diary when she'd been looking earlier. She'd been too obsessed to notice anything but the laxative packets. Abby appeared to have calmed down a little bit.

'Tell me how long this has been going on, Abby. Be honest,' Leonie commanded her.

Abby didn't meet her eyes. Shuffling from foot to foot, she stood outside her bedroom door still in her school uniform. 'Not long,' she said. 'I read about them but they didn't work, so there! Those were old packets you saw.'

'Please tell me that you won't do it again,' Leonie begged. 'If you want, we could get counselling for you. I know there are eating-disorder groups . . .'

'I don't have an eating disorder!' snapped Abby. 'I was just experimenting, right. I don't have to explain everything to you, you know. I'm not a child,' she said, her tone scathing.

'I know, love,' Leonie said weakly. She tried to touch Abby but the girl jerked away from her. 'Don't be angry with me, Abby. I don't want to treat you like a child, but what you've been doing is dangerous and I'm your mother. It's my job to take care of you. I can't stand by and watch you destroy yourself. I need to know that you won't take laxatives again, and I need to know if you've done anything else . . .' Her voice failed her briefly. '. . . If you've been making yourself sick.'

'I haven't done anything else,' Abby answered sullenly. 'Don't you believe me?' she hissed.

Leonie stared at her for a long time. 'If you promise you're telling me the truth, then yes, I believe you. But if you have, we can get over it, together, as a family.' Her eyes were wet with tears. She wanted to hug Abby, the way she'd done when the twins were toddlers. Abby had been so affectionate, a scrap of a thing who loved cuddles and kisses. 'I can get the number of the eating-disorder group and we can deal with this problem together.'

Abby's eyes narrowed. 'I've got the answer,' she snapped. 'Listen, Mom, I don't want to be here, I could go and live with Fliss and Dad. They'd love to have me, and I bet I wouldn't be so much of a *problem* for them,' she said, eyes like knives.

Leonie stared at her, hurting so bad she could barely think straight. Abby was speaking as if she was already in America. Calling her 'Mom' instead of Mum the way she'd always said it. And she hadn't said she'd go to her father and Fliss – it had been the other way round. Fliss first, then Ray. He wasn't the lure that drew her to America, it was the slim, elegant, charming Fliss. Leonie had never cared that the beautiful American woman had married her ex-husband. They'd been apart for so long, Fliss was welcome to him. But she would die if Fliss took her children away.

'You're not a problem, Abby,' she said brokenly. 'I love you, I couldn't bear it if you went to live somewhere else. I just want what's best for you, don't you understand?'

'Leave me alone,' Abby said. 'That's what's best for me.'

She whirled round and went back into her room, slamming the door so hard that the surrounds shook.

Leonie prepared dinner on automatic pilot, her mind in turmoil as she figured out what to do. She felt too shattered to phone her mother or Ray, even though she knew she needed moral support. She wanted some time alone to think about Abby's behaviour.

Abby emerged from the room that evening, white-faced and red-eyed. Leonie knew instinctively that she was sorry for all the things she'd said. Leaving the vegetables she'd been straining, she crossed the kitchen and pulled her daughter into her arms.

'Oh, Mum,' sobbed Abby, crumpling against her mother's body, 'I'm so sorry. I hate myself for what I said to you. I love you so much, I was upset. Please believe me.'

'Hush, hush,' said Leonie softly, stroking Abby's hair. 'I love you too, Abby. I want to help you. Will you let me? Please don't push me away.' She held Abby's face in her hands and looked at her questioningly. 'Will you promise me not to touch laxatives again, please?'

Abby nodded mutely, her eyes brimming. 'I'm sorry, Mum.'

Leonie hugged her again. 'It's all right, darling, we'll get through it together. It's all right.'

Of course, it wasn't all right. At every meal, Leonie tried her best to keep her eyes away from Abby's plate but she was inexorably drawn to it, watching anxiously as every mouthful was forked up, and straining her ears each time Abby went near the bathroom, listening for signs of vomiting.

'Stop watching me,' hissed Abby on Saturday evening as she picked at her dinner.

Tension loomed over the entire weekend. Amazingly, Danny, who was working flat-out on a project, didn't seem to notice. Abby consistently avoided her mother so that Leonie was forced to engineer a moment alone to ask how she was feeling.

'Fine,' exploded Abby. 'I told you I'm not doing it any more, so can't you just accept that?'

On Monday morning, the twins left for school and Leonie rang the surgery to say she'd be in late. She had a phone call to make.

The woman on the eating disorder helpline was called Brenda and had heard it all before. Her soft, friendly voice and non-judgemental manner were a balm to Leonie's bruised soul. She judged herself badly for not noticing Abby's problem, therefore she expected everyone else to judge her badly too.

But Brenda swept aside the idea of blame or guilt: 'It's great that you finally know how Abby feels,' she said once she'd been told the story. 'You can help. Before, you couldn't. Surely that's positive.'

'I suppose,' Leonie said numbly.

'Trust is an important part of how you cope from now on,' Brenda explained in her kind, matter-of-fact manner. 'There's no use you watching over Abby like a hawk, forcing her to eat up her dinner or insisting she has large portions. That'll just make her more secretive than ever.'

'But what do I do?' cried Leonie. 'I want to help but I feel so helpless. She's pushing me away.'

'That's common. Don't think it's just you. She's upset and hurt. She wants to hurt someone back, and she's trying to keep you away from her so she can remain in control of what she's doing. If she lets her guard down, she thinks she won't be in control.'

'She was always so good, the best kid imaginable,' Leonie said in anguish. 'If anyone was destined to develop this, I would never have thought of Abby. Her twin, Melanie, is much more interested in how she looks, in clothes and boys. Mel's the gorgeous, feminine one. Abby's reliable and easy-going.'

'Perhaps,' Brenda said delicately, 'she got tired of being reliable. It may be hard living in her sister's shadow.'

'You're right.'

'It sounds as if you have caught this in the early stages, although you can never be sure. People with eating disorders are very successful at hiding it.' Brenda laughed. 'I should know, I was anorexic for five years and bulimic for eight.'

On the other end of the phone, Leonie gasped.

'I know you're surprised,' Brenda added, 'but think about it: the best person to help someone with an eating disorder is someone who's actually gone through it all themselves. You cannot force your daughter to eat. All you can do at this stage is provide her with support and help her to deal with it. You're doing fine.'

She recommended some books that would be useful and added

that if there was any way Leonie could get Abby along to a meeting, then it would be a wonderful help. 'Some of the girls come here for the first time and they're scared stiff. They don't know anyone else who feels the way they do, they feel utterly alone. They rarely say anything at the first meeting, they just sit and stare, amazed that they're in a room full of people who've gone through the same thing. Try and bring your daughter, Leonie.'

'I'll do my best,' Leonie promised.

She could barely concentrate on work.

'Has Hugh asked you to marry him or something?' Angie enquired laconically when Leonie produced the wrong rabbit for neutering during morning surgery. 'This is a female.'

'Sorry,' Leonie said, scooping the bewildered, struggling rabbit up again. 'Migraine, that's all.'

'Do you want to go home?' Angie asked sympathetically.

Leonie shook her head. The last thing she wanted to do was go home and spend the afternoon on her own, alone with all her miserable thoughts about Abby.

After lunch, she went into one of the upstairs offices and braced herself to phone Ray. He had to be told.

Ray was in a bad mood and, once Leonie had reassured him – untruthfully – that there was nothing wrong, he spent five minutes muttering about the appalling weather in Boston. 'Damned climate,' he grumbled.

'Yeah,' said Leonie absently. 'It's cold here too. Listen, Ray,' she said heavily, 'we've got to talk.'

'You mean there *is* something wrong,' he said.

'I hate to simply phone up and say, "Ray, there's something terribly wrong,"' Leonie muttered.

'Tell me,' he said.

She'd expected Ray to be upset and even tearful. What she *hadn't* expected was for him to get furious with her.

'For Chrissake, Leonie, how the hell did it happen without you knowing? You can't turn on the TV here without hearing about kids with anorexia or bulimia. Schools and parents are totally aware of it and you apparently haven't a clue!'

'That's not fair,' protested Leonie. 'By its very nature, it's a secretive illness. I love the kids, I'd do anything for them. I hope you're not accusing me of neglecting them!'

'You certainly took your eye off the ball this time,' Ray snapped.

'They've just come back from Cannes with you. How come you didn't notice?' she shrieked at him.

'Four days is nothing,' he said curtly. 'I've got to go. I've a ten o'clock. I have a day, you know. I'll call tonight to talk to Abby. I think it'd be a good idea if she came to stay with Fliss and me for a while. We can keep an eye on her. Fliss is great with Abby. They had a fantastic time in Cannes.'

He hung up, leaving Leonie horrified.

Desperate for reassurance, she phoned Emma but got her voice mail. A polite woman in Hannah's office said she was out. She didn't try Hugh. This was something she felt she couldn't talk to Hugh about. Bloody Jane had been such a perfect teenager, according to him, that Leonie couldn't bear to tell him what had been happening with Abby.

Feeling very alone, Leonie buried her face in her hands and sobbed her heart out. How was she ever going to cope with this? Why had she been so interested in herself that she'd neglected her beloved kids?

She went home early and took Penny out for a walk, despite the fact that the so-far balmy May afternoon had been transformed into a raging gale with hailstones like bullets hurtling down. Leonie didn't mind the weather: it suited her current mood of introspective self-loathing. She *deserved* hailstones whipping against her face and the wind threatening to whisk her off her feet. Bad mothers couldn't expect anything else. Penny, on the other hand, loved the wind. She held her head aloft and sniffed ecstatically, breathing in scents that no human nose could identify. She danced along, landing heavily in puddles, with Leonie stomping along behind her, head down against the gale.

As they reached the heavy black gates at the end of Doug Mansell's drive, Penny, accustomed to meeting his two collies on their evening walks, decided she'd pay them a visit now. Ignoring Leonie's demands that she come back here immediately, she trotted confidently up the drive to see her friends. Leonie groaned but set out after her quickly. It might be nice to talk to Doug, she thought. They often walked together in the evenings now, talking about everything and nothing. It was a companionable, easy relationship. Doug could be very funny in a dry way and once he'd let his guard down with Leonie and the kids, he did so wholeheartedly. He'd been to dinner loads of times and appeared to enjoy the banter of the Delaney household. He'd been giving Danny driving lessons in his jeep and had promised that when the girls were old enough, he'd teach them too. 'I better get the pacemaker fitted first,' he'd kidded Mel, who was not mechanically inclined and who viewed driving as a method of getting out and about to meet more guys than she could on the bus.

Leonie didn't tell Hugh about these cosy dinners. She felt he might interpret them incorrectly. It was hard to explain her friendship with Doug because it was totally unlike any other friendship she'd ever had. Not romantic, obviously, but, well . . . It was about companionship and camaraderie. You couldn't explain that.

She went round the back to the kitchen door because she knew Doug would either be there or in his studio beside the kitchen. He opened the door without her having to knock on it, alerted to her presence by the demented barking of three dogs, all desperate to play with each other.

'Sorry to butt in, but Penny decided she wanted to see Alfie and Jasper,' she said.

Doug screwed up his face in mock disgust: 'You mean you wouldn't bother to come and see me unless Penny wanted a date?' he demanded. But seeing how Leonie's face crumpled at his remark, his looked immediately contrite. 'What's wrong, Leo?' he asked in concern. He was the only person who called her that and she liked it. It was special, private.

She told him everything. It was a relief to talk to someone about it all. She'd felt too raw and hurt to tell Angie, and she hated telling her mother, because she'd be so upset. But Doug was a good person to tell things to. He installed her in the comfiest of the small couches in the warm kitchen, gave her hot, sweet tea and the Italian biscuits he always seemed to have on hand. After listening to the whole story calmly, feeding the three slavering dogs biscuit crumbs, he said that Ray had over-reacted and ought to be shot. 'It's very easy to tell you where you're going wrong from three thousand miles away,' he remarked. 'Ray feels guilty as hell because he's not here, so he gets that off his chest by snapping at you. You don't have to take that, Leo.'

'I've failed as a mother,' she wailed.

Doug was stern, the hooded eyes severe. 'You haven't failed. You have three great kids, but they're not saints. They make mistakes – we all do, Leo. If Mel, Abby and Danny were three plaster saints, they'd be boring individuals who'd never amount to anything in the world. But they're not. They're funny, clever, sensitive – too sensitive, in Abby's case – people who are feeling their way in life. They're not kids any more. You have to accept that. You can be there for them when they make mistakes, but you can't stop them making those mistakes. Right,' he said, seeing Leonie's bottom lip wobbling, 'lecture over. I believe in you, Leo, and so do the kids. The twins and Danny would go to hell and back for you. That's because of all the sacrifices you made for them. Don't forget that.'

She nodded.

Doug eyed the three dogs, who were now splayed out on the kitchen floor, exhausted after playing a frenzied game of tag with each other all over the downstairs of the house. 'Penny has had enough exercise for one day. I'll drive you home and if you show me which bit of the freezer you keep that amazing lasagne in, I'll make dinner. Deal?'

'Deal.'

Fliss rang late that night when Doug had gone home and the twins were going to bed. Leonie felt her hackles rise at the sound of the other woman's voice, the same way Penny's hackles rose when she spotted a cat other than her housemate, Clover.

'Leonie, this is a terrible experience for you and for the whole family. I feel just awful for you.'

'Well, thanks, Fliss,' said Leonie woodenly, hating Fliss for having access to this most private family secret.

'Ray told me he lost it with you earlier and I wanted to apologize because he had no right to do that,' Fliss continued. 'We've been talking it over and we came up with a solution that might be appropriate for everyone.'

'Really?'

Without losing any of her calmness, despite Leonie's sarcastic tone, Fliss continued: 'Ray and I think it would be good for Abby if she came to stay with us for a while – and Mel too. I think it'd be a mistake to part them.'

'What? That's ridiculous,' Leonie said. 'They've just gone back to school after taking two extra days to go to France. They can't miss any time now. They've got their end-of-year exams.'

'It's only transition year. Besides, they were due to come in August anyway,' Fliss interrupted. 'They'll just be coming a few months early. It would be so good for Abby to have a change of scenery to take her mind off what's been going on.'

'Even though it is their transition year,' Leonie said hesitantly, 'the school probably won't want them to miss the exams.'

'You could always say it's about parental access,' Fliss suggested. 'I'm not that familiar with family law cases, but I know it's not unusual for kids to take time out to live with the other parent for a while. Even two or three months could make a difference for Abby.'

'Two or three *months*!' gasped Leonie, horrified. 'I was thinking more of a couple of weeks. I'd be lost without them.'

'Yeah, I guessed you'd feel that way.' Fliss was very gentle. 'Leonie, I'm not trying to take your girls away from you. They're your kids, they love you. Nobody can take that away. This isn't about that, it's about Abby. You are the best support she could have, but right now, I believe that breaking the cycle of what she's been doing is the best thing for her. She needs another environment. You know her father would love to have her here – and Mel, too.'

Leonie knew she had to get off the phone quickly or she'd burst into tears.

'Let me think about it, Fliss,' she said abruptly and hung up. Then she did burst into tears.

* * *

Doug offered to drive them to the airport. 'You won't be in any fit state to drive anywhere,' he told Leonie candidly.

She knew he was right. In the three days since she'd told the girls about the trip, she hadn't been able to do anything right. She'd taken time off work because it was quite possible she'd make an awful mistake in the surgery and be responsible for the demise of some poor animal. Angie had been wonderfully sympathetic when she heard about Abby.

'Change of scenery is probably a good idea for both Abby and you,' she said. 'When the girls are gone, why don't you and Hugh go away for a week? Drive down to Kerry or Clare and do absolutely nothing but eat, drink and go for tramps in the woods. You deserve a break, and if Hugh is boring, you can go off with that tramp from the woods!'

But Leonie wasn't in the mood for joking or a holiday, any holiday. She wanted to crawl into her lair and hibernate to lick her wounds.

It was ten in the morning and the twins' flight was leaving at half two. Leonie wanted to make sure they were there on time for the lengthy US immigration process. How ironic, she thought, that she was rushing to make sure they caught a flight she didn't really want them to be on.

'Ready, girls?' she called with false gaiety.

Mel and Abby had been up since seven, in a frenzy of last-minute packing, hair-washing and even one final, triumphant phone call to Mel's long-time enemy, Dervla Malone to boast about flying to Boston while she was heading off to school for double French followed by netball practice in the rain.

'Nearly,' called Mel. 'I can't close this suitcase. Can you come in and help, Mum?'

Rolling her eyes at Doug, who was patiently reading the newspaper in the kitchen with a slavish Penny at his feet, Leonie went into the girls' room.

'Surprise!' they chorused, waving an envelope and two oddly shaped presents at her.

'Wine,' said Mel unnecessarily, as she presented a bottle-shaped present.

'And this is something to cuddle when you're lonely,' Abby said quietly, handing over the other present.

Leonie felt a lump in her throat. 'Oh, girls,' she said tearfully, 'I'm going to miss you both so much.'

Abby threw herself at her mother. 'I know it's my fault we're going, and I love going, but I'm sorry it's hard for you,' she said jerkily.

They clung together, Leonie desperately trying not to cry.

'Aren't you going to open your presents?' asked a dry-eyed Mel happily.

Leonie praised the bottle of wine to the heavens. It was a lovely Burgundy, expensive she was sure of it. 'How did you pair manage to buy alcohol?' she asked. 'You're under-age.'

'Doug helped us. He said what you'd like and helped us pick it.'

Leonie was touched. What a kind man Doug was. The kids adored him and he'd promised to give Abby painting lessons. He'd roared laughing the day before when Mel artlessly said she'd love to have her portrait painted, but not by him because in his pictures everybody looked fat and ugly.

Leonie opened the second present. It was a furry toy, a cuddly dog with big brown eyes like Penny's and reddish fur.

'It's lovely,' she cried.

'Isn't it?' sniffed Abby. 'I know you'll be lonely, so this is to make you think of us.'

Leonie caressed Abby's cheek lovingly. 'As if I could forget about you two for one minute,' she said fondly. 'Thank you both. We better get going, Doug will go mental if we don't leave soon.'

Abby grinned. 'That's the nice thing about Doug,' she said, 'no matter what happens, he never goes mental.'

Leonie managed to keep a firm hold on her emotions all through the car journey and while they had a cup of coffee in the cafeteria.

'Don't forget to study,' she said. 'The only reason the school is letting you go is if you work hard and have counselling, Abby.'

Ray had arranged a private tutor to give the girls lessons during their six weeks away and Abby had agreed to see an eating-disorder counsellor. It was only the promise of that, during a lengthy discussion with the headmistress about Abby's problems and her father's legal right of access, that had made the head agree to let both girls go.

'If it wasn't transition year, there is no way both girls would be able to take that much time off without having to stay back a year,' Sister Fidelma had said. 'They have exams coming up and I know people think transition-year exams aren't important, but they are.'

Leonie had explained passionately that Abby's state of mind was more important than any attendance record or summer exams.

'The Department of Education might not agree,' Sister Fidelma said testily. But she had nevertheless made all the arrangements. Leonie had remarked to Doug that you'd swear she was sending her daughters off as apprentices in a Thai sex-shop instead of a visit to their father in Boston.

'And don't leave the kitchen in a mess like you do at home,' Leonie warned. 'It's not fair on Fliss. And please phone,' she added.

'Of course we will,' Mel said, impatient to be off.

'They should probably go through now,' Doug said gently. 'The immigration process takes a while.'

Leonie could only nod, she was incapable of speech. She and Doug walked the twins to the security barrier leading to the departure gates, where they were to meet the Aer Lingus representative helping them through immigration because they were minors.

Both girls kissed Doug goodbye.

'Look after Mum, will you?' asked Abby.

'Of course,' he replied.

Abby turned to Leonie.

'Bye, Mum,' she said.

'Goodbye,' Leonie replied, her strength disappearing. She sobbed, not able to help herself, reaching out blindly to grab Mel and Abby.

The three of them hugged each other tightly before Mel broke away.

'Don't panic, Mum,' she said, 'we'll be back before you know it.'

She took Abby's hand and pulled her away. 'Let's go. I hate goodbyes.'

They waved until they were out of sight. Doug put one strong arm around Leonie's heaving body. 'They're only going for six weeks, you know,' he said. 'They'll be back. Now come on, let's get out of here. I'm bringing you out to dinner somewhere posh tonight and we've got to walk the dogs first.'

She had stopped crying by the time he parked outside the cottage an hour later.

'I'm coming in to make you some hot tea,' he said.

'Better make it hot whiskey,' Leonie snuffled through her bunged-up nose.

'That's a deal.'

Good as his word, Doug boiled the kettle and made her a strong hot whiskey. When she was finished drinking it, he got up.

'Leonie, I'm not letting you sit here moping all day. Get your walking gear on and I'll be back in ten minutes with Jasper and Alfie. We're going to walk some of the Wicklow Way and when you're too knackered to walk any more, we're going to dinner in the Hungry Monk.'

'You're so bossy,' she grumbled.

His stern face softened into a smile. 'It's working, though, isn't it?'

It was a glorious day. As they walked past acres of the sulphur yellow gorse that covered the Wicklow hills, Leonie brooded. She answered Doug in monosyllables until he got fed up with her moping.

'I'm only going to say this once, Leo. You're a great mother. Those kids love you. They're growing up, that's all, with all the pain growing up involves. So stop moping and pull yourself together.'

'Well why do I feel like such a bloody awful mother, then?' she demanded angrily. 'I feel so fucking furious.'

Hugh would have been shocked if he'd heard her swear, but Doug wasn't in the least put out.

'Why?'

'Why? That's a stupid bloody question, Doug,' she hissed.

'You're not God,' he said calmly. 'Things happen that are outside your control and you've got to learn to deal with them. *I've* had to. Do you think I wanted to get burned in a fire and have the woman I loved dump me because she couldn't cope with a disfigured shell of a man who was no longer the darling of the art gallery scene?'

Leonie was too astonished to say anything. Doug had never spoken about his past before. She'd discovered that he was a famous, critically acclaimed artist but they never talked about that. He sometimes showed her his paintings and Leonie loved them all, especially the wild, fierce landscapes that leapt from the canvas into your heart.

'I had no control over that,' Doug said solemnly. 'I had to deal with it. You must too, or you'll be eaten up with bitterness and resentment. I'm not letting that happen to you, Leo. Now come on, we've still got three miles to go.'

Doug marched on resolutely, leaving even Leonie with her long legs, hurrying to keep up.

Three hours later, they sat in a dark corner of the Hungry Monk in Greystones, tearing into the bread rolls and drinking gin and tonics.

'I'm ravenous,' Leonie said. Her limbs ached pleasurably from their six-mile hike and she felt relaxed for the first time since she'd found those awful laxatives under Abby's bed. 'Exercise is definitely better than booze for making you relax.'

Doug, with his head in the wine list, laughed. 'Exercise *and* booze are the best yet.'

They ate amazing fat mussels, corn-fed chicken and sinful potatoes laced with cheese and cream. After a bottle of red wine, they moved on to an Australian dessert wine with the apple dessert they shared, happy to sit and listen to the chatter of the other diners. Feeling reckless, Leonie decided she'd have an Irish coffee to round things off.

'You'll regret it in the morning,' Doug warned. 'Mixing your drinks like that will give you a murderous hangover.'

'No it won't, silly,' she said, happy now that she was physically tired and mentally a bit dopey thanks to alcohol. If she had one more drink, she'd sleep like a baby and wouldn't spend the night worrying about her beloved twins.

Languorously tipsy, Leonie found the courage to ask Doug about what he'd said earlier.

'I never ask you about your past,' she said, 'but you did bring it up. Tell me. After all,' she added, 'you know everything there is to know about me and mine.'

Doug fiddled with the stem of his wine glass. 'I don't like talking about it,' he said gloomily.

'It's only me,' Leonie protested.

'Well, seeing as it's you,' he said. 'This is not a story with a happy ending, you know.'

'Pish posh,' said Leonie dismissively. 'Spill the beans, Mansell. I know you too well for this coyness.'

'Did you ever think of investigative journalism as a career?' he enquired.

Leonie giggled. 'You have to learn to ask leading questions when you've got three kids, otherwise you'd never know who their friends are or what they were up to.'

For once, Doug didn't grin back. He looked sombre as he started his story: 'I was going to be married to a woman I'd been seeing for three years. I'd lived with a few people over the years,' he explained, 'but I'd never wanted to marry anyone until I met Caitlin. She was a sculptor and it seemed like the marriage made in heaven. I'd have my studio and she'd have hers right beside it.' He took a gulp of wine, his eyes opaque. 'One night we were out late and we decided to stay in town with a friend of mine who lived over his gallery in this second-floor flat. An electric heater caught fire downstairs. I woke up and couldn't find Caitlin. There was smoke everywhere, I thought maybe she'd gone down to try and get out that way, even though there was a fire escape. I got burned down there.'

'What happened to her?' Leonie asked, horrified.

Doug shrugged wryly. 'She'd decided to go home to her own place earlier. Left me a note, she said, because she hated sleeping in the flat and had to get up early, so she went home at about three. You don't notice notes on the pillow when the room is filled with smoke,' he said with heavy irony. 'Afterwards, she couldn't cope. It was a mixture of guilt that I'd been burned because of her and the fact that she loves beautiful things.' The old bitterness that Leonie hadn't seen on his face for a long time returned, twisting his mouth into a grim shape. 'I wasn't beautiful any more. Caitlin loved touching things; she'd run her hands over my face with her eyes closed as if she was reading Braille. As a sculptor, she saw with her fingers. She didn't like what she saw any more.'

How horribly cruel, Leonie thought. This Caitlin couldn't have loved Doug very much if she left him over that.

'That's when you moved in here,' Leonie prompted.

'I'd planned a reclusive life of painting and then this local woman fell over outside my house and that was it: so much for privacy,' he joked. 'I can't get rid of her, actually.'

He pretended to consider this. 'Ah no, that's not true. If she wasn't around, I'd miss her. She drives me mad but she's great fun.'

Leonie blushed.

Doug waved at a waitress. 'Could you order us a taxi, please?' he asked.

In the taxi home, Leonie drifted off to sleep. She woke up as the car pulled up outside the cottage and found herself leaning comfortably against Doug's bony shoulder.

'Wake up, sleepy head,' he said, gently shaking her.

'God, sorry,' she muttered sleepily.

Doug got out of the taxi and helped her out. 'You all right?' he asked.

She nodded. 'See you tomorrow.' And then she reached up and did something she'd never done before: kissed him. His beard felt funny against her lips, funny but nice. Doug was nice too. Happy in her alcohol haze, she patted his cheek lovingly before turning to meander up the drive.

The sound of Penny barking woke her the following morning. It sounded like the Rank Organization man with the gong was in her bedroom, banging it for all he was worth.

'Stop it, Penny,' moaned Leonie, pulling a pillow over her head. Her head ached and her mouth felt dry. The night before drifted in and out of her mind. The Hungry Monk, lovely food, Doug being sweet to her, his story about the fire and . . . oh no. She sat up abruptly. She'd kissed him goodnight. How awful. He'd hate that, he'd think she was coming on to him. Ohmigod no! And she had a man in her life, too. She had Hugh. It wasn't as if she was desperate for a man. No, but she still had to act like some middle-aged slapper who threw herself at her friends because she was drunk.

After a while, thirst got her out of bed. Struggling into her towelling dressing gown, she shuffled along to the kitchen, her slippers slapping against her heels. Danny was listening to the radio at top blast, making toasted sandwiches and creating a mess of crumbs, squelches of dropped mayonnaise and melted cheese.

Penny immediately sat at his feet adoringly, waiting for scraps.

'You look terrible, Mum,' Danny said cheerfully.

'Would you mind turning the radio down,' Leonie said in a feeble voice, 'and make me some tea.'

'Tea?' roared Danny wickedly, knowing she was hungover.

Leonie shot him a murderous look. 'Next time you come home from the Micro Club plastered and I make you drink a pint of water and put you to bed, I'll remind you how cruel you were to me today.'

'Only kidding, Mum,' he said. 'Tea coming up.'

Outside the kitchen window, she could see Clover standing on the sill, staring in at them with an outraged expression on her feline face. She obviously hadn't been fed.

'Feed Penny and Clover, too,' Leonie added. She got to her feet. 'I've got to make a phone call.'

As she rang Doug, she quailed at the thought of how he might react.

'I'm sorry, was I awful last night?' she asked as soon as he picked the phone up, not wanting to know the answer.

Doug laughed heartily. 'Terrible,' he agreed. 'I had to stop you dancing on the table in the Hungry Monk, and as for what you tried to do with the cream from your Irish coffee . . . Well,' he said, deadpan, 'I don't think they'll ever accept a booking from us again.'

'Oh God,' she groaned.

'I'm kidding, you fool. You were fine,' he said. 'Apart from the bit . . .'

Leonie held her breath. He was about to say *apart from the bit where you tried to snog me.*

Instead, he said, '. . . where I had to watch you stagger up the drive to your front door. The taxi driver and I were taking bets on how long it'd take you to get your door keys out of your handbag. I should have walked up with you,' he said. 'Sorry.'

'That's all right,' said Leonie with relief. 'I shouldn't have had that last Irish coffee. It sent me right over the edge.'

Danny came in with a pot of tea.

'I have to go. I'll see you soon,' she said to Doug. 'Thanks for last night.'

'Oh, I forgot to tell you, Mum,' Danny said, helping himself to one of the chocolate biscuits he'd put on the tray with the tea. 'The girls phoned this morning, early. They got there safely last night so they rang to say they were fine.'

'Why didn't you wake me?' wailed Leonie.

'You were asleep,' protested Danny, injured.

'I'll ring them now,' she said frantically.

'They're going out for the day, Mel said,' Danny pointed out. 'Fliss is bringing them shopping. To some market or something, I can't remember exactly. You know Mel, dead excited about shopping.'

'Did you speak to Abby?' his mother asked in a small voice.

'Yeah. She sounded excited too. I'm going out, Mum,' he added. 'I'll probably be late tonight. See you.'

'See you,' echoed Leonie sadly.

When Hugh phoned later, she was delighted to hear from him. She'd spent such a lonely day in the house. Penny had done her best to comfort her, shoving her cool wet nose into her mistress's hand occasionally, saying, *I'm here*. But Leonie felt so inconsolable that even her beloved Penny couldn't cheer her up.

Hugh's phone call, therefore, was welcome. Perhaps he'd rung to tell her there was a change of plan and that they were going out after all.

'Are you still bringing Jane to the theatre?' she asked hopefully.

'Yes,' Hugh said. 'She's so excited about it. Poor love is all cut up about that awful ex-boyfriend of hers.'

'I'm sorry,' Leonie said untruthfully. She wished Hugh had cried off from his trip with his daughter. Leonie could have done with some company tonight. But kids had to come first, she thought dully. Except Jane wasn't a kid.

'You don't suppose there's any way Jane would cope if you cried off tonight and came to see me instead?' Leonie said daringly.

Hugh sounded horrified. 'I can't, Leonie,' he said in shocked tones. 'That bastard of a boyfriend was stringing her along for ages, she's so upset about him. She needs me.'

But what about me? Leonie wanted to cry. I need you too. My daughters have gone and they're more precious to me than some boyfriend-of-three-weeks is to bloody Jane. But she said nothing.

CHAPTER TWENTY-FIVE

Three months later

Felix's proposal became the stuff of interviews. Another fact to be sculpted into a media sound-bite. The lovely story of how he'd arrived at her house with fifty bouquets (a smidgen of exaggeration was de rigueur for interviews, Felix explained) and a huge diamond, only to end up waiting outside for hours for his beloved to arrive, whereupon he'd nearly developed hypothermia and had needed half an hour in front of the fire before his teeth had stopped chattering.

Hannah was heartily sick of their life becoming fodder for interviews. At least their Caribbean wedding hadn't made eight pages in *Hello!* (although Hannah reckoned it was only because Bill, Felix's agent had failed to get what she considered a suitable offer from the magazine), but several Sunday newspapers had featured some of the photos. Hannah had been very critical of herself in the simple ankle-length Ben de Lisi gown with her hair trailing down her back and flowers entwined in it. She'd felt fat and pregnant beside Bill, who turned out to be a chain-smoking, over-the-top Londoner who felt a day was wasted if she hadn't screamed at someone that they were a 'fucking idiot!'

Short, thin to the point of emaciation, and with big hair the colour of damson jam, Bill turned more heads than the bride did when she arrived at the beachside wedding in a cream trousersuit with nothing on underneath. Apart from the bouffant hair, she looked very Bianca Jagger.

Hannah, who'd been brought up to believe that it was rude to upstage the bride by wearing white or cream, was furious. She'd felt perfectly dressed beforehand. Her skin was a golden colour and gleamed with a healthy sheen thanks to a silken moisturizer with hints of gold in it.

'She's a cow,' she longed to hiss to somebody as she stood beside the pretty altar which was decked out in all manner of exotic blossoms. But there was nobody to hiss to. They were on St Lucia and the guest list consisted of herself, Felix, Bill, her assistant – a lanky young bloke who practically never spoke even when Bill screamed at him – and the official who was going to marry them.

Hannah would have killed to have just one close friend with her on this special day. Even Gillian from the office would have been welcome: just someone she could talk to normally.

By the time Felix had finished his telling of it, the wedding had become a last-minute decision and they'd simply left their home with just the clothes they were standing up in (which didn't quite explain Hannah's exquisite dress that had to be ordered three weeks in advance and altered twice to cope with her ever-growing five-months-pregnant belly) and hopped on a plane to the Caribbean.

> *Just like the romantic charmer he's playing in his new series, Felix Andretti couldn't resist marrying his fiancée, Hannah, in the most idyllic manner possible. Instead of spending months organizing church, flowers and the reception, two months ago Felix whisked brunette Hannah off to St Lucia where they married in a simple beachside ceremony with just two close friends as witnesses.*
>
> *'We wanted it to be as simple and pure as possible,' Felix says earnestly, unable to tear his eyes away from his stunning Irish wife. 'I'm a romantic sort of guy and I'd always thought that when I met the right woman, I'd want to get married immediately with no fuss. Marriage is sacred to me and the idea of marrying outdoors with the ocean and nature all around made sense: you're at one*

> *with nature and the one you love. We were both barefoot on the sand. I'll never forget it. It was just a wonderful spur-of-the-moment thing.'*
>
> *The couple spent their honeymoon enjoying lazy days swimming and taking moonlit walks along the same beach where they'd got married, mere steps away from their lovely hotel, the charming Rex St Lucian. Felix even tried his hand at scuba diving while Hannah, who's pregnant with the couple's first baby, lounged around enjoying the sunshine.*

Hannah could barely cope with reading the glowing report in the magazine. Felix had gone scuba diving all right, leaving her alone with bloody Bill for days on end. As Bill's notion of having a good time meant knocking back as many rum-based cocktails as possible, she didn't make a very lucid companion.

Some days, Bill held off drinking long enough to play a quick game of tennis with the hotel's handsome pro, before ending up in the buffet having the odd lettuce leaf with a bottle of chilled white wine. Hannah, who felt too hot to sunbathe, spent most of her time in the air-conditioned bedroom, looking out at the happy couples beside the pool.

She bet she was the only honeymooner in the place who'd spent most of her time on her own.

On their last day there, she'd begged Felix to forget his scuba diving so they could have one day together, perhaps drive around the island and have lunch somewhere . . .

'I've paid for today,' Felix protested. 'It'd be a waste of money to miss the last dive.'

'It was a waste of money asking me to come with you! You could have saved by not bringing me, since you haven't spent five minutes with me since we got here!' Hannah screamed, throwing an ashtray at him.

Felix ducked and the ashtray crashed loudly into the wall, leaving a big dent in it.

'Now look what you've done,' he said in exasperation.

Hannah burst into tears.

'If you're going all hormonal on me, I'm leaving,' he muttered.

She went for a facial in a hotel nearby and then sat and drank an iced tea at the poolside bar before going for a short walk along the beach. It was too hot to stay outside for long, so she bought some magazines, and went back to her room. She'd just lie down on the bed and have a snooze . . .

Felix woke her up at seven. 'Come on, darling, let's have dinner. I'm ravenous.'

Disorientated, Hannah couldn't remember where she was for a moment. But Felix was here, wasn't he? His skin glowing with a deep golden tan, his hair bleached white in the sun, he looked better than ever. A white linen shirt and beige linen trousers hung elegantly on his lean frame. His teeth were brilliant white against the dark skin, his mouth a sensuous slash on his face. He leaned forward and kissed her. Hannah could smell the tang of salt water and the unmistakable scent of tanned flesh. Sleepily, she let him undo the buttons of her sundress and cup the newly heavy breasts in his hands. His tongue, hot and slick, moved over her skin, tasting and nibbling, sending her reeling with pleasure.

'We'll have dinner later,' Felix pronounced as he slid the dress off and slipped his hands into her cotton panties.

A woman recognized Felix at Birmingham airport. He and Hannah were waiting for their luggage and talking about whether they'd go for a quick sandwich or not before heading to Felix's mother's house. It was a good three-quarters of an hour away by taxi and they were both famished, having not eaten since the meal on the plane from St Lucia. Even for the figure-conscious Felix, a small packet of cheese-flavoured nibbles on their connecting flight from Heathrow didn't constitute lunch. Then a middle-aged woman in a neat navy blazer and cream skirt came racing up excitedly, pulling a tiny trolley case behind her.

'You're the bloke off the telly! Off *Bystanders*, aren't you? The carpenter who lives in the flat downstairs to the two girls.'

Felix smiled boyishly at her. 'Yes,' he said. 'I am.'

The woman blossomed under his smile. She roared to her friend to come over too. Soon, the three of them were talking animatedly, with Felix signing autographs with the easy expertise of someone who'd been doing it for years. He chatted away to the women as if they were all great friends, asking them questions and answering theirs.

Hannah stood to one side and watched in amusement. Felix had such charm, she thought proudly. He had the two fans eating out of his hands.

She kept an eye out for their luggage and listened in on the conversation.

'Is she your girlfriend?' asked the first woman, who was now identified as Josephine.

Hannah whipped her head round and grinned.

'No,' Felix said, pride in his voice, 'she's my wife.'

'Lovely looking, too,' said Josephine admiringly.

Hannah felt about six feet tall. She'd done her best to look good, on the grounds that she'd be meeting her beloved's mother for the first time. She'd worn her rather chic red Jasper Conran dress that used to cling to her svelte curves becomingly, along with long suede boots and a new square gleaming leather handbag that cost four times more than any handbag she'd ever owned. The dress was straining around her belly now, even though it was cut generously, so she'd draped a beautiful black and white shawl she'd bought in St Lucia over one shoulder to take people's eyes away from her bump.

The effect was elegance personified and Felix adored it. He'd never said that his mother would adore it or her, though. In fact, there hadn't been many mentions of his mother at all and Hannah was beginning to feel a bit nervous about meeting Mrs Andretti.

'Must go, Josephine and Lizzie,' Felix said now to the two fans. 'I can see our luggage on the conveyor belt.'

With 'good luck' ringing in their ears, Hannah and Felix collected their belongings and left the airport. 'Mum is bound to start cooking when we arrive,' Felix said, explaining why he'd decided they shouldn't bother with a sandwich at the airport. 'Even if you arrive announced, she gets the frying pan out.'

'You mean you haven't told her we're coming?' Hannah asked in surprise as she settled herself in the back of the taxi. She was sure when Felix declared he was bringing her to meet his mother that he'd actually *told* the poor woman he'd just got married and was planning to turn up with a wife in tow.

'No,' he said cagily. 'We're not that sort of family, not into big get-togethers.'

Felix rarely mentioned his family – second-generation Spanish parents, from what Hannah could gather. In fact, she'd learned that from his *TV Times* biography when *Bystanders* began its six-week run. He'd never discuss them with her, merely saying they weren't close. 'They're my past, you're my future,' he'd say mysteriously.

She'd assumed that they were traditionally Spanish, valuing the family and keen on marvellous family feasts where all generations got together. Felix's problem had obviously been that nobody in the family felt acting was a proper job. They couldn't think that now, Hannah decided. Felix's career was on the up. She thought of telling his mother about how successful he was, and the notion of bringing this estranged family back together gave her a warm glow. She'd even secretly studied a Spanish–English phrase book, trying to pick up the odd word so his family wouldn't think she was rude by not knowing any of their language.

'What will I call your mum?' she asked, deciding to keep quiet about Felix's having neglected to tell his family they were coming.

'Vera,' he said.

'That's not very Spanish,' Hannah joked.

'Hannah, love, before we get there, I've got to explain something. Actors take stage names, you know that. Cary Grant was Archibald something or other and John Wayne's real first name was Marion. I changed my name, right?'

'You mean you're not partly Spanish?' she asked. 'It was in the *TV Times*.'

'No.' He shrugged. 'I thought it was a good idea at the time because I'm so blond. You know, the blond Spaniard, I thought I'd get remembered for it – and I have been. But that's the official line, right? My real name,' he said in a whisper, 'is Loon, not Andretti.'

Hannah gaped at him. After going out for months, after getting married, she was only now learning about the real Felix. If he was Felix. She quailed at the thought that he wasn't called Felix either. 'What's your first name?' she asked hesitantly.

'Phil.'

'Phil Loon,' she said slowly. 'I think I prefer Felix, certainly. I can't imagine calling you anything else.'

'Look, my name is Felix Andretti, full stop,' he said firmly. 'I'm just telling you my old name because you're going to meet my family. My mother's never forgiven me for changing it, but you could hardly be an international star of stage and screen and be called Loon. Imagine the fun the critics would have with that: Loon-ey tunes every time I was in something. No, siree.'

'So I'm Mrs Loon,' Hannah said reflectively. She giggled at the improbability of it all.

'I've changed it by deed poll now, so it's official,' Felix snapped. 'Stop making a laugh of it, right?'

'But your accent,' Hannah continued, 'you don't sound totally English. You have a hint of something else . . .' She paused. Felix did sound faintly exotic, as if he'd learned English at public school but had spent his youth in some far-off land.

'Elocution lessons,' he said tightly. 'And I never said I was personally Spanish, just that my family originally came from there. It wasn't a lie, really. I can always say people took me up wrong if it gets out.'

Felix's mother lived in a small semi-detached house in a modern housing estate outside Birmingham. Women with pushchairs clutching children by the hand congregated around the small primary school at the end of the road when the taxi drove up. Opposite the house was a green area with a children's playground and plenty of lush shrubbery.

'It's pretty,' said Hannah, admiring the newish houses with their fashionable picture windows, pointy-roofed porches and decorative brickwork.

'I didn't grow up here, obviously,' Felix said, paying the driver. 'She moved here after we all left home.'

'What about your dad?'

'He's dead.'

'Oh.' Hannah dragged out her small case and realized she'd learned more about her fiancé and his family in the past hour than she had in their entire time together.

Felix rang the bell and the door was opened by a tall blonde woman who filled the doorway with her bulk. In a navy silky tracksuit, she had to weigh all of twenty stone. Her facc was hard, a fact emphasized by the platinum colour of her hair. This woman could not be Felix's mum.

'Hiya, Ma,' said Felix, his vowel sounds curiously flattening out. 'This is Hannah, we've just got married and you're going to be a granny again soon.'

'You better come in then,' said Vera Loon. 'June,' she yelled, nearly deafening Hannah, 'put the kettle on.'

June turned out to be Felix's sister, a dark version of her gorgeous brother. Slim and with the same beautifully chiselled features, she could have modelled in any glossy magazine. But it was obvious that all her time was spent looking after the three boisterous boys who were running riot in their granny's kitchen.

'Congratulations,' June said in a friendly way when she heard the news. 'He's a quiet one, our Phil. Never tells anyone anything.'

He never told me he was called Phil, Hannah wanted to say but didn't.

'Come here, boys,' Vera said. 'Meet your new auntie. You're very brown, love. Been away?'

The three boys were introduced, tea and cake was produced, and everyone sat down at the kitchen table.

Vera was less daunting when she was sitting down and wasn't eyeing you up and down like an airport scanner, Hannah decided.

'I don't know why he couldn't have brought you home before now,' Vera sighed. 'Just like his father, secretive.'

'I was working,' Felix said sulkily.

He looked out of place here, Hannah thought. He wasn't the sort of man you could imagine in a three-bedroomed semi with an ordinary kitchen and a couple of holy pictures on the walls. Felix did look exotic, different. Yet he wasn't, was he? He was an ordinary man with an ordinary family. She wondered briefly what else he'd concealed from her and the rest of the world? Was there more to Felix Andretti than met the eye – or less?

She drank her tea and admired the boys while Felix prowled restlessly around the room, apparently bored. He didn't join in the stilted conversation and made no attempt to rough-house with his nephews, Hannah noticed.

'It's a pity you didn't want us at the wedding,' Vera added sorrowfully. 'I love a nice day out. Tell us when the baby's due, love?'

Hannah's heart leapt for this woman who clearly knew her glamorous son was ashamed of his roots. She patted Vera's hand kindly. 'December,' she said with a smile. 'Of course we'd have wanted you at the wedding,' she said, forgetting that she hadn't been keen on the idea of a big family wedding either. 'It all happened so quickly, what with the baby and everything, we didn't have time to ask you. Felix would have loved it if you'd been there.'

Felix kicked her under the table.

'We got married abroad,' he said quickly. 'You know, to avoid the papers following us. We flew back from St Lucia this morning, actually.'

'We'd love to go abroad,' June said, holding her youngest, three-year-old Tony, squirming on her lap as he gobbled up chocolate biscuits. 'Tony Senior and I haven't been abroad since our honeymoon. Portugal,' she added to Hannah. 'I love Portugal, but with three kids and me not working any more, it's hard to afford foreign holidays. We had Clark the year after we were married, then Adam eighteen months later, and then Tony.'

'What did you work at?' Hannah asked.

'A hairdresser.'

'With your looks, you could be a model,' Hannah pointed out. 'You're beautiful.'

June shuddered. 'Having all those people looking at me, telling me I'm too fat or too old – no way. Phil loves it, but I wouldn't.'

Chalk and cheese, Hannah thought with a little smile. Felix would kill to have everyone looking at him, while his sister was horrified at the notion. Families were strange. United by blood but so utterly different.

'Why'd you go on telling them they'd have to visit us when we get settled?' Felix snapped a few hours later when they were in yet another taxi going to a local hotel.

'They're your family,' she protested. 'You can't forget about them.'

'You've conveniently forgotten yours,' he snarled.

'That's a lie!' Hannah said hotly. 'You'll meet my mother soon and as for my father, as I've told you, he's an alcoholic. Believe me, you wouldn't want him at any function where there was free drink.'

'So it's all right to leave your father out of the fun, but not to leave my family out, is that it?' he said.

They argued all the way to the hotel, Hannah bitterly pointing out that he'd even managed to insult his mother by refusing to spend the night at her home.

'She's got a spare bedroom,' Hannah said. 'She was dying to have us stay, specially since you haven't been home in ages.'

'I didn't want to sleep there when I could be in a nice four-star hotel,' Felix retorted.

'Far from bloody four-star hotels you were reared!' she shouted at him.

'Not any more, sweetie pie,' he hissed. 'Now I'm a fucking star and I've got to behave like a star.'

'Yeah? Well, I can promise you one thing,' Hannah hissed back at him. 'If that's the way you behave as a *fucking* star, there won't be any fucking at all, got it?'

Hostilities were suspended the next day when they visited Vera's again for lunch before heading to the airport. Hannah was gratified to see that Felix was behaving a bit better to his poor mother, even going so far as to invite her to Dublin for a weekend 'sometime . . .'

'We'd love to have you and June and the kids to stay,' Hannah said earnestly as they left. 'I mean that. Our place is a bit small right now, but we'll be moving somewhere bigger and we'd really love to see you then.'

'I can see you mean it, Hannah love,' Vera smiled. 'Look after that son of mine, will you? I'm happy that he's got himself a decent woman at last. And take care of yourself, love, won't you. He's a handful, our Phil, always was.'

'Your mum's lovely,' Hannah said on the way to the airport.

'Yeah, well, you try living with her,' Felix remarked, staring moodily out the window.

Hannah gave up and left him to his sulks. His humour didn't improve until they were in the air when the stewardess smiled and asked him for his autograph '. . . for my sister.'

For you, you mean, Hannah thought grimly as Felix gave the stewardess his most dazzling smile.

Back in Dublin, Felix was his old self, charming, affectionate and funny. 'I'm a bit tense when I go home,' he admitted, holding Hannah's left hand as they drove to her flat. 'I didn't mean to take it out on you, it's just . . . you know, family history. You think I'm being a bastard, but you just don't understand what's happened.'

'How can I know if you won't tell me?' Hannah protested. 'Don't keep secrets from me, Felix.'

'It's not a secret, it's just boring family stuff. Forget about it.'

And with that she had to be content.

CHAPTER TWENTY-SIX

Hugh threw the holiday brochures down on to the coffee table.

'Well, at least *look* at them, Leonie,' he said angrily.

She glared up at him from her position in the armchair, Harris, the Jack Russell, curled up in her arms.

'I've told you, Hugh,' she said, trying to be patient, 'I can't arrange a holiday right now. The girls are due back and they'll need me.'

'They've been gone for two and a half bloody months, they can cope without you for a week at least. Your mother can look after them,' Hugh said dismissively.

Harris wriggled his silky little head and Leonie stroked his velvety ears. He looked like a little bat lying upside down, belly exposed, head lolling back and the bat ears hanging down. He had the most mischievous eyes, little pools of naughtiness.

'They're not kids, they can look after themselves, you know,' Hugh continued.

She could feel the first stirrings of temper deep inside her.

'I haven't been away for a year and neither have you,' Hugh went on. 'Just a week in Italy later this month; maybe two weeks. It'll be black with tourists in August but we'll have a great time.'

'I know it sounds lovely,' Leonie began. It was hard when everyone and their granny were talking about summer holidays and you had nothing planned. But she hadn't felt like taking a break with the twins away and Hugh's idea that they should go away together had come at a bad time. The girls were due home next week and she ached to see them. Every day that passed was a day nearer to her hugging them and telling them she loved them so much. 'I can't leave the girls on their own now,' she pointed out.

'They're happy enough away from you to last for a couple of months without you. They were only supposed to go for six weeks,' Hugh said sharply.

That hurt. The fact that Mel and Abby had wanted to be away from her for nearly three whole months pained Leonie more than she dared tell anyone.

'They may as well stay with us when we go to Charlie's ranch in Texas this summer,' Ray had said on the phone in early July when the girls' six weeks was up. 'They could learn how to ride and have fun. It's only a few more weeks. Abby is blossoming. She's doing so well, why not let them stay, Leonie?'

Mel and Abby had begged to be allowed to stay. '*Please, please*, Mom,' they'd pleaded.

She had given in and then cried for two days afterwards, feeling betrayed by her darling daughters who wanted to spend time away from her. It was different with Danny. He was older and more independent. He'd announced that he was spending a month with pals backpacking around Europe and Leonie hadn't minded. She'd worried and fretted, naturally, afraid he'd come to harm, or be mugged, or get mixed up with drugs or something. But he was twenty since May and it wasn't her job to rein him in any more. Without him and the girls, the cottage was like a morgue. Penny was depressed and even Herman the hamster had gone into a decline, not playing on his wheel or anything.

Even the lure of Portofino in the sweltering heat couldn't drag Leonie away from home once her beloved twins returned.

'I can't go now,' she said reluctantly. 'If only you'd thought of it earlier, we could have gone and come back by now.'

'I'm down on the roster for holidays at the end of this month,' snapped Hugh. 'Anyway, that's not the issue. It's Melanie and Abigail. They're not babies any more. You've got to let them go.'

'That's a bit rich coming from you,' Leonie retorted.

'What do you mean by that?' he demanded.

'Oh, come on, you don't need me to spell it out, do you?' she said, angry now. 'You've got a twenty-two-year-old daughter and you wouldn't let her make her damned bed if you could possibly do it for her! Jane is totally ruined, spoilt. You give her money all the time, even though she has a perfectly good job, and you run to help her at the drop of a hat. Look at that time she got a flat tyre going to a party and you left me sitting like a fool in the restaurant to rush off and change it for her! That's not normal! My girls are still teenagers, they're not even sixteen yet. *You're* the one treating a grown-up woman like a little girl.'

Hugh was staring at her furiously. 'I love Jane –' he began.

'Tell me something I don't know!' shrieked Leonie. 'It's obsessive, it's not normal. And then you accuse *me* of not being able to let my kids go. The words pot, kettle and black come to mind.'

'You have no right to talk to me like that.' Hugh's face was choleric.

'Why not? You think you've the right to say anything to me about my kids, but nobody is allowed to breathe a word about yours. No, not both of them, actually,' Leonie said suddenly, 'only Jane. Poor Stephen never gets a look in.'

The doorbell chimed at that instant. Hugh looked out the window and the stricken look disappeared from his face. 'It's Jane,' he hissed. 'Perhaps we can keep this argument to ourselves?'

'Suits me,' Leonie snapped back.

Jane waltzed in, arms full of bags, with the dogs dancing around her feet.

'Hello, Leonie,' she said, almost friendly. 'I was out in Liffey Valley shopping and I thought I'd drop in on Dad on the way home.'

Leonie stared at the carrier bags. Five bags, all jammed with clothes. All purchased by a woman who still hadn't paid her father back for booking her holiday on his credit card.

'What did you buy?' asked Hugh in his indulgent daddy voice.

Jane beamed and pulled out a lycra black dress that would have looked tarty on a nun. Leonie tried and failed to imagine Jane wearing it. Leonie could never figure out why Jane deliberately bought clothes that did nothing for her shape.

'Bit revealing,' Hugh said, eyeing the garment up and down. 'I suppose you're going to wow them at the office dinner in that?'

They both laughed conspiratorially.

'Do you remember that last party when you picked us up from Buck's and we were all plastered? And when you brought me back to Mum's, you had to carry me up the stairs?' Jane began.

She did that every single time they met, Leonie noticed: started a conversation designed to exclude Leonie. As if to say, *Look at us, we have a history, we talk about things you know nothing of.*

Jane chattered away on the 'Do you remembers . . .' for a few more minutes, shooting Leonie the odd sly glance of triumph.

Leonie picked up Harris again and cuddled him close to her. He favoured her with a couple of devoted licks.

'What dinner dance?' she said, attempting to be polite for Hugh's sake. She couldn't care less about any office dinner and thought the dress was seriously unsuitable for any professional occasion, unless the profession in question involved dancing sordidly around a pole on a stage in front of lots of drunken, drooling men.

'We have a big party every summer,' Jane explained, in the condescending tones of a professor explaining quantum physics to a three-year-old. 'It used to be a barbecue but some of us complained that we wanted a proper do.' She smirked. 'We're having it in the Great Room in the Shelbourne this year. I can't wait.'

Leonie would like to see those photos. The Shelbourne and black lycra hooker dresses didn't match up in her mind.

'I was about to make coffee,' Hugh said. 'Do you want a cup?'

'Yeah,' said Jane, sitting down on the couch and picking up the holiday brochures.

'You going on holiday, Dad?' she yelled after him.

The demon in Leonie's head woke up. 'No,' she said sweetly, 'your father and I are trying to pick a holiday together. He wants us to go to Italy but it's a bad time for me.'

It was gratifying to see Jane's cold little eyes widen in horror.

'Maybe September,' she said thoughtfully. 'I've always wanted to drive along the Italian coast in a sports car. Your dad would love that, wouldn't he?'

She felt marginally guilty for being bitchy to a kid, but then Jane was hardly a kid. She was a kid the same way that girl in *The Exorcist* was.

'I don't know if he'd like that,' Jane said coolly. 'In September, we always used to rent a cottage in West Cork. Him, me and Stephen.'

'But you haven't done that for years,' Leonie said, 'have you?'

'Done what?' said Hugh, coming back into the room with a tray of coffee-filled mugs.

'Gone to West Cork,' said Jane wistfully. 'Oh, Daddy, can't we go again this year? That trip with the girls was nice but to be totally relaxed, we need a week in Clonakilty or somewhere. Pub lunches, traditional music sessions at night, walking on the beach . . . please, let's go?'

She looked like a child, Leonie thought. A child of divorced parents who'd spent years successfully playing one off the other. That was what Leonie had been afraid would happen to Mel, Abby and Danny when she and Ray split up: that they'd become experts at playing on both parents' guiltometers, lowering their eyes at opportune moments and saying, 'Dad would let me do that . . .' Luckily, it hadn't happened that way. But Jane displayed all the symptoms. The only strange thing was, she'd been almost an adult when Hugh and his wife had split up. And she wasn't using her wiles to manipulate them. She only wanted to manipulate Hugh so she could have him all to herself.

Hugh was now considering a cottage in West Cork. 'You could come then, couldn't you, Leonie?'

Without Jane, it would have been an appealing proposition. Leonie was very fond of Stephen and would have enjoyed a holiday with him along. But not with Ms Spoilt.

'I'd have to bring Mel and Abby,' she said thoughtfully.

'I thought it would be just us, Dad,' pouted Jane.

'Leonie needs a break, Janie,' he replied lovingly. 'Maybe the girls could stay with their granny for the week,' he suggested.

Leonie stared at him coldly. 'My family aren't good enough for West Cork, is that it?' she said, her earlier anger and hostility re-emerging.

'It's not that,' Hugh said earnestly. 'The cottage we always go to isn't very big, that's all.'

'Renting a bigger one isn't an option, then?' Sarcasm dripped from every word Leonie spoke.

'We always go to the same one,' Jane said, eyes shining.

Leonie wondered what it was about Jane that made her hand itch to slap her.

Hugh said nothing, not a word about how of course they'd rent a bigger cottage, and what a fool he'd been to suggest Mel and Abby staying anywhere else.

'Fine.' Leonie dislodged a disgruntled Harris from her lap and got up. She ignored Jane and addressed Hugh. 'Go to West Cork, Hugh. You need a holiday. I'm afraid I won't be going with you. I'll phone you. Sometime.'

She picked up her handbag and swept out as regally as she could.

Hugh and the three dogs followed her into the small porch. 'Don't be like that, Leonie,' he begged. 'We could talk about the holiday. The girls might not want to come. It'll seem boring to them after a grand holiday in Boston.'

'You're amazing, Hugh. And I don't mean that in a congratulatory way.' She was wearing heels today so she was much taller than him. She stared down her nose at him now. 'My children come first in my life and if you don't understand that, you don't understand very much about me. I wouldn't dream of going on a "family holiday" without my own family. How dare you even suggest it. Goodbye, Hugh.'

She didn't wait for him to speak, just opened the door and stormed down the drive. She raged against him all the way home. Other drivers seeing her on the dual carriageway must have thought she was mad, talking to herself and gesticulating furiously.

At home, she phoned Hannah, desperate to talk to someone.

Hannah was unpacking boxes in her new house in London and was delighted to be diverted.

'I hate this house,' she moaned to Leonie. 'The kitchen is hideous and dark, and the hall looks as though it was decorated with blue paint left over from a 1940s mental hospital. I hate being on my own here.'

'Where's Felix?'

'Gone out,' Hannah said darkly. 'Tell me your news,' she added abruptly. 'Mine is too boringly depressing.'

'Join the club,' Leonie said sadly.

In her misery, she told Hannah all the little painful things she'd deliberately never mentioned before. About how Hugh thought multiple orgasms were what happened to him when they made love three times. About the time Hugh had cancelled a date because Jane had phoned him with tickets to a rugby match.

'The scheming little cow,' Hannah growled. 'You don't get tickets like that at the last minute. She must have known before, she simply waited until he'd set up a date with you and then sprang her surprise.'

And Leonie spilled the beans about the night Hugh had brought her for a special four-month anniversary dinner in Thornton's only to have Jane ring the restaurant in hysterics over some trauma. They'd paid the bill, left most of their main course, and Hugh had dropped Leonie at the DART while he hotfooted it over to Jane's flat to comfort her. She'd never told anyone that: it felt too shameful, as if she was second rate and would never be first.

'I mean, what did I do wrong?' Leonie asked tearfully. 'Where did I make the mistake with Hugh? I thought we were so good for each other.'

'Don't ask me,' Hannah said. 'I'm no expert on men.'

Leonie laughed, as if it were a joke. 'Yeah, right,' she said. 'The stunning Mrs Andretti who's the pride of the society pages with her gorgeous husband, the man she caught when nobody else could.'

'I swear I only caught Felix because he'd decided he needed a wife,' Hannah said fiercely. 'He had everything else, he needed a wife. Now he's got a pregnant wife, which is very useful for impressing TV and film companies who don't want an unstable, drug-using party-goer starring in their multi-million pound production. They want a reliable family man with huge financial commitments who won't wreck the budget by getting slammed in jail for doing too much coke in the loos at parties.'

'What do you mean?' Leonie was aghast at the anger in Hannah's voice. It was like hearing that Paul Newman and Joanne Woodward weren't the most happily married couple in the world after all. Felix and Hannah adored each other, for God's sake. Didn't they?

'Nobody ever understands Felix, did you know that, Leonie? That's what he said to me the other night,' Hannah said bitterly. 'Up till then, I thought that I understood him, but apparently not. He's been wheeling me around in front of him at parties, telling every journalist he meets about his great love affair, and the reality is that he's so happy to be back in London that he's never home. We lived in Bill's flat for two weeks and I never set eyes on either of them. We moved here on Monday and he hasn't unpacked one box.' Her voice quivered. 'I'm the new publicity angle in his life, for God's sake!'

'You don't mean that, Hannah,' said Leonie, ever the comforter.

'Maybe I don't. If you need a holiday, why don't you and the twins come to stay with me?' Hannah suggested, brightening up. 'Mel and Abby wouldn't mind sleeping bags, would they?'

'No,' Leonie said, thinking that after a luxury holiday in the US, sleeping bags would be very low down the list of Mel and Abby's idea of fun. 'That's lovely of you, Hannah. I'd love it. I'll talk to the girls when they get home. Are you sure Felix wouldn't mind us descending upon him?'

Hannah sounded glum again: 'Felix won't mind. He's never here.'

When they'd finished talking, Leonie hung up sadly. She'd phoned Hannah hoping for comfort and ended up feeling scared for her friend. Hannah was normally so upbeat and now she sounded so down, so depressed, so bitter. It couldn't be a hormonal thing. Men loved to blame every nuance of a woman's mood on hormones, but that was way too simple. Hannah had sounded seriously depressed. Not for the first time, Leonie wished that Hannah hadn't moved away.

She decided to phone Emma to cheer herself up.

Kirsten answered. 'Hi, Leonie,' she said when Leonie introduced herself. 'Em's upstairs. I'll just get her.'

'Hi,' Emma said in over-bright tones when she finally picked up the phone. 'Hold on, Leonie, I'll bring the phone into the other room.'

Leonie could hear a door shut firmly.

'I couldn't talk in the hall in case Kirsten heard me,' Emma whispered.

'Why? What's up?'

'Kirsten's left Patrick.'

'What!'

'Or rather, I should say she left before he threw her out. She had an affair and he found out about it. I think she was flirting madly with everyone for ages and Patrick must have noticed. They were fighting all the time and I didn't have a clue why. But I guess she finally stopped flirting and actually did the bold thing with some guy they both know. Now it's all over, between her and Patrick, I mean. She turned up here this morning with eight suitcases and her favourite pillow, saying the marriage was over.'

'How awful,' Leonie said, aghast. 'She didn't sound upset on the phone, but then, that's the first time I've ever talked to her so I can't tell.'

'She's not upset,' Emma whispered. 'I think she's on tranquillizers or something. Either that, or she expects Patrick to storm up in half an hour and whisk her home, saying he can't bear to be without her.'

'Do you think he will?'

'No. She's really screwed it up this time. Patrick is a lovely guy but he won't stand for that. It's dreadful,' she added reflectively, 'they were great together. Patrick was perfect for Kirsten. He indulged her but he was always the boss. Still, if she's living here, she can help me with Mum. She hates being on her own, so I'm spending a lot of time with her. Kirsten will be able to lend a hand, I hope. Then again, maybe not. She has to leave the house when Mum starts crying, which she does a lot now, poor love.'

'Between you, me and Hannah, we're a right threesome,' Leonie remarked. 'I've broken up with the man of my dreams, you're struggling to cope with your entire family's problems and Hannah is in the depths of despair.'

'What's wrong with Hannah?' asked Emma sharply. She didn't understand how there could be anything wrong with Hannah. Wasn't she pregnant? What more could a woman ask for? Typical bloody Hannah – always wanting to have her cake and eat it too.

'She's a bit miserable about Felix, that's all,' Leonie said, instantly feeling guilty for even mentioning it. Hannah and Emma had barely talked recently. It was obvious that Emma couldn't cope with seeing Hannah so deliriously pregnant. In turn, Hannah was irritated by the fact that Emma didn't do something about having a baby of her own. It was up to Leonie to keep the peace between them, something which was increasingly difficult to do.

'Why?'

'He's a bit useless when it comes to unpacking the boxes,' Leonie said lightly.

'Is that all?' Emma sniffed. 'She doesn't have much to worry her, does she?'

Dispirited by both her phone calls, Leonie decided there was nothing for it: she'd drop in on Doug.

Putting Penny's lead on, she walked briskly down to his house.

He emerged from his studio with tired eyes, his old jeans covered with paint.

'Fancy a walk?' she asked brightly.

He grinned. 'Great idea. I'll be ready in two minutes. We could do a few more miles on the Wicklow Way.'

The answering-machine light was flashing hysterically when she got home from the walk with Doug and the three delirious dogs. Hugh had left four messages, each more anxious than the one before.

'I'm sorry, Leonie. We've got to talk,' he said each time.

Talk to a bloody psychiatrist! she hissed as she pressed the delete button. The walk had calmed her down, although she hadn't told Doug what had happened. He was very intuitive, so he had probably figured out that something was wrong. But he would never pry.

Hugh rang again that night.

Leonie was reasoned and calm this time, having regretted her earlier outburst.

'I respect the fact that you have children, Hugh,' she said, cutting off his 'I'm sorry, Leonie,' before he could even say it. 'And in the same way, you've got to respect the fact that I have too.'

'I do,' he protested.

'You don't seem to,' she said sadly. 'I know that when people of our age meet, we have a lot of emotional and physical baggage, but we've got to learn to cope with that. I find it hard to deal with Jane and you, apparently, find it hard to deal with my children.'

'I don't,' he repeated.

'Hugh, you didn't want the girls to go on holiday with us.' Leonie couldn't think of anything more hurtful than that. 'We're a package deal, Hugh. You get me, you get the kids too. It's that simple.'

'Other people's children are hard to deal with,' Hugh said. 'The only child I ever really got on with was Jane. Even with Stephen I wasn't great. I'm not good with kids.'

'That's a cop out,' she said frostily. 'I made an effort with Jane even though she hates my guts. You won't even try with my children. How often did you want to come here and have dinner with us? Once, that's all. You preferred to meet in town or at your place, and now I know why.'

'Jane doesn't hate you,' Hugh said, still stung by Leonie's remarks about his daughter.

Leonie lost her temper. 'Wake up and smell the coffee, Hugh! She hates any woman who tries to take you away from her. Are you honestly telling me that she doesn't?'

'She's sensitive about my dating someone,' he said.

If it hadn't been such a serious conversation, Leonie would have laughed out loud. Jane, sensitive?

'Hugh, if you think it's because she's sensitive, that's your business,' Leonie said, resisting the impulse to say that Jane was an obsessive, manipulative, control freak who needed a sharp injection of reality to make her cop on. 'I think we should cool things for a bit, step back and consider our relationship.'

'Why?' he demanded. 'That's code for breaking up, you know it, Leonie.'

'It's not. It's giving us time to think. You need to decide if you want to date a woman with three children and I need to decide if I want to date you.'

There was a pause. 'You're very hard about this, Leonie.'

'I'm not being hard,' she said. 'I'm being realistic. I actually worried over whether Penny would get on with your dogs. I should have been worried about whether you'd get on with Abby, Mel and Danny, and how I'd get on with Jane and Stephen. And, crucially,' she paused, 'how they'd feel about us.'

'We can't break up over something so silly,' Hugh blustered.

'It's not silly and we're not breaking up. We're taking time out,' Leonie pointed out. 'I'll phone you in a couple of weeks when we're all feeling less emotional.'

'But what about our holiday?' Hugh wailed.

'Go with Jane.'

When she hung up, Leonie thought about how she felt. Would she burst into tears and head straight for the gin? No. She smiled grimly. She wasn't emotional at all. Hugh had been a nice idea: a lovely man to go on dates with, see films with and have sex with. But he'd been nothing more than that. He wasn't the one to fill her with passion and longing. If he had been, she'd have been sobbing her heart out now. She'd have fought tooth and nail to loosen Jane's stranglehold over him. And he'd have understood how much she loved her kids. He wasn't the One after all.

She went into the kitchen and decided what to cook for dinner. Poor Hugh, she thought as she chopped up vegetables for a stir-fry, he'd never escape from the claustrophobic embrace of Jane. He longed for love and she'd frighten off any woman who dared to get close to him.

Hannah sat on a cushion on the sitting-room floor, carefully unwrapping ornaments from tissue paper. She'd unwrapped everything from the kitchen and had painstakingly put every cup, plate, saucer and bowl away, after carefully washing out the cupboards first. Now she was working on the sitting-room boxes. There were so many of them. How did she have so much stuff?

The front door slammed and the china she'd left on the floor rattled with the vibration.

'Hannah!' roared Felix. 'Are you home?'

Where the hell else would I be? Hannah growled. I don't know anybody, all my friends are in Ireland and I don't have a car. Where am I going to go?

'In here,' she called.

Two hands appeared at the door, one holding a big pink gift bag, the other, an enormous bouquet of lilies.

Then Felix appeared, his handsome face lit up with a giant grin. 'Pressies for you, my love. Because you're the most wonderful woman in the world.'

In spite of herself, Hannah smiled. He strolled over to her, bent down and presented her with the bouquet. She inhaled the wonderful scent.

'There's more,' Felix said, handing her the pink gift bag. Inside was a bottle of champagne which she held up and waggled at him. 'I can't drink, you dope,' she said mildly.

'That's for me,' laughed Felix, taking it from her. 'The rest is for you.'

The rest was a bottle of Chanel's Allure, one of her favourite perfumes, a box of hand-made chocolates that would go straight on to her already swelling tummy, Hannah grinned, and finally, a sliver of amber silk that shimmered as she held it up to admire it. A slinky, short nightdress that must have cost an arm and a leg. An arm and a leg they didn't have. Since the backing had collapsed for the film Felix was supposed to be making in September, money was even tighter than ever.

'Felix,' she said, lost in admiration, 'we can't afford this.'

'Yes we can, my love,' he said, sitting on the floor beside her and nuzzling her neck. 'We're in the money again. They've approved a second series of *Bystanders* and the wages have gone mega.'

'Oh, Felix,' she said gratefully. 'That's fantastic. I was so worried about money . . .'

'And about me, I suppose,' he said ruefully. 'I know, I'm sorry. I'm a bastard to live with when I'm out of work. I've been horrible, but I'm going to make it up to you. Forgive me?'

She nodded tremulously.

Felix began to pull her cardigan off. 'Let's see what this wonderful nightie looks like on,' he murmured.

'Felix, we can't!' said Hannah. 'It's still light. The curtains are open. Anyone could come up the path and see us.'

His laughter was rich and earthy. 'Won't that be fun?'

He dozed off afterwards on the couch, strands of blond hair falling across the perfect profile. Hannah never ceased to be amazed by his ability to sleep anywhere. He could doze off on a plane while she was fretting at the turbulence. He'd even fallen asleep on the Tube with her when they were only travelling from Green Park to Covent Garden. She covered him with his jumper and got up slowly to put the flowers in water.

Her eyes were soft with love as she gazed at him. She loved him, for all his moods and melancholy. It had to be the artistic temperament. The insecurity of acting combined with the soul-searching required for every role: it had to have a lasting effect on a person. That was Felix's problem, Hannah decided. She had to learn to cope with that. You couldn't be an actor's wife and become emotional each time he became depressed. Other people might feel that they never quite knew where they stood with Felix, but not her. She was his wife, the one he brought flowers and love gifts to. They understood each other perfectly. Walking quietly so she wouldn't wake him, she went down to the below-stairs kitchen. She was sure she'd unpacked a vase, but where was it?

CHAPTER TWENTY-SEVEN

Doug insisted on driving Leonie to the airport to pick up Mel and Abby.

'I can't take you away from your work,' she said, knowing he was close to finishing an important painting he'd been working on.

'I was in at the start of this Delaney family drama and I want to be in at the finish,' Doug said. 'Anyway, I need to go into town to see my friend with the gallery. If you come with me, we can have lunch and then go to the airport, killing two birds with one stone.'

'If you're sure . . .' Leonie hesitated.

'What are you like?' he demanded. 'I've said I'm sure. Unless you want Hugh to go with you?'

'No,' mumbled Leonie. She still hadn't said anything about Hugh and the break-up to Doug. She felt so foolish. Doug would be horrified to think that Hugh wasn't interested in the twins. He adored them and he wasn't even dating her. Leonie shuddered. It was appalling to think she'd gone out with a man who didn't care for her children.

'See you at half eleven tomorrow then,' Doug said.

She almost didn't recognize him when he arrived the next day. In all the time she'd known Doug, she'd never seen him out of his shabby old jeans and lumpy jumpers the colour and consistency of wet cement. Today, he looked startlingly different. His wild auburn hair was tamed and brushed neatly back, and he wore a dark grey suit with a deep blue shirt that looked incredible with his hair. A sober steely grey tie completed the ensemble. Leonie stared at the urbane man about town in front of her. He looked so polished and elegant. You'd hardly notice his scars now: they were fading wonderfully. Ever since Leonie had read about the vitamins and minerals which help the body heal, she'd been forcing Doug to take a handful of tablets every morning. He joked that he rattled when he walked, but they, or something, were certainly working on the scars.

'I'm not welded into my old work clothes, you know,' Doug said, a mischievous glint in his eyes as Leonie goggled at him. 'I do have other clothes and, occasionally, I like to dress up.'

'But . . . you look so different!'

'Better?'

She angled her head. 'You look fantastic,' she said, 'but I love your old stuff. I'd never have felt so relaxed with you if I'd met you first like this,' she added. 'As the queen of jumble-stall grunge, I would have been far too intimidated to talk to you in your finery.'

'This was Caitlin's favourite suit,' he said reflectively. 'She hated my sloppy work clothes, insisted I clean the paint off and dress up in the evenings. She thought suits were very sexy. Does Hugh wear suits?' he enquired suddenly.

'Don't mention Hugh, would you?' Leonie groaned.

'Having a fight?'

She nodded. It was easier to let him think that than get into complicated explanations.

In the city, Doug parked outside a gallery in Ballsbridge.

'It will take me a few minutes to bring the canvasses in,' he said. 'Why don't you go in and browse around.'

'I'll help,' she offered.

'You will not,' he said firmly. 'They're heavy. Go on and browse. I'll be with you in a few minutes.'

While Doug and a man from the gallery with mad bouffant hair and a pink tie brought in the paintings, Leonie wandered around, admiring vivid oils and gentle, dreamy watercolours and spiky, aggressive sculptures in the middle of the floor. Everything was very expensive. Doug's paintings would probably be even more costly. Hugh had told her that Doug Mansell paintings were a serious investment.

'You could buy a cheap one from him,' Hugh had said, eyes lighting up as he planned a bit of money-making, 'and in a few years sell it for a tidy profit.'

Leonie had been horrified: make money from a friend? No way.

She was peering at a large modern picture and trying to figure out exactly what it was supposed to be, when the gallery door slammed loudly. Leonie's head swivelled round to see a petite blonde woman march in.

Vivacious would be how you'd describe her, Leonie thought idly. And energetic. Energy fizzled out of the woman like bubbles from champagne. From behind a weird piece of sculpture, Leonie admired the woman's extravagantly red trouser suit, perilously high funky boots and her short, spiky blonde hair. She didn't dye that herself, Leonie thought, with an expert eye. The woman reached Doug and then leaned up to take his face in her hands and kiss him.

Leonie's eyes widened. It couldn't be . . .

'Hello, Caitlin. I didn't think you'd be here,' Doug said evenly.

'I heard you were coming in,' Caitlin answered in a Marlboro rasp.

Leonie did her best to melt into the background. She admired a horrible daub of a painting and tried not to eavesdrop. But she couldn't help it. This was the woman who'd destroyed Doug when she left him.

'How have you been?' Caitlin asked, one small hand still touching Doug's arm.

She was much shorter than Doug, and had to arch her slender neck to look up at him. Vivacious, definitely, with that expressive little face and huge dark eyes. She never stopped moving, one foot tapping constantly as she spoke.

'I missed you, you know,' she said.

'Did you? You never called. You knew where I was living,' Doug answered.

Leonie felt her heart ache for him. He'd longed for Caitlin and she'd abandoned him. The bitch.

Caitlin angled her body closer to his, one hand sneaking up to touch the lapels of his jacket in an intimate gesture. 'You wore my favourite suit,' she said softly, looking up at him.

'Yes.'

One word could say so much. He'd worn it for Caitlin, Leonie knew.

She couldn't take any more of the tortured eye contact between the two of them.

'Bye, darling,' she said, blowing a kiss to the surprised gallery man. 'I'm just popping next door to have a coffee. I'll be back later.'

Rising to the occasion, he blew her a dramatic kiss back. 'Fine, sweetie, see you then.'

Skirt whirling, she left, whisking past Doug as if she didn't know him. It wouldn't be fair to muddy the waters for him. If he wanted Caitlin back, he might not want her to know about his friendship with Leonie.

Not, Leonie thought forlornly as she ordered a decaf and a doughnut in the coffee shop, that there *was* anything to their relationship other than pure friendship. She stirred her coffee miserably, suddenly realizing that she wished there *was* something more to it. Doug was lovely, kind, her friend. She wanted him to be more than a friend. Much more. And she'd had her chance but now she'd blown it.

Don't be stupid, he was never interested in you anyway, she told herself firmly. What could she offer a man who'd gone out with someone like Caitlin, a little bombshell who was well under forty, had a fantastic career into the bargain, and who didn't have to buy granny shoes to fit her huge feet?

She'd bet her life savings that Caitlin didn't have a wardrobe of sloppy leggings and sweatshirts for her fat days. No, if Caitlin had two wardrobes one would be a '*Wow, I'm feeling sexy*' wardrobe and the other a '*My God, I'm bloody gorgeous*!' wardrobe.

She sipped her coffee and stared out the window, longing for Doug to appear and tell her he'd sent Caitlin off with a flea in her perfectly shaped little ear. She'd drunk her second cup and eaten all of her bun when the gallery man appeared at the door. Spotting her, he waved dramatically and sashayed over, his pink tie shimmering into purple under the strip lighting.

'Leonie, is it?' he said.

She nodded.

'Doug asked me to give you this and apologize on his behalf for not being able to bring you to the airport.' He put a fifty-pound note on the table. 'He's sorry he can't bring you, but Mademoiselle Caitlin is having hysterics and he's calming her. "Diva" is not the word for the lady.' The gallery man shuddered distastefully. 'I'd slap her myself, but Doug wouldn't like it and I'm so fond of him.'

Leonie was only half listening. She'd tuned out when she'd heard that Doug couldn't give her a lift because he was comforting Caitlin. Doug was very reliable. He'd never let you down, not in a million years. Except for someone he really loved, someone he'd been away from for a few years and had now been reunited with.

Leonie felt her eyes brimming. She shoved the money back across the table. 'No thanks,' she said, as bravely as she could. 'I don't want it. I've loads of money. Doug was only doing me a favour,' she added.

'Really?' The gallery man's eyes were shrewd under their discreet coating of mascara. 'Don't be a fool, dearie,' he advised. 'I was a fool once and look at me now. Alone. Say your piece, that's my advice.'

Leaving the money on the table, he sashayed off.

Leonie grabbed the money and her bag and rushed out the door. She ran away from the gallery, panting in the August sunshine as she passed lines of cars sitting idly at the traffic lights. Her aim was to be as far away as possible so that she didn't have to catch sight of Doug clutching Caitlin in a loving embrace. Finally, she reached the top of the road and ran round the corner. There was a taxi rank nearby, she remembered.

She was hot and sweating when she finally fell into a taxi, foundation running down her cheeks and her amber silk shirt stuck to her body. Whatever deodorant she'd sprayed on earlier had given up the ghost. But Leonie didn't care. She sat in the back of the car, staring out of the window morosely.

The driver attempted to talk to her but when she answered in monosyllables, he gave up. They were nearing the airport when Leonie realized that she looked a sight, and quickly pulled out her make-up kit to repair the damage. She was an hour early, so she sat in the arrivals hall, and leafed through a magazine, not really seeing the articles. Doug, oh Doug. Why didn't I realize it earlier, she thought in despair. It was too late now.

Most of the passengers from the Boston flight had come out before Mel and Abby burst through the sliding doors, tanned, healthy and glowing, with a mountain of luggage and numerous carrier bags.

'Mum!' they shrieked when they saw her.

Leonie hugged them both, tears falling down her face with delight.

'I'm so pleased to see you,' she said, half laughing, half crying.

'Us too,' they chorused.

'You both look wonderful,' she cried. And they did.

Mel looked fantastic: gloriously brown and beautiful, long dark hair held back in a plait, smart in black nylon trousers and a swirly pink T-shirt with a lilac cardigan tied carelessly around her slim waist. But it was Abby who took her mother's breath away. She'd shot up and was now taller than Mel. The extra height had elongated her body, making it sexily curved instead of stocky. She wore clinging faded jeans that showed off her long legs, along with a tight T-shirt in turquoise, which brought out the electric colour of her amazing eyes. Silver and turquoise American Indian bracelets rattled from her arms and she wore a silver choker round her tanned neck. Her hair, bleached by the sun, feathered around her shoulders and hung down her back. The look was relaxed, *Thelma and Louise*-style, and it suited her perfectly.

'Abby, you look fantastic,' Leonie said, standing back and admiring the beloved duckling who really had grown into a swan.

'I feel fantastic,' Abby said with a broad grin. 'I feel me, not anyone else.'

'She's been reading those self-help books non-stop,' giggled Mel. 'I can't find my inner power no matter what I do!'

'You only find your inner power when you see a good-looking guy,' Abby teased.

As if by magic, a group of young guys weighed down with rucksacks walked past them and shot admiring glances at both girls. Mel, used to it, pouted prettily at them. But it was Abby's reaction that astonished Leonie. She looked at the men with a confident grin and then flicked her head away laughing, her hair shimmering round her shoulders. She exuded self-assurance, Leonie realized. Her baby had come home as an adult.

They talked non-stop in the taxi home.

'I thought Doug was picking us up?' Mel said.

'He couldn't make it,' Leonie said brightly. 'Now, tell me everything.'

Boston had been brilliant, Texas was better. Fliss's father, Charlie, had a ranch in the Panhandle but also had a house near Taos in New Mexico, 'this beautiful, cutesy little place where you can go skiing in winter,' Mel said dreamily. 'It was seriously amazing. Full of these New Age types, which Abby loved. She went out with one, Kurt his name was.'

Once, Abby would have gone puce if her twin had revealed such a thing. Now, she grinned and played with the suede thong that circled one tanned wrist. 'He was a friend, that's all, Mom. Mel wants everyone to be going out. That is *so* last year, Mel.'

At home, Penny went crazy with excitement, her golden body quivering with delight as she licked the twins and sniffed their suitcases ecstatically.

'We missed you,' Abby crooned, sitting cross-legged on the floor with the dog.

Clover ignored the welcoming party and chose to sit on top of the kitchen cupboards, watching the proceedings like a reigning monarch bored with her subjects.

Leonie had half-expected the girls to be disappointed to be home, but they seemed thrilled, delightedly exclaiming how much they'd missed the place, and how irritating it was being ultra-tidy all the time.

'Fliss is, like, obsessed with tidiness,' Mel said. 'You'd hate it, Mom.'

Leonie smothered a giggle.

Mel immediately went off to phone her friends/enemies to tell them what a fabulous time she'd had, how brown she was and what incredible new clothes she'd got, clothes that you'd never be able to buy in Ireland, naturally.

Abby unpacked several small coloured boxes of herb and fruit teabags and offered to make a restorative brew for her mother. She'd given up regular tea and coffee, she told Leonie. She didn't pollute her body with things like that any more. 'You are what you eat,' she said, explaining that fresh, healthy foods were so much better than any processed stuff. 'Lemon is wonderfully revitalizing, I find,' she said as she boiled the kettle, 'although my favourite is cranberry and orange.'

Leonie sat on a kitchen chair and admired her tall, self-assured daughter.

'You look beautiful, Abby,' she said with a catch in her throat. 'I'm so proud of you.'

'Try this,' Abby said, proffering a cup of cranberry tea.

'Lovely,' Leonie said.

'I was abusing my body,' Abby explained, 'I put the wrong things into it and I didn't listen to it. That's why I was depressed and hated myself. But I feel wonderful now.'

Her face glowed, Leonie thought. Her eyes sparkled and she was full of life, confident and happy.

Remembering the confused, angry girl who'd gone away just three months before, Leonie said a small silent prayer of thanks. And she thanked Fliss too. Whatever Fliss had done for Abby, Leonie was truly grateful.

'Fliss has been great, obviously,' she said.

'It wasn't Fliss,' Abby said emphatically. 'It was you, Mom. You did it for me. You've always been so strong and I couldn't be. I was lost in trying to look like someone else. I . . .' she searched for the right words, 'wanted to look like Mel and talk like Fliss but be me. And you can't do that.'

She laughed at the stupidity of the very idea. 'We all owe it to ourselves to be ourselves. The course taught me that. I went to the eating-disorder counsellor for a while, and it was great, but when we went to Taos, I heard about this course. It was about healing and empowering yourself. Mel thinks it's mad, but it was just what I needed. You have to let go of all these silly notions you have of who you are and learn about who you really are. We had to talk about the people who inspired us and –' Abby's eyes were shining – 'I talked about you, Mom.'

Leonie's eyes gleamed too, with tears.

'I told them how you'd been brave to split up with Dad because you knew it wasn't right, because you owed it to you, to Dad and to us, to be with the right person. And I told them all the sacrifices you make for us. I know, Mom, you buy second-hand clothes so we've got lovely new stuff. Don't think I wasn't aware of it. I just never appreciated it before, I guess. When I was away from you, I did.'

'Oh, Abby.' Leonie reached out and took Abby's silver-ringed hand in hers. 'I thought you couldn't wait to get away from me to spend time with Fliss.'

'I couldn't wait to get away from myself,' Abby admitted. 'I was bulimic, Mom. I made myself sick, I'm sorry. I know I lied to you.'

Leonie couldn't speak but held Abby's hand even tighter.

'I can't believe how stupid I was,' Abby continued. 'I mean, you could have a heart attack from bulimia. It ruins your teeth and your gums, hurts your throat from vomiting all the stomach acid up, and it doesn't even work. All it does is destroy you on the inside.' She took a deep breath. 'It was hard telling you that, Mom, because I lied to you. But it's important to face these things.'

She sounded so grown-up, so in control of herself.

'Abby, promise you'll never do it again,' Leonie begged.

Abby put her arms gently round her mother. 'I won't, Mom. I won't for you and I won't for me, you have my word. To stop being bulimic, you've got to do it for yourself. That's what healing is all about. It's not always easy, you know, but I can do it. Especially when I have you with me.'

They sat around the kitchen table all evening, laughing and talking about the holiday. As usual, Mel had photos and, also as usual, she'd decapitated most of her subjects.

She seemed younger than her twin, Leonie realized. Abby had grown so much for so many reasons, while Mel had never had to. She'd have to suffer at some stage, go through the pangs she'd effortlessly avoided now. Leonie knew Abby would be there for her when it happened.

'Mom, I'm hungry,' Abby said, prowling around the kitchen and opening cupboards. 'Do we have any rocket, pesto and pine nuts?'

Leonie laughed heartily. 'No. We'll have to go to the supermarket tomorrow. Does your new healthy-eating plan mean I'll be cooking four different types of meals every day?'

Abby stuck her tongue out wickedly. 'I'll have you eating my way before long, you wait and see.'

'She will,' Mel confirmed. 'She won't let me have double chocolate-chip ice cream any more.'

That night, Leonie got ready for bed feeling as if a giant load had been lifted from her shoulders. Abby was well, more than well, actually. Blooming. That was the most important thing in the world. So what if Leonie had a small ache in one corner of her heart over Doug. She had her girls, her beloved girls. What else did she need? She'd made the mistake of getting involved with Hugh and not noticing what was wrong with Abby. That wouldn't happen again. Men would not be a part of her life in the future, she decided emphatically. Who needed them anyway?

The next day, the three of them went shopping for clothes and school uniforms. School started in a week and Mel needed a new jumper, while Abby needed a new skirt as she'd shot up too much for the other one to fit. When they'd bought everything, they went to the latest Merchant Ivory movie and then to a Mexican restaurant to have something to eat. While she was with the twins, Leonie could forget about Doug. But they came home to find he'd left a brief message on the answerphone saying he'd ring back. Leonie spent the evening waiting for the phone to ring. She didn't know quite how Doug was going to explain what had happened but she still wanted to hear his voice, to hear him say 'Leo' in that tender way of his. The phone rang all right: for the girls, endlessly. Doug didn't phone. He was obviously lost in love and deliriously happy with Caitlin, Leonie decided sadly.

She felt oddly dispirited as she went into work the next day. She should have been thrilled: Mel and Abby were home, delighted to see her, and Danny was due back the following week. But she felt a bit miserable.

'What's up with you?' Angie enquired, as Leonie dumped her belongings and pulled on her nurse's uniform.

'Nothing,' Leonie said, taking the clipboard with the day's instructions on it. There were two dogs booked in for spaying that morning and Angie was doing exploratory surgery on a cat who was suspected of eating an entire reel of thread and a needle.

'Is it the girls?' Angie asked delicately.

'No, they're great. They had a lovely time but they're happy to be home,' Leonie answered. 'Abby looks amazing and she's so happy.' Leonie's voice trailed off. She didn't want to talk about it. Hell, she didn't *know* what was annoying her.

She inspected the surgery's inhabitants. Three cats, one of whom was on a drip, four dogs who'd been operated on the day before and were due to go home, and Henry, a pigeon with a broken wing who glared at her from his cage, outraged to be confined in this way. To prove his point, he picked up his birdseed and threw it out of the cage on to the floor. Normally, this would have made Leonie laugh. Today, she glared back at him. 'Bad boy, Henry,' she said.

Angie answered a phone call from an owner concerned about their dog, while Leonie, Helen and Louise, the other nurses on duty, began bringing the dogs out for a constitutional in the back yard.

'I know it hurts, you poor thing,' Leonie crooned to a sweet nine-month-old boxer bitch who'd been spayed the day before and who was whimpering as she walked shakily out of her cage. The boxer leaned against Leonie, shivering and desperate for reassurance. Leonie hugged her until the frantic shaking stopped. 'You'll be going home today,' she murmured, petting the dog's soft ears.

When all the dogs had been let out and their cages cleaned, she and Louise started on the cats.

Finally, all the animals had been seen to and it was time for morning surgery. Because the receptionist was late, Leonie had to man the desk. She hated working on reception when it was busy and today the place was jammed. People and animals were crowded into the reception area, with dogs howling in misery and a lot of frightened mewing from cats in carriers. By the time the receptionist got there, apologizing profusely because she'd had a flat tyre, Leonie had processed ten people, taken four phone calls, and calmed a hysterical woman who arrived with a vomiting cat.

'It's OK,' Leonie said woodenly.

Relieved of reception duty, she took over from Helen, who was assisting Angie in the operating room. Angie was removing impacted teeth from a poodle, a tricky job. Silently, Leonie took up her position beside the poodle's head, monitoring the dog's breathing and colour. The dog's tongue was a healthy shade of pink, meaning it was doing fine under the anaesthetic.

'Jeez, Leonie, you look like you lost a shilling and found sixpence,' Angie said, without looking up.

'I'm fine.'

'If you're fine, I'm the Queen of Sheba,' Angie announced. 'Tell me what's wrong, for God's sake.'

'Oh I don't know. Something depressed me . . .' Leonie said.

'Hugh?' Angie asked as she triumphantly dropped the extracted tooth into a little dish.

'No. Something happened the other day when I went into town with Doug on the way to pick the twins up from the airport.'

'Ah yes, the reclusive Doug. I saw him the other day,' Angie said. 'You wouldn't kick him out of bed for eating crisps.'

'Angie, you're disgraceful! He's been through so much.'

'And you fancy comforting him?' Angie remarked shrewdly.

'No, I don't. He's a friend, that's all.'

'What was that Shakespeare said about people protesting too much?' Angie went to work on another tooth.

'He *is*,' Leonie insisted.

'And why didn't you get an attack of the miseries when darling Hugh got the big E?'

There was no answer to that.

'Tell me what happened,' Angie ordered.

Leonie did.

'And he hasn't phoned since?' Angie said in outrage.

Leonie shook her head.

'You know what you have to do, don't you?' Angie added. 'See him and tell him how you feel.'

'Don't be daft,' Leonie began. Then backtracked: 'Anyway, I don't feel anything. I was just hurt he hadn't rung to apologize. Well, he did ring, but I wasn't there and he hasn't rung back since.'

'Delaney, don't bullshit me,' Angie barked. 'I know damn well you're crazy about him. You see him every second day, go for long walks with him, have endless cups of coffee in his studio . . . Now don't tell me that's not love, even if it's only just occurred to you that it is. Hell, you saw ten times as much of Doug as you ever saw of bloody Hugh. *Of course* you're in love with him.'

'I didn't know I was,' Leonie said quietly. 'It was when I saw him and Caitlin together that it hit me. I hated her for hurting him so much.'

'Well, *tell him*!'

'How can I tell him when he's obviously with her? What should I do – stomp up to the house and demand to be heard, with her standing in the background mocking me for even imagining I could go out with him? You should have seen her, Angie,' she groaned. 'She's bloody perfect.'

'Not if she dumped him as callously as you say she did.' Angie gave the poodle an injection of antibiotic to help fight infection, then she picked him up to bring him back to his cage. 'You've got to say something to Doug or you'll kick yourself for the rest of your life.'

'Guess I'll just have to kick myself,' Leonie muttered, cleaning up after the operation.

The following week, Danny came home from his trip with a rucksack full of filthy clothes and a million tales of his travels. The twins went back to school, buoyed up with their own tales of travels. Leonie was permanently busy, what with trying to get back into the early-morning routine, along with doing extra hours in work as one of the other nurses was sick and they all had to fill in. She shouldn't have had a moment to think about Doug, but she managed it. She kept thinking of their walks in the mountains, the long talks they'd enjoyed sitting in Doug's kitchen and that wonderful dinner in the Hungry Monk when they'd been so relaxed with each other. She'd never been that relaxed with Hugh, she realized. Even during lovemaking. Or perhaps *especially* during lovemaking. Sometimes, she let herself think what it would be like to make love with Doug, to feel his beard brushing against her breasts as he kissed her . . . Stop it! Furious with herself for moping like a teenager, she took Penny on long, exhausting walks to burn off her nervous energy. She didn't walk past Doug's house: she went in completely the other direction so there was no chance of bumping into him and Caitlin, entwined besottedly with Jasper and Alfie gambolling at their feet. Penny, however, wanted to go their usual way and meet her canine pals, but Leonie dragged her away.

On Friday evening, she got home from her walk to find Doug's jeep parked on the drive.

'Doug's here!' yelled Mel unnecessarily as Leonie arrived.

'Great,' lied Leonie. She hated facing him but there was no option. Fixing a bright smile on to her face, she went into the sitting room where Doug was watching television with Danny.

Doug immediately got up. 'I need to talk to you,' he said.

'Sorry, can't,' Leonie trilled. 'I've got a date with Hugh,' she lied.

'No you haven't . . .' began Danny.

Leonie silenced him with a killer look.

'About last week, I'm so sorry, Leonie. Caitlin turned up and I had to talk to her . . .'

'Fine,' Leonie said brightly, backing out of the room. 'Whatever. I have to go. Bye.'

She ran to her bedroom and slammed the door shut. Then she fell on to the bed, mindless of the fact that she was still wearing her filthy walking clothes, and burst into tears.

He phoned on Saturday.

'Say I'm out,' Leonie whispered.

'She says to tell you she's out,' Danny told Doug.

Leonie rolled her eyes. Tactful it wasn't. Well, it might give him the message that their friendship was over, Leonie decided. If Doug was going to be superglued to the nauseous Caitlin for the rest of his life, Leonie didn't want to have to witness it.

On Sunday, she was walking Penny when she spotted Doug's jeep coming down the road. Frantic to avoid him, she leapt into a nearby field, to Penny's delight. The sheep in the field looked horrified. 'We'll only be here a moment,' Leonie reassured them from her hiding place just inside the gate.

Life went on as usual. Abby enquired why Doug hadn't been round to dinner since they'd got back from America.

'I don't know,' Leonie lied. 'He's busy with a painting, I think.'

Abby gave her mother a knowing look. 'And you expect me to believe that?' she said.

Leonie groaned. 'Not you, too. It's like being on *Oprah* and being advised by the audience on what to do with your life.'

'You're not happy, Mom,' Abby said. 'Anybody can see that.'

'I'm tired, Abby, that's all. Now, if you'll excuse me, I've got to put some washing in the machine.'

Another week limped by. Leonie was on auto pilot for most of it. It was her weekend on in the surgery and on Saturday, the place was jammed with clients and shivering animals. Leonie was monitoring a neutered rabbit when the phone rang for Angie.

'Keep an eye on the rabbit, will you?' Leonie asked Louise. 'I have to get Angie.'

She went into the second surgery and stopped dead. There, holding a quivering and howling Jasper on the examining table, was Doug. He looked harassed, his hair was windswept and he was wearing his walking clothes. He looked tired. Too much sex, she thought grimly.

'What's wrong with Jasper?' she asked immediately.

Recognizing his old friend, Jasper wagged his plumy tail weakly.

'Poor love,' she said, stroking his head.

'He's hurt his paw. The dew claw has been ripped away from the flesh.' Angie was preparing to numb the area.

Jasper howled with the pain and howled even louder when Angie approached him. She had that vet smell, Leonie knew, the smell all dogs hated.

'There's a phone call for you,' Leonie told her. 'Mrs McCarthy, about her cat. It's urgent.'

'Right. I'll be back in a moment.'

Angie left the room.

'Why have you been avoiding me?' Doug asked quietly.

Leonie wouldn't look at him. She kept her head facing Jasper, who had stopped howling but was pleading with her to let him get out of this horrible place.

'I haven't been avoiding you,' Leonie said sharply. 'I've been busy with my life, the way you've been busy with yours.'

'I haven't been busy,' Doug replied. 'I've been lonely and depressed. There's been nobody dropping round at all hours making sure I take my vitamins or dragging me out of the studio to get some fresh air. Nobody to invite me to dinner and feed me home-made lasagne. Nobody to laugh with and talk to.'

Leonie found she'd been holding her breath. She exhaled slowly and shakily. 'What about Caitlin?' she asked. 'The love of your life has come back, you don't need boring old me to make you coffee or talk to. You've got Ms Wonderful to do that with you.'

Before he could reply, Angie swept back into the room. Jasper whimpered again.

'Sorry about that,' she said, staring at Leonie, who was very pale around the mouth.

'I must go,' Leonie said and ran from the room.

She hid in the loo for a few minutes until she was sure she had overcome the desire to cry. Then she went back to look after the rabbit. They were short-staffed today and there were so many animals to keep an eye on; she couldn't leave it all to Louise and Helen.

She'd just closed the rabbit's cage a few minutes later when Angie appeared, followed by Doug and Jasper, who was panting happily and holding up his front paw which was now expertly bandaged.

'You're not allowed in here,' Leonie yelped. 'Jasper's better now. You should go home.'

Angie took Jasper's lead from Doug, who advanced until he was standing very close to her. She could smell the distinctive scent of oil paints and there was a smudge of yellow ochre on his shirt.

'You can fix his paw,' Doug said, 'but you can't fix my heart.'

Leonie stared tremulously up at him.

All the nurses were watching. Even the animals in the cages were interested. Watching humans having a heart-melting drama was more fun than watching the nurses approach with injections and rectal thermometers.

'Doug, what are you on about?' Leonie said, desperately trying to control her emotions.

'You – I'm on about you. You've been avoiding me for two weeks. You won't go for walks with me and you never come to the studio for coffee any more.'

'This is hardly the place to talk about it,' she squeaked.

'You won't talk to me at home, so I had to come here.'

'And you hurt poor Jasper to get me to talk to you?' she enquired.

'No, Jasper knew I was desperate and when he came home today limping, it was the ultimate sacrifice.'

Even at a moment like this, Doug could make her laugh.

'I've never met anybody who can jump to conclusions like you do,' he added.

'That's true,' Louise interjected.

Leonie gasped at the injustice of it all.

'You were convinced that German Shepherd's leg was broken when it wasn't,' Louise pointed out.

'That's not jumping to conclusions, that's imagining the worst-case scenario so you can make the correct decision. I'd prefer to over-react than under-react,' Leonie said.

'You over-reacted when you saw me with Caitlin,' Doug said softly. 'I couldn't bring you to the airport because I had to comfort her. She was in bits because she wanted us to get back together and I told her it was out of the question, that I was in love with someone else.'

Leonie felt tears prickle behind her eyes.

Jasper, getting bored, howled.

'Quiet, Jasper,' warned Angie. 'This is better than *Coronation Street*.'

Everyone laughed. Doug reached out and pulled Leonie towards him. 'I love you, Leonie. If I have to tell you in front of an audience, I will, because I'm crazy about you and that's the only way you'll believe me.' He raised his voice. 'I, Doug Mansell, am madly in love with Leonie Delaney, mother-of-three, big softie and jumper-to-conclusions.'

The audience clapped and the animals who weren't recovering from anaesthetics joined in, howling, barking, yelping and flapping their wings.

'Really?' Leonie said, leaning against him weakly.

Doug kissed the top of her head because her face was buried against his shirt.

'Really. I've spent the past week trying to talk to you and if it hadn't been for Abby, I wouldn't have said anything because you made me think you were still with that bastard Hugh.'

'Abby?'

'She's been plotting with me. If Jasper hadn't rushed things by hurting his paw, I'd have been round this evening to drag you away. Abby is packing a suitcase and I was going to whisk you off to Kilkenny for a romantic few days away. Mount Juliet, two days in a beautiful country estate.'

The audience sighed at the romance of it all.

'I figured the masterful approach was the best, seeing as you refused to even talk to me.'

'I'll kill Abby, the little wretch. She could have told me,' Leonie said.

'You can't. She's looking after the dogs for us,' Doug said. 'Will you come?'

Leonie rubbed the paint off his shirt, then patted his beard. 'Yes, I'd love to.'

The girls sighed again.

'We can't disappoint them,' Doug said, a wicked glint in his eyes. 'They need a kiss for the end of the matinee performance.' And he kissed her so hard that Leonie had to lean against the medicine cupboard to stop herself from falling over.

CHAPTER TWENTY-EIGHT

Seven months later

As she listened to the six o'clock news on the kitchen radio, Emma cut the steaming chicken breast into small pieces and then ladled a large spoon of mashed potato on to the plate. She'd made some gravy for her father's dinner but knew it would be a mistake to give any to her mother. Gravy went the same way as things like baked beans or dark pasta sauces: all over either Emma or the floor. It was an inexplicable fact that the only occasions Anne-Marie became upset at meal times were when she was eating something with the capability to stain. With pale foods, she fed herself quietly with the plastic fork or meekly let herself be fed. With bolognaise sauce, she became agitated and hurled her fork across the room, splattering the furniture and walls till the place resembled a bit of modern art. It was like feeding a child, Emma had thought on many occasions. An adult-sized child who could be surprisingly strong.

'Mum,' she called now, putting the plate on the kitchen table along with a cup of lukewarm tea. 'Mum, dinner is ready.'

When her mother didn't appear, she went looking. Anne-Marie was in the dining room vigorously attempting to open the patio doors. It was her favourite occupation after pacing around the house restlessly and only the fact that the doors were permanently locked with the key carefully hidden meant she couldn't escape. Three months ago, when she'd disappeared one night and had been – mercifully – discovered by the next-door neighbours standing crying in their front garden, Emma had insisted that all the doors and windows remained locked.

Jimmy, shattered by his wife's sudden disappearance from their bed at three in the morning, had nodded mutely. The house was now a mini-Colditz. Anne-Marie had proved herself to be remarkably resourceful at climbing out of wide-open windows. Complicated window locks that allowed windows to be opened no more than a fraction were the only option. Child-proof fasteners on the cupboards and drawers were another innovation, along with a plastic cover for the front of the video after she broke the previous one by sticking a tape in backwards which jammed the mechanism. It would be awful during the hot months of the summer, Emma knew, when they'd long to throw open all the windows. But Emma wondered what would have happened by then. Would her mother still be living at home? She was deteriorating so fast, Emma was sure her father wouldn't be able to cope for much longer. Not that he was coping that well now.

Today, a cool Friday evening in March, Anne-Marie was in a calm mood and patted Emma's arm gently as she was led into the kitchen for her dinner. Emma put sugar in the tea, then sat down beside her mother to see whether she needed help or not. Or not was this evening's answer. Attacking her meal hungrily, Anne-Marie stared into space as she chewed. Her once-pretty face was now devoid of expression a lot of the time, except when she was unaccountably afraid. Those times, her big eyes were wide with some unspoken fear. Fear was one of the few emotions left to her these days. Today, her face was a blank canvas, her eyes glazed over and the muscles slack as she chewed slowly with her mouth open. Emma had never realized how much a person's face relied upon emotions until her mother had become ill. She'd assumed your face was your face, sometimes lit up with thoughtfulness or happiness, always marked with some sort of expression even when you were mentally miles away.

But watching a woman succumbing to the horrible grip of Alzheimer's made it clear to her: the brain was everything. When that was slowly being eaten away by the ruthless progression of the illness, the face became just another body part. All the humour or intelligence seemed to have faded away. Anne-Marie didn't talk much any more; except for murmured ramblings or the occasional angry moments when she threw things and then cried pitifully for Jimmy.

She still said people's names out loud and she recognized them – Emma, Kirsten, Jimmy, and Pete especially for some reason. But putting the right name to the face was often beyond her. She called Emma 'Kirsten' most of the time, which Emma no longer minded. She was thinking ahead to the time when her mother wouldn't recognize her and wouldn't be able to call her anything.

'She'll know you're important to her but she won't actually know who you are any more,' the kind Alzheimer specialist had explained to them all on the sobering day three months previously when he'd made his diagnosis.

Of all of them, Jimmy had been the most shocked by those words. Emma had long since read every book about progressive dementias that she could lay her hands on. She knew all the painful details, from the slow, gradual loss of faculties to the final indignities of incontinence, and liquid meals if, as sometimes happened, the patient stopped being able to swallow. With her usual forbearance, she'd forced herself to read every horrible detail.

Kirsten refused to look at any of the books her sister bought, while Jimmy had resolutely insisted that there was nothing wrong that couldn't be cured.

An operation, he said gruffly, that's what was needed.

He'd built a lovely conservatory for this doctor once and the man knew all about brain surgery. That was it.

They trekked to see a neurological specialist who had looked candidly at Emma across the room and kindly tried to explain to Jimmy O'Brien that it was unlikely that any surgery could help his wife. He could probably have explained what was wrong with her but, instead, recommended them to the gentle, helpful Alzheimer expert who'd managed to impart his dreadful news as compassionately as he knew how.

Only an autopsy would confirm his suspicions, he explained, because of the nature of dementias. But he was pretty certain Anne-

Marie O'Brien had Alzheimer's. She would eventually need twenty-four-hour nursing care.

Jimmy had looked as if he might cry for the first time in his life. His big shoulders were slumped in defeat, he wasn't the booming, hearty Father Christmas any more, but a broken shell of a man. Kirsten looked out of the consulting room window, her face impenetrable. Only Emma had talked to the specialist, discussing what they should do for the present, what sort of treatment, if any, Anne-Marie would benefit from, and what nursing homes he could recommend. Jimmy and Kirsten went outside: Jimmy to sit with his wife, who'd been outraged to be left with the specialist's nurse while the rest of them went in for a chat; Kirsten for a forbidden cigarette.

It was easier to talk frankly without them in the room.

'My father has trouble dealing with this,' Emma said.

'It's hard for everyone. I can't think of many people who would find it easy,' the specialist replied. 'The difficulty is that you will be the person coping until the others come to terms with your mother's illness. Your sister also has trouble with it . . . ?' he probed gently.

Emma nodded. Now was not the time to get into Kirsten's blinkered view of life. Like the naughty toddler who thought that if they covered their eyes and couldn't see you, you could no longer see them, Kirsten believed that nothing could hurt her unless she actually looked it straight in the eye.

'In practical terms,' Emma began, getting out a notebook to record exactly what he said, 'where do we go from here? How long is my mother likely to continue the way she is now?'

At the time, she was often agitated and, while talkative, couldn't remember conversations or incidents or even meals. Minutes after having lunch, she'd angrily complain that she was being starved and wanted something to eat.

The specialist explained that it was impossible to work that out. The illness progressed at different speeds. Some people stayed at one level for ages; others, like Anne-Marie, became worse with dizzying speed.

He pointed out that Alzheimer's worked along a step system: a person could be on one level for a while, then drop to the next step, never to go back up. The descent was irreversible.

Drugs could help in the early stages but, ultimately, the progression continued. Because Anne-Marie was a young patient, she could live many years with the illness. Moreover, as she was energetic and had a tendency to move around a lot, caring for her could ultimately be harder than for an older, less mobile person. She would need a secure, specialized unit which would inevitably be expensive. If she became more agitated than she was now, he would advise admitting her to the psychiatric hospital to try and help her with drug therapy which would at least help her to sleep.

'Some people wear themselves out walking constantly; others want to eat all the time because they forget they've been fed, and then they put on huge amounts of weight. Every patient is different, each one is unique. But,' he leaned forward in his chair, 'the patient isn't the only patient, if you understand what I mean. The whole family is affected by Alzheimer's. The family needs to be looked after and often that's where the biggest problems occur. The principal carer has a lot to put up with. Will you be the principal carer?'

'I don't know,' she said honestly. 'I have a job and, up till now, my father was trying to work from home on the phone. I'd drop in every evening to see how things were going. But the past month, he's had to take time off because my mother wouldn't let him leave in the morning.'

The specialist nodded. 'She's afraid. Think about it: she looks at her house and she doesn't always recognize it. She knows she's alone but she has no concept of for how long or when someone she knows is coming back. It's terrifying. She needs someone with her all the time, I'm afraid.'

It had been a long hard road since they'd been given the diagnosis. A combination of family and friends had chipped in to help look after Anne-Marie. Emma spent most Saturdays with her mother and dropped in three times a week in the evenings, cooking and cleaning. Her father now worked part-time, leaving the bulk of the work to his second-in-command, while two neighbours sat with Anne-Marie for a couple of mornings each week, to give Jimmy time to work.

Kirsten turned up on Sundays to help, but was no good during the week as she said she was worn out with her new job as a dentist's receptionist. Even awful Aunt Petra rolled up on Friday mornings to sit in the house, although Emma wasn't sure if this was a good idea or not, as Aunt Petra had a bad hip and osteoporosis and was likely to break something going up and downstairs after the constantly moving Anne-Marie.

What they really needed was some qualified help, Emma felt. Her mother was no longer sleeping well and was reaching the point where she needed more specialized care than a well-meaning band of friends and family doing their best.

But Jimmy wouldn't hear of it; it was as if he'd managed to convince himself that nothing too awful could really be happening if they didn't have specialist care for his wife. Having family and friends around meant things were all right, weren't they? Once there was a care worker or nurse in the house, then he would have to give in and admit that there was no light at the end of the tunnel.

Stubborn as usual, he and Emma had had several rows about this.

'We're not having any nurse,' he'd said angrily. 'There's no need. I can look after your mother myself.'

But you're not looking after her yourself, Emma wanted to say. You've already got help and you need more. Hating herself for not saying it, she left. Over eight months of therapy had taught her that when she found herself unable to say what she wanted to, it was wiser to simply leave. That way her father would know she was angry and didn't agree with him, even if she wasn't strong enough to say so to his face.

As a stand, it wasn't emphatic enough but it was something. She poured her mother some more tea, making sure the cup was out of her reach until enough milk had been added to make it suitably lukewarm.

Anne-Marie took it and drank it straight down, spilling a little down the front of the pink pleated blouse she'd adored when she bought it in a sale in Ashley Reeves years before.

'Twenty pounds down from fifty!' Anne-Marie had crowed

delightedly that day, waving the pretty blouse with the mother-of-pearl buttons. 'It'll go beautifully with my grey skirt.'

Emma wiped away a tear from the corner of her eye at the memory of those days and sighed. Heartache and tiredness fought for supremacy. Exhaustion won. It was the second outfit her mother had spilled food on that day. More clothes to wash.

Emma had been bringing her parents' clothes home to wash them herself because Jimmy really wasn't much good with the washing machine. The amounts were getting bigger all the time and Emma was struggling desperately to keep up. Anne-Marie had been so conscious of how she looked; always immaculate and beautifully dressed and made up. Emma was determined to make sure she stayed that way, no matter what.

She wondered briefly whether a nurse would apply Anne-Marie's beloved make-up every day the way she tried to. Probably not. Make-up would be far down the list and yet it was strangely important.

They desperately needed a nurse, someone qualified to step in some of the time. It was expensive, Emma knew, but her father wasn't a poor man. He could afford to pay for some nursing care. Except that lack of funds wasn't behind his stubborn resistance to the idea.

'Anyone home?' called Kirsten's voice from the hall. 'It's me.'

'We're in the kitchen.'

Kirsten ambled into the kitchen, threw her jacket on a chair and slumped down beside Emma, not going near their mother to greet or kiss her.

The months she'd been parted from Patrick had certainly changed her: she'd lost that expensive sheen that came from having a husband well off enough to provide endless hair and beauty treatments as well as ensuring that she didn't have to work.

Now her job as a dental receptionist meant she no longer had the money to have her hair constantly cut and coloured, and the twice-weekly manicures were a thing of the past. Her hair was longer, honey-streaked with darkening roots, and her make-up was patchy after a long day at work and no time to run to the loo every five minutes and primp. Only her flamboyant leopard-skin handbag and large engagement ring were signs of the old Kirsten.

Patrick was fighting tooth and buffed nail to keep his fortune from Kirsten's grasp, but he hadn't asked for the ring back.

'What's up, Sis?' she asked. 'I don't suppose there's any tea going? I could murder a cup.'

'In the pot,' Emma said. 'Say hello to Mum.'

'Hi, Mum,' Kirsten said without any real feeling. She dragged herself to her feet with the weary air of a post-twenty-six miles marathon runner and investigated the teapot. 'This is cold,' she announced. 'I'll make more.'

'What are you doing here?' Emma asked, irritated by her sister's lack of interest in their mother.

'At a loose end. Thought I'd drop in and see what you were up to tonight. Maybe you'd fancy a movie or something.'

Emma suppressed the desire to snap that if Kirsten had time to spare, she could have used it in looking after their mother more often. That wasn't fair. They had to have a life beyond caring for her. And Kirsten was lonely since the break up of her marriage.

She no longer had the money to run with her old crowd. Popping off to New York for a spot of shopping or Meribel for skiing wasn't an option any more, nor was running up huge bills in ritzy restaurants. Too embarrassed to drift back to the friends she'd known before she got caught up with the rich, trendy crowd, Kirsten appeared to live a rather solitary life and had taken to dropping in on Emma and Pete a lot, bringing the newest video release and giant tubs of Pringles.

'We've nothing planned,' Emma said. 'Pete's working late and we were going to have a takeaway. Why don't you join us?'

'Yeah,' Kirsten said, 'maybe I will.'

When her mother had finished eating, Emma escorted her upstairs for the difficult ceremony of changing her blouse. Anne-Marie coped with being fed quite well most of the time and didn't seem to mind having her teeth brushed, although she swallowed more toothpaste than she spat out. But having her clothes changed was like a red matador to a bull. As soon as one button was undone, she began to rage at Emma, pulling her arm away and squealing as if she was being hurt.

'Jimmy,' she roared plaintively. 'Make her stop!'

'Mum,' Emma said as calmly as she could while dodging blows, 'we're just changing your blouse. You know you hate wearing anything dirty . . .'

'Jimmy,' roared her mother louder.

Where was bloody Kirsten when you needed her, Emma fumed.

'Jimmy, Jimmy, Jimmy . . .'

The front door slammed and heavy footsteps pounded up the stairs.

'What are you doing with her?' screeched Jimmy O'Brien, appearing at the door, his face like thunder.

Anne-Marie, hearing more yelling, began to scream even louder.

'Jimmy, Jimmy! Help me!'

'I'm here!' he yelled back, trying to hug his wife. But she, upset now, dragged herself away from him.

'What have you done to her?' he accused Emma.

Tired after the long morning and afternoon looking after her mother, Emma just sank back on to the bed. 'Nothing,' she said dully. 'Trying to change her blouse because she got dinner on it.'

'That bloody blouse doesn't matter,' Jimmy yelled.

Something in Emma snapped. She'd taken a half-day from the office so her father could have an entire day to work. She was tired after working until nine the day before on paperwork she wouldn't have time to do today. And it had been an exhausting afternoon with her mother successfully emptying a bottle of toilet cleaner all over the landing, which had taken ages to clean up.

Those bottles were not childproof, no matter what they said on the label.

Now she stared at her father, feeling the white heat of fury racing through her veins. 'The blouse is very important,' she said, her voice low and calm so it wouldn't upset her mother any further. 'Mum likes to look nice. It's always been very important to her. The problem is that I am not trained in changing the clothes of somebody like Mum. Only a trained carer would be able to do it without upsetting her, as you know.'

Jimmy started to interrupt. 'Listen to me –'

But Emma couldn't. She got up and left the room to her father's outraged demands that she get back there immediately, young lady.

She found Kirsten eavesdropping at the bottom of the stairs.

'Way to go, Sis. I take it we're leaving?'

Emma nodded grimly. She couldn't allow herself to speak.

Arriving home, she got out of the car and waited for Kirsten, a throbbing headache growing behind her eyes. She wanted to scream and yell at herself for being such a coward, for not telling her bloody father exactly what he could do with his nastiness, bad manners and total unappreciation for all she did. She'd had the chance to say all those things and she'd certainly been angry enough but, yet again, she'd failed. Impotence was her middle name. Along with weak-willed, stupid and plain old pathetic. Elinor would not be impressed.

'You look miserable,' Kirsten said when she slid elegantly out from behind the steering wheel of her car, bearing the inevitable Pringles and a giant bar of Toblerone. 'I hope it's not because you're planning to phone Dad up and apologize for walking out on him in mid-flow. He hates to lose the audience when he's warming up for the big fight. You are a bad girl.'

Her sister grinned weakly. Kirsten always managed to defuse things with her blithe unconcerned manner.

'The only thing I'm planning to do tonight is watch whatever terrible movie you get out of the video shop and stuff my face with pizza.'

Pete took one look at Emma's taut little face when he got home and said they were all going out to dinner.

'To hell with the budget,' he said, hugging Emma. 'You need cheering up and I don't need you to tell me why.'

They went to a small Italian restaurant and gorged on home-made pasta and wonderful ripe red wine, finishing up with complimentary glasses of grappa because Kirsten had smiled so beguilingly at the owner that he had to pull up a chair and talk to them, making cow eyes at Kirsten.

It was when Emma was weaving her way tipsily back to the table after a trip to the ladies that she overheard Kirsten and Pete deep in heated conversation as they waited for the bill.

'I'd like to smash his bloody face in, you know,' Pete was saying, unusual venom in his kind voice. 'When I think of the amount of time she spends with your mother, looking after her, doing bloody everything . . . For Emma's sake, I never say anything because I think she can do without another bossy bastard in her life, but one day I'm going to tell your father exactly what I think of him!'

'Don't hold yourself back on my account,' Kirsten said lightly. 'He's not on my list for the Nobel Peace Prize either and he adores me. Emma's problem is that she's got to confront him herself. I don't know why she hasn't done it years ago.'

Despite the insulation of wine and grappa, Emma felt miserable again. It was no good bolstering herself with alcohol to hide how she was feeling. She was kidding herself. Only confronting her father would help. But there were so many terrible things happening to him right now that it would be cruel to fight with him. It wasn't his fault that she hadn't had the courage to stop him browbeating her years ago. She couldn't kick him when he was down.

'Will I stay in the bathroom longer to give you pair more time to talk about me?' she enquired, walking to the table and dropping a kiss on Pete's bald head.

'Sorry, love, we were only talking about your damned father,' Pete said guiltily. 'I know you don't want me to interfere, but I'd prefer to say something to him. It's not right the way he treats you and I can't stand it any longer. You're like some indentured servant to him and it's about time somebody stood up to him and said so.'

'Oh, Pete.' Emma sighed. 'Poor Dad has so much to cope with right now, with Mum being ill. We can't say anything. Let me handle it, please?'

Kirsten and Pete shrugged in unison.

The next day, Emma drove reluctantly to her parents' house. It was a glorious sunny morning with not a cloud in the sky. Just the sort of day when she and Pete liked to laze around in the garden, enjoying the sun and getting lost in the weekend supplements, reading bits out to each other and cooking lazy food like scrambled eggs. Or perhaps visiting the garden centre to see what new plants they could buy and kill. Neither of them were very good gardeners; their handkerchief-sized plot of lawn was patchy, to say the least, and the petunias which the garden-centre assistant had sworn blind would flourish anywhere, were all depressed and stunted. Only the little purple flower that Emma suspected was a virulent weed was doing well. It already covered the rockery, surrounding her purple heathers, and was about to make a hostile takeover of the bulbs which were struggling to sprout above ground.

Instead, she had to spend three or four hours looking after her mother because her father had an appointment for lunch with an old pal. She felt guilty at how much she dreaded the day ahead of her.

How did nurses and care staff do it, she wondered miserably as she sat at a red traffic light with the windows rolled down, enjoying the last bit of fresh air she'd get for hours because there was no way Anne-Marie could be trusted with any window open. Surely it was an impossible job to care for people whose minds were slipping away and who veered between wild mood swings that could make you laugh or cry?

It was different when you weren't related to the person, Emma supposed. It mustn't hurt so much when an Alzheimer patient shouted angrily at you if they were just that: a patient, instead of the mother who had cared for you as a child.

Her father was waiting for her inside the hall door, his jacket on and the car keys in his hand. He looked agitated.

'You're late,' was all he said, as he marched past her. 'I haven't made her any lunch. She's having a bad day.'

This turned out to be an understatement. Emma found her mother locked in her bedroom surrounded by the contents of her wardrobe, Jimmy's wardrobe and all their drawers. Socks, shirts, blouses, trousers, handkerchiefs lay in heaps around her. Anne-Marie, dressed only in a slip and tights, was making piles of things on the bed, carefully placing garments on top of each other in a perilous heap until they fell over and she started again.

Her long, once-cared for hair was tangled and unwashed, her face was make-up-less and she didn't wear any of the jewellery she so loved. Not an earring or her wedding and engagement rings, which she'd never taken off. She wouldn't have left her bedroom in the morning without making sure she was wearing at least her pearl studs and a necklace. And the only time Emma could remember seeing her mother with her hair that messy had been years ago when she'd been ill with a virulent flu.

Emma felt her eyes brim with tears.

Two hours and several tantrums later, Anne-Marie was dressed in a navy blue dress, with her pale hair gleaming and her make-up carefully applied. She admired herself in the hall mirror while Emma cooked some pasta for their lunch.

Whatever bad mood Anne-Marie had been in, she'd recovered. Now she sang to herself in a high voice, occasionally dancing into the kitchen to smile sweetly at her daughter. They had lunch and then retired to the sitting room where Emma switched on the TV. A black-and-white movie was just starting.

'Mum, sit with me and we'll watch this,' Emma said, patting the cushions on the couch.

Her mother sat obediently beside her. Anne-Marie rarely looked at the television any more but she loved old films, particularly musicals. Now she curled up beside Emma and watched the beginning of *Now Voyager*.

If anyone had seen them, they'd have thought it was a touching tableau of a mother and daughter watching a film together, Emma thought wistfully. In reality, it was different. Would she ever have her own daughter to sit and watch television with? Maybe not.

But why not? Emma sat up straighter on the couch. What was stopping her? She didn't know if she was infertile or not. Until she found out for certain that she couldn't have a baby, why mourn as if she couldn't? Life was too precious to waste in an agony of not knowing. Anne-Marie began to sing her own tuneless song and Emma stroked her arm. If ever there was proof that life was too precious to waste, it was her mother. She should have had years left to enjoy her life; instead, she was locked in this terrible illness, her life as good as over.

Emma couldn't waste the rest of her life. She wouldn't. Fired up with sudden, glorious enthusiasm and feeling like St Paul on the road to Damascus, she was desperate to tell Pete.

It took him a while to answer the phone. 'I fell asleep reading the papers,' he admitted. 'I was so tired.'

Emma smiled.

'What's up, Em?' he asked, yawning. 'Is your mum all right?'

'Do you remember when we talked about having tests done to see why I wasn't getting pregnant?'

'Yes,' said Pete hesitantly.

'Do you still want to do it?' Emma asked, her heart thumping.

'Absolutely.' He'd never sounded more sure of anything.

'First thing on Monday morning, I'm going to the doctor,' Emma announced. 'I want a baby, Pete. I've been stupid putting this off for so long, but I didn't think it was the right time with Mum so sick. It's the right time now, though.'

'Oh, Em, I love you, you daft thing,' Pete said. 'What made you decide now?'

'Sitting here with Mum did it,' she explained. 'Her life is just slipping away, day by day, and here am I wasting mine because I can't face the truth. If we can't have a baby, we'll adopt. Anything is better than doing nothing, which is what I've done for years. I've been so stupid.'

'Don't be so hard on yourself, Em,' he said.

'I'm not, but I have wasted time. You need to be on the adoption list for years before you get the go-ahead to adopt a baby from abroad; I've wasted too much time already.'

'Let's see if we can have our own baby, first. I've been reading about that IVF thing. There's a twenty per cent success rate, mind you, so if it doesn't work the first time, we'll try, try and try again.'

'It's not cheap,' Emma said.

'If I have to sell my body to finance it, I will,' joked Pete. 'Seriously, love, we'll manage. This is the most important thing in the world. We'll borrow the money if we have to, I don't care.'

'You're wonderful, do you know that?' Emma said.

'Ditto. Come home soon and we can practise getting my specimen in the paper cup!'

It was well after seven before Jimmy came home. Emma was exhausted and longed to go home to Pete so they could make plans. She was eager for it to be Monday morning so she could start on her quest to discover what was wrong with her. Whatever it was, she was sure they'd overcome it. She and Pete were going to be parents, that was definite.

Jimmy was in a foul mood. 'Did you not make any dinner for me?' he demanded as soon as he realized that there was nothing inviting waiting in the oven for him.

Emma stared at him. He was unbelievable.

'No,' she said coolly. 'I didn't make any dinner for you because I assumed you'd be home long before this.'

'That's marvellous. I reared you and you can't even make me a bit of dinner. Listen to me, my girl . . .'

'No,' Emma said sharply. 'You listen to me. I have been here all afternoon on my day off looking after Mum and the first thing you do when you get back is shout at me. It's just not good enough.'

'Don't take that tone with me, young lady!' Jimmy roared.

For once in her life, Emma didn't quail. This was a day for firsts. She'd made a momentous decision to do something about a baby, now she needed another momentous event.

'Don't talk to me like that,' she said, ice in every word. 'Because if you do, I'm walking out that door and I'm not coming back, and then you're going to find out exactly how much I do for you.'

'Rubbish,' he shouted at her.

'When you have to look after Mum full-time without my back up, when you have to clean this house for yourself and wash and iron your own clothes, perhaps then you'll be sorry, Dad.'

'Kirsten would do it in a flash,' he snapped.

'Kirsten wouldn't be bothered,' she replied witheringly. 'She has her own life and she figured out how to say no to you years ago. I've only just learned.'

She picked up her handbag. 'I won't be back until you've apologized,' she said.

Jimmy's face lost some of its bluster. 'What about your mother?'

'We need to discuss nursing care, whether you like it or not.'

'I don't like it,' growled her father, 'and it's my decision.'

'I'm afraid it's not your decision alone. It's mine and Kirsten's too. It's getting to the point where we can't look after Mum on our own. Either you get carers to come to the house, or she needs to go to a nursing home where she'll get specialized care. And you can stop the bullying, Dad, it doesn't work any more.' She ignored her father's furious mouthing. 'And *never* talk to me like that again. I'm looking after Mum because I love her, not because of you.'

She drove home fast, pushing her foot to the floor in an attempt to get rid of the nervous energy she was experiencing.

She waited for the guilt to come, the overwhelming sense that she'd failed everyone who loved her by giving in to an appalling display of temper and ungratefulness. Nice girls didn't fight with their fathers. But it didn't happen; she didn't feel any guilt, only a glorious sense of release.

She'd been seething with anger and resentment for all her life but had kept it to herself. Anger was bad, unfeminine, destined to make people hate you. Or so she'd thought.

Today, she'd discovered that wasn't true at all. Pete, whom she loved, would be delighted with her for standing up to their father. Did it matter if her father was angry with her? He'd been angry with her since the day she was born, for no apparent reason. She'd given him a valid one, that was all. And he needed her more than she needed him. She didn't need him at all. It was a heady feeling.

She found Pete making dinner and she ran to him, throwing her arms around him.

'You haven't changed your mind, have you?' he asked anxiously.

'Far from it,' Emma said. 'It's been quite a day.'

The next day, they lazed late in bed.

'It's nice to have you to myself,' Pete said, wrapping his body around hers.

'I suppose I have been spending a lot of time with Mum,' Emma sighed. 'I hope she's OK. It's her I feel guilty about.'

'Your father is the one responsible for all this,' Pete said. 'He's abused you and the only way to teach him a lesson is to be tough. Tough love.'

'He can't cope and he can't admit it,' Emma said.

'That's his problem. You can't take the troubles of the world on your shoulders, Emma. You've been at his beck and call since you were born. It doesn't mean you're a bad daughter just because you need your own life away from that bully.'

She snuggled against him, enjoying the feel of his body against hers.

'It's sad,' she explained. 'I'd have sympathy for anyone in Dad's situation but I can't reach him. Our relationship is so bad, I'll never be able to do that.'

'You look after your mother,' Pete pointed out. 'Making sure that she's well taken care of is the most important thing. Don't let him use that to manipulate you.'

'I won't.'

In the end, Kirsten got involved.

'I can't believe you're doing this,' Emma said a week later as they drove to the hotel where they were going to meet their father and the carers they were to interview for the position of looking after Anne-Marie.

'He's never off the phone to me,' Kirsten complained. 'He can't use the washing machine, that was the first problem. He broke the Hoover yesterday and, as for the microwave, forget it. I told him I wasn't his bloody slave and he could learn how to do it himself. And,' she smirked, 'I gave him a piece of my mind for being so nasty to you. Told him you'd been a far better daughter to him than I ever had and that he didn't deserve to see you ever again.'

'You didn't!' Emma was lost in admiration. 'That was sweet of you.'

'Well, if he's got you to lean on, he won't be on the phone to me all the time, so there was a certain personal motive behind my sweetness,' she admitted.

Emma laughed. Kirsten never changed.

'It's been an awful week,' Kirsten protested. 'I had to get him off my back somehow. Still, it worked. He's finally realized that he can't look after Mum on his own, mainly because you did so much.'

Jimmy seemed to have diminished when they saw him standing in the hotel lobby. He looked smaller, thinner. Emma felt the old guilt that she shouldn't have left him on his own to look after Anne-Marie.

Kirsten poked her in the ribs. 'No getting all maudlin and apologetic,' she warned. 'Dad has to apologize to *you*, not the other way round. Mum's illness doesn't allow him to be an even worse bastard than he already is.'

Apologies weren't Jimmy's forte.

'Hello, girls,' he muttered. 'I said I'd meet them in the bar. We should go in.'

'Don't you have something to say, Dad?' Kirsten enquired.

He looked Emma in the eye for the first time. 'I'm sorry,' he said gruffly. 'I wasn't fair on you the other day.'

'Apology accepted,' she said formally. That was as good as it was ever going to get. Her father would never acknowledge that he had more than just the other day to apologize for. But it was her own fault for being such a victim. She'd let him walk all over her. Still, if they could get on well enough to look after Anne-Marie together, that was good enough.

'Shall we go into the bar?' she said brightly. She wanted to get this over with. Now that she felt she'd made a new start with her father, she was dying to tell Kirsten her news: that she and Pete were on the baby trail and nothing was going to stop them having one. Nothing.

The results were unexpected. There was nothing wrong with either of them. Pete's sperm count was excellent and Emma had no blockages, scarring or obvious reasons why she'd never conceived.

'There is absolutely no reason why you can't have a baby,' the specialist said. 'We call it unexplained infertility.'

It sounded so inconclusive, so unconvincing. Emma found it incredible that in a world of modern science where everything was transplantable and where mice could grow human ears on their backs, infertility like hers could be inexplicable. But unexplained infertility left her with that most precious commodity: hope.

'Some people in your position wait and hope, but as you've waited and hoped for quite a while, you could try the IVF option,' the specialist said encouragingly.

Outside the clinic, Pete had held her hand so tightly that it hurt. She could see him biting his lip and knew he was afraid to even look at her, afraid that she'd go to pieces. Yet for some unaccountable reason, she didn't feel upset: she felt relieved. As if a millstone had been cut from the rope where it hung around her neck. Her inability to have a baby was inexplicable, not something she'd done, not some flaw within her traitorous body, not a problem that couldn't be fixed. The cleverest minds had told her so. The fear and dread of the result was out of her hands.

After years of being scared to discover the truth, she now knew it. And it was cathartic, like a balm to her soul. Because unexplained infertility meant hope.

'Pete . . .' She swung around to face him, stroking his tense face, feeling the soft skin where he'd shaved a few hours before. 'I'm not upset, love, really I'm not.'

He didn't believe her; she could see that. His normally open, smiling face was racked with grief for both of them. But Pete hadn't read every book and magazine article on infertility the way Emma had. He assumed that this result was the worst thing, but it wasn't.

'Don't you see, Pete, we can start again,' she pleaded. 'We've been messing around for so long, wondering what was wrong, afraid to talk about it and afraid to talk about the future. But now,' she smiled a smile of genuine pleasure, 'they can't find anything wrong. That's what unexplained infertility means. I don't have anything they can see. That may mean I can never have a baby or it may mean I can. Let's try IVF. We've as good a chance as anyone else has. They've got a twenty per cent success rate, as you told me. I don't mind gambling if you don't.'

For a moment, Pete stared at her, then his face cracked into a beaming smile. Picking her up, he whirled her around, kissing her fervently and yelling, 'I love you,' at the top of his voice.

Clinging to him, Emma threw back her head and whooped, not caring that passers-by were looking at the happy couple who looked as if they were re-enacting a movie scene about young lovers.

'Where do we go?' demanded Pete. 'Let's do it now, right this minute, immediately!'

CHAPTER TWENTY-NINE

Claudia threw her dummy at Hannah. With the phone still cradled between her ear and shoulder, Hannah picked the dummy up, dumped it in the sterilizer, removed another one and handed it to Claudia. Seeing the look in her mother's eyes, Claudia, who was very clever for four months old, decided to hold on to the dummy. She twinkled endearingly at her mother, scrunching up her cherub face and letting the liquid brown eyes so like her father's take the crossness out of Hannah's expression. Before Claudia had been born, Hannah thought dummies were the work of the devil and lazy mothers. No child of hers would ever have one. After two months of constant screaming, one kind neighbour she'd met in the park had told her to forget her high-principled ideas and hit the chemist immediately for a six-pack. 'Peace and principles are two very different things,' the woman had said. 'I swore I'd never use them, and look at my lot. They'll be doing college finals with them in their mouths.' Hannah took her advice and peace reigned.

Now Claudia sucked happily, big eyes watching her mother intently.

'We need another waitress,' Hannah said again to the man who ran A & E Catering. 'One isn't enough. We've got fifty people coming tonight, as you well know because you're supplying the food. One waitress is ludicrous.'

He gave her the usual bullshit and Hannah rolled her eyes. Why

Felix had insisted on using these people was beyond her. Just because his new best friend had recommended them was no reason to entrust their first big party to them. But he insisted it was a good idea.

'Hannah, I've been at three parties lately where they've worked, trust me,' he said bluntly.

As she hadn't been to the same three parties because Claudia's colic meant the au pair couldn't manage, Hannah had no comeback. The au pair couldn't manage very much. Neither, it seemed, could A & E Catering. Felix had told her grandly about plans for a seafood buffet with splendid raspberry tarts as dessert, like the last party he'd been at. The catering company had said that the woman who oversaw seafood buffets was on holiday and would she not settle for hams, cheese, the odd quiche and exotic fruit meringue?

Now the problem was the number of staff. Somebody had overbooked and there was only one waitress available for the party. Hannah, who thought it was all too expensive anyway and would have much preferred to cancel the bloody party, had no intention of being the second waitress, which was what would happen unless she could twist the caterers' arms.

'Look,' she said finally, 'I want two waitresses or consider yourself fired.'

She hung up.

'Mercedes!' she yelled.

Mercedes was the au pair, an indolent French charmer who could have been on the front of *Vogue* and was clearly biding her time au pairing until she was asked. A tall, sylph-like nineteen with endless legs, she had long platinum-blonde hair she could sit on and big blue eyes that must have looked wanton from the day she was born. Now she swayed into the kitchen, pink kitten heels clacking on Hannah's terracotta tiles, a vision in black jeans and a pink gingham shirt with the ends tied carelessly about her tiny waist.

'*Oui*,' she breathed.

'Can you take Claudia for a walk?' Hannah asked. 'I have a few more phone calls to make and she's restless.'

'But I must do my nails,' Mercedes said plaintively.

Hannah's own nails were unpainted and likely to stay that way because she still had to do so much before the party Felix wanted, a party they couldn't afford.

'Mercedes, please,' begged Hannah. 'You can have all of tomorrow off.'

For a brief, dizzying moment, Hannah remembered running an office, hiring and firing at will. Now she was reduced to begging the au pair for help. Mercedes was supposed to work for six hours, five days a week, the days to be organized between employer and employee. But after that first month coaxing Mercedes out of the desolation of homesickness for Marseilles, Hannah had crossed the line from employer to mother-figure and Mercedes now behaved exactly the way Hannah suspected she behaved at home: on the phone at all hours, by turn melancholy and jubilant, depending on which boyfriend had phoned, and uninterested in emptying out the dishwasher. She loved Claudia, which was wonderful, but hated nappy-changing and feeding. Getting her to take Claudia out for a walk was like getting NATO chiefs to reach a unanimous decision.

The promise of Saturday off did it. Mercedes liked nothing better than spending Saturdays with her au pair friends, idling away hours drinking coffee in Covent Garden, being eyed up by handsome young men and spending money their parents had sent on flirty little outfits from French Connection and Monsoon.

'*Oui*,' Mercedes said grudgingly, and because she was a kind girl, added, 'Are you going to the 'airdresser, 'Annah? I'll keep Claudia for the afternoon.'

Hannah could have kissed her. Once she'd decided to help, Mercedes was generous.

Claudia was the only one who didn't like this plan. She scrunched up her face and bawled, hurling her bottle at Mercedes this time and making enough noise to frighten the cat.

Hannah picked her up and cuddled her tightly as the wails subsided. As she held Claudia's heaving body close to hers, she marvelled again at the intensity of her feelings for her daughter. From the very second she'd been born, love for Claudia had overwhelmed Hannah like a volcanic eruption pouring ceaselessly out of a crater. She adored each dark curl on her daughter's head, was obsessed with every breath she took, even sitting beside the cot when Claudia had been very small, listening to every inhalation, as if watching the tiny chest rise and fall could keep Claudia safe. Under the circumstances, it was a miracle that Claudia had remained so sweet and sunny-natured thus far. But despite her adoration, Hannah was terrified of spoiling Claudia, and the little girl had learned that her beloved mother occasionally had to do things and go places that didn't include her.

She wasn't in the mood today. Snuggling closer to Hannah, Claudia sniffed plaintively.

'I hope she's not getting something,' Hannah said anxiously, immediately toying with the idea of cancelling her hairdresser's appointment.

'She's fine,' Mercedes said, taking a protesting Claudia away from her mother. 'We'll go to the common and play. Won't we, *ma cherie*?' Mercedes said in baby-speak to Claudia.

The baby's eyes lit up at the attention.

She looked so adorable in her red woollen cardigan and blue spotty dungarees. 'Go with Ruth from next door, won't you?' said Hannah. You never knew what sort of weirdo would approach a young girl with a pushchair. She'd become paranoid about security and felt much safer when the next-door nanny went walking with Claudia, Mercedes and her charge, a one-year-old bruiser named Henry who was training Claudia how to have terrible tantrums one minute and smile angelically the next.

'Perhaps we should get a dog, a guard dog,' Hannah had said worriedly to Felix when they moved to the house in Clapham. Claudia wasn't even born at the time and Hannah had read a terrible story about a woman who'd had to run away from a crazed man in a park near her home when she was wheeling her twin boys out.

'You're such a worrier,' Felix had remarked, patting her belly. 'We're not Tom Cruise and Nicole Kidman, you know. Nobody is going to kidnap our baby.'

Even so, Hannah did her best to ensure that when Mercedes went out with Claudia, they went with somebody else. She wasn't frightened of meeting someone scary when she was on her own with Claudia: mainly because Hannah knew she'd savage anyone, man or beast, who tried to harm a hair of her precious baby's head. Mother love could be a terribly violent thing.

Claudia grizzled a bit as Hannah put on her red woollen hat and matching coat. It was a glorious Friday in April but Hannah was paranoid about chills and it was a bit windy out on the common. Convinced that Claudia was buttoned-up safely from both the wind and mad men on the common, she let them off, reminding Mercedes to phone her in the hairdresser's if there was a problem.

It was wonderful to have a few precious hours to herself, she thought as she let herself out of the house ten minutes later. The sun shone on the small terraced white houses on the road, and the scent of next door's yellow jonquils filled Hannah's head as she shut the door. Their house wasn't the large, airy Edwardian mansion in Chelsea that Felix had promised her when he'd persuaded her to live in London. There was nothing airy about it. Tall and narrow, there was a basement kitchen, two pretty reception rooms on the ground floor, and three pokey bedrooms on the second floor. If the attic hadn't been floored, Hannah didn't know where Felix would have put his clothes.

Still, it was a pretty little house and would be even prettier if they had any money to spend on doing it up. They'd had the living room wallpapered in an apple green and cream patterned paper Felix had fancied and it had worked out so expensive that they'd been forced to abandon plans to redo the dark red kitchen.

It all came back to money. Felix hadn't worked for two months now and, due to his reckless spending when he was working, they were a bit strapped for cash. Which was one of the reasons why Hannah wasn't keen on the idea of tonight's party.

'You don't get it, do you?' Felix had said crossly. 'This sort of entertaining is vital for my career. Bill's bringing this important casting director with her. She could do things for me.'

Hannah knew when she was beaten. Felix's career was everything, especially since hers was on the backburner. But they needed to cut back on something. Mercedes was an expense they could do without. Hannah hadn't wanted an au pair at all, saying she'd prefer to look after Claudia by herself, but Felix had insisted that people 'like them' always had some sort of help. She could get out more and maybe go back to work, he'd suggested.

However, an intense desire to be with Claudia meant her work was confined to two mornings a week working at a local charity shop, which her mother had insisted was good for getting her out of the house.

'You don't want to turn into one of those wives who have no life outside the four walls of your kitchen,' Anna Campbell had said wisely. 'Without my job, I'd have been ga-ga years ago.'

She spent an enjoyable hour in the hairdresser, reading magazines she wouldn't normally buy and savouring a cup of sugary coffee. The small local salon always did a wonderful job of washing and blowdrying her hair. Felix went to Nicky Clark for his streaks but they couldn't both afford to go there.

'To think I believed this was natural,' Hannah laughed, running her fingers through his silky blond hair the day she discovered he had it professionally coloured.

'I was very fair as a child,' Felix protested, sounding hurt at the notion that Hannah felt he wasn't really the gilded creature she'd married.

She kissed him affectionately. 'I won't tell anyone, I promise.'

He'd had his hair done the day before and was now out meeting Bill in the Groucho Club, looking as if he was successful and gainfully employed instead of overdrawn and worried. Bill was a terrible woman for boozing and Hannah prayed she'd stay off the Black Label until she got to the party. Otherwise, she'd be pinching men's bottoms at a rate of knots. Bill went through men faster than Claudia went through nappies. At least if she was bringing a famous and influential casting director to the party, she would be on her best behaviour. Hopefully.

On impulse, Hannah stopped at the chemist on the way home and treated herself to pillarbox red lipstick and matching nail varnish. She'd been very drab lately, slopping around in her old threadbare jeans and never bothering much with make-up or such niceties as painting her nails. Some days it was a miracle that she managed to brush her hair. Felix was such a sweetie, he never complained when she came to bed in a crumpled giant T-shirt and socks instead of some beautifully ironed silken slip of a thing designed to be whipped off.

But then he knew how tired she'd been after having Claudia. Caring for a baby who refused to sleep at night for more than two hours at a time until the last week, had knocked the stuffing out of Hannah. Sex and a beauty routine seemed to matter very little when you were so tired you could barely see straight.

Tonight, she'd remind Felix of the glamorous, sensual woman he'd married, Hannah vowed as she paid for the cosmetics. A smile lifted the corners of her generous mouth as she thought about it. And when the party was over, she'd bring him upstairs, cross her fingers that Claudia would sleep, and seduce him. Slowly, sexily, the way he loved.

'What are they coming for?' demanded Felix, pulling Hannah into the kitchen as soon as she had led Freddie and Michelle from next door into the sitting room and gone off to get them a glass of wine.

'They're our neighbours,' Hannah whispered angrily, 'and unless you want warfare along the road, you have to ask neighbours to parties. If Bill gets twisted and starts running up and down the street naked with a glass of whiskey in her hand and a rose up her bum, it's better to have the neighbours on our side, don't you think?'

Felix scowled. He hadn't a leg to stand on. Bill had arrived home with him from the Groucho Club, much later than he'd promised and minus the famous casting director. Felix had been mildly drunk (he was far too ambitious to ever let his bleached hair down) but Bill was completely plastered, no matter how she tried to hide it. Hannah was an expert at gauging drunkenness. She'd shoved a cup of strong coffee into Bill's hand, sent her into the garden to cool off, and had made Felix feed her a plate of the Spanish ham that the caterers were taking out of refrigerated packs. That had been an hour ago. Now the guests were beginning to trickle in, starting with their neighbours who all had small children and liked going to parties early because toddler alarm calls at five every morning meant they were too exhausted to stay out late.

'Circulate,' hissed Hannah to her handsome husband, who was now admiring his reflection in a shiny silver platter.

'None of my people are here yet,' he replied, adjusting the collar on the chocolate brown DKNY shirt that went so well with his eyes and golden skin.

'Do you mean that all the neighbours are my boring friends and that the thrilling act-or types, who won't get here for hours, are your friends?' Hannah said angrily.

'Keep your hair on,' Felix said. 'I'll mingle. Just rescue me if I get stuck.'

Hannah followed him in with the wine and watched as he greeted Freddie and Michelle as if he'd been counting the hours till their arrival. Michelle flushed pink when he kissed her hello like she was Claudia Schiffer's prettier little sister instead of a clever, rounded banker who moaned to Hannah that she was fed up to the teeth with Weight Watcher's spaghetti.

'Freddie!' said Felix warmly. 'When are you going to stop bullshitting me and give me that game of squash? You promised to fit me in.'

He was so charming, Hannah reflected, watching the tableau. People adored him; he could light up a room, not to mention what he could do to a woman's eyes. No wonder he was so magical on film.

As the best, if somewhat bittersweet, review had put it: 'Felix Andretti has a screen presence which draws your eyes to him. If he's on the screen, you're watching this magnetic man. It is star quality, but is it acting quality? Time will tell, but keep an eye out for his name.'

Hannah had been horrified by the review. And scared. Her great fear had always been that Felix was such a beautiful creature he'd succeed to a certain level within the business but no further, simply because he wasn't a good enough actor despite his matinee-idol looks. With his lofty dreams of both critical and commercial success, it would kill him. This review seemed to confirm her fears, but Felix and Bill had been in raptures over it.

'Acting, schmacting,' Bill had crowed as they enjoyed a celebratory lunch in a chi-chi bistro on the King's Road. 'You've got star quality, babe. That's what this business is all about.'

The condensation ran down the white wine glasses as Hannah stood inside the door and watched Felix ooze star quality.

Freddie and Michelle giggled like schoolkids at his jokes, as did the other people in the room who'd gravitated towards him instinctively.

'Were you taking those glasses of wine to anybody in particular?' demanded the waitress.

A & E Catering had come up with two waitresses, one competent and friendly, the other a surly girl who wasn't much older than sixteen and looked as if she'd been dragged away from a particularly brilliant episode of *Friends* to waitress at this boring party.

It was Ms Surly speaking.

'It's OK,' Hannah said, smiling in the hope that the girl might summon up a smile in return. 'I'll bring them.'

'Suit yourself,' said the girl before stomping off.

'Darling,' called Felix, giving her a look she recognized as his 'rescue me' plea. 'Come here with the wine before we all expire from thirst.'

She made her way over to the group and Felix handed out the drinks before wrapping his free arm around her waist in a gesture as much of pride as possession.

'Isn't she wonderful?' he said warmly. 'I don't know what I'd do without her.'

'Wonderful,' chorused the Felix acolytes.

It was Hannah's turn to flush. She hated it when he did that, made her feel like a possession on display. She remembered a party at one actor's house when she'd been heavily pregnant and Felix had pushed her round in front of him like a talisman, as if to say 'Aren't I a wonderful family man?'

Of course, he couldn't really have been doing that. She'd been such a slave to her hormones at the time that she'd discounted her initial notion as pregnancy blues.

Yet it felt like it now. She was a part of Felix's resumé, along with his stint in badly financed theatre shows, his year in America and the rep *Hamlet* in modern clothes set in Chicago. Her place on the CV was that of sweet Irish wife who looked after their adorable little daughter and their cosy Clapham home. The domestic bliss section of every actor's life, without which they 'simply wouldn't be able to cope', as they told every interviewer.

'I must answer the doorbell,' she said hurriedly.

'Did it ring?' asked Michelle in surprise. 'I thought yours made the same noise as ours, and I didn't hear it.'

Blessedly, the bell rang loudly.

'There it goes again,' Hannah lied.

Freddie laughed at Michelle. 'One sip of wine and she doesn't know whether she's coming or going!'

Hannah escaped to let the newcomers in and to rest her hot forehead against the cool wall in the upstairs bathroom. There must be something wrong with her. She checked on Claudia and Mercedes. The baby was asleep, cherubic with those naughty eyes closed.

'Would you like something to eat?' she asked Mercedes, who looked shocked at the idea.

After nine, Mercedes never touched more than a crispbread. Which was why she was so slim, Hannah thought, a hand straying to her tummy, which had never quite regained its once-enviable slimness after Claudia's birth.

The buffet went down a treat, along with the endless bottles of Roda wine. The acting fraternity turned up en masse and went through the food like a plague of locusts, especially enjoying knocking back the after-dinner champagne that Felix had apparently ordered without telling Hannah.

'Good drink is the mark of a good party,' breathed one of Felix's pals drunkenly as he helped himself to another red wine-sized glass of champagne with the eagerness of a wino opening a new bottle of Thunderbird.

A waste of a good party, Hannah thought bleakly as she surveyed the scene of destruction that was the kitchen and thought of how much money the whole thing had cost them. Every time another cork popped, she winced and remembered their overdraft. It would have been bearable if Bill's important friend had turned up to admire Felix and subsequently cast him in some career-making TV show or film.

But she hadn't arrived and now that it was after eleven, it didn't seem likely she would.

The guests were almost all hard-up talent rather than wealthy, powerful behind-the-scenes people. The most powerful person in the room turned out to be a beautifully preserved actress who seemed to have been in every British film made in the previous ten years and who was clearly there because she fancied Felix.

To Hannah's relief, he didn't appear interested and even bitchily confided in her that the actress's gorgeous young husband was in fact gay.

'At her age, it's the best she can get,' he'd said dismissively.

Hannah was so consoled by the knowledge that Felix wasn't interested in the other woman, that she never said a word about how ageist and sexist his remarks were.

She noticed, sourly, that he spent ages talking quietly in a corner with Sigrid, a Danish actress who'd had a small part in his last TV series. A taut and lean brunette with short spiky hair and a personality to match, she was amazingly dressed in tight suede trousers under which her body seemed to lean towards Felix as they stared deliberately over each other's shoulders, talking fiercely.

Hannah chatted to other guests, laughed at old jokes and poured out wine, all the while watching her husband out of the corner of her eye. He and Sigrid never even looked at each other but there was something between them, some unmistakable sense that they were closer than mere colleagues. But they weren't touching or anything. Was she imagining it?

Even when someone spilled a glass of red on the tapestry cushion that she'd meant to hide because it wasn't Scotchguarded, Hannah didn't mind. She was too busy watching Felix, feeling nervous knots in her stomach.

When she returned from rescuing the cushion with a pound of salt in the kitchen, Felix was chatting to another group of people, one arm loosely round the shoulders of a woman she knew he disliked. Perhaps that was the clue, she thought with the shock of sudden comprehension.

He let himself publicly touch people he didn't like and ostentatiously refrained from touching anyone he did.

She was relieved when Sigrid left shortly afterwards with the man she'd arrived with. But the nagging feeling in the pit of her stomach wouldn't go away.

'Everything all right, darling?' Felix asked casually when Sigrid had gone, patting Hannah's arm.

'Fine,' she said.

He smiled almost maniacally at her: she was tired of the party and he was on a high, thrilled that these people had come to see him, buoyed up on a mixture of drink and excitement.

He kissed her on the cheek and was gone, flirting, charming, enchanting everyone. The golden boy who captured every eye in the room.

By ten past twelve, she was exhausted from the combination of being hostessy with worrying that the party would upset Claudia, whom she'd checked on all evening. Most of the partygoers had gone except for the hard-core acting fraternity who were used to staying up late and who were now sitting round the kitchen table, stuck into the Scotch Bill had unearthed behind the tea towels in a kitchen cupboard.

When Hannah went into the kitchen after saying goodbye to some guests, the hard-core were happily ripping apart a period television series in which none of them had been given parts.

'Derivative crap,' sneered one.

'I hate that corset and yes-your-ladyship stuff,' said Bill. 'I mean, didn't they have sex in Jane Austen's time? You'd never bloody know it.'

Hannah wondered if anyone would notice if she sloped off to bed.

Claudia had slept throughout the whole thing, in spite of the odd rowdiness, so she'd be awake as usual at half five. Hannah knew Felix wouldn't have the energy to get up to her, and Mercedes, who'd been wonderful all evening and had taken Claudia's cot into her room to make sure she was all right, was deservedly having the day off.

That was it, Hannah decided. She'd nip into Mercedes' room and remind the poor girl that she'd take Claudia in the morning so Mercedes could have a lie-on. Felix must be in the loo or something, but he'd figure out she had gone to bed and would look after his guests without her.

She tiptoed upstairs, deeply grateful that the party was over. It had taken so much planning, mainly because of the inefficiencies of the caterers. And she'd been cleaning the house for a week. Mercedes was hopeless when it came to putting on rubber gloves and doing things with cream cleanser. She'd shuddered expressively when Hannah had even suggested it.

Poor Mercedes. She'd miss her Gallic charm.

Hannah was mentally working out how much they'd save by not paying an au pair when she came to Mercedes' room. There was a lot of muffled noise coming from inside and she instantly assumed that Claudia was awake and demanding attention. Knocking perfunctorily, she didn't wait as she usually did for Mercedes to say, 'Come in.' Hannah was extremely conscious that Mercedes was entitled to her privacy but this was the first time she had ever left Claudia's cot in the au pair's room for the evening. Thinking that she'd relieve Mercedes of the baby was foremost on her mind when she pushed the door open.

Only it wasn't an over-tired Claudia stretched out on Mercedes' bed, wriggling as her nappy was changed and grizzling for her mother.

It was Felix, only a pair of boxer shorts covering his long, lean limbs. His Next boxers, Hannah noticed, astonished at the details which seemed clear to her at this traumatic moment.

He didn't look upset. On the contrary, he looked mildly surprised, as if he'd just woken up in their own bed and it had been Hannah herself beside him in bra and knickers, instead of the nubile body of Mercedes looking wonderful in matching ivory undies.

Claudia was mercifully slumbering in her cot, cherubic face peaceful in sleep, one small hand clutching the cuddly black sheep she refused to be parted from. Hannah would never have forgiven Felix if he'd screwed their au pair with the baby watching. That would have been unforgivable. Not that the current state of affairs was forgivable, but it was marginally more so because of Claudia's slumber.

''Annah, I am so sorry,' cried Mercedes, distraught. 'I never meant to, I am too fond of you, you must believe me. There was no plan – it just 'appen.'

I wonder how often it has 'appened before, Hannah thought wildly.

'How did it happen, then?' Hannah asked coldly, looking at Felix instead of Mercedes, who was, after all, an impressionable nineteen-year-old and could hardly be blamed for her employer's adultery.

Felix's face went blank when he was in the wrong, a sort of bare canvas on which he could paint the correct expression. It was blank now, waiting to see what barbs his wife would fire so he could react correctly.

'I'm waiting, Felix,' Hannah said, 'for an explanation from you.'

As if realizing that she wasn't taking the traditional 'blame the other woman' line, Felix adjusted his face accordingly.

'I'm sorry, Hannah,' he said. 'I was drunk. I came in to check on Claudia and Mercedes was here. She came on to me . . .'

'I did not!' squealed Mercedes hotly. 'You 'ave been after me since I get here. I only give in because you pester me!'

'Lying bitch!' hissed Felix. 'Don't believe a word she's saying, Hannah,' he implored. 'She's been like a cat on heat ever since she arrived.'

At this, Claudia woke up and, on seeing her favourite people glaring angrily at each other, started bawling. Mercedes looked at Hannah briefly as if asking would she pick her up. But Hannah shook her head imperceptibly and reached for her squirming daughter.

'How's my pet?' she crooned, snuggling Claudia's curly head against her breast and marvelling that she could speak normally to her daughter after what had just happened. The bawling continued.

'Felix, perhaps you could move the cot into our bedroom.'

He smirked at Mercedes. I won, he seemed to be saying. She believed me. Mercedes' face fell and her full lower lip wobbled.

Hannah ignored all this and carried Claudia into what the estate agent had described as the 'master bedroom'. Slightly less box-like than the other two bedrooms, there was only room for a bed, a pine dressing table, two tiny bedside tables and a chair. The master must have been very small, Hannah always thought. She would never have described such a small room as the master bedroom when it sounded so stupid, she'd thought. With the cot in there, she wouldn't have room to move.

Once Felix had transferred Claudia's cot and all her belongings, he went to sit on their big double bed with its flowery yellow duvet.

'Don't even think about it, Felix,' Hannah warned, keeping her voice low because she was trying to calm Claudia. 'You can sleep somewhere else tonight. I'm sure there's someone who'll oblige – maybe Sigrid, if Mercedes is too pissed off to let you back in her bed.'

His head shot up and he looked warily at Hannah, speculating as to how much she knew or guessed.

'How dumb do you think I am?' she asked harshly. 'No, don't answer that because it's obvious that I am a bit dumb. I failed to notice what you were getting up to under my roof and I failed to notice you screwing probably half the actresses in London.'

'I haven't . . .' he began.

'Don't bother either apologizing or making excuses.' Hannah walked around the room, gently rocking Claudia. 'Now get out and look after your guests.'

Knowing when he was beaten, Felix left. A few moments later, a soft knock on the door and a little voice signalled the arrival of Mercedes.

''Annah, can I come and explain?'

'Go away, Mercedes, you can explain in the morning,' Hannah said wearily.

When she went downstairs half an hour later to get some milk for Claudia, the kitchen was empty. The stragglers were in the living room playing charades, porn-movie-title charades from the sound of it. Filthy laughter erupted when someone loudly guessed *Dirty Cowgirls Do Downtown Delhi*.

Hannah warmed milk for both herself and her daughter. Somehow the idea of hot milk appealed to her, probably because it was one of her mother's favourite remedies. If you had a sick stomach, hot milk with ginger was a favourite. For flu, hot milk with the strange addition of black pepper was the remedy. Whether it worked or not, Hannah didn't know, but she still associated hot milk with comfort.

When Claudia finally drifted off to sleep in her cot, Hannah pulled off her clothes and lay back against the yellow pillows wearing just her knickers, sipping the dregs of her milk. They were the black lycra and net ones she'd never worn before and had chosen because of her planned seduction of Felix. How ironic that when she'd been thinking of how she could give her beloved husband a reminder of their once-amazing love life, he'd been thinking of what opportunity he'd have to screw their au pair. Hannah tried to banish the image of him and Mercedes lounging on the bed, with the graceful insouciance of models in a Calvin Klein perfume commercial.

She didn't want to think about what had just happened, didn't want to have to face the painful lessons it was teaching her. Instead, she wanted to be able to talk to Leonie or her mother or Emma and cry. She wanted more comfort than a mug of hot milk.

For some irrational reason, she thought of David James. His strong face and those big shoulders came to her mind. You could cry into those shoulders, bury your head in their solidity and lean against them while gentle, strong arms held you tightly, saying comforting things. Not like Felix's arms. Terrified of bulking up like a Schwarzenegger, Felix stuck to smaller weights in the gym, wanting his physique to be lean and honed rather than strong and masculine. She couldn't imagine herself sobbing into his shoulders. Felix was the sort of man that women sobbed over and not to.

David had tried to warn her and she hadn't listened. Who could she turn to now?

Morning came with painful slowness and, for once, Hannah had her eyes open before Claudia began mumbling and grumbling in her cot, cooing baby talk to Harvey the sheep. Hannah reckoned she'd managed about three fitful hours of sleep, punctuated by sweaty moments when she'd sat up in bed, dizzy from the memory of the night before. Felix consumed her nightmares; his lean, naked body curled around a succession of female ones, sometimes Sigrid, sometimes Mercedes, sometimes other anonymous beauties who laughed scornfully at Hannah and waggled pert, un-stretchmarked bodies at her.

She got Claudia up, kissing the wriggling pink baby who squirmed as she was being dressed. Hannah merely pulled on her old jeans again and dragged a marl grey T-shirt over her head. She ran a brush through her hair and cleaned her teeth, but nothing else. What was the point of going for glamour when your husband didn't give a shit?

She peeped into the sitting room and saw Felix asleep on the couch. Bastard.

In the kitchen she made Claudia a bottle. It had been so much easier when she'd breastfed but her milk had unaccountably dried up after a month and she'd been forced to bottle-feed Claudia.

'I'll be able to help more now that you're not breastfeeding,' Felix had volunteered. That was a laugh, Hannah thought grimly. Felix's help involved changing Claudia's nappy whenever there was a press photographer around. Otherwise, he restricted his help to cuddles during bathtime and other occasions when the baby was clean. Laboriously feeding her a bottle was too boring for him because Claudia was a slow feeder.

Hannah managed to grab a cup of coffee and a piece of toast in between feeding Claudia and tidying up. She'd filled and emptied the dishwasher twice when Mercedes came tentatively into the kitchen.

Mercedes clearly hadn't slept much either and her normally dewy complexion was grey with tiredness under the Dior foundation. Her big brown eyes were red-rimmed and she was obviously consumed with remorse. Even so, she still looked immaculate, a red polka-dot scarf tied jauntily round her neck to enliven the plain white fitted shirt and black trousers she wore.

''Annah, I am so sorry, please believe me,' Mercedes said, twisting her hands anxiously.

She really was sorry. It was weird that her au pair appeared to care more about how hurt Hannah was than her own husband.

If Felix had really given a damn, he'd have been up by now, begging her not to leave him. As if she would, she thought hopelessly.

'Mercedes, I think you better go home. I'll phone your parents . . .'

'No,' shrieked the girl. 'You can't tell them!'

'I wasn't planning to tell them,' Hannah said. 'I'll just say that we have to let you go and tell them what flight you'll be on. Did Felix use a condom?' she asked bluntly. She didn't want to send Mercedes home pregnant. She felt sure it would contravene the employer/au pair guidelines.

The girl blushed. 'Yes.'

'I hope you don't get pregnant,' Hannah sighed. 'You really should see your doctor when you go home.' How strange, it was as if she and Mercedes were discussing an ordinary sexual encounter, not one where her own husband was involved.

'It was safe,' Mercedes said, still red.

'Good. This whole situation is complicated enough without adding any more complications.' Hannah found the Yellow Pages and opened it on the airline section. She shoved it and the phone towards Mercedes. 'Mr Andretti will pay for your flight home, I have no doubt. It's the least he can do. We're going out for a walk,' she added and left the room with Claudia in her arms.

When she got back, Mercedes and her belongings were gone, along with a tearful note saying she was sorry, so sorry.

Hannah folded the note thoughtfully and put it in her pocket. She'd been fond of Mercedes.

Felix was in the sitting room, watching football and drinking a glass of red wine. She was amazed that there was anything left to drink in the house after the party. She was sure Bill would have unearthed all the hidden booze, with her uncanny ability to sniff out alcohol.

'Hi, babe,' Felix said unconcernedly as Hannah put Claudia on a mat on the carpet for a wriggle and set her baby gym beside her. Claudia loved the gym: she whacked the bells and kicked the fluffy balls with delight, gurgling all the time.

Felix was still glued to the football. Hannah felt the rage grow deep inside her. She'd been on automatic pilot since last night, determined to cope with Felix's hideous betrayal as calmly as she could. But his laid-back attitude pierced her heart. How *could* he sit there as if nothing had happened, as if he hadn't screwed their au pair with the baby watching, as if he hadn't practically admitted to screwing half the actresses in London?

'Have you got nothing to say for yourself?' she said bitterly.

Felix shrugged and flicked back a strand of silky blond hair as if to say, 'About what?'

'How could you?' she yelled at him, losing her head. 'How could you sleep with someone else? I loved you, Felix. Wasn't that enough for you?'

'Don't be so fucking bourgeois,' Felix snapped. 'Everybody does it.'

'Bourgeois!' screeched Hannah. 'Is that what you call it when you believe in fidelity? Because if it is, then I'm the most bloody bourgeois person I know!'

'Don't give me that crap!' he said, curling his lip. 'You can't tell me you haven't played around. Until we became serious, you had a thing going with David James, didn't you, huh? Don't lie to me, I know you did. You were two-timing me. He as near as dammit told me to leave you alone.'

'He did what?'

Felix laughed at her. 'Not so cocky, now, are you, Hannah dear? David told me that if I hurt you, he'd rip my throat out. I may not be a Mensa member but even I can figure out what he meant by that.'

Hannah was mute. 'But, but . . .' she stammered after a moment. 'He didn't, *we* didn't . . .'

'Oh yeah, *right*.'

'We didn't,' she insisted. 'I didn't even know he liked me.'

'And why did he pluck you from the office manager's job and make you a junior agent, then? Because you were the most gifted person he'd ever met in his life or because he wanted to get into your knickers?'

She recoiled at the crudity. How typically Felix: to hit her while she was down. 'You're saying that my talent had nothing to do with my promotion, that David was cynically using me and that he'd demote me back to my old position when he'd got his leg over,' she said calmly, hating Felix for what he'd said. 'How flattering, Felix. It's nice to know that you appreciate my finer qualities and have respect for my abilities. To think I gave up that good job to marry a man who sees me as a useless bimbo.' She favoured him with the lethal, stern look she'd used to great effect for so many years. 'The only person who cynically uses anyone round here is you, Felix. You married me because you thought a pregnant wife would be useful, another string to your bow.'

She waited for him to deny it but he didn't. He merely sat looking at her with cool disinterest.

Claudia began to wail at the shouting around her. Hannah picked her up and cuddled her, murmuring soothing baby noises and holding her close.

'If you couldn't wait for our first anniversary before you started screwing around, I've got to ask why did you marry me, Felix?' she asked quietly. 'Mercedes wasn't the first, was she? Why did you need someone else? I thought I was enough for you.'

He rolled his eyes. 'Will you stop with all this psychoanalysis stuff, Hannah. We got married, we are married, end of story. People screw around in marriage, it's not the end of the world. Life isn't *Gone with the Wind*, you know. It doesn't all end happily ever after.'

'It didn't end happily in *Gone with the Wind*,' Hannah said in a strange high voice.

'Whatever. You married me and you're stuck with me. This is the way I am. I can't change,' he said.

'But I thought you loved me,' she repeated blindly.

'I do love you, I just wanted to fuck somebody else,' Felix explained. 'Haven't you ever wanted to do that?'

'No,' she whispered, 'I haven't. You are enough for me.'

'Jesus, you women and your obsession with what's enough! It's like red wine,' he said, holding up his glass. 'Just because I like it, doesn't mean I want to drink it all the time. Sometimes I like whiskey or champagne.'

'What am I, then? The dregs? Cheap wine of the screw-top bottle variety?' she said, starting to cry.

Felix downed his wine in one gulp and headed for the door. 'If you're going to carry on like that, I'm leaving. I'll stay with Bill for a few days, let you cool down.'

She wanted to beg him not to go but, miserable as she was, she knew she couldn't completely degrade herself. She could hear him upstairs, throwing stuff into a bag. Within ten minutes, he was gone and Hannah allowed herself to cry properly. Claudia joined in.

When they'd both stopped, Hannah felt as worn out as if she'd swum fifty lengths. She made herself a cup of tea and considered her options.

She longed to phone Leonie, to hear her friend's kind, comforting and sensible advice. Leonie would know what to do. She always did. But Hannah couldn't phone her. She was too raw and hurt. It would be painful and humiliating to admit what had happened. Instead, she cleaned the house, tidying up the worst excesses of the partygoers. She scrubbed and polished, working until her arms ached with cleaning. Claudia watched and dozed. Eventually, Hannah stopped and sat down on the couch to watch *Blind Date*. The opening music had just ended when the phone rang and Hannah leapt to it, hoping it was Felix, phoning to declare his undying love and to apologize, both of which were highly unlikely. It was her mother. Anna Campbell always phoned on a Saturday night before she went to bingo with her friends. It was a comforting ritual they'd got into, discussing their week and sorting out the world's problems.

'Hello, Hannah,' said her mother, who was not the sort of person given to saying 'Hello, darling.'

Hannah burst into tears.

'It's Felix, isn't it?' Anna said matter-of-factly.

Hannah sobbed more loudly. It was a few minutes before she could control her sobs enough to tell the whole sorry tale. She left nothing out. Her instinct to keep the most humiliating bits to herself had left her, like Felix.

'Come home, Hannah,' said Anna Campbell when she'd heard everything. 'You're banging your head against a brick wall. Do it. I should have done it years ago, but I never had the courage. You're young, you've got the child to think of, leave him.'

Hannah leaned her head against the cool of the wall. 'I can't just leave,' she said weakly.

'Why not? Because he's everything you ever wanted?' Anna sounded sour. 'What will you do the next time? Because there will be a next time, you know.'

'What would I do?' Hannah said in desperation.

'Your boss would give you back your job, wouldn't he?' Anna said. 'You've always said he was one man you could trust in any situation.'

'David James, you mean?' Hannah fell silent. She could hardly ask

David, of all people. She'd spurned his advances in every sense of the word. He'd obviously been crazy about her and she'd rubbed his face in it. He'd even given her a career when she had nothing else and she'd turned her back on that too. He'd done his best to protect her by warning Felix not to hurt her, dear David. He'd be the last person she could ring, even if she wanted to. And she wanted to.

'Why don't you phone him, Hannah? You can stay with me for a week or so to get you back on your feet and then go back to work. Leonie would have you, or that nice Donna you talked about. You could get a place for yourself and Claudia in no time, and a crèche. I don't know why you think you can't.'

'I can't explain,' Hannah said in exasperation. She felt too shattered to think straight, never mind make such a cataclysmic decision. 'I can't do it,' she said tiredly. The *Blind Date* music played in the background. They'd been talking for an hour.

'Your phone bill will be horrendous, Mum, and you'll miss bingo,' she said. 'I'll phone tomorrow.'

'To hell with bingo,' her mother said.

'I'll phone tomorrow,' Hannah repeated. She didn't want to be told what to do any more. She wanted to lick her wounds in peace. She wanted to have a bath and rinse away all the horrible things that had been happening.

The wrapper said it was a butterball, scented with vanilla, ylang ylang and with a helping of cocoa butter to soften your skin.

Hannah carefully unwrapped the bath bomb from its plastic covering and dropped it into the bath. It immediately began to fizz in the water, releasing a glorious scent of vanilla into the air, like freshly baked cakes mixed with the soft scent of a baby's skin. She breathed it in and sighed. Her body ached for a hot bath. She never had time for them any more. Claudia was so demanding that a two-minute shower snatched between naps was the extent of Hannah's beauty routine. She hadn't conditioned her hair in weeks purely because it took too long to rinse the conditioner out of it. And as for face masks, forget it. Having a bath with a butterball bomb in it was the ultimate in sensual excitement these days. The hairdresser had tut-tutted about the state of her hair yesterday. Yesterday, before the party, it seemed a hundred years ago.

Opening the bathroom door, she gingerly crept into her bedroom and peered into the cot. Claudia was lying on her back, covers bunched up around her feet and one fat little hand crammed against her mouth. In sleep, she was like a cherub from a medieval painting: her dark hair curled around her head, her cheeks rosy and her expression angelic. Awake, she was very keen on having her own way, with the most beguiling smile in the world when she was happy. The rush of love hit Hannah again like an express train. She would never have believed you could love somebody so much. She simply couldn't bear to be away from Claudia. They spent hours playing together, Hannah patiently showing her toys and objects, Claudia delightedly crowing when she got to bite something. She bit everything, from towels to fingers, and had a remarkably strong grip for a small baby. In fact, Hannah was worried that the kitten would find her tail in Claudia's strong little hand and that neither would enjoy the experience. She loved the kitten but wished Felix had thought about it when he bought it. Kittens and babies were not necessarily the best housemates. But Felix didn't care about the effect of his actions: he just did things and let other people pick up the pieces.

Satisfied that Claudia was asleep, Hannah stripped off her jeans and sweatshirt and underwear and sank gratefully into the steaming water. Drifting mentally as the hot water soothed the aches in her body, she faced the pain. Felix had betrayed her and would probably do it again. In choosing Mercedes, he'd shown his contempt for Hannah.

It hit her like a flash of lightning, a *coup de foudre*, as Mercedes would say. If she stayed, she'd be doing what her mother had done. *Sticking it out for the sake of the children.* Hadn't Hannah railed against her mother for just that? Railed against the reasoning that insisted on maintaining the status quo, at no matter what personal cost. Ever since she'd been old enough to hear her father knocking over the furniture when he staggered home, drunk out of his mind, Hannah had wondered why her mother hadn't left – or thrown him out. The answer was that Anna Campbell's generation didn't believe in that type of thing. They married for life – a life sentence as Hannah saw it. Her plan had always been to escape that sort of life and control her own destiny. Having a career and being independent was the only way out of marital slavery, and yet she'd followed her mother's path as faithfully as if they were identical twins: getting involved with two men who'd used and abused her, both of whom had taken away her self-belief and left her like a hollowed-out gourd, empty and useless. First Harry, then Felix. If Harry hadn't walked away, she'd have still been with him. Hoping they'd get married and settle down, when, in reality, Harry was incapable of settling down.

And now Felix was using her and humiliating her. If she stayed, he'd continue to do it, confident that he'd get away with any number of indiscretions, knowing that Hannah would be waiting for him dutifully, a sweet wifey who'd never walk out. No, she thought with growing horror, no way. The only way to break the pattern was to take control and leave him. No matter how much it hurt, no matter how much she longed for him. She was crazy about Felix, she longed for him physically, yearned for his smile, hungered to be with him when they were apart. But it was one-sided. She knew that in relationships there was always one who loved more. And that was the one who wasn't in control. She was that person and Felix would make the most of it. Unless she left him now. Otherwise, both she and Claudia would suffer. She couldn't let her daughter grow up in a family where the notion of respect was nothing more than a sham. She imagined Claudia at twenty, talking about her childhood memories and recalling Daddy screwing other women when Mummy was out and he thought Claudia was too young to take notice.

She got out of the bath and wrapped herself in her old blue towelling dressing gown. In the bedroom, Claudia gurgled at her mother, waking up and demanding love and attention. Hannah picked her up and marvelled at Felix's incredible eyes staring out at her from Claudia's cherubic baby face. He'd always be part of her life because of Claudia. Which was only right. Hannah didn't believe in separating a parent from their child. But he wouldn't be a part of *her* life, not in that way. She'd be destroyed if he was.

'How would you like to go to Connemara?' Hannah crooned to Claudia, who smiled her gummy smile.

Leonie was washing her hair when the phone rang. Streams of shampoo bubbles rushed down her neck as she squeezed her hair quickly and wrapped a towel around her head turban-style. She raced to the phone, panting in her eagerness. It might be Doug, after all. He'd been in Dublin all day and she was dying to talk to him. It still amazed her how much she missed him when they weren't together. They were planning a quiet Saturday night in with the twins, a video and a takeaway. She couldn't wait.

'Hello?' she said breathlessly, feeling the trails of water disappearing down her neck and into her sweater.

'Hi, Leonie, it's Emma. Can you talk?' said Emma in her lovely husky voice.

'Course, love. How are you?' Leonie said, using the corner of the towel to dry her neck. She sat down on the small stool beside the phone. Her hair could wait. She hadn't spoken to Emma for at least a week.

'I'm fine,' Emma said. 'Actually, I'm more than fine, I'm absolutely delirious. You'll never guess what's happened.'

'What?'

'Are you sitting down?'

'Yes,' Leonie said nervously. 'It's good news, isn't it?'

'The best.' Even over the phone, Emma's triumph was apparent. 'I'm pregnant.'

Leonie squealed. 'OhmiGod! That's incredible, Emma. I'm so happy for you.'

She felt the tears swell up in her eyes. Darling Emma had wanted this for so long; she'd gone through hell trying to get pregnant and she'd be such a wonderful mother. 'I'm so thrilled, that's wonderful news.'

'I know.' On the other end of the line, Emma's own eyes were brimming too. 'I never ever thought this would happen, Leonie. I'd wondered would I ever be pregnant. Even when we decided to get on the IVF programme, I didn't know if it would work.'

As Emma spoke, her fingers idly stroked her still totally flat belly lovingly.

'How far are you gone?' Leonie asked anxiously.

'Six weeks,' Emma said. 'Imagine, me six weeks pregnant and not knowing it until a few days ago.' She laughed joyously. 'Let me tell you all about it.'

She and Pete had made their appointment with the IVF clinic for the following month and Emma had been immersing herself in the literature she'd been sent. She wanted to know everything before their appointment, so she read and re-read about the strain the treatment put on couples, about how her ovaries would be stimulated with hormone injections and about precisely how her eggs would be collected. It all sounded daunting.

The literature recommended starting the IVF cycle at a time when work wasn't too busy. Emma couldn't imagine a busier time in Krisis-Kids: they were about to move to bigger premises and, because of a horrific child-abuse case which had gripped the nation over the past few weeks, the counsellors and Edward were in great demand to talk about the charity's work.

The phones had never stopped hopping, the publicity department was in chaos because Finn had been struck down by food poisoning, and Emma had been coping with his work as well as her own. By Thursday morning, she was exhausted and couldn't summon up the energy to get out of bed when the clock went off at half six.

'I'm shattered. I can't get up yet,' she murmured to Pete, snuggling up against him, savouring the warmth of his solid body next to hers. It was a chilly morning and she couldn't face braving the cold and stripping off for her shower.

'Five minutes more,' Pete said sleepily, pulling her close to him.

Emma's body fitted into the curve of his, spooned against him. Pete slid one hand under her T-shirt to caress her bare skin. It wasn't an erotic gesture, more of a comforting, loving one. Emma snuggled closer to him, enjoying the feeling of his warm hands stroking her.

Pete's fingers found the curve of one breast. He stroked her softly, fingers splaying out over the sensitive skin of her nipples, skin that seemed suddenly very tender.

'Have you been doing those bust exercises again?' Pete teased gently. 'You're getting very bosomy in your old age.'

'What?' asked Emma, feeling as if she'd been doing a jigsaw puzzle and it had all begun to fall into place. She sat up in the bed, barely noticing the cool of the room compared to the cosiness under the duvet.

'Only teasing,' Pete said hastily. 'You just felt bigger, that's all.'

'B-but . . . they are bigger,' Emma stuttered, ripping her T-shirt off to stare down at her chest. She touched herself; there was no doubt about it: her breasts looked bigger and they felt different. Sensitive, almost painfully sensitive.

'Are they bigger?' she demanded.

Pete sat up too and looked at her. 'They don't look that different, but they *feel* bigger,' he said. 'Why?'

Emma spoke calmly: 'Bigger breasts and sensitive nipples are one sign of pregnancy.'

Pete grabbed her in excitement. 'Emma!' he yelled with delight.

'No, hang on, Pete,' she warned. 'Let's not make the same mistake I always make. I've been down this particular road before. Let's check it out for sure before we start.'

Her heart thumping, she swung herself off the bed and went into the bathroom. At the bottom of the cabinet, hidden in an old toilet bag, was a pregnancy tester.

'Where did you get that?' asked Pete, leaning against the bathroom door.

'From an earlier, obsessed version of my life,' she said wryly.

Together, they read the instructions. One pink dot meant you weren't pregnant, two meant you were.

'Let's hope for two pink dots,' Pete said earnestly, his eyes shining.

Emma hugged him. 'Let's do it.'

When she'd peed on the tester, they left it on the bathroom floor, then sat on the edge of the bed and cuddled. They were both too uptight to shower or dress. Emma couldn't look at her watch because the seconds went so slowly. Three minutes the box said; the longest three minutes of her life.

'It's ready,' Pete said finally, staring at his watch. They both stayed on the bed as if glued to it.

'I can't look,' Emma said huskily. 'I can't. I've wanted this for so long, I can't bear it.'

He held her so tightly it hurt. Emma could feel Pete's heart beating through the thin fabric of his T-shirt. He was as tense as she was, every muscle strained with waiting and longing.

'I'll look,' he said manfully.

She nodded tightly, afraid to speak in case she broke down.

Slowly, Pete went into the bathroom and picked up the tester.

Emma waited, breath held. He was an age. She watched his broad back as he stood with the tester in one hand.

'Pete?' she said.

'Two pink dots!' he roared and turned so she could see the tears streaming down his face. 'Two dots! Emma, my love, we're going to have a baby!'

Leonie had to use her sleeve to wipe the tears away.

'That's so wonderful, Emma,' she said tearfully. 'I'm so very happy for both of you.'

'Thank you,' Emma said, beaming. 'I just had to tell you. We're keeping it to ourselves for a few months. The doctor says I'm six weeks along, so I think we'll make it public in another six. I'm so happy, I have to stop myself smiling all the time or people will think I'm some sort of idiot on drugs.'

'Smile as much as you want to,' Leonie advised, 'you deserve to. When are you pair coming down here for the celebration dinner?'

'Probably next month,' Emma giggled, 'because Pete has set himself a schedule of doing up the house, and especially the nursery, that would exhaust the most ardent DIY person. He's already bought paint and wallpaper for the nursery.'

Leonie laughed delightedly.

'Why don't you and Doug come to us for dinner next weekend?' Emma urged.

'We'd love to. It's a pity Hannah won't be there,' Leonie added. 'We could have a proper Egypt reunion then.'

'I feel so guilty about Hannah,' Emma said. 'I couldn't cope when she got pregnant with Claudia and I wasn't very nice to her. The night you phoned me saying she'd had Claudia, I got plastered,' she admitted. 'Pete had to literally put me to bed.'

'Hannah understood how you felt,' Leonie said kindly. 'She knew how much you longed for a baby. Anyway,' she added briskly, 'that's all behind us now. The next question is: when are you and I going shopping for pregnancy clothes?'

Emma sighed with happiness. 'What are you doing next Saturday?'

CHAPTER THIRTY

On Tuesday, the movers took four hours to pack everything up, stopping only for one tea break and a packet of biscuits. They were so efficient, although when she'd phoned first thing on Monday morning to book them, she'd impressed upon them that speed was of the essence. If they thought it was odd to be hired at such short notice, nobody said anything. Probably they'd been there for many marriage break-ups, Hannah thought wryly.

She was maudlin as she remembered how happily she'd packed her belongings up seven months before, when she'd been so sure that she and Felix had a glorious future ahead of them. Now the only thing they shared was Claudia. Poor darling Claudia. Hannah had never meant her to be the product of a broken home. She knew how hard Donna had worked to look after little Tania on her own, and how tough it had been for Leonie. Single parents didn't get an easy time. But it was better to be single and have respect for yourself than stay married and grow slowly more resentful as the years went on. It could only be good for Claudia this way. At least she'd never see her parents hating each other, having affairs in retaliation and bitching about the other one behind their back.

The moving lorry was only half-way down the road when Hannah made her final round of the house. She'd left Felix the bed, all his personal belongings, and the dining-room suite. He'd bought that. The couch, kitchen table and most of the ornaments, pictures, bookcases and table lamps had belonged to her. Michelle from next door had adopted the kitten. Hannah hadn't thought she'd be able to manage a cat box as well as Claudia on the trip home and if she left the poor little thing, Felix would probably forget to feed it.

She rang for a taxi and twenty minutes later she was on her way to Heathrow, weighed down by two large suitcases, all Claudia's baby paraphernalia, including her pushchair, and a rucksack. The taxi driver helped her into the cab with all her stuff, but at Heathrow, once he'd put it all on a trolley for her, she was on her own.

She remembered flying to Paris a month after Claudia had been born. It was a junket for Felix's film, the one he'd been making in Ireland when they first met. They'd flown first class and there had been people helping all the time: the lovely stewardesses on the flight, and the film publicity people who all cooed at Claudia, petting her, asking to hold her and appearing thrilled when they were allowed to burp her. Insulated by love and helpers, Hannah had barely noticed the journey.

Today, she noticed every minute. Claudia bawled her head off during check-in and bawled even more when she caught sight of the security staff in their uniforms. Hannah's plan to feed her and rock her to sleep for the flight receded into the distance as Claudia's howls reverberated around the airport. Still dragging the pushchair, baby bag and rucksack, Hannah struggled along to the departure lounge where nobody wanted to hear a baby roar at the top of her voice.

'Has Daddy been giving you lessons on projecting your voice?' Hannah asked her daughter, when Claudia's range extended all the way from gates 82 to 90.

She didn't stop on the flight but continued to scream for the entire fifty-five minutes. Hannah managed to drink about a quarter of a glass of water before Claudia spilled it. 'Please don't cry, darling,' Hannah begged, feeling like crying herself. This was a nightmare. Why did she think she could manage on her own? She should have phoned Leonie. She'd have flown to London to help her come home, and she'd have been there at the airport to meet her, smiling and beaming, with Doug happily by her side.

Only you had to be proud, didn't you, Campbell? Hannah hadn't told anyone she was coming home because she was too ashamed. Ashamed because they'd all been right and she'd been wrong. Emma had seen through Felix from the start. So had David James. Only dear blindly romantic Leonie had honestly thought true love could flower from true lust. Only Leonie and Hannah, of course. She'd fallen for that notion hook, line and sinker herself and now she had only herself to blame.

That was why she was getting a taxi to an anonymous hotel room tonight instead of spending it with her dear friends, because she was so mortally embarrassed.

As soon as the plane landed, Claudia cheered up. 'It's because she's happy to be home,' smiled the old man beside them.

'She was born in London,' Hannah said, relieved that Claudia had stopped crying. 'She's never been to Ireland before.'

'The mother country,' said the man fondly.

Hannah nodded, thinking that Claudia's sudden silence was probably a combination of getting wind up and exhaustion.

After another wearying twenty minutes where at least Claudia slept, Hannah collected the luggage, piled it on to a trolley and staggered like a drunk out into the arrivals hall. Pushing the pushchair with one hand and pulling the trolley behind her with the other, she was so preoccupied with not hitting anyone, that she almost missed the tall man watching out for her anxiously.

'Hannah! And this must be baby Claudia.'

In her astonishment, Hannah took a step backwards and crashed into another trolley.

'Sorry,' she muttered. David smiled at her. Wearing an ochre-coloured jacket over jeans, he looked at once both comfortingly familiar and foreign. Used to Felix's lean sinewy body, David looked very big and solid. His salt-and-pepper hair was sleeked back and the narrow eyes were a little unsure, as if he wasn't sure she'd be happy to see him. How wrong could you be.

'Your mother phoned me and said you could do with being picked up from the airport,' he said.

Hannah smiled for what felt like the first time that day.

'Forceful lady, your mother,' he said.

'Incredible,' Hannah agreed.

'Let me.' David took control of the trolley and steered it to the car park. They didn't speak. Hannah, because she was too tired for conversation. At David's car, he quickly loaded all the luggage. Hannah sat in the back with Claudia on her lap because there wasn't a car seat. Claudia woke up and yawned. Seeing David, she smiled gummily at him.

'Aren't you a lovely girl,' he said, chucking her under the chin. Claudia rewarded him with one of her beaming smiles.

'She's adorable,' David said. 'Now, are we all set?'

'Yes,' Hannah said. 'I've booked into Jury's Hotel.'

'Actually, you're booked into your friend Leonie's,' David said apologetically.

Hannah was dumbstruck again. 'My mother?' she asked.

'If she ever needs a job, I could do with a woman with her organizational skills,' he said.

Hannah had to laugh. 'I suppose she's already rung Jury's and cancelled my booking.'

'I wouldn't be at all surprised,' he agreed.

Claudia was happy. She gurgled along to the radio as they sped in the direction of Wicklow. David didn't ask about Felix or about why Hannah had suddenly returned to Ireland without him. Her mother must have said something about her marriage breaking up, but David wouldn't pry. He was too kind. Hannah stole a glance sideways. David's profile wasn't the thing of aesthetic beauty that Felix's was. Where Felix was all long, perfect lines, like a statue of Italian marble, David was solid and unyielding, as if hewn directly from granite. There was something terribly masculine about him compared to Felix's almost feminine beauty. And sexy; he was definitely sexy in that fiercely male way. Hannah found herself wishing she'd made more of an effort in her travelling clothes. Jeans on their third day and her scarlet woollen coat weren't exactly exciting garments.

'Have you spoken to Leonie?' Hannah asked.

'Yes. She hopes you haven't eaten, because she's making a huge dinner for us all.'

'I'm sorry you got roped into all this,' Hannah said. 'You've wasted half a day already.'

'It's not a waste,' David replied. He turned to smile at her and the corners of his eyes crinkled up with warmth. Hannah felt herself relax. She remembered all the wonderful times they'd laughed and joked in his office, sharing coffee and forbidden chocolate biscuits. She felt safe with David, that was it. In Felix's company, she'd always felt as if she was standing on the edge of a glacier, ready to ski down into its vast, dangerous depths. With David, she felt protected, sheltered. Like sitting by the fire in a log cabin listening to the snow outside.

He switched the radio to a classical channel and the gentle music soon sent both Claudia and Hannah to sleep.

They awoke to the sound of Penny barking maniacally. The entire Delaney clan appeared to be waiting for them outside Leonie's cottage, Mel looking like minxy jail bait in her school uniform, Abby slender in paint-splattered dungarees. Danny, Doug, Leonie and two other dogs, which had to be Doug's famous Alfie and Jasper, gathered around David's car.

'Hannah, darling, how lovely to see you,' cried Leonie. Hannah found herself enfolded into her friend's welcoming arms. She breathed in the scent of Opium perfume and felt instantly at home.

'Don't let the dogs bark, Danny,' ordered Leonie. 'They'll scare Claudia.'

But Claudia, who was being cuddled by Abby, showed no sign of nerves at the barking. Instead, she was staring wide-eyed at the three hounds, pointing her chubby fingers excitedly and then stuffing them into her mouth. When Penny attempted to sniff her dangling feet, she went into a spasm of delighted giggling.

'She loves them, don't you, sweetie?' Abby crooned.

Hannah was hugged by everyone and Claudia had to be admired and told she was the most beautiful baby in the world before the procession could reach the house. A glorious aroma of cooking filled the air.

'Doug has been making dinner,' Leonie said proudly. 'He does the most incredible lamb with rosemary.'

'An artist in the kitchen as well as in the studio,' Doug deadpanned, grabbing Leonie's waist from behind. She laughed and leaned back in his embrace. He nuzzled her cheek and Leonie closed her eyes at the caress, utterly at peace.

Hannah felt her heart lift just looking at them. They were so happy together. Leonie's face literally filled with joy every time she touched Doug, and he was the same. They were forever touching, small intimate gestures that telegraphed their love to the world. Happiness had taken years off Leonie too: she looked ten years younger.

Leonie had borrowed a cot for Claudia, so while she and Hannah sorted out the baby's things, the rest of the family waited hungrily in the kitchen, clamouring for food.

'Is it really over with Felix or is this a cooling-off period?' Leonie asked, sitting down on the bed while Hannah changed Claudia's nappy.

'It's over,' Hannah said. 'It probably never should have started. We were so different, I don't know why I fell in love with him at all.' She burst into tears again. It was so final being here. She'd left Felix. She was at home again. It was all over. She felt shocked now, like a disaster survivor when all the screaming and shouting is done.

Leonie cradled her and muttered soothing words in her ear. Eventually, Hannah stopped crying.

'Dinner's ready,' called Doug.

'About time too,' yelled Danny.

'I shouldn't have organized a big dinner with everyone here,' Leonie fretted. 'You're not ready for it.'

Hannah shook her head. 'It's just what I need, actually. I've got out of the habit of meeting people. Felix was always dashing off to parties and receptions. He used to bring Bill with him most of the time. I didn't fit in. His friends weren't my friends, it wasn't my type of life. I miss talking to the people I love.'

'I'm sorry,' Leonie said. 'I feel as if I've let you down. I should have visited, I should have known what you were going through . . .'

Claudia howled, irate at being ignored for so long. Hannah picked her up. 'You couldn't have done anything then, Leonie,' she said. 'I wasn't happy, but I'd have stayed with Felix no matter what. It took finding him in bed with the au pair to make me wake up. What a wake-up call that was.'

Leonie was horrified.

Hannah grinned at her expression. 'If you read about it in the paper, you wouldn't believe it,' she said. 'Come on, Doug's wonderful dinner will be cold. I'm suddenly starving. I'll tell you the sordid details later.'

The lamb was incredible. Hannah sat beside David and ate with gusto. Claudia was passed around the table like a doll, cuddled and kissed, before being moved on to the next person. She adored all the attention, giggling coyly one minute and waving her fat little hands imperiously the next. Doug kept everyone's glasses filled up with wine or mineral water, while Danny heaped great mounds of mashed potato on to their plates.

'I couldn't eat another bite, I'm stuffed,' Hannah protested when he tried to give her a third helping.

'I mashed it myself,' Danny wheedled, spoon hovering. 'It's a special recipe.'

'You want to see the amount of butter he puts in it,' Abby remarked. 'It's fifty per cent potato and fifty per cent butter.'

'My figure can do without butter,' Hannah laughed, patting her belly.

'Nonsense, you need fattening up,' David said. 'Wait till I have you back in the office. I'll force feed you chocolate biscuits during our coffee sessions.'

Hannah just stared at him. 'What do you mean?' she said.

'You are coming back to work with me, aren't you?' he asked.

'I didn't know . . . I didn't think,' she stammered.

'Do you think I'm going to let some other rascally auctioneer steal you away from me?' he said loudly. Then in a quieter voice, he said: 'Please, Hannah. We need you . . . I certainly do.'

Under the table, she reached out and took his hand. He gripped hers tightly.

'Thank you,' she whispered.

'Don't thank me,' he said softly. 'I'm doing it for strictly selfish reasons.'

Hannah found that she couldn't speak, so she merely held his hand under the table, only letting go when Claudia arrived back at David. 'Hello, you scamp,' he said, sitting her on his knee.

Claudia burped loudly then smiled at him. 'I know what we'll do,' David told her. 'You come and work for me and your mummy will come in too, to look after you. You'll be the boss, naturally – a senior agent – and you can help Mummy with her exams.'

Claudia blew bubbles up at him.

Hannah laughed at them both. 'Usually when she does that, she's contemplating getting sick all over you.'

David cuddled Claudia. 'We don't mind, darling, do we?'

Emma arrived as they were having coffee. 'Sorry I couldn't make dinner,' she said to Leonie before hugging Hannah. She took Claudia from David. 'Isn't she beautiful,' she crooned. 'Hello, Claudia, I'm your auntie Emma, your mum's friend.'

Claudia looked surprised and then sicked up a gurgle of white goo. Emma crowed with laughter and Claudia, happy now she'd been sick, started laughing too.

'Aren't you gorgeous,' Emma said. 'She's got your lovely hair, Hannah,' she added.

There was obviously something going on here that she didn't know about, Hannah thought, surprised; Emma adored children, she knew that. But she found it hard to cope with other people's children because they reminded her so painfully of her own inability to have any. But here was Emma, laughing and giggling with Claudia, not looking strained or tearful as she held her.

'You girls go into the sitting room and gossip,' Doug said. 'We'll tidy up.' He couldn't resist kissing Leonie goodbye tenderly as she left.

'Talk about lovebirds,' teased Emma.

Leonie grinned fit to burst.

'You're looking pretty happy yourself,' Hannah remarked to Emma.

It was her turn to beam. 'Well, I have some exciting news for you, Hannah,' Emma began. 'Pete and I booked in for IVF treatment, we were due to start next month. I've been taking my folic acid and doing yoga, you name it.' She smiled. 'I was the best prepared, hopeful candidate in the world. And, you wouldn't believe it . . .' She paused.

Hannah waited in disbelief. Leonie was smiling, she knew whatever Emma was about to say next, obviously.

'I'm pregnant!' Emma said happily. 'Six weeks, that's all. Most people wouldn't have noticed, I'm sure. You know me, if I'm one day late, I buy a testing kit. But I didn't this time. I never even thought of it at first but my boobs suddenly got so incredibly sensitive. It was amazing, my own personal pregnancy tester.'

'That's incredible,' Hannah said, feeling the tears of joy in her eyes. 'I'm so delighted for you.'

'Thank you,' beamed Emma. 'I know what happened. I stopped panicking about it. We were going to have IVF and it was out of our hands. I had hope. I read that lots of people conceive naturally after going through the IVF programme and not getting pregnant. It was a bit like that, really.

'Elinor, my therapist, says I had lots of unresolved issues that were literally blocking out everything else. Once they were gone, I just got pregnant like that.' She picked up Claudia and hugged her joyously. 'I'm so happy, it's fantastic. The only sad thing is that Mum will never know her first grandchild.'

They were all silent for a moment.

'How is she?' Hannah asked, feeling guilty because she didn't know what had been going on in Emma's life. She knew that Anne-Marie was much worse and that she had carers looking after her a lot of the time, but that was it.

'She has her good days and her bad days,' Emma said. 'She's on a new Alzheimer drug and it has helped her, actually. She knows who we all are and she's much calmer, but she's going downhill,' she paused sadly. 'You have to learn to deal with it. It's heart-breaking. But I think what's been happening makes the baby even more special. It's like we're slowly losing my mother but gaining another person. Death, rebirth, the whole cycle goes on and on.'

'That sounds like the sort of thing Abby's always saying,' Leonie remarked.

'You have to become a philosopher when you cope with illness,' Emma explained. 'Otherwise you'd go mad wondering, "Why her, why us?" You have to accept it and deal with it.'

'I'm sorry I've been so out of touch with you,' Hannah said, touching Emma's hand gently. 'You've been through so much and I wasn't any help at all.'

Emma patted Hannah's hand affectionately. 'We're friends, we're not supposed to be joined at the hip,' she said. 'It was partly my fault, anyway,' she admitted. 'I couldn't cope with you being pregnant with this little pet.' She kissed the top of Claudia's head. 'That's a terrible thing to have to admit, but I believe in saying what I think nowadays. Therapy,' she pointed out, 'is wonderful for that. The night you had Claudia, when Leonie rang me to tell me, I drank an entire bottle of red wine with misery. I felt so hopeless. So I pushed you out of my life, Hannah. I'm not proud of it but I'm going to make it up to you.'

'You don't have to make anything up to me,' Hannah said genuinely. 'But I can be of benefit to you. I've got some lovely maternity clothes you could borrow.'

'I can't wait to have to wear them,' Emma sighed. 'I keep turning sideways and looking at myself in the mirror to see if there's a bump yet. I'm longing for a belly, stretch marks, you name it. I've waited so long for this baby. I want to exult in it.'

'Is Pete over the moon?' Hannah asked.

'He's already decorated the nursery,' Emma grinned. 'Only kidding! He's bought paint, wallpaper and a Disney border, though.'

They all laughed.

'If you want anyone to stencil an Egyptian motif in the nursery, don't forget to ask me,' Leonie said.

'Of course,' giggled Emma. 'Nobody else knows, apart from Kirsten,' she added. 'We didn't want to tell anyone until three months are up.'

'Claudia needs friends now she's going to be living here,' Hannah said, taking the baby from Emma. 'She and your little mite can be pals.'

'If it's a girl, they sure will be,' Emma said fervently. 'She'll need her girlfriends. Where would I be without mine?'

'Stuck in an Egyptian prison cell for murdering your father,' teased Leonie.

'Don't remind me,' Emma groaned. 'Although he's being very nice to me these days. Kirsten says it's so I'll continue doing his washing, but it's a start.'

'Maybe we should all go on holiday again soon,' Leonie said thoughtfully. 'Doug wants to go away.'

'Italy,' suggested Emma. 'We could rent a house in the summer. With all of us, it would work out quite cheap. Pete and I will be economizing, I'm afraid.'

'Me too,' said Hannah. 'I can't see Felix being reliable when it comes to maintenance money for Claudia.'

'David's well off, isn't he?' said Emma archly.

Hannah scowled at her. 'I've only just left my husband,' she said, 'don't go setting me up with strange men. It's a bit soon.'

Emma and Leonie exchanged glances.

'I think I'll ask that nice David if he fancies a holiday this year,' Emma said. 'Those villas are cheaper if you have lots of people going. I'm sure *somebody* will let him bunk down in their bedroom.'

Hannah threw a cushion at her.

'I swear, I am never going on holiday with you two again,' she insisted.

The next morning was sunny but the ground was frosty. The tyres of David's car crunched on the gravel as he drove out of Leonie's.

'I shouldn't be letting you do this,' Hannah said. 'It's a hell of a long drive to Connemara and you're missing more work.'

'Four hours at the most,' David replied, eyes on the road. 'It's only half eight, we'll be there in time for lunch.'

'That's only the journey down. I feel terrible about this. I could have got the train,' she said. 'Claudia is a great traveller,' she lied.

'I wanted to drive you,' David said.

'You didn't need to,' she answered.

'Hannah, why do you think I'm doing this?' he demanded. 'Why did I come to the airport? Because I'm crazy about you, that's why.'

'Stop the car,' she commanded.

Surprised, David pulled over on to the grass verge.

Claudia, who'd been asleep in the car seat Leonie had dug out of the attic, woke up and began to bawl.

'You get used to it,' Hannah remarked as the wails increased. Then she leaned over and kissed David firmly on the mouth. In an instant, his arms were around her and he was kissing her back furiously. He tasted wonderful and he felt wonderful too. Different from Felix. Solid and comforting, the way she'd known he would be. His mouth was soft but not gentle, he kissed passionately, intensely. Hannah felt herself melt in response.

She pulled away reluctantly and stared at him.

'It's going to take time,' she warned. 'I've left Felix but he still hasn't left me, if you know what I mean. I can't forget about him in an instant.'

'We can take it slowly,' David said, eyes roaming over her face lovingly.

'Really slowly,' she repeated.

'Like this.' David pulled her into his arms again and lowered his mouth to hers. Claudia roared louder. 'You're right,' he said in wonder, stopping kissing her for a moment, 'you *do* get used to it.'